THE COSSACK CHARGE

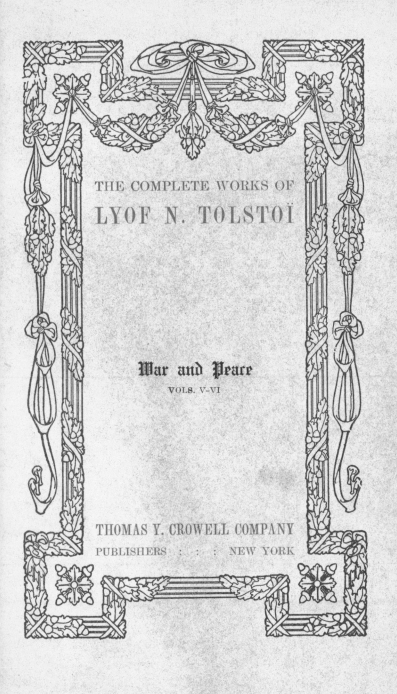

THE COMPLETE WORKS OF
LYOF N. TOLSTOÏ

War and Peace

VOLS. V–VI

THOMAS Y. CROWELL COMPANY
PUBLISHERS : : : NEW YORK

WAR AND PEACE

VOL. V

CONTENTS

PART XI

CONTENTS

PART XII

CONTENTS

PART XIII

CONTENTS

WAR AND PEACE

PART ELEVENTH

CHAPTER I

THE human intellect cannot grasp the idea of absolutely uninterrupted motion. Man can begin to understand the laws of any kind of motion only when he takes into consideration arbitrarily selected units of such motion. But at the same time from this arbitrary division of unbroken motion into measurable units flows the greater part of human errors.

Take, for instance, the so-called "sophism" of the ancients, to prove that Achilles would never overtake a tortoise which had the start of him, even though Achilles ran ten times more swiftly than the tortoise. As soon as Achilles had passed over the distance between them, the tortoise would have advanced one-tenth of that distance; Achilles runs that tenth, the tortoise advances a hundredth, and so on *ad infinitum*.

This problem seemed to the ancients unsolvable. The fallacy of the reasoning that Achilles would never overtake the tortoise arose from this: simply, that intermitted units of motions were arbitrarily taken for granted, whereas the motion of Achilles and the tortoise were continuous.

By assuming ever smaller and smaller units of motion, we only approach the settlement of this question, we never really attain to it. Only by assuming infinitesimal quantities, and the progression up to one-tenth, and by taking the sum of this geometrical progression, can we attain the solution of the question. The new branch of mathematics which is the science of reckoning with infinitesimals enables us to deal with still more complicated problems of motion, and solves problems which to the ancients seemed unanswerable.

This new branch of mathematics, which was unknown to the ancients, and applies so admirably to the problems of motion, by admitting infinitesimally small quantities, — that is, those by which the principal condition of motion is reëstablished, — namely, absolute continuity, in itself corrects the inevitable error which the human mind is bound to make when it contemplates the separate units of motion instead of continuous motion.

In searching for the laws of historical movements precisely the same things must be observed. The progress of humanity, arising from an infinite collection of human wills, is continuous.

The apprehension of the laws of this onward march is the aim of history.

But in order to discover the laws of continuous motion in the sum of all the volitions of men, human reason assumes arbitrary and separate units. History first studies an arbitrary series of uninterrupted events, and contemplates it separate from the others, albeit there is and can be no beginning of an event, but every event is the direct outgrowth of its predecessor.

Secondly, history studies the deeds of a single man, a tsar, a colonel, as representing the sum of men's volitions, when in reality the sum of men's volitions is never expressed in the activities of any one historical personage.

The science of history is constantly taking ever smaller and smaller units for study, and in this way strives to reach the truth. But, however small the units which history takes, we feel that the assumption of any unit separate from another, the assumption of a *beginning* of any phenomenon whatever, and the assumption that the volitions of all men are expressed in the actions of any historical character, must be false *per se*.

Every deduction of history falls to pieces, like powder, without the slightest effort on the part of criticism, leaving nothing behind it, simply in consequence of the fact that the criticism chooses as the object of its observation a more or less interrupted unit ; and it has always the right to do this, since every historical unit is always arbitrary.

Only by assuming the infinitesimal unit for our observation, — as the differential of history, — in other words, the homogeneous tendencies of men, and by attaining the art of integrating (calculating the sum of these infinitesimal differentials), can we expect to attain to the laws of history.

The first fifteen years of the nineteenth century in Europe exhibit an extraordinary movement of millions of men. Men abandon their ordinary vocations, rush from one end of Europe to the other, rob, slaughter one another ; they are filled with triumph and with despair, and the whole course of their lives is for a number of years changed, and undergoes a powerful movement, which at first goes on increasing and then slackens.

"What is the cause of this movement, or by what laws did it take place?" asks the human mind.

The historians, replying to this question, bring to our notice certain acts and speeches of certain dozens of men, in one of the buildings of the city of Paris, and call these acts and speeches "the Revolution"; then they give a circumstantial account of Napoleon, and of certain sympathizers and enemies of his, tell about the influence which certain of these individuals had upon the others, and they say : —

"This was the cause of this movement, and here are its laws."

But the human mind not only refuses to put credence in this explanation, but declares, up and down, that this manner of explanation is fallacious, for the reason that, according to it, a feeble phenomenon is taken as the cause of a mighty one. The sum of human volitions produced both the Revolution and Napoleon, and only the sum of these volitions sustained them and destroyed them.

" But in every case where there have been conquests there have been conquerors ; in every case where there have been revolutions in a kingdom there have been great men," says history.

"Indeed, in every case where conquerors have appeared, there have been wars," replies human reason ; but this does not prove that the conquerors were the cause of the wars, or that it is possible to discover the laws of war in the personal activity of a single man.

In every case when I, looking at my watch, observe that the hand points at ten, I hear the bells ringing in the neighboring church ; but from the fact that in every case when the hand reaches ten o'clock, the ringing of the bells begins, I have no right to draw the conclusion that the position of the hands is the cause of the motion in the bells.

Every time when I observe an engine in motion, I hear the sound of the whistle, I see the valves open and the wheels in motion ; but from this I have no right to conclude that the whistle and the movement of the wheels are the cause of the movement of the engine.

The peasants say that in late spring the cold wind blows because the oak tree is budding, and it is a fact that every spring a cold wind blows when the oaks are in bloom. But, although the cause of the cold wind blowing during the blossoming-time of the oaks is unknown to me, I am unable to agree with the peasants in attributing the cause of the cold winds to the burgeoning buds on the oaks, for the reason that the force of the wind is wholly outside the influence of the oak buds. I see only a coincidence of conditions, which is found in all the phenomena of life, and I see that, no matter how carefully I may contemplate the hands of the watch, the valves and wheels of the engine, and the oak buds, I shall never learn the cause that makes the church-bell chime, the engine to move, and the wind to blow in the spring. To discover this, I must entirely change my point of view, and study the laws that regulate steam, bells, and the wind.

History must do the same thing.

And experiments in this have already been made.

For, studying the laws of history, we must absolutely change the objects of our observation, leave kings, ministers, and generals out of the account, and select for study the homogeneous, infinitesimal elements that regulate the masses. No one can say how far it is given to man to attain by this path an understanding of the laws of history; but evidently on this path only is there any possibility of grasping the laws of history, and the human intellect has not, so far, devoted to this method the one-millionth part of the energies that have been expended by historians in the description of the deeds of individual tsars, colonels, and ministers, and in the elucidation of their combinations, resulting from these deeds.

CHAPTER II

THE forces of a dozen nations of Europe invaded Russia.

The Russian army and the people, avoiding collision, withdraw before the enemy to Smolensk, and from Smolensk to Borodino. The French army, with continually increasing impetus, advances upon Moscow, the goal of its destination.

As it approaches the goal, its impetus increases, just as the velocity of a falling body increases as it approaches the earth. Behind it are thousands of versts of devastated, hostile country; before it, only a few dozen versts separate it from its goal. Every soldier in Napoleon's army is conscious of this, and the invading force moves forward of itself by its own momentum.

In the Russian army, in proportion as it retreats, the spirit of fury against the enemy becomes more and more inflamed; during the retreat it grows concentrated and more vigorous.

At Borodino the collision takes place.

Neither the one army nor the other is dispersed, but immediately after the collision, the Russian army recoils, as inevitably as a ball recoils when struck by another in the impetus of full flight. And just as inevitably the colliding ball moves a certain distance forward (although it loses its force by the collision).

The Russians retire one hundred and twenty versts — beyond Moscow; the French advance as far as Moscow, and there come to a standstill.

During the five weeks that follow, there is not a single battle. The French do not stir.

Like a mortally wounded wild beast, which licks its profusely bleeding wounds, the French remain for five weeks at Moscow, making no attempts to do anything. Then, suddenly, without new reason, they fly back; they take the road to Kaluga, and, after one victory, since the field of Malo-Yaroslavets is theirs, they retreat still more rapidly, without risking any important battle, to Smolensk, beyond Smolensk, beyond Vilna, beyond the Berezina, and so on.

On the night of September 7 Kutuzof and the whole Russian army were persuaded that they had won the battle of Borodino. Kutuzof even thus reported to his sovereign.

Kutuzof gave orders to prepare for another battle to finish with the enemy, not because he wanted to deceive any one, but because he knew that the enemy had been beaten; and this fact was likewise known by all of the participants in the battle.

But that night, and the next day, reports one after another began to come in, of the unprecedented losses sustained, of the army being reduced to one-half, and another battle seemed physically impossible.

It was impossible to give battle, when their condition was as yet unknown, their wounded uncared for, their dead uncounted, fresh missiles not furnished, new officers not replacing those killed, and their men unrefreshed by food and sleep.

Moreover, the French army, immediately after the battle, the next morning, by the law of momentum, its force increasing inversely according to the square of the distance, had already begun to move of itself against the Russian army.

Kutuzof wanted to renew the attack on the following day, and all his army desired this. But the desire to make an attack is not enough. There must also be the possibility of doing it; and in this case possibility was lacking.

It was impossible to prevent retreating one day's march; in the same way, it was impossible to prevent retreating a second day's march, then a third; and finally, when, on September 13, the army reached Moscow, notwithstanding all the force of rising sentiment in the ranks of the army, the force of circumstances obliged them to retire beyond the city, and they made this one last retrograde movement and abandoned Moscow to the enemy.

To those who are wont to think that generals plan their wars and battles in the same way as we, seated tranquilly in our libraries, with a map spread before us, make up combinations and ask ourselves what measures we should have taken in such and such a war, the questions arise, Why did not Kutuzof, in beating a retreat, stop in this place or in that? — why did he not occupy some position before Fili? — why did he not at once take the road to Kaluga, leaving Moscow to itself? and so on.

Men wonted to think in this way forget or do not know the inevitable conditions by which every commander-in-chief must act. His occupation has nothing at all analogous to what we fondly imagine it to be as we sit comfortably in our libraries, picking out, with the aid of a map, a campaign with a given number of troops on the one side and the other, and in a given locality, and beginning at some given moment.

The general-in-chief is never, at the *beginning* of an action, surrounded by conditions such as we always have when we consider the action. The commander-in-chief is always at the center of a series of hurrying events, so that he is not in a condition, for a single instant, to comprehend the whole significance of what is going on. The action is imperceptible, unfolding from instant to instant; and at every instant of this uninterrupted, continuous succession of events, the commander-in-chief is at the center of a complicated game of intrigues, labors, perplexities, responsibilities, projects, counsels, dangers, and deceits, and is obliged to reply to an infinite number of contradictory questions which are submitted to him.

Military critics assure us, in the most serious manner, that Kutuzof should have led his troops along the Kaluga road, before ever he thought of retreating to Fili; that such a course was even suggested to him. But a commander-in-chief has, especially at a decisive moment, not one project alone, but a dozen projects to examine at once. And all of these projects, based on strategy and tactics, are contradictory to one another. It is the office of the commander-in-chief, so it would seem, simply to select some one of these projects that are suggested; but even this he cannot do. Time and events will not wait.

Let us suppose that on the tenth of September it is proposed to Kutuzof to cross over to the Kaluga road, but that at the same moment an aide from Miloradovitch gallops up, and asks whether they shall at once engage with the French or retire. This question must be decided instantly. But the order to retire prevents us from the *détour* along the Kaluga highway.

Immediately after the aide comes the commissary and asks where the stores are to be transported; the chief of ambulance wishes to know where the wounded shall be carried; a courier from Petersburg brings a letter from the sovereign, declaring the abandonment of Moscow to be impossible; a rival of the commander-in-chief, who is trying to undermine his authority, — there are always several such, not one alone, — presents a new plan diametrically opposed to that favoring retreat by the Kaluga road.

The commander-in-chief is thoroughly exhausted, and needs sleep and refreshment. But a respectable general who has been passed over without a decoration comes to make a complaint; the inhabitants implore protection; an officer who has been sent out to recon-

noiter returns and brings a report directly contrary
to that brought by the officer who had been sent out
before him; a spy and a captive and a general who has
made a reconnoitering tour all describe in a different
way the position of the enemy.

Men who are not accustomed to consider, or who
forget the inevitable conditions controlling the activity
of every commander-in-chief, show us, for example, the
situation of the troops at Fili, and take for granted that
the commander-in-chief had till September 13 to decide
the question as to the abandonment or defense of Moscow; whereas, in the position of the Russian army,
within five versts of Moscow, this question could not
even arise.

At what point, then, was this question decided?

It was decided at Drissa, at Smolensk, still more palpably, on September 5, at Shevardino, at Borodino on
the seventh, and every day, every hour, and every minute of the retreat from Borodino to Fili.

CHAPTER III

YERMOLOF, who had been sent by Kutuzof to reconnoiter a position, came back to the field-marshal and
said, "It was impossible to fight in that position and
they must retreat."

Kutuzof looked at him in silence.

"Give me your hand," said he; and, turning it round
so as to feel his pulse, he said:—

"You are ill, my dear![1]   Think what you are saying."

Not even yet could Kutuzof comprehend that it was
possible to retire beyond Moscow without a battle.
Kutuzof got out of his carriage on the Paklonnaya[2]
Hill, six versts from the Dorogomilovskaya barrier, and
sat down on a bench at the edge of the road.   A portentous array of generals gathered around him.   Count Rostopchin, who had driven out from Moscow, joined them.

All this brilliant society, dividing itself into little

[1] *Galubchik.*   [2] Salutation.

circles, was discussing together the advantages and dis-
advantages of the position, the condition of the forces,
the various plans proposed, the state of Moscow, and
about military matters in general.   All felt that this was
a council of war, although they had not been convened
for the purpose, and though it was not called so.   All
conversation was confined to the domain of these general questions.   If any one communicated or heard
private news, it was in a whisper, and such digressions
were immediately followed by a return to the general
questions; not a jest, not a laugh, not even a smile
was exchanged among all these men.

All, though it evidently required an effort, tried to
maintain themselves to the height of the occasion.   And
all these groups, engaged in conversation, strove to
keep close to the commander-in-chief — the bench on
which he sat was the center of these circles — and they
spoke so that he might overhear them.

The commander-in-chief listened, and occasionally
asked for a repetition of what was said around him ;
but he did not himself mingle in the conversation, and
he expressed no opinion.   For the most part, after
listening to what was said in any little group, he would
turn abruptly away with a look of disgust, as if what
they said was not at all what he wanted to hear.

Some talked about the position chosen, criticizing
not the position so much as they did the intellectual
characteristics of those who had selected it.   Others
tried to prove that a mistake had been made before,
that they should have accepted battle two days before ;
still others were talking about the battle of Salamanca,
which a Frenchman, named Crossart, who had just
arrived in a Spanish uniform, described to them.

This Frenchman was discussing the siege of Sara-
gossa with one of the German princes serving in the
Russian army, and laying it down that Moscow could
be defended in the same way.

In a fourth group, Count Rostopchin was declaring
that he, together with the Moscow city troop,[1] was

---

[1] *Druzhina.*

ready to perish under the walls of the capital, but that still he could not help regretting the uncertainty in which he had been left, and that if he had only known about this before, things would have been different. ....

A fifth group, making a display of the profundity of their strategical calculations, talked about the route which our troops ought to have taken.

A sixth group talked sheer nonsense.

Kutuzof's face kept growing more and more troubled and melancholy. From all these scraps of conversation he drew one conclusion : that to defend Moscow was a physical impossibility in the full meaning of the words ; that is, so far it was an impossibility that if any commander-in-chief should be senseless enough to issue the order to give battle, confusion would ensue, and no battle would take place ; it would not take place for the reason that all the high nachalniks not only pronounced the position untenable, but, as they talked, they gave their opinions only in regard to what was to ensue after the abandonment of this position, which was taken for granted. How could these generals lead their troops upon a field of battle which they regarded as untenable?

The nachalniks of lower rank, even the soldiers (who also had their opinions), in the same way, considered the position impossible, and, therefore, they could not be expected to fight when they were morally sure that they were going to be defeated. If Benigsen still urged the defense of this position, and the others still were willing to discuss it, this question, nevertheless, had no significance in itself ; the only significance was the pretext which it offered for quarrels and intrigues. Kutuzof understood this.

Benigsen, having selected a position, hotly insisted on the defense of Moscow, thereby making a show of his Russian patriotism. Kutuzof, as he listened to him, could not help frowning. Benigsen's motive was to him as clear as day : in case of disaster and failure he would lay the blame on Kutuzof, who had led the troops, without a battle, to the Sparrows Hills ; while, in the event of success, he would claim all the credit of it for himself; but if he refused to make the attempt, he would wash his hands of the crime of abandoning Moscow.

But the old man was not at the present occupied with this intrigue. One single, terrible question occupied him. And from no one could he obtain an answer to this question. The question now merely consisted in this:—

"Have I allowed Napoleon to reach Moscow, and when did I do it? When was this decided? Was it yesterday, when I sent to Platof the order to retreat, or was it day before yesterday, in the evening, when I was sleepy, and ordered Benigsen to make his own dispositions? Or was it before that?.... But when, when was this terrible deed decided? Moscow must be abandoned! The troops must retire, and this order must be promulgated!"

To issue this terrible order seemed to him tantamount to resigning the command of the army. But, though he loved power, and was used to it (the honor granted to Prince Prozorovsky, to whose staff he was attached while he was in Turkey, annoyed him), still he was persuaded that the salvation of Russia was predestined to be accomplished by him; and, only for this reason, against the sovereign's will, and in accordance with the will of the people, he had been placed in supreme command. He was convinced that he alone could, in these trying circumstances, maintain himself at the head of the army; that he was the only one in all the world who was able to view without horror the invincible Napoleon as his opponent, and he was overwhelmed at the mere thought of the command which he was obliged to give. But it was essential to come to some decision; it was essential to cut short these discussions around him, which were beginning to assume altogether too free a character.

He called to him the senior generals:—

"*Ma tête, fut elle bonne ou mauvaise, n'a qu'à s'aider d'elle-même* — my judgment, whether good or bad, must be its own reliance," said he, as he got up from the bench; and he drove to Fili, where his horses were stabled.

CHAPTER IV

A COUNCIL was convened at two o'clock, in the largest and best room of the muzhik Andreï Savostyanof's cottage. The men, women, and children belonging to the muzhik's large household were huddled together in the living-room [1] across the entry. Only Andreï's granddaughter, Malasha, a little girl of six summers, whom his serene highness had caressed and given a lump of sugar, while he was drinking tea, remained in the large room, on the stove. Malasha coyly and gleefully looked down from the stove on the faces, uniforms, and crosses of the generals who came one after the other into the izba and took their places on the wide benches in the "red corner," under the holy pictures.

The "little grandfather" [2] himself, as Malasha secretly called Kutuzof, sat apart from the rest, in the "dark corner," behind the stove. He sat far back in a camp-chair, and kept grumbling and pulling at his coat-collar, which, though it was turned back, seemed to choke him.

The men, as they came in one at a time, paid their respects to the field-marshal. He shook hands with some of them; he nodded to others. Adjutant Kaïsarof was about to draw up the curtain at the window, over against Kutuzof, but the general fiercely waved his hand at him; Kaïsarof understood that his serene highness did not wish his face to be seen. Around the muzhik's deal table, whereon lay maps, plans, lead-pencils, sheets of paper, were gathered so many men that the servants had to bring in still another bench and set it down near the table.

On this bench sat the late comers: Yermolof, Kaïsarof, and Toll. Under the images, in the place of honor, sat Barclay de Tolly, with the George round his neck, and with pale, sickly face and lofty brow, between which and the bald head there was no dividing line. For two days he had been suffering from an attack of

---

[1] *Chornaya izba* (black hut), the back room.　　[2] *Dyedushka.*

ague, and at this very moment he was chilled and shaking with fever.

Next him sat Uvarof, and in a low tone of voice (and they all spoke that way) was making some communication with quick gestures.

The little round Dokhturof, arching his brows and folding his hands on his paunch, was attentively listening.

On the other side sat Count Ostermann-Tolstoï, with fearless features and gleaming eyes, leaning his big head on his hand, and seemed lost in thought.

Rayevsky, with a look of impatience, was, as usual, engaged in twisting his black curls forward into lovelocks, and now gazed at Kutuzof, now at the front door.

Konovnitsuin's reliable, handsome, good face was lighted by a shrewd and friendly smile. He was trying to catch Malasha's eyes, and was winking at her and making the little one smile.

All were waiting for Benigsen, who had made a pretext of wishing once more to examine the position so as to eat his sumptuous dinner in peace. They waited for him from four o'clock till six; and all that time they refrained from any deliberation, but talked in undertones about irrelevant matters. Only when Benigsen entered the izba did Kutuzof leave his corner and approach the table, but even then he took care that the candles placed there should not light up his face.

Benigsen opened the council with the question : —

"Shall the holy and ancient capital of Russia be deserted without a blow being struck, or shall it be defended ?"

A long and general silence followed. All faces grew grave, and in the silence could be heard Kutuzof's angry grunting and coughing. All eyes were fixed on him. Malasha also gazed at the "little grandfather." She was nearer to him than any of the others, and could see how his face was covered with frowns ; he seemed to be ready to burst into tears. But this did not last long.

"*The holy, ancient capital of Russia !*" he suddenly repeated, in a gruff voice, repeating Benigsen's language, and thereby making them feel the false note in these words. "Permit me to tell you, your illustrious-ness, that this question has no sense for a Russian." (He leaned forward with his heavy body.) "It is im-possible to put such a question, and such a question has no sense. The question for which I have convened these gentlemen is a military one. That question is as follows:—The salvation of Russia is her army. Would it be more to our advantage to risk the loss of the army and of Moscow too by accepting battle, or to abandon Moscow without a battle? It is on this question that I wish to know your minds."

He threw himself back into his chair again.

The discussion began.

Benigsen refused to believe that the game was yet played out. Granting the opinion of Barclay and the others, that it was impossible to accept a defensive battle at Fili, he, being thoroughly imbued with Russian patriotism and love for Moscow, proposed to lead the troops during the night, over from the right to the left flank, and on the next day to strike a blow at the right wing of the French.

Opinions were divided; discussion waxed hot over the pros and cons of this movement. Yermolof, Dokh-turof, and Rayevsky concurred with Benigsen's views. Whether they were dominated by a sense that some sacrifice was necessary before the capital was aban-doned, or whether it was personal considerations that influenced them, still the fact was, all these generals seemed unable to comprehend that this advice could not alter the inevitable course of events, and that Moscow was already practically abandoned.

The other generals understood this, and, setting aside the question of Moscow, they merely discussed the route which the army in its retrograde march should take.

Malasha, who, with steady eyes, gazed at what was going on before her, understood the significance of this council in an entirely different way. It seemed to her that the trouble was merely a personal quarrel between the "little grandfather" and "long-skirts," as she called Benigsen. She saw that they got excited when they talked together, and in her heart she clung to the "little grandfather's" side.

In the midst of the discussion she remarked the keen, shrewd glance which he cast upon Benigsen, and immediately after, much to her delight, she noticed that the "little grandfather," in saying something to "long-skirts," offended him. Benigsen suddenly flushed, and angrily walked across the room. The words which had such an effect upon Benigsen were spoken in a calm, low tone, and merely expressed Kutuzof's opinion as to the advisability or inadvisability of Benigsen's suggestion; that is, to lead the troops during the night, from the right to the left flank, so as to attack the right wing of the French.

"Gentlemen!" said Kutuzof, "I cannot approve of the count's plan. Transfers of troops in the immediate proximity of the enemy are always dangerous, and military history confirms this view. Thus, for example,"— Kutuzof paused as if he was trying to call up the desired example, and gave Benigsen a frank, naïve look, — "yes, suppose we should take the battle of Friedland, which I presume the count remembers was .... well .... about as good as given away simply for the reason that our troops attempted to cross from one flank to the other while the enemy were in too close proximity.".....

A silence followed, lasting for a minute, but seeming an age to all present.

The discussion was again renewed; but there were frequent interruptions, and there was a general feeling that there was nothing more to be said.

During one of these lulls in the conversation, Kutuzof drew a long sigh, as if he were preparing to speak. All looked at him.

"*Eh bien, Messieurs, je vois que c'est moi qui payerai les pots cassés* — I see that I must bear the brunt of it," said he. And slowly getting to his feet he approached the table : "Gentlemen, I have listened to your views. Some of you will be dissatisfied with me. But" — he hesitated — "I, in virtue of the power confided to me by the sovereign and the country, I command that we retreat."

Immediately after this, the generals began to disperse with that solemn and silent circumspection which people observe after a funeral. Several of the generals, in low voices, but in an entirely different key from that in which they had spoken during the council, made some communication to the commander-in-chief.

Malasha, who had long since been expected at the supper-table, cautiously let herself down backwards from the loft, clinging with her little bare toes to the projections of the stove, and, slipping between the legs of the officers, darted out of the door.

Having dismissed the generals, Kutuzof sat for a long time with his elbows resting on the table and pondering over the same terrible question : —

"When was it, when was it, that it was finally decided Moscow must be abandoned? When took place that which decided the question? and who is to blame for it?"

"I did not expect this, I did not expect it," said he aloud to his aide, Schneider, who came to him late that night. "I did not expect this. I did not dream of such a thing!"

"You must get some rest, your serene highness," said Schneider.

"It's not done with yet! They shall *chaw* horse-flesh yet like the Turks," cried Kutuzof, not heeding him, and thumping his fat fist on the table. "They shall .... as soon as ...."

CHAPTER V

In contradistinction to Kutuzof, though at the same time, and in an event of even greater importance than the retreat of the army without fighting, — namely, in the abandonment and burning of Moscow, — Rostopchin, who has been considered the responsible agent for this action, behaved in an entirely different manner.

This event, — the abandonment of Moscow and its destruction by fire, — after the battle of Borodino, was just exactly as inevitable as the retirement of the troops beyond Moscow, without fighting.

Every man in Russia might have predicted what took place, not indeed by basing his deductions on logic, but by basing them on that sentiment which is inherent in ourselves and was inherent in our forefathers.

What happened in Moscow likewise happened — and that too without Count Rostopchin's proclamations — in all the cities and villages of the Russian land, beginning with Smolensk. The nation unconcernedly awaited the arrival of the foe, displaying no disorder, no excitement, tearing no one in pieces, but calmly awaiting their fate, conscious that, even at the most trying moment, they should find they had the power to do whatever was required of them. And as soon as the foe approached, the more wealthy elements of the population departed, leaving their possessions behind them; the poorer classes stayed, and burned and destroyed what was abandoned.

The conviction that things must be as they are has always been and still is inherent in the Russian mind. And this conviction — nay, more, the presentiment that Moscow would be taken — pervaded Russian and Moscovite society in the year 1812. Those who started to abandon Moscow as early as July and the beginning of August showed that this was what they expected. Those who fled, taking with them whatever they could, and abandoning their houses and the half of their possessions, acted thus in obedience to that latent patriotism which is expressed not in phrases, nor in the slaughter of children for the salvation of the fatherland, and in other unnatural deeds, but is expressed imperceptibly, simply, organically, and, accordingly, always produces the most powerful results.

"It is disgraceful to flee from danger; only cowards will fly from Moscow," it was said to them. Rostopchin, in his placards, declared that it was ignominious to leave Moscow. They were ashamed to be branded as cowards, they were ashamed to go; but still they went, because they knew that it had to be so.

What made them go?

It is impossible to suppose that Rostopchin frightened
them by the atrocities committed by Napoleon in conquered lands. They fled, and the first to flee were the
wealthy, cultivated people, who knew perfectly well that
Vienna and Berlin were left intact, and that there, during Napoleon's occupation, the inhabitants led a gay life
with the fascinating Frenchmen, who at that time were so
beloved by Russian men and particularly Russian women.

They went, because for Russians there could be no
question whether it would be good or bad to have
the French in control of Moscow. It was impossible
to exist under the dominion of the French; that was
worse than aught else. They began to escape even
before the battle of Borodino, and after the battle of
Borodino with greater and greater rapidity, not heeding
the summons to remain and protect the city, notwithstanding the statements of the governor-general of
Moscow as to his intention of taking the Iverskaya
Virgin and going forth to fight, and notwithstanding the
balloons which were destined to bring destruction upon
the French, and notwithstanding all the nonsense which
Count Rostopchin wrote about in his proclamations.

They knew that the army ought to fight, and that, if
it could not, then it was no use for them to go out with
their fine ladies and their household serfs to Tri Gorui [1]
to do battle with Napoleon, but that it was necessary
for them to make their escape, however much they might
regret leaving their property to destruction.

They fled, and gave never a thought to the majestic
significance of this splendid and rich capital abandoned
by its inhabitants, and unquestionably doomed to be
burned (for it is not in the nature of the Russian populace not to sack, not to set fire to empty houses); they
fled each for himself; but, at the same time, merely as
a consequence of their fleeing, was accomplished that
majestic event which will forever remain the crowning
glory of the Russian people.

That noble lady who, even as early as the month of
June, took her negroes and her jesters, and went from

[1] Three Hills.

Moscow to her country place near Saratof, with a vague consciousness that she was no slave to Bonaparte, and with some apprehension lest she should be stopped by Count Rostopchin's orders, was simply and naturally doing the mighty act that was to prove the salvation of Russia.

Count Rostopchin himself, now putting to shame those who fled, now transferring the courts outside the city, now distributing good-for-nothing arms to a drunken mob, now displaying the holy pictures, now forbidding Avgustin to remove the relics and ikons, now seizing all the private conveyances that were in Moscow, now conveying on one hundred and thirty-six carts the balloon constructed by Leppich, now hinting that he should set Moscow on fire, now declaring that he had burnt his own house, now writing a proclamation to the French in which he solemnly reproached them for having destroyed his Foundling Asylum; now taking the glory of the burning of Moscow, now disclaiming it; now ordering the people to capture all spies and bring them to him, now reproaching the people for doing that very thing; now sending all the French out of Moscow, while, at the same time, leaving in the city Madame Aubert-Chalmé, whose house was the center of the whole French population of Moscow; and now, without a shadow of excuse, ordering the honorable director of the posts, the venerable Kliucharef, to be arrested and banished; now collecting the populace on the Tri Gorui, in order to do battle with the French, and now, in order to get rid of this same mob, giving them a man to slaughter, while he himself slipped out from a rear gate; now declaring that he would not survive the misfortune of Moscow, now writing French verses[1] in albums to commem-

---

[1] *Je suis né tartare ;*
Je voulais être romain ;
Les français m'appelèrent barbare,
Les russes Georges Dandin.

I was born a Tatar; I wanted to be a Roman; the French called me a barbarian, the Russians George Dandin. — AUTHOR'S NOTE. (George Dandin, a character in one of Molière's plays, is the type of a peasant raised to the nobility, and marrying a rich wife, who proves unfaithful.)

orate the part that he took in these deeds, — this man did not appreciate the significance of the deed accomplished, but he merely desired to do something himself, to astonish some one, to accomplish something patriotically heroic ; and, like a child, he sported over the majestic and inevitable circumstance of the abandonment and burning of Moscow, and strove with his puny little hand now to encourage, now to stem, the current of that tremendous popular torrent which was carrying him along with it.

CHAPTER VI

ELLEN, who had returned with the court from Vilna to Petersburg, found herself in a trying and delicate situation.

At Petersburg, Ellen enjoyed the special protection of a grandee who held one of the most important offices in the empire.

But at Vilna she had become intimate with a young foreign prince. When she returned to Petersburg, the prince and the grandee were both in town ; both claimed their rights, and Ellen found that she had to face a new problem in her career : to preserve her intimacy with both without offending either.

What would have seemed difficult and even impossible for any other woman did not cause the Countess Bezukhaya even a moment's hesitation, thereby proving that it was not in vain she enjoyed the reputation of being a very clever woman. If she had tried to hide her actions, to employ subterfuge in escaping from an awkward position, she would, by that very method, have spoiled her game by confessing herself guilty. But Ellen, on the contrary, openly, after the manner of a truly great man, who can do anything that he pleases, assumed that she was in the right, as she really believed, and that all the rest of the world were in the wrong.

The first time when the young foreign personage permitted himself to reproach her, she, proudly holding high her beautiful head, and looking at him over her shoulder, said steadily : —

"Here is an example of man's egotism and cruelty! I might have expected it. A woman sacrifices herself for you, and this is her reward! What right have you, monseigneur, to hold me to account for my friendships, for my affections? This man has been more than a father to me."

The personage began to make some answer. Ellen interrupted him : —

"Well, then, grant it!" said she, "perhaps he has for me other sentiments than those of a father; but that is no reason why I should shut my door to him. I am not a man that I should be ungrateful. I would have you understand, monseigneur, that in all that touches my private feelings, I am accountable only to God and my conscience," she said, in conclusion, and pressed her hand to her beautiful, heaving bosom, with a glance toward heaven.

"But, for God's sake, listen to me."

"Marry me and I will be your slave."

"But it is impossible."

"You are too proud to stoop to marriage with me, you...." said Ellen, bursting into tears.

The personage tried to console her. Ellen, through her tears, declared (as if she had forgotten herself) that no one could prevent her from marrying; that there were examples — at that time there were few examples, but she mentioned Napoleon and other men of high degree; that she had never been to her husband what the name of wife implies; and that she had been led to the altar as a sacrifice.

"But laws, religion...." murmured the personage, beginning to yield.

"Laws, religion!.... Why were they ever invented, if they could not help in such a case as this?"

The exalted personage was amazed that such a simple line of reasoning had never entered his mind, and he applied for advice to the holy brethren of the Society of Jesus, with whom he stood in intimate relationship.

A few days later, at one of the enchanting *fêtes* which Ellen gave at her *datcha*, or suburban residence, on the Kamennoï Ostrof, M. de Jobert, *un Jésuite à robe courte*, a fascinating man, no longer young, with hair as white as snow, and with dark, glittering eyes, was presented to her; and for a long time, as they sat in the garden in the brilliant light of the illuminations, and listening to the sounds of music, he conversed with her about love to God, to Christ, to the Sacred Heart of Mary, and about the consolations vouchsafed in this life and the life to come by the one true Catholic religion.

Ellen was touched, and several times the tears stood in the eyes of both of them, and her voice trembled.

The dance for which a partner came to engage Ellen interrupted her interview with her future *directeur de conscience;* but in the evening of the following day M. de Jobert came alone to Ellen's, and from that time he was frequently at her house.

One day he took the countess to the Catholic church, and there she remained on her knees before the altar, to which she was brought.

The elderly, fascinating Frenchman laid his hands on her head, and, as she herself afterwards declared, she became conscious of something like the fanning of a cool breeze which entered her soul. It was explained to her that this was *la grâce*.

Then an *abbé à robe longue* was introduced to her. He heard her confession, and granted her absolution from her sins.

On the next day they brought her a casket in which was contained the Holy Communion, and they left it in her house for her use.

After a few days Ellen, to her satisfaction, learned that she had now entered the true Catholic Church, and that shortly the Pope should be informed about it, and would send her a certain document.

All that happened at this time around her and within her; all the attention lavished on her by so many clever men, and expressed in such agreeable, refined forms; and the dove-like purity in which she now found herself,

—these days she constantly wore white gowns with white ribbons, — all this afforded her great satisfaction, but she did not for a moment allow this satisfaction to prevent her from the attainment of her ambitions.

And, as it always happens that in a matter of *finesse* the stupid man obtains more than the clever, she, comprehending that the object of all these words and labors consisted chiefly in making her pay for the privilege of conversion to Catholicism by turning over certain moneys for the advantage of Jesuit institutions, concerning which they had dropped various hints, — Ellen, before turning this money over, insisted on their execution in her behalf of the various formalities which would free her from her husband.

In her idea, the significance of any religion consisted only in observing certain conventionalities, while at the same time allowing the gratification of human desires.

And, with this end in view, during one of her interviews with her spiritual guide, she strenuously insisted on his answering her question, how far she was bound by her marriage.

They were sitting in the drawing-room, by the window. It was twilight. Through the window wafted the fragrance of flowers. Ellen wore a transparent white gown, through which showed her bosom and shoulders. The abbé, well-fattened, with plump face smooth-shaven, pleasant, forceful mouth, and white hands folded on his knees, was sitting close to Ellen, and, with a slight smile on his lips and eyes, decorously devouring her beauty, was looking from time to time into her face, and explaining his views on the question that occupied them.

Ellen, with an uneasy smile, looked at his flowing locks, his smooth-shaven, dark-shaded, plump cheeks, and each moment expected some new turn to the conversation. But the abbé, though he evidently appreciated his companion's beauty, was carried away by the skill which he used in his arguments.

The course of reasoning employed by the director of conscience was as follows : —

"In your ignorance of the significance of what you took upon yourself, you plighted your troth to a man who, on his side, by entering into marriage without believing in the religious sacrament of marriage, committed sacrilege. This marriage had no complete significance, such as it should have. But, nevertheless, your vow binds you. You have broken it. What have you committed thereby, *péché veniel* or *péché mortel?* Venial sin, because what you have done has been without evil intent. If you now, for the sake of having children, should enter into a marriage bond, your sin might be forgiven you. But this question resolves itself into two : first.... "

"But I think," said Ellen, suddenly losing patience and beaming on him with her fascinating smile, "I think that, now that I have entered into the true faith, I cannot remain bound by what was imposed on me by a false religion."

The *directeur de conscience* was astonished at this solution, which had all the simplicity of Columbus's egg. He was delighted by the unexpected rapidity with which his teachings had met with success, but he could not refrain from following out the train of thought which he had elaborated with so much pains.

"Let us understand each other, *comtesse*," he said, with a smile, and he proceeded to refute his spiritual daughter's reasoning.

CHAPTER VII

ELLEN understood that the matter was very simple and easy from the religious standpoint, but that her spiritual directors stood out against it simply because they were apprehensive of the way it might strike the temporal powers.

And, consequently, Ellen resolved that it was necessary for society to be prepared for this eventuality. She aroused the old grandee's jealousy, and told him exactly what she had said to her first suitor ; in other words, she made him understand that the only way of establishing his rights over her was to marry her.

The aged personage, at the first moment, was just as much astonished as the young personage had been at this proposal of marrying during the husband's lifetime. But Ellen's imperturbable assurance that this was as simple and natural as the marriage of a virgin, had its effect even on him. If there had been noticed the slightest symptom of vacillation, shame, or underhandedness on Ellen's part, then her game would have undoubtedly been lost; but, on the contrary, she, with simple and good-natured innocence, told her nearest friends (and that was all Petersburg) that both the grandee and the prince had proposed to her, and that she was in love with both of them, and afraid of paining either.

The rumor was instantly bruited through Petersburg — not that Ellen desired to obtain a divorce from her husband; if this report had been current, very many would have protested against such a lawless proceeding — that the unhappy, interesting Ellen was in perplexity as to which of the two men she should marry.

The question was not at all how far this was permissible, but which party was the most desirable, and how the court looked on it. There were, to be sure, a few obdurate people, who were unable to rise to the height of this question, and who saw in this project a profanation of the marriage sacrament; but such people were few, and they held their peace, while the majority were merely interested in the question which Ellen would choose, and which choice would be the better. As to the question whether it were right or wrong to marry a second time during the lifetime of the first husband, nothing was said, because this question had been evidently settled for people "who were wiser than you and me" (so they said), and to express any doubt of the correctness of such a settlement of the question was to run the risk of showing one's stupidity and one's ignorance of society.

Marya Dmitrievna Akhrasimova. who had gone that

summer to Petersburg to visit one of her sons, was the only one who permitted herself frankly to express her opinion, though it was in direct contravention to that of society in general. Meeting Ellen one time at a ball, Marya Dmitrievna stopped her in the middle of the ball-room, and in her loud voice, which rang through the silence, she said :—

"So you propose to marry again while your husband is alive! Perhaps you think you have discovered something new!.... You have been forestalled, matushka. This thing was invented long ago. In all the . . . . they do the same thing."

And with these words Marya Dmitrievna, with that characteristic, threatening gesture of hers, turned back her flowing sleeves, and, glancing sternly around, passed through the room.

Marya Dmitrievna, although she was feared, was regarded in Petersburg as facetious, and therefore, in the words which she spoke to Ellen, they merely took notice of her use of the coarse word, and repeated it in a whisper, supposing that therein lay all the salt of her remark.

Prince Vasili, who of late had grown peculiarly forgetful, and repeated himself a hundred times, said to his daughter whenever he chanced to see her :—

"Ellen, I have a word to say to you," he would say to her, drawing her to one side and giving her hand a pull. "I have heard rumors of certain projects concerning — you know who. Well, my dear child, you know that my paternal heart would rejoice to feel .... you have had so much to endure. .... But, dear child, ... consult only your own heart. That is all that I have to say."

And, hiding the emotion that always overmastered him, he would press his cheek to his daughter's and go away.

Bilibin had not lost his reputation of being a clever man, and as he had been a disinterested friend of Ellen's, one of those friends whom brilliant women always manage to attach to them, — men who may be relied on never to change from friend to lover, — he once, *en petit comité*, gave Ellen the benefit of his views in regard to all this business.

"Listen, Bilibin," said Ellen, who always called all such friends as Bilibin by their last names, — and she laid her white hand, blazing with rings, on his coat-sleeve; "tell me as you would a sister, what ought I to do? Which one of the two?"

Bilibin knitted his brows, and sat reflecting with a smile on his lips.

"You do not take me by surprise, do you know," said he. "As a true friend I have thought and thought about your affairs. You see, if you marry the prince" (that was the young man), — he bent over his finger, — "you lose forever your chance of marrying the other one, and, besides, you offend the court. As you are aware, there is some sort of relationship. But if you marry the old count, you will make his last days happy, and then as the widow of the great . . . . the prince will not make a misalliance in contracting a marriage with you."

"Here is a true friend!" cried Ellen, radiantly, and once more laying her hand on Bilibin's sleeve. "But the trouble is that I love both of them; I should not wish to pain either of them. I would sacrifice my life to make both of them happy," said she.

Bilibin shrugged his shoulders as much as to say that even he himself could not endure such a grievous thing.

"*Une maîtresse-femme!* That is what is called stating the question squarely. She would like to have all three as husbands at once!" thought Bilibin. "But tell me how your husband is going to look on this matter," he asked, trusting to the solid foundation of his reputation, and therefore having no fear of hurting himself by such an artless question. "Will he consent?"

"Ah! He loves me so!" cried Ellen, who had somehow conceived the notion that Pierre also loved her! "He will do anything for me!"

Bilibin again puckered his forehead, so as to give

intimation of the approaching *mot*. "Even divorce?" he asked.

Ellen laughed.

Among those who permitted themselves to doubt the legality of the proposed marriage was Ellen's mother, the Princess Kuragina. She was constantly tortured by jealousy of her daughter, and now when the object that especially aroused this jealousy was the one dearest to the princess's heart, she could not even endure the thought of it. She consulted with a Russian priest in regard to how far divorce and marriage during the life of the husband were permissible, and the priest informed her that this was impossible, and to her delight pointed out to her the Gospel text, where it is strictly forbidden to marry again during the life of a husband.

Armed with these arguments, which seemed to her irrefutable, the princess drove to her daughter's early one morning, so as to find her alone.

After listening to her mother's objections, Ellen smiled a sweet but satirical smile. "Here it is said in so many words," said the old princess. "He who ever shall marry her who is put away ...."

"Ah, *maman*, don't talk nonsense. You do not understand at all. In my position I have duties," interrupted Ellen, changing the conversation into French, since it always seemed to her that the Russian brought out a certain lack of definiteness in this transaction of hers.

"But, my dear ...."

"Ah, *maman!* Can't you understand that the Holy Father, who has the right to grant dispensations ...."

At this instant the lady companion who lived at Ellen's came in to announce that his highness was in the drawing-room and wished to see her.

"No, tell him that I do not wish to see him, that I am furious with him because he has broken his word!"

"*Comtesse*, there is a pardon for every sin!" said a fair young man, with a long face and long nose, who came into the room.

The old princess arose most respectfully and courtesied; the young man who came in paid no attention whatever to her. The princess nodded to her daughter and sailed out.

"Yes, she is right," mused the old princess, all of whose convictions were dissipated by the sight of his highness. "She is right. But how was it we did not know this in those days which will never return, when we were young? And it is such a simple thing," mused the old princess, as she took her seat in her carriage.

Toward the beginning of August, Ellen's affairs were entirely settled, and she wrote her husband — who was so fond of her as she thought — informing him of her intention of marrying N. N., and that she had embraced the one true religion, and begging him to fulfil all the indispensable formalities of the divorce, in regard to which the bearer of her letter would give due particulars : —

"And so I pray God, my dear, to have you in His holy and mighty protection.
                              "Your friend,
                                        "ELLEN."

This letter was brought to Pierre's house at the very time when he was on the field of Borodino.

CHAPTER VIII

TOWARD the end of the battle of Borodino, Pierre, fleeing for the second time from the Rayevsky battery, joined a throng of soldiers hurrying along the ravine to Kniazkovo, and came to the field lazaret, and there seeing blood, and hearing cries and groans, he hurried on, mingling with the throngs of soldiers.

The one thing Pierre now desired with all the powers of his soul was to escape as soon as possible from these terrible scenes through which he had lived that day, to return to the ordinary conditions of every-day life, and to sleep calmly in his own bed in his own room. He was conscious that only by getting back to ordinary conditions would he be able to understand himself and all that he had seen and experienced. But these ordinary conditions of life were non-existent.

Although cannon-balls and bullets were not whistling along this part of the road where he was walking, still there was on all sides of him what he had seen on the battle-field. There were the same suffering, tortured, and sometimes strangely indifferent faces, the same gore, the same military cloaks, the same sounds of firing although softened by distance, but still causing ever new horror, and, besides, this suffocating heat and dust.

Procéeding three versts along the Mozhaïsk highway, Pierre sat down on the edge of it.

Twilight had settled down on the earth, and the roar of artillery had died away. Pierre leaned his head on his hands and sat in this posture for a long time, watching the shadows trooping by him in the dusk. It seemed to him all the time as if a cannon-shot were flying down on him with that terrible screech. He trembled and got up. He had no idea how long a time he had been delaying there.

Late in the night, three soldiers, dragging along some brushwood, started a fire near him and made themselves at home. These soldiers, looking askance at Pierre, kindled their fire, put their kettle on it, crumbled hard-tack into it, and laid on their salt pork.

The agreeable savor of appetizing viands and of frying mingled with the odor of the smoke. Pierre stood up and drew a sigh. The soldiers — there were three of them — were eating and conversing together, and paid no heed to Pierre.

"Well, what corps are you from?" suddenly asked one of the soldiers, addressing Pierre, and evidently, by this question, wishing to signify, and Pierre understood it so, "If you want something to eat we will give it to you; only tell us if you are an honest man."

"What? I? I?".... stammered Pierre, feeling it incumbent on him to belittle his social position so far as possible, so as to be nearer and more accessible to the soldiers: —

"I am at present an officer of the militia; only I have

missed my corps; I went into the battle and got sepa
rated from my men."

"To think of it!"[1] said one of the soldiers.

One of the others shook his head.

"Well, have something to eat, if you like our mess,"
said the first, and, after licking off the wooden spoon, he
handed it to Pierre.

Pierre sat down by the fire and began to eat the pot-
tage which was in the kettle, and which seemed to him
the most palatable of anything he had ever tasted in his
life.   While he greedily bent over the kettle, fishing
out great spoonfuls and swallowing them down one after
another, his face was lighted by the fire, and the soldiers
silently studied him.

"Where do you want to go?   Tell us that!" asked
one of them again.

"I want to go to Mozhaïsk."

"You are a barin, I suppose?"

"Yes."

"And what's your name?"

"Piotr Kirillovitch."

"Well, Piotr Kirillovitch, come on, we'll show you
the way."

In utter darkness the soldiers and Pierre went toward
Mozhaïsk.

The cocks were already crowing when they came near
the town and began to climb the steep slope that led to
it.   Pierre went on with the three men, entirely forgetting that his tavern was below, at the foot of the hill,
and that he had already gone beyond it.   He would not
have remembered it at all — he had got into such a state
of apathy — if half-way up the hill he had not accidentally fallen in with his equerry, who had been searching
for him in the town, and was on his way back to the
tavern.   His equerry recognized Pierre by his hat, which
gleamed white in the darkness.

"Your illustriousness," he exclaimed, "we have been
in perfect despair!   What!   Are you on foot?   Where
have you been, please?"

[1] *Vish tui.*

"Oh, yes!" replied Pierre.

The soldiers paused.

"So, then, you have found your men, have you?" asked one of them.

"Well, good-by!¹ Piotr Kirillovitch; it's all right, is it?".... "Good-by, Piotr Kirillovitch!" cried the other voices.

"Good-by," said Pierre, and he started back with his equerry to the tavern.

"I ought to give them something," thought Pierre, feeling in his pocket. "But no, it is not necessary," said some voice within him.

There was no room for Pierre anywhere in the tavern; all the beds were taken. Pierre went out into the yard, and, wrapping himself, lay down in his calash.

CHAPTER IX

PIERRE had hardly laid his head on his extemporized pillow before he felt himself going off to sleep; but suddenly, with almost the vividness of reality, he heard the *bumm! bumm! bumm!* of the firing, he heard cries, groans, the thudding of missiles, he smelt blood and gunpowder; and a feeling of horror and the terror of death took possession of him.

He opened his eyes in a panic, and lifted his head from his cloak. All was quiet in the dvor. Only at the gates, talking with the dvornik, and splashing through the mud, some one's man was walking up and down. Over his head, under the dark under side of the shed roof, the pigeons were fluttering their wings, startled by the movement which he had made in raising himself. The whole dvor was full of that powerful barnyard odor, which, at that instant, delighted Pierre's heart — the odor of hay, of manure, and of tar. Through a chink in the shed roof he could see the clear, starry sky.

"Thank God, there is no more of *that*," said Pierre to himself, again covering up his head. "Oh! what a

¹ *Prashchavaĭ.*

terrible panic, and how shameful to give way to it.   But they .... *they* were calm and firm even to the very end," his thoughts ran on.   *They*, in Pierre's soliloquy, meant the soldiers who had been in the battery, those who had given him food, and those who had worshiped before the ikon.   *They* — he had never known them till now — *they* were clearly and sharply separated from all other men.

"To be a soldier, a simple soldier," thought Pierre, as he fell off to sleep.   "To enter into that common life with all my being, to learn the secret of what makes them what they are!   But how to get rid of this super- fluous, devilish weight of the external man?   Once I might have been such.   I might have run away from my father's house, as I wanted to do.   I might even after my duel with Dolokhof have been sent off as a common soldier."

And before Pierre's imagination arose the dinner at the club, when he challenged Dolokhof, and his visit to the Benefactor at Torzhok.   And here Pierre recalled the Masonic lodge at Torzhok.   This lodge was in- stalled at the English Club.   And some one whom he knew well, some one intimately connected with his life, and dear to him, was sitting at the end of the table. Yes, it was he!   It was the Benefactor!

"Yes, and did he not die?" mused Pierre.   "Yes, he was dead ; I did not know that he was alive.   And how sorry I felt that he was dead, and how glad I am that he is alive again!"

On one side of the table sat Anatol, Dolokhof, Nes- vitsky, Denisof, and others of the same sort, — the cate- gory of these men was just as clearly defined in his dream in Pierre's mind as the category of the men whom he had spoken of as *they ;* and these men — Anatol, Dolokhof, and the rest — were shouting and singing at the top of their voices ; but above their shouts he could hear the benefactor's voice talking incessantly, and the ring of his voice was as significant and continuous as the roar of the battle-field, but he was soothed and comforted by it.

Pierre did not comprehend what the Benefactor was saying, but he knew — the category of his thoughts was so clear in his dream — that the Benefactor was talking about goodness, and the possibility of being the same manner of man as *they* were. And *they* came from all sides and surrounded the Benefactor with their simple, good, steadfast faces. But, although they were good, they did not look at Pierre, did not know him. Pierre was anxious to attract their attention and to talk. He started to get up, but his legs were cold and uncovered.

He was ashamed of himself, and was going to cover his legs, from which his cloak had actually slipped off. While Pierre was covering himself up again, he opened his eyes and saw the same shed, the same beams, the same dvor, but everything was enveloped in a bluish light, and sparkled with dew or frost.

"Daybreak!" thought Pierre. "But this is not what I want. I must listen, hear, and understand the Benefactor's words."

He again wrapped himself in his cloak, but there was no longer any Masonic lodge; the Benefactor was gone. There were simply thoughts, clearly expressed in words, thoughts which either some one spoke or which Pierre himself imagined.

When he afterwards came to recall these thoughts, although they were evidently superinduced by the impressions of the day, Pierre was convinced that some one outside of himself spoke them to him.

Never, so it seemed to him, while awake, had he been able to think such thoughts or to express them in such language.

"The hardest thing for man to do is to subordinate his freedom to the laws of God," said the voice. "Simplicity is submission to God; thou canst not escape from Him. And *they* are single-hearted. *They* do not talk, they act. Speech is silver, but silence is golden. Man can never get the mastery, as long as he is afraid of death. Whoso feareth not death, all things shall be added unto him. If it were not for suffering, man would not know his limitations, would not know himself. The hardest thing," continued Pierre, either thinking or hearing in his dream, "consists in being able to unite in the soul the knowledge of all things. To unite all things?" Pierre was asking. "No, not to unite. It is impossible to unite thoughts; but to coördinate; that is what is necessary! Yes, to coördinate, to coördinate," said Pierre, repeating the word over to himself with inward enthusiasm, conscious that by just these words, and by these only, could be expressed what he desired to express, and have the question decided that was forever tormenting him.

"Yes, coördinate, time to coördinate."

"We must make a start, we shall be too late,[1] your illustriousness," repeated some voice at his ear. "Must make a start, we shall be too late!"

It was the voice of the equerry trying to rouse Pierre. The sun was shining full in Pierre's face. He looked at the muddy yard of the dvor, in the center of which, around the well, soldiers were watering lean horses, and from the gates of which trains were starting away. Pierre turned away with disgust, and, closing his eyes, made haste to roll over again on the carriage-seat.

"No, I do not wish this, I do not wish to see this or to understand it; I wish to comprehend what was revealed to me while I was dreaming. Just one second more, and I should have understood it all. Now, what must I do? To coördinate, yes, but how coördinate all things?"

And Pierre found to his dismay that the whole structure of what he had seen and thought out in his dream had been demolished.

His equerry, the coachman, and the dvornik all told Pierre that an officer had come with tidings that the French were moving on Mozhaïsk, and that our forces were retreating.

Pierre got up, and, giving orders to have his horses

---

[1] Pierre's confusion of dreaming and waking ideas is caused by the similarity between "*sapriagat*," to unite, join, coördinate, and "*zapriagat*," to hitch up, harness horses.

harnessed and to overtake him, started to walk through the town.

The troops were in full retreat, leaving about ten thousand wounded. These wounded could be seen in the yards and windows of the houses, and thronging the streets. The streets where stood the telyegas that were to carry away the wounded were full of cries, curses, and the sounds of blows.

Pierre overtook a wounded general of his acquaintance, and offered him a seat in his calash, and they drove on toward Moscow together. On the road Pierre heard of the death of his brother-in-law and of the death of Prince Andreï.

CHAPTER X

On the tenth of September Pierre arrived at Moscow. Near the barrier he was met by one of Count Rostopchin's aides.

"Well, we have been searching for you everywhere," said the aide. "The count wants very much to see you. He begs that you will come to him immediately on very important business."

Pierre, without even going first to his own house, called an izvoshchik and drove to the governor-general's.

Count Rostopchin had only that morning come to town from his suburban datcha at Sokolniki. The anteroom and reception-room of the count's residence were full of officials who had come at his summons or to get orders. Vasilchikof and Platof had already had an interview with the count, and had informed him that it was impossible to defend Moscow, and that it must be abandoned. This news was concealed from the inhabitants, yet the chinovniks, the heads of the various departments, knew that Moscow would soon be in the hands of the enemy just as well as Count Rostopchin knew it; and all of them, in order to shirk responsibility, came to the governor-general with inquiries as to what they should do in their respective jurisdictions.

Just as Pierre entered the reception-room, a courier from the army left the count's room.

The courier made a despairing gesture in answer to the questions directed to him, and passed through the room.

On entering, Pierre, with weary eyes, gazed at the various chinovniks, old and young, military and civil, who were waiting in the room. All seemed anxious and ill at ease.

Pierre joined one group of chinovniks, among whom he saw an acquaintance. After exchanging greetings with Pierre they went on with their conversation.

"Whether they exile him or let him come back, there's no telling; you can't answer for anything in such a state of affairs."

"Well, here is what he writes," said another, calling attention to a printed broadside which he held in his hand.

"That's another thing. That's necessary for the people," said the first speaker.

"What is that?" asked Pierre.

"This is the new placard."

Pierre took it and read as follows:—

His serene highness, the prince, in order to effect a junction as soon as possible with the troops coming to meet him, has passed through Mozhaïsk and occupied a strong position where the enemy will not find it easy to reach him. Forty-eight cannon, with ammunition, have been sent to him from here, and his serene highness declares that he will shed the last drop of his blood in defense of Moscow, and that he is ready to fight even in the streets. Brothers, do not be surprised that the courts of justice have ceased to transact business; it was best to send them to a place of safety, but the evil-doer shall have a taste of the law all the same. When the crisis comes, I shall want some gallant fellows, from both town and country. I shall utter my call a day or two before, but it is not necessary yet. I hold my peace. An ax is a good weapon; a boar-spear is not bad, but best of all is a three-tined pitchfork; a

Frenchman is no heavier than a sheaf of rye. To-morrow, after dinner, I shall take the Iverskaya to the Yekaterininskaya Hospital, to the wounded. There we will bless the water; they will all the sooner get well, and I now am well; I have had a bad eye, but now I see out of both."

"But military men," said Pierre, "have told me that it was perfectly impossible to fight in the city, and that the position ...."

"Well, yes, that is just what we were talking about," interrupted the first chinovnik.

"But what does he mean by saying: 'I have had a bad eye, but now I see out of both'?" asked Pierre.

"The count has had a stye," replied the aide, with a smile, "and he was very much disturbed when I told him that people were calling to ask what was the matter with him. But how is it, count?" said the aide, abruptly, addressing Pierre, with a smile. "We have heard the rumor that you have some domestic tribulations.... that the countess, your wife ...."

"I have heard nothing," replied Pierre, indifferently; "what have you heard?"

"Oh, well, you know, stories are often invented. I am only saying what I heard."

"But what have you heard?"

"Well, they say," replied the aide, with the same smile, "that the countess, your wife, is about to go abroad. Of course, it is all nonsense ...."

"Perhaps so," said Pierre, heedlessly glancing around. "But who is that?" he asked, referring to a short old man in a clean blue coat, and with an enormous beard as white as the driven snow, eyebrows the same, and a florid complexion.

"He? That's a merchant: that is, he is the tavern-keeper Vereshchagin. — Perhaps you have heard that story about the proclamation?"

"Ah! and so that is Vereshchagin," exclaimed Pierre, gazing into the old merchant's calm, self-reliant face, and trying to discover in it any characteristics of a traitor.

"Yes, that is the very man. That is, he is the father of the one who wrote the proclamation," said the aide. "The young man is in jail, and it looks as if it would go hard with him."

A little old man with a star, and another official, a German, with a cross suspended around his neck, joined the group.

"You see," proceeded the aide with his story, "it is a puzzling piece of business. This proclamation appeared a couple of months back. It was brought to the count. He ordered it investigated. Gavrilo Ivanuitch here looked into it; this proclamation passed through as many as sixty-three hands. We go to a certain man: 'Whom did you get this from?'.... 'From so-and-so.'.... Off to him: 'Whom did you get this from?' and so on, till it was traced to Vereshchagin — an ignorant little merchant. They ask him: 'Whom did you have this from?' And here you must understand that we know whom he got it from; from no one else than the director of posts. There had been for some time connivance between them. But he says: 'I didn't get it from any one. I wrote it myself.' They threatened and entreated; he stuck to it — wrote it himself. Well, now, you know the count," said the aide, with a proud, gay smile. "He flew into a terrible rage, but just think of it, — 'such cunning, falsehood, and stubbornness'!".....

"Ah! the count wanted them to implicate Kliucharef, I understand," said Pierre.

"Not at all," said the aide, startled. "They had sins enough to lay against Kliucharef without this; that was why he was sent away. But the truth of the matter was, that the count was very indignant..... 'How could you have written it?' asked the count. He picked up from the table this Hamburg paper. 'Here it is. You did not write it, but you translated it, and you translated it atrociously, because even in French you are an idiot, don't you know?'.... Now, what do you think?'.... 'No,' says he, 'I have never read any papers, I composed it.'.... 'Well, if that is so, you are a traitor and I will have you tried and hanged. Confess! from whom did you receive it?'.... 'I have never seen any papers. I composed it myself!'.... And so it hung fire. The count called the father also. He stood by his own. And they handed him over to the court, and, it seems, they condemned him to penal labor. Now the father has come to intercede for him. But what a wretched chap! You know the kind.... these merchants' sons, a regular macaroni! a seducer! got a few lessons, and thinks himself a shade better than any one else.[1] That is the kind of a fellow he is. And his father keeps an inn there by the Kamennoï Bridge.... you know there's a big picture of Almighty God, who is represented with a scepter in one hand and the imperial globe in the other.... well, he took this picture home for a few days, and what do you think he did? He found a beastly painter who.... "

CHAPTER XI

In the midst of this new anecdote, Pierre was summoned to the governor-general.

Pierre went into Count Rostopchin's cabinet. Rostopchin, scowling, was rubbing his forehead and eyes with his hand as Pierre entered. A short man was saying something, but as Pierre approached he stopped and left the room.

"Well, how are you, mighty warrior?" exclaimed Rostopchin, as soon as this man had gone. "We have heard about your gallantry. But that is not to the point just now. My dear, *entre nous*, are you a Mason?" asked Count Rostopchin in a stern tone, as if there were something wrong in that, but that he was ready to grant his forgiveness.

Pierre made no reply.

"*Mon cher*, I have been told, but I know that there are Masons and Masons, and I hope that you don't belong to that set who, under the appearance of saving the human race, are doing their best to ruin Russia."

"Yes, I am a Mason," replied Pierre.

[1] Literally: "thinks that the devil is not his brother any more."

"Well, then, look here, my dear, I think that you are not ignorant of the fact that Messrs. Speransky and Magnitsky have been sent somewhere into exile; the same thing has happened to Mr. Kliucharef, and the same thing has happened to others besides, who, under the appearance of erecting Solomon's temple, have been trying to overturn the temple of their country. You can understand that there are reasons for this, and that I could not have sent off the director of posts here if he had not been a dangerous man. Now I am informed that you provided him with a carriage to take him from the city, and also that you received from him papers for safe-keeping. I like you and I do not wish you ill, and, as I am more than twice your age, I advise you as a father to cut short all dealings with this sort of people, and to leave Moscow as speedily as possible."

"But wherein, count, was Kliucharef to blame?" asked Pierre.

"That is my affair to know, and not yours to ask me," cried Rostopchin.

"He was accused of having circulated Napoleon's proclamation, but it was not proved against him," said Pierre, not looking at Rostopchin; "and Vereshchagin ...."

"That is just the point," interrupted Rostopchin, scowling suddenly, and speaking much louder than before. "Vereshchagin is a traitor and a renegade, who has received the punishment which he richly deserves," said Rostopchin, with that heat and ugliness characteristic of men at the recollection of an insult. "But I did not summon you to criticize my actions, but to give you some advice, or a command if you prefer that term. I beg of you to cut short your dealings with such gentlemen as Kliucharef and to leave town. I'll knock the folly out of any one, no matter who it is;" but, apparently discovering that he was almost shouting at Bezukhoï, who was not as yet in any respect to blame, he added in a mixture of French and Russian, cordially seizing Pierre's hand, "We are on the eve of a public disaster, and I have no time to make civil speeches to all who come to see me. My head is sometimes in a whirl..... Now then, my dear, what are you doing .... you personally ? "

"Nothing at all," replied Pierre, not lifting his eyes and not altering the expression of his thoughtful face.

The count frowned.

"Take the advice of a friend, my dear. Decamp, and as soon as possible; that is all that I have to say to you. Fortunate is he who has ears to hear. Good-by, my dear. Oh, here," he shouted, as Pierre was about to leave the room, "is it true that the countess has fallen into the paws of the *saints pères de la Société de Jésus?*"

Pierre made no reply, and scowling, and angry as he had never been seen before, he left Rostopchin's.

When he reached home it was already dark. Eight different people came to see him that evening, — the secretary of a committee, the colonel of his battalion, his overseer, his majordomo, and several petitioners. All had business with Pierre which he was obliged to settle. Pierre could not understand at all, he was not interested in such matters, and he gave only such replies to all questions as would soonest rid him of these people.

At last, when he was left alone, he broke the seal of his wife's letter, and read it.

"*They* — the soldiers in the battery; Prince Andrei killed .... the old man .... simplicity is submission to God. Suffering is necessary .... the significance of things .... must take apart and analyze .... my wife is going to take another husband .... one must forget and learn ...."

And, going to his bed, he threw himself down without undressing, and immediately fell asleep.

When he awoke the next morning, his majordomo came to inform him that a police officer had come directly from Count Rostopchin to find whether Count Bezukhoï had gone or was going.

A dozen different persons who had business with Pierre were waiting for him in the drawing-room. Pierre made a hasty toilet, but, instead of going down to those who were waiting for him, he went down by the back steps and thence out through the gates.

From that time forth until after the burning of Moscow, no one of Bezukhoï's household, in spite of all their search for him, saw anything more of Pierre or knew what had become of him.

CHAPTER XII

THE Rostofs remained in the city up to the thirteenth of September, the day before the enemy entered Moscow.

After Petya had joined Obolyensky's Cossack regiment, and gone to Byelaya Tserkov, where this regiment was recruiting, a great fear came upon the countess. The thought that both of her sons had gone to the war, that both had left the shelter of her wing, that to-day or to-morrow either one of them, or perhaps even both of them, might be killed, as had been the case with the three sons of a friend of hers, for the first time now this summer recurred with cruel vividness to her mind.

She endeavored to induce Nikolaï to come home to her; she herself wanted to go to Petya, to send him to some place of safety in Petersburg; but both schemes seemed impracticable. Petya could not be recalled unless his regiment should be recalled, or unless he should be transferred to some other working regiment. Nikolaï was off somewhere with the army, and since his last letter, in which he described his meeting with the Princess Mariya, nothing had been heard from him.

The countess could not sleep nights, and even when she dozed she saw in her dreams her sons slain.

After many plans and discussions, the count at last found a means of consoling the countess's apprehensions. He had Petya transferred from Obolyensky's regiment to Bezukhoï's, which was mobilizing near Moscow. Although Petya remained in the military service, still the countess by this transfer had the consolation of seeing at least one of her sons, as it were, under her wing, and she cherished the hope of arranging matters so that he would not be sent away any more, and would always be assigned to such places in the service that he would not be exposed in battle.

As long as Nicolas alone was in danger, it seemed to the countess — and it even caused her a pang of remorse — that she loved her eldest more than her other children; but when her youngest, the mischievous, badly-trained Petya, who was forever breaking things in the house, who was always in everybody's way, this snub-nosed Petya with his merry dark eyes, his fresh, ruddy complexion, and the down just beginning to cloud his cheeks, went off *yonder*, to mingle with terrible, coarse, grown-up men, who were fighting, and finding a real pleasure in doing such things, — then it seemed to the mother that she loved him more, far more than all of her children. The nearer the time came for her rapturously awaited Petya to return to Moscow, the more the countess's uneasiness increased; she even began to imagine that she should never attain that happiness. The presence not only of Sonya, but even of her beloved Natasha, even her husband's presence, irritated the countess.

"What do I care for them? I want no one else but Petya," she would say to herself.

Early in September the Rostofs received a second letter from Nikolaï. He wrote from the government of Voronezh, where he had been sent after horses. This letter did not calm the countess. In spite of her assurance that one of her sons was out of danger, she began to worry all the more about Petya.

Although almost all the Rostofs' acquaintances had left Moscow, even as early as the first of September, although they all tried to persuade the countess to start as soon as possible, she would not hear to such a thing as going until her treasure, her idolized Petya, should return.

Petya came on the ninth of September. The sixteen-year-old officer was not pleased by the morbidly passionate affection with which his mother welcomed him. Although she hid from him her purpose not to let him fly again from under her maternal wing, Petya fathomed her thoughts, and instinctively fearing lest he should be too soft, and a "mamma's pet" (as he himself expressed it), he treated his mother coldly, avoided her, and during his stay in Moscow devoted himself exclusively to Natasha, for whom he had always cherished a peculiarly brotherly affection, almost as chivalrous as a lover's.

When the ninth of September arrived, thanks to the count's characteristic slackness, nothing was as yet ready for the journey, and the carts which they expected from their estate at Riazan and their pod-Moskovnaya to convey from the city all their movable property did not arrive until the twelfth.

From the ninth until the twelfth of September, all Moscow was in a stir and ferment of excitement. Each day there poured past the Dorogomilovskaya barrier, and scattered through the city, thousands of those who had been wounded in the battle of Borodino, and thousands of teams, laden with the inhabitants and their belongings, passed out through the other barriers.

In spite of Rostopchin's placards, or independently of them, or in direct consequence of them, the strangest and most contradictory rumors were current throughout the city. One said that no one would be permitted to depart; another, on the contrary, declared that the ikons had been removed from the churches, and that all the inhabitants were to be sent away, whether they would or not. One said that, since Borodino, there had been another battle, in which the French had been beaten; another declared, to the contrary, that the whole Russian army had been annihilated. One said that the Moscow militia, together with the clergy, had started for Tri Gorui; another whispered that Avgustin had been forbidden to go away, that traitors had been caught, that the peasantry were in revolt and were attacking those who started, and so on, and so on.

But these were merely rumors, and in substance both those who fled and those who were left — although this was even before the council at Fili, when it was definitely decided to abandon Moscow — all felt, even though they did not express it, that Moscow would assuredly be abandoned, and that they must make all haste to pack up and save their effects.

There was a feeling that everything was about to go to pieces, and that a sudden change was imminent, but up to the thirteenth no change ensued. Just as a criminal, led out to punishment, knows that he is about to be killed, but still looks around and straightens his ill-fitting cap, — so Moscow involuntarily pursued its habitual life, although it knew that the time of its destruction was at hand, when all the conventional conditions of its existence would be suddenly snapped short.

During those three days preceding the occupation of Moscow by the French, all the Rostof family were absorbed in their various worldly occupations. The chief of the family, Count Ilya Andreyitch, was constantly flying about the city, picking up on all sides the flying rumors, and while at home making superficial and hasty arrangements for hastening their departure.

The countess superintended the packing of the things, but she was in a sad state of dissatisfaction with every one, and kept tagging after Petya, who avoided her, and she was devoured by jealousy of Natasha, with whom he spent all his time.

Sonya was the only one who looked after the practical side of affairs : the packing of the things. But Sonya had been peculiarly melancholy and silent of late. The letter in which Nicolas had spoken of the Princess Mariya had caused the countess to express in her presence the most joyful auguries : she declared that in the interview of Nicolas and the Princess Mariya she saw God's providence.

" I never felt happy at all," said the countess, " when Bolkonsky was engaged to Natasha, but I always wished that Nikolinka might marry the princess, and I had a presentiment that it would turn out so. And how good that would be ! "

Sonya felt that this was true, that the only possibility

of retrieving the fortunes of the Rostofs was for Nikolaï "to make a rich marriage," and that the princess was an excellent match.

But still it was very bitter to her. In spite of her grief, or possibly in consequence of it, she took upon her all the difficult labor of arranging for packing up and stowing away, and was busy from morning till night.

The count and countess addressed themselves to her when they had any orders to give.

Petya and Natasha, on the other hand, not only did not help their parents, but for the most part were a hindrance and a burden to all in the house. And almost all day long the house echoed with their footsteps dancing about, their shouts and merry laughter. They laughed and enjoyed themselves, not because there was any reason for laughter, but their hearts were full of life and joy, and because everything that they heard seemed to them a reason for laughter and gayety.

Petya was gay because, having left home a lad, he had returned — as every one told him — a gallant young hero ; he was gay because he was at home, because he had come from Byelaya Tserkov, where there had been not even a remote prospect of taking part in a battle, and had come to Moscow, where any day they might have fighting ; and above all he was gay because Natasha, to whose moods he always was very susceptible, was gay also.

Natasha was gay because she had been melancholy quite too long, and now nothing reminded her of the reason of her previous melancholy, and she was well ! Moreover, she was gay because there was a man who flattered her — flattery was an absolutely essential lubricant if her machinery was to move with perfect freedom — and Petya flattered her.

Chiefly they were gay because the war had come to the very gates of Moscow, because there was a possibility of fighting at the barriers, because they were giving out guns, because there were running about and departures this way and that, because some great event was in the very air, and this is always provocative of good spirits in men, especially in the young.

CHAPTER XIII

On Saturday, the eleventh of September, everything in the Rostofs' house seemed topsy-turvy. All the doors were open, all the furniture was carried off or out of place, mirrors and paintings were taken down. The rooms were full of packing-boxes and littered with hay, wrapping-paper, and pieces of twine. Muzhiks and household serfs trod over the parquetry floors with heavy steps as they lugged the things. In the dvor there was a throng of peasants' carts, some of which were already loaded and corded up, and some still empty.

The voices and footsteps of the enormous retinue of servants and of the muzhiks who had come with the teams rang through the house and the court.

The count had been out since early morning. The countess, who had a headache as a consequence of all the bustle and noise, was lying down in the new divan-room, her head wrapped up in vinegar compresses. Petya was not at home; he had gone to see a comrade with whom he proposed to change from the militia into the regular army. Sonya was busy in the dining-room, packing up the glassware and china.

Natasha was sitting on the floor, in her own dismantled room, amid a heap of dresses, laces, and ribbons, and holding lifelessly in her hands an old ball-dress — the very one — how out of style it was! — which she had worn to her first Petersburg ball. Her conscience pricked her for doing nothing while all the rest in the house were so busy, and several times since morning she had tried to take hold and help; but her heart was not in the work, and she could not and would not do anything at all, unless she could do it with all her heart, with all her might.

She had started to assist Sonya in packing the china, but soon desisted and went to her room, to dispose of her own things. At first she found it very good fun to distribute her dresses and ribbons among the maids;

but afterwards, when what was left had to be really packed up, it began to bore her.

"Dunyasha, you will put them in for me, that's a darling![1] won't you?"

And when Dunyasha willingly agreed to do it all for her, Natasha sat down on the floor, and picked up her old ball-dress, and she began to think of something very different from what ought now to have occupied her. She was aroused from the brown study into which she had fallen by the chatter of the maids in the adjoining room, and by the sounds of their hurried steps as they ran from this room toward the rear of the house. Natasha got up and looked out of the window.

An enormous train of wounded men had come to a halt in the street.

The maids, the lackeys, the housekeeper, the old nurse, the cooks, the coachmen, the postilions, the scullions, all were standing at the gates, gazing at the wounded.

Natasha, throwing a white handkerchief over her hair, and holding the ends with both hands, ran down into the street.

The former housekeeper, the old Mavra Kuzminishna, broke through the crowd collected at the gates, and, going up to a cart shaded by a reed cover, entered into conversation with a pale young officer, who was stretched out in it. Natasha advanced a few steps, and stood timidly, still holding her handkerchief, and listening to what the old "keywoman" said.

"Well, I suppose you haven't any kith or kin in Moscow, have you?" asked Mavra Kuzminishna. "You would be so much more comfortable in a room somewhere.... here, for instance, in our house. The folks are going off."

"I don't know as it would be permitted," replied the officer, in a feeble voice. "There's our commander, yonder — you see?" and he indicated a stout major, who was walking back along the street, past the line of carts.

[1] *Galubushka.*

Natasha, with startled eyes, looked into the wounded officer's face, and immediately went to meet the major.

"Can some of the wounded be taken into our house?" she asked.

The major, with a smile, raised his hand to his vizor.

"What would you like, mamzel?" he asked, squinting his eyes, and smiling.

Natasha calmly repeated her question, and her face and her whole manner, although she still kept hold of the ends of her handkerchief, were so serious, that the major ceased to smile; and, after first stopping to consider, as if he were asking himself how far this were admissible, at last gave her an affirmative answer.

"Oh, yes, certainly they can," said he.

Natasha bowed slightly, and returned, with swift steps, to Mavra Kuzminishna, who was still standing by the officer, and talking with him with compassionate sympathy.

"They can, he said they could," whispered Natasha.

The covered cart in which the officer was lying was driven into the Rostofs' yard, and a dozen carts, with their loads of wounded, by invitation of the inhabitants, were taken in at different yards and driven up to the steps of the houses on the Povarskaya Street.

Natasha was evidently pleased by having something to do with new people, remote from the ordinary conditions of life. She and Mavra Kuzminishna made as many more of the wounded come into the dvor as possible.

"Still, we must ask your papasha," Mavra Kuzminishna said.

"Not at all, not at all; what difference can it possibly make? Just for one night, we could sleep in the drawing-room. We can let them have all our rooms."

"What queer notions you do have, young lady! Even if we gave them the wing and the unfinished rooms, we should have to ask permission!"

"Well, I will go and ask."

Natasha ran into the house, and on tiptoes passed through the half-open door of the divan-room, where there was a strong scent of vinegar and Hoffmann's drops.

"Are you asleep, mamma?"

"Oh! how can I sleep?" said the countess, waking from a doze into which she had dropped.

"Mamma, darling,"[1] said Natasha, kneeling before her and leaning her cheek close to her mother's, "I am sorry; forgive me for waking you up, I will never do it any more. — Mavra Kuzminishna sent me .... some wounded men have been brought here, some officers. Will you let them come in? They don't know where to take them; I know you will let them come," said she, hurriedly, without stopping to breathe.

"What officers? Who has been brought here? I don't understand at all!" said the countess.

Natasha began to laugh; the countess responded with a feeble smile.

"I knew that you would let them come .... well, then, I will go and tell them," and Natasha, kissing her mother, jumped up, and hurried off.

In the hall she met her father, who had come home with bad tidings.

"Here we are still!" cried the count, with involuntary vexation. "The club is already closed, and the police are going."

"Papa, it does not make any difference, does it? I have invited some wounded men to be brought in?" asked Natasha.

"Why, of course not," said the count, distractedly. "But that's not the trouble. I beg of you to have done with trifling, and to help get packed up, so we can go, go, go to-morrow."

And the count proceeded to give the majordomo and all the servants the same order.

Petya came back to dinner, and communicated his budget of news.

He told how that day the people had got arms at the Kreml, that, though Rostopchin had declared he would give the alarm two days in advance, still there was no

---

[1] *Galubchik.*

question that he had ordered the whole populace to go
out fully armed the next day to Tri Gorui, and that
there was going to be a great battle there.

The countess, with timid dismay, looked at her son's
bright, excited face while he was saying this. She knew
that if she said a word that might be interpreted as asking
Petya not to go to that battle — for she knew that his heart
was full of joy at the prospect of such a battle — then
he would have something to say about *men*, about *honor*,
about the *fatherland* — something so absurd, so like a
man, so contrary to all reason — against which there
was no reply to be made, and her hopes would be dashed ;
and therefore trusting so to arrange it as to attain
her end, and take Petya with her, as her defender and
protector, she said nothing to him, but, after dinner,
called the count aside, and with tears besought him to
start as soon as possible, that very night if it were possible. With the feminine, artless cunning of love, she
who till then had boasted of her absolute freedom from
timidity declared that she should die of alarm, if she
did not go that very evening.

There was no pretense about it : she was really afraid
of everything.

CHAPTER XIV

MADAME SCHOSS, who had been over to her daughter's,
still more enhanced the countess's fear by her account
of what she had seen in Miasnitskaya Street, at a wine-
shop. As she was returning along the street, her way
home was blocked by a throng of the drunken populace,
surging around the shop.

She took an izvoshchik and came home by a round-
about route, and the izvoshchik had told her that the
crowd had been staving in the casks in the wine-shop,
and that they had been permitted to do so.

After dinner all the household of the Rostofs, in a
perfect transport of zeal, set themselves to the task of
packing up their effects and preparing for the departure.

The old count, suddenly taking a hand in affairs, from dinner-time forth ceased not to trot back and forth between the dvor and the house, incoherently shouting to the hurrying servants, and urging them to still greater haste. Petya remained in the dvor, giving orders there. Sonya knew not what to do under the count's contradictory orders, and entirely lost her head. The men, shouting, scolding, and making a fearful racket, hastened through the rooms and bustled about in the courtyard.

Natasha, with that zeal that was so characteristic of her, suddenly also put her hand to the work. At first her interference with the task of packing was resented. All that was ever expected of her was quips, and now they were in no mood for such things; but she was so earnest and eager in claiming their submission to her will, she was so grave, and came so near weeping because they would not listen to her, that at last she won the victory and their confidence.

Her first achievement, which cost her enormous efforts and gave her the power, was the packing of the rugs. The count had in his house some precious Gobelins and Persian carpets. When Natasha first put her hand to the work two great chests stood open in the ball-room; one was filled almost to the top with china, the other with rugs. There was still a great quantity of china standing about on the tables, and they were bringing still more from the store-rooms. It was necessary to begin still a third fresh packing-case, and some of the men had been sent after one.

"Sonya, wait, we can get it all in as it is," said Natasha.

"Impossible, baruishnya! it has been tried already," said the butler.

"No, wait and see, please."

And Natasha began rapidly to take out of the packing-case the plates and dishes wrapped up in paper.

"The platters must be put in there with the rugs," said she.

"But there are rugs enough as it is for all three of the boxes!" exclaimed the butler.

"Now wait, please." And Natasha began swiftly and skilfully to unpack. "Those are not needed," said she of some Kief-ware plates. "But those are to be put in with the rugs," said she of some Dresden dishes.

"There, now, let it alone, Natasha; there, that 'll do, we 'll get it packed!" exclaimed Sonya, reproachfully.

"Ekh! baruishnya!" exclaimed the majordomo. But Natasha would not yield; she took out everything and proceeded rapidly to pack them up again, deciding that there was no need at all of taking the cheap, ordinary carpets and the superfluous tableware.

When everything was taken out they began to pack up again. And in fact after everything of little value which it was not worth while to take with them had been removed, all that had any value could be put into the two packing-cases. But it was found impossible to close the lid of the box that held the rugs. It could be done by taking out one or two things, but Natasha was bound to have it done in her own way. She arranged the things, and rearranged them, pressed them down, and compelled the butler and Petya, whom she called in to help her pack, to sit on the cover, and she herself put forth all her strength with the energy of despair.

"There, that's enough, Natasha," said Sonya; "I see you are right, only take out the top one."

"I don't wish to," cried Natasha, with one hand pushing back her disheveled locks from her sweaty face and pressing down the rugs with the other. "Now press down, Petya, push! Vasilyitch, keep pressing down!" cried she. The rugs gave way and the cover was shut.

Natasha, clapping her hands, actually squealed with delight, and the tears gushed from her eyes. But this lasted only a second. She immediately applied herself to something else, and by this time they had begun to repose the most implicit confidence in her; even the count was not indignant when he was informed that Natalya Ilyinishna had countermanded some order of his, and the household serfs came to her to ask: Should they cord up the loads or not, or was not the team full enough? Thanks to Natasha's clever management great progress was made in the work; articles of little account were left out, and the most precious things were packed in the most practical form possible.

But, in spite of the efforts of all the people, the labor of packing was not completed that night, though they worked till late. The countess went to bed, and the count, deferring the start till morning, also retired.

Sonya and Natasha, without disrobing, went to sleep in the divan-room.

That night another wounded man had been brought through the Povarskaya, and Mavra Kuzminishna, who happened to be standing down by the gates, had him brought into the Rostof house. This wounded man, according to Mavra Kuzminishna, was evidently a man of great distinction. He was carried in a calash entirely covered with the apron and with the hood let down. On the box with the driver sat a very dignified old valet. The calash was followed by a team with the doctor and two soldiers.

"Come into our house, come in. The folks are all going; the whole house will be deserted," said the old woman, addressing the aged servant.

"Well," said the valet, sighing, "we did not know where to take him. We have our own house in Moscow, but it's far off and no one in it."

"We beg it as a favor; our folks have always a houseful, so please come," said Mavra Kuzminishna. "What! is he very bad?" she added.

The valet spread open his hands.

"We did not know as we could get him here. I must ask the doctor." And the valet sprang down from the box and went to the other team.

"Very good," said the doctor.

The valet returned to the calash, looked into it, shook his head, bade the driver turn into the dvor, and he himself remained standing by Mavra Kuzminishna.

"Merciful Saviour!"[1] she exclaimed.

[1] *Gospodi Iisuse Khriste!* Lord Jesus Christ!

Mavra Kuzminishna invited them to carry the wounded man into the house.

"The folks won't say anything," she went on. But it was necessary to avoid carrying him up-stairs, and therefore the wounded man was taken into the wing and placed in the rooms formerly occupied by Madame Schoss.

The wounded officer was Prince Andreï Bolkonsky!

CHAPTER XV

THE last day of Moscow dawned.

It was bright, inspiriting autumn weather. It was Sunday. Just as on ordinary Sundays, the bells on all the churches rang for mass. It seemed as if even now no one realized what was coming upon Moscow.

Only two symptoms of the crisis in society showed the position in which Moscow was placed : the rabble, that is to say, the poorer classes, and the prices of commodities. Factory operatives, household serfs, and muzhiks in a portentous throng, wherein mixed and mingled officials, seminarists, noblemen, had early that morning gone out to Tri Gorui. Having reached there, they did not wait for Rostopchin, but, coming to the conclusion that Moscow was to be abandoned, this mob scattered through Moscow, among the wine-shops and *traktirs*, or taverns.

Prices that day also indicated the posture of affairs. The prices for weapons, for gold, for teams and horses, kept going higher and higher, while the prices for paper money and for city luxuries kept depreciating, so that by the middle of the day there were instances of costly wares like cloth being carried off by izvoshchiks for nothing, while as high as five hundred rubles were paid for a muzhik's horse; but furniture, mirrors, and bronzes went begging.

In the dignified old house of the Rostofs', the overturn of the former conditions of existence found very feeble expression. As far as the servants were concerned, it only happened that during the night three out of all the enormous retinue ran away; but nothing was stolen, and the prices of things were well shown by the fact that the thirty teams brought from the country represented an enormous fortune, which many men coveted, and for which tremendous offers were made to the Rostofs.

Although great sums of money were offered for these teams, nevertheless, during the evening of the twelfth and on the morning of the thirteenth of September, there was a constant stream of denshchiks, and other servants, sent by wounded officers, as well as the wounded men themselves who had been accommodated at the Rostofs' and at neighboring houses, begging the Rostofs' servants to obtain for them these teams so that they could escape from Moscow.

The majordomo, to whom these men applied with such petitions, although he pitied the wounded, gave a decided refusal, declaring that he should not dare to propose such a thing to the count. However hard it was to leave the wounded behind, it was self-evident that, if one team were given up, there would be no reason for refusing another, and another, and finally all their teams and even their private carriages. Thirty teams would not save all the wounded, and, in the universal calamity, it was out of the question that each person should not think of himself and his family first. Thus the majordomo thought in behalf of his barin.

On waking up on the morning of the thirteenth, Count Ilya Andreyitch softly left his chamber, so as not to arouse the countess, who had fallen asleep only toward morning, and in his lilac-colored silk dressing-gown went down to the front steps.

The teams, ready loaded, stood in the yard. The traveling-carriages were at the door. The majordomo was standing by the entrance, conversing with an elderly denshchik, and a pale young officer with his arm in a sling. The majordomo, seeing the count, made a stern and significant sign to the officer and the man, that they should go.

"Well, is everything ready, Vasilyitch?" asked the

count, rubbing his bald spot, and looking good-naturedly at the officer and the man, and nodding to them. The count was fond of new faces.

"About ready to hitch up, your illustriousness."

"Well, that is excellent! But here, the countess will soon be awake, and then God speed us.[1] — Well, sir?" said he, turning to the officer. "You will make yourself at home in my house, will you?"

The officer drew nearer. His pale face suddenly flushed a brilliant crimson.

"Count, do me the favor, ... allow me .... for God's sake .... let me creep into one of your wagons. I have no luggage with me here .... I would as soon go in the cart .... "

The officer had not finished speaking, before the man came up to the count, to prefer the same request in behalf of his master.

"Oh, yes, yes, yes," cried the count, hastily. "I am very, very glad. Vasilyitch, you make the arrangements; have one or two of the telyegas unloaded .... say that one yonder .... well .... any one that seems most advisable .... " said the count, couching his orders in vague phrases.

But at the same instant the eager expression of gratitude on the officer's face confirmed him in his determination. The count glanced around: the courtyard, the gates, the windows of the wing, were all crowded with wounded men and their attendants. The eyes of all were riveted on the count, and they were coming toward the steps.

"Please, your illustriousness, come into the picture-gallery; what do you wish done in regard to the pictures?" asked the majordomo.

The count went with him into the house, at the same time repeating his injunctions not to refuse any of the wounded who begged to be taken.

"There, now, something can be unloaded," he added, in a low, mysterious voice, as if he feared some one would overhear him.

[1] *S Bogom.*

At nine o'clock the countess awoke, and Matriona Timofyevna, her former lady's-maid, who now exercised in the countess's behalf the duties of chief of police,[1] came to inform her old mistress that Marya Karlovla was greatly incensed, and that it was an impossibility for the young ladies' summer dresses to be left behind!

When the countess made inquiries why Madame Schoss was incensed, it appeared that her trunk had been taken from the cart, and that they were unloading all of the teams ; that they were making ready to take on and carry away with them the wounded whom the count, in his simple-hearted kindness, had promised to rescue.

The countess had her husband summoned.

"What does this mean, my love? I hear they are unloading the things again."

"You see, *ma chère*, ... I was going to tell you, *ma chère* grafinyushka .... the officer came to me .... and begged me to let them have a few of the teams for the wounded. Of course, this is all worth a good deal, but how could we leave them behind? Just think! .... It's a fact, they're in our yard .... we invited them in. .... You see, I think .... we really ought, *ma chère* .... so now, *ma chère* .... let 'em go with us .... what is the hurry, anyway?" ....

The count spoke timidly, as he always did when there was any money-transaction on foot. The countess was accustomed to this tone, which always preceded any project that was going to eat up his children's fortunes, as for instance the starting a picture-gallery, new orangeries, the arrangement of private theatrical performances, or music ; and she was accustomed, and had long considered it her duty, to oppose anything that was suggested in this tone of voice.

She put on her set, tearful face, and said to her husband : —

"Listen, count ; you have brought things to such a pass that we are n't worth anything, and now all our property — *our children's* — all that's left — you want

---

[1] *Shef zhendarmof.*

to make way with. Why, you yourself said that what was in the house was worth a hundred thousand! I will not consent, my love, I will not consent! Do as *you* please! It's for the government to look after the wounded. They know it. Look across the street there at the Lopukhins'; everything was carried off clean three days ago. That's the way men do! We alone are idiots! If you don't have any pity on me, at least remember your children!"

The count made a gesture with his hands, and, saying nothing further, left the room.

"Papa! what is the matter?" asked Natasha, who had followed him to her mother's room.

"Nothing! none of your concern!" replied the count, testily.

"No, but I heard what you were saying," said Natasha. "Why isn't mamenka willing?"

"What business is it of yours?" cried the count.

Natasha went to the window and pondered. "Papenka! Berg has come!" said she, looking out of the window.

CHAPTER XVI

BERG, the count's son-in-law, was now a colonel, wearing the Vladimir and the Anna around his neck, and occupied in the same pleasant and sinecure post, as assistant to the chief of the staff of the assistant chief of staff of the first division of the second corps.

On the thirteenth of September he drove in to Moscow from the army.

There was nothing to call him to Moscow, but he had observed that all were asking leave of absence to go to Moscow and seemed to have private business there. He considered it essential for him also to go and inquire after his wife's family and affairs.

Berg drove up to his father-in-law's house in his elegant little drozhsky drawn by a pair of plump roans, exactly like those belonging to a certain prince. He gave a keen look at the teams drawn up in the court; and, as he came to the steps, he took out a clean handkerchief and tied a knot in it.

Berg passed from the anteroom into the drawing-room with slow, dignified steps, and embraced the count, and kissed Natasha's hand, and Sonya's, and made haste to inquire after his mamasha's health.

"Who thinks about health nowadays? Tell us," said the count, "tell us about the army. Will they retire or will there be another battle?"

"The Everlasting God, papasha," said Berg, "can alone decide the fate of the fatherland. The army is afire with the spirit of heroism, and even now the leaders, so to speak, are collected in council. What will be is not known. But I can tell you in general, papasha, the heroic spirit, the truly antique valor, of the Russian army, which they — I mean it " — he corrected himself — "showed, or rather displayed, in that battle of the seventh instant, words are not sufficient to describe. I tell you, papasha," — here he gave himself a slap on the chest, just as he had seen a general do in telling this story, though he was rather late in bringing it in effectively, because he should have given himself the slap on the chest at the words *Russian troops* — "I will tell you frankly that we, the leaders, not only were not obliged to urge on the soldiers or do anything of the sort, but, rather, we found it hard work to restrain their ardor — their, their — yes, their gallant and antique onslaughts," said he, eloquently. "General Barclay de Tolly exposed his life everywhere in front of the troops, I tell you! Our corps was posted on the slope of a hill. You can imagine!"

And here Berg related all that he remembered of the various reports that he had heard at the time.

Natasha did not take her eyes from him, which confused Berg, for she seemed to be searching his face for the answer to some question.

"Such heroism as was displayed by the Russian troops in general, it is impossible to imagine or to praise sufficiently," said Berg, glancing at Natasha, and smiling in answer to her fixed look, as if he was anxious to win her good graces. "Russia is not in Moscow, she is in the hearts of her sons. Isn't that so, papasha?" asked Berg.

At this moment the countess came out from the divan-room with a weary and dissatisfied face. Berg sprang up, kissed her hand, inquired after her health, and, expressing his sympathy by a shake of the head, remained standing by her side.

"Yes, mamasha, I will tell you frankly these are melancholy, trying times for every Russian. But why be so disturbed? There is still time for you to get away safely"....

"I don't understand what the servants are up to," said the countess, addressing her husband. "I have just been told that not a thing is ready yet. You see how necessary it is for some one to take full charge. Now here we really miss Mitenka. There will never be any end to it!"

The count was about to make some reply, but evidently restrained himself. He got up from his chair and went to the door.

Berg just then took out his handkerchief as if to blow his nose, and, catching sight of the knot that he had tied, grew thoughtful and shook his head in a melancholy and significant manner.

"I have a great favor to ask of you, papasha," said he.

"Hm?".... returned the count, stopping short.

"I was just passing Yusupof's," said Berg, with a laugh. "The overseer, who is an acquaintance of mine, came running out, and urged me to buy something. I went in just out of curiosity, and there I found a pretty little chiffonnier [1] and toilet. You know how Vierushka has always wanted one, and how we have actually quarreled over it." — Berg involuntarily took a tone of self-congratulation over his comfortable little establishment, as he began to speak about the chiffonnier and the toilet. — "And it is such a beauty! It is full of drawers, and has an English secret panel, don't you know! And Vie

[1] *Shifonyerotchka.*

rotchka had wanted one so long! And so I wanted to surprise her. I saw you had so many of these muzhiks in the yard. Let me have one, please. I will pay him handsomely, and...."

A frown passed over the count's face, and he began to clear his throat.

"Ask the countess; I am not giving the directions."

"If it is inconvenient, no matter about it," said Berg. "Only I wanted it very much for Vierushka's sake."

"Akh! go to the devil — all of you, to the devil, to the devil, and to the devil!" cried the old count. — "My head is in a whirl!"

And he flew out of the room.

The countess burst into tears.

"Yes, indeed, mamenka, it is a very trying time!" said Berg.

Natasha followed her father out of the room, and at first started to go to him; but then, seeming to collect her thoughts, she hastened down-stairs.

Petya was standing on the steps, busy providing with arms the men who were to escort the family from Moscow. In the dvor the teams still stood corded up. Two of them had been unloaded, and in one the young officer had already taken his place, assisted by his denshchik.

"Do you know what the trouble was?" asked Petya of Natasha. Natasha understood that Petya referred to the dispute between their father and mother. She made no reply.

"Because papenka wanted to give up all the teams to the wounded!" said Petya. "Vasilyitch told me. In my opinion...."

"In my opinion," suddenly interrupted Natasha, almost screaming, and turning her wrathful face full upon Petya — "in my opinion, this is so mean, so shameful, so .... so .... I can't express it! Are we miserable Germans?"

Her throat swelled with convulsive sobs, and, fearing lest she should break down and waste the ammunition of her wrath, she turned on her heel and flew impetuously up-stairs.

Berg was sitting down near the countess, and trying, like a dutiful son, to console her. The count, with his pipe in his hand, was striding up and down, when Natasha, her face distorted with indignation, dashed into the room, and hurried to her mother with rapid steps.

"This is shameful! This is abominable!" she cried. "It cannot be that you have given such an order."

Berg and the countess looked at her in fear and bewilderment. The count paused by the window, and listened.

"Mamenka, it must not be! see what they are doing in the yard!" she cried. "They are to be left!"

"What is the matter? Who are to be left? What do you want?"

"The wounded men, that's who! It must not be, mamenka!.... This is not like you at all! No, mamenka, dearest little dove![1] Mamenka! what do we want of all those things that we are going to take away? only look out into the yard!.... Mamenka!.... This must not, cannot be." ....

The count still stood by the window without turning his face away, as he listened to Natasha's words.

Suddenly he blew his nose, and leaned over toward the window.

The countess gazed at her daughter, saw her face tinged with shame for her mother's sake, saw her agitation, understood now why it was her husband would not look at her, and then glanced around her with a troubled face.

"Akh! you may do as you please. Am I interfering with any one?" she exclaimed, not willing even yet to give in suddenly.

"Mamenka, dear little dove, forgive me!"

But the countess pushed her daughter away, and went over to the count.

"*Mon cher*, you give what orders are necessary. You see, I know nothing about this at all!" said she, guiltily dropping her eyes.

"The eggs.... the eggs are teaching the old hen,"

[1] *Galubushka.*

exclaimed the count through his happy tears, and he embraced his wife, who was glad to hide her face crimson with shame against his heart.

"Papenka, mamenka! Shall I give the orders? May I?" .... asked Natasha. "We will still take all that we really need," said Natasha.

The count nodded assent, and Natasha, with the same swift steps with which she would run when she used to play *goryelki*, or tag, flew across the room into the anteroom, and down-stairs into the courtyard.

The men gathered around Natasha, and they would not put any faith in the strange command which she gave them, until the old count himself came down, and, in the name of his wife, ordered them to give up all the wagons to the wounded, and to carry the boxes and trunks back to the storerooms.

After they had comprehended the meaning of the order, the men with joyful eagerness addressed themselves to the new task. This did not any longer seem strange to the menials, but, on the contrary, it seemed to them that it could not be ordered otherwise; just the same as, a quarter of an hour before, it did not seem strange to any one that the wounded men were to be left and the things carried away, but seemed to them that it could not be ordered otherwise.

All the household, as if grieved because they had not got at this work more expeditiously, took hold of it with a will, and made place for the wounded. The wounded men dragged themselves down from their rooms, and their pale faces lighted up with joy as they gathered around the teams.

The rumor spread to the adjoining houses that the teams were going to start from the Rostofs', and still more of the wounded came crowding into the Rostofs' yard from the other houses.

Many of the wounded begged them not to remove all the things, but simply to let them sit on top. But the work of unloading having once begun, it could not stop. It was a matter of indifference whether all the things were left or only half of them. The courtyard was littered up with the unladen chests and boxes full of china, bronzes, paintings, mirrors, which had been so carefully packed up the night before, and still the work went on of taking off this thing and that, and giving up one team after another.

"We can take four more," said the overseer. "Here, I will give up my team! but then, what should I do with them?"

"Well, give them the one that has my trunks," said the countess; "Dunyasha can sit with me in the carriage."

So they gave up also the wardrobe wagon,[1] and let the wounded from two neighboring houses have the use of it. All the household and the servants were full of happy excitement. Natasha had risen to a state of enthusiastically happy emotion such as she had not experienced for a long time.

"How shall we tie this on?" asked some of the men, who were trying to fasten a chest on the narrow footboard of one of the carriages. "We ought to give up a whole team to it!"

"What does it contain?" asked Natasha.

"The count's books."

"Leave it, Vasilyitch will take care of it. We don't need them."

The britchka was full; there was some question where Piotr Ilyitch was to go.

"He can sit on the coachman's box. Get up there on the box!" cried Natasha.

Sonya was also indefatigably at work; but the object of her labors was diametrically opposed to the object of Natasha's. She was looking out for the things which had to be left behind, labeling them by the countess's desire, and doing her best to have as much taken as could be.

[1] *Garderobnaya povozka.*

CHAPTER XVII

By two o'clock, the four equipages of the Rostofs, loaded and packed, stood at the door. The teams with the wounded, one after the other, filed out of the gate. The calash in which Prince Andreï was carried passed in front of the entrance, and attracted the attention of Sonya, who was engaged with the maid in trying to arrange a comfortable seat for the countess in her huge, lofty coach, which stood at the door.

"Whose calash is that?" asked Sonya, putting her head out of the carriage window.

"Why, don't you know, baruishnya?" replied the maid. "It's the wounded prince; he spent the night at our house, and is also going with us."

"But who is he? What is his name?"

"It's our former lover, Prince Bolkonsky!" replied the lady's-maid, with a sigh. "They say he's going to die."

Sonya sprang out of the carriage and hastened to the countess. The countess, already dressed for the journey, in shawl and hat, was weariedly walking up and down through the drawing-room, waiting for the household to assemble so as to sit down, with closed doors, and have prayers read before setting forth on the journey. Natasha was not in the room.

"*Maman!*" exclaimed Sonya, "Prince Andreï is here! wounded and dying. He is going with us!"

The countess opened her eyes wide with terror, and, seizing Sonya's arm, looked around.

"Natasha!" she exclaimed.

Both for Sonya and for the countess this news had at the first moment only one significance. They knew their Natasha, and the horror at the thought how this news would affect her crowded out all sympathy for the man whom they both loved.

"Natasha does not know it yet; but he is going in our party," said Sonya.

"Did you say he was dying?"

Sonya bent her head.

The countess threw her arms around Sonya and burst into tears.

"The ways of the Lord are past finding out!" she said to herself, with the consciousness that in everything that was then taking place an All-powerful Hand was in control of what had been concealed from the eyes of men.

"Well, mamma, all is ready. — What is the matter with you?" asked Natasha, suddenly coming into the room, with flushed and eager face.

"Nothing," said the countess. "If we are ready, then let us be off."

And the countess bent over to her reticule, in order to hide her disturbed face. Sonya hugged Natasha and kissed her.

"What is the matter? What has happened?"

"Nothing .... noth...."

"Something wrong, and about me? What is it?" asked the sensitive Natasha.

Sonya sighed, and made no reply.

The count, Petya, Madame Schoss, Mavra Kuzminishna, and Vasilyitch came into the room, and, shutting the door, all sat down, and remained for some seconds in silence, not exchanging glances.

The count was the first to rise, and, drawing a loud sigh, he began to cross himself toward the holy pictures. All did likewise. Then the count began to embrace Mavra Kuzminishna and Vasilyitch, who were to be left in Moscow, and while they fondled his hand and kissed him on the shoulder, he lightly patted them on the back, muttering some vague, affectionately consoling phrases.

The countess went to the oratory, and Sonya found her there on her knees in front of the "images," which were left here and there on the wall. The most precious images, as family heirlooms, had been taken down and carried off.

On the stairs and in the yard, the men who were to accompany the teams, furnished with daggers and sabers, delivered out to them by Petya, and with their trousers tucked into their boots, and their coats tightly girt around them with girdles and belts, were exchanging farewells with those who were to stay behind.

As always happens at starting on a journey, many things were forgotten or not properly packed; and the two haïduks had been long standing on either side of the open door, by the carriage steps, ready to help the countess in, while the maids were bustling about with cushions and parcels to stow away in the coaches and the calash and the britchka.

"They are forever and forever forgetting something!" exclaimed the countess. "Now see here. You know I can't sit that way." And Dunyasha, setting her teeth together, and making no reply, though an expression of indignation contracted her face, flew into the carriage to rearrange the cushions.

"Akh! what a set of people!" exclaimed the count, shaking his head.

The old coachman, Yefim, with whom alone the countess would consent to travel, sitting high on his box, did not even deign to glance around at what was going on behind him. He knew by thirty years' experience that it would be still some time before they said to him their "*S Bogom* — Let us be off" — and that, even after the order to start was given, he would still be stopped two or three times, while they sent back for things forgotten; and that even then he would be stopped again, and the countess herself would thrust her head out of the window, and ask him in the name of Christ the Lord — *Khristom Bogom* — to drive more cautiously down the slopes. He knew this, and therefore, with even greater patience than his horses, — especially more than the off chestnut, Sokol,[1] which stood pawing with his hoofs, and champing his bit, — he waited for what should be.

At last all were in their places; the steps were done up, the door shut with a bang, a forgotten box sent for, the countess put her head out and made the stereotyped remark. Then Yefim deliberately removed his hat from

[1] Hawk.

his head, and proceeded to cross himself. The postilion and all the people did the same. "*S Bogom* — God with us," cried Yefim, as he put on his cap. "Off we go!"

The postilion cracked his whip. The near pole-horse strained on the collar, the lofty springs creaked, and the great coach swayed. As it started, the footman leaped up on the box. The carriage went jolting along as it rumbled out from the dvor upon the uneven pavement; the other vehicles also followed jolting along, and the procession turned up the street. All in the carriages, the calash, and the britchka crossed themselves as they passed the church opposite. The servants remaining in Moscow followed on both sides of the street, escorting them.

Natasha had rarely known such a feeling of keen delight as she experienced now, sitting in the coach, next the countess, and gazing out at the walls of abandoned, excited Moscow slowly moving past. She from time to time put her head out of the window and gazed forward and back at the long string of wagons containing the wounded accompanying them. Almost at the very front of the line she could see Prince Andreï's covered calash. She did not know who was in it, and yet every time when she surveyed their train her eyes turned instinctively to this calash. She knew that it was at the front.

A number of carriage trains like the Rostofs' had turned out into Kudrina Street, from Nikitskaya, from Preisen, from Podnovinsky, and when they reached the Sadovaya there were already a double row of vehicles and trains moving along.

As they passed the Sukharef tower, Natasha, glancing with curiosity at the throng of people coming and going, suddenly uttered an exclamation expressive of delight and amazement.

"Ye saints![1] Mamma! Sonya! look, there he is!"

"Who? who?"

"Look! for pity's sake,[2] Bezukhoï!" exclaimed Natasha, putting her head out of the carriage window, and

[1] *Batiushki.*   [2] *Yeï Bogu.*

staring at a tall, stout man in a coachman's kaftan —
evidently a gentleman in disguise, to judge by his gait
and carriage — who was walking along with a sallow,
beardless little old man in a frieze cloak under the arch
of the Sukharef tower.

"Indeed,[1] it's Bezukhoï, in the kaftan, walking with a
little old man! Indeed it is!" exclaimed Natasha.
"Look! look!"

"Why, no! It can't be. How can you say such
absurd things!"

"Mamma!" cried Natasha, "I'll wager my head that
it is he. I assure you it is. Stop! stop!" she cried to
the coachman. But the coachman could not stop, because a whole file of wagons and vehicles came in from
Meshchanskaya, and shouted to the Rostofs to drive on
and not delay the others.

But, although he was now at a much greater distance
from them all, the Rostofs now recognized Pierre, or the
man in the coachman's kaftan that looked like Pierre,
pacing along the street with dejected head and solemn
face, side by side with the little beardless man who had
the appearance of a footman. This little old man remarked the face thrust forth from the carriage-window
and trying to attract their attention, and he respectfully
nudged Pierre's elbow, and said something to him, pointing to the carriage.

It was some time before Pierre realized what he said,
he seemed to be so deeply sunken in thought. At last,
when his attention was roused, he looked in the indicated
direction, and, recognizing Natasha, gave himself up for
a second to the first impression and ran nimbly over to
the carriage.

But, after taking a dozen steps, some thought, apparently, struck him, and he paused.

Natasha put her head out of the window and beamed
with a sort of quizzical affectionateness.

"Piotr Kiriluitch, come here! You see, we recognized
you. This is marvelous!" she cried, giving him her
hand. "What does this mean? Why are you so?"

[1] *Yeï Bogu.*

Dan:
you do
get this
one don't
you?!?

"What did I say, Boris?...These new uniforms
are a crock!"

Pierre took the proffered hand, and, as he walked along, — for the carriage was still moving, — he awkwardly kissed it. "What is the matter with you, count?" asked the countess, in a voice expressing amazement and sympathy.

"I .... I .... Why? .... don't ask me," said Pierre, and he glanced at Natasha, whose eyes, beaming with delight, — he felt them even though he did not look into them, — overwhelmed him with their charm.

"What are you going to do? stay behind in Moscow?"

Pierre made no reply.

"In Moscow?" he repeated questioningly. "Yes, in Moscow. Farewell."

"Akh! I wish I were a man, I would certainly stay behind with you. Akh! how nice that would be!" exclaimed Natasha. "Mamma, if you will let me, I will stay."

Pierre gave Natasha an absent look, and was about to say something, but the countess interrupted him.

"We heard you were in the battle."

"Yes, I was," replied Pierre. "To-morrow, there is to be another battle...." he began to say, but Natasha interrupted him.

"What is the matter with you, count? You are n't like yourself."....

"Akh! don't, don't ask me, don't ask me, I myself don't know. To-morrow .... but no! Farewell, farewell," he went on. "Terrible times!" and, moving away from the carriage, he passed along on the sidewalk.

Natasha for a long while still kept her head out of the window, beaming on him with an affectionate and somewhat quizzical smile of joy.

CHAPTER XVIII

PIERRE, during the two days since his disappearance from home, had been living in the late Bazdeyef's deserted rooms.

This was how it happened.

On waking up the morning after his return to Moscow and his interview with Count Rostopchin, it was a long time before Pierre could realize where he was and what was required of him. When he was informed that among those who were waiting to see him in his reception-room there was the Frenchman who had brought him the letter from the Countess Yelena Vasilyevna, there suddenly came over him that feeling of embarrassment and hopelessness to which he was peculiarly prone.

It all at once came over him that everything was now at an end, that ruin and destruction were at hand, that there was no distinction between right and wrong, that there was no future, and that there was no escape from this condition of things. With an unnatural smile on his lips, and muttering unintelligible words, he first sat down awhile on his divan; then he got up, went to the door, and looked through the crack into the reception-room; then, making a fierce gesture, he tiptoed back and took up a book. The majordomo came for the second time to tell Pierre that the Frenchman who had brought the letter from the countess was very anxious to see him, "if only for a little minute," and that a messenger had come from I. A. Bazdeyef's widow to ask him to come for the books, since Madame Bazdeyeva had herself gone to the country.

"Oh, yes, immediately .... wait .... or no, no .... go and say that I will come immediately," said Pierre to the majordomo.

But, as soon as the majordomo had gone, Pierre took his hat, which lay on the table, and left his cabinet by the rear door. There was no one in the corridor. Pierre passed along the whole length of the corridor to the stairs, and, scowling, and clasping his head in both hands, he went down to the first landing. The Swiss was standing at the front door. From the landing which Pierre had reached, another flight of stairs led to the rear entrance. Pierre went down this and came out into the yard. No one had seen him. But on the street, as soon as he left the gates, the coachmen waiting with their equipages, and the dvornik, or porter, saw the count, and took off their hats to him. Conscious of their glances fastened on him, Pierre acted like an ostrich which hides its head in the sand so as not to be seen; he dropped his head, and, hastening his steps, ran out into the street.

Of all the business which faced Pierre that morning, the business of assorting Iosiph Alekseyevitch's books and papers seemed to him most needful.

He took the first izvoshchik that happened to come along, and ordered him to drive to the Patriarch's Pools,[1] where the widow Bazdeyeva lived. As he kept glancing about on all the caravans of people, making haste to escape from Moscow, and balanced his obese frame so as not to be tipped out of the rickety old drozhsky, Pierre experienced the same sort of reckless enjoyment felt by a truant boy. He entered into conversation with the driver.

The driver informed him that arms had been that day distributed to the populace in the Kreml, and that on the morrow they were all going out to the Tri Gorui barrier, and that a great battle would take place there.

On reaching the Patriarch's Pools, Pierre had to make some little search for Bazdeyef's house, as he had not been there for some time. He approached the wicket door. Gerasim, the same sallow, beardless little old man whom Pierre had seen five years before at Torzhok, with Iosiph Alekseyevitch, came out at his knock.

"Any one at home?" asked Pierre.

"Owing to present circumstances, Sofya Danilovna and her children went yesterday to their Torzhok country-seat, your illustriousness."

"Nevertheless, I will come in; I must assort the books," said Pierre.

"Do, I beg of you; the brother of the late lamented — the kingdom of heaven be his! — Makar Alekseyevitch — is left here, as you will deign to know — he is very feeble," said the old servitor.

[1] *Patriarshiye Prudui.*

Makar Alekseyevitch was, as Pierre well knew, Iosiph Alekseyevitch's half-witted brother, who was addicted to drink.

"Yes, yes, I know. Come on, come...." said Pierre, and he entered the house.

A tall, bald, red-nosed old man, in a dressing-gown, and with galoshes on his bare feet, was standing in the reception-room. When he saw Pierre he testily muttered something, and shuffled off into the corridor.

"He once had great intellect, but now, as you will deign to observe, he has weakened," said Gerasim. "Would you like to go into the library?"

Pierre nodded assent.

"The library remains just as it had been left, with seals on everything. Sofya Danilovna gave orders that if you sent any one they were to have the books."

Pierre went into the same gloomy cabinet into which, during the Benefactor's life, he had gone with such trepidation. It was now dusty, and had not been touched since Iosiph Alekseyevitch's death; it was gloomier than ever.

Gerasim opened one of the shutters, and left the room on his tiptoes. Pierre crossed the floor, went to one of the bookcases in which manuscripts were kept, and took out one of the most important of the documents of the order at that time. These were some of the original acts of the Scotch branch, with observations and explanations in the Benefactor's handwriting.

He took a seat at the dust-encumbered writing-table, and spread the manuscripts in front of him, opened them, then shut them, folded them up, and, finally, pushing them away, rested his head on his hands and fell into deep thought.

Several times Gerasim cautiously came and looked into the library, and found Pierre still in the same attitude. Thus passed more than two hours. Gerasim permitted himself to make a little stir at the door so as to attract his attention; Pierre heard him not.

"Do you wish me to send away the driver?"

"Akh! yes," said Pierre, starting from his reverie

and hastily jumping to his feet. — "Listen," he added, taking Gerasim by his coat-button, and looking down on the little old man with glittering, humid eyes, full of enthusiasm — "Listen, do you know that to-morrow there is to be a battle?"

"They say so," replied Gerasim.

"I beg of you not to tell any one who I am. And do what I tell you." ....

"I will obey," replied Gerasim. "Do you wish something to eat?"

"No, but I want something else. I want a peasant's dress and a pistol," said Pierre, unexpectedly reddening.

"I will obey," said Gerasim, after thinking a moment.

All the rest of this day Pierre spent alone in the Benefactor's library, restlessly pacing from one corner of the room to the other, as Gerasim could hear, and sometimes talking to himself, and he spent the night in a bed made ready for him there.

Gerasim, with the equanimity of a servant who has seen many strange things in his day, accepted Pierre's residence without amazement, and seemed well satisfied to have some one to wait on. That same evening, without even asking himself what was the reason therefor, he procured for Pierre a kaftan and hat, and promised on the following day to get the pistol that he wished.

Makar Alekseyevitch, twice that afternoon, shuffling along in his galoshes, came to his door and halted, looking inquisitively at Pierre. But, as soon as Pierre turned round to him, he wrapped his dressing-gown around him with a look of injured annoyance, and hastily made off.

Pierre, dressed in his coachman's kaftan, procured and refitted for him by Gerasim, and accompanied by the old man, was on his way to get the pistol at the Sukharef tower, when he fell in with the Rostofs.

CHAPTER XIX

On the night of September 13, Kutuzof's order for
the Russian troops to retire through Moscow to the
Riazan highway was promulgated.

The vanguard moved in the night. The troops marching at night took their time and proceeded slowly and
in good order; but at daybreak the troops that reached
the Dorogomilovsky Bridge saw in front of them, on
the other side, endless masses of troops, packed together,
hurrying across the bridge and toiling along the street
and avenues, blocking them up, while others were pressing on them from the rear.

And an unreasonable haste and panic took possession
of the troops. The whole mass struggled forward to
the bridge, and across the river by the bridge, by the
fords, and by boats. Kutuzof gave orders to be driven
round by back streets to the other side of Moscow.

By ten o'clock on the morning of the fourteenth, only
some of the troops of the rear-guard were left, with
ample room in the Dorogomilovsky suburb. The bulk
of the army was by that time fairly on the other side of
Moscow and beyond Moscow.

At this time — ten o'clock on the morning of September 14 — Napoleon stood, surrounded by his troops, on
the Poklonnaya Hill, and gazed at the landscape opened
out before him.

From the seventh until the fourteenth of September
— from the battle of Borodino until the entry of the
enemy into Moscow — every day of that anxious, of
that fateful, week was distinguished by unusual autumn
weather, which always fills people with surprise, when
the sun, though moving low, burns more fiercely than
in the spring; when every object stands out in the thin,
clear atmosphere, dazzling the eye; when the lungs expand and are refreshed by taking in the fragrant autumn air; and when, during the mild dark nights, golden
stars slip from the skies — a constant source of terror
and delight.

On September 14, at ten o'clock in the morning, the weather was still the same. The brilliancy of the morning was enchanting. Moscow, from the Poklonnaya Hill, was spread out spaciously, with its river, its gardens and churches, and, as it seemed, still alive with its own life, with its cupolas palpitating like stars in the rays of the sun.

At the sight of this strange city, with the fantastic forms of its unusual architecture, Napoleon experienced that somewhat envious and uneasy curiosity which men are wont to experience at the sight of unusual forms of a foreign life, such as they have never known. Apparently, this city was alive with all the energy of its special life. By those vague signs whereby even at a distance one can infallibly distinguish a live body from a corpse, Napoleon, from the top of the Poklonnaya Hill, could feel the palpitation of life in the city, and felt, as it were, the breathing of that mighty and beautiful body.

Every Russian, looking at Moscow, feels that she is his *mother;* every foreigner, looking on her, even though he cannot appreciate this feeling for the motherhood of the city, must feel the feminine character of this city, and Napoleon felt it.

"*Cette ville asiatique aux innombrables églises, Moscou la Sainte. La voilà donc enfin, cette fameuse ville ! Il était temps.* — There she is at last, this Asiatic city with its numberless churches — Holy Moscow. It was time !" said Napoleon, and, dismounting, he commanded to have spread before him the plan of that Moscow, — and he had his interpreter, Lelorme d'Ideville, summoned.

" *Une ville occupée par l'ennemi ressemble à une fille qui a perdu son honneur,*" he said to himself, repeating the remark that he had made to Tutchkof at Smolensk. And it was as a "deflowered virgin" that he looked on this Oriental beauty, never seen before by him, now lying prone at his feet. Strange it was to himself that at last his long desire, which had seemed impossible, was to be gratified. In the clear morning light, he contemplated now the city and then the plan, and studied the characteristics of this city, and the certainty that he should possess it excited him and filled him with awe.

"Could it have been otherwise?" he asked himself. "Here she is — this capital at my feet, awaiting her fate. Where now is Alexander, and what thinks he now? Strange, beautiful, magnificent city! And how strange and splendid this moment!"

And then thinking of his warriors, he said to himself, "In what a light I must appear to them! This is the reward for all these men of little faith," he mused, as he gazed about him on those who were near him, and at the troops coming up the hill and falling into line.

"One word from me, one movement of my hand, and destroyed is the ancient capital of the tsars. *Mais ma clémence est toujours prompte à descendre sur les vaincus.* I must be magnanimous and truly great. — But, no, it can't be true that I am at Moscow ...." this doubt suddenly occurred to him. "Yet there she lies, at my feet, her golden cupolas and crosses gleaming and palpitating in the rays of the sun. But I will show mercy to her! On yon ancient memorials of barbarism and despotism I will inscribe the mighty words of justice and mercy.... this will be the most cruel thing of all to Alexander; I know him." (It seemed to Napoleon that the principal significance of what had taken place lay in the settlement of his personal dispute with Alexander.) "From the heights of the Kreml .... yes, that Kreml yonder .... yes, I will grant him the laws of justice, I will show him the meaning of true civilization. I will compel the generations of boyars to remember with affection the name of their conqueror. I will tell the deputations that I have had, and still have, no desire for war, that I waged war only on the false policy of their court, that I love and reverence Alexander, and that I will grant conditions of peace in Moscow worthy of myself and my peoples. I have no desire to take advantage of the fortunes of war to humiliate an esteemed monarch. 'Boyars,' I will say to them, 'I have no wish for war;

my desire is for the peace and prosperity of my subjects.'
However, I know that their presence will inspire me,
and I will speak to them as I always speak, clearly,
triumphantly, and majestically. But can it be true that
I am at Moscow? Yes, lo! there she is. ....

"*Qu'on m'amène les boyards* — Have the boyars
brought to me," he said, addressing his suite.

A general with a brilliant staff instantly galloped off
after the boyars.

Two hours passed. Napoleon ate his breakfast, and
then took up his position on the same spot on the Poklonnaya Hill, and waited for the deputation. His speech
with the boyars was already clearly outlined in his fancy.
This discourse should be full of dignity, and of that
grandeur which Napoleon understood so well.

Napoleon himself was fascinated by this tone of magnanimity which he fully intended to use toward Moscow.
In his fancy he named a day for a reception in the
palace of the tsars — at which all the Russian grandees
would mingle with the grandees of the French emperor.
He mentally named a governor, such a one as would be
able to influence the population in his favor. As he
happened to know that Moscow had many religious
establishments, he decided, as he thought it over, that
all these institutions should experience his bounty. He
thought that just as in Africa he was bound to put on a
burnoose and attend a mosque, so here in Moscow he
must be gracious after the manner of the tsars. And,
in order completely to win the hearts of the Russians, he,
like every Frenchman, unable to conceive any sentiment
without some reference to *ma chère, ma tendre, ma
pauvre mère*, he decided that on all these establishments he should order to be inscribed in great letters: *ÉTABLISSEMENT DÉDIÉ À MA CHÈRE MÈRE:*
"no, simply, *MAISON DE MA MÈRE*," he decided in
his own mind. "But am I really at Moscow? Yes,
there she is before me; but why is it that the deputation of the citizens is so long in appearing?" he
wondered.

Meantime, in the rear ranks of the emperor's suite, a

whispered and excited consultation was taking place among his generals and marshals. Those who had been sent to drum up a deputation returned with the tidings that the city was deserted, that all had departed or were departing from Moscow. The faces of the generals grew pale and anxious. They were not frightened because Moscow was abandoned by its inhabitants, — serious as that event might well appear to them, — but they were afraid of the responsibility of explaining the fact to the emperor; how, how could it be done without exposing his majesty to that terrible position which the French call *ridicule*, to explain to him that he had vainly waited for the boyars all this time, that there was a throng of drunken men in the city, and that was all!

Some declared that it was necessary, in the circumstances, to get up a deputation of some sort or other; others combated this notion and insisted that they must tell the emperor the truth, after first skilfully and cautiously preparing his mind for it.

"We must tell him, nevertheless," said the gentlemen of the suite. "*Mais, messieurs....*"

The position was all the more difficult from the fact that the emperor, now that he had fully considered his schemes of magnanimity, was patiently pacing back and forth before the plan of the city, looking from time to time, with hand shading eyes, down the road to Moscow, and smiling with gayety and pride.

"*Mais c'est impossible!*" exclaimed the gentlemen of the suite, shrugging their shoulders, and not venturing to pronounce the terrible word which all understood: *le ridicule*.

Meantime, the emperor, wearied of his fruitless waiting, and, by his quick, theatrical instinct, conscious that the "majestic moment," by lasting too long, was beginning to lose its majesty, waved his hand.

A single report of a signal-gun rang forth, and the troops which inclosed Moscow on all sides moved toward Moscow by the Tverskaya, Kaluzhskaya, and Dorogomilovskaya barriers. Swifter and swifter, one after another, at double quick or on galloping steeds, moved the troops, hidden in clouds of dust raised by their trampling feet, and making the welkin ring with the commingling roar of their shouts.

Carried away by the movement of the troops, Napoleon rode along with them to the Dorogomilovskaya barrier, but there again he paused, and, dismounting, walked for a long time down the Kammerkolezhsky rampart, in expectation of the deputation.

CHAPTER XX

Moscow meantime was deserted.

There were still people there; five-sixths of all the former inhabitants were still left, but it was deserted. It was deserted just in the same sense as a starving beehive which has lost its queen bee.

In the queenless hive, life has practically ceased, but at a superficial view it seems as much alive as others.

Just as merrily in the bright rays of the midday sun the bees hum around the queenless hive, just as they hum around the other living hives; the honey smell is carried just as far away; the bees make their flights from it just the same. But it requires only a glance into it to understand that there is no longer any life in that hive. The bees do not fly in the same way as from the living hives. The bee-master recognizes a different odor, a different sound. When he taps on the walls of such a hive, instead of that instantaneous, friendly answer which had been the case hitherto, the buzzing of ten thousand bees, lifting their stings threateningly, and the swift fanning of wings producing that familiar, airy hum of life, he is answered by an incoherent buzzing, a faint rumbling in the depths of the empty hive.

From the apertures comes no more, as formerly, that fine, winy fragrance of honey and pollen, nor wafts thence that warm breath of garnered sweets, but the odor of the honey is mingled with the effluvium of emptiness and decay.

No more you find at the entrance the guardians of

the hive, trumpeting the alarm, curling up their stings, and making ready to perish for the defense of the swarm.   No more that equable and gentle murmur of palpitating work, like the sound of bubbling waters, but instead you hear the incoherent, fitful buzz of disorder. Back and forth around the hive, coyly and cunningly, fly the black, oblong, honey-coated plunderer bees ; they sting not, rather they slip away from peril.   Before, they never flew in unless they were laden, but when they flew out again they were stripped of their burden of bee-bread ; now they fly off laden with honey.

The bee-master opens the lower compartment and looks into the bottom of the hive.   Instead of black bunches of juicy bees bustling with labor, clinging to one another's legs, and hanging down to the very *ūs* (as the bottom board of the hive is called), and with the ceaseless murmur of labor constructing the waxen walls, now stupefied, shriveled bees crawl here and there aimlessly across the floor and on the walls.

Instead of a floor neatly jointed with propolis and swept by winnowing wings, he sees it littered with crumbs of cells and bee-dirt, half-dying bees scarcely able to move their legs, and bees entirely dead and left unscavengered.

The bee-master opens the upper compartment and looks at the top of the hive.

Instead of compact rows of bees filling all the cells of the honeycomb and warming the larvæ, he sees, to be sure, the artistic, complex edifice of the comb, but no longer in that state of perfection which it had shown before.   All is neglected and befouled.   Dusky robber wasps make haste to thrust their impertinences stealthily among the works ; his own bees, shriveled, curled up, withered, as if old age had come upon them, languidly crawl about, disturbing no one, wishing for naught, and balked of all consciousness of life.   Drones, bumble-bees, beetles, and bee-moths come blundering in their flight against the walls of the hive.   Here and there among the cells filled with honey and dead larvæ can be heard occasionally an angry *briuzhzh ;* now and then a pair of bees, through old custom and instinct, try to clear out the cell, and, zealously exerting all their feeble forces, drag forth the dead bee or dead drone, themselves not knowing why they do so.

In another corner two aged bees lazily fight, or clean themselves, or feed each other, not knowing whether friendship or enmity impels them. In still a third place, the throng of bees, crowding one another, fall on some victim and strike and suffocate it. And there a weakened or injured bee falls slowly and lightly, like eiderdown, from above on the heap of the dead.

The bee-master breaks open some of the waxen cells, in order to see the brood. Instead of the compact black circles with thousands of bees crouched back to back and contemplating the lofty mysteries of generation, he sees hundreds of downcast, half-dead, unconscious skeleton bees. Almost all of them have died unconsciously, as they sat in the holy of holies, which they had been guarding, and which they now guard no more. From them arises the effluvium of decay and death.

Only a few of them stir feebly, try to lift themselves, fly indolently and settle on the hostile hand without strength left to sting it ere they die — the rest that are dead shower down like fish-scales.

The bee-master shuts up the compartment, puts a chalk mark on the stand, and, when the time comes, knocks it open and drains out the honey.

In the same way Moscow was deserted, when Napoleon, weary, uneasy, and in bad humor, walked back and forth at the Kammerkolezhsky ramparts, waiting for the deputation — a ceremony which, although one of mere show, he nevertheless affected to consider absolutely indispensable.

It was only out of thoughtlessness that in the various quarters of the city men still stirred about, keeping up the ordinary forms of life, and not themselves realizing what they were doing.

When at last Napoleon was informed, with proper circumlocution, that Moscow was deserted, he gave his informant a fierce look, and, turning away, continued his silent promenade.

"Have my carriage brought!" he said.

He took his seat in it by the side of his aide-de-camp and rode into the suburb.

"*Moscou déserté! Quel événement invraisemblable!* — How incredible!" he muttered to himself.

He did not enter the city proper, but put up at a hotel in the Dorogomilovsky suburb.

Le coup de théâtre avait raté — His theatrical climax had fallen through.

CHAPTER XXI

THE Russian troops poured across Moscow from two o'clock in the morning until two o'clock in the afternoon, and they had taken with them the last fleeing inhabitants and the wounded.

The largest division of the troops during the movement passed over the Kamennoï, Moskovoretsky, and Yauzsky bridges.

While they were flowing in two streams around the Kreml and over the two former, — the Stone and Moscow River bridges, — a tremendous mob of soldiers, taking advantage of the delay and crush, ran back from the bridge, and stealthily and noiselessly sneaked by Vasili Blazhennui [1] and through the Borovitskiya gates into the city, to the Krasnaya Ploshchad, or Red Place, where they knew, by their keen scent, that they might without much difficulty lay their hands on what did not belong to them.

A similar throng of men, as if in search of cheap bargains, also thronged the Gostinnui Dvor — Moscow's great bazaar — in all its alleys and passageways. But absent were the persistent, softly wheedling voices of the shopkeepers; absent the peddlers and the varie-

[1] Vasili Blazhennui, the many-bulbed, turreted, fasceted, and fantastic cathedral of Saint Basil, built by Ivan the Terrible, who, in order that it should not be reduplicated, is said to have had the architect's eyes put out.

gated throng of women purchasers. Nothing was to be seen but uniforms and the cloaks of weaponless soldiers, silently entering without burdens and returning to the ranks laden with spoil.

Merchants and bazaar-men — a few of them — ran about amongst the soldiers, like crazy men, opening and closing their shops, and themselves helping the gallant soldier lads to carry off their wares.

On the square in front of the Gostinnui Dvor stood drummers beating to arms, but the rattle of the drums had not its usual effect to call back the soldier plunderers, but on the contrary drove them to run farther and farther from its signal.

Among the soldiers, in the shops and the passageways, could be seen men in gray kaftans and with shaven heads.

Two officers, one with a scarf over his uniform, and riding a thin, dark-gray steed, the other in a cloak and on foot, stood at the corner of Ilyinka Street, engaged in conversation. A third officer dashed up to them.

"The general orders that they be all driven out instantly at any cost. Why, there was never the like of it seen! Half of the men have left the ranks. — Where are you going? — And you, too?" he cried, first to one and then to three infantry soldiers, who, without weapons, and holding up the tails of their overcoats, were sneaking past him to rejoin their ranks. "Halt, you dogs!"

"Yes, but please try to collect them," replied the other officer. — "You can't do it! the only way is to march more rapidly, and then the ones in the rear could n't drop out, that 's all."

"But how move faster, or move at all, when there 's a halt and a jam at the bridge? Why not post sentinels, and keep them from breaking ranks?"

"Forward and drive them out!" cried the senior officer.

The officer in the scarf dismounted, beckoned up the drummer, and went with him under the arch. A number of soldiers started away on the run. A merchant with red pimples on his cheeks, around his nose, and with an expression of cool, calculating composure on his oily face, came to the officer with all the haste compatible with his elegant dignity, and, wringing his hands : —

"Your nobility," said he, "do me a favor; give me your protection. As far as any small trifles go we shall be only too glad to accommodate you, you know .... if you please I will bring you some cloth instantly .... glad enough to give a gentleman a couple of rolls, it 's a pleasure to us because we feel .... but this, this is out-and-out robbery! Please! if they had only set a guard, or at any rate let us know in time to shut up ...."

A number of merchants gathered around the officer.

"Eh! it 's a waste of breath to whine like that!" said one of them, a lean man with a grave face. "Men with their heads off don't weep for their hair! — Let 'em have what they want!"

And he made an energetic gesture, and came to the officer's side.

"It 's fine talk for you, Ivan Sidoruitch!" exclaimed the first merchant, angrily. — "I beg of you, your nobility!"

"Fine talk!" echoed the lean man. "I have yonder three shops, and a hundred thousand worth of goods. How can we have protection when the troops are off? 'God's powers are not ours.'[1]"

"I beg of you, your nobility," persisted the first merchant, making a low bow. The officer stood in uncertainty, and his face showed his irresolution.

"But, after all, what affair is it of mine?" he suddenly cried, and went with swift strides toward the front of the line.

In one shop, that was open, resounded blows and curses, and, just as the officer reached the door, a man in gray coat and with shaven head was flung out violently.

This man, all doubled up, slunk past the merchants and the officers. The officer flew at the soldiers who

[1] *Bozhyu Vlast' nie rukami sklast'.*

were in the shop. But just at that instant the terrible yells of a tremendous throng were heard on the Mosko-voretsky Bridge, and the officer hurried across the square.

"What is it? What is the matter?" he demanded; but his comrade had already spurred off in the direction of the outcry, past Saint Basil's. The officer mounted and set out after him. When he reached the bridge he saw two cannon unlimbered, the infantry running along the bridge, several carts overturned, a number of frightened faces, and soldiers roaring with laughter.

Near the cannon stood a team drawn by a pair of horses. Behind the team, between the wheels, four greyhounds, with collars on, were leashed together. The team was loaded with a mountain of household effects, and on the very top, next a baby's high-chair with its legs turned up in the air, sat a peasant woman uttering the most piercing, piteous squeals.

The officer was told by his comrades that the yells of the throng and the woman's squeals arose from the fact that General Yermolof, when he rode up to this mob and learned that the soldiers were scattered about plundering the shops because of the crowd of citizens encumbering the bridge, had ordered the cannon to be unlimbered, and to clear the bridge as an example. The crowd, trying to escape, overturning the teams, running into each other, yelling desperately, had cleared the bridge; and the troops were allowed to proceed.

CHAPTER XXII

THE city proper, meantime, was deserted. Almost no one was on the streets. The house-gates and shops were all locked up. Here and there, in the vicinity of drinking-saloons, could be heard occasional shouts of revelry or drunken singing. Not a carriage passed along, and rarely were heard the steps of pedestrians.

In the Povarskaya it was perfectly still and deserted. The enormous courtyard of the Rostofs was littered with wisps of straw and the droppings of the horses; not a soul was visible.

In the house itself, abandoned with all its costly contents, two human beings were in the great drawing-room. These were the porter, Ignat, and the groom, Mishka, Vasilyitch's grandson, who had been left behind with the old man, in Moscow. Mishka had opened the clavichord, and was drumming on it with one finger. The porter, with his arms akimbo, and with a smile of self-satisfaction, was standing in front of the mirror.

"Wan't that smart? Hey? Uncle Ignat?" asked the lad, suddenly beginning to pound with both hands on the keys.

"Just listen!"[1] replied Ignat, the smile that answered his smile in the glass growing ever broader and broader with amazement.

"You unconscionable creatures! Aren't you ashamed of yourselves?" suddenly exclaimed the voice of Mavra Kuzminishna, who had stolen noiselessly into the room. "Eka! what a conceited simpleton, grinning at his own teeth! That's the way you take hold! There's nothing put away yon, and Vasilyitch clean beat out! Have done with this!"

Ignat, hitching up his belt, ceased to smile, and, submissively dropping his eyes, left the room.

"Little auntie,[2] I was playing very softly!" said the lad.

"I'll *softly* you! You little scamp!" cried Mavra Kuzminishna, shaking her fist at him. "Go, get ready the samovar for your granddad!"

Mavra Kuzminishna, whisking the dust from the clavichord, closed it, and with a heavy sigh left the drawing-room and locked the door behind her.

On reaching the dvor, Mavra Kuzminishna paused to consider where she should next turn her steps; whether to drink tea with Vasilyitch in the wing, or to the store-room to finish putting away what was still left to put away.

Swift steps were heard coming down the quiet street.

[1] *Ish tui.*   [2] *Tyotinka.*

The steps halted at the wicket gate; a hand rattled the latch, and tried to open it.

Mavra Kuzminishna went to the gate.

"Who is wanted?"

"The count, Count Ilya Andreyitch Rostof."

"Who are you?"

"An officer. I should much like to see him," said a pleasant, gentlemanly voice, a Russian voice.

Mavra Kuzminishna opened the wicket. And into the dvor walked a chubby-faced officer of about eighteen, with a strong family resemblance to the Rostofs.

"They have gone, batyushka. They were pleased to go yesterday afternoon," said Mavra Kuzminishna, in an affectionate tone.

The young officer, standing in the gateway, as if undecided whether to come in or to go away, clucked his tongue.

"Akh! what a shame!" he exclaimed. "I ought to have come yesterday..... Akh! what a pity!"....

Mavra Kuzminishna, meantime, had been attentively and sympathetically scrutinizing the familiar Rostof traits in the young man's face, and his well-worn cloak and the run-down boots that he wore.

"But what do you want of the count?" she asked.

"Now I declare!.... What can I do?" exclaimed the young man, in a tone of vexation, and took hold of the wicket with the intention of going away. Then he paused again irresolutely.

"You see," said he, suddenly, "I am a relative of the count's, and he has always been very good to me. Just look here, do you see?" — he glanced down at his cloak and boots with a frank, gay smile. — "And I'm getting out at elbows, and I have n't a copper; so I was going to ask the count...."

Mavra Kuzminishna did not allow him to finish speaking. "You just wait a wee minute,[1] batyushka!" said she. "Just one wee minute."

And the instant the young officer had let go of the latch, Mavra Kuzminishna turned about, and, with her

[1] *Minutotchka.*

old woman's gait, she rapidly waddled across the back of the dvor to the wing where her own rooms were.

While Mavra Kuzminishna was trotting off to her room, the officer walked up and down the dvor, dropping his head, contemplating his ragged boots, and slightly smiling.

"What a shame that I have missed my dear little uncle. But what a nice old woman! Where did she go to? And I should like to know what is the nearest way for me to reach my regiment; it must have got to the Rogozhskaya gate by this time," said the young officer to himself.

Mavra Kuzminishna, with a terrified and, at the same time, resolute face, and carrying in her hand a checkered handkerchief tied into a knot, came hurrying back from her room. Before she had gone many steps she untied the handkerchief, and took out of it a "white note" of twenty-five rubles assignats, and hastily handed it to the officer.

"If his illustriousness were at home, of course, he would help a relative, but as it is perhaps .... these times .... " Mavra Kuzminishna faltered, and grew confused; but the officer had no scruples, and showed no haste, but he grasped the bank-note, and thanked Mavra Kuzminishna.

"Christ be with you — *Khristos s vami, batyushka* — God save you!" exclaimed Mavra Kuzminishna, making a low obeisance, and going down to the gate with him.

The officer smiled as if amused at himself, and, shaking his head, started off down the deserted streets, almost at a run, in order to overtake his regiment at the Yauzsky Bridge.

But Mavra Kuzminishna stood long with tears in her eyes in front of the closed wicket gate, contemplatively shaking her head, and conscious of an unusual gush of motherly affection and pity for the young officer, whom she had never seen before.

CHAPTER XXIII

In an unfinished house, in the Varvarka, the lower part of which was occupied by a wine-shop, were heard drunken shouts and songs. On benches, by the tables, in the small filthy room, sat a dozen or more factory hands. All of them were tipsy, sweaty, with clouded eyes, and they were singing with wide, yawning mouths and bloated cheeks. They were singing, each on his own account, laboriously, with all their might and main, apparently not because they felt like singing, but simply to show that they were intoxicated and were on a spree.

One of them, a tall, fair-complexioned young fellow, in a clean blue *chuïka*, or peasant coat, was standing up as their leader. His face, with its delicate, straight nose, would have been handsome had it not been for the thin, compressed, constantly twitching lips, and the clouded, ugly-looking, unchanging eyes. He stood over them as they sang, and, apparently possessed by some fancy, he solemnly, and with angular motion, waved his white arm, bare to the elbow, while he tried to spread his dirty fingers to an unnatural extent. The young fellow's sleeve was constantly coming down, and he kept tucking it up again with his left hand, as if it were especially important to keep that white, blue-veined, restless arm entirely bare.

While they were in the midst of the song, the sound of a scuffle and of blows was heard on the steps leading to the entry. The tall young man waved his hand. "That'll do!" he cried imperatively; "a fight, boys!" and he, while still trying to keep his sleeves tucked up, hastened out to the steps.

The factory hands staggered after him. The factory hands, who had that morning been singing in the dram-shop under the leadership of the tall young fellow, had brought the tapster some hides from the factory, and exchanged them for wine. Some blacksmiths, from a neighboring smithy, hearing the rumpus in the dram-shop, and supposing that it had been violently broken open, thought that they would like to take a hand also.

A quarrel had ensued on the steps. The tapster was brawling with one of the smiths at the very door, and just as the factory hands arrived on the scene, this blacksmith tore himself free from the tapster, and fell face down on the sidewalk.

A second blacksmith forced his way into the door, and was pressing up against the tapster with his chest.

The young fellow with the sleeve rolled up, as he came out, dealt the obstreperous blacksmith a heavy blow in the face, and cried savagely : —

"Boys ! they 're killing ours ! "

By this time the first blacksmith had picked himself up, and dashing off the blood from his bruised face, he set up a lachrymose yell : —

"Police ! murder !.... A man killed ! Help ! "

"Oï batyushki ! they 're murdering a man ! There 's murder going on ! " screamed a woman, running out from the gates of the adjoining house. A throng of the populace collected around the bleeding blacksmith.

"Is n't it enough for you to plunder the people, and rob them of their last shirt," cried some voice, addressing the tapster, "but you have to kill a man ? You murderer ! "

The tall young fellow, standing on the steps, rolled his bleary eyes first on the tapster, then on the smiths, apparently trying to make up his mind which first he was in duty bound to take up the quarrel with.

"Murderer ! " he suddenly cried to the tapster. "Tie him, boys ! "

"I should like to see you tie me ! " yelled the tapster, defending himself against the men who started to lay hands on him ; and snatching off his cap, he flung it on the ground. As if this action had some mysterious, ominous significance, the factory hands who had surrounded the tapster paused irresolute.

"I 'm for order, brother, I understand very well. I 'm going for the police. You suppose I won't go ? All

rioting to-day was particularly forbidden!" cried the
tapster, picking up his cap.

"Come on, then, let's go!" and "Come on, then, let's
go!" cried first the tapster, and then the tall young
man, and they moved down the street, side by side.
The bloody-faced blacksmith fell in with them. The
factory hands and a motley crowd of people followed
them, talking and shouting.

At the corner of Moroséïka Street, opposite a great
house with closed shutters and a shoemaker's sign-
board on it, stood a score of journeymen shoemakers
with dismal faces — lean, weary-looking men, in khalats
and torn blouses.

"He ought to settle his men's accounts!" exclaimed
a thin master workman with a Jewish beard and knitted
brows. "But now he's sucked our very blood, and
thinks it's quits! He's led us by the nose, yes, he has
for a whole week. And now he's got us to the last
post, and has skipped himself."

When the master workman saw the bloody-faced man
and the crowd, he ceased speaking, and all the boot-
makers, with eager curiosity, joined the hurrying crowd.

"Where's the crowd going?"

"Why, everybody knows! We're going to the authorities!"

"Say! Is't true that ours is beaten?"

"You thought so, did you! See what the men's saying!"

Questions and answers were exchanged. The tapster, taking advantage of the growing mob, stepped
aside from the people, and returned to his dram-shop.

The tall young man, not noticing the disappearance
of his enemy the tapster, and waving his bare arm, went
on speaking vociferously, attracting general attention.
The crowd huddled close around him preëminently, supposing that he might be able to give some reasonable
answer to the questions that interested them all.

"He talk about order! talk about laws! Why, we
must depend on the authorities! Ain't I right, orthodox believers?" cried the tall young fellow, almost

noticeably smiling. "Does he think there ain't any authorities? How could we get along without authorities? If it were n't for them, why, we 'd .... there 'd be no end of plundering!"

"What empty talk!" cried some speaker in the crowd. " So they are going to desert Moscow, are they? They have been making fun of you, and you believed it all!.... How many of our soldiers are going? So you think they 'll let him in, do you? .... That 's what the authorities is for!.... Just listen to him! What baby talk he 's giving us!"

Such were the remarks made by the crowd as they pointed to the tall young fellow.

Near the walls of the Kitaï Gorod[1] another small knot of men were gathered around a man in a frieze cloak, who held a sheet of paper in his hands.

"The ukase! the ukase! He 's reading the ukase! he 's reading the ukase!" cried various voices in the throng, and the populace rushed toward the reader.

The man in the frieze overcoat was reading Rostopchin's "placard" of September eleventh. When the crowd gathered round him he became, as it were, confused, but, at the demand of the tall young fellow, who forced his way up to him, once more, with a slight tremor in his voice, he began at the beginning of the placard.

" *To-morrow morning early I am going to his serene highness the prince*," he read.

"His serene highness!" repeated the tall young fellow, triumphantly, with a smile on his lips, and a frown on his brow.

" *In order to talk things over with him, to act and to help the troops exterminate the villains. We 'll knock the wind out of them*," pursued the reader, and paused.

"Has he seen him?" cried the tall young fellow, tri-

---

[1] The so-called "China Town" of Moscow: "perhaps derived from Kataï-gorod in Podolia, the birthplace of Helena, mother of Ivan IV., who founded the Kataï of Moscow, inclosing the bazaars and palaces of the nobles, and separated from the Kreml by a vast space called the Red Place, or Place Beautiful." — A. RAMBAUD.

umphantly. "He's kept clear of him the whole distance!"

"*And we shall send these guests of ours to the devil.
I shall be back to dinner to-morrow, and will then set to
work and we'll give it to these rascals hot and heavy, and
wipe 'em out of existence.*" [1]

The final words were read by the reader amid utter
silence. The tall young fellow gloomily dropped his
head. It was evident that no one understood those final
words. Especially the sentence "I shall be back to dinner to-morrow" offended the good sense of the reader
and the hearers as well. The feeling of the populace
was pitched to a high key, and this was too simple and
unnecessarily commonplace; it was exactly what each
one of them might have said, and therefore what a
ukase emanating from the supreme authority had no
business to say.

All stood in melancholy silence. The tall young fellow pursed his lips and swayed slightly.

"Why not go and ask him?" .... "There is he himself!" .... "How would you ask him?" .... "Why not?"
.... "He will explain it to us."

Such were the remarks heard in different parts of the
crowd, and general attention was directed to the drozhsky of the chief of police, driving across the square accompanied by two mounted dragoons.

The chief of police had gone that morning by the
count's orders to set fire to the boats, and, as it happened, this errand had procured for him a goodly sum
of money which at that very moment was in his pocket.
When he saw a great throng of people hurrying toward
him, he commanded the driver to pull up.

"What is this crowd?" he shouted to the men who
came up timidly ahead of the others, and paused near
the drozhsky. "What is this crowd? I should like to
know," asked the chief of police, who had received no
answer.

"Your nobility, they ...." began the man in the frieze
cloak who had been the reader, "your nobility, they ....

[1] *Sdielayem, dedielayem i otdielayem.*

they have heard the most illustrious count's proclamation and are willing to serve, and they don't value their lives, and this is n't a riot at all, as the most illustrious count...."

"The count has not gone, he is in town, and arrangements will be made for you. Drive on — pashol...." cried he to the coachman. The crowd stood quietly pressing around those who had heard what the official said, and looking at the receding drozhsky.

Just then the chief of police glanced around in terror, said something to his coachman, and his horses were sent off at a sharper trot.

"Fooled, boys! Go for him!" cried the tall young fellow. .... "Don't let him escape!" .... "Make him give an account!" .... "Hold him!" cried various voices, and the men started on the run after the escaping drozhsky.

The crowd following the chief of police hurried along with a roar of voices to the Lubyanka.

"How is this? The gentry and the merchants have all gone off, and we are betrayed! What! are we dogs, that we are left?" was said by more than one in the crowd.

CHAPTER XXIV

On the evening of September 13, after his interview with Kutuzof, Count Rostopchin, offended and wounded because he had not been invited to the council of war, and because Kutuzof paid no attention to his offer to take part in defense of the capital; amazed at the discovery that he had made while at the camp, that the tranquillity of the capital and the patriotic disposition of its inhabitants were regarded not merely of secondary importance, but rather as absolutely trivial and insignificant, — offended, wounded, and amazed by all this, Count Rostopchin had returned to Moscow.

After finishing his dinner, the count, without undressing, lay down on his couch, and at one o'clock was awakened by a courier who brought him a letter from

Count Kutuzof. This letter stated that, as the troops were to retire beyond Moscow along the Riazan highway, the count would be doing a favor if he would send a number of policemen to conduct the troops across the city.

This was no news to Rostopchin. Not only during his conference with Kutuzof on the Poklonnaya Hill, but ever since the battle of Borodino, when all the generals who came to Moscow declared with one voice that it was impossible to give battle, and when, by the count's consent, the crown treasure had been sent out of the city every night, and already half of the inhabitants had left, Count Rostopchin was well aware that Moscow was to be abandoned; but, nevertheless, this news, conveyed in the form of a simple note, containing Kutuzof's command and received at midnight, in the midst of his first sleep, amazed and annoyed the count.

Afterwards, in explaining his action at that time, Count Rostopchin wrote in several instances that he had two objects of especial importance in view, — "to maintain good order in Moscow, and to expedite the departure of the inhabitants."

If we grant this twofold object, any of Rostopchin's actions would be irreproachable.

Why were not the precious things of Moscow carried away, — weapons, cartridges, powder, stores of grain? Why were thousands of the inhabitants treacherously informed, to their ruin, that Moscow was not to be abandoned?

"To preserve tranquillity in the capital," is Count Rostopchin's explanation and answer.

Why were packages of unnecessary papers from the court-house, and Leppich's balloon, and other articles, sent out?

"In order to leave the city empty," again says Count Rostopchin's explanation.

Only grant the premise that this and that threatened the city's tranquillity, and every sort of procedure would be justifiable. ....

All the horrors of the Terror were based merely on the attempt to preserve the tranquillity of the people.

On what was based Count Rostopchin's effort to keep the Moscow populace tranquil in 1812? What reason was there for supposing that any tendency toward popular disturbance existed in the city? The citizens had left, the troops retreating filled Moscow. Why should this have led to any riots among the people?

Neither in Moscow alone nor anywhere in all Russia, during the invasion of the enemy, was there anything like an insurrection. On the thirteenth and fourteenth of September, more than ten thousand inhabitants remained in Moscow, and, except in the crowd collected in the governor-general's dvor, and that at his own instigation, there was no trouble.

Evidently there would have been still less reason to expect excitement among the populace if, after the battle of Borodino, when the abandonment of Moscow was evident or at least probable, Rostopchin, instead of stirring up the people by the distribution of arms and placards, had taken measures to remove all the treasure, the gunpowder, the projectiles, and the specie, and fairly explained to the people that the city was to be abandoned.

Rostopchin, a hot-tempered, sanguine man, who had always been employed in the higher administrative circles, though he had genuine patriotic feeling, had not the slightest comprehension of that populace which he thought he directed. From the earliest occupation of Smolensk by the enemy, Rostopchin, in his imagination, conceived that he was to play the part of director of the popular sentiment in the heart of Russia. Not only did it seem to him — as it seems to every administrator — that he was ruling the external affairs of the inhabitants of Moscow, but it seemed to him that he directed their impulses by means of his proclamations and "placards" composed in that flippant style which is insulting to the people, and which they do not comprehend when they hear it from their superiors. The beautiful *rôle* of director of the popular sentiment was so pleasing to Rostopchin, he stuck to it so assiduously, that the imperative necessity for him to step down and out of it, — the imperative necessity of abandoning Moscow, with any heroic climax, took him by surprise ; and the ground on which he had been standing was suddenly cut out from under, and he really knew not what to do.

Although he foresaw it, still with all his soul he refused to believe, until the last moment, that Moscow was to be abandoned, and he did nothing with that end in view. The inhabitants left the city against his will. If he sent out the court records, it was only because the officials insisted upon it, and the count consented against his better judgment.

He himself was wholly occupied in that *rôle* which he had taken upon himself. As often happens with men endowed with a vivid imagination, he had long before known that Moscow would have to be abandoned, but he knew it only by his reason, and his whole soul revolted against the belief because he was not yet carried by his imagination to the height of this new position.

All his activity, assiduous and energetic as it was, — how far it was profitable and reacted upon the populace, is another question, — all his activity was directed simply toward arousing in the inhabitants the feeling which he himself experienced — of patriotic hatred against the French, and confidence in himself.

But when the event assumed its actual historical proportions, when it seemed trivial to express his hatred merely in words against the French, when it was no longer possible to express this hatred by a conflict, when self-confidence began to appear disadvantageous in face of the one great question that concerned Moscow, when the whole population like one man, flinging away their possessions, streamed out of Moscow, proving by this act of negation all the power of the popular sentiment, — then the *rôle* which Rostopchin had selected seemed suddenly absurd. He suddenly felt himself alone, weak, and ridiculous, with nothing solid to stand upon.

On being wakened from sound sleep and receiving a

cold and imperative note from Kutuzof, Rostopchin felt all the more excited because he felt that he was to blame. Everything that had been expressly intrusted to him was left in Moscow — all the crown treasures that he should have had removed out of the city. There was now no possibility of getting them away.

"Who is to blame for this? Who let it come to this?" he mused. "Of course it was not I. As far as I was concerned, everything was all ready. I held Moscow as in a vise. And this is the pass to which they have brought things. Knaves! traitors!" he exclaimed mentally, not having a very clear idea who these knaves and traitors were, but feeling that he was in duty bound to hate these traitors, whoever they were, that were to blame for the false and ridiculous position in which he found himself.

All that night Rostopchin gave out instructions to all who came for them from every part of Moscow. His intimates had never seen the count so gloomy and irascible.

"Your illustriousness, a messenger from the Chancery Department: the director asks instructions".... "from the Consistory".... "from the Senate".... "from the University".... "from the Foundling Asylum".... "the suffragan has sent to".... "wants to know".... "What orders are to be given to the fire brigade?".... "the superintendent of the prison".... "the director of the Lunatic Asylum."

Thus all night long without cessation men came to the count for their orders. To all these queries the count gave curt and surly answers, which show that any regulations of his were now unnecessary, that all the preparations which he had so carefully elaborated some one had now rendered nugatory, and that this *some one* would have to shoulder all the responsibility for what was now taking place.

"Well, tell that blockhead that it is his business to guard his papers," he replied to the query from the Chancery Department. "Well, now, what is that rot about the fire brigade? If they have horses, let 'em go to Vladimir!".... "Don't leave them for the French."

"Your illustriousness, the overseer of the Lunatic Asylum is here; what orders do you give to him?"

"What orders? Let 'em all out, that's all.... let the lunatics loose in the city. When lunatics are at the head of our armies, God means for these to be out!"

When asked what to do with the convicts who were in the jail, the count wrathfully shouted to the inspector: "What? Did you expect me to give you a couple of battalions as escort, when there are n't any to be had? Let 'em out; that's all."

"Your illustriousness, there are the politicals, Mieshkof and Vereshchagin."

"Vereshchagin! Is n't he hanged yet?" cried Rostopchin — "bring him to me."

CHAPTER XXV

By nine o'clock A.M., when the troops were already on the way across Moscow, no one any longer came to ask the count what dispositions were to be made. All who could leave had left on their own responsibility; those who remained behind decided for themselves what it was necessary for them to do.

The count commanded his horses to be brought round to take him to Sokolniki, and he was sitting in his cabinet with folded arms, scowling, sallow, and taciturn.

To every administrator in quiet, stormless times, it seems that only by his efforts the population committed to his care lives and moves, and in this consciousness of his indispensable services he finds the chief reward for his labors and efforts.

It is easy to see that, as long as the historical sea is calm, the pilot-administrator in his fragile craft, who holds by his boat-hook to the ship of State, and while moving, must imagine that it is by his efforts the ship which he is steering moves. But only let a storm arise, the sea grow tempestuous and toss the ship itself, and then any such illusion is impossible. The ship drives on in its own prodigious, independent course, the boat-hook is not sufficient for the tossing ship, and the pilot is suddenly reduced from the position of director, the fountain-head of force, to a humiliated, useless, and feeble man.

Rostopchin realized this, and this was what vexed his soul.

The chief of police, who had been stopped by the throng, came to the count at the same time as his aide, who brought word that the horses were ready. Both were pale; and the chief of police, having reported the accomplishment of his commission, informed the count that in the dvor was a vast throng of people desiring to see him.

Rostopchin, not answering a single word, got up and with swift strides passed into his luxurious, brilliant drawing-room, went to the balcony door, took hold of the latch, then dropped it again and crossed to the window, from which the whole throng could be seen.

The tall young fellow with a sullen face was standing in the front row, gesticulating and making some remark. The bloody-faced blacksmith with angry eyes stood next him. Through the closed windows could be heard the roar of their voices.

"Carriage ready?" asked Rostopchin, leaving the window.

"It is, your illustriousness," said the aide.

Rostopchin again went to the balcony door.

"Now what do they want?" he asked of the chief of police.

"Your illustriousness, they declare that they have come by your orders, ready to go out against the French; they are shouting something about treason! But it is a riotous mob, your illustriousness. I escaped with my life. Your illustriousness, may I be bold enough to suggest .... "

"Be good enough to withdraw; I know what is to be done, without your advice," cried Rostopchin, savagely. He stood by the balcony door, looking down at the throng. "This is what they have brought Russia to! This is the way they have treated me!" brooded

Rostopchin, feeling uncontrollable rage rising in his heart against whoever might be considered as the cause of what had taken place. As often happens with hot-tempered men, he was overmastered by rage, but he was still in search of some scapegoat on whom to vent it.

"Look at that populace, the dregs of the people," he said to himself in French, as he gazed down at the mob. "The plebs stirred up by *their* folly! They must have a victim," came into his head, as he gazed at the tall young fellow gesticulating his arms. And this idea came into his head precisely for the reason that he himself wanted a victim, an object for his wrath.

"Carriage ready?" he demanded a second time.

"It is, your illustriousness. What orders do you give in regard to Vereshchagin? He is waiting at the stairs," replied the aide.

"Ah!" cried Rostopchin, as if struck by some unexpected thought.

And, quickly throwing the door open, he went with resolute steps out on the balcony. The talking suddenly hushed; hats and caps were doffed, and all eyes were turned on the count.

"Good-morning, boys!" cried the count, hurriedly, and in a loud voice. "Thank you for coming. I will be down directly, but, first of all, we must settle the account with a villain. We must punish the villain who is the cause of Moscow's ruin. Wait for me!"

And the count retired from view, slamming the door behind him.

An approving roar of satisfaction ran through the throng.

"Of course he'll settle with all villains!".... "You talk about the French!".... "He'll bring things to order!" said the people, as if reproaching each other for their little faith.

In a few minutes an officer came hastily out of the rear door, gave some order, and a line of dragoons was formed. The throng eagerly rushed from the balcony toward the steps. Rostopchin, coming out on the porch,

angrily, with swift steps, looked around him, as if searching for some one.

"Where is he?" asked the count.

And, at the instant the words left his mouth, he saw
coming around the corner of the house, between two
dragoons, a young man, with a long, thin neck, and with
one-half of his head shaven, though the hair had begun.
to grow again. This young man was dressed in a tattered foxskin short tulup lined with blue cloth — it had
once been a stylish garment — and dirty, hempen convict drawers, stuffed into fine boots, covered with mud
and run down at the heels. On his slender, weak legs,
he dragged along heavy iron shackles, which made his
gait difficult and irresolute.

"Ah!" exclaimed Rostopchin, hastily turning his
eyes away from the young man in the foxskin jacket,
and pointing to the lower step of the porch.

"Stand him there!"

The young man, with clanking chains, heavily dragged
himself to the spot indicated ; and, after pulling up with
his finger his jacket collar, which pinched him, and twice
stretching out his long neck and sighing, he folded in
front of his belly submissively his slender hands, which
were not those of a man accustomed to work.

Silence prevailed for several seconds, until the young
man had fairly taken his position on the steps. Only
in the rear of the crowd, where the people were trying
to press forward, were heard grunts and groans and
jostling and the shuffling of moving feet.

Rostopchin, waiting until the prisoner was in the
designated place, frowned, and passed his hand over his
face.

"Boys!" cried he, in a voice ringing out with metallic clearness, "this man, Vereshchagin, is the scoundrel
who has lost us Moscow!"

The young man in the foxskin jacket stood in a submissive attitude, with his wrists crossed on his abdomen,
and slightly stooping. He hung his head with its
mutilation of shaven hair ; his thin young face wore a
hopeless expression. At the first words spoken by the

count, he slowly raised his head and glanced at the count, as if wishing to say something, or, at least, to get his eye. But Rostopchin looked not at him. On the young man's long, slender neck, behind his ear, a vein stood out like a whipcord, tense and livid, and his face suddenly flushed.

All eyes were fastened on him. He returned the gaze of the throng, and, as if he found some cause for hope in the expression of the faces, he gave a timid and pitiful smile, and, again dropping his head, shifted his feet on the step.

"He is a traitor to his Tsar and his country; he has sold himself to Bonaparte; he alone out of all the Russians has shamed the name of Russian, and by him Moscow has been destroyed," cried Rostopchin in a steady, sharp voice; but suddenly he gave a swift glance at Vereshchagin, who continued to stand in the same submissive attitude. This glance seemed to set him beside himself. Raising his hand, he shouted, stepping almost down to the crowd : —

"Take the law into your own hands ! I give him over to you !"

The throng made no answer, and merely pressed together more and more densely. To be crushed together, to breathe in that infected atmosphere, to be unable to stir, and to expect something unknown, incomprehensible, and terrible, was above human endurance. The men standing in the front row, who saw and heard all that was taking place before them with startled, wide-staring eyes and gaping mouths, exerted all their force, and resisted with their backs the forward thrust and pressure of the rear ranks.

"Kill him !.... let the traitor perish and not shame the name of a Russian !" yelled Rostopchin. "Kill him ! I order it !"

The mob, hearing not the words but the venomous sounds of Rostopchin's voice, groaned, and moved forward, then instantly stood still again.

"Count !" exclaimed, amid the momentary silence which had instantly ensued, Vereshchagin's timid, but at the same time theatrical, voice, — " Count, there is one God over us ...." said Vereshchagin, lifting his head ; and again the thick vein on his slender neck filled out with blood, and the red flush spread over his face and died away.   He had not said what he meant to say.

" Kill him ! I order it ! " shouted Rostopchin, suddenly growing as pale as Vereshchagin.

" Draw sabers ! " commanded the officer to the dragoons, himself unsheathing his saber.

Another and still more violent billow rolled through the crowd, and, running up to those in the front rows, it seemed to lift them, and, reeling, broke against the very steps of the porch.   The tall young fellow, with a petrified expression of face, and with his hand arrested in mid-air, stood almost next Vereshchagin.

" Cut him down ! " came the whispered command of the officer to the dragoons ; and, suddenly, one of the dragoons, his face distorted with rage, gave Vereshchagin a blow on the head with his dull broadsword.

" Ah ! " cried Vereshchagin, who gave a short cry of amazement, and looked around in terror and as if he could not understand why this was done to him.   The same groan of amazement as before ran through the throng.   " O Lord — O Gospodi ! " exclaimed some voice.

But, instantly following the cry of amazement uttered by Vereshchagin, he gave a piteous shriek of pain, and that shriek was his undoing.

The barrier of humane feeling stretched to the highest tension, and holding back the mob, suddenly broke. The crime was begun, and it had to be accomplished. The lugubrious groan of reproach was swallowed up in a fierce and maddened roar of the mob.   Like the seventh and last wave which wrecks the ship, this final, irresistible billow, impelled from the rear, was borne through to those in front, overwhelmed them, and swallowed up everything.

The dragoon who had used his sword was about to repeat his blow.   Vereshchagin, with a cry of horror, warding off the stroke with his arm, leaped among the people. The tall young fellow, against whom he struck, grasped his slender neck with his hands, and with a savage yell fell together with him under the trampling feet of the frenzied crowd.

Some beat and mangled Vereshchagin ; others, the tall young fellow. And the cries and yells of the surging multitude and of the men who were trying to rescue the tall young fellow only the more excited the virulence of the mob. It was long before the dragoons were able to extricate the tall factory hand, who was half beaten to death, and covered with blood. And it was long, in spite of all the hot haste with which the throng strove to finish the work which they had begun, before those men who were beating, trampling, and mangling Vereshchagin were able to kill him ; but the throng pressed them on every hand, and at the center it was like a solid mass rocking and swaying from side to side, and gave them no chance either to finish with him or to let him go.

"Finish him with an ax, hey ? " .... "They 've crushed him well." .... "The traitor! he sold Christ." .... "Is he alive yet ? " .... "He 's a tough one ! " .... "He gets his deserts." .... "Try it with a bar ! " .... "Is n't he dead yet ? "

Only when the victim ceased to struggle, and his shrieks gave way to the measured, long death-rattle, did the mob begin hastily to avoid the spot where lay the corpse covered with gore. Each one came up, gave a look at what had been done, and, full of horror, remorse, and amazement, pressed back.

"O Lord, men are like wild beasts ! wonder any one was spared ! " exclaimed some voice in the crowd.

"And a young fellow too ! " .... "Must be a merchant's son." .... "What a mob ! " .... "They say he 's the wrong one." .... "What do you mean .... the wrong one ? " .... "O Lord ! " .... "Some one else was beaten to death too ! " .... "They say he just escaped with his life ! " .... "Oh, what people ! " .... "Ain't it a sin to be afraid of ? "

These remarks were made by the same men, as with painfully pitiful faces they looked at the dead body with the face smeared with blood and begrimed with dust, and the long, slender neck half backed off.

A zealous police official, thinking it unbecoming to have a corpse encumbering his excellency's yard, ordered the dragoons to drag it forth into the street. Two dragoons seized the body by the mutilated legs and hauled it out. The blood-stained, dust-begrimed, dead, shaven head, rolling on the long neck, was dragged along thumping on the ground. The mob surged away from the corpse.

At the moment that Vereshchagin fell, and the mob with a savage yell burst forward and rushed over him, Rostopchin turned suddenly pale, and, instead of going to the rear stairs, where his horses were waiting for him, he, without knowing where or wherefore, started with sunken head and swift steps along the corridor that led to the rooms on the ground floor. The count's face was pallid, and he could not keep his lower jaw from trembling as if he had an ague.

"Your illustriousness, this way.... where are you going?.... this way if you please!" exclaimed a trembling, frightened voice behind him.

Count Rostopchin was in no condition to answer, and, obediently wheeling about, he took the direction whither he was called. At the rear entrance stood his calash. Even here the distant roar of the excited mob reached his ears. Count Rostopchin hastily sprang into the carriage, and ordered the coachman to drive to his suburban house at Sokolniki.

When they reached the Miasnitskaya, and the yells of the mob were no longer heard, the count began to feel qualms of conscience. He remembered now with dissatisfaction the excitement and terror which he had displayed before his subordinates. " *La populace est terrible, elle est hideuse,*" he said to himself in French. "They are like wolves, which can be appeased only with flesh."

" *Count, there is one God over us !* "

Vereshchagin's words suddenly recurred to him, and a disagreeable feeling of chill ran down his back. But this feeling was only momentary, and Count Rostopchin smiled a scornful smile at himself.

"I had other obligations," he said to himself. "The people had to be appeased. Many other victims have perished, and are perishing for the public weal."

And he began to consider the general obligation which he had toward his family, the capital committed into his keeping, and his own safety — not as Feodor Vasilye-vitch Rostopchin — he understood that Feodor Vasilye-vitch Rostopchin would sacrifice himself for the public good — but as the governor-general and the repository of power, and the authorized representative of the Tsar.

"If I were only Feodor Vasilyevitch, my line of con-duct would have been very differently drawn, — *aurait été tout autrement traçé,* — but as I was, I was in duty bound to preserve my life and the dignity of the governor-general."

Slightly swaying on the easy springs of his equipage, and no longer hearing the terrible sounds of the mob, Rostopchin grew calmer physically, and, as always hap-pens, simultaneously as physical calm returned, his reason furnished him arguments for moral tranquillity.

The idea that ·soothed Rostopchin was not new. Never since the world began and people began to slaugh-ter one another has man committed crime against his fellow without soothing himself with this idea. This idea is the public good — the hypothetical weal of other men. The man not carried away by his passions never knows what this weal is, but the man who has com-mitted a crime always knows very well what constitutes it. And Rostopchin now knew.

He not only did not reproach himself for what he had done, but he even found reason for self-congratula-tion that he had so happily succeeded in taking advan-tage of this fortuitous circumstance for punishing a criminal, and at the same time pacifying the mob.

"Vereshchagin was tried and condemned to **death,**"

said Rostopchin to himself — though Vereshchagin had only been condemned by the senate to hard labor. "He was a spy and a traitor; I could not leave him unpunished, and, besides, I killed two birds with one stone — I offered a victim to pacify the people, and I punished an evil-doer."

By the time he reached his suburban house, and began to make his domestic arrangements, he had become perfectly calm.

At the end of half an hour the count was driving behind swift horses across the Sokolnichye Pole, with his mind perfectly oblivious to what had happened, and thinking only of events to come. He was on his way now to the Yauzsky Bridge, where he had been told Kutuzof was to be found.

Count Rostopchin was preparing mentally the angry and caustic reproaches with which he intended to load Kutuzof for so deceiving him. He would give that old court fox to understand that the responsibility for all the misfortunes which would flow from the abandonment of the capital, from the destruction of Russia (as Rostopchin supposed it to be), would redound upon his old gray head, which was so entirely lacking in brains. While Rostopchin was thinking over what he should say to him, he angrily straightened himself up in his calash, and looked fiercely about him on all sides.

The Sokolnichye Pole was deserted. Only at one end, near the poorhouse and lunatic aslyum, could be seen a few groups of men in white raiment and several individuals of the same sort, who were hastening across the "field," shouting something and gesticulating.

One of these men ran so as to cut off Count Rostopchin's calash. The count and his coachman and the dragoons all gazed with a dull sense of terror and curiosity at these liberated lunatics, and especially at the one who was running toward them.

The lunatic, unevenly bounding along on his long, thin legs, and with his white khalat flying out behind him, was running with all his might, not taking his eyes from the count, yelling something in a hoarse voice and signaling for the carriage to stop. His gloomy and impassioned face, overgrown with uneven blotches of beard, was haggard and sallow. His dark, agate-colored eyes, with their saffron whites, rolled frenziedly.

"Stop! Hold on, I say!" he cried in piercing tones, and panting, he began again to shout with extravagant intonations and gestures.

He came up with the calash, and ran along by the side of it.

"Thrice have they killed me, thrice have I risen from the dead. They have stoned me, they have crucified me. I shall rise again.... I shall rise again.... I shall rise again. They have torn my body to pieces. They have overthrown the kingdom of God. Thrice shall I tear it down, and thrice shall I build it again!" he yelled, raising his voice higher and higher.

Count Rostopchin suddenly paled, just as he had paled when the mob threw itself on Vereshchagin. He looked away. "Dri.... drive faster!" he called to the coachman in a trembling voice. The calash sprang forward with all the speed of the horses; but still for a long time the count could hear, growing more and more distant, that senseless, despairing cry, while before his eyes all he could see was the amazedly frightened, bloody face of the "traitor" in the fur jacket.

This vision was now so vivid that Rostopchin felt it was deeply etched into the very substance of his heart. He now clearly realized that he should never outlive the bloody trace of this recollection; but that, on the contrary, this terrible remembrance, the longer he lived, even to the end of his days, would grow more and more cruel, more painful.

He heard, so it seemed to him, even now the ring of his own words: "Kill him! If you don't, you shall answer to me for it with your heads!"

"Why did I say those words?" he asked himself, almost despairingly. "I need not have said them," he thought, "and then *nothing* would have happened."

He saw the face of the dragoon that gave the blow change from terror to ferocity, and the glance of silent, timid reproach which that young man in the foxskin jacket gave him.

"But I did it not for myself. I was obliged to per-form that part. The populace .... the traitor .... the pub-lic good .... " he said to himself.

The troops were still crowding the bridge over the Yauza. It was sultry. Kutuzof, with contracted brows and dismal, sat on a bench near the bridge, and was playing with his whip in the sand, when a calash drove up to him in hot haste. A man wearing a gen-eral's uniform and a plumed hat, and with wandering eyes expressing a mixture of wrath and terror, got out, and, approaching Kutuzof, began to say something to him in French.

This was Count Rostopchin.

He told Kutuzof that he had come to him because Moscow and the capital were no more, and the army was all that was left.

"It would have been different if your serene highness had not told me you would not abandon Moscow without giving battle; then this would not have happened at all," said he.

Kutuzof glanced at Rostopchin, and, apparently not taking in the full significance of the words addressed to him, he seemed to be exerting all his energies to read the peculiar expression that was written in the face of the man addressing him.

Rostopchin grew confused, and stopped speaking. Kutuzof shook his head slightly, and, not taking his inquisitive glance from Rostopchin's face, he said in a low tone : —

"No, we are not giving up Moscow without a struggle!"

Whether Kutuzof was thinking of something entirely aloof when he said those words, or said them on pur-pose, knowing their absurdity, at all events Rostopchin made no reply, and hastily turned away from him.   And, strange enough! the governor-general of Moscow, the haughty Count Rostopchin, taking a whip in his hand, went to the bridge, and began to shout, and hurry along the teams which were blocked together there.

CHAPTER XXVI

At four o'clock in the afternoon, the troops under Murat entered Moscow. In front rode a detachment of Würtemberg hussars ; next followed the king of Naples in person, mounted, and surrounded by a large suite.

Near the center of the Arbat, in the vicinity of the church of Nikola Yavlennui,[1] Murat reined in, and waited for a report from the van as to the state of the city fortress, "*le Kremlin.*" Around Murat gathered a small knot from among the citizens that had remained in Moscow. All gazed with shy perplexity at this long-haired, foreign "nachalnik," so gorgeously bedizened with feathers and gold.

"Say ! that one's their tsar, ain't he ?" queried low voices.

The interpreter approached the knot of men.

"Hats off !" .... "Hats !" men were heard saying as they in the throng admonished one another.

The interpreter addressed himself to an old porter, and asked if it were far to the Kreml. The porter, hearing the strange Polish accent with which the man spoke, and not comprehending that he was speaking to him in Russian, did not understand what was said to him, and slipped behind the others.

Murat beckoned up the interpreter, and commanded him to ask where the Russian army was. One of the citizens made out what was asked, and several voices suddenly began to reply to the interpreter. A French officer came galloping back from the van, and reported to Murat that the fortress gates were closed, and that probably there was an ambuscade.

"Very good," said Murat, and, addressing one of the gentlemen of his suite, he commanded him to have four light field-pieces brought up, and to batter down the gates.

The artillery set forth on the gallop from the column

[1] St. Nicholas of the Miraculous Apparition.

that was just behind Murat, and crossed the Arbat. On reaching the end of the Vozdvizhenka, or Holy-Rood Street, the artillery stopped, and deployed on the square. Several French officers took command of the cannon, aiming them, and scrutinizing the Kreml through their field-glasses.

The bells began to ring for vespers in the Kreml, and this sound confused the French. They supposed that it was an alarum. Several of the infantry soldiers ran toward the Kutafya gates. Beams and planks barricaded the gates. Two musket-shots rang sharply out from behind the gates as soon as the officer and his detachment started to approach. The general, standing by the cannon, shouted some command to the officer, and the officer and one of the soldiers hastened back to him. Three more musket-shots rang out from the gates. One shot wounded a French soldier in the leg, and a strange yell from a few throats was heard behind the barricade.

From the faces of the French — general, officers, and men — simultaneously, as if at word of command, vanished their former expression of gayety and calm, and in its place came an obstinate, concentrated expression of readiness for battle and suffering. For all of them, from marshal down to the most insignificant soldier, this place was no longer the Vozdvizhenka, Mokhovaya, Kutafya, and Troitskiya gates, but it was the new locality of a new battle-field, in all probability destined to be deluged with blood; and all prepared for this battle.

The yells from the gates ceased. The cannon were pointed. The artillerists blew up their lighted slow-matches. The officer gave the command: *feu!* fire! and two hissing sounds of canister-shot followed one after the other. The grape clattered on the stones of the gateway, on the beams and the barricade, and two puffs of smoke floated away over the square.

A few seconds later, when the echoes of the reports had died out along the stone walls of the Kreml, a strange noise was heard over the heads of the French.

An enormous flock of jackdaws arose above the walls, and cawing, and flapping their countless wings, circled around in the air. At the same instant a single human yell was heard in the gates, and through the smoke appeared the figure of a hatless man in a kaftan. He held a musket, and aimed it at the French. "*Feu !*" cried the artillery officer a second time, and at exactly the same instant rang out one musket-shot and two cannon-shots.

Smoke again concealed the gates.

Behind the barricade no one any longer moved, and the French infantry soldiers and their officers again approached the gates. At the gates lay three men wounded and four dead. Two men in kaftans were in full flight down along the walls to Znamenka.

"*Enlevez-moi ça* — Clear 'em away," said the officer, indicating the beams and the corpses ; and the French, finishing the wounded, flung the corpses down behind the fence. "*Enlevez-moi ça*" was all that was said about them, and they were flung away, and afterwards were removed so as not to foul the air. Only Thiers consecrates to their memory a few eloquent lines : —

These wretches had taken possession of the sacred stronghold, seized firearms from the arsenal, and attacked the French. A few of them were put to the sword, and the Kreml was purged of their presence.[1]

Murat was informed that the way was clear. The French poured through the gates, and began to set up their camp in the Senatskaya Square. The soldiers flung chairs out of the windows of the senate-house into the square, and used them as fuel for their fires.

Other divisions crossed through the Kreml, and took up their stations along the Moroseïka, Lubyanka, Pokrovka. Still others settled themselves in the Vozdvizhenka, Znamenka, Nikolskaya, and Tverskaya. Finding nowhere any hospitality, the French settled down, not

---

[1] *Ces misérables avaient envahi la citadelle sacrée, s'étaient emparé des fusils de l'arsenal, et tiraient (ces misérables) sur les français. On en sabra quelques-uns, et on purgea le Kremlin de leur presence.*

in "quarters," as they usually would in a city, but, as it were, in a camp pitched inside the city limits.

The French, though ragged, hungry, weary, and reduced to one-half of their original numbers, entered Moscow in regular military order. It was a jaded, exhausted, but still martial and redoubtable army.

But it was such only until the moment when the soldiers of that army were distributed in their lodgings. As soon as the men of the various regiments began to scatter among the rich and deserted mansions, then the martial quality disappeared forever, and the men were neither citizens nor soldiers, but were changed into something betwixt and between, called marauders.

When, five weeks later, these same men marched out of Moscow, they were still no longer troops. They were a throng of marauders, each one of whom brought or carried away with him a quantity of articles which seemed to him precious or necessary.

The object of each of these men, as they left Moscow, was not, as formerly, to prove themselves warriors, but to preserve what they had obtained. Like the monkey which has thrust its paw into the narrow neck of the jug, and grasped a handful of nuts, and will not open its fist lest it lose its prize, thus destroying itself, — the French, on leaving Moscow, were evidently doomed to perish, in consequence of lugging their plunder with them, since to relinquish what they had taken as plunder was as impossible as it was impossible for the monkey to let go of its handful of nuts.

Ten minutes after each regiment of the French host made its entry into any given quarter of Moscow, there was not left a single soldier or officer. Men in capotes and gaiters could be seen in the windows of the houses, boldly exploring the rooms. In cellars and store-rooms, the same men were making free with provisions and stores. In the yards the same men were tearing open or breaking down the barn and stable doors. They kindled fires in kitchens, and with sleeves rolled up they baked, kneaded, and cooked, they frightened or confused or wheedled women and children. There were a host of these men everywhere in the shops and in the houses; but army there was none.

On that day, order after order was issued by the French commanders, with the object of preventing the troops from scattering about through the city — stern rescripts against offering violence to the inhabitants, or marauding, and insisting on a general roll-call at evening; but, in spite of such precautions, the men, who just before had constituted an army, wandered about through the rich, deserted city, which still abounded in comforts and enjoyments.

As a famished herd of cattle go huddled together over a barren field, but instantly become uncontrollable and scatter as soon as they come into rich pasture-lands, so did this army separate and scatter irreclaimably through the opulent city.

There were no citizens in Moscow, and the soldiers were absorbed in it (like water in sand), and, bursting all restraint, radiated out in every direction from the Kreml, which was their first objective point.

Cavalrymen, coming to some merchant's mansion, abandoned with all its treasures, and finding stabling sufficient for their own horses and others besides, nevertheless proceeded to take possession of the one adjoining, because it seemed better still.

In many cases, a man or group of men would take possession of several houses, and scratch the name of the claimant in chalk on the doors, and quarrel and even come to blows with men of other regiments.

Such soldiers as failed to find accommodations ran along the streets inspecting the city, and when word was given out that the whole city was abandoned, they made haste to find and take whatever was valuable. Officers went to collect their men and were involuntarily drawn into the same proceedings.

In the Karetnui Riat, or carriage mart, there were shops full of equipages ; and here the generals crowded, selecting calashes and coaches.

Such inhabitants as were left invited the French commanders to lodge in their houses, thereby hoping to escape from being plundered.

There was an abundance of wealth, and there seemed to be no end to it. Everywhere, in a circle from the place first occupied by the French, there were places, as yet unknown and unexplored, where, as it seemed to the French, there must be still greater riches. And Moscow even more and more absorbed them into itself. Just as the consequence of pouring water upon dry earth is that the water disappears and the dry earth as well, so in exactly the same way the consequence of a hungry army pouring into a well-furnished, abandoned city was its destruction, and the destruction of the opulent city, and filth follows; conflagrations and marauding follow.

The French attributed the burning of Moscow to the savage patriotism of Rostopchin — *au patriotisme féroce de Rostopchine;* the Russians, to the savagery of the French. In last analysis, responsibility for the burning of Moscow was not due and cannot be attributed to any one person or to any number of persons.

Moscow was burned because it was in a condition when every city built of wood must burn, independently of the question whether they had or had not one hundred and thirty wretched fire-engines. Moscow had to burn because its inhabitants had deserted it, and as inevitably as a heap of shavings on which live coals are dropped must burn.

A wooden city, which has its conflagrations almost every day in spite of the police and the proprietors, careful of their houses, could not fail to burn when the inhabitants were gone and their places taken by soldiers, who smoked their pipes, made camp-fires of senators' chairs in the Senatskaya Square, and cooked their meals there twice a day.

Even in times of peace, when troops are quartered in certain places in villages, the number of fires is immediately increased. How much greater must the probabilities of conflagration be in a deserted city built of wood and occupied by a foreign army!

Le patriotisme féroce de Rostopchine and the savagery of the French were not to blame for this. The burning of Moscow was due to the soldiers' pipes, to the cook-stoves, the camp-fires, to the negligence of hostile troops, when houses were occupied by men not their owners.

Even if there were incendiaries (which is very doubt-ful, since there was no reason for setting fires, and to do such a thing would have been hard and risky), they could not be considered as the cause of the conflagra-tion, since it would have taken place without them.

However flattering it was for the French to blame Rostopchin's savage patriotism, and for the Russians to blame the villain Bonaparte, or, in later times, to place the heroic torch in the hands of their own people, it is impossible not to see that such an immediate cause of the conflagration had no real existence, because Mos-còw had to burn, as every wooden town, every factory, and every house would be burned when abandoned by its owners and strangers had taken possession and were cooking their victuals in it.

Moscow was burned by its citizens, — that is true; not, however, by the citizens who remained, but by those who went away.

Moscow, occupied by the enemy, did not remain intact like Berlin, Vienna, and other cities, simply because the inhabitants did not come forth to offer the French the bread and salt — *Khlyeb-sol* — of hos-pitality, and the keys of the city, but left it.

CHAPTER XXVII

THE *soaking*-up of the French into Moscow, spread-ing out star-wise, reached the quarter where Pierre was now living, only in the evening of September 14.

After the two days which Pierre had spent solitary, and in such an unusual manner, he had got into a state of mind that bordered on insanity. His whole being was possessed by one importunate idea. He himself knew not how or when it came about, but this idea had such mastery of him that he remembered nothing of the past, had no comprehension of the present, and what he saw and heard seemed as if it had happened in a dream.

Pierre had left his home simply and solely to escape from the complicated coil of social demands which held him, and from which he could not, in his situation at the time, tear himself away. Under the pretext of wishing to arrange the late owner's books and papers, he had gone to Iosiph Alekseyevitch's house simply because he was in search of some alleviation from the demands of life; and his recollections of Iosiph Alekseyevitch were connected in his mind with that world of eternal, tranquil, and solemn thoughts which were diametrically opposed to the confused coil in which he felt himself entangled.

He sought a quiet refuge, and actually found it, in Iosiph Alekseyevitch's library. When, in the dead silence of the room, he sat down and leaned his elbows on his late friend's dust-covered writing-table, the recollections of the last few days began one by one to rise before him, calmly, and in their proper significance, especially that of the battle of Borodino, and that irresistible sense of his own insignificance and falseness in comparison with the truth, simplicity, and forcefulness which had so impressed him in that class of men he called *They*.

When Gerasim aroused him from his brown study, the thought occurred to Pierre that he was to take a part in the supposed popular defense of Moscow. And, with this end in view, he had immediately sent Gerasim to procure for him a kaftan and pistol, and explained to him his intention of concealing his identity and remaining in Iosiph Alekseyevitch's house.

Afterward, in the course of the first day spent alone and idly, — for, though he several times tried, he could not put his mind on the Masonic manuscripts, — the thought of the cabalistic significance of his name in connection with that of Bonaparte's occurred vaguely to him; but this thought which he had before con-

ceived, that *l' Russe Besuhof* was predestined to overthrow the power of the *Beast*, now came to him only
as one of the illusions which thronged his imagination,
without logical connection, and vanished without leaving any trace.

When, after the purchase of the kaftan, — with the
purpose merely of taking part in the popular defense
of Moscow, — Pierre met the Rostofs, and Natasha
had said to him : "What are you going to do? stay
behind in Moscow? .... Akh ! how nice that would
be !" the thought had flashed through his mind that
truly it would be good, even if Moscow were captured,
for him to remain in Moscow and fulfil his predesti-
nation.

On the following day, with the sole idea not to spare
himself, and not to keep aloof from anything in which
they took part, he went to the Tri Gorui barrier. But
when he reached home again, convinced that no attempt was to be made to defend Moscow, the consciousness suddenly came over him that what had
hitherto seemed merely a possibility had now become
absolutely imperative and unavoidable. It was his duty
to remain in Moscow *incognito*, to fire at Napoleon and
to kill him : either he must perish himself, or put an
end to the misery which afflicted all Europe, and was
caused, as Pierre reasoned, by Napoleon alone.

Pierre knew all the particulars of the German student's attempts on Bonaparte's life in Vienna in 1809,
and he was aware that the student had been shot.
And the danger to which he was about to expose his
life in carrying out his purpose filled him with still
stronger zeal.

Two feelings of equal intensity irresistibly attracted
Pierre to execute his project. The first was the feeling that sacrifice and suffering were demanded from
him as a penalty for the consciousness of the general
wretchedness — that feeling which, on the seventh,
had impelled him to go to Mozhaïsk and even into
the very thick of the conflict, and now drove him
from his home to sleep on a hard divan, and to share

Gerasim's meager fare, instead of enjoying the com
forts and luxuries to which he was accustomed.

The second was that vague, exclusively Russian scorn
for all things conventional, artistic, human, for all that is
counted by the majority of men to be the highest good
in the world.

It was in the Slobodsky palace that Pierre had for the
first time in his life experienced this strange and
bewitching feeling, when he suddenly arrived at the
consciousness that wealth and power and life — everything that men get and cherish with such passionate
eagerness, even if it is worth anything — are of no
consequence compared to the enjoyment which is the
concomitant of their sacrifice.

It is this feeling that impels the volunteer to drink up
his last kopek, the drunkard to smash mirrors and
glasses without any apparent cause, although he knows
that it will cost him his last coin to pay for them ; the
feeling which impels a man, committing (in the common
acceptation of the word) crazy actions, to put forth all
his personal force and strength, thereby testifying to the
existence of a higher justice outside of human conditions and ruling life.

From that very day when Pierre for the first time experienced this feeling in the Slobodsky palace, he had
been constantly under its influence ; but now only he
found full satisfaction for it. Moreover, at the present
moment, Pierre was kept up to his intention, and deprived
of the possibility of renouncing it, by what he had already done in that direction. His flight from home,
and his kaftan, and his pistol, and his announcement to
the Rostofs that he should stay in Moscow, all would be
meaningless — nay, it would be contemptible and ridiculous, Pierre knew that by instinct — if, after all, he
should do what the others had done, and leave Moscow.

Pierre's physical condition, as was always the case,
corresponded with his moral. The coarse, unusual food,
the vodka which he had been drinking those days, the
abstinence from wine and cigars, the dirty, unchanged
linen, the two almost sleepless nights which he had

spent on the short, pillowless divan, all this had reduced
Pierre to a state not far removed from lunacy.

It was already two o'clock in the afternoon; the
French had already entered Moscow. Pierre knew it,
but, instead of acting, he thought only of his enterprise,
considering all its minutest details. In his imagination
he did not dwell with such keenness of vision on the act
itself of firing the shot, or on the death of Napoleon, but
he imagined with extraordinary vividness, and with a
melancholy delight, his own ruin and his heroic courage.

"Yes, one for all! I must accomplish it or perish!"
he said to himself. "Yes, I will go up to him.... and
then suddenly.... with a pistol.... or would not a dagger
be better?" — mused Pierre. — "However, it is immaterial. — ' Not I, but the hand of Providence punishes
thee!'.... I will exclaim." Pierre was rehearsing the
words which he should utter as he killed Napoleon. —
"'Well, then, take me, punish me,'" Pierre went on to
say, still further imagining the scene, and drooping his
head with a melancholy but firm expression of countenance.

While Pierre, standing in the middle of the room, was
thus musing, the library door was suddenly flung open,
and the figure of Makar Alekseyevitch appeared on the
threshold, absolutely changed from his former attitude
of wild shyness.

His khalat was flung open. His face was flushed and
distorted. He was evidently drunk. Seeing Pierre, he
was for the first moment confused; but, remarking signs
of confusion in Pierre, he immediately expressed his
satisfaction, and came into the middle of the room, tottering on his thin legs.

"They 're scared!" he exclaimed in a hoarse, confiden-
tial voice. "I tell you: ' We won't surrender.' That 's
what I say.... Right ?.... Hey, mister ?"

He deliberated for a moment; then, suddenly catching sight of the pistol on the table, he grasped it with
unexpected quickness and ran into the corridor.

Gerasim and the dvornik, who had followed at Makar
Alekseyevitch's heels, stopped him in the entry and tried

to take away the pistol. Pierre came out into the corridor, and looked with pity and disgust on the half-witted old man. Makar Alekseyevitch, scowling with the effort, clung to the pistol, and screamed in his hoarse voice something that he evidently considered very solemn.

"To arms! Board 'em![1] You lie! you shan't have it," he yelled.

"There, please, that 'll do. Have the goodness to put it up, please. Now please, barin ...." said Gerasim, cautiously taking Makar Alekseyevitch by the elbows and trying to force him back to the door.

"Who are you? Bonaparte?" screamed Makar Alekseyitch.

"That is not right, sir. Please come into your room; you are all out of breath. Please let me have the pistol."

"Away with you, you scurvy slave! Touch me not! Do you see this?" yelled Makar Alekseyitch, brandishing the pistol. "Board 'em!"

"Look out!" whispered Gerasim to the dvornik. They seized Makar Alekseyitch by the arms and dragged him to the door.

The room was filled with the confused sounds of the scuffle and the hoarse, drunken sounds of the panting voice.

Suddenly a new and penetrating scream of a woman was heard from the steps, and the cook ran into the entry.

"Here they are! Oh, ye saints of my sires! .... Oh, God! here they are! Four of them on horseback!" .... she cried.

Gerasim and the dvornik let go of Makar Alekseyitch's arms, and in the silence which suddenly ensued the pounding of several hands was heard on the outside door.

[1] *Na abordage!*

CHAPTER XXVIII

PIERRE, deciding for himself that, until the time came for the fulfilment of his project, it was best not to disclose his identity, or his knowledge of French, stood in the half-opened door leading into the corridor, intending instantly to go and hide himself as soon as the French entered. But the French came in, and Pierre had not stirred from the door; an indefinable curiosity seized him.

There were two of them. One was an officer, tall, gallant-looking, and handsome; the other evidently a soldier, or his servant, short and stubbed, lean and sunburned, with sunken cheeks and a stupid expression of face. The officer, resting his weight on a cane, and limping a little, came forward. Having advanced a few steps, the officer, as if deciding that the rooms were good, halted, and turned round to some soldiers who appeared in the doorway, and in a tone of command shouted to them to put up their horses. Having attended to this, the officer, with a gallant gesture, lifting high his elbow, twisted his mustache and then touched his cap.

"*Bonjour la compagnie!*" he cried cheerily, with a smile, and glancing round.

No one made any answer.

"*Vous êtes le bourgeois?* — Are you the master of the house?" asked the officer, addressing Gerasim. Gerasim, with a scared, questioning look, stared at the officer.

"*Quarteer, quarteer — logement!*" exclaimed the officer, surveying the little man from top to toe, with a condescending and benevolent smile: "The French are jolly boys. *Que diable! Voyons!* Don't get touchy, old man!" he added, slapping the startled and silent Gerasim on the shoulder. "*A ça! Dites donc, on ne parle donc français dans cette boutique?* — Tell me, isn't French spoken in this establishment?" he added, glancing around and catching Pierre's eyes. Pierre slunk aside from the door.

The officer again addressed himself to Gerasim. He tried to make the old man show him the rooms in the house.

"Barin gone .... no understand ! .... my .... you .... your " .... stammered Gerasim, striving to make his words more comprehensible by speaking in broken Russian.

The French officer, with a smile, waved his hands in front of Gerasim's nose, giving him to understand that he did not understand him, and he limped again to the door where Pierre was standing. Pierre started to go away in order to hide from him, but just at that instant he saw through the open door of the kitchen Makar Alekseyitch peering out, with the pistol in his hand. With the cunning of a madman, Makar Alekseyitch gazed at the Frenchman, and, raising the pistol, aimed.

"Board 'em ! " cried the drunken man, and cocked the pistol.

The French officer, hearing the shout, turned round, and at that instant Pierre flung himself on the drunkard. But, before Pierre had time to seize and throw up the pistol, Makar Alekseyitch got his fingers on the cock and a sharp report rang out, deafening them all and filling the passage with gunpowder smoke. The Frenchman turned pale and sprang back to the door.

Pierre seized the pistol and flung it away and ran after the officer, and (then forgetting his intention of not revealing his knowledge of French) began to speak with him in French.

"You are not wounded ? " he asked, with solicitude.

"I think not," replied the officer, examining himself. "But I had a narrow escape that time," he added, pointing at the broken plastering on the wall. "Who is that man ? " he demanded, giving Pierre a stern look.

"I am really greatly distressed at what has just happened," said Pierre, speaking fluently, and entirely forgetting the part he was going to play. "He is crazy, an unfortunate man who did not know what he was doing."

The officer turned to Makar Alekseyitch and seized him by the collar. Makar Alekseyitch, thrusting out his lips, swayed as if he were sleepy, and stood leaning against the wall.

"Brigand! you shall answer for this!" said the Frenchman, taking off his hand. "It's in our nature to be merciful after victory, but we do not forgive traitors," he added, with a look of gloomy solemnity on his face, and with a graceful, energetic gesture.

Pierre continued in French to urge the officer not to be too hard on this half-witted drunkard. The Frenchman listened in silence, without a change in his scowling face, then suddenly turned to Pierre with a smile. He looked at him for a few seconds without speaking. His handsome face assumed a tragically sentimental expression, and he held out his hand: "*Vous m'avez sauvé la vie! Vous êtes français!* — You have saved my life! You are French!" he said. For a Frenchman this inference was beyond question. To do a magnanimous action was alone possible to a Frenchman, and to save the life of *Monsieur Ramball, capitaine du* 13*me leger,* was unquestionably the greatest deed of all.

But, reasonable as this inference was or the conviction which the officer based upon it, Pierre felt it incumbent upon him to disclaim it.

"*Je suis russe,*" he said rapidly.

"Tititi! tell that to others," said the Frenchman, smiling and raising a warning finger. "By and by you can tell me all about it. *Charmé de rencontrer un compatriote. Eh bien!* What shall we do with this man?" he added, already addressing Pierre as if he were his brother.

Even though Pierre was not a Frenchman, having once granted him that appellation, — the highest in the world, — he could never disavow it, said the French officer's whole tone, and the expression of his face.

In reply to the last question, Pierre once more explained who Makar Alekseyitch was, explained that just before their arrival this witless drunkard had got hold of the loaded pistol, and they had just been trying to get it away from him; finally, he begged him to let his behavior pass without punishing him.

The Frenchman swelled out his chest and made a regal gesture with his hand : —

" *Vous m'avez sauvé la vie. Vous êtes français. Vous demandez sa grâce? Je vous l'accorde. Qu'on emmène cet homme !* — You ask me to pardon him. I will. Take this man away ! " exclaimed the French officer, rapidly and energetically, and, linking his arm with that of Pierre, the man whom for having saved his life he admitted into fellowship with the French, he went with him into the house.

The soldiers who had been in the dvor, when they heard the pistol-shot, hastened into the entry, asking what was up, and expressing their readiness to punish the offenders ; but the officer sternly repressed them.

"You shall be called when you are needed," said he.

The soldiers flocked out. The man who had meantime explored the larder came back to the officer and reported finding soup and roast mutton, and asked if he should bring it.

" *Capitaine, ils ont de la soupe et du gigot de mouton dans la cuisine,*" said he. "*Faut-il vous l'apporter?*"

" *Oui, et le vin !* " said the captain.

CHAPTER XXIX

As the French officer and Pierre went in together, Pierre felt that it was his duty once more to assure the captain that he was not French, and that he wanted to go ; but the French officer would not even hear to such a thing. He was so extremely polite, courteous, and good-natured, and so genuinely grateful for having had his life preserved, that Pierre had not the heart to refuse him, and therefore sat down with him in the dining-room, which happened to be the first which they entered.

At Pierre's asseveration that he was not a Frenchman, the captain, evidently not comprehending how it could enter the heart of man to refuse such a flattering designation, shrugged his shoulders, and declared that if he were resolutely bent on passing for a Russian, he might do so, but still, nevertheless, he was eternally bound to him by the feeling of gratitude for saving his life.

If this man had been gifted with the slightest capacity for entering into the feelings of others, and had guessed Pierre's sentiments, Pierre would undoubtedly have left him ; but this man's impermeability to everything except his own personality quite won Pierre.

"*Français ou prince russe incognito,*" said the Frenchman, scrutinizing Pierre's fine but soiled linen, and the ring on his finger, " I owe you my life, and I offer you my friendship. A Frenchman never forgets an insult or a favor. That is all I have to say."

In the tones of this officer's voice, in the expression of his face, in his gestures, there was so much affability and good-breeding (in the French use of the terms), that Pierre, giving back unconsciously smile for smile, pressed the proffered hand. " *Capitaine Ramball du 13me leger, décoré pour l'affaire du 19me,*" he went on to say, introducing himself with a smile of exuberant self-satisfaction curling his lips under his mustaches. "Would you not tell me, now, with whom I have the honor of conversing so agreeably instead of being in the ambulance with that madman's pistol-ball in me ? "

Pierre replied that he could not tell him his name, and reddened as he tried to think of some name, to invent some reason for not giving his own; but the Frenchman hastily interrupted him.

" I beg of you ! " said he. " I appreciate your scruples ; you are an officer .... an officer of rank, perhaps. You have borne arms against us .... it is not my affair. I owe my life to you. That is enough for me. I am wholly at your service. You are a gentleman ? " he added, with just a shade of question.

Pierre nodded assent.

" Your given name, please ; I ask nothing more. Monsieur Pierre, you say .... excellent ! — That is all that I wish to know."

When the mutton and omelet, the samovar, vodka, and wine which the French had obtained from a Russian cellar and brought with them, had been set on the table, Ramball invited Pierre to share in this repast, and instantly he himself fell to, ravenously and hastily attacking the viands like a healthy hungry man, chewing lustily with his sound, strong teeth, constantly smacking his lips, and exclaiming, *"Excellent, exquis!"*

His face grew flushed and sweaty. Pierre was hungry, and participated with great satisfaction in this dinner.

Morel, the servant, brought a saucepan full of warm water, and set in it a bottle of red wine. He also brought a bottle of kvas which he had found in the kitchen, and wanted to experiment with.

This beverage was already known to the French, and had received a name. They called kvas *limonade de cochon,* — pig's lemonade, — and Morel had taken possession of this *limonade de cochon* which he had found in the kitchen.

But as the *capitaine* possessed wine that had been plundered somewhere as he passed through the city, he left the kvas to Morel, and devoted himself to a bottle of Bordeaux. He wrapped the bottle up to the neck in a napkin, and poured the wine out for himself and Pierre. Hunger alleviated and the wine enlivened the captain more and more, and during all the dinner-time he chattered without cessation.

"Yes, my dear Mr. Pierre, I owe you a handsome taper for having saved me from that ....that madman. ....You see I have balls enough in my body as it is. There's one" — he touched his side — "received at Wagram, and two at Smolensk," — he indicated the scar on his cheek. "And this leg, you see, can't walk. I received that on the seventh, in the great battle of the Moskva. Ye gods! that was fine! You ought to have seen it! It was a deluge of fire. You blocked out a tough job for us! I should n't blame you for boasting about it! by the Devil, I should n't! And on my word, in spite of the cough which I contracted, I should be willing to begin it all over again. I pity those who did n't see it!"

"I was there!" said Pierre.

" What! really? Well, then, so much the better,"
said the Frenchman. "You are glorious enemies, all
the same. The great redoubt held her own, by all the
powers. And you made us pay dear for it. I got in it
three times, just as sure as you see me. Three times
we were right on the guns, and three times we were
knocked over like pasteboard soldiers! Oh, it was fine,
Mr. Pierre! Your grenadiers were superb, by heavens!
Six times running I saw them close up ranks and march
out as if they were going to a review! Fine fellows!
Our king of Naples, who is a perfect dab at such things,
cried, 'Bravo!' Ah! ha! good soldiers — quite our
match!" said he, with a smile, after a moment's silence.
" So much the better, so much the better, Mr. Pierre!
Terrible in battle....gallant with the fair ones!"—
he winked and smiled, — "that's the Frenchman, Mr.
Pierre, ain't that so?"[1]

The captain was so naïvely and good-naturedly jovial,
frank, and self-satisfied that Pierre himself almost winked
as he looked at him.

Apparently the word "gallant" reminded the captain
of the state of Moscow.

" By the way, tell me now, is it true all the ladies
have left Moscow? A strange notion! What had they
to be afraid of?"

[1] " *Oui, mon cher M. Pierre, je vous dois une fière chandelle de m'avoir
sauvé — de cet enragé. — J'en ai assez, voyez-vous, de balles dans le corps.
En voilà une à Wagram et deux à Smolensk. — Et cette jambe, comme
vous voyez, qui ne veut pas marcher. C'est à la grande bataille du 7 à la
Moscowa que j'ai reçu ça. Sacré Dieu, c'était beau! Il fallait voir ça;
c'était un deluge de feu. Vous nous avez taillé une rude besogne; vous
pouvez vous en vanter, nom d'un petit bonhomme! Et, ma parole, malgré
la toux, que j'ai gagné, je serais prêt à recommencer. Je plains ceux qui
n'ont pas vu ça." — " J'y ai été." — " Bah, vraiment! eh bien, tant mieux.
Vous êtes de fiers ennemis, tout de même. La grande redoute a été ténace,
nom d'un pipe! Et vous nous a' fait crânement payer. J'y suis allé trois
fois, tel que vous me voyez. Trois fois nous étions sur les canons et trois fois
on nous a culbutié et comme des capucins de cartes. Oh! c'était superbe,
M. Pierre! Vos grenadiers ont été superbes, tonnerre de Dieu! Je les
ai vu six fois de suite serrer les rangs et marcher comme à une revue.
Les beaux hommes! Notre roi de Naples, qui s'y connait, a crié: ' Bravo!'
Ah! ah! soldats comme nous autres! Tant mieux, tant mieux, M.
Pierre! Terribles en batailles — galants avec les belles, voilà les Fran-
çais, M. Pierre, n'est ce pas?"*

"Would n't the French ladies leave Paris if the Russians marched in?" retorted Pierre.

"Ha! ha! ha!" The Frenchman burst into a gay, hearty laugh, and slapped Pierre on the shoulder. "Ah! that is a good one," he went on to remark. "*Paris? .... Mais Paris, Paris*" ....

"*Paris la capitale du monde!*" said Pierre, finishing his sentence.

The captain looked at Pierre. It was a habit of his in the middle of a sentence to hesitate and give one a steady look from his laughing, friendly eyes.

"There, now, if you had not said that you were Russian, I would have wagered you were Parisian. You have something about you" .... and, having said this compliment, he again paused and looked.

"I have been at Paris. I spent some years there," said Pierre.

"Ah! that is very evident. Paris! A man who does n't know Paris is a barbarian. You can tell a Parisian by the smell two leagues off! *Ça se sent à deux lieux.* Paris is Talma, la Duchesnois, Potier, la Sorbonne, *les boulevards!*" and, perceiving that his conclusion was somewhat inconsequential, he made haste to add: "There is only one Paris in the world. You have been in Paris, and you remain Russian! Well, I do not esteem you the less for it."

Under the influence of the wine which he had drunk, and after the days spent in solitude with his somber thoughts, Pierre could not help experiencing a certain satisfaction in talking with this jolly and good-tempered gentleman.

"To return to your ladies: they are said to be pretty. What a crazy notion to go and bury themselves in the steppes, when the French army is at Moscow! What a chance they have missed! Your muzhiks! that 's another thing! but you are civilized beings, and ought to know us better than that. We have captured Vienna, Berlin, Madrid, Naples, Rome, Warsaw — all the capitals of the world. We are feared, but we are loved. There 's no harm in knowing men like us. And then the emperor...." he began, but Pierre interrupted him.

"*L'empereur,*" repeated Pierre, and his face suddenly assumed a gloomy expression of confusion — "*Est ce que l'empereur?*" ....

"The emperor! He is generosity, clemency, justice, order, and genius itself! That's what the emperor is! I, Ramball, tell you so. I, the very person before you, was his enemy eight years ago! My father was a count and an *émigré*. .... But this man was too much for me. He conquered me. I could not resist the spectacle of the glory and grandeur with which he was loading France. When I understood what he wanted, when I saw that he was making a perfect bed of laurels for us, do you know, I said to myself : 'There's a sovereign for you,' and I gave myself to him. And that's the whole story. Oh, yes, my dear sir, he is the greatest man of the ages past or to come."

"Is he at Moscow?" asked Pierre, stammering, and with a guilty countenance.

The Frenchman looked at Pierre's guilty face, and smiled. "No, he will make his entrance to-morrow,"[1] said he, and went on with his stories.

Their conversation was interrupted by a noise of many voices at the gate, and by Morel coming in to explain to the captain that some Würtemberg hussars had made their appearance and wanted to stable their

[1] "*Pour en revenir à vos dames, on les dit bien belles. Quelle fichue idée d'aller s'enterrer dans les steppes, quand l'armée française est à Moscou ! Quelle chance elles ont manqué, celles-là ! Vos moujiks, c'est autre chose ; mais vous autres gens civilisés, vous devriez nous connaître mieux que ça. Nous avons pris Vienne, Berlin, Madrid, Naples, Rome, Varsovie — toutes les capitales du monde. — On nous craint, mais on nous aime. Nous sommes bons à connaître. — Et puis l'empereur. — L'empereur ! C'est la générosité, la clémence, la justice, l'ordre, le génie : voilà l'empereur ! C'est moi, Ramball, qui vous le dit. Tel que vous me voyez, j'étais son ennemi, il y a encore huit ans. Mon père a été comte émigré. — Mais il m'a vaincu, cet homme. Il m'a empoigné. Je n'ai pas pu resister au spectacle de grandeur et de gloire dont il couvrait la France. Quand j'ai compris ce qu'il voulait, quand j'ai vu qu'il nous faisait une litière de lauriers, voyez-vous, je me suis dit : Voilà un souverain. Et je me suis donné à lui. Oh, oui, mon cher, c'est le plus grand homme des siècles passées et à venir.*" — "*Est-il à Moscou ?*" — "*Non, il fera son entre demain.*"

horses in the same dvor, which was preëmpted by the captain's horses.

The difficulty arose principally from the fact that the hussars did not understand what was said to them.

The captain commanded the old non-commissioned officer to be brought into his presence, and, in a stern voice, he began to question him : To what regiment did he belong ? Who was his chief ? and, By what authority he permitted himself to take possession of quarters that were preëmpted ?

In reply to the first two questions the German, whose knowledge of French was but slender, named his regiment and his superior ; but in reply to the last, which he did n't understand, he began to explain, in German interlarded with a few words of broken French, that he was the billeter of his regiment, and that he had been ordered by his colonel to take possession of all the houses in the row.

Pierre, who knew German, interpreted for the captain what the Würtemberger said, and he repeated the captain's answer in German to the hussar. When at last he understood what was meant, the German yielded, and withdrew his men. The captain went to the steps and gave some orders in a loud voice.

When he returned to the room, Pierre was still sitting in the same place as before, with his hands clasped on top of his head. His face expressed suffering. He was actually suffering at that moment. When the captain went out and Pierre was left alone, he suddenly came to his senses, and realized the position in which he found himself. Crueily as he felt the fact that Moscow was captured and that these fortunate victors were making themselves at home in the city, and patronizing him, still it was not this which chiefly tormented Pierre at the moment. He was tortured by the consciousness of his own weakness. The few glasses of wine he had drunk, the conversation with this good-natured man, had destroyed that darkly determined mood in which Pierre had been living for a day or two, and which was indispensable for the fulfilment of his purpose.

Pistol and dagger and kaftan were ready. Napoleon would make his *entrée* on the morrow. Pierre felt that it was right and profitable to kill the " evil-doer," but he felt that now he should not accomplish his purpose.

Why?

He knew not, but he had the presentiment that he should not carry out his intention. He struggled against this consciousness of his weakness, but vaguely felt that he should not get the mastery of it, that his former dark thoughts about vengeance, assassination, and self-sacrifice had scattered like dust at the first contact with his fellow-men.

The captain, slightly limping and whistling some tune, came back into the room.

The Frenchman's chatter, which had before amused Pierre, now annoyed him. And the tune that he was whistling, and his gait, and his habit of twirling his mustache, — all now seemed offensive to Pierre.

" I will go instantly, I will have nothing more to say to him," thought Pierre. He thought this, but still he kept his seat in the same place. A strange feeling of weakness rooted him to his place; he felt the desire, but he was unable to get up and go.

The captain, on the contrary, seemed very merry. He paced two or three times up and down the room. His eyes flashed, and his mustaches slightly worked, as if he were smiling all by himself at some merry conceit of his. "*Charmant!*" he suddenly exclaimed, "*le colonel de ces Wurtembourgeois! c'est un allemand: mais brave garçon, s'il en fut. Mais allemand!* — He's a German, but he's a good fellow, all the same."

He sat down opposite Pierre. "*À propos, vous savez donc l'allemand, vous?* — So you know German, do you?"

Pierre looked at him and made no reply.

"*Comment dites-vous asile en allemand?*"

"*Asile,*" repeated Pierre, "asylum in German? — *Unterkunft!*"

"*Comment dites-vous?*" again asked the captain, quickly, with a shade of distrust in his voice.

"*Unterkunft!*" repeated Pierre.

"*Onterkoff,*" said the captain, and looked at Pierre for several seconds with mischievous eyes. "*Les allemands sont de fières bêtes, n'est ce pas!* — Germans are beastly conceited, are n't they! — *M. Pierre?*" he added by way of conclusion. "*Eh bien, encore une bouteille de ce Bordeau Moscovite, n'est ce pas? Morel! va nous chauffer encore une petite bouteille, Morel!* — Warm up another bottle for us!" gayly cried the captain.

Morel brought candles and another bottle of wine. The captain looked at Pierre by the light of the candles, and was evidently struck by his new friend's distracted face. With genuine concern and sympathy expressed in his eyes, he went over to Pierre and bent down over him.

"*Eh bien, nous sommes tristes,*" said he, touching Pierre's arm. "Have I hurt your feelings? No, truly, have n't you something against me?" he insisted. "Perhaps it 's due to the state of things."

Pierre made no answer, but looked affectionately into the Frenchman's eyes. This expression of sympathy was grateful to him.

"On my word of honor, without reference to my gratitude to you, I feel a genuine friendship for you. Can I do anything for you? I am entirely at your service. It is for life or for death! I tell you this with my hand on my heart!" said he, slapping himself on the chest.

"No, thank you," said Pierre.

The captain kept his eyes on him, just as he looked at him when he was learning what the German for "refuge" was, and his face suddenly beamed.

"Ah! in that case, I drink to our friendship," he gayly cried, pouring out two glasses of wine.

Pierre took his, and drained it. Ramball drank his, again pressed Pierre's hand, and then leaned his elbows on the table in thoughtful, melancholy pose: "Yes, my dear friend, see the caprices of fortune!" he began. "Who would ever have said that I was going to be a soldier and captain of dragoons in the service of Bonaparte, as we called him a little while ago! And yet, here I am in Moscow with him. I must tell you, my dear fellow," he continued, in the solemn and measured voice of a man who is getting ready to spin a long yarn : "I must tell you our name is one of the most ancient in France ...."

And, with the easy-going and simple frankness of a Frenchman, the captain told Pierre the story of his ancestors, his childhood, youth, and manhood, giving all the particulars of his ancestry, his estates, and his relationships. *"Ma pauvre mère,"* of course, played an important *rôle* in this story.

"But all that is only the stage setting of life ; the real thing is love. Love ! is n't that so, Mr. Pierre ? " said he, growing more animated. "Have another glass."[1]

Pierre drank it up, and poured out for himself still a third glass.

"Oh, les femmes, les femmes !" and the captain, with oily eyes, gazing at Pierre, began to talk about love and about his gallant adventures. He had enjoyed a very great number of them, as it was easy to believe from a glance in the officer's handsome, self-satisfied face, and the enthusiastic eagerness with which he talked about women.

Although all of Ramball's adventures had that characteristic of vileness in which the French find the exclusive charm and poetry of love, still the captain told his stories with such honest conviction that he was the only one who had ever experienced and understood

---

[1] *"Vous ai-je fait de la peine? Non, vrai, avez-vous quelque chose contre moi? Peut-être rapport à la situation? Parole d'honneur, sans parler de ce que je vous dois, j'ai de l'amitié pour vous. Puis-je faire quelque chose pour vous? Disposez de moi! C'est à la vie et à la mort. C'est la main sur le cœur que je vous le dis."* — *"Merci !"* — *"Ah ! dans ces cas je bois à notre amitié. Oui, mon cher ami, voilà les caprices de la fortune! Qui m'aurait dit que je serai soldat et capitaine de dragons au service de Bonaparte comme nous l'appellions jadis. Et cependant me voilà à Moscou avec lui. Il faut vous dire, mon cher, que notre nom est l'un des plus anciens de la France.* — *Mais tout ça ce n'est que la mise-en-scène de la vie ; le fond c'est l'amour. L'amour ! N'est ce pas, M. Pierre ! — Encore un verre !"*

all the delights of love, and he gave such alluring descriptions of women that Pierre listened to him with curiosity.

It was evident that *l'amour* which the Frenchman so loved was not that low and simple sensual passion which Pierre had once experienced for his wife, nor yet that romantic flame which was kindled in his heart by Natasha, —both of which kinds of love Ramball held in equal contempt, —one being, according to him, *l'amour des charretiers,* carter's love; the other, *l'amour des nigauds,* booby's love: *l'amour* which the Frenchman worshiped consisted preëminently in unnatural relations toward women, and in combinations of incongruities which gave the chief charm to the passion.

Thus the captain related a touching story of his love for a bewitching marquise of thirty-five, and, at the same time, for a charming innocent maiden of seventeen, the daughter of the bewitching marquise. The struggle of magnanimity between mother and daughter, ending with the mother sacrificing herself and proposing that the daughter should become her lover's wife, even now, though it was a recollection brought up from a long-buried past, moved the captain.

Then he related an episode in which the husband played the lover's part, while he—the lover—played the part of husband, and then several comical episodes from his *souvenirs d'Allemagne,* where *"asile"* was *Unterkunft,* where *les maris mangent de la choux croute* — where husbands eat sauer-kraut, and where *les jeunes filles sont trop blondes !*

Finally, his latest episode in Poland, which was still fresh in the captain's recollections, for he told it with eager gestures and a flushed face, consisted in his having saved a Polyak's life (as a general thing, in the captain's narrations, the episode of life-saving was an important feature), and this Polyak had intrusted to him his most fascinating, bewitching wife—"*Parisienne de cœur*"—while he himself entered the French service. The captain was fortunate, the bewitching Pole wanted to run away with him, but, moved by generosity, he had restored the wife to the husband, saying : *"Je vous ai sauvé la vie et je sauve votre honneur !"* In pronouncing these words, the captain rubbed his eyes, and gave himself a little shake, as if to drive away his weakness at such a touching recollection.

While listening to the captain's yarns, Pierre, as was apt to be the case, late in the evening, and under the influence of the wine, took in all that the captain had to say, comprehended it all, and, at the same time, connected it with a whole series of personal recollections, which somehow suddenly began to rise up in his mind. As he listened to these stories of love, his own love for Natasha occurred to him, with unexpected suddenness, and as he unrolled, in his imagination, the pictures of this love, he mentally compared them with Ramball's.

Thus, when he followed that story of the struggle between love and duty, he saw, with wonderful vividness, in all its details, his last meeting with the object of his love, near the Sukharef tower.

At that time the meeting had not made any special impression upon him ; he had not once since thought of it. But now it seemed to him that this casual meeting had something very significant and poetic.

"Piotr Kiriluitch ! Come here ! I recognized you !"

He now heard her saying those words ; he had before him a vision of her eyes, her smile, her traveling-hood, a lock of hair escaping from it, — and something very touching and tender connected itself with the whole scene.

Having finished his tale about the bewitching *Polka*, the captain asked Pierre if he had ever experienced anything like self-sacrifice for love, or jealousy of a woman's husband.

Aroused by this question, Pierre raised his head, and felt it incumbent upon him to pour out the thoughts that filled his mind. He began to explain in what a different manner he understood love for a woman. He declared that in all his life he had loved and should love only one woman, and that this woman could never be his.

" *Tiens !* " exclaimed the captain.

Pierre explained that he loved this woman when he was very young; but he did not then dare to aspire to her, because she was too young, while he was an illegitimate son without name. Afterward, when he had received a name and fortune, he could not think of her, because he loved her too much, regarded her too far above all the world, and accordingly too far above himself.

When he reached this part of his confession, Pierre turned to the captain, and asked him if he understood him.

The captain made a gesture, as much as to say that if he did not understand him, still he would beg him to proceed: "*L'amour platonique, nuages,*" he muttered.

Either from the wine which he had drunk, or from the need that he felt of pouring out all his heart, or from the thought that this man would never know any of the personages of his story, or from everything combined, Pierre's tongue became unloosened. And with thick utterance, and bleary eyes looking into space, he related his whole story; about his marriage and the history of Natasha's love for his best friend, and the change that had taken place in her, and all his simple relations to her. And, under a little pressure from Ramball, he disclosed what at first he had concealed, his position in society, and even told him his name.

What amazed the captain more than anything else was the fact that Pierre was very rich, that he had two palaces in Moscow, and that he had given up everything, and, instead of fleeing from Moscow, had remained in the city, concealing his name and rank.

It was already very late that night when they went out into the street. It was mild and bright. At the left of the house already gleamed the ruddy glare of the first fire, that on the Petrovka, which was the beginning of the conflagration of Moscow.

At the right, high up in the sky, stood the young, slender sickle of the moon, and over against the moon could be seen that brilliant comet which was connected in Pierre's mind with his love.

At the gates stood Gerasim, the cook, and two Frenchmen, laughing and talking, each in a language incomprehensible to the other.

They were gazing at the ruddy glow which could be seen across the city.

There was nothing terrible in a small fire at a distance in the vast city.

As he looked up at the high, starry heavens, at the moon, at the comet, and at the glare of the conflagration, Pierre experienced an agreeable emotion.

"Now, how beautiful this is! What more is needed?" he asked himself.

And suddenly, when he remembered his resolve, his head grew giddy, he felt so badly that he had to cling to the fence not to fall.

Without saying good-night to his new friend, Pierre, with tottering steps, left the gates, and, returning to his room, lay down on his divan, and instantly fell asleep.

CHAPTER XXX

THE glare of the first fire that broke out, on the fourteenth of September, was witnessed from various roads and with various feelings by the escaping and departing citizens and the retreating troops.

The Rostofs were spending that night at Muitishchi, about twenty versts from Moscow. They had started so late on the thirteenth, the road was so encumbered with trains and troops, so many things had been forgotten, for which men had to be sent back, that they had determined to spend the night at a place five versts from Moscow.

On the next morning they awoke late, and again there were so many delays that they got no farther than Bolshiya Muitishchi. At ten o'clock the Rostof family and the wounded men whom they had brought with them were all quartered among the dvors and cottages of the great village. The servants, the Rostofs' drivers, and the denshchiks of the wounded men, having arranged for their comfort, had eaten their suppers, fed their horses, and were come out on the steps.

In a neighboring cottage lay a wounded aide to Rayevsky, with a broken wrist; and the terrible anguish which he felt made him groan piteously all the time, and these groans sounded terribly in the darkness of the autumn night. The first night this aide, had been quartered at the same place with the Rostofs. The countess declared that she could not close her eyes on account of his groaning, and at Muitishchi she had taken a worse room so as to be farther away from this wounded man.

The night was dark, and one of the servants had noticed, from behind the high body of a carriage standing near the gate, a small glare of a second conflagration. One had already been noticed some time before, and all knew that that had been the village of Maluiya Muitishchi, set on fire by Mamonof's Cossacks.

"Look at that, boys! another fire!" said the denshchik. The attention of all was attracted to the glare.

"Oh, yes, they say Maluiya Muitishchi has been set on fire by Mamonof's Cossacks."

"They? No! that's not Muitishchi; it's farther off. See there! That must be Moscow!"

Two of the men came down from the porch, went behind the carriage, and climbed up on the rack.

"It's too far to the left for Muitischi — 'way round on the other side."

Several men came and joined the others.

"See how it flares up!" said one. "Yes, gentlemen, that fire's in Moscow — either in the Sushchevskaya or in the Rogozhskaya."

No reply was made to this conjecture. And for some time all these men looked in silence at the distant flames of this new conflagration, which seemed to be spreading.

An old man, the count's valet (*Kammerdiener*, as they called him), Danilo Terentyitch, came out to the crowd and shouted to Mishka: —

"What are you staring at, you blockhead? — The count is calling, and no one there; go put his clothes away."

"I only came out after some water," said Mishka.

"Now, what do you think, Danilo Terentyitch — is your idea that fire's in Moscow?" asked one of the lackeys.

Danilo Terentyitch made no reply, and again they all stood for a long time silent.

The glare spread and wavered over a wider and wider stretch of the horizon.

"God have mercy! The wind and the drought!" said a voice at last.

"Just look! how far it has gone! O Lord! I think I can see the jackdaws! Lord, have mercy on us sinners!"

"They'll put it out, never fear!"

"Who's to put it out?" Danilo Terentyitch's voice was heard asking. He had not spoken till then. His tone was calm and deliberate. "Yes, that is Moscow, boys," said he. "Our white-walled matush...."

His voice broke, and he sobbed like an old man.

And as if all were waiting for this, before they could realize the meaning which this glare that they saw had for them, sighs were heard, ejaculations from prayers, and the old kammerdiener's sobs.

CHAPTER XXXI

THE kammerdiener returned to the house, and informed the count that Moscow was burning.

The count put on his dressing-gown and went out to look. With him went Sonya and Madame Schoss, who had not yet undressed. Natasha and the countess were alone in their room. Petya was now parted from his family; he had gone on ahead with his regiment, which had its rendezvous at Troïtsa.

The countess wept when she heard that Moscow was on fire. Natasha, pale, with fixed eyes, was sitting on a bench under the holy pictures — in the same place where she had taken her seat when they first came in — and paid not the slightest attention to her father's report. She listened to the aide's incessant groaning, which could be heard three houses off.

"Akh! how horrible!" exclaimed Sonya, coming in from out of doors, chilled and scared. "I think all Moscow is on fire; it's a terrible blaze! Natasha, come here and look. You can see it now from this window!" she exclaimed, evidently wishing to rouse her cousin from her thoughts.

But Natasha looked at her as if not comprehending what she wanted, and again she turned her eyes toward the stove.

Natasha had been in that state of petrifaction since early that morning, from the moment when Sonya, to the amazement and annoyance of the countess, without any reason for doing so, had felt obliged to tell Natasha that Prince Andreï was wounded, and was with them in their train. The countess was more angry with Sonya than she had ever been before. Sonya had wept and begged for forgiveness, and now, as if she were striving to atone for her error, she was assiduous in waiting on her cousin.

"Look, Natasha! what a terrible fire it is!" said Sonya.

"What fire?" asked Natasha. "Oh, you mean Moscow?"

And, evidently wishing not to offend Sonya by refusing, but to get rid of her, she turned her head to the window, and glanced out in such a way that she evidently could see nothing, and immediately resumed her former position.

"But you did n't see, did you?"

"Yes, truly, I did!" exclaimed Natasha, in a tone that implied her desire to be left in peace.

Both the countess and Sonya understood that for Natasha, Moscow, or the burning of Moscow, or anything else, in fact, had no significance.

The count had again withdrawn behind the partition and gone to bed. The countess went up to Natasha, smoothed her head with the back of her hand, as she used to do when her daughter was ill, then she touched her forehead with her lips, to see whether she were feverish, and kissed her.

"Are you chilly? You are all of a tremble! You had better go to bed!" said she.

"Go to bed? Oh, yes, very good! I will go to bed. I will in a moment," said Natasha.

Since Natasha had been told that morning that Prince Andreï was severely wounded and was traveling with them, she had only at first asked, Where?.... how?.... is he dangerously wounded? and could she see him?

But when she was told that it was impossible for her to see him, that he was severely wounded, but that his life was not in danger, she, evidently putting no faith in what they told her, and convinced that no matter what questions she asked she would receive the same answer, had ceased to ask questions or even to speak. All the way, Natasha had sat motionless in her corner of the carriage, with wide, staring eyes, with that expression which the countess knew so well, and dreaded; and now she sat in the same way on the bench. She was planning some scheme, she was coming to some decision, or else had already made up her mind, — this the countess knew; but what it was she knew not, and this alarmed and tormented her.

"Natasha, undress! Come, darling, get into bed with me." (The countess was the only one who had a regular bed; Madame Schoss and the two young ladies slept on the floor, on straw.)

"No, mamma, I will lie here on the floor!" said Natasha, testily, and, going to the window, she threw it open. The aide's groaning was heard more distinctly through the open window. She thrust her head out into the damp night air, and the countess saw how her slender neck was swollen with her repressed sobs and throbbed against the window-frame. Natasha was aware that Prince Andreï was not groaning. She knew that Prince Andreï was in the same row of cottages where they were, in the next izba, with only a wall between; but this terrible incessant groaning made her sob. The countess exchanged glances with Sonya.

"Go to bed, darling, go to bed, sweetheart!" said the countess, giving Natasha a gentle touch on the shoulder. "Go to bed now."

"Oh, yes, ... yes, I will go to bed at once .... at once," said Natasha, hastily beginning to undress, and breaking the strings of her petticoats. After taking off her dress and putting on her dressing-jacket, she curled up her feet and sat down on the bed that had been prepared on the floor, and, pulling her short, thin braid down over her shoulder, she began to braid it over again.

Her long, slender fingers swiftly, deftly unbraided it, then braided it up again and tied it with a ribbon. Natasha's head turned as usual first to the window and then in the other direction, but her eyes, feverishly opened, gazed fixedly straight ahead.

When her preparation for the night was accomplished, she quietly dropped down on the sheet spread over the hay, on the side next the door.

"Natasha, you take the middle!" said Sonya.

"No, I'll stay here," replied Natasha. "Do lie down," she added, in a tone of annoyance. And she buried her face in the pillow.

The countess, Madame Schoss, and Sonya hastily undressed and went to bed. The night lamp alone was left burning in the room. But out of doors it was light as day from the fire at Maluiya Muitishchi, two versts distant; and from across the street at the tavern which Mamonof's Cossacks were rifling came the drunken shouts of men, and the aide's groans were incessant.

Natasha listened for a long time to all these sounds without and within, and did not stir. At first she heard her mother's muttered prayer, and sighs, the creaking of the bed as she moved, Madame Schoss's well-known piping snore, Sonya's gentle breathing. Then the countess spoke to Natasha. Natasha made no reply.

"I think she's asleep, mamma," softly replied Sonya.

The countess, after a little interval of silence, spoke again, but this time no one answered her.

Soon after, Natasha heard her mother's measured breathing.

Natasha did not move, though her little bare foot, peeping out from under the bed-covering, was chilled by the uncarpeted floor.

A cricket, as if proud of watching over all, chirped in a crevice. A cock crowed at a distance, and was answered by another nearer. The shouts had ceased in the tavern; the only other sound was the aide's incessant groaning. Natasha sat up in bed.

"Sonya, are you asleep?.... Mamma?" she whispered.

No one answered.

Natasha slowly and cautiously arose, crossed herself, cautiously set her light, slender, bare foot on the cold, dirty floor. The boards creaked. She ran nimbly as a kitten for a few steps, and took hold of the cold latch of the door.

It seemed to her as if something heavy were knocking with regular strokes on all the walls of the izba. It was her heart beating and almost bursting with terror and love.

She opened the door, crossed the threshold, and set foot on the damp, cold earth of the passageway. The all-enveloping coolness refreshed her. She touched a sleeping man with her bare foot, stepped over him, and opened the door into the izba where Prince Andreï was lying. It was dark in this room. On a bench in the corner, just back of the bed, whereon something lay, stood a tallow candle, which in burning had taken the form of a great mushroom.

Natasha, ever since that morning, when she learned about Prince Andreï's wound and that he was with them, had made up her mind that she must see him. She knew not why this was necessary, but she knew that the interview would be painful, and therefore she was all the more certain that it was inevitable.

All that day she had lived in the sole hope of being able to see him that night. But now, when the moment had actually come, she was filled with horror at the thought of what she was going to see. How was he mutilated? How much of him was left? *Was he like the aide's incessant groans?* Yes, he must be. In her imagination he was the very embodiment of these horrible groans.

When she caught sight of an ill-defined mass in the corner, and took his knees thrust up under the bed-clothes for his shoulders, she imagined some horrible body, and in her terror she paused. But an unexpected force compelled her forward. She cautiously took one step, then another, and found herself in the middle of the small room filled with luggage. On the bench in the corner under the holy pictures lay another man, — this was Timokhin, — and on the floor lay two other men, — these were the doctor and the valet.

The valet sat up and whispered something. Timokhin, suffering from pain in his wounded leg, was not asleep, and stared with all his eyes at this strange apparition of a young girl in her white nightgown, dressing-sack, and nightcap.

The sleepy and startled words of the valet, "What do you want? Who is it?" merely caused Natasha to step the more quickly to what was lying in the corner. However terribly unlike the form of man that body was, she still must see it. She passed by the valet; the candle flared up, and she clearly saw Prince Andreï with his arms stretched out over the spread, and looking just as she had always known him.

He was the same as ever. But the flushed face, his gleaming eyes gazing at her with ecstasy, and especially his delicate, boyish throat, relieved by the opened shirt-collar, gave him a peculiarly innocent, babyish appearance such as she had never seen in him.

She went to him, and threw herself on her knees with the swift, pliant grace of youth.

He smiled, and extended to her his hand.

CHAPTER XXXII

A week had passed since Prince Andreï had come to himself in the field lazaret of Borodino. Almost all of this time he had been in a state of unconsciousness. His feverish condition, and the inflammation of his intestines, which had suffered a lesion, were, in the opinion of the surgeon who attended him, destined to carry him off. But on the seventh day he ate a morsel of bread and drank some tea with appetite, and the doctor remarked that his fever had diminished.

Prince Andreï had regained his consciousness in the morning. The first night after they left Moscow had been pretty warm, and Prince Andreï had not been moved from his calash; but at Muitishchi he himself had asked to be taken into a house and given some tea. The anguish caused by moving him into the izba caused Prince Andreï to groan aloud, and to lose consciousness again. When they had placed him on the camp-bed, he lay for a long time motionless, with closed eyes. Then he had opened them, and asked in a whisper : —

"May I have tea ?"

Such a memory for the small details of life had amazed the surgeon. He felt of his pulse, and, to his surprise and regret, discovered that his pulse was better. The doctor remarked it with regret, because from his experience he was certain that Prince Andreï could not live, and that if he were to live on he would only have to die a little later in terrible agony.

The red-nosed major of his regiment, Timokhin, had been also brought to Moscow with him, wounded in the leg in the same battle of Borodino. They were accompanied by the surgeon, the prince's valet, his coachman, and two denshchiks.

They had handed Prince Andreï his tea. He drank it eagerly, looking with feverish eyes straight ahead at the door, apparently trying to understand and remember something.

"I don't want any more. Is Timokhin there?" he asked. Timokhin crept along on the bench toward him.

"I am here, your illustriousness."

"How is the wound?"

"Mine? It's all right. But you?"

Prince Andreï again lay thinking, as if trying to remember something.

"Can't you get me the book?" he asked.

"What book?"

"The New Testament."

"The New Testament? I have n't one."

The doctor had promised to get one for him, and began to inquire of the prince how he felt. Prince Andreï answered reluctantly but intelligibly to all the doctor's questions, and then said that he would like a bolster, for he felt uncomfortable, and his wound was very painful. The doctor and valet took off the cloak which covered him, and, scowling at the putrid odor of the gangrene spreading through the wound, began to examine the terrible place.

The surgeon had found the state of things very unsatisfactory, made some different disposition of the bandages, and turned the wounded man over, so that it made him groan again; and the agony caused in turning him back again had caused him to lose consciousness; he had begun to be delirious. He kept insisting that they should fetch for him as quickly as possible the book that he had wanted, and place it in such and such a place.

"What would it cost you?" he asked. "I have n't one — please get me one! — let me have it for a little minute!" he had pleaded, in a pitiful voice.

The doctor went into the entry to wash his hands.

"Akh! it's terrible, truly!" he had said to the valet, who was pouring water for him over his hands. "Only look at him for a moment. Why, it's such agony that I am amazed that he endures it."

"Well, we have to take what is sent us! O Lord Jesus Christ!" ejaculated the valet.

Prince Andreï, for the first time, had realized where

he was and what was the matter with him, and remembered that he had been wounded, and how, when the
carriage stopped at Muitishchi, he had asked to be taken
into the izba. His mind grew confused again from the
pain, but he had come to himself, for a second time, in
the izba, as he was drinking the tea ; and then once
more, as he went over all his experience, he more vividly
than anything else recalled that moment at the field
lazaret when, at sight of the sufferings of the man whom
he so hated, new thoughts, that gave promise of happiness, came to him.

And these thoughts, though obscure and vague, had
now again taken possession of his mind. He remembered that a new happiness had come to him, and that
this happiness was somehow connected with the Gospel.
Therefore he had asked for the New Testament.

But the new position in which his wound had been
placed, and the turning him over, had again confused
his thoughts ; and when, for the third time, he awoke to
a consciousness of life, it was in the absolute silence of
night.

All were asleep around him. A cricket was chirping
in another room ; some one was shouting and singing
in the street ; cockroaches were rustling over the table,
the holy pictures, and the walls ; a fat fly came blundering against his pillow, and buzzed around the tallow
candle with the mushroom arrangement that stood near
him.

His mind was not in its normal condition. The
healthy man ordinarily thinks, feels, and remembers a
countless collection of objects at one and the same time ;
but he has the power and strength to choose one series
of thoughts or phenomena, and to give to this series all
his attention.

The man in health, no matter how deep may be his
thoughts, can put them aside at a moment's notice in
order to speak a courteous word to any one coming in,
and then immediately resume them again.

Prince Andreï's mind was not in a normal condition
in this respect. All its forces were more keen and ac-

tive than ever, but their activity was entirely outside of his will. They were simultaneously under the control of the most heterogeneous thoughts and visions.

Sometimes his mind began suddenly to work, and with an energy, clearness, and subtlety such as it had never shown when he was in health. And then just as suddenly, in the midst of this fabrication of his brain, some unexpected vision would interpose and interrupt, and he would not have the strength to return to it.

"Yes, a new happiness not to be taken from man was revealed to me," he said to himself, as he lay in the semi-obscurity of the quiet izba, and looked up with feverishly wide-open and fixed eyes. "A happiness to be found outside of material forces, outside of exterior, material influences, the happiness of the spirit alone, of love. Every man can understand it, but God alone can adjudge it and prescribe it. But how does God prescribe this law? Why did the Son?"....

And suddenly the course of his thoughts was broken off, and Prince Andreï heard, but he could not tell whether he really heard it or whether it was his delirium, — he heard a low lisping voice constantly rehearsing in measured rhythm: "*i piti — piti — piti*" — and then again "*i ti-ti*," and then "*i piti — piti — piti*," and then once more "*i ti-ti*."

At the same time, while this whispered music was ringing, Prince Andreï felt that over his face, over the very center of it, was rising a strange sort of airy edifice of delicate little needles or shavings. He felt — but this was trying to him — that it was necessary for him to keep in perfect equilibrium, so that the growing edifice might not crumble; but nevertheless it fell down, and then slowly rose again to the sounds of this whispered, rhythmic music.

"It is growing, it is growing! it is stretching up and growing!" said Prince Andreï to himself.

At the same time that he heard the whispered music, and with the perception of that upstretching and rising edifice of needles, Prince Andreï could see by fits and starts the ruddy circle of the candle-light, and could hear the rustling of the cockroaches and the buzzing of the fly which blundered against his pillow and his face. And whenever the fly struck his face it produced a burning sensation; but at the same time he was amazed because when it touched the domain occupied by that structure of needles it did not affect it.

Then, moreover, there was something else singular. This was something white by the door; it was a statue of the sphinx, which also crushed him.

"But maybe that is my shirt on the table," thought Prince Andreï, "but these are my legs, and that is the door, but why does that structure rise up and stretch out so, and that *piti — piti — piti i ti-ti i piti — piti — piti?* — That is enough.... please stop," begged Prince Andreï, as if addressing some one. And suddenly again his thoughts and feeling became extraordinarily clear and distinct.

"Yes, love," he thought, with perfect distinctness, "but not that love which loves for a purpose, for a personal end, but that love which I for the first time experienced when, dying, I saw my enemy, and could still love him. I experienced the feeling of love which is the very substance of the soul, and which needs no object. And even now I experience that blessed feeling. To love one's neighbors, to love one's enemies. Always to love — to love God in all his manifestations. To love one's friends is human love; but to love one's enemies is divine. And this is what made me experience such bliss when I felt that I loved that man! What has become of him? Is he living, or....

"Love in its human form may pass over into hate; but divine love cannot change. Nothing, not even death, can destroy it. It is the very substance of the soul. But how many people have I hated in my life! And none have I ever loved more warmly or hated more bitterly than her!"

And he vividly pictured Natasha, not as she had formerly seemed to his imagination, through her charming personality alone; but, for the first time, in her spiritual nature. And he understood her feelings, her suffering, her shame, and her repentance.

He now for the first time realized all the cruelty of his renunciation, saw the cruelty of his break with her.

"If I might only see her once again .... once again look into her eyes, and tell her .... "

"*I piti — piti — piti — i ti-ti i piti — piti — bumm !*" went the fly. ....

And his attention was suddenly diverted to that other world of delirious activity in which such strange things took place. In this world, just the same as before, that edifice arose and crumbled not, the candle burned with its red halo, the same shirt-sphinx[1] lay by the door; but, in addition to all this, there was a squeaking sound, there was the odor of a cooling breeze, and a new white sphinx appeared, standing in front of the door. And this sphinx had a pallid face, and the sparkling eyes of that same Natasha of whom he had but just been thinking.

"Oh! how trying this incessant hallucination is!" said Prince Andreï to himself, striving to banish this vision from his imagination. But the face still stood in front of him in all the vividness of reality; nay, this face approached him.

Prince Andreï was anxious to return to the former world of pure thought, but he could not, and the delirium compelled him into its thraldom. The low whispering voice continued its rhythmic lisping, something like a weight oppressed him, and the strange vision stood in front of him.

Prince Andreï summoned all his energies so as to become master of himself; he moved, and suddenly in his ears there was a humming, his eyes grew clouded, and, like a man plunged in water, he lost consciousness.

When he came to his senses, Natasha, the veritable living Natasha, whom of all people in the world he had been most anxious to love with that new, pure, divine love just revealed to him, was before him, on her knees!

[1] *Rubashka-sfinks.*

He realized that this was the living, actual Natasha; and he felt no surprise, but only a gentle sense of gladness.

Natasha, on her knees before him, held back her sobs and gazed at him timidly but intently; she could not stir. Her face was pale and motionless; only the lips quivered slightly.

Prince Andreï drew a sigh of relief, smiled, and stretched out his hand.

"You?" he asked. "What happiness!"

Natasha, still on her knees, with swift but cautious movement bent over to him, and, cautiously taking his hand, bent her face down to it and began to kiss it, scarcely touching it with her lips.

"Forgive me!" she murmured, lifting her head and gazing at him. "Forgive me!"

"I love you!" said Prince Andreï.

"Forgive...."

"What have I to forgive?" asked Prince Andreï.

"For.... give me for .... what I .... did!" continued Natasha, almost inaudibly, in a broken whisper, and she began to kiss his hand faster than before, scarcely touching it with her lips.

"I love thee better, more dearly than before," said Prince Andreï, lifting her face with his hand so that he might look into her eyes.

Those eyes, overflowing with blissful tears, looked at him timidly, compassionately, and with the ecstasy of love. Natasha's face was thin and pale, the lips swollen; it had no trace of beauty; it was frightful. But Prince Andreï did not notice that; he saw her sparkling eyes, and they were beautiful.

Voices were heard behind them. Piotr, the prince's valet, now thoroughly awake, aroused the doctor. Timokhin, who had not been asleep at all on account of the pain in his leg, had not noticed what had been going on, and, solicitously covering himself, curled himself up on the bench.

"What does this mean?" asked the doctor, sitting up. "Please go, young lady!"

At the same time the maid sent by the countess to fetch her daughter knocked at the door.

Like a somnambulist awakened in the midst of her dream, Natasha left the room, and, returning to her own izba, fell sobbing on her bed.

From that day forth, during all the rest of the Rostofs' journey, at all their halts and resting-places, Natasha stayed by the wounded Bolkonsky's side, and the doctor was forced to confess that he had never expected to see in a young girl such constancy or such skill in nursing a wounded man.

Terrible as it seemed to the countess to think that the prince might (or, as the doctor said, probably would) die during the journey, in her daughter's arms, she had not the heart to refuse Natasha.

Though, in consequence of the now reëstablished relationship between the wounded prince and Natasha, it occurred to them that in case he recovered the engagement might be renewed, no one — Natasha and Prince Andreï least of all — spoke about it.

The undecided question of life and death hanging over, not Bolkonsky alone, but over Russia as well, kept all other considerations in the background.

CHAPTER XXXIII

PIERRE awoke late on the fifteenth of September. His head ached; his clothes, in which he had slept without undressing, hung heavy on him, and his mind was burdened by a dull consciousness of something shameful which he had done the night before.

This shameful act was his talk with Captain Ramball.

It was eleven o'clock by his watch, but it seemed peculiarly dark out of doors. Pierre got up, rubbed his eyes, and, seeing the pistol with its carved handle, which Gerasim had replaced on the writing-table, Pierre remembered where he was, and what was before him on that day.

"But am I not too late?" he queried. "No, probably *he* would not make his *entrée* into Moscow later than twelve o'clock."

Pierre did not allow himself to think what was before him, but he made all the greater haste to act.

Having adjusted his attire, Pierre took up the pistol and made ready to go. But then the thought for the first time occurred to him how he should carry his weapon through the street otherwise than in his hand. It was hard to hide the great pistol even under the flowing kaftan. Nor was it possible to keep it out of sight in his belt or under his arm. Moreover, the pistol had been discharged, and Pierre had not had time to reload it.

"Well, the dagger is just as good," said he to himself, though more than once, while deliberating over the accomplishment of his undertaking, he had come to the conclusion that the chief mistake made by the student in 1809 consisted in his trying to kill Napoleon with a dagger.

But as Pierre's chief end consisted not so much in fulfilling the scheme which he planned as it did in proving to himself that he had not renounced his purpose, and was doing everything to fulfil it, Pierre hastily seized the blunt and notched dagger in its green sheath, which he had bought together with the pistol at the Sukharef tower, and concealed it under his waistcoat.

Having belted up his kaftan and pulled his hat down over his eyes, Pierre, trying to make no noise and to avoid the captain, crept along the corridor and went into the street.

The fire which he had looked at so indifferently the evening before had noticeably increased during the night. Moscow was burning in various directions. At one and the same time the carriage-market, the district across the river,[1] the Gostinnui Dvor, the Povarskaya, the boats on the Moskva river, and the timber-yards by the Dorogomilovsky bridge were on fire.

Pierre's route took him by cross-streets to the Povar-

[1] The *Zamoskvoretchye.*

skaya, and thence along the Arbat to Saint Nikola Yavlennoi, where, in his imagination, he had determined should be the place for the execution of his project. Most of the houses had their doors and window-shutters nailed up. The streets and alleys were deserted. The air was full of smoke and the smell of burning. Occasionally he met Russians with anxiously timid faces, and Frenchmen of uncitified, military aspect, who walked in the middle of the street. All looked with amazement at Pierre. The Russians were impressed not only by his great height and stoutness, but by the strange, gloomily concentrated and martyr-like expression of his face and figure, and they stared at him because they could not make out to what rank of life he belonged. The French followed him in amazement because Pierre, unlike the other Russians, paid absolutely no attention to them, instead of looking at them in trepidation or curiosity.

At the gates of one house three Frenchmen, trying to talk to some Russian servants, who could understand nothing of what they said, stopped Pierre and asked him if he knew French.

Pierre shook his head and went on his way. In another cross-street the sentinel mounted by a green caisson challenged him, and it was not until Pierre heard his threatening call repeated, and the click of his musket, which the sentinel took up, that he realized that he must go round on the other side of the street.

He heard nothing and saw nothing of what was going on around him. With a sense of nervous haste and horror, he took with him, like something terrible and alien to him, that project of his, and feared — taught by his experience of the night before — that something would distract him. But it was not Pierre's destiny to reach his destination in the same frame of mind. Moreover, even if there had occurred nothing to detain him, his project could not now have been carried out, for the reason that Napoleon, some four hours previously, had passed through the Dorogomilovsky suburb, across the Arbat, into the Kreml, and now was seated in the gloomiest frame of mind in the imperial cabinet of the Kreml palace, issuing detailed and urgent orders in regard to the measures to be taken at once for quenching the fires, preventing pillage, and reassuring the inhabitants.

But Pierre knew nothing about this : wholly absorbed in the actual, he was tormenting himself as men do who recognize that their undertaking is impossible, not because of its difficulties, but because it is so entirely unsuited to their nature.   He was tormented by his fear that at the decisive moment he should weaken, and in consequence of it lose his self-respect.

Although he saw nothing and heard nothing, he instinctively took the right road and made no mistake in following the cross-streets that led him into the Povarskaya.

But in proportion as Pierre approached the Povarskaya the smoke grew denser and denser, and he even began to feel the heat from the fire.   Occasionally, he could see tongues of flame behind the roofs of the houses.   More people were found on the streets, and these people were more excited and anxious.   But Pierre, though he was conscious that something extraordinary was going on around him, did not realize that he was approaching the conflagration.

As he followed along a foot-path that skirted a large open space, bordered on one side by the Povarskaya, on the other by the park attached to Prince Gruzinsky's mansion, Pierre suddenly heard near him the pitiful shrieks of a woman.   He stopped as if wakened out of a dream, and raised his head.

On one side of the foot-path, on the dry, dusty grass, was piled up a heap of household furniture : feather-bed, samovar, sacred pictures, and trunks.   On the ground, next the trunks, sat a lean, elderly woman, with long, projecting upper teeth.   She was dressed in a black cloak and a cap.   This woman rocked herself to and fro, and was muttering as she wept and sobbed.   Two little girls, ten or twelve years old, dressed in short, dirty skirts and little cloaks, gazed at their mother with an expression of perplexity on their pale, frightened faces.

A little boy of seven, in a chuĭka and cap altogether too big for him, was weeping in his old nurse's arms. A dirty, bare-legged servant-girl was sitting on a trunk, and, having let down her pale blond plait, was pulling out the scorched hairs, smelling of them as she did so. The husband of the family, a short, round-shouldered little man, in undress uniform, with wheel-like little side-whiskers, and love-locks brushed smoothly from under his cap, with impassive face, was sorting the trunks piled one on top of the other, and trying to get some clothes out.

The woman almost threw herself at Pierre's feet when she saw him.

"Oh, good father! Oh, orthodox Christian! Help, save her!.... Oh, dear sir![1].... Whoever you are, help!" she cried, through her sobs. "My little daughter!.... my daughter!.... My youngest daughter has been left behind!.... She is burning up! Oh! oh! oh! oh, why did I nurse thee?.... Oh! oh! oh!"

"There! that'll do, Marya Nikolayevna," expostulated her husband, in a mild voice, but evidently merely so as to make a good impression on the stranger. "Sister must have got her. If not, it's all over with her by this time," he added.

"Monster! Villain!" angrily screamed the woman, suddenly ceasing to weep. "There's no heart in you! You have no pity for your own child! Any other man would have snatched her from the fire. But you are a monster.... and not a man, and not a father..... But you, sir, you are noble!" cried the woman, addressing Pierre, speaking rapidly, and sobbing. "The row was on fire; ours caught. The girl cried: 'We are on fire.' We tried to save what we could. Whatever we could lay our hands on, we carried out..... This here is what we saved..... The holy picture[2] and our wedding-bed — all the rest was lost. We got the children, all but Katitchka! Oh! oh! oh! oh, Lord!" and again she burst into tears. "My darling little one! she's burnt up! she's burnt up!"

---

[1] *Galubchik.*   [2] *Bozhye blagoslovenye :* literally, God's benediction.

"But where was it, where was she left?" asked Pierre.

By the expression of his excited face, the woman realized that this man might help her.

"Batyushka! Father!" she cried, clasping him around the legs. "Benefactor! set my heart at ease!.... Aniska, go, you nasty hussy! show him the way," she cried to the girl, and angrily opened her mouth, by this action still more exposing her long teeth.

"Lead the way, lead the way .... I .... I .... I will do what I can," stammered Pierre, in a panting voice.

The dirty-looking girl came out from behind the trunk, put up her braid, and, with a sigh, started off down the foot-path, with her stubbed, bare feet.

Pierre had, as it were, wakened suddenly to life after a heavy swoon. He raised his head higher, his eyes were filled with the spark of life, and, with rapid strides, he followed the girl, passed her, and hurried along the Povarskaya. The whole street was shrouded in clouds of black smoke. Tongues of flame here and there darted out from it. A great throng of people were packed together in front of the fire. In the middle of the street stood a French general, and he was saying something to those around him. Pierre, accompanied by the girl, was going toward the place where the general stood, but French soldiers halted him.

"*On ne passe pas* — You cannot pass!" cried a voice.

"This way, uncle,"[1] cried the girl; "we'll go round by this side-street, through Nikulini."

Pierre turned back, and almost ran as he hastened in her footsteps, so as to overtake her. The girl scurried along, turned down a cross-street at the left, and, passing by three houses, turned into the gates of a house at the right.

"There it is .... right there!" cried the girl, and, running across the yard, she opened a wicket door in the deal fence, and, stepping back a step, pointed out to Pierre a small wooden "wing," where the flames were burning bright and hot. One side was already fallen

---

[1] *Dyadinka*, diminutive of *dyadya*.

in ; the other was burning, and the flames were bursting out from the broken windows and from under the roof.

When Pierre reached the wicket he was suffocated by the heat, and involuntarily drew back.

" Which .... which is your house ? " he asked.

" Oh ! oh ! okh ! " howled the girl, as she pointed to the wing. "That one there ; that was our home.[1]

" Are you burnt up, O Katitchka ! our treasure ! my darling little mistress ! Oh ! okh ! " howled Aniska, at the sight of the fire, feeling that it was necessary for her to express also her feelings.

Pierre edged toward the burning wing, but the heat was so powerful that he was obliged to make a wide circle around the building, and he came out next a large house which was as yet burning only on one side of the roof. A great crowd of Frenchmen were swarming around it.

Pierre could not at first understand what these Frenchmen were doing, who appeared to be dragging something, but, when he saw one of them strike a peasant with the flat of his saber, and take away from him a foxskin shuba, Pierre had a dim idea that pillaging was going on there ; still the idea merely flashed through his mind.

The noise of the crackling and the crash of falling walls and ceilings, the hissing and snapping of the flames, and the excited cries of the people, the spectacle of billowing, whirling clouds of smoke now thick and black, now dotted with gleaming sparks, now lighted up with solid, sheaf-shaped red and golden-scaled flames lapping the walls, the sense of the heat and the smoke, and the swiftness of motion, all served to produce upon Pierre the usual exciting effect of fires. This effect was peculiarly powerful upon him, because suddenly, at the sight of this fire, he felt himself liberated from the oppression of his thoughts. He felt young, gay, agile, and resolute. He ran round the wing from the burning house, and tried to force his way into that part of it that was still standing,

[1] She calls *kvartira* (quarters) *fatera.*

when suddenly he heard, over his very head, several voices shouting, immediately followed by the rush and metallic ring of some heavy body falling near him.

Pierre looked round and saw, in the windows of the house, some Frenchmen who had just flung out a chest of drawers, full of some metallic articles. Other French soldiers, standing below, were running to the chest of drawers.

"Well, what does this fellow want here?"[1] cried one of the Frenchmen, seeing Pierre.

"A child in this house? Have n't you seen a child?" asked Pierre, in French.

"Hold! What's he prating about! Go to the devil!" replied a voice; and one of the soldiers, evidently fearing that it was Pierre's intention to rob them of the silver and bronzes that were in the drawers, came up to him in a threatening manner.

"A child?" cried the Frenchman from above. "I heard something squealing in the garden. Perhaps 't was the poor man's little brat. Must be humane, you know."

"Where is he? Where is he?" asked Pierre.

"There! There!" cried the Frenchman from the window, pointing to the garden behind the house. "Wait, I'm coming right down." And, in fact, in a moment the Frenchman, a black-eyed fellow with a spot on his cheek, and in his shirt-sleeves, sprang out from the window of the first story, and, giving Pierre a slap on the shoulder, ran with him down into the garden. "Hurry up, boys," he cried to his comrades. "Beginning to grow warm."

Running behind the house, on the sand-strewn path, the Frenchman gave Pierre's arm a pull and pointed to the circle. On a bench lay a little maiden of three years, in a pink dress.

"There's your brat. Ah! a little girl! So much the better," said the Frenchman. "Good-by, old fellow. Must be humane. We are all mortal, you see."[2]

---

[1] "*Eh bien! qu'est ce qu'il veut, celui-là?*"

[2] "*Un enfant dans cette maison? N'avez-vous pas vu un enfant?*" — "*Tiens! qu'est ce qu'il chante, celui-là? Va te promener.*" — "*Un*

And the Frenchman with the spot on his cheek
hurried back to his comrades.

Pierre, choking with delight, started back to the girl,
and was going to put the little one in his arms.   But
the little one, pale like her mother, and sick with the
scrofula, — a disagreeable-looking child, — seeing the
strange man, set up a screech and tried to run away.
Pierre, however, seized her, and took her in his arms.
She screamed in a desperately angry voice, and with
her slender little arms struggled to tear herself away
from Pierre, and to bite him with her slobbery mouth.
Pierre was seized by a feeling of horror and repulsion,
such as he would have felt at contact with any nasty
little animal.   But he forced himself not to throw the
child down, and hastened with her back to the great
house.   He found it impossible to return the same way;
the girl, Aniska, had disappeared, and Pierre, with a
feeling of pity and disgust, holding to his heart as tenderly as he could the passionately screaming and wet
little girl, ran through the garden to find another exit.

CHAPTER XXXIV

WHEN Pierre, making his way round by yards and
alleys, brought his burden back to Prince Gruzinsky's
garden, on the corner of the Povarskaya, he did not at
first recognize the place which he had left when he went
after the child — it was so swarming with people and
with household furniture.   Besides the Russian families
taking refuge here with their treasures, there were also
many French soldiers, in various garb.

Pierre paid no attention to them.   He was in haste
to find the chinovnik's family, so as to restore the little

*enfant ?   J'ai entendu piailler quelque chose au jardin.   Peut-être c'est son
moutard au bonhomme.   Faut être humain, voyez vous." — " Où est-il ?
Où est-il ?" — " Par ici !   Par ici !   Attendez ! je vais descendre.   Dé-
pêchez-vous, vous autres.   Commence à faire chaud. — Voilà votre moutard.
Ah, une petite ! — tant mieux.   Au revoir, mon gros.   Faut être humain.
Nous sommes tous mortels, voyez-vous !"*

girl to her mother, and then go and rescue some one else. It seemed to him that he had still very much to do, and as speedily as possible. Heated with the fire and his exertion in running, Pierre at that moment experienced more keenly than ever that feeling of youth, energy, and resolution which had taken possession of him when he started to rescue the child.

The little girl was calmer now, and, clinging to Pierre's kaftan, she sat on his arm, and like a little wild animal looked around her.

Pierre occasionally looked down at her and smiled. It seemed to him that he saw something touchingly innocent in that scared and sickly little face.

Neither the chinovnik nor his wife was to be seen in the place where they had been before. Pierre, with rapid strides, wandered round among the people, scrutinizing the various faces that he met.

His attention was accidentally attracted to a Georgian or Armenian family, consisting of a handsome man of very advanced age, with a face of Oriental type, and dressed in a new dyed tulup and new boots, an old woman of the same type, and a young woman. This very young woman seemed to Pierre the perfection of Oriental beauty, with her dark brows delicately arched, and her long face of remarkable freshness of complexion and genuine but expressionless beauty. Amid the indiscriminate heap of household articles on the green, she, in her rich satin mantle and bright lilac kerchief covering her head, reminded one of a delicate hot-house flower flung out into the snow. She sat on a parcel behind the old woman, and with her motionless, big, dark, oblong eyes, shaded by long lashes, looked at the ground.

Evidently she was conscious of her beauty, and it filled her with alarm. This face struck Pierre, and, in spite of his haste as he passed along the fence, several times he glanced round at her.

On reaching the fence and still not finding those of whom he was in search, Pierre paused and looked around.

Pierre's figure, with the child in his arms, was now

even more remarkable than before, and a number of Russians, both men and women, gathered round him.

"Have you lost any one, dear man?".... "You are a noble, are n't you?".... "Whose child is that?" were among the questions put to him.

Pierre explained that the child belonged to a woman in a black mantle, who had been sitting in that very spot with her children; and he asked if no one knew who she was, and where she had gone.

"It must be the Anferofs," said an old deacon, addressing a pock-marked woman. "Lord, have mercy! Lord, have mercy!" he added, in his usual bass.

"Where are the Anferofs?" asked the woman. "The Anferofs started early this morning. This may be Marya Nikolayevna's or the Ivanofs'."

"He said a woman, but Marya Nikolayevna is a lady,"[1] said a household serf.

"Surely you must know her—long teeth, a thin woman," said Pierre.

"Certainly, it's Marya Nikolayevna. They went into the garden as soon as these wolves came down on us," said the peasant woman, pointing to the French soldiers.

"O Lord, have mercy!" again ejaculated the deacon.

"Go down yonder, then. You'll find them. She's there. She was all beat out; she was crying," said the peasant woman. "She is over there. You'll find her."

But Pierre heard not what the woman said. For several seconds he had been watching anxiously what was going on a few steps away. He was looking at the Armenian family and a couple of French soldiers who had approached them. One of these soldiers, a little, nimble man, wore a blue overcoat belted with a rope. He had a nightcap on his head, and was barefooted.

The second, who especially attracted Pierre's attention, was a long, lank, round-shouldered, white-haired man, slow in his movements, and with an idiotic expression of countenance. He was clad in a frieze

[1] *Baruinya.*

capote, with blue trousers, and Hessian boots which had come to holes.

The little bootless Frenchman in the blue overcoat had gone up to the Armenians, and, after making some remark, had seized the old man by the legs, and the old man had immediately begun to pull off his boots in great haste.

The other one had taken up his position in front of the pretty Armenian girl, and, with his hands thrust deep in his pockets, was staring at her in perfect silence, without moving.

"Take it, take the child!" exclaimed Pierre, addressing the peasant woman in imperative tones, holding out the little girl. "Take her and give her back to them!" he cried, and set the screaming child on the ground, and then turned once more to look at the Frenchmen and the Armenian family.

The old man was, by this time, barefooted. The little Frenchman had appropriated his second boot, and was knocking the two together. The old man with a sob made some remark, but Pierre merely glanced at him; his whole attention was attracted to the Frenchman in the capote, who, slowly swaggering, had by this time approached the young woman, and, drawing his hands from his pockets, was just taking her by the neck.

The beautiful Armenian girl continued sitting in the same impassive posture, with her long lashes drooping, and apparently neither saw nor felt what the soldier was doing to her.

By the time Pierre had taken the several steps that separated him from the Frenchmen, the lank marauder in the capote had already snatched her necklace from the Armenian girl's neck, and the young woman, clasping her hands around her throat, uttered a piercing shriek.

"*Laissez cette femme!* — Let this woman alone!" roared Pierre in a furious voice, clutching the lank, stooping soldier by the shoulder, and flinging him off. The soldier fell flat, picked himself up, and ran away. But his comrade, throwing down his booty of boots, drew his cutlass, and advanced threateningly against Pierre. "See here! None of your nonsense!" he cried.

Pierre was in that rapt state of fury which, when it came upon him, made him oblivious of everything, and multiplied his strength tenfold. He threw himself upon the barefooted Frenchman, and, before the fellow had time to use his cutlass, he had knocked him over, and was belaboring him with his fists.

The people gathered around with an approving yell, but just at that instant appeared around the corner a mounted squad of French uhlans. The uhlans came up to Pierre and the Frenchman at a trot, and surrounded them. Pierre remembered nothing of what followed. He only remembered that he was pounding some one, that he himself was pounded, and that, finally, he became conscious that his arms were bound; that a crowd of French soldiers were standing round him, and searching his clothes.

"He has a dagger, lieutenant," were the first words that Pierre comprehended.

"Aha, armed!" said the officer, and he turned to the barefooted soldier who had been taken at the same time with Pierre.

"Very good; you shall tell all this at the court-martial," said the officer. And immediately he turned to Pierre.

"*Parlez-vous français, vous?*"

Pierre glared around him with bloodshot eyes, and made no reply. Evidently, his face must have seemed very terrible, because the officer gave a whispered order, and four other uhlans detached themselves from the squad and stationed themselves on each side of Pierre.

"*Parlez-vous français?*" asked the officer a second time, keeping at a respectful distance from him. "Bring the interpreter."

A little man in the dress of a Russian civilian came forth from the ranks. Pierre instantly knew by his attire and his accent that he was a Frenchman from some Moscow shop.

"He does not look like a man of the common people," said the interpreter, eying Pierre.

"Oh, ho! it seems to me he has the appearance of being one of the incendiaries," said the officer. "Ask him who he is," he added.

"Who are you?"[1] demanded the interpreter. "You should reply to the authorities," said he.

"I will not tell you who I am. I am your prisoner. Take me away," suddenly exclaimed Pierre, speaking in French.

"Ah, ha!" exclaimed the officer, scowling. "Come on."

A crowd had gathered around the uhlans. Closest of all to Pierre stood the pock-marked peasant woman with the little girl. When the squad started she sprang forward.

"Where are they taking you, my good friend?"[2] she demanded. "The little girl! what shall I do with the little girl if she isn't theirs?" insisted the woman.

"What does this woman want?" asked the officer.

Pierre was like one drunk. His rapt state of mind was still more intensified at the sight of the little girl whom he had saved.

"What does she want?" he exclaimed. "She has brought my daughter, whom I just saved from the flames," he explained. "Adieu!" and he himself, not knowing why he should have told this aimless falsehood, marched off with resolute, enthusiastic steps, surrounded by the Frenchmen.

This patrol of French horsemen was one of those sent out by Durosnel's orders, to put a stop to pillaging and especially to apprehend the incendiaries who, according to the general impression prevalent that day among the French, were the cause of the conflagrations. After riding up and down several streets, the squad had gathered in some half-dozen Russians — a shop-keeper, two seminarists, a muzhik, and a man-servant — and a few marauders.

---

[1] The interpreter says *Ti kto?* instead of *Tui kto?*
[2] *Galubchik tui moi*, little pigeon thou mine.

But of all the suspects the most suspicious of all seemed Pierre. When they were all taken to the place of detention, — a great mansion on the Zubovsky Val, — where the guardhouse was established, Pierre was given a special, separate room, under a strong guard.

PART TWELFTH

CHAPTER I

IN Petersburg at this time in the highest circles was raging with greater virulence than ever before the complicated battle between the parties of Rumyantsof, the French, Marya Feodorovna, the tsesarevitch, and others, absorbing, as always, the energies of the court drones. But Petersburg life went on in its old channels —tranquil, sumptuous, engrossed only in phantoms and reflections of life; and any one in the current of this life needed to exercise great energy to recognize the peril and the difficult position in which the Russian nation was placed. There were the same levees and balls, the same French theater, the same court interests, the same official interests, and the same intrigues.

Only in the very highest circles were any efforts made to realize the difficulties of the actual situation. It was told in a whisper how differently the two empresses behaved in such trying circumstances. The Empress Maria, concerned for the safety of the charities and educational establishments of which she was the patroness, made her arrangements to have all these institutions transferred to Kazan, and the effects of these institutions had already been removed.

The Empress Elizabeth,[1] on the other hand, when the question arose, what she wished done, deigned to reply with that genuine Russian patriotism characteristic of her, that she had no orders to give in regard to the governmental institutions, since that was the province of the sovereign; while, as far as what de-

[1] Yelizavieta Alekseyevna, the consort of the emperor, in contradistinction to the empress dowager, Marya Feodorovna.

pended upon her personally, she was pleased to declare that she should be the last to leave Petersburg.

On the seventh of September, the same day as the battle of Borodino, Anna Pavlovna gave a reception, the flower of which was to be the reading of a letter from his eminence the metropolitan, sent to the sovereign together with a sacred picture of his holiness Saint Sergii. This letter was considered a model of patriotic, spiritual eloquence. It was to be read by Prince Vasili himself, who was renowned for his skill as a reader. (He had even read at the empress's!) His art of reading consisted in pouring out the words, now in a loud tone and now in a sweet tone, now giving a desperate roar, now a tender murmur, absolutely independent of the significance of the words, so that it was wholly a matter of chance whether the roar or the murmur fell on one word or another.

This reading, like everything that happened at Anna Pavlovna's receptions, had a political significance. This particular evening there were to be present a number of important persons whom it was necessary to put to shame for attending the French theater, and to stir to a patriotic state of mind.

Already a considerable number of guests had gathered, but Anna Pavlovna did not yet see in her drawing-room all whose presence was deemed necessary, and accordingly she still delayed the reading and permitted general conversation.

The chief item of news that day in Petersburg was the Countess Bezukhaya's illness. The countess had been unexpectedly taken ill several days before; she had missed several assemblies of which she was the adornment, and rumor had it that she received no one, and that, instead of the famous Petersburg doctors who had usually prescribed for her, she had intrusted her case to an Italian doctor, who was treating her by some new and extraordinary method.

All knew perfectly well that the charming countess's illness arose from the difficulty of marrying two husbands at once, and that the Italian's treatment consisted in the removal of these difficulties; but in Anna Pavlovna's presence no one even dared to think about this; it was as if it were not known by any one.

"They say the poor countess is very ill. The doctor says it is angina pectoris."

"Angina? Oh, that is a terrible illness."

"They say the rivals are reconciled, thanks to this angina." The word *angine* was pronounced with great unction.

"The old count, I am told, is very pathetic. He wept like a child when the doctor told him that it was a dangerous case."

"Oh, it would be a terrible loss! She's a bewitching creature!"

"You were speaking of the poor countess," said Anna Pavlovna, joining the group. "I sent to hear how she was. They informed me that she was a little better. Oh, unquestionably she is the most charming woman in the world," said Anna Pavlovna, with a smile at her own enthusiasm. "We belong to different camps, but that does not prevent me from esteeming her as she deserves. She is very unhappy," added Anna Pavlovna.

Supposing that Anna Pavlovna by these words slightly lifted the veil of mystery that shrouded the countess's illness, one indiscreet young man allowed himself to express his amazement that physicians of repute had not been called, but that a charlatan, who might very easily administer dangerous remedies, was treating the countess.

"You may be better informed than I am," suddenly said Anna Pavlovna, with a cutting tone, to the inexperienced young man. "But I have been told on very good authority that this doctor is a very learned and very skilful man. He is private physician to the queen of Spain."

And having thus annihilated the young man, Anna Pavlovna turned to Bilibin, who, in another circle, having wrinkled up his skin, and evidently made ready to smooth it out again preliminary to getting off a witticism, was speaking about the Austrians.

"I find it charming," said he, referring to a diplomatic document which had been sent to accompany some Austrian standards captured by Wittgenstein — the hero of Petropolis, *le héros de Pétropol,* as he was called in Petersburg.

"What, what is that?" said Anna Pavlovna, turning to him with a view to causing a silence, so that the *mot,* which she had already heard, might be more effective.

And Bilibin repeated the following authentic words of the diplomatic despatch which he himself had drawn up.

"'The emperor returns the Austrian flags,'" said Bilibin, "'friendly flags gone astray, which he found off the usual route.'"

"Delightful, delightful!" exclaimed Prince Vasili.

"The route to Warsaw, perhaps," said Prince Ippolit, unexpectedly, in a loud voice.

All looked at him without understanding what he meant by that. Prince Ippolit also looked round with a complacent smile. He had just as little idea as the rest had of what the words he had spoken meant. All through his diplomatic career, he had more than once observed that a few words thus unexpectedly thrown in seem very smart, and at every chance he made such remarks, the first that came to his tongue. "It may turn out well," he thought, "but even if it is n't a success, still they will be able to make something out of it."

In fact, the awkward silence that ensued was broken by the appearance of the insufficiently patriotic individual whom Anna Pavlovna was expecting and hoped to convert, and she, with a smile, and threatening Prince Ippolit with her finger, beckoned Prince Vasili to the table, and, placing two candles and the manuscript before him, invited him to begin.

General silence : —

"*Most gracious Sovereign and Emperor,*" declaimed Prince Vasili, sternly, and gave his audience a look as much as to ask, 'Who had anything to say against that?' But no one spoke. "*Our chief capital city, Moscow, the new Jerusalem, receives ITS Christ,*" — he gave a sudden emphasis on the pronoun *ITS.* "*Like as a mother embracing her fervently devoted sons, and catching sight through the gathering murk of the splendid glory of thy realm, she sings in her rapture, 'Hosanna! Blessed is he that cometh!'*"

Prince Vasili uttered these final words in a voice suggestive of tears.

Bilibin attentively gazed at his finger-nails; and several evidently felt abashed, and seemed to be asking, 'What have we done amiss?' Anna Pavlovna, in a whisper, went on with the next sentence like an old woman repeating the prayer at communion:— "*If the insolent and brazen Goliath,*" she began.

Prince Vasili read on:—

"*If the insolent and brazen Goliath from the confines of France bring his homicidal horrors upon the lands of Russia, humble faith, that sling of the Russian David, shall smite unexpectedly the head of his bloodthirsty pride. This image of Saint Sergii, the ancient zealot of our country's good, is sent to your imperial majesty. I regret that my failing powers prevent me from rejoicing in the sight of your beloved face. Earnest prayers I shall raise to heaven: may the Almighty increase the generation of the righteous, and fulfil your majesty's pious hopes.*"

"*Quel force! Quel style!*" were the encomiums passed upon reader and author alike.

Animated by this discourse, Anna Pavlovna's guests for a long time still discussed the condition of the country, and made various predictions about the result of the battle which it was known was to be fought about that time. ·

"*Vous verrez* — you will see," exclaimed Anna Pavlovna. "We shall have news to-morrow; it's the sovereign's birthday. I have a happy presentiment."

CHAPTER II

ANNA PAVLOVNA'S presentiment was in fact jus·
tified.

On the following day, during the Te Deum chanted
at the palace in honor of the emperor's birthday, Prince
Volkonsky was called out from the chapel and handed
an envelop from Prince Kutuzof. This contained
Kutuzof's report written from Tatarinovo on the day of
the battle. Kutuzof wrote that the Russians had not
fallen back· a step, that the French had lost far more
than ours, that he made his report in all haste from the
field of battle, without having had time, as yet, to receive all details.

Of course it was a victory. And instantly, without
dismissing the audience, a thanksgiving was sung to the
Creator for His aid and for the victory.

Anna Pavlovna's presentiment was justified; and
throughout the city there reigned, all the morning, joyfully festive enthusiasm. All considered the victory
complete, and many went so far as to talk about Napoleon himself being a prisoner, and of his overthrow and
the choice of a new sovereign for France.

Remote from the scene of action, and in the midst of
court life, it was thoroughly difficult to realize events in
all their completeness and force. Involuntarily, events
in general group themselves around some special incident. Thus, in the present instance, the chief joy of
the courtiers was included not so much in the fact that
the Russians had won a victory, as in the fact that the
news of this victory had arrived precisely on the sovereign's birthday. It was a sort of successful surprise.

In Kutuzof's report mention was also made of the
losses suffered by the Russians, and especially singled
out for mention were Tutchkof, Bagration, Kutaïsof.
Accordingly, also, the melancholy side of the occurrence, as it presented itself there, in the Petersburg
world, was made concrete in the one fact of Kutaïsof's
death. All knew him; he was a favorite with the sov-

ereign; he was young and interesting. On this day all who met said to each other: —

"How wonderfully it all came about! Right in the midst of the mass! And what a loss, Kutaïsof! Akh! what a pity!"

"What did I tell you about Kutuzof?" now exclaimed Prince Vasili, with the pride of a prophet. "I always said that he was the only one capable of beating Napoleon."

But on the following day no news was received from the army, and the general voice began to be anxious. The courtiers suffered from the painful state of ignorance in which the sovereign was left.

"What a position for the sovereign!" said the courtiers; and before the third day had passed they already began to pass judgment on Kutuzof, who was regarded as the cause of the sovereign's uneasiness.

Prince Vasili on that day ceased to boast of his *protégé* Kutuzof, and maintained a discreet silence when the commander-in-chief was mentioned.

Moreover, on the evening of this same day, as if all things conspired together to alarm and disquiet the inhabitants of Petersburg, another terrible piece of news was announced. The Countess Elena Bezukhaya suddenly died of that terrible disease which her friends found it so pleasant to name.

Officially, in all the great coteries it was declared that the Countess Bezukhaya had died of a terrible attack of *angine pectorale*, but in select circles details were forthcoming: how *le médecin intime de la reine d'Espagne* had prescribed for Ellen small doses of some medicine so as to bring about certain effects; and how Ellen, worried because the old count had some suspicion of her, and because her husband, to whom she had written (that miserable, depraved Pierre), did not reply to her, suddenly took an overdose of the drug prescribed, and died in agony before help could be got to her. It was said that Prince Vasili and the old count had at first blamed the Italian; but the Italian had showed them such letters from the late unfortunate countess that they had instantly let him go.

Gossip in general was confined to these three un-happy events: the ignorance in which the sovereign was left, the loss of Kutaïsof, and Ellen's death.

On the third day after Kutuzof's despatch had been received, a landed proprietor arrived at Petersburg from Moscow, and soon the whole city was ringing with the news that Moscow was abandoned to the French.

This was terrible! What a position it placed the sovereign in! Kutuzof was a traitor, and Prince Vasili, while receiving *visites de condoléance* for the death of his daughter, speaking of that same Kutuzof whom he had but shortly before been praising (it was pardonable that in his grief he should forget what he said before), declared that it was idle to expect anything else from a blind and lewd old man.

"I am only amazed that the fate of Russia should have been intrusted to such a man!"

This news being as yet unofficial, there was still room for doubt, but on the following day the following des-patch came from Count Rostopchin:—

Prince Kutuzof's aide brought me a letter wherein he de-mands of me police officers to conduct the army to the Riazan road. He protests his regret at abandoning Moscow. Your majesty, Kutuzof's act decides the fate of the capital and of your empire. Russia will thrill when she learns of the abandon-ment of that city, which is the focus of the greatness of Russia, where lie the ashes of your ancestors. I follow the army. I have sent everything away. It remains for me only to weep for the misfortune of my fatherland.

On receiving this letter, the sovereign sent Prince Volkonsky with the following rescript to Kutuzof:—

Prince Mikhaïl Iliaronovitch! Since September 9 I have had no report from you. Meantime I have received, by the way of Yaroslavl, under date of September 13, from the governor-general of Moscow, the melancholy tidings that you and the army have decided to abandon Moscow. You may imagine the effect which these tidings produced upon me, and your silence deepens my amazement. I send General-Adjutant Prince Vol-konsky with this to learn from you the condition of the army and what reasons compelled you to such a melancholy decision.

CHAPTER III

NINE days after the abandonment of Moscow, a messenger from Kutuzof arrived in Petersburg with the official confirmation of the abandonment of Moscow. This
courier was the Frenchman Michaud, but, though a foreigner, yet a Russian in heart and soul — as he himself
declared.

The sovereign immediately gave the courier audience
in his cabinet in his palace on the Kamennui Ostrof.
Michaud, who had never seen Moscow before this campaign, and could not speak Russian, nevertheless felt
greatly agitated when he appeared before "*notre très-
gracieux souverain*" (as he expressed it in a letter) with
the tidings of the burning of Moscow — the flames of
which lighted up his way. Though the source of Mr.
Michaud's chagrin must have been very different from
that from which the grief of the Russian people proceeded, Michaud drew such a melancholy face, as he was
ushered into the sovereign's cabinet, that the sovereign
instantly asked him : —

"Are you bringing me bad news, colonel ?"

"Very bad, sire," replied Michaud, with a sigh, and
dropping his eyes, "*l'abandon de Moscou !*"

"Can they have surrendered my ancient capital without a battle ?" exclaimed the emperor, an angry flush
suddenly rising in his face.

Michaud respectfully delivered the message with which
he had been intrusted by Kutuzof ; to wit, that it was
a sheer impossibility to accept an engagement at Moscow, and that as but one choice was left, to lose both
the army and Moscow, or Moscow alone, the field-marshal had felt it his duty to choose the latter alternative.

The sovereign listened in silence, not looking at
Michaud.

"Has the enemy entered the city ?" he demanded.

"Yes, your majesty, and it is a heap of ashes by
this time. When I left it, 't was all on fire," said Michaud, resolutely ; but when he glanced at the emperor,

Michaud was horror-struck at what he had said. The sovereign was breathing with quick, labored respirations; his lower lip trembled, and his handsome blue eyes for an instant overflowed with tears.

But this lasted only a moment. The sovereign suddenly scowled as if he was annoyed at himself for his weakness. And, raising his head, he turned to Michaud, with a steady voice : —

"I see, colonel, from all that is happening to us," said he, "that Providence demands great sacrifices of us .... I am ready to submit to His will; but tell me, Michaud, how did you leave the army which saw my ancient capital thus abandoned without striking a blow? Did you see no signs of discouragement?"

Michaud, seeing this calmness of his "very gracious sovereign," instantly recovered his own presence of mind; but he was not yet ready to reply to the emperor's straightforward and unequivocal question, which demanded a straightforward answer.

"Your majesty, will you allow me to speak freely, like a loyal soldier?" he asked, for the sake of gaining time.

"Colonel, that is what I always demand," said the emperor. "Conceal nothing from me; I wish to know absolutely how matters stand."

"Your majesty," said Michaud, with a shrewd but scarcely perceptible smile on his lips, having now collected himself sufficiently to formulate his answer in a graceful and respectful *jeu de mots :* "Your majesty, I left the whole army, from the chiefs down to the last soldier, without exception, in a state of terrible, desperate fear." ....

"How is that?" interrupted the sovereign, darkly frowning. "Will my Russians allow themselves to be cast down by misfortune? .... Never!"

This was all that Michaud wished so as to complete his *jeu de mots.*

"Your majesty," said he, with a sprightly but respectful expression, "their only fear is that your majesty, through kindness of heart, will be persuaded to

make peace. They are burning to fight," said the ac-
credited representative of the Russian people, "and to
prove to your majesty by the sacrifice of their lives how
devoted they are." ....

"Ah!" said the sovereign, reassured, and with an
affectionate gleam flashing from his eyes, as he tapped
Michaud on the shoulder, "you relieve me, colonel."

The sovereign then dropped his head and remained
for some time lost in thought.

"Very well! Return to the army," said he, drawing
himself up to his full height, and turning to Michaud
with a gentle but majestic gesture. "And tell our
brave men, tell all my good subjects everywhere you
go, that when I have no soldiers left, I will place myself at the head of my beloved nobles and of my worthy
peasants, and thus I will exhaust the last resources of
my empire. It will furnish me yet with more than my
enemies think," said the sovereign, growing more and
more moved. "But if ever it were written in the
decrees of Divine Providence," he went on to say, raising to heaven his beautiful, kindly eyes, gleaming with
emotion, "that my family should cease to reign on the
throne of my ancestors, then, after having exhausted
all the means that are in my power, I will allow my
beard to grow to here," — the sovereign placed his hand
half-way down his chest, — "and I will go and eat potatoes
with the humblest of my peasants sooner than sign the
shame of my country and of my beloved nation, whose
sacrifices I can appreciate."

Having said these words in a voice full of emotion,
the sovereign suddenly turned round, evidently to hide
from Michaud the tears that filled his eyes, and walked
to the end of his cabinet. After standing there a few
moments, he came back to Michaud with long strides,
and gave his arm a powerful squeeze below the elbow.
His handsome, kindly face was flushed, and his eyes
flashed with decision and wrath : —

"Colonel Michaud, forget not what I have said to you
here ; perhaps some day we shall recall it with pleasure
— either Napoleon or I," said the sovereign, laying his

hand on his chest. "We can no longer reign together. I have learned to know him ; he shall never deceive me again !"

. And the sovereign, with a frown, relapsed into silence.

Michaud, though a foreigner, yet a Russian in heart and soul, felt at that solemn moment *"enthousiasmé"* by all that he had just heard (as he said afterwards), and in the expressions that followed, he uttered not only his own feelings but also the feelings of the Russian people, whose representative he considered himself.

"Sire !" said he, "your majesty at this moment seals the glory of the nation and the safety of Europe."

The sovereign with an inclination of the head dismissed Michaud.

CHAPTER IV

AT the time when Russia was half conquered, and the inhabitants of Moscow were fleeing to distant provinces, and levy after levy of the militia was rising for the defense of the fatherland, we, who were not alive at the time, involuntarily imagine that all the men of Russia, from small to great, were solely occupied in sacrificing themselves, in saving the country, or in bewailing its ruin.

Stories and descriptions of that period, all without exception, speak of self-sacrifice, love for the fatherland, the desperation, sorrow, and heroism of the Russians.

In reality this was not so at all. It merely seems so to us from the fact that we are occupied with the general historical interest of the time, and fail to see all those personal human interests which occupied men and women. But, in reality, those personal interests seemed to the men of that day so much more significant than the general interests, that the general interests were never felt at all, and were scarcely regarded. The majority of the men of that time paid no attention at all to the general course of events, and were merely guided by

the personal interests of that time.   And those very
men were the most important factors of that time.

Those who strove to comprehend the general course
of events, and were anxious by their self-sacrifice and
heroism to take part in it, were the most useless members of society.   They saw everything in a wrong sense ;
and all that they did, in spite of their good intentions,
proved to be profitless waste, like the regiments organized by Pierre and Mamonof, which pillaged the Russian villages, or like the lint picked by high-born young
ladies, which never reached the wounded, and so on.

Even those who, in their fondness for subtilities and
the expression of their feelings, talked about the actual
state of Russia, involuntarily gave to their speeches the
stamp of their impressions, or pretenses, or falsehoods,
or profitless criticisms and animosities against men who
were blamed for that for which no one could really be
held responsible.

In historical events more strictly than elsewhere holds
the prohibition against tasting the fruit of the tree of
knowledge.   Only unconscious activity brings forth fruit,
and a man who plays a part in any historical event never
realizes its significance.   If he tries to realize it, he is
astounded by its inutility.

The significance of the event which was at that time
taking place in Russia was proportionately incomprehensible according to the part which any man took in it.
In Petersburg and the provinces remote from Moscow,
ladies and men in militia uniforms mourned over Russia
and the capital, and talked about self-sacrifice and other
such things ; but in the army which was retreating from
Moscow, almost nothing was said or thought about Moscow ; and as they looked at the conflagration no one
dreamed of wreaking vengeance on the French, but they
thought of the next quarter's pay, about the next halting-
place, about Matrioshka the sutling-wench,[1] and the like.

Nikolaï Rostof, without any pretense of self-sacrifice,
but fortuitously, the war having surprised him while he
was still in the service, took a genuine and continuous

[1] *Marketantka.*

part in the defense of his country, and accordingly looked without despair and without somber forebodings on what was then happening in Russia.

If any one had asked him what he thought about the condition of Russia at the time, he would have replied that it was not for him to think about it, that Kutuzof and the others were for that, but he had heard that more regiments were mobilizing, and that there would be still more fighting, and that if nothing happened it would not be astonishing if in a couple of years he were given a regiment.

It was because he took this view of affairs that he not only felt no regret at being deprived of participation in the last engagement, having received word that he was appointed commander of a remount expedition to Voronezh after horses for his division, but was even perfectly delighted, and took no pains to hide it from his comrades, who were generous enough to sympathize with him.

A few days before the battle of Borodino, Nikolaï received his money and papers, and, sending a hussar on in advance, he started for Voronezh by post-relays.

Only a man who has experienced this, that is, who has spent several months in succession in the atmosphere of military campaign life, can comprehend the delight which Nikolaï experienced when he passed beyond the region affected by the foraging parties, provision trains, and ambulances of the army; when he ceased to see soldiers, army wagons, the dirty traces of a camp, and caught sight of villages, with peasant men and women, landholders' mansions, fields with grazing cattle, post-station-houses with their sleepy agents, he felt such joy as if he saw it all for the first time in his life.

One thing especially kept him in a perpetual state of surprise and delight, and this was the sight of young and healthy women, who did not each have a dozen officers tagging after her all the time, and women who found it a flattering novelty to have an officer, as he passed by, joke with them.

In the most jovial frame of mind, Nikolaï reached

Voronezh at evening, put up at the inn, ordered all that he had so long been in want of at the front, and on the next day, after getting a clean shave, and putting on his long unused dress uniform, he went to pay his respects to the city officials.

The commander of the militia was a civil general, an old man who evidently took great delight in his military title and rank. He received Nikolaï sternly, — thinking that this was proper in a military man of his importance, — and questioned him in a very significant way, approving or disapproving as if it was his special prerogative, and as if he was the judge of how the general course of the war was directed.

Nikolaï was so happy that this merely amused him.

From the commander of the militia he went to the governor. The governor was a lively little man, very friendly and simple-hearted. He told Nikolaï of several establishments where he might obtain horses, recommended to him a horse-dealer in the city and a landed proprietor twenty versts from the city who kept good horses, and he promised him any sort of coöperation.

"Are you Count Ilya Andreyevitch's son? My wife used to be very good friends with your mother. On Thursdays I always have a reception : to-day is Thursday; do me the favor to come informally," said the governor, as Nikolaï took his leave.

Immediately on leaving the governor's, Nikolaï took post-horses, and, accompanied by his quartermaster, drove rapidly the twenty versts so as to see the stud owned by the landed proprietor.

Nikolaï found everything jolly and comfortable during this his first visit at Voronezh, and, as is usually the case when a man is in a good frame of mind, everything was easily and satisfactorily settled.

The landed proprietor whom Nikolaï went to see was an old bachelor, formerly a cavalryman, a connoisseur of horses, a huntsman, the master of spiced vodka [1] a hundred years old, of old Hungarian, and of beautiful horses.

[1] *Zapekanka :* vodka and honey boiled with spices.

Nikolaï, in two words, bought, for six thousand rubles, seventeen stallions, "assorted," as he expressed it, "for the show pieces of his remount." After a good dinner, and drinking considerable of admirable Hungarian, Rostof, exchanging kisses with the proprietor, with whom he was already on the most intimate terms of friendship, drove back over the horrible road (which, however, did not affect his spirits), constantly urging his postilion to do his very best to get him back to the governor's in time for the reception.

Having changed his clothes, scented himself, and wet his hair down with cold water, Nikolaï, though rather late, but with the proverb "better late than never" ready for use, appeared at the governor's.

It was not a ball, and it was not formally announced that there would be dancing; but Katerina Petrovna, as all knew, would play some *valses* and *écossaises* on the clavichord, and there might be some dancing; and all the guests took this for granted, and came in ball costumes.

Provincial life in 1812 was pretty much the same as ever, with this only difference, that it was unusually gay in the little city, owing to the presence of a number of wealthy families from Moscow, and to the fact that, as in everything that was done in Russia at this time, there was unprecedented luxury observable (the sea being but knee-deep to drunken men), while the small talk that is a necessity among people, and which, hitherto, had been concerned merely with the weather and petty gossip, now turned on the state of Moscow, the war, and Napoleon.

The society which met at the governor's was the best society of Voronezh.

There were any number of ladies, there were several of Nikolaï's Moscow acquaintances; but there was not a man who could in any way compare with the Georgiev-sky cavalier, the gallant hussar, the good-natured, well-bred Count Rostof!

Among the men was an Italian, who had been an officer in the French army, and was now a prisoner, and

Nikolaï felt that this prisoner's presence still further enhanced his consequence as a Russian hero. It was a kind of a trophy! Nikolaï felt this, and it seemed to him that this was the way they all regarded the Italian, and so he treated him cordially, but with a certain dignity and reserve.

As soon as Nikolaï entered the room in his hussar's uniform, diffusing around him an odor of perfumes and of wine, and he himself said, and heard others say, again and again, the words *vaut mieux tard que jamais*, — better late than never, — he became the center of the gathering; all eyes were fixed on him, and he immediately felt that the position of general favorite which he had taken in the province was exceedingly appropriate to him, and pleasant, and, after such long deprivation, really intoxicating in its agreeableness. Not only at the post-stations, the taverns, and the residence of the landed proprietor, were the servant-maids flattered by his attentions, but here, at the governor's reception, it seemed to Nikolaï that there was an inexhaustible array of young married women and pretty girls who were impatient to have him give them a share of his attention.

The ladies and young girls coquetted with him, and the old people, from the very first moment, took it on themselves to find a wife for this madcap young hussar, and bring him to his senses. Among the latter was the governor's wife herself, who received Rostof like a near relative, and called him " Nicolas " and addressed him with the familiar *tui*, "thou."

Katerina Petrovna, as was expected, began to play her *valses* and *écossaises*, and the dancing began, and, by his graces in this accomplishment, Nikolaï still more captivated all the governmental society. He surprised every one by his peculiarly free and easy manner of dancing. Even Nikolaï was somewhat surprised at himself by his manner of dancing that evening. He had never danced so at Moscow, and he would have been disposed to call such extravagance of freedom unbecoming, and " bad form," had he not felt the necessity on him of surprising them all by something extraordinary, something which they must be taught to regard as the proper thing in capitals, but as yet unknown in the provinces.

All that evening, Nikolaï devoted the most of his attentions to a blue-eyed, plump, and pretty little blonde, the wife of one of the governmental officials. With that naïve persuasion with which young men flatter themselves that other men's wives were created especially for their diversion, Rostof stayed by this lady, and treated her husband in a friendly, somewhat *conspiratical* way, as if it were to be quite taken for granted, though as yet nothing had been said about it, that they would get along splendidly, that is, Nikolaï with this man's wife!

The husband, however, it seemed, did not share in this persuasion, and did his best to treat Rostof with marked coldness. But Nikolaï's unaffected frankness was so unbounded, that more than once the husband was obliged, in spite of himself, to give way to Nikolaï's geniality.

Toward the end of the evening, however, in proportion as his wife's face grew more and more flushed and excited, her husband's face grew ever more and more set and melancholy, as if there was a common fund of vivacity shared by the two so that in proportion as it waxed in the wife, it waned in the husband.

CHAPTER V

NIKOLAÏ, with a beaming smile on his lips, sat in his easy-chair, leaning over as near as possible to the pretty blondinka, whispering mythological compliments into her ear.

Briskly shifting his legs in their tight riding-trousers, exhaling the odor of perfumes, and contemplating his lady and himself, and the handsome shape of his calves under his top-boots, Nikolaï was telling the pretty blonde that it was his plan, while he was there at Voronezh, to run away with a certain lady.

"Who is she?"

"Charming, divine! Her eyes"— Nikolaï looked closely at his neighbor— "are blue; her lips, coral; her complexion" — he gave a significant look at her shoulders — "her form, Diana's!"....

The husband joined them, and asked his wife gloomily what she was talking about.

"Ah! Nikita Ivanuitch," exclaimed Nikolaï, politely rising. And, as if he were anxious for Nikita Ivanuitch to share in his jokes, he confided to him his intention of eloping with a certain pretty blonde.

The husband smiled chillingly, the wife rapturously. The governor's worthy wife came up to them with a disapproving look on her face.

"Anna Ignatyevna is desirous of seeing you, *Nicolas*," said she, and by the tone in which she mentioned the name Anna Ignatyevna, Rostof instantly realized that Anna Ignatyevna was a very important individual. "Come, let us go, Nicolas. You permit me to call you so, don't you?"

"Oh, yes, *ma tante*. But who is she?"

"Anna Ignatyevna Malvintseva. She had heard of you through her niece.... how you rescued her!.... Can you guess?"....

"But was she the only one I rescued there?" said Nikolaï.

"Her niece, the Princess Bolkonskaya. She is here with her aunt in Voronezh. Oho! how he reddens! What does that mean, now?"....

"I could not imagine, ... there, there, *ma tante!*"

"Pretty good, pretty good! Oh, what a boy you are!"

The governor's wife led him to a tall and very stately old lady with a blue toque, who had just finished a hand at cards with the most consequential personages of the city. This was Madame Malvintseva, the Princess Mariya's aunt on her mother's side, a rich, childless widow, who had always lived in Voronezh. She stood settling her card account when Rostof was brought to her. She blinked her eyes with a stern and important expression, gave him a glance, and went on berating the general who had won her money.

"Very glad to see you, my dear," said she, extending her hand. "Pray come and see me."

After speaking a few words about the Princess Mariya and her late father, whom, evidently, Madame Malvintseva had not loved, and asking a few questions as to what news Nikolaï had to give about Prince Andreï, who also seemed not to enjoy her good graces, she dismissed him, repeating her invitation to visit her.

Nikolaï promised, and again reddened as he took his leave of the widow.

At the remembrance of the Princess Mariya, Rostof experienced a feeling of bashfulness, even of fear, which he could not understand.

After leaving Madame Malvintseva, Rostof intended to return to the dancing again, but the little gubernatorsha laid her plump little hand on his sleeve, and said that she wanted to have a talk with him, and led him into the divan-room, which was instantly evacuated by those who were in it and who did not want to be in her way.

"You must know, *mon cher*," said the governor's wife, with a serious expression on her good little face, "I have found exactly the right wife for you; do you want me to arrange the match?"

"Who is it, *ma tante*?" asked Nikolaï.

"I propose the princess. Katerina Petrovna advises Lili; but that's not my idea — I say the princess. What do you say? I am sure your *maman* would be very thankful. Truly, she is a charming girl, and, after all, she is not so very plain!"

"Indeed, she is n't!" exclaimed Nikolaï, in an injured tone. "As for myself, *ma tante*, I do as a soldier should: I never offer myself, and I never refuse anything," said Nikolaï, before he had time to think what he was saying.

"But remember! This is no joke."

"What is no joke?"

"Yes, yes," said the governor's wife, as if speaking to herself. "And see here, *mon cher*, you are quite too attentive to that other lady, *la blonde*. Really, her hus-band is to be pitied."

"Oh, no ; he and I are very good friends," replied Nikolaï, who, in his simplicity of soul, never once dreamed that such a gay way of whiling away time could be aught else than gay to any one.

"What foolish nonsense did I speak to the governor's wife ?" Nikolaï suddenly asked himself while at supper. "She is trying to make a match .... but Sonya ?" ....

And on bidding the governor's wife good-night, when she with a smile said to him, "Now remember...." he drew her to one side.

"*Ma tante*, I have something which I really ought to tell you.... "

"What can it be, my boy ? Come in and let us sit down here."

Nikolaï suddenly felt a desire and an irresistible im-pulse to confide in this almost perfect stranger all his private thoughts — thoughts which he would never have told his mother, his sister, his friend. Afterwards, when he remembered this outburst of needless, inexplicable frankness, which nevertheless had very important con-sequences, it seemed to him as it always seems to peo-ple — that he had acted very foolishly; this outburst of frankness, together with other trivial circumstances, had for him and for his whole family portentous results.

"This is what I mean, *ma tante*. *Maman* has for a long time been anxious for me to marry a rich young lady. But the idea of marrying for money has always been extremely repugnant."

"Oh, yes, I understand," assented the governor's wife.

"But the Princess Bolkonskaya : that is another thing. In the first place, I will tell you honestly, she pleases me very much ; I like her extremely. And besides, after meeting her in such a way, in such a terrible position, the thought has often occurred to me that it was fate. You may remember, *maman* long, long ago thought about this, before I ever happened to meet her, and somehow it happened so; we never met. And then when my sister Natasha was engaged to her brother, why, of course, then it became out of the question to think of marrying her.[1]   And now, just as Natasha's engagement is broken off, it must needs happen that I meet her ; well, it 's all .... this is the trouble .... I have never told any one about this, and I shall never speak of it again.   Only to you."

The governor's wife gave his elbow an encouraging pressure.

"You know Sophie, my cousin.   I love her, and I have promised to marry her, and I shall marry her. .... And so you see there is nothing to be said about this other matter," explained Nikolaï,. disconnectedly and reddening.

"*Mon cher! mon cher!* how can you have such ideas? Why, you know Sophie has nothing, and you yourself have told me that your papa's affairs were in a wretched state.   And your *maman?*   This would kill her, surely ! Then, Sophie, if she is a girl with any heart, what a life it would be for her !   Your mother in despair, your property all dissipated ! .... No, *mon cher*, you and Sophie must see things as they are."

Nikolaï made no reply.   It was pleasant for him to hear this reasoning.

"Still, *ma tante*, this cannot be," said he, with a sigh, after some little silence.   "Then, do you suppose the princess would marry me ? and besides, she is in mourning.   How can such a thing be thought of ?"

"What ? do you suppose I would have you marry her instantly ?   *Il y a manière et manière !* — there are ways and ways ! " said the governor's wife.

"What a match-maker, *ma tante !* " said Nikolaï, kissing her plump hand.

[1] The marriage sacrament according to the Greek Church makes marriage relationship blood relationship.

CHAPTER VI

THE Princess Mariya, on arriving at Moscow after her meeting with Rostof, had found there her nephew and his tutor, and a letter from Prince Andreï, who enjoined on them to go immediately to Voronezh, to her Aunt Malvintseva.

The labors consequent on this move, her anxiety for her brother, the regulation of her life in her new home, new acquaintances, the education of her nephew, — all this tended to quench in the Princess Mariya's heart that seductive longing which had tormented her during her father's illness, and after his death, and especially after her meeting with Rostof.

She was unhappy.

The impression of her father's loss, associated in her mind as it was with the ruin of Russia, now, after a month spent in the conditions of a calm, equable life, grew more and more vivid to her. She was anxious; the thought of the perils to which her brother was exposed — the only man who was closely related to her — constantly tormented her.

She was occupied with the instruction of her nephew, but she felt all the time that she was peculiarly unfitted for it. Nevertheless in the depths of her soul there was a certain sense of quietude arising from the consciousness that she had crushed out the personal hopes and dreams that had sprung up in her heart, and were connected with the appearance of Rostof.

When, on the day following her reception, the governor's wife went to call upon Madame Malvintseva, after a private conversation with her in regard to her scheme (making the reservation that, though under present circumstances it was impossible to think of a formal courtship, still the young people might be brought together and made acquainted), and when, after receiving the aunt's approval, the gubernatorsha spoke in the Princess Mariya's presence of Rostof, praised him, and told how he had reddened at the mere mention of the prin cess's name, the Princess Mariya experienced a feeling not of pleasure but of pain ; her inward calm had entirely vanished, and again arose her desires, doubts, self-re-proaches, and hopes.

During the two days that intervened between hear-ing this news and her interview with Rostof, the Prin-cess Mariya did not cease to think how she ought to behave toward him. At one moment she made up her mind that she would not go into the drawing-room when he came to call on her aunt, that it was not be-coming for her to receive callers when she was in deep mourning ; then again she thought that it would be rude after all that he had done for her ; then it occurred to her that the governor's wife and her aunt must have some designs on her and Rostof, — their glances, and certain words they had dropped, it seemed to her, con-firmed this supposition, — then she said to herself that nothing but her inborn depravity made her have such thoughts ; they could not help remembering that, in her situation, she not having yet taken off her "weep-ers," such a wooing would be an insult to her, as well as to her father's memory.

Assuming that she should go down to meet him, the Princess Mariya tried to imagine the words which he would say to her, and which she should say to him, and at one moment these words seemed undeservedly cold, at the next they seemed to possess too great significance.

More than all else she was apprehensive that on meeting him she should show that bashfulness which she was certain would take possession of her, and be-tray her as soon as she saw him.

But when on Sunday, after mass, the lackey an-nounced at the drawing-room door that Count Rostof had come, the princess showed no symptoms of con-fusion ; only a faint tinge of color suffused her cheeks, and her eyes shone with a new, luminous light.

"You have seen him, auntie?"[1] asked the Princess Mariya in a tranquil voice, surprised herself that she could be outwardly so calm and natural.

[1] *Tiotushka ;* diminutive of *tiotka.*

When Rostof entered the room, the princess for a moment dropped her head, as if for the purpose of allowing the guest time to exchange greetings with her aunt, and then at the very moment that Nikolaï came toward her, she raised her head, and with radiant eyes met his glance.

With a movement full of grace and dignity, she arose with a joyful smile, offered him her slender, delicate hand, and spoke to him in a voice which for the first time vibrated with new, deep, womanly tones.

Mlle. Bourienne, who was in the drawing-room, looked at the Princess Mariya in wonder and perplexity.   She herself, though a most accomplished coquette, could not have manœuvered better on meeting a man whom she wished to fascinate.

"Either black is becoming to her, or really she has grown pretty; I certainly never remarked it so before," said Mlle. Bourienne to herself.

If the Princess Mariya had been in a position to think at that moment, she would have been even more amazed than was Mlle. Bourienne at the change that had taken place in her.   From the instant that she saw that kind face, so beloved, a new power of life took possession of her, and compelled her, irrespective of her own will, to speak and to act.   Her face from that moment that Rostof entered was suddenly transformed.

Just as the complicated artistic work on the sides of a painted or carved lamp-shade comes out with sudden and unexpected details of beauty when a light is lighted in it, though before it had seemed coarse, dark, and meaningless, so was the Princess Mariya's face unexpectedly transformed.   For the first time all that pure, spiritual, inward travail which she had gone through for so many years was laid open to the light.   All that inward travail, which had left her so dissatisfied with herself, — her suffering, her yearnings after the right, her submission, love, self-sacrifice, — all this now shone forth in her luminous eyes, in her gentle smile, in every feature of her tender face.

Rostof saw all this so clearly that it seemed to him

he had known her all his life. He felt that the being before him was different, was better, than all that he had hitherto met, and, what was more important, was better than himself.

Their conversation was extremely simple and insignificant. They talked about the war, involuntarily, like every one else, exaggerating their grief at the event; they talked about their last meeting, whereupon Nikolaï tried to turn the conversation to something else; they talked about the good gubernatorsha, about their parents.

The Princess Mariya did not speak of her brother, deflecting the subject to another topic as soon as her aunt spoke about Andreï. It was evident that, while there might be some pretense in her expressions of grief in the miseries of Russia, her brother was an object too near to her heart, and she would not and could not talk about him. Nikolaï remarked this, for, with a keenness of observation that was not at all characteristic of him, he remarked all the little shades of the princess's nature to the effect of greatly intensifying his conviction that she was a being entirely out of the common.

Nikolaï, exactly the same as the princess, had changed color and become confused when her name was mentioned in his presence, and even when he thought about her; but in her presence he felt perfectly unhampered, and by no means confined himself to the set speeches which he had made ready in advance, but spoke whatever came into his head.

During Nikolaï's short call there were, as always happens where a number of people are together, moments of silence, and during one of these Nikolaï made up to Prince Andreï's little son, petted him, and asked him if he would like to be a hussar. He took hold of the boy's hands, spun him around, and glanced at the Princess Mariya. Her tender, happy, and timid eyes followed the little lad whom she loved while he was in the arms of the man whom she loved. Nikolaï also remarked this look, and evidently understanding its significance, he flushed with gratification, and with good-natured jollity began to kiss the little fellow.

The Princess Mariya, owing to her mourning, was not going into society, and Nikolaï felt that it was unbecoming for him to repeat his call on them; but the governor's wife, nevertheless, continued her task of match-maker, and, taking occasion to repeat to Nikolaï all the flattering things that the Princess Mariya had said about him, and *vice versa*, she insisted that he should declare himself to the princess.

In order to bring about this explanation, she arranged a meeting between the young people at the archbishop's, before mass.

Although Rostof had told the governor's wife that he would not come to any explanation with the Princess Mariya, still he promised to be present.

Just as at Tilsit he had not allowed himself to doubt whether what had been enjoined on all was good or not, so now, after a short but genuine struggle between his wish to arrange his life in his own way and a peaceful submission to circumstances, he chose the latter alternative, and gave himself up to that power which, as he could not help feeling, was irresistibly drawing him away. He knew that, having plighted his troth to Sonya, if he confessed his feelings for the Princess Mariya, it would be nothing else than base. And he knew that he would never do anything base. But he knew also (not so much knew it as felt it in the depths of his heart) that if he gave himself up into the control of men and of circumstances and let them guide him, he not only would do nothing wrong, but would rather do something very, very important, so important that nothing like it would ever again recur to him in his life.

After his meeting with the Princess Mariya, although his manner of life continued to be the same outwardly, still all his former pleasures lost for him their zest, and he frequently found himself thinking of the Princess Mariya; but he never thought of her as he had always, without exception, thought of the various young ladies whom he had met in society, nor even as he had for long and sometimes even enthusiastically thought of Sonya.

Like almost every pure young man, when he thought about any young lady as his possible wife, he strove to make her fit the condition of marital existence, as he imagined it — the white capote, the wife behind the samovar, his wife's carriage, wee bits of children, *maman* and papa, their relations to her, and so forth, and so forth ; and these representations of the future gave him pleasure.

But when he thought about the Princess Mariya, whom they were trying to make a wife for him, he could not make the representations of his future married life in any way concrete. Even when he tried everything seemed incoherent and false. All that remained in his mind was a kind of dread.

CHAPTER VII

THE terrible news of the battle of Borodino, of our losses in dead and wounded, and the still more terrible tidings of the loss of Moscow, were received in Voronezh toward the end of September.

The Princess Mariya, learning only from the bulletin that her brother was wounded, and having no definite information about him, determined to go in search of him. This was what Nikolaï heard. He himself had not seen her again.

On learning of the battle of Borodino and the abandonment of Moscow, Nikolaï, while not giving himself up to feelings of despair, anger, or desire for vengeance or the like, still suddenly began to feel bored and out of place at Voronezh ; his conscience almost reproached him, and he felt awkward. All the talk that he heard seemed to him hypocritical ; he knew not what judgment to pass on events, and he was conscious that not until he returned to his regiment would things become clear to him again. He made haste to accomplish his purchase of horses, and oftentimes without any just cause became impatient with his servant and the quartermaster.

Several days before Rostof's departure, a solemn service was held in the cathedral, in honor of the victory that had been won by the Russian troops, and Nikolaï was present. He was standing a little behind the governor, and, though his gravity was worthy of the occasion, he was thinking of the most varied subjects, even while he listened to the service. When the Te Deum was ended, the governor's wife called him to her.

"Have you seen the princess?" she asked, with her head indicating a lady in black who stood behind the choir.

Nikolaï instantly recognized the Princess Mariya, not so much by her profile, a glimpse of which could be seen under her hat, as by that feeling of shyness, fear, and pity which instantly came over him. The Princess Mariya, evidently absorbed in her thoughts, was crossing herself for the last time before she should leave the church.

Nikolaï looked into her face with amazement. It was the same face which he had seen before, there was the same general expression of gentle, inward, spiritual travail; but now it was lighted up by a very different sort of light. It had a touching expression of sorrowfulness, entreaty, and hope.

As had been the case with Nikolaï before when he was in her presence, he, without waiting for the gubernatorsha's advice to join her, without asking himself whether it were right or proper for him to address her there in the church, instantly went to her and said that he had heard of her sorrow, and that he sympathized with her with all his heart. She had hardly caught the first sound of his voice, when suddenly a bright light flashed into her face, giving witness at one and the same time of her sorrow and her joy.

"I only wanted to tell you this, princess," said Rostof, "that if Prince Andreï Nikolayevitch were not alive, it would be instantly announced in the bulletins, since he is a regimental commander."

The princess looked at him, not comprehending his words, but delighting in the expression of sympathy and sorrow in his face.

"And I have known so many cases where a wound caused by a splinter (in the bulletins it said by a shell) was either fatal immediately, or, if not, very trifling," said Nikolaï. "You must hope for the best, and I am certain...."

The Princess Mariya interrupted him: —

"Oh, this would be so hor...." she began, but her emotion overmastered her, and, without completing the word, she bent her head with a graceful motion (like everything that she did in his presence), and, giving him a grateful look, rejoined her aunt.

The evening of that same day, Nikolaï accepted no engagements out, but remained at his lodgings in order to square up certain accounts with the horse-dealers.

Having completed his business, it being too late to go anywhere, but too early to retire for the night, Nikolaï long walked up and down his solitary room, thinking over his life, which was an unusual thing for him to do.

The Princess Mariya had produced on him an agreeable impression when he saw her near Smolensk. The fact that he had met her then in such extraordinary circumstances, and that she was the very one whom his mother had once recommended to him as an eligible heiress, caused him to regard her with peculiar interest.

When he came to see her again at Voronezh, this impression was not only agreeable, but it was powerful. Nikolaï was struck by that peculiar moral beauty which he for the first time observed in her.

He was ready to take his departure, however, and it had not occurred to him to regret the fact that in leaving Voronezh he was depriving himself of the chance of seeing the princess. But his meeting with her that morning at church (Nikolaï was conscious of this) had sunk deeper into his heart than he could have foreseen, and deeper than he would have wished for his peace of mind.

That pale, gentle, sorrowful face, those luminous eyes,

those quiet, graceful movements, and, above all, that profound and sweet expression of sorrow pervading all her being, troubled him and aroused his sympathy.

Rostof could not endure to see in men the expression of a lofty spiritual life, — that was the reason he did not like Prince Andreï, — he scornfully called it philosophy, *day-dreaming;* but in the Princess Mariya, especially in that sorrow which brought forth all the depth of that spiritual world so marvelous to Rostof, he felt an irresistible attraction.

"She must be a marvelous girl! A real angel!" said he to himself. "Why am I not free? Why was I in such haste with regard to Sonya?"

And involuntarily he began to institute a comparison between the two : the poverty in one, the abundance in the other, of those spiritual gifts which Nikolaï himself had not, and which therefore he prized so highly.

He tried to imagine what would be if he had been free. How would he have made his proposal to her, and if she had become his wife! But no, he could not imagine it.

A strange feeling of dread came over him, and nothing clear presented itself to his imagination. Now he had long ago drawn the picture of his future with Sonya, and it was all clear and simple, for the reason that it had been thought out, and he knew all that was in Sonya; but it was impossible to formulate any scheme of life with the Princess Mariya, because he did not understand her, but only loved her.

His visions of Sonya had something about them that was jolly and frivolous. But it was always hard and rather terrible to think of Princess Mariya.

"How she was praying!" he mused, following his recollections. "It was evident her whole soul was in her prayer. Yes, that is the prayer that removes mountains, and I am sure that her prayer will be fulfilled. Why cannot I pray for what I need?" he asked himself. "What do I need? My freedom, to be released from Sonya. — She said what was true," he was recalling the gubernatorsha's words — "'Nothing but misfortune would come of my marrying her.' Confusion, grief to *maman* .... business .... confusion, terrible confusion! Yes, and I don't love her. I don't love her as I ought. My God! save me from this terrible inextricable state of things!" he began, trying to offer a prayer. "Yes, prayer moves the mountain, but faith is needful, and one should not pray as Natasha and I used to pray when we were children, that the snow would change into sugar, and then run out of doors to see whether our prayer was answered. No, but I cannot pray about trifles now," said he, as he laid his pipe down in the corner, and, folding his hands, stood in front of the holy pictures. And touched by his recollection of the Princess Mariya, he began to pray as he had not prayed for a long, long time. The tears were standing in his eyes and swelling his throat when Lavrushka suddenly came in with documents in his hand. "Idiot — durak! — what do you come sneaking in for when you were n't called?" exclaimed Nikolaï, abruptly changing his position.

"From the governor," said Lavrushka, in a sleepy voice — "a courier came; letter for you."

"All right, thanks! Begone!"

Nikolaï had two letters. One was from his mother, the other from Sonya. He recognized them by their handwriting, and he opened Sonya's first. He had only read a few lines when his face grew pale and his eyes opened wide in terror and delight.

"No, it cannot be!" he exclaimed aloud. He could not sit still, but with the letter in his hand began to pace the room. He glanced through the letter, then read it, once and a second time, and, shrugging his shoulders and opening out his hands, he stood still in the middle of the room with open mouth and set eyes.

The very thing which he had just been praying for with the faith that God would fulfil his prayer was granted; but Nikolaï was amazed by this, as if it had been something extraordinary, and as if he had never expected it, and as if the very thing which had so quickly eventuated proved that this had come, not by the will of God, to whom he had offered his petition, but from ordinary chance.

This apparently unsolvable knot which fettered Rostof's freedom was cut by this letter from Sonya — so unexpected (as it seemed to Nikolaï) and unsolicited. She wrote that the recent unfortunate events, the loss of almost all the Rostofs' property in Moscow, and the more than once expressed desire of the countess that Nikolaï should marry the Princess Bolkonskaya, and his own silence and coldness of late, — all taken together had caused her to decide to release him from his promise and give him perfect freedom. She wrote:

It was too trying for me to think that I might be a source of sorrow or dissension in a family which has loaded me with benefits, and my love has for its one single aim the happiness of those whom I love. And therefore I beseech you, Nicolas, to consider yourself perfectly free, and to know that, in spite of all, no one could love you more truly than your Sonya.

Both letters were written from Troïtsa.

The second letter was from the countess. In this there was given a full description of the last days in Moscow, their departure, the fire, and the loss of all their property. In this letter also, among other things, the countess wrote that Prince Andreï was among the wounded whom they had brought away with them. His condition was very critical, but now the doctor declared that there was more hope. Sonya and Natasha were attending him as watchers.

On the following day, Nikolaï took this letter, and went to see the Princess Mariya. Neither Nikolaï nor the princess said a word as to the significance of the fact that Natasha was attending the sufferer; but, thanks to this letter, Nikolaï suddenly felt drawn closer to the princess, almost as if he were a relative.

On the next day, Rostof escorted the Princess Mariya to Yaroslavl, and not long after rejoined his regiment.

CHAPTER VIII

SONYA's letter to Nikolaï, coming so opportunely in answer to his prayer, had been written from Troïtsa.

This was the way it happened.

The old countess had become more and more occupied by the idea of Nikolaï marrying a rich wife. She knew that Sonya was the chief obstacle in the way of this. And Sonya's life in the countess's home had been made more and more trying of late, especially since Nikolaï wrote of meeting the Princess Mariya at Bogucharovo.

The countess lost no opportunity of addressing Sonya with insulting or cruel insinuations.

A few days before their departure from Moscow, however, the countess, exacerbated and excited by all that was happening, had called Sonya to her, and, instead of loading her with reproaches and demands, had begged her with tears in her eyes to have pity on her, and, as a return for all that had been done for her, to release Nikolaï from his engagement.

"I shall never be content until you have given me this promise."

Sonya sobbed hysterically, promised through her sobs that she would do anything, that she was ready for any sacrifice; but she did not give the promise in so many words, and in her heart she found it impossible to consent to do what they required of her. It was necessary for her to sacrifice herself for the happiness of the family which had fed and educated her.

To sacrifice herself for the happiness of others was second nature to Sonya. Her position in the household was such that it was only on the road of sacrifice that she could show her worth, and she was accustomed to sacrifice herself, and loved to do so.

But hitherto, in all her acts of self-sacrifice, she had enjoyed the pleasant consciousness that in thus sacrificing herself, she was by this very act enhancing her value in her own eyes and the eyes of others, and was becoming more worthy of Nicolas, whom she loved above all else in the world.

But now her sacrifice was to consist in renouncing all that had promised to be the reward of her sacrifice, the whole meaning of life. And for the first time in her life she had bitter feelings against those very people who had loaded her with benefits only to torment her the more. She began to hate Natasha, who had never been called upon to experience any such trial, who had never been required to sacrifice herself, but who had obliged others to sacrifice themselves for her, and yet was loved by all.

And for the first time Sonya felt that her gentle, pure love for Nicolas was growing into a passion which was mightier than law and virtue and religion; and under the influence of this feeling Sonya, who had been involuntarily taught by her life of dependence to be reserved, replied to the countess in general, indefinite terms, avoided having anything further to say to her, and made up her mind to wait until she should see Nikolaï again, with the idea, not of giving him his freedom, but, on the contrary, of binding him to her forever.

The labors and terror incident to those last days that the Rostofs spent in Moscow put out of mind the gloomy thoughts that had been weighing her down. She was glad to find an escape from them in practical activity. But when she learned of Prince Andreï's presence in the house, notwithstanding the genuine pity which she felt for him and for Natasha, she was seized by a blithe and superstitious presentiment that God did not wish her to be separated from Nicolas.

She knew that Natasha had never loved any one besides Prince Andreï, and that she still loved him. She knew that, now being brought together in such terrible circumstances, their mutual affection would be renewed, and that then it would be impossible for Nikolaï to marry the Princess Mariya, on account of the relationship which would be entailed on them. Notwithstanding the horror of all that had taken place during the last days and during the early part of their journey, this feeling, this consciousness of the interference of Providence in her personal affairs, had rejoiced Sonya's heart.

The Rostofs made their first halt at the Troïtskaya Lavra, or Trinity Monastery.

At the hostelry of the Lavra, the Rostofs were assigned three large rooms, one of which was taken by Prince Andreï. The wounded man that day was much better. Natasha had been sitting with him. In the adjoining room the count and countess were engaged in a polite conversation with the father superior, who had come to pay his respects to his old acquaintances and benefactors. Sonya was also sitting with them, and was tormented by curiosity as to what Prince Andreï and Natasha were talking about, for she could hear the sounds of their voices. The door of Prince Andreï's room had been left open.

Natasha, with agitated face, came running out, and not heeding the monk, who arose to meet her and offered her his right hand under his flowing sleeve, went straight to Sonya, and took her by the arm.

"Natasha! what is the matter? Come here!" said the countess.

Natasha submitted to the priest's blessing, and the father superior advised her to go for help to God and his saint.

As soon as the father superior was gone, Natasha took her cousin's hand, and drew her into the empty room.

"Sonya! is he going to live? Say yes!" said she. "Sonya! How happy I am, and how unhappy! Sonya darling,[1] it is all just as it used to be. If only he would live!.... he can't get well.... because.... be.... cause...."

And Natasha burst into tears.

"Yes! he will. I have been sure of it! Glory to God! He will get well!"

Sonya was no less agitated than Natasha, not only because of her friend's suffering and sorrow, but also because of her own private thoughts, which she shared with no one. Sobbing, she kissed Natasha, and tried to soothe her.

[1] *Galubchik.*

"If only he *would* get well!" she said to herself. Having had a good cry and a talk together, and wiping away their tears, the two friends went to Prince Andreï's door. Natasha, carefully opening it, glanced into the room. Sonya stood next her at the half-open door.

Prince Andreï lay bolstered up high on three pillows. His white face was calm, his eyes closed, and apparently he was breathing regularly.

"Akh! Natasha!" Sonya almost screamed, suddenly seizing her cousin's hand, and starting away from the door.

"What .... what is it?" asked Natasha.

"Let me tell you! this .... this!" .... said Sonya, with pallid face and trembling lips.

Natasha gently closed the door, and went with Sonya to the window, no longer remembering what had been said to her.

"Do you remember," began Sonya, in a frightened and solemn voice, — "do you remember when I looked for you at the mirror .... at Otradnoye, on Twelfth Night? .... Do you remember what I saw?" ....

"Yes, yes," replied Natasha, opening her eyes wide, and having a dim remembrance that at that time Sonya had said something about Prince Andreï, whom she claimed to have seen lying down.

"Do you remember?" continued Sonya: "I saw then and told you all — you and Dunyasha. I saw him lying on a bed," said she, at every detail waving her hand with outstretched finger, "and his eyes were closed, and he was covered with a pink spread, and his arms were folded," pursued Sonya, convinced that all these details, which she had just before seen, were the very same that she had *seen* at that time.

Really, at that time she had seen nothing, but she had related as having seen what first entered her mind; but what she had imagined then seemed to her the reality, like any other remembrance. What she had said then about his looking at her and smiling, and being covered with something blue and red, she did not remember, but was firmly persuaded that she had then said and seen

VOL. V. — 14

how he was covered with something pink, indeed a pink coverlet, and that his eyes were closed!

"Yes, yes, certainly it was pink," said Natasha, who also at the present time remembered that the color mentioned had been pink, and in this fact she found the chief wonder and mystery of the prediction.

"But what does this mean?" queried Natasha, thoughtfully.

"Oh, I'm sure I don't know! How extraordinary it all is!" exclaimed Sonya, clasping her head with her hands.

In a few minutes, Prince Andreï rang, and Natasha went to him; but Sonya, experiencing an emotion and excitement such as she had rarely experienced, still stood by the window, thinking over all the strangeness of what had happened.

There happened to be on that day an opportunity to send letters to the army, and the countess was writing to her son.

"Sonya," said the countess, lifting her head from her letter as her niece passed her, — "Sonya, won't you write Nikolenka?" asked the countess, in a gentle, trembling voice; and by the look in her weary eyes, which the countess gave her over her spectacles, Sonya read what she meant by those words. In that look was expressed a prayer, and fear of a refusal, and shame that she was obliged to ask such a thing, and readiness for implacable hatred in case of refusal.

Sonya went to the countess, and, kneeling down beside her, kissed her hand.

"I will write," said she.

Sonya was softened, excited, and touched by all that had happened on that day, especially by the mysterious accomplishment of the divination which she had just seen. Now, when she knew that, in case of Natasha's engagement to Prince Andreï being renewed, Nikolaï could not marry Princess Mariya, she had a sense of joy in the return of this condition of self-sacrifice in which she was in the habit of living. And with tears in her

eyes and with a blissful consciousness of having accomplished a magnanimous action, she, though several times
interrupted by the tears which clouded her velvety dark
eyes, wrote the touching letter, the receipt of which had
so amazed Nikolaï.

CHAPTER IX

At the guard-house where Pierre was conducted, the
officer and soldiers who had him in charge treated him
like an enemy, but at the same time with consideration.
In their treatment of him there seemed to be some
suspicion that he might prove to be a man of very great
importance, and the unfriendliness was due only to the
remembrance of the personal struggle which they had
just had with him.

But on the following morning, when the guard was
relieved, Pierre was made aware that for the new guard
— officers and men alike — he had not that importance
which he had enjoyed with those who captured him.
And indeed this great, portly man, in peasant's kaftan,
the new guards did not know as that energetic man who
had fought so desperately with the marauder and with
the horse patrol, and had spoken that solemn phrase
about the saving of the child, but they saw in him merely
No. 17 of the Russian prisoners who had been taken
and held by order of men high in command.

If there was anything special in Pierre, it was certainly his appearance, devoid of timidity, and full of
intense, concentrated thought, and the elegant French
which he spoke, to the amazement of the French themselves. Nevertheless, on this day Pierre was put in
with the other suspects that had been captured, for the
reason that the special room which had been given him
first was required by an officer.

All the Russians locked in with Pierre were men of
the very lowest station. And all of them, recognizing
that Pierre was a barin, shunned him, and all the more

from the fact that he spoke French. Pierre with a certain melancholy listened to their sarcasms at his expense.

On the following evening Pierre learned that all these prisoners (and apparently he himself in the number) were to be tried for incendiarism. On the third day Pierre and the rest were conducted to a house where were a French general with a white mustache, two colonels, and several other Frenchmen with chevrons on their arms.

Pierre, the same as the rest, was subjected to a series of questions, put with that shrewdness and precision that affect to be superior to all human weaknesses and are characteristic of all ordinary dealings with prisoners at the bar. Who was he? Where had be been? For what purpose? and so forth.

These questions, putting aside the essence of the vital fact, and excluding the possibility of getting at the truth, were like all questions put at legal examinations, having for their object the laying down of a sort of gutter in which examiners wish the answers of the victim to trickle so that he may be brought to the requisite point; namely, incrimination!

The moment he began to make any remark that did not satisfy this end, the "gutter" was applied, and the water made to flow in the desired direction.

Moreover, Pierre experienced what is always experienced by men on trial: a sense of perplexity, of wonder why all these questions are asked. He had a feeling that it was only out of condescension, or possibly courtesy, that the expedient of the question-gutter was made use of. He knew that he was in the power of these men, that it was merely brute force that had brought him where he was, that only might[1] gave them the right to demand of him answers to their questions, that the sole aim of this court was to prove him guilty.

And therefore, as they had the power and the desire to convict him, there was no need of the expedient of

[1] The simple style of the original is shown by the fact that one word — *vlast'* — stands for power, brute force, and might.

the interrogatory and the court. It was evident that all his answers were taken as proof of his guilt.

To the question what he was doing when he was arrested, Pierre replied with a certain tragic force that he was restoring to its parents a child which he had rescued from the flames — *qu'il avait sauvé des flammes*.

Why had he fought with the marauder? Pierre replied that he was protecting a woman, that the defense of an insulted woman was the duty of every man, that....

They interrupted him; this was irrelevant.

Why had he been in the yard of the burning building, where the witnesses had seen him?

He replied that he had gone out to see what was happening in Moscow.

He was again interrupted; he had not been asked where he was going, but *why* he was in the vicinity of the fire.

Who was he? they asked, reiterating their first question; he replied once more that he could not tell them that.

"Write that down; it looks bad. Very bad," sternly said the white-mustached general with the florid complexion.

On the fourth day fires broke out on the Zubovsky Rampart.

Pierre and thirteen others were removed to the Kruimsky Brod, or Crimean Ford, and placed in the coach-house of a merchant's mansion. As they marched along the streets, Pierre was suffocated by the smoke, which seemed to him to be settled down over the whole city. In various directions fires could be seen. Not even then did Pierre understand the significance of the burning of Moscow, and he looked upon these fires with horror.

In the coach-house of this solitary mansion by the Kruimsky Brod, Pierre spent four days more, and during this time he learned, from the talk of the French soldiers, that the decision of the marshal regarding the prisoners confined there was expected each day.

Pierre could not learn from the soldier what marshal it was. Evidently for the soldier the term marshal connoted some elevated and mysterious link in the chain of power.

These days up till the twentieth of September, on which the prisoners were put through a second examination, were very trying for Pierre.

CHAPTER X

On the twentieth of September, an officer of very great importance, to judge by the respect shown him by the guards, came into the coach-house to see the prisoners. This officer, who apparently belonged to Napoleon's staff, had a list in his hand, and called a roll of all the Russians, designating Pierre as *celui qui n'avoue pas son nom* — the man who refuses to give his name.

Surveying the prisoners with a look of lazy indifference, he ordered the officer of the guard to see that they were decently clad and ordered before they were brought into the marshal's presence.

Within an hour, a file of soldiers appeared, and Pierre and thirteen others were taken out to the Dievitchye Pole.[1]

It was a bright, sunny day after rain, and the air was extraordinarily clear. The smoke did not hang low, as it had on that day when Pierre was removed from the watch-house of the Zubovsky Val. It rose in columns in the clear atmosphere. No flames were visible, but on all sides arose these columns of smoke, and all Moscow, as far as Pierre could see, was one conflagration. On all sides were ruins, with stoves and chimneys, and here and there the devastated walls of stone houses.

Pierre gazed at the fires, but could not recognize any part of the city. Here and there could be seen churches still standing. The Kreml, undevastated,

[1] Virgin's Field.

gleamed white in the distance, with its cupolas and Ivan Veliki.[1]

Near by gleamed jocund the cupola of the Novo-dievitchy monastery, and with unusual clearness could be heard the sound of the chimes. This sound of the chimes reminded Pierre that it was Sunday, and the Festival of the Nativity of the Mother of God. But it seemed as if there was no one to celebrate this festival. Everywhere was the ravage of the flames, and only rarely were any of the Russian populace to be seen, and these were ragged, panic-stricken folk, who concealed themselves at sight of the French.

Evidently, the Russian nest was wrecked and ruined; but Pierre had a dim consciousness that after the overthrow of this old order of life, in place of this ruined nest, there would be established the new and entirely different but stable French order. He felt it at the sight of these soldiers who marched gallantly and blithely in perfectly unbroken ranks as they escorted him and the other offenders along; he felt it at the sight of an important French official in a two-horse calash, driven by a soldier, coming toward him; he felt it by the inspiriting sounds of the martial music which came across from the left of the field; and especially he felt it and realized it by the way in which the French officer had that morning read off the list containing the names of the prisoners.

Pierre had been taken by certain soldiers, carried to one place, then transferred to another with a dozen other men; it seemed as if they might have forgotten about him, have confused him with others. But no! the answer that he had given during the investigation returned to him in the form of an appellation: *celui qui n'avoue pas son nom* — the man who refuses to give his name.

And under this appellation, terrible to Pierre, he was

---

[1] The Tower of Ivan Veliki, or John the Great, "a goodly steepill of hewen stoen in the inner Castell of Musco," built by Boris Godunof, 1600. It is 320 feet high, and provided with a chime of 34 bells, the largest of which weighs 64 tons.

now conducted somewhere, with the undoubted conviction written on all faces that he and the rest of the prisoners were the very ones required, and that they were
being taken to the proper place. Pierre felt himself an
insignificant chip falling into the wheels of a machine
which he knew nothing about, but which acted with
absolute regularity.

Pierre and the other prisoners were conducted to the
right-hand side of the Dievitchye Pole, to a large white
house with an immense garden not far from the monastery. This was Prince Shcherbatof's house, which Pierre
had often been in, and which now, as he ascertained from
the talk of the soldiers, was occupied by the marshal, the
Prince d'Eckmühl.

They were taken to the porch, and led into the house
one at a time. Pierre was the sixth. Through the
glass gallery, the entry, the anteroom, rooms all well
known to Pierre, he was led into a long, low cabinet,
at the door of which stood an aide-de-camp.

Davoust, with his spectacles on his nose, sat by a
table at one end of the room. Pierre came close to
him. Davoust, without raising his eyes, evidently consulted a document placed in front of him. Without even
raising his eyes, he asked in a low voice: "*Qui êtes
vous ?* — Who are you ?"

Pierre said nothing, from the reason that he had not
the power to utter a word. Davoust, in Pierre's eyes,
was not simply a French general: for Pierre, Davoust
was a man notorious for his cruelty. As he looked into
Davoust's icy face, like that of a stern teacher who is
willing to be patient for a time and wait for a reply,
Pierre felt that every second of delay might cost him
his life, but he knew not what to say. He could not
make up his mind to repeat what he had said at the first
examination; to divulge his name and station was at
once dangerous and shameful.

Pierre said nothing.

But before he had time to come to any decision Davoust
raised his head, pushed his spectacles up on his forehead,
squinted his eyes, and gave Pierre a fixed stare.

"I know this man," said he, in an icy tone, evidently meant to alarm Pierre. The chill which before had been running up and down Pierre's back clutched his head as in a vise.

"General, you cannot possibly know me; I have never seen you...."

"He is a Russian spy," interrupted Davoust, turning to another general who happened to be in the room and had not before been observed by Pierre. And Davoust looked away.

With an unexpected rumbling in his voice, Pierre suddenly began to speak rapidly.

"No, monseigneur," said he, unexpectedly remembering that Davoust was a duke. — "No, monseigneur, you cannot have known me. I am an officer of militia, and I have not been out of Moscow."

"Your name?" demanded Davoust.

"Bezukhoï."

"Who will prove that you are not lying?"

"Monseigneur!" cried Pierre, in a tone that betrayed not offense but expostulation.

Davoust raised his eyes and stared at Pierre. For several seconds they looked into each other's eyes, and this look was what saved Pierre. In this look there was established between these two men, above and beyond all the conditions of war and the court-room, the relations of a common humanity. Both of them at that one moment became confusedly conscious of an infinite number of things, and realized that they both were children of humanity, — that they were brothers.

For Davoust, who had only just raised his head from the list where the acts and lives of men were represented by numbers, Pierre at first glance was only an incident, and Davoust would have had him shot without his conscience regarding it as a wicked deed; but now he already began to see that he was a man. He deliberated for an instant.

"How will you prove the truth of what you tell me?" asked Davoust, coldly.

Pierre remembered Ramball, and mentioned his regi

ment and name and the street where his lodgings would be found.

"You are not what you say you are," reiterated Davoust.

Pierre, in a trembling, broken voice, began to adduce proofs of the correctness of his representation.

But at this instant an aide entered and made some report to Davoust. Davoust suddenly grew radiant at the news communicated by the aide-de-camp, and began to button up his coat. He had evidently forgotten Pierre's existence.

When the aide reminded him of the prisoner, he frowned, and nodded in Pierre's direction, and ordered him to be led away. But where was he to be led? Pierre had no idea, whether back to the coach-house or to the place prepared for the execution, which, as he had crossed the Dievitchye Pole, his comrades had pointed out to him.

He turned his head and looked back, and saw that the aide was making some inquiry.

"*Oui, sans doute;*" but what this "Yes, of course," meant, Pierre had no idea.

Pierre had no idea how long he was kept walking or whither he was taken. In a condition of absolute stupor and abstraction, conscious of nothing around him, he mechanically moved his legs together with the others until they were all halted, and then he also halted.

During all this time one thought filled his mind. This thought was: Who had in last analysis condemned him to be executed? It was not the same men who had examined him at the court-martial; there was not one man among them who would have been willing, or, in all probability, could have done so. It was not Davoust, who had looked at him with such a human look. One instant more and Davoust would have understood that they were making a mistake, but that moment was disturbed by the aide who had come in. And this aide evidently would not have willingly done anything wrong, but he could not help it. Who, then, was it that was the final cause of his being punished, killed, deprived of life — he, Pierre, with all his recollections, yearnings, hopes, ideas? Who was doing this?

And Pierre felt that it was no one.

It was the order of things, the chain of circumstances.

This order of things was somehow killing him, — Pierre, — depriving him of life, destroying him.

CHAPTER XI

FROM Prince Shcherbatof's house, the prisoners were conducted directly down along the Dievitchye Pole, to the left of the Dievitchy monastery, and were brought into a kitchen-garden where stood an upright post. Back of the post a great pit had been dug, the fresh earth was piled up at one side, and around the pit and the pillar in a semicircle stood a great throng of people. The throng consisted of a few Russians and a great number of Napoleonic troops out of military rank; Prussians, Italians, and French, in various uniforms. At the right and left of the post stood files of French troops in blue uniforms with red epaulets, in gaiters and shakoes.

The condemned were stationed in the same order as that which they had occupied on the list, — Pierre was number six, — and they were brought up to the post. A number of drums were beaten suddenly on two sides, and Pierre felt that at these sounds a part of his very soul was, as it were, torn from him. He lost the faculty of thinking and considering. He could only see and hear. And he had only one desire left, and that was that the terrible thing that had to be done should be done as speedily as possible. Pierre glanced at his comrades and observed them.

Two men at the end were shaven-headed convicts. One was tall, thin; the other, dark, hirsute, muscular, with a flattened nose. Number three was a domestic serf,[1] forty-five years old, with grayish hair and a plump, well-fed body. The fourth was a very handsome muzhik,

[1] *Dvorovui.*

with a bushy, reddish beard, and dark eyes. Number five was a factory hand, a sallow, lean fellow of eighteen, who wore a khalat.

Pierre listened to the French soldiers asking how the men should be shot : one at a time, or two at a time.

"Two at a time," replied the senior officer, in a tone of cool composure.

A stir ran through the rank and file of the soldiery, and it was plain to see that all were making ready, and making ready not as men do who make haste to do something which all comprehend, but rather as men make haste to finish some unusual task, which must be done, yet is unpleasant and incomprehensible.

A French official with a scarf on directed his steps to the right-hand side of the file of the condemned, and read the sentence in Russian and in French.

Then two couples of the French soldiers advanced to the prisoners, and, by direction of the officer, pinioned the two convicts who stood at the end. The convicts were halted at the post, and while they were bringing the death-caps looked silently around them, as a disabled wild beast at bay glares on the hunter approaching.

One kept crossing himself, the other scratched his back and tried to force his lips to smile. The soldiers, with hasty hands, began to bind their eyes, to put on the death-caps, and fasten the men to the post.

A dozen musketeers, with their guns in their hands, stepped forth with firm, measured steps, and came to a halt eight paces from the post.

Pierre looked away so as not to see what was going to take place. Suddenly was heard a crash and a rattle, which seemed to Pierre louder than the most terrific thunderclap, and he looked round. There was a smoke, and some Frenchmen, with pale faces and trembling hands, were doing something at the pit.

Two others were led out. In the same way, with the same eyes, these two also gazed at them all, vainly, with their eyes alone — for their lips were silent — begging for help, and evidently not comprehending and not realizing what was going to be. They could not believe, because they alone knew what their life was for them, and therefore they understood not and believed not that it could be taken from them.

Pierre wished not to look, and again turned his head away; but again his ears were assailed as by a terrible explosion, and, at the same time, he saw the smoke, the blood of some one, and the pale, frightened faces of the Frenchmen again occupied, with something near the post, — with trembling hands pushing one another.

Pierre, breathing heavily, glanced around him, as if to ask, "What is the meaning of this?"

The same question was expressed in all the eyes that met Pierre's.

On all the faces of the Russians, on the faces of the French soldiers and officers, all without exception, he read the same fear, horror, and battle which were in his heart.

"Yes, who is really doing this? They all suffer just exactly as I do. Who is it? who?" Such was the question that flashed through Pierre's mind.

"*Tirailleurs du 86me, en avant* — Squad of the 86th, forward," some one commanded.

The man who was fifth on the list, and stood next to Pierre, was led out — alone!

Pierre did not comprehend that he was saved; that he and all the others had been brought out simply to be witnesses of the execution. With ever increasing horror, but with no realizing sense either of joy or relief, he watched what was going on.

The fifth man was the factory workman in the khalat. The moment they laid their hands on him he seemed overwhelmed with terror, and clung to Pierre. Pierre shuddered, and shook him off.

The factory hand could not walk. He was seized under the arms and dragged away, yelling something. When they brought him to the post, he suddenly became quiet. An idea suddenly seemed to occur to him. Whether he realized that it was idle to scream, or felt that it was impossible that these men should really mean to kill him, — at all events, he stood by the post waiting for his eyes to be bandaged, just as the others had done, and like the wild beast at bay glared around him with flashing eyes.

Pierre could not bring himself to turn away or close his eyes. His curiosity and emotion, shared with the whole throng at the spectacle of this fifth execution, had arisen to the highest pitch. Like the other four, this new victim was composed. He wrapped his khalat around him, and rubbed one bare foot against the other.

When they proceeded to bind his eyes, he himself arranged the knot on the back of his head, as it was too tight for him. Then when they placed him with his back to the blood-sprinkled post, he leaned back against it, but then, apparently finding it uncomfortable in that position, he straightened himself up, and, standing on even feet, he coolly stood with his back to it.

Pierre did not take his eyes from him, or lose his slightest motion.

Some command must have been given; the command must have been followed by the reports of eight muskets. But Pierre, in spite of all his subsequent efforts to remember, heard not the slightest report from the firearms. He only saw how the factory hand, for some reason, suddenly leaned with all his weight on the ropes, how blood showed in two spots, and how the ropes themselves from the weight of the suspended body gave way, and the factory hand, unnaturally lolling his head, and his legs doubling under him, sat down.

Pierre ran up to the post. No one detained him. The pale, terror-stricken men were doing something or other about the factory hand. One old, mustached French soldier, as he untied the ropes, could not prevent his lower jaw from trembling. The body was laid on the ground. The soldiers clumsily and in all haste dragged it behind the post, and proceeded to push it into the pit.

They all, evidently, were well assured that these men were criminals, and that it was necessary as quickly as possible to put out of sight all traces of their crime.

Pierre glanced into the pit, and saw that the factory hand lay there with his knees drawn up near to his head and one shoulder higher than the other. And this shoulder was convulsively but regularly falling and rising. But already shovelfuls of earth were falling on his whole body.

One of the soldiers sternly, impatiently, wrathfully, called to Pierre to come back. But Pierre heard him not, and stood by the post, and no one drove him away.

When now the pit was all filled up, a word of command was heard. Pierre was brought back to his place, and the French troops, standing in files on both sides of the post, faced about, and marched by the post in measured step.

The twenty-four men whose muskets had been emptied, standing in the midst of the square, ran to their places, as their companies marched by them.

Pierre gazed with lack-luster eyes at these men who two by two left the circle. All but one had rejoined their companies. A young soldier with a deathly pale face, and wearing a shako on the back of his head, had grounded his musket, and still stood in front of the pit, in the spot where he had fired. He staggered like a drunken man a few steps forward, then back, and could scarcely keep from falling. An old soldier, a non-commissioned officer, ran from the ranks, and, seizing the young soldier, drew him back to his company. The throng of Russians and French began to disperse. All went off in silence, with dejected heads.

"*Ça leur apprendra à encendier* — This 'll teach 'em to set fires," said one of the Frenchmen.

Pierre glanced at the speaker, and saw that he was a soldier who wanted to get some consolation from what had been done, but could not. Without finishing what he had begun to say, he waved his hand, and went on his way.

CHAPTER XII

AFTER the execution, Pierre was parted from the others, and placed by himself in a small, dilapidated church which had been burned.

Just before evening, a non-commissioned officer of the guard, accompanied by two soldiers, came into the church, and explained to Pierre that he was reprieved, and was to be put into the barracks of the prisoners of war.

Without comprehending what was said to him, Pierre got up and went with the soldiers.

He was conducted to some huts at the upper part of the field, constructed of burned planks, beams, and scantling, and introduced into one of them. Pierre found himself in the dark, surrounded by a score of various men. He looked at these men, without comprehending who they were, why they were there, or what they wanted of him. He heard the words that they spoke, but he saw no connection or coherence in them; he did not comprehend their meaning. He answered their questions, but he had no idea who listened to him, or how his answers were received. He looked at the faces and forms, and they all alike seemed to him meaningless.

From the moment that Pierre had looked on that horrid massacre perpetrated by men who did not wish to do it, the mainspring by which everything had been coördinated and kept alive in his mind seemed to have been torn away, and everything had crumbled into a heap of incoherent dust. Although he made no attempt to explain how it happened, his faith in the beneficent ordering of the universe, in the human soul, and in his own and in God, was destroyed.

Pierre had passed through such a mental crisis before, but never one of such violence as this. Before, when doubts of this kind had come on Pierre, they had had their origin in his own wrong-doing. And then Pierre had felt in the depths of his heart that his salvation from such despair and doubt was in himself. But now he was conscious that it was not his own fault that the universe had collapsed before his eyes, leaving only incoherent ruins. He felt that it was not in his power to return to faith in life.

Around him in the darkness stood a number of men ; apparently they found something in him to interest them. They told him things, they asked questions of him ; then they led him somewhere, and at last he found himself in a corner of the hut, together with certain men who were talking and laughing together. " Here, now, my brothers, ... this very prince *who* .... " (special stress was laid on the word "who") some one was saying in the opposite corner of the balagan.

Pierre sat motionless and silent on the straw next the wall, now opening and now closing his eyes. But as soon as he closed his eyes he saw before him the factory workman's face, terrible, especially terrible, from its very simplicity, and the still more terrible faces of the reluctant executioners, with their anxious looks. And he would again open his eyes and stare inanely into the darkness around him.

Next him sat a little man all doubled up, whose presence Pierre was made aware of from the very first by the strong odor of sweat which emanated from him every time he moved. This man was engaged in doing something to his feet, and though it was so dark Pierre could not see his face, he felt conscious that this man kept looking at him. By straining his eyes to suit the darkness, Pierre made out that this man was baring his feet. And Pierre began to grow interested in the way he did it.

Having unwound the long band which was twisted around one foot and leg, he carefully rolled it up, and then went to work on the other foot the same way, constantly glancing at Pierre. While one hand was hanging up the first leg-wrapper, the other had instantly begun to undo the one on the other leg. Having thus bared his feet with precise but flowing, well-directed motions whereby no time was lost, the man spread out his foot-gear on the pegs which were driven in just above his head, took out his pocket-knife, pared off something, shut up his knife, thrust it under his pillow, and, having settled himself more comfortably, he clasped his raised knees with both hands and stared straight at Pierre.

For Pierre there was something agreeable, soothing, and satisfying in these well-regulated motions, and in this man's making himself so at home in his corner, — even in the odor emanating from him; and Pierre, without dropping his eyes, returned his gaze.

"Well, have you seen pretty hard times, barin? hah?" suddenly asked the little man.

And there was such an expression of gentleness and simple-hearted goodness in the man's singsong voice that Pierre would have instantly replied, but his jaw trembled and the tears came into his eyes. The little man at the same second, not giving Pierre time to betray his confusion, went on in the same pleasant voice : —

"Ah, my dear friend,[1] don't repine," said he, in that gentle, singsong, affectionate tone with which old Russian peasant women talk, "don't repine, my friend. An hour to suffer, but an age to live! That's the way it is, my dear! But we live here, thank God, without offense. There's bad men and there's good men as well," said he, and, while still speaking, he got up on his knees with an agile motion, arose, and, coughing, went somewhere.

"Here, you little rascal,[2] you've come, have you!" Pierre heard the same caressing voice at the other end of the hut, saying, "You remembered me, did you? There, there! that'll do!"

And the soldier, pushing off a puppy that was jumping up on him, returned to his place and sat down. He carried in his hand something wrapped up in a rag.

"Here's something to eat, barin," said he, returning to his former respectful tone, and, unwrapping the bundle, he gave to Pierre several baked potatoes. "We

[1] *E sokolik* (little hawk).   [2] *Ish shelma.*

had porridge for dinner. But potatoes are excellent."

Pierre had eaten nothing all day, and the smell of the potatoes seemed to him extraordinarily pleasant. He thanked the soldier and began to eat.

"Well, how is it?" asked the soldier, with a smile, and taking one of the potatoes,—"do you relish it?" — He again got out his jack-knife, laid the potato on his palm, and cut it into halves, sprinkled salt on from the rag, and offered it to Pierre. "Potatoes excellent," he reiterated. "Eat it that way!"

It seemed to Pierre that he had never eaten any viands that tasted more appetizing.

"No, it makes no difference to me, one way or the other," said Pierre. "But why did they shoot those poor wretches? .... The last one was n't twenty."

"*Tts! tts!*" .... said the little man. "A sin!—a sin!" he quickly added; and as if words were always ready to his lips, and winged to fly away very unexpectedly from them, he added :—

"How was it, barin, that you stayed in Moscow?"

"I did not think they would come so soon. It was by accident I stayed," replied Pierre.

"And how came they to take you? Was it from your own house, my dear?" [1]

"No; I was going to the fire, and then they seized me, and tried me as an incendiary."

"Where the tribunal is, there is injustice," said the little man, sententiously.

"Have you been long here?" asked Pierre, as he munched the last potato.

"I? Since Sunday. I was taken from the hospital in Moscow."

"So you were a soldier, were you?"

"One of Apsheron's regiment. I was dying of fever. No one had ever told us anything about it. There were twenty of us lying there. We had no idea of such a thing .... did n't dream of it!"

"Well, are you bored at being here?"

---

[1] *Sokolik,* darling (little hawk).

"How can I help being, my dear?[1]   My name is Platon; surname, Karatayef," he added, evidently so as to make Pierre's intercourse with him less formal. "They always called me sokolik in the army.   How can one help being bored, my dear?   Moscow is the mother of our cities!   How can one look on and see her destruction and not be blue?   'The worm gnaws the cabbage, but perishes before it;' that's the old folks' saying," he added quickly.

"How, how did you say that?" asked Pierre.

"I?" asked Karatayef.   "Oh, I say, 'Not by our wit, but as God sees fit,'"[2] said he, thinking he was repeating the former proverb.   And immediately he went on : —

"And you have property, have n't you, barin?   And have a house?   Your cup must be full.   And have a wife?[3]   And old folks alive?" he asked.

And Pierre, though he could not see because it was so dark, still knew that the soldier's lips were curved in a respectful smile of friendliness as he asked these questions.

He was evidently grieved to learn that Pierre had no parents, especially no mother.

"A wife for advice, a wife's mother for a welcome, but nothing sweeter than one's own matushka!" said he.   "But have you any children?" he proceeded to inquire.   Pierre's negative reply again evidently grieved him, and he hastened to add : "Well, you are young yet; God may give them.   Only you should live in good understanding ...."

"It's all the same to me now," said Pierre, involuntarily.

"Ekh!   My dear man!" exclaimed Platon.   "There's no getting rid of the beggar's sack nor of the prison cell!"   He got into a more comfortable attitude, cleared his throat, and was evidently preparing to spin a long yarn.   "This was the way, my dear friend,[4] I lived when I was at home," he began.   "We had a rich estate ....

1 *Sokolik*, darling (little hawk).
2 *Nye nashim umom a Bozhyim sudom.*
3 *Khozyaïka*, mistress of the house.
4 *Druk moï liubeznui.*

much land .... peasants lived well, and we in the house too, glory to thee, O God! My own batyushka would go out and mow. Lived well, as *Christians* should! But it happened .... "

And Platon Karatayef related a long story about how he went into another man's grove after fire-wood, and the watchman had caught him; how he had been flogged, tried, and sent off as a soldier.

"Well, my dear friend," [1] said he, his voice altered by his smile, "it seemed a misfortune; on the contrary, good thing! My brother would have had to go if it had n't been for my sin. But my younger brother had five children, while, you see, I had only a wife to leave. I had a little girl once, but God took her back before I went soldiering. I went home on leave once. I will tell you about it. I see they live better than they did before. Yard full of live stock; women at home; two brothers off at work. Only Mikhaïlo, the youngest, at home. And my batyushka, he says, says he, 'All my children's alike to me; no matter which finger you pinch, it hurts just the same. And if they had not taken Platon, Mikhaïlo 'd had to go.' He took us all in front of the 'images' — would you believe it? — and made us stand there. 'Mikhaïlo,' says he, 'come here. Bow down to the ground before him; and you, woman, bow down; and you, little ones, bow down, all of you! Have you understood?' says he. And that 's the way it is, my dear friend. 'No escaping Fate.' [2] And we are always declaring, 'This is not good, or this is all wrong.' But our happiness is like water in a net; put it in, and it 's full; take it out, and it 's empty! That 's the way it is."

And Platon shifted his seat on his straw.

After a little space of silence, Platon arose: "Well, I suppose you 'd like to go to sleep?" said he, and he began to cross himself, muttering, "Lord Jesus Christ! Saint Nikola! Frola and Lavra! Lord Jesus Christ,

---

[1] *Sokolik.*

[2] Literally, Fate, destiny, seeks heads. A variant of the proverb reads "If Fate does not find the man, the man goes to Fate."

Saint Nikola! Frola and Lavra, Lord Jesus Christ —
have mercy upon us and save us!" he said in conclusion, bowed down to the very ground, got up, drew a
deep sigh, and lay down on his straw. "Now, O God!
let me 'sleep like a stone and rise like a loaf,'"[1] he exclaimed, and lay down, covering himself with his soldier's
coat.

"What was that prayer you were repeating?" asked
Pierre.

"Heh?" said Platon. He was already dozing. "Repeated what? I was praying to God. Don't you say
your prayers?"

"Certainly I say my prayers," replied Pierre. "But
what was that about Frola and Lavra?"[2]

"Why," swiftly replied Platon, "that's the horses'
saints. For we must have pity on the cattle," said
Karatayef. "Oh, you rascal! you have come back,
have you? You want to get warm, do you, you nice
little bitch?" said he, fondling the puppy at his feet,
and, turning over again, instantly fell asleep.

Outside in the distance were heard the sounds of
wailing and yells, and through the cracks in the hut the
glare of the fire could be seen, but within it was dark
and still. It was long before Pierre could go to sleep;
and he lay in his place in the darkness with wide-open
eyes, listening to Platon's measured snoring, as he lay
near him, and feeling that that formerly ruined world
was now arising again in his soul, in new beauty and
with new and steadfast foundations.

CHAPTER XIII

THE *balagan*, or hut, where Pierre was confined, and
where he spent four weeks, contained twenty-three
soldiers, three officers, and two chinovniks, — all prisoners.

Afterwards all of them seemed to be misty memories

---

[1] *Kalachik* (kalatch), a sort of pretzel, or light loaf.
[2] *Frola* and *Lavra :* Flora and Laura.

to Pierre; but Platon Karatayef forever remained in Pierre's mind as a most powerful and precious recollection, the very embodiment of all that was good and worthy and truly Russian.

When, on the following day, at dawn, Pierre saw his neighbor, the first impression of something rotund was fully confirmed; Platon's whole figure, in his French overcoat belted with a rope, in his forage-cap and bast shoes, was rotund. His head was perfectly round; his back, his chest, his shoulders, even his arms, which he always carried as if he were ready to throw them around something, were round; his pleasant smile and his large, thick brows and his gentle eyes were round.

Platon Karatayef must have been more than fifty, to judge by his stories of campaigns in which he had taken part as a soldier. He himself had no idea, and could never have told with any accuracy, how old he was. But his teeth, brilliantly white and strong, were always displayed in two unbroken rows whenever he laughed, — which he often did, — and not one was not good and sound. There was not a trace of gray in beard or hair, and his whole frame had the appearance of agility and especially of steadfastness and endurance.

His face, in spite of a multitude of delicate round wrinkles, gave the impression of innocence and youth; his voice was agreeable in its melodious singsong. But the chief peculiarity of his speech consisted in its spontaneity and shrewdness. He evidently never thought of what he said or what he was going to say. And from this arose the irresistible persuasiveness that was found in the rapidity and certainty of his intonations.

His physical powers and activity were so great during the early part of their term of captivity that it seemed as if he knew not what weariness or ill-health meant. Every morning and evening, as he lay on his couch of straw, he would say, "Lord, let me sleep like a stone and rise like a loaf."

When he got up in the morning he always shrugged his shoulders in a certain way and said, "Turn over when you lie down, shake yourself when you get up."

And, in point of fact, all he had to do was to lie down, and instantly he would be asleep like a stone; and all he had to do was to shake himself, and without a second's delay he would be ready to take up anything, just as children, when they are once up, take to their toys.

He was a jack-at-all-trades, but neither very good nor very bad at any. He could bake, cook, sew, cut hair, cobble boots. He was always busy, and only when it came night did he allow himself to enjoy social converse, though he enjoyed it, and to sing. He sang his songs, not as singers usually sing, knowing that they will be heard; but he sang as the birds sing, evidently because it was just as much a necessity for him as it was for him to stretch himself or to walk. And these sounds were always gentle, soft, almost like a woman's, plaintive, and his face, while he was engaged in this, was very grave.

During his captivity he let his beard grow, and evidently discarded everything extraneous which was foreign or military, and involuntarily returned to his former condition of the peasant and man of the people.

"'A soldier on leave is a shirt made out of drawers,'" he would quote. He was not fond of talking about his soldiering days, although he had no regret for them, and often declared that during all his term in the service he had not once been flogged. When he had stories to tell he much preferred to confine them to old and evidently precious recollections of the time when he was a serf — *Khristianin*, Christian, he called it, instead of *Krestyanin!*

The proverbs of which he made so much use were not that generally coarse and vulgar slang which soldiers are apt to employ, but were genuine popular "saws," which seem perfectly insignificant when taken out of connection, but which suddenly acquire a meaning of deep wisdom when applied appositely.

He often said things that were diametrically opposed to what he had said before, but yet each statement would be correct. He loved to talk, and talked well, embellishing his discourse with affectionate diminutives and proverbs, which, it seemed to Pierre, the man himself improvised; but the chief charm of his narrations arose from the fact that the simplest events, those which Pierre himself had seen without taking account of them, assumed a character of solemn beauty.

He liked to listen to the yarns — though they were all of a single stamp — which a certain soldier used to tell evenings, but above all he liked to listen to tales of actual life.

He smiled blithely while listening to such tales, suggesting words and asking questions conducive to bringing out all the beauty of what was related to him.

Special attachments, friendships, loves, as Pierre understood them, Karatayef had none; but he liked all men, and lived in a loving way with all with whom his life brought him into contact, and especially with men — not any particular men — but with such as were in his sight. He loved his dog; he loved his comrades, the French; he loved Pierre, who was his companion; but Pierre felt that Karatayef, in spite of all that affectionate spirit which he manifested toward him, — and which he could not help giving as a tribute to Pierre's spiritual life, — not for one moment would grieve over separation. And Pierre also began to have the same feeling toward Karatayef.

Platon Karatayef was, in the eyes of all the other prisoners, a most ordinary soldier. They called him *sokolik*, "little hawk," or *Platosha*, good-naturedly quizzed him, made him do odd jobs for them.

But for Pierre, he remained forever what he had seemed to him the first night, — the incomprehensible, "all round," and eternal personification of the spirit of simplicity and truth.

The only thing that Platon Karatayef knew merely by rote was his prayer. When he talked, he, it would appear, would have no idea where, having once begun, he should finish.

When Pierre sometimes missed the sense of what he said, and would ask him to repeat himself, Platon would not be able to remember what he had spoken only the minute before, just as in the same way he could not give Pierre the words of his favorite song. The words were: *Rodimaya, beryozanka i toshnenko mnye*, — Mother, little birch tree, sick at heart am I, — but there was no coherent sense in those words. He could not remember or define words apart from the context.

Every word he spoke and everything that he did was the manifestation of that, to him, incomprehensible activity, his life. But his life, as he himself looked at it, had no sense as a separate existence. It had sense only as it was a part of the great whole of which he was constantly conscious. His words and deeds flowed from him as regularly, unavoidably, and spontaneously as the fragrance exhales from a flower. He could not comprehend either the object or the significance of words or deeds taken out of their proper connection.

CHAPTER XIV

The Princess Mariya, having learned from Nikolaï that her brother was with the Rostofs at Yaroslavl, immediately, in spite of her aunt's dissuasion, made her arrangements to join him, not alone, but with her nephew.

She did not ask herself whether this would be hard or easy, feasible or impossible, and she cared not to know; it was her duty not only to be with her brother, who perhaps was dying, but also to put forth her utmost endeavors to bring his son to him, and she was bound to go.

If Prince Andreï himself did not send her word, it was to be explained, the princess was certain, either because he was too feeble to write, or because he felt that the long, roundabout journey would be too hard and perilous for her and his son.

In a few days the Princess Mariya was ready for the journey. Her outfit consisted of the vast, princely coach in which she had made the journey to Voronezh, a britchka, and a baggage wagon. She was accompanied by Mlle. Bourienne, Nikolushka with his tutor, the old nurse, three maids, Tikhon, a young footman, and a haïduk whom her aunt sent with her.

To go by the usual route, by way of Moscow, was not even to be thought of, and therefore the round-about journey which the princess had to take through Lipetsk, Riazan, Vladimir, Shuya, was very long, and, by reason of the dearth of post-horses, very difficult, and in the vicinity of Riazan, where, so it was said, the French had begun to appear, even perilous.

During this trying journey, Mlle. Bourienne, Des-salles, and the Princess Mariya's servants were amazed at her steadfastness and activity. She was the last of all to retire, she was the first of all to rise, and no difficulties sufficed to daunt her. Thanks to her activity and energy, which inspirited her companions, at the end of the second week they reached Yaroslavl.

During the last part of her stay in Voronezh, the Princess Mariya had experienced the keenest joy of her life. Her love for Rostof no longer tormented her or excited her. This love filled her whole soul, had made itself an inseparable part of her being, and she no longer struggled against it. Of late, the Princess Mariya had persuaded herself — though she never said this in so many words even to herself — that she loved, and was loved in return. She was convinced of this at her last meeting with Nikolaï, when he came to explain that her brother was with his parents.

Nikolaï had not intimated by a single word that now, in case of Prince Andreï's restoration to health, the former relations between him and Natasha would be renewed, but the Princess Mariya saw by Nikolaï's face that he knew it was possible and had thought of it.

And, nevertheless, his relations toward her, so considerate, so gentle, and so affectionate, not only underwent no change, but he was apparently delighted, because now the kinship between him and the Princess Mariya gave him greater freedom in manifesting to her his friendship-love, for such the princess sometimes considered it to be. The Princess Mariya knew that this, in her case, was love for the first and last time in her life, and she felt that she was loved, and she was happy and calm in this state of things.

But this happiness did not prevent her from feeling grief in all its force for her brother; on the contrary, this spiritual composure, in one sense, permitted her greater possibility of giving herself up completely to this feeling for her brother.

This feeling was so intense at the first moment of her departure from Voronezh that her attendants were convinced, as they looked into her anguished, despairing face, that she would assuredly fall ill on the way; but the difficulties and trials of the journey, which employed so much of her energies, saved her for the time being from her grief, and imparted strength to her.

As is always the case during a journey, the Princess Mariya had no other thought than about the journey, and forgot the object for which it was undertaken. But, as she approached Yaroslavl, when the possibilities before her recurred to her mind, and she realized that it was to be that very evening and not at the end of days, the Princess Mariya's agitation reached its utmost limits.

When the haïduk, who had been sent forward to find where in Yaroslavl the Rostofs were quartered, and how Prince Andreï was, rode back and met the great traveling-coach at the barriers, he was horror-struck to see the princess's terribly pallid face, as she put it out of the window.

" I have found out all about it, your ladyship[1]; the Rostofs are on the square, at the house of the merchant Bronnikof. Not very far from here, right on the Volga," said the haïduk.

The Princess Mariya looked into his face anxiously and inquiringly, not understanding why he did not reply to the question that chiefly occupied her : —

" How is my brother ? "

Mlle. Bourienne asked this question for the princess.

" How is the prince ? " asked she.

[1] *Vashe siyatelstvo*, illustriousness.

" His illustriousness is with them in the same house."

"Of course, then, he must be alive," thought the princess, and she softly asked : —

" How is he ? "

"The servants say he is still in the same condition."

The princess did not dream of asking what he meant by being "in the same condition," and, imperceptibly giving a swift glance at the seven-year-old Nikolushka, who was sitting next her and rejoicing in the sight of the city, she dropped her head and did not look up again until the heavy carriage, rumbling, jolting, and swaying, stopped. The steps were let down with a clatter. The door was thrown open. At the left was water — the great river; at the right a door-step; on the door-step were servants and a young, ruddy-faced girl, with a long, dark switch of hair, who wore what seemed to the Princess Mariya a disagreeably hypocritical smile.

This was Sonya.

The princess got out and mounted the steps; the hypocritically smiling young girl said, "This way, this way ;" and the princess found herself in the anteroom, in the presence of an elderly woman, with an Eastern type of face, who, with a flurried expression, came swiftly to meet her.

This was the old countess.

She threw her arms around the Princess Mariya and began to kiss her.

"My child !" she exclaimed, "I love you, and I have known you for a long time."

In spite of all her agitation the princess realized that this was the countess, and that she must say something to her. She, without knowing how she did it, murmured a few polite words in French, in the same tone in which those spoken to her were said, and then she asked : —

" How is he ? "

"The doctor says that there is no danger," said the countess ; but even while she made that remark she sighed and raised her eyes to heaven, and in this action contradicted what she had just said.

"Where is he? May I see him? May I?" asked
the princess.

"Directly, princess, directly, dear friend!—Is this
his son?" she asked, turning to Nikolushka, who had
come in with Dessalles. "There will be room enough
for us all. It is a large house.—Oh, what a lovely little
boy!"

The countess took the princess into the drawing-room.
Sonya engaged in conversation with Mlle. Bourienne.
The countess fondled the boy. The old count came
into the room to pay his respects to the princess.

The old count had completely altered since the princess had seen him the last time. Then he was a lively,
jovial, self-confident little old man; now he seemed like
a melancholy wreck of himself. As he talked with the
countess he kept looking round, as if he were asking all
present whether he was doing the proper thing. After
the destruction of Moscow and his property, being taken
out of the ruts in which he was accustomed to run, he
had apparently lost his bearings, and felt that there was
no longer any place for him in life.

In spite of her one desire to see her brother as speedily
as possible, and her annoyance because at the moment
when she might be gratifying this desire, and seeing
him, she was obliged to exchange courtesies with
these people, and to listen to pretended praise of her
nephew, still the princess kept a close watch on everything around her, and felt that it was incumbent upon
her to conform to the new order of things into which
she had fallen. She knew that it was a necessity, and,
hard as it was, still she kept her temper.

"This is my niece," said the count, introducing Sonya.
"You have not met her, have you, princess?"

The princess turned to her, and, trying to overmaster
the feeling of hostility which this young lady caused in
her heart, she gave her a kiss. But it was made hard
for her because of the want of harmony between all
these people and what was in her own heart.

"Where is he?" she asked again, addressing no one
in particular.

"He is down-stairs. Natasha is with him," replied Sonya, coloring. "They've sent word to him. I think you must be tired, princess."

Tears of vexation arose to the princess's eyes. She turned away, and was going once more to ask the countess how she could go to him, when light, impetuous, one might almost say jocund, steps were heard in the adjoining room. The princess glanced round and saw Natasha almost running, — that same Natasha who, when she had last seen her in Moscow, had so completely failed to please her.

The princess had scarcely glanced into the face of this Natasha before she perceived that this was a genuine sympathizer in her grief, and hence her friend. She went to meet her, and, throwing her arms around her, melted into tears on her neck.

As soon as Natasha, who had been sitting by Prince Andreï's bedside, learned of the princess's arrival, she had quietly left the room, and with the same swift, and, as it seemed to the Princess Mariya, jocund steps, hurried to meet her.

On her agitated face there was only one expression when she came into the room — the expression of love, unbounded love for him, for his sister, for everything that was near and dear to this beloved man, the expression of pity, of sympathy for others, and a passionate desire to give herself up entirely to find help for him. It was evident that, at that moment, there was no room in Natasha's soul for thoughts about herself, or about her relations toward him.

The sensitive Princess Mariya, at the first glance into Natasha's face, realized all this, and, with a bitter sweetness, she wept on her neck.

"Let us go to him; come, Marie!" exclaimed Natasha, leading her into the next room.

The Princess Mariya looked up, wiped her eyes, and was about to ask Natasha a question. She felt that from her she could ask and learn all that she wanted to know.

"How...." she began to ask, but suddenly paused.

She felt that her question could not be asked or
answered in words. Natasha's face and eyes would
tell her everything more clearly and with profounder
meaning.

Natasha looked at her, but, it seemed, she was in too
great fear or doubt, either to tell or not to tell all that
she knew ; she seemed to feel that, in presence of those
lucid eyes, searching the very depths of her soul, it was
impossible not to tell the whole truth, everything as she
herself saw it. Natasha's lip suddenly trembled, the
ugly wrinkles grew more pronounced around her mouth,
and she burst into tears, and hid her face in her hands.

The Princess Mariya understood all.

But still she hoped, and she asked in words in which
she had no faith : —

" But how is his wound ? What is his general condition ? "

" You .... you .... will see for yourself," was all that
Natasha could manage to say.

The two waited for some time down-stairs, next his
room, so as to finish crying, and to go to him with composed faces.

" How has his whole illness gone ? Has the change
for the worse been of recent occurrence ? When did
this take place ? " asked the Princess Mariya.

Natasha had told her that during the first part of the
time there was danger from his fever and suffering, but
that at Troïtsa this had passed off, and the doctor had
only feared Anthony's fire. But even this danger of
mortification had been avoided. When they reached
Yaroslavl, the wound began to suppurate (Natasha
understood all about suppuration and such things),
and the doctor said that the suppuration might take
its normal course. There had been some fever. The
doctor declared that this fever was not ominous. "But
two days before," Natasha said, "*this* had suddenly
come upon him." — She restrained her sobs. — "I don't
know why, but you will see how he is."

" Has he grown weaker ? Has he grown thin ? "
asked the princess.

"No, not exactly, but thinner. You will see. Ah,
Marie! he is too good; he cannot, cannot live ....
because .... "

CHAPTER XV

WHEN Natasha, with her ordinary composure, opened
the door of his room, allowing the princess to enter
before her, the Princess Mariya felt that the sobs were
already swelling her throat. In spite of her preparations, her endeavors to compose herself, she knew that
she should not be able to see him without tears.

The Princess Mariya comprehended what Natasha
meant by the phrase, "*Two days before, this had suddenly come upon him.*" She realized what it meant that
he had suddenly grown softened; this sweetness and
humility were the symptoms of death. As she entered
the doorway, she already saw in her fancy that face of
her Andriusha, which she had known in childhood,
gentle, sweet, full of feeling, sensitive, in a way which
in later days had rarely shown itself, and which had,
therefore, always made such a vivid impression on her.
She knew that he would speak to her those subdued,
affectionate words, like what her father had spoken
just before he died, and that she would not be able to
endure it, and would burst into tears before him.

But sooner or later it had to be, and she entered the
room. The sobs rose higher and higher in her throat,
as, with greater and greater distinctness, with her near-
sighted eyes, she distinguished his form and searched
his features, and then she saw his face and met his eyes.

He lay on a divan, propped up with pillows, and
wrapped in a squirrel-skin khalat. He was thin and
pale. One thin, transparently white hand held his
handkerchief; with the other he was, by a gentle
motion of the fingers, caressing his soft whiskers which
had been allowed to grow. His eyes were turned
toward the visitors.

When the Princess Mariya saw his face and her eyes

met his, she suddenly modified the haste of her steps, and felt that her tears were suddenly dried and her sobs relieved. As she caught the expression of his face and eyes, she suddenly grew awestruck, and felt that she was guilty.

"But what am I guilty of?" she asked herself.

"Because thou art alive, and art thinking of the future, while I?"—was the reply of his cold, stern look.

In that look of his, not outward from within, but turned inward upon himself, there was almost an expression of hostility, as he slowly turned his eyes on his sister and Natasha. He exchanged kisses with his sister, and shook hands as usual.

"How are you, Marie? How did you get here?" he asked, but his voice had the same monotonous and alien sound that was in his look. If he had uttered a desperate cry, this cry would have filled the Princess Mariya with less horror than the sound of his voice. "And have you brought Nikolushka?" he asked, in the same slow, indifferent way, and evidently finding it hard to recollect.

"How are you now?" inquired the Princess Mariya, amazed, herself, at her question.

"That you must ask of the doctor," he replied; and evidently collecting his strength, so as to be more gracious, he said with his lips alone (it was evident that he did not think at all of what he was saying), "*Merci, chère amie, d'être venue*—Thank you for coming!"

The Princess Mariya pressed his hand. He almost noticeably frowned at the pressure of her hand. He was silent, and she knew not what to say. She now understood what had come over him two days before. In his words, in his tone, especially in this glance of his, this cold, almost hostile look, could be perceived that alienation from all that is of this world, that is so terrible for a living man to witness. He evidently found it difficult to understand the interests of life, but at the same time one could feel that this was so, not because he was deprived of the power of remembrance, but because his mind was turned to something else, which the living comprehend not and cannot comprehend, and which was absorbing him entirely.

"Yes, see what a strange fate has brought us together again!" said he, breaking the silence, and indicating Natasha. "She has taken care of me all the time."

The Princess Mariya heard him and understood not what he said. He, the sensitive, gentle Prince Andreï, how could he say this of her whom he loved and who loved him? If he had had any thought of living he could never have made such a remark in such a coldly insulting tone. If he had not known that he was going to die, how could he have failed to pity her, how could he have said such a thing in her presence! The only explanation could be that to him it was a matter of indifference and wholly of indifference, because something else, something far more important, had been revealed to him.

The conversation was cold, desultory, and interrupted every instant.

"Marie came through Riazan," said Natasha.

Prince Andreï did not remark that she had spoken of his sister as Marie. But Natasha, having called her so, for the first time noticed it herself.

"Well, what about it?" he asked.

"They told her that Moscow was all on fire, all burned up, and that ...."

Natasha paused; it was impossible for her to speak. He was evidently making an effort to listen, and still could not.

"Oh, yes, burned," said he. "Too bad!" and again he looked straight ahead, smoothing his whiskers abstractedly with his fingers.

"And so you met Count Nikolaï, did you, Marie?" suddenly asked Prince Andreï, evidently trying to say something pleasant. "He wrote home that he was very much in love with you," he pursued very simply and calmly, evidently not being strong enough to realize all the complicated significance which his words had for the living. "If you love him also, then it would be a very good thing .... if you were to marry," he added a little more rapidly, as if rejoiced to find at last words which he had been long trying to find.

The Princess Mariya heard his words, but they had for her no meaning, except as they showed how terribly far he was now from all earthly interests.

"Why speak about me?" she asked composedly, and glanced at Natasha. Natasha, conscious of this glance, did not look at her.

Again all were silent.

"André, do you wa...." suddenly asked the princess, in a trembling voice — "do you want to see Nikolushka? He is always talking about you."

Prince Andreï for the first time smiled, though almost imperceptibly; but his sister, who knew his face so well, observed to her horror that this was not a smile of pleasure or of affection for his son, but one of quiet, sweet irony at his sister's employing, as he supposed, this final means of bringing him back to conscious emotion.

"Yes, very glad to see Nikolushka. Is he well?"

When they brought to Prince Andreï his little Nikolushka, who gazed in terror at his father, but did not weep, because no one else was weeping, Prince Andreï kissed him, and evidently knew not what to say to him.

When Nikolushka was led away again, the Princess Mariya returned to her brother, kissed him, and, unable to control herself longer, burst into tears.

He gazed at her steadily.

"Are you crying for Nikolushka?" he asked.

The princess, weeping, nodded affirmatively.

"Marie, you know the New Tes...." but he suddenly stopped.

"What did you say?"

"Nothing. But you must not weep here," he added, looking at her with the same cold look.

When the Princess Mariya burst into tears, he understood that she was weeping because Nikolushka would be left fatherless.

By a great effort of self-mastery he tried to return to
life and look upon things from their standpoint.

"Yes, it must seem very sad to them," he thought,
"but how simple this is! — the fowls of the air sow not,
neither do they reap, yet your heavenly Father feedeth
them," he said to himself, and that was what he was
going to say to the princess; "but no, they understood
that in their way; they will not comprehend it. They
cannot comprehend that all these feelings which they
cherish, all these ideas which seem to us so important, are of *no consequence*. We cannot understand each
other." And so he held his peace.

Prince Andreï's little son was seven years old. He
scarcely knew how to read. He really knew nothing.
He went through much subsequent to that day, acquir-
ing knowledge, the habit of observation, experience; but
if he had at that time enjoyed the mastery of all that he
acquired later, he could not have had a deeper, truer
comprehension of the significance of that scene between his father, the Princess Mariya, and Natasha,
than he had then. He understood it perfectly, and, not
shedding a tear, he left the room, silently crept up to
Natasha, who followed him, and shyly looked at her out
of his beautiful, dreamy eyes; his short lip trembled;
he leaned his head against her and wept.

From that day he avoided Dessalles, avoided the
countess, who petted him, and either stayed alone by
himself or timidly joined the Princess Mariya and Natasha, whom he, as it seemed, liked better than his
aunt, and quietly and shyly stayed by them.

The Princess Mariya, on leaving her brother, perfectly comprehended what Natasha's face had told her.
She said nothing more about any hope of saving his
life. She took turns with her in sitting by his divan,
and she ceased to weep; but she prayed without ceasing, her soul turning to that eternal, searchless One,
whose presence so palpably hovered over the dying
man.

CHAPTER XVI

PRINCE ANDREÏ not only knew that he was going to die, but he also felt that he was dying, that he was already half-way toward death.

He experienced a consciousness of alienation from everything earthly, and a strange beatific exhilaration of being. Without impatience and without anxiety, he waited for what was before him.

That ominous Eternal Presence, unknown and far away, which had never once ceased, throughout all his life, to haunt his senses, was now near at hand, and, by reason of that strange exhilaration which he felt, almost comprehensible and palpable.

* * * * * *

Before, he had feared the end. Twice he had experienced that terribly tormenting sense of the fear of death, of the end, and now he did not realize it.

The first time he had experienced that feeling was when the shell was spinning like a top before him, and he looked at the stubble-field, at the shrubbery, at the sky, and knew that death was before him.

When he waked to consciousness, after his wound, and in his soul, for an instant, as it were, freed from the burden of life that crushed him, had sprung up that flower of love eternal, unbounded, independent of all life, he no longer feared death, and thought no more of it.

During those tormenting hours of loneliness and half-delirium which he had spent since he was wounded, the more he pondered over this new source of eternal love which had at first been concealed from him, the more he became alienated from the earthly life, though the process was an unconscious one.

To love everything, all men, always to sacrifice self for love's sake, meant to love no one in particular, meant not to live this mundane life. And the more he imbued himself with this source of love, the more he let go of life, and the more absolutely he broke down that terrible impediment which, if love be absent, holds between life and death.

When, during this first period, he remembered that he must die, he said to himself, "Well, then, so much the better."

But after that night at Muitishchi, when in his semi-delirium she whom he had longed for appeared before him, and when he, pressing his lips to her hand, had wept gentle tears of joy, then love for one woman imperceptibly took possession of his heart and again attached it to life. And joyful but anxious thoughts began to recur to him. As he remembered the moment at the field lazaret, when he had seen Kuragin, he could not now renew that former feeling; he was tortured by the question: "Is he alive?" But he dared not make the inquiry.

His illness had followed its physical course, but what Natasha had spoken of as *having come over him* happened two days before the Princess Mariya's arrival. This was the last moral combat between life and death, and death had been victorious. It was the unexpected discovery that he still prized his life, which presented itself in the guise of his love for Natasha, and the last victorious attack of horror before the unknown.

It was evening. As was usually the case after dinner, he had been in a slightly feverish condition, and his mind was preternaturally acute. Sonya was sitting by the table. Suddenly, a realizing sense of bliss took possession of him.

"Ah! she has come!" he said to himself.

In point of fact, Sonya's place was occupied by Natasha, who had just come in with noiseless steps.

Ever since the time when she had begun to be his nurse, he had always experienced this physical sense of her presence.

She sat in the easy-chair, with her side toward him, shading his eyes from the candle-light, and knitting stockings. (She had learned to knit stockings because one time Prince Andreï had told her that no one made such admirable nurses for the sick as old nurses, who are always knitting stockings, because there is something very soothing in the operation of knitting.) Her slender fingers swiftly plied the occasionally clicking needles, and the pensive profile of her bended head was full in his sight. She moved — the ball of yarn rolled from her lap. She started, glanced at him, and, shading the candle with her hand, with a cautious, lithe, and graceful movement, she bent over, picked up the ball, and resumed her former position.

He looked at her without stirring, and noticed that after she had picked up the ball she had wanted to draw a long breath, with her full bosom, but had refrained from doing so, and had cautiously masked her sigh.

At the Troïtskaya Lavra they had talked over the past, and he had told her that in case he lived he should eternally thank God for his wound, which had brought him back to her; but from that time they had not spoken of the future.

"Can it possibly be?" he was now musing, as he looked at her and listened to the slight steely click of her knitting-needles, "can it be that Fate has so strangely brought us together again only that I may die?.... Can it be that the true meaning of life was revealed to me only that I might live in a lie? I love her more than all else in the world. But what can I do if I love her?" he asked himself, and he suddenly, in spite of himself, groaned, as he often did, out of a custom acquired while he had been suffering.

Hearing this sound, Natasha laid down her stocking, bent nearer to him, and, suddenly noticing his beaming eyes, she went over to him and bent down to him.

"Have n't you been asleep?"

"No; I have been looking at you this long time. I knew by feeling when you came in. No one except you gives me such a sense of gentle restfulness .... such light! I feel like weeping from very joy."

Natasha moved still closer to him. Her face was radiant with solemn delight.

" Natasha, I love you too dearly ! More than all in the world ! "

" And I ? " She turned away for an instant. " Why ' too dearly ' ? " she asked.

" Why too dearly ?.... Well, tell me what you think — what you think in your heart, in the depths of your heart ! shall I get well ? How does it seem to you ? "

" I am sure of it, sure of it," Natasha almost screamed, with a passionate motion seizing both his hands.

He was silent.

" How good it would be ! " And, taking her hand, he kissed it.

Natasha was happy and agitated ; and instantly she remembered that this was all wrong, that he needed to be kept perfectly quiet.

" But now you have not been asleep," said she, calming her delight. " Try to get a nap .... please."

He had relinquished her hand, after pressing it once again, and she had gone back to the candle and resumed her former position. Twice she had looked at him ; his eyes had met hers. She had set herself a stint on the stocking, and resolved that she would not look up until she had finished it.

In point of fact, soon after this he had closed his eyes and gone to sleep. He had not slept long, but had awakened suddenly with a start in a cold perspiration.

During his nap, his mind had been still occupied with the constant subject of his thoughts of late — life and death. And more than anything else of death. He felt that it was near.

" Love? What is love ? " he asked himself.

" Love stands in the way of death. Love is life. All, all that I understand, I understand solely because I love. All is, all exists, simply and solely because I love. All is summed up in this alone. Love is God ; and death for me, who am a tiny particle of love, means returning into the universal and eternal source of love."

These thoughts had seemed consoling to him. But they were only thoughts. There was something lacking in them, something that was exclusive and personal –

there was no basis of reality.   And he was a prey to the same restlessness and lack of clearness.

He had fallen asleep.

It had seemed to him, in his dream, that he was lying in the same room in which he was actually lying, but that he was not wounded, but quite well.   Many different persons, insignificant, indifferent, appear before him. He is talking with them, discussing something of no earthly consequence.   They are preparing to go somewhere.   Prince Andreï dimly comprehends that all this is mere waste of time, and that he has something of real importance to accomplish, but still he goes on talking, filling them with amazement at his words, which are witty but devoid of sense.

Gradually, but imperceptibly, all these persons begin to disappear, and his attention is wholly occupied by the question of a closed door.   He gets up and goes to the door, with the intention of pushing the bolt and closing the door.

Everything depends on whether he succeeds or not in closing it.   He starts, he tries to make haste, but his legs refuse to move, and he knows that he will not have time to close the door, but still he morbidly puts forth all his energies.   And a painful anguish of fear takes hold of him.   And this fear is the fear of death : behind the door *It* is standing.

But by the time that he feebly, awkwardly drags himself to the door, this *something* horrible, pushing its way from the other side, breaks through.   Something that is not human — Death — is pushing the door open, and he must keep it shut.   He clutches the door, exerts his final energies, — not indeed to shut it, for that is impossible, but to hold it ; his energies, however, are weak and maladroit, and, crushing him with its horror, the door opens and again closes.

Once more the pressure came from without.   His last, superhuman energies were vain, and both wings of the door noiselessly swung open.   *It* came in, and it was Death.

And Prince Andreï was dying.

But at the very instant that he was dying, Prince Andreï remembered that he was asleep, and at the very instant that he was dying, he made one last effort and awoke.

"Yes, that was *death*. I died — I woke up. Yes, death is an awakening."

This thought had suddenly flashed through his soul, and the veil which till then had covered the unknown was lifted from before his spiritual eyes. He felt as it were a deliverance from the bonds which before had fastened him down, and that strange buoyancy which from that time forth did not forsake him.

When he had awakened in a cold sweat and stirred on his divan, Natasha had gone to him and asked him what was the matter. He had made no reply, and, not understanding what she had said, had given her a strange look.

This was what had taken place two days before the Princess Mariya's arrival. From that day, as the doctor said, his wasting fever had taken a turn for the worse, but Natasha had no need to depend on what the doctor said; she could see for herself those terrible moral symptoms which no longer allowed room for doubt.

From that time forth had begun for Prince Andreï, simultaneously with the awakening from his dream, the awakening from life. And, considering the length of life, this seemed to him no slower than the awakening from the dream when compared to the length of his nap.

There was nothing terrible and nothing cruel in this relatively slow awakening.

The last days and hours glided away peacefully and simply. Both the Princess Mariya and Natasha, who stayed constantly by his side, felt this. They wept not, they trembled not, and the last part of the time, as they themselves realized, they were watching, not the man himself, — for he was no more, he had gone from them, — but simply the most immediate remembrance of him, simply his body.

The feelings of both were so strong that the external

terrible side of death had no effect on them, and they found it unnecessary to give vent to their grief. They wept neither in his presence nor when away from him, and they never talked about him together. They felt that they could not express in words what was real to their understandings.

They both saw how he was sinking, deeper and deeper, slowly and peacefully, away from them into the *whither*, and they both knew that this was inevitable and that it was well. He was confessed and partook of the sacrament. All came to bid him farewell.

When his little son was brought, he kissed him and turned away, not because his heart was sore and filled with pity (the Princess Mariya and Natasha understood this), but simply because he supposed that this was all that was required of him. But when he was told that he should give him his blessing, he did what was required of him, and looked around as if to ask whether it was necessary to do anything more.

When the last gentle spasm shook the body, as it was deserted by the spirit, the princess and Natasha were present.

"It is over!" said the Princess Mariya, after his body had lain motionless and growing cold for several moments. Natasha came to the couch, looked into his dead eyes, and made haste to close them. She closed them and kissed them not, but reverently touched that which had been the most immediate remembrance of him.

"Where has he gone? Where is he now?"

When the mortal frame, washed and clad, lay in the coffin on the table, they all went in to say farewell, and all shed tears.

Nikolushka wept from the tormenting perplexity that tore his young heart.

The countess and Sonya wept from sympathy for Natasha, and because he was no more.

The old count wept because very soon, as it seemed to him, he also would have to take this terrible step.

Natasha and the princess also wept now, but they

wept not because of their own personal sorrow : they wept from a reverent emotion which took possession of their souls in presence of the simple and solemn mystery of death, which had been accomplished before their eyes.

PART THIRTEENTH

CHAPTER I

THE association of cause and effect is something beyond the comprehension of the human mind. But the impulse to search into causes is inherent in man's very nature. And the human intellect, unable to search the infinite variety and complicated tangle of conditions accompanying phenomena, — every one of which may seem to be the ultimate cause, — seizes on the first and most obvious coincidence, and says, "This is the cause!"

In historical events, where the acts of men are the object of investigation, that which first suggests itself seems to be the will of the gods; then the will of those men who stand in the forefront of historical prominence — historical heroes.

But it requires only to penetrate into the essence of any historical event, that is, the activity of the whole mass of the people who took part in the event, to become convinced that the will of the historical hero not only did not guide the actions of the masses, but, on the contrary, was itself constantly guided.

It would seem as if it were a matter of indifference whether the significance of an historical event is explained in one way or another. But between the man who should say that the nations of the West marched against the East because Napoleon wished them to do so, and the man who should say that this happened because it had to happen, there is as wide a difference as between men who are convinced that the earth stands fixed and that the planets move around it, and those who assert that they know not what holds the earth, but they know that there are laws which govern the motion of the earth and the other planets.

The causes of historical events can be nothing else than the only cause of all causes. But there are laws which govern events, and some of them are unknown to us, and some of them we have investigated. The discovery of these causes is possible only when we repudiate the idea that these causes may be found in the will of a single man, exactly in the same way as the discovery of the laws governing the motions of the planets became possible only when men repudiated the notion of the fixity of the earth.

After the battle of Borodino and the occupation of Moscow by the enemy and its destruction by fire, the most important episode of the war of 1812, according to the historians, was the movement of the Russian army from the Riazan road toward the camp of Tarutino by way of the Kaluga road, the so-called flank movement beyond Krasnaya Pakhra.

Historians ascribe the glory of this stroke of genius to various individuals, and do not agree on any one to whom it belongs. Foreign historians, even the French historians, in speaking of this "flank movement," recognize the genius of the Russian generals.

But why military writers and everybody else suppose that this flank movement was the perspicacious invention of any single person, which thus saved Russia and overthrew Napoleon, is something hard to understand.

In the first place it is hard to understand in what consists the perspicacity and genius displayed by this movement; for it does not require a great intellectual effort to see that the best position for an army when not enduring attacks is where there is the greatest abundance of supplies. And any one, even a dull boy of thirteen, might suppose that in 1812 the most advantageous position for the Russian army after the retreat from Moscow was on the road to Kaluga. Thus it is impossible in the first place to understand by what arguments historians persuade themselves that they see perspicacity in this manœuver.

In the second place it is still more difficult to understand exactly how historians attribute the salvation of the Russians and the destruction of the French to this manœuver; for if this "flank movement" had been carried out under other conditions, preceding, accompanying, or following, it might have brought about the destruction of the Russian army and the salvation of the French. Even though the situation of the Russian army began to improve from the time this movement was effectuated, still it does not follow that this movement was the cause of it.

This flank movement not only might not have brought any advantage, but might even have been fatal to the Russian army had there not been a coincidence of other conditions.

What would have happened if Moscow had not been burned? If Murat had not lost sight of the Russians? If Napoleon had not remained inactive? If at Krasnaya Pakhra the Russian army had followed the advice of Benigsen and Barclay, and given battle?

What would have happened if the French had attacked the Russians when they were on the march beyond Pakhra?

What would have happened if Napoleon, after approaching Tarutino, had attacked the Russians with even a tenth part of the energy with which he had attacked at Smolensk?

What would have happened if the French had marched toward Petersburg? —

In any one of these suppositions, the flank movement, instead of being the salvation of Russia, might have been a disaster.

In the third place, most incomprehensible of all it is that those who make a study of history are unwilling to see that it is impossible to attribute the flank movement to any particular person, that no one could ever have foreseen it, that this manœuver, like the retreat to Fili, never presented itself to anybody in its totality; but, step by step, event by event, moment by moment, it came about as the result of an infinite number of most heterogeneous conditions, and it appeared clearly in its totality only when it had been consummated and was an accomplished fact.

At the council of war held at Fili among the Russian generals the predominant opinion was for retreat by the most direct and obvious route, the Nizhni-Novgorod road. This is proved by the fact that the majority of votes at the council were thrown in favor of this plan, and above all by the conversation that occurred after the council between the commander-in-chief and Lanskoï, who was in charge of the commissary department.

Lanskoï informed the commander-in-chief that the army stores were concentrated principally along the Oka in the governments of Tula and Kazan, and that in case of retreat on Nizhni, the army would be separated from its stores by the great river Oka, which, during the first stages of winter, it would be impossible to cross with supplies.

This was the first indication of the necessity for renouncing the plan of a direct retreat to Nizhni, which at first had seemed the most natural.

The army kept farther to the south, on the road to Riazan, so as to be nearer its base of supplies.

Afterward the inactivity of the French, who seemed even to have lost sight of the Russian army, the work of protecting the arsenal at Tula, and above all the advantage of proximity to its supplies, compelled the Russian army to move still farther to the south along the Tula road.

When at length Pakhra had been passed by this desperate movement along the Tula road, the chiefs of the Russian army thought of halting at Podolsk, and there was not the slightest thought of taking up a position at Tarutino ; but an infinite number of circumstances — the reappearance of the French army, which before had lost the Russians out of sight, and plans of battle, and above all the abundance of stores at Kaluga — compelled our army to swerve still more to the southward,

and, taking a route right through the midst of its abundance, to cross over from the Tula road to the Kaluga
road and approach Tarutino.

Just as it is impossible to answer the question when
Moscow was abandoned, so it is impossible to tell when
and by whom it was decided to go to Tarutino.

Only when the troops had already reached Tarutino,
by reason of an infinite number of differentiated efforts,
then men began to persuade themselves that this had
been their wish and their long predetermination.

CHAPTER II

THE celebrated flank movement consisted simply in
this: The Russian army, which had been retreating
straight back as the invaders pushed forward, turned
aside from the straight direction when they saw the
French no longer pursuing, and naturally took the direction in which they were attracted by an abundance of
supplies.

If there had not been men of genius at the head of
the Russian army, if it had been merely an army without generals, it could have done nothing else than return
to Moscow, describing a semicircle in that direction
where there were more provisions and where the country was richer.

The change of route from the Nizhni road toward the
Riazan, Tula, and Kaluga roads was so natural that the
foragers of the Russian army took that very direction,
and that very direction was the one in which Kutuzof
was ordered from Petersburg to conduct his army.

At Tarutino, Kutuzof received almost a reproach
from the sovereign because he had led his army in the
direction of Riazan, and he was ordered to take up the
very position relative to Kaluga which he was already
occupying at the time when he received the letter from
the sovereign.

The Russian army, like a ball which had been rolling
in the direction of the blow given it all through the

campaign and especially at the battle of Borodino, assumed its natural position of stable equilibrium as soon as the force of the blows diminished and no new ones were communicated.

Kutuzof's merit lay not in what is called "a stroke of genius" in making a strategical manœuver, but simply in the fact that he was the only one who understood the meaning of what was taking place about him.

He alone understood what the inactivity of the French army signified, he alone persisted in declaring that the battle of Borodino was a victory for the Russians. He alone — the very man who, it would seem, from his position as commander-in-chief, ought to have been disposed to favor objective measures — used all his power to restrain the Russian army from undertaking useless battles.

The beast wounded at Borodino lay where it had been left by the escaping huntsman; but whether it was alive, or whether it still had strength left, or whether it was hiding itself, the huntsman knew not.

Suddenly was heard this wild beast's cry.

The cry of this wounded beast, — the French army, — the premonition of its approaching doom, was the sending of Lauriston to Kutuzof's camp with a request for peace

Napoleon, with his conviction that whatever it occurred to him to do was as right as right could be, wrote to Kutuzof the first words that entered his mind. They had no sense whatever.

Prince Kutuzof [he wrote], I send you one of my general aides to discuss with you on various matters of interest. I wish your highness to repose confidence in what he will say, *especially when he expresses the sentiments of esteem and respect which I have long felt for you personally. This letter having no other purpose, I pray God, prince, that He have you in His holy and beneficent care.*

(Signed) NAPOLEON.

MOSCOW, October 30, 1812.[1]

---

[1] *Monsieur le Prince Koutouzov! J'envoie près de vous un de mes aides-de-camp généraux pour vous entretenir de plusieurs objets intéres-*

"I should be cursed by posterity if I were regarded as the first to move toward any compromise. *Such is the present spirit of our people,*" replied Kutuzof, and he continued to put forth all his energies to keep his troops from a battle.

During the month spent by the French army in the pillage of Moscow, and by the Russian army in tranquil recuperation at Tarutino, a change had taken place in the relative strength of the two armies, — their spirit and effective, — in consequence of which a preponderance of strength began to show itself on the side of the Russians.

Although the condition of the French army and its effective were unknown to the Russians, yet, as soon as the relative position was changed, the inevitability of an attack was shown by a multitude of symptoms.

These symptoms were the sending of Lauriston and the abundance of provisions at Tarutino, and the reports coming in from all sides of the inactivity and disorderliness of the French, and the filling-up of our regiments with recruits, and the fine weather, and the long rest accorded to the Russian soldiers, and the general impatience caused among the troops by the long rest, and their desire to finish the work for which they had been brought together, and the curiosity about what was going on in the French army, which had been lost from sight so long, and the audacity with which now the Russian outposts skirmished around the French stationed at Tarutino, and the news of easy victories over the French won by Russian muzhiks and "partisans," and the jealousy aroused by this, and the desire of vengeance kindled in every man's soul from the moment that the French occupied Moscow, and, above all, the indefinite but genuine consciousness which filled the heart of

sants. Je désire que votre Altesse ajoute foi à ce qu'il lui dira, surtout lorsqu'il exprimera les sentiments d'estime et de particulière considération que j'ai depuis longtemps pour sa personne. Cette lettre n'étant à autre fin, je prie Dieu, Monsieur Prince Koutouzov, qu'Il vous ait en Sa sainte et digne garde.

(Signé) NAPOLEON.

Moscou, le 30 Octobre, 1812.

every soldier that the relative positions were reversed and the superiority was on our side.

The material relations were changed, and the attack was becoming inevitable. And instantly, just as the chime of bells in the clock begin to strike and to play when the hand has accomplished its full circuit of the hour, so in the higher circles, by the correspondingly essential correlation of forces, the increased motion was effectuated, — the whizzing of wheels and the playing of the chimes.

CHAPTER III

THE Russian army was directed by Kutuzof and his staff, and by the sovereign, who was at Petersburg.

Even before news of the abandonment of Moscow had reached Petersburg, a circumstantial plan of the whole war had been drawn up and sent to Kutuzof for his guidance. Although the plan was made with the pre-supposition that Moscow was still in our hands, it was approved by Kutuzof's staff and accepted as the basis of action.

Kutuzof merely wrote that plans made at a distance were always hard to carry out. And then further in-structions, meant to solve the difficulties that might arise, were sent, and individuals were charged to watch his movement and to send back reports.

Moreover, at this time great changes were made in the staff of the Russian army. They had to fill the places of Bagration, who had been killed, and of Barclay, who, considering himself insulted, had resigned.

They debated with perfect seriousness what would be best : to put A in the place of B, and B in the place of D, or, on the contrary, to put D in the place of A, and so on ; as if anything else than the pleasure given to A and B could depend on this.

In the army staff, owing to the animosity between Kutuzof and Benigsen, his chief of staff, and the pres-ence of the sovereign's inspectors, and these changes, there arose a much more than usually complicated play of party intrigues ; by all possible plans and combina- tions A was undermining the authority of B, and D that of C, and so on.

In all these operations the object of their intrigues was for the most part the war which all these men thought they were conducting, but all the while the war was going on independently of them in its own destined way, that is, never conforming to the schemes of these men, but resulting from the real relations of masses. All these schemes, crossing and conflicting, merely represented in the higher spheres the faithful reflection of what had to be accomplished.

On October 14, the sovereign wrote the following letter, which was received by Kutuzof after the battle of Tarutino : —

Prince Mikhaïl Ilarionovitch ! —

Since September 14, Moscow has been in the hands of the enemy. Your latest reports are dated October 2 ; and in all this time not only nothing has been done in the way of a dem- onstration against the enemy and to deliver the first capital, but according to your last reports you have been retreating again. Serpukhof is already occupied by a detachment of the enemy, and Tula, with its famous arsenal so indispensable to the army, is in peril.

From General Winzengerode's report, I see that a body of the enemy, of ten thousand men, is moving along the Peters- burg road. Another of several thousand men is marching upon Dmitrovo. A third is advancing on the road to Vladimir. A fourth, of considerable size, is between Ruza and Mozhaïsk. Napoleon himself, on the seventh, was at Moscow.

Since, according to all this information, the enemy has scat- tered his forces in strong detachments, since Napoleon himself is still at Moscow with his Guard, is it possible that the strength of the enemy before you has been too great to prevent you from taking the offensive ?

One might assume, on the contrary, with certainty, that he would pursue you with detachments, or at least by an army corps far weaker than the army which you command.

It seems as if, profiting by these circumstances, you might with advantage have attacked an enemy weaker than yourself, and exterminated him, or, at least, by obliging him to retire, have regained a great part of the province now occupied by the enemy, and at the same time have averted the peril of Tula and our other cities of the interior.

On your responsibility it will rest if the enemy send a considerable body of troops to Petersburg to threaten this capital, which is almost destitute of troops ; for, with the army confided to you, if you act with firmness and celerity, you have all the means needed to avert this new misfortune.

Bear in mind that you are still bound to answer before an insulted country for the loss of Moscow !

You have already had proof of my readiness to reward you. This good-will shall not grow less, but I and Russia have a right to demand from you all the zeal, fortitude, and success that your intellect, your military talents, and the gallantry of the troops under your command assure us.

But while this letter, which shows how the state of things was regarded in Petersburg, was on its way, Kutuzof could no longer restrain the army which he commanded from taking the offensive, and the battle had already been fought.

On October 14, a Cossack, Shapovalof, while on patrol duty, killed one hare and shot at another. In pursuing the wounded hare, Shapovalof struck into the forest at some distance and stumbled upon the left flank of Murat's army, which was encamped without outposts.

The Cossack laughingly told his comrades how he had almost fallen into the hands of the French. A cornet who heard this tale told it to his commander.

The Cossack was sent for and questioned. The Cossack chiefs wished to profit by this chance to get horses ; but one of them, who was acquainted at headquarters, told a staff general what had occurred.

Latterly, the relations of the army staff had been strained to the last degree. Yermolof, several days before, had gone to Benigsen and implored him to use all his influence with the commander-in-chief in favor of assuming the offensive.

"If I did not know you," replied Benigsen, "I should think that you did not wish what you were asking for.

I have only to advise anything and his serene highness will do exactly the contrary."

The news brought in by the Cossacks being confirmed by scouts sent out, it became evident that the time was ripe for action.

The strained cord broke, and the clock whizzed and the chimes began to play. Notwithstanding all his supposed power, his intellect, his experience, and his knowledge of men, Kutuzof — taking into consideration Benigsen's report sent directly to the sovereign, and the one desire expressed by all of his generals, and the sovereign's supposed wishes, and the information brought by the Cossacks — could no longer restrain a movement that was inevitable, and gave the order for something that he regarded as useless and harmful, consented to an accomplished fact!

CHAPTER IV

Benigsen's note and the report of the Cossacks about the uncovered left flank of the French were only the last symptoms that it was absolutely inevitable to give the order for the attack, and the attack was ordered for October 17.

On the morning of the sixteenth Kutuzof signed the order for the disposition of the troops. Toll read it to Yermolof, proposing to him to take charge of the further arrangements.

"Very good, very good, but I can't possibly attend to it now," said Yermolof, and left the room.

The plan of attack drawn up by Toll was very admirable. Just as for the battle of Austerlitz it had been laid down in the "disposition": *die erste Kolonne marschirt* this way and that way, *die zweite Kolonne marschirt* this way and that way, so here also, only not in German, it was prescribed where the first column and the second column should march.

And all these columns, on paper, were to unite at a designated time and at a designated place, and annihilate the enemy. Everything was beautifully foreseen and provided for as in all "dispositions," and as in all "dispositions," not a single column was in its place at the right time.

When the proper number of copies had been made of the order, an officer was summoned and sent to Yermolof, to give him the papers that he might do the business.

A young cavalry officer, Kutuzof's orderly, delighted with the important commission, hastened to Yermolof's lodgings.

"He is out," replied Yermolof's servant.

The cavalry officer went to the lodgings of the general in whose company Yermolof was frequently found.

"No, — and the general is also out."

The cavalry officer, mounting his horse, went to still another.

"No, gone out."

"Hope I shan't be held accountable for the delay. What a nuisance!" said the officer to himself. He rode entirely around the camp. One man declared that Yermolof had been seen driving off somewhere with some other generals; another said that he was probably at home again.

The officer, without even taking time to eat his dinner, searched till six o'clock. Yermolof was nowhere to be found, and no one knew where he was. The officer took a hasty supper at a comrade's, and started off once more, this time in search of Miloradovitch, who was with the advance-guard.

Miloradovitch also was not at home, but there he was told that Miloradovitch was at a ball given by General Kikin, and that Yermolof was probably there also.

"And where is that?"

"Over yonder at Yetchkino," said a Cossack officer, indicating the estate of a landed proprietor at some distance.

"But how is that? It's beyond the lines!"

"Two regiments of ours were sent up to the lines, and they're having a spree there this evening; that's just the mischief of it! Two bands, three choirs of regimental singers."

The officer crossed the lines to Yetchkino. While still a long way off, as he rode toward the mansion, he heard the jovial reckless sounds of the soldiers' choragic song.

"*Vo-oluziakh — vo-oluziakh!*" rang the meaningless words of the song, mingled with whistling and the sounds of the torban,[1] occasionally drowned out by the roar of voices.

These jolly sounds made the officer's heart beat faster, but at the same time he was terribly alarmed lest he should be blamed for having been so long in delivering the weighty message which had been intrusted to him.

It was already nine o'clock in the evening. He dismounted and climbed the steps of the great mansion, which had been preserved intact, though it was situated between the French and the Russians. Servants were flying about in the dining-room and the anteroom with wines and refreshments. The singers stood under the windows.

The officer was shown in, and he suddenly caught sight of all the most distinguished generals of the army gathered together, and in their number he recognized Yermolof's tall, well-known figure. All the generals wore their uniform-coats unbuttoned; their faces were flushed and full of excitement, and they were laughing noisily as they stood round in a semicircle. In the middle of the "hall" a handsome, short general with a red face was skilfully and vigorously dancing the triepaka.

"Ha! ha! ha! bravo! aï da! — Nikolaï Ivanovitch! ha! ha! ha!"....

The officer felt that to come in at such a moment with an important order he should be doubly in the wrong, and he wanted to wait; but one of the generals caught sight of him, and, understanding why he had come, spoke to Yermolof. Yermolof, with a frowning face, advanced to the officer, and, after listening to his

---

[1] A kind of musical instrument.

story, took from him the paper, without saying a word.

"Perhaps you think that it was a mere accident that he had gone off?" said a staff comrade that evening to the cavalry officer, in reference to Yermolof.

"'T was a joke! it was all cut and dried. It was to play it on Konovnitsuin. See what a stew there 'll be to-morrow!"

CHAPTER V

On the following day, Kutuzof was awakened early in the morning, prayed to God, dressed, and, with the disagreeable consciousness that he was obliged to direct an engagement of which he did not approve, took his seat in his calash, and from Letashevka, five versts behind Tarutino, drove to the place where the attacking columns were to rendezvous. As he was driven along he kept dozing and awakening again, all the time listening if he could hear the sounds of firing at the right, and if the battle had begun.

But as yet all was silent. A damp and gloomy autumn morning was only just beginning to dawn. On reaching Tarutino, he noticed some cavalrymen who were leading their horses to water across the road along which the calash was driven. Kutuzof looked at these cavalrymen, stopped the calash, and asked to what regiment they belonged. These cavalrymen belonged to the column which should long before have been far forward in ambush.

"A mistake, perhaps," thought the old commander-in-chief.

But when he had driven a little farther, Kutuzof saw some infantry regiments with stacked arms, the soldiers in their drawers, cooking their kasha and getting firewood.

An officer was summoned. The officer reported that no orders had been received about any attack.

"How could it...." Kutuzof began, but he instantly

checked himself, and ordered the senior officer to be brought to him.

He got out of his calash, and walked back and forth, with sunken head, drawing long sighs as he silently waited. When Eichen, the officer of the general staff, who had been sent for, appeared, Kutuzof grew livid with rage, not because this officer was to blame for the blunder, but because he was a convenient scapegoat for his wrath. Trembling and panting, the old man, who was falling into that state of fury which sometimes would cause him to roll on the ground in his paroxysm, attacked Eichen, threatening him with his fists, screaming, and loading him with the grossest abuse. Another officer who happened to be present, Captain Brozin, though in no respect to blame, came in also for his share.

"These wretched dogs! Let 'em be shot! Scoundrels!" he hoarsely screamed, gesticulating and reeling. He suffered physical pain. He, the commander-in-chief, "his highness," who, as every one believed, held more power than any one in Russia had ever before possessed, how came he, he, to be placed in such a position — to be made the laughing-stock of the whole army!

"Was it all in vain that I tried so hard to pray for to-day, all in vain that I passed a sleepless night and planned and planned?" he asked himself. "When I was a mere little chit of an officer,[1] no one would have dared to turn me into ridicule so .... but now?" ....

He suffered physical pain, as if from corporal punishment, and he could not help expressing it in cries of pain and fury; but soon his strength began to fail him, and he took his seat in his calash, looking around with the consciousness that he had said much that was unseemly, and silently rode back.

His fury was spent, and returned no more; and, feebly blinking his eyes, Kutuzof listened to Benigsen, Konovnitsuin, and Toll, — Yermolof kept out of sight for a day or two, — and their excuses and words of justification, and their urgent representations that the

[1] *Malchishka-ofitser.*

movement which had so miscarried should be postponed till the following day.   And Kutuzof was obliged
to consent.

CHAPTER VI

On the following evening, the troops made their
rendezvous in the designated places, and moved during
the night.

It was an autumn night, with dark purple clouds, but
no rain.   The ground was moist, but there was no mud,
and troops proceeded noiselessly; the only sound was
the occasional dull clanking of the artillery.   The soldiers were stringently forbidden to talk above a whisper,
to smoke their pipes, to strike a light; the horses refrained from neighing.   The mysteriousness of the
enterprise enhanced the fascination of it.   The men
marched blithely.   Several of the columns halted, stacked
their arms, and threw themselves down on the cold
ground, supposing that they had reached their destination; others — the majority — marched the whole night,
and came to a place which was obviously not their
destination.

Count Orlof-Denisof with his Cossacks — the smallest
detachment of all the others — was the only one who
reached the right place and at the right time.   This
detachment was halted at the very skirt of the forest,
on the narrow foot-path that led between the villages of
Stromilova and Dmitrovskoye.

Before dawn, Count Orlof, who had fallen asleep, was
aroused.   A deserter from the French camp had been
brought in.   This was a Polish non-commissioned officer
from Poniatowsky's corps.   This non-comissioned officer
explained in Polish that he had deserted because he had
been insulted in the French service, that he ought long
before to have been promoted to be an officer, that he
was the bravest of them all, and therefore he had given
them up, and was anxious to have his revenge on them
He declared that Murat was spending the night only

a verst from there, and that if they would give him an escort of a hundred men he would take him alive.

Count Orlof-Denisof consulted with his comrades. The proposal was too attractive to be refused. All offered to go; all advised to make the attempt. After many discussions and calculations, Major-General Gre-kof, with two regiments of Cossacks, decided to go with the non-commissioned officer.

"Now mark my word," said Count Orlof-Denisof to the Pole, as he dismissed him, "in case you have lied, I will have you hanged like a dog; but if you have told the truth — a hundred ducats!"

The non-commissioned officer with a resolute face made no reply to these words, leaped into the saddle, and rode off with Grekof, who had swiftly mustered his men.

They vanished in the forest.

Count Orlof, pinched by the coolness of the morning, which was now beginning to break, excited and made anxious by the responsibility which he had incurred in letting Grekof go, went out a little from the forest and began to reconnoiter the enemy's camp, which could be seen now dimly in the light of the dawn and the dying watch-fires.

At Count Orlof's right, on an open declivity, our columns were to show themselves. Count Orlof glanced in that direction; but, although they would have been visible for a long distance, these columns were not in sight. But in the French camp, it seemed to Count Orlof-Denisof, who also put great confidence in what his clear-sighted aide said, there were signs of life.

"Akh! too late!" said Count Orlof, as he gazed at the camp.

Just as often happens when a man in whom we have reposed confidence is no longer under our eyes, it suddenly seemed to him clear and beyond question that the Polish non-commissioned officer was a traitor, that he had deceived them, and the whole attack was going to be spoiled by the absence of the two regiments which this man had led off no one knew where. "How could they possibly seize the commander-in-chief from among such a mass of troops!" "Of course he lied, that scoundrel!" exclaimed the count.

"We can call them back," said one of the suite, who, exactly like Count Orlof-Denisof, felt a distrust in the enemy on seeing the camp.

"Ha? So?.... What do you think? Shall we let them go on, or not?"

"Do you order them recalled?"

"Yes, recall them, recall them," cried Count Orlof, coming to a sudden decision, and looking at his watch. "It would be too late; it's quite light."

And the adjutant galloped off through the forest after Grekof. When Grekof returned, Count Orlof-Denisof, excited both by the failure of this enterprise and by his disappointment at the non-arrival of the infantry columns, which had not even yet showed up, and by the proximity of the enemy — all the men of his division experienced the same thing — decided to attack.

He gave the whispered command: "To horse!"....

They fell into their places. They crossed themselves. — "S Bogom!.... Away!"....

"Hurra-a-a-a-ah!" rang through the forest, and the sotnias or Cossack companies, one after another, as if they were poured out of a sack, flew, with lances poised, across the brook against the camp.

One desperate, startled yell from the first Frenchman who saw the Cossacks, and all in the camp, suddenly awakened from their dreams, fled undressed in all directions, abandoning their artillery, their muskets, and their horses.

If the Cossacks had followed the French without heeding what was back of them and around them, they would have captured Murat and his whole effective. This was what the officers wanted. But it was an impossibility to make the Cossacks stir when once they had begun to occupy themselves with the booty and their prisoners. No one would heed the word of command.

Fifteen hundred prisoners were captured, thirty-eight

cannons, flags, and — what was more important than all
for the Cossacks — horses, saddles, blankets, and various articles. They must needs oversee all this, secure
the prisoners and the cannon, divide the spoils, shout,
and even quarrel among themselves; with all this the
Cossacks were busying themselves.

The French, finding that they were no longer pursued, came to their senses, formed their lines, and began to fire. Orlof-Denisof was all the time expecting
the infantry columns, and refrained from further offensive action.

Meantime, according to the "disposition" by which
die erste Kolonne marschirt, and so on, the infantry
forces of the belated columns, commanded by Benigsen
and led by Toll, had set out according to orders, but, as
always happens, had come out somewhere, but not at
the place where they ought to have been.

As it always happens, the men who had started out
blithely began to straggle. Tokens of dissatisfaction
were shown; there was the consciousness that a blunder
had been made; they started back in another direction.

Aides and generals were galloping about, shouting,
scolding, and quarreling, and declaring that they were
wrong, and that they were too late, and trying to find
some one to reprimand, and so on, and finally they all
waved their hands, and marched on simply for the purpose of going somewhere.

"Come, let us go somewhere!"

And in fact they went somewhere, but some of them
went in the wrong direction, and those who went in the
right direction arrived so late that they did no good in
coming, but simply became targets for musket-shots!

Toll, who in this battle played the part that Weirother
played at Austerlitz, diligently galloped from place to
place, and everywhere found everything at loose ends.
For instance, he found Bagovut's corps in the woods
just before it was quite daylight, when this corps should
have been with Orlof-Denisof long before. Exasperated
and excited by the failure of the movement, and supposing that some one must be to blame for this, Toll dashed

up to the corps commander and began sternly berating him, declaring that he ought to be shot for this.

Bagovut (an old general, gallant but placid), who was also exasperated by all these delays, this confusion, and by contradictory orders, fell into a fury, much to the surprise of every one, for it was contrary to his nature, and said disagreeable things to Toll.

"I will not be lectured by any one! I and my men can die as well, as bravely, as others!" said he, and he moved forward with only one division.

When he reached the field, swept by the French fire, the gallant and excited Bagovut, not stopping to consider whether (at such a time and with only one division) his participation in the action would be advantageous or not, marched straight ahead and led his troops under the fire. Peril, shot, and shell were the very things he required in his angry mood. One of the first bullets killed him; succeeding bullets killed many of his men. And his division remained for some time needlessly under fire.

CHAPTER VII

MEANTIME, at the front another column should have been attacking the French, but Kutuzof was present with this column. He knew perfectly well that nothing but confusion would result from this battle, which was undertaken against his will, and he held back his troops to the best of his ability. He did not stir.

Kutuzof rode silently on his gray cob, indolently replying to those who proposed to attack: —

"All of you have the word 'attack' on your tongue, but don't you see that we can't make complicated manœuvers!" he said to Miloradovitch, who asked permission to move forward.

"You weren't smart enough this morning to take Murat alive: you were quite too late; now there is nothing to be done," he replied to another.

When the report was brought to Kutuzof that there

were now two battalions of Poles back of the French, where before, according to the report of the Cossacks, there had been no troops, he gave Yermolof a side glance. He had not spoken to him since the day before.

"This is the way they ask to make attacks; all sorts of plans are proposed, and when you come to it, nothing is ready, and the enemy, warned, take their measures."

Yermolof screwed up his eyes and slightly smiled as he overheard those words. He understood that the storm had passed, and that Kutuzof would content himself with this innuendo. "He is entertaining himself at my expense," said Yermolof in a low tone, touching Rayevsky's knee.

Shortly after this, Yermolof approached Kutuzof, and respectfully made his report:—

"It is not too late yet, your highness; the enemy have not moved. If you will only give the order to attack! If you don't, the guards will not have smelt gunpowder!"

Kutuzof made no reply; but, when he was informed that Murat's troops were in retreat, he ordered the attack, but at every hundred paces he halted for three-quarters of an hour.

The whole battle was summed up in what Orlof-Deni-sof's Cossacks did; the rest of the troops simply lost several hundred men absolutely uselessly.

In consequence of this battle, Kutuzof received a diamond order, Benigsen, also, some diamonds and a hundred thousand rubles; the others, according to their ranks, also received many agreeable tokens, and after this battle some further changes were made in the staff.

"That is the way it *always goes with us* — everything at cross-purposes," said the Russian officers and generals, after the battle of Tarutino, just exactly as is said at the present day, giving to understand that there is some stupid person responsible for this blundering way, whereas *we* should have done it in quite another way.

But the men who talk that way either know not what they are talking about, or purposely deceive themselves.

Any battle — Tarutino, Borodino, Austerlitz — is

fought in a different way from what those who planned for it suppose it will be. That is the essential condition.

An infinite number of uncontrollable forces — for never is a man more uncontrollable than in a battle, where it is a matter of life or death — influence the direction of a battle, and this direction can never be foreseen and will never be governed by the direction of any one force whatever.

If many forces act in different directions on any particular body at the same time, then the direction in which this body will move cannot be that of any one of the forces ; but it will always take a middle direction which is a combination of these forces — which in physics is called the diagonal of the parallelogram of forces.

If we find in the writings of the historians, and especially of the French historians, that they make wars and battles conform to any prescribed plan, then the only conclusion which we can draw from this is that their descriptions are not to be relied on.

The battle of Tarutino evidently failed of attaining the object which Toll had in mind, — to lead the troops into the battle in proper order according to the " disposition " ; or the object which Count Orlof may have had in mind, — to take Murat prisoner ; or that which Benigsen and many others may have had, — of destroying the whole corps at a single blow ; or the object of the officer who wished to fall in the battle and distinguish himself ; or that of the Cossack who was desirous of getting more booty than he got, and so on.

But if the object of the battle was what actually resulted, and which, at that time, was the chief desire of all the Russians, — the driving of the French from Russia and the destruction of their army, — then it is perfectly clear that the battle of Tarutino, precisely in consequence of its absurdity, was the very thing that was necessary at that period of the campaign.

It is hard, nay, it is impossible, to imagine a more advantageous outcome of that battle than what actually resulted from it. With the very slightest effort, in spite of the most extraordinary confusion, with the most insignificant loss, the most important results of the whole campaign were attained ; a change from retreat to advance was made, the weakness of the French was manifested, and that impulse was communicated to the Napoleonic army which alone was needed to make them begin their retreat.

CHAPTER VIII

NAPOLEON enters Moscow after the brilliant victory *de la Moskowa ;* there can be no doubt that it is a victory, since the French remain masters of the field of battle !

The Russians retreat and give up their capital. Moscow, full of provisions, arms, ammunition, and infinite riches, falls into the hands of Napoleon.

The Russian army, twice as weak as the French, during a whole month makes not a single effort to assume the offensive.

Napoleon's situation was most brilliant. It would seem that no extraordinary genius was demanded, either to fall, with doubly superior forces, on the remains of the Russian army and exterminate it ; or to offer advantageous terms of peace ; or, in case his offer were rejected, to make a threatening movement against Petersburg, or even, in case of non-success, to return to Smolensk, or to Vilna, or to remain in Moscow, — in a word, to retain the brilliant position which the French army held.

To do this only the simplest and easiest way was necessary, not to allow the army to pillage, to prepare winter clothing (there would have been enough in Moscow for the whole army), and to make systematic collection of provisions, which, according to the French historians, were abundant enough to supply the French troops for half a year.

Napoleon, this genius of geniuses, who had, as historians assure us, the power to control his army, did nothing of the sort.

He not only did nothing of the sort, but on the con trary he used his power to select out of all possible measures open to him the one that was most stupid and the most disastrous.

Of all that Napoleon might have done, — to winter at Moscow, to go to Petersburg, to move on Nizhni-Novgorod, to return by a more northerly or southerly route, following Kutuzof's example, — what could be imagined more stupid or more disastrous than what Napoleon actually did ? Which was this : —

To remain in Moscow till October, allowing his sol-diers to pillage the city ; and then, after deliberating whether or not to leave a garrison behind him, to leave Moscow, to approach Kutuzof, not to give battle, to move to the right as far as Malo-Yaroslavetz again without seeking an opportunity of making a route of his own, and, instead of taking the course followed by Kutuzof, to retreat toward Mozhaïsk along the devas-tated Smolensk highway. A plan more absurd than this, more pernicious to the army, could not be imag-ined, as is fully proved by the results.

Let the ablest masters of strategy, granting that Napoleon's design was to destroy his army, conceive any other plan which would so infallibly and so inde-pendently of any action on the part of the Russian army have so completely destroyed the French army as what Napoleon did.

Napoleon, with all his genius, did this. But to say that Napoleon destroyed his army because he wished to destroy it, or because he was very stupid, would be just as false as to say that Napoleon led his troops to Mos-cow because he wished to do so and because he was a man of great intelligence and genius.

In both cases, his personal action, which was of no more consequence than the personal action of any sol-dier, only coincided with the laws by which phenomena took place.

It is absolutely false, simply because the conse-quences did not justify Napoleon's action, for historians to say that his powers grew weaker at Moscow.

He employed all his intellect and all his power to do the best thing possible for himself and his army, just as he had always done before, and as he did afterwards in 1813. Napoleon's activity at this time was no less amazing than it was in Egypt, in Italy, in Austria, and in Prussia.

We know not sufficiently well the real state of activity of Napoleon's genius in Egypt, where forty centuries looked down on his greatness, for the reason that all his great exploits there are described for us only by the French.

We cannot rate at its proper value his genius in Austria and in Prussia, for with regard to his activity there we must draw our information from French and German sources ; but the surrender of army corps without striking a blow, and of forts without a siege, could not fail to incline the Germans to regard his genius as the only explanation of the victorious campaign which he carried on in Germany.

But, glory to God, we Russians have no reason for acknowledging the genius of Napoleon in order to hide our shame. We paid for the right to look at facts simply as they are, and this right we will not yield !

Napoleon's activity at Moscow was as astonishing and full of genius as it was everywhere else. From the time he entered Moscow until he left it, order upon order and plan upon plan emanated from him. The absence of the inhabitants and of deputations, even the burning of the city, disturbed him not. He forgot not the welfare of his army, or the activity of the enemy, or the good of the people of Russia, or the administration of affairs at Paris, or diplomatic combinations concerning the possible conditions of peace.

CHAPTER IX

In relation to military matters, Napoleon, immediately on entering Moscow, gives strict orders to General Sebastiani to watch the movements of the Russian army, sends troops in various directions, and orders Murat to pursue Kutuzof. Then he proceeds diligently to fortify the Kreml. Then he traces on the whole map of Russia a brilliant plan for the rest of the campaign.

In relation to diplomatic matters Napoleon sends for the robbed and despoiled Captain Yakovlef, who had not succeeded in getting away from Moscow, and gives him a detailed exposition of all his political views, and of his magnanimity, and, having written a letter to the Emperor Alexander, in which he counts it his duty to inform his friend and brother that Rostopchin has behaved very badly at Moscow, he sends Captain Yakovlef with it to Petersburg. Having in the same way expressed in detail his views and his magnanimity before Tutolmin, he sends this little old man also to Petersburg to enter into negotiations.

In relation to judicial affairs, Napoleon, immediately after the conflagrations, gives orders that the guilty shall be found and executed ; and, to punish the malefactor Rostopchin, orders his houses to be set on fire.

In relation to administrative affairs, Napoleon grants a constitution to Moscow, organizes the municipal government, and publishes the following : —

INHABITANTS OF MOSCOW!

Your miseries are great, but His Majesty the Emperor and King desires to put an end to them.

Terrible examples have taught you how he punishes disobedience and crime. Severe measures have been taken to put an end to disorder and to restore general security.

A paternal administration, composed of men from among yourselves, will constitute your municipality, or city government. This will care for you, for your needs, for your interests.

The members thereof will be distinguished by a red scarf, which they will wear over the shoulder, while the mayor [1] will wear, in addition to the scarf, a white belt.

But when not on duty the members will wear simply a red band around the left arm.

The municipal police is established on the lines of its former

[1] *Gradskii golova*, head of the city.

organization, and, thanks to its vigilance, the best of order already exists.

The government has named two commissioners-general, or *politseï-meïsters*, and twenty commissioners, or *tchastnui pristafs*, assigned to different portions of the city. They will be recognized by the white band worn around the left arm.

A number of churches of different denominations are open, and divine service is there celebrated without hindrance.

Your fellow-citizens are daily returning to their dwellings, and orders have been given that they shall find the aid and protection due to their misfortune.

Such are the measures which the government is using to restore order and mitigate your position; but to attain this end, you must coöperate with it, you must forget, if possible, the misfortunes which you have endured, you must cherish the hope of a less cruel destiny, must be convinced that an inevitable and infamous death awaits all those who make any assault on your persons or the property that remains to you, and you must not doubt that they will be guarded, for such is the will of the greatest and most just of all monarchs.

Soldiers and citizens, of whatever nation you may be! — reëstablish public confidence, that source of happiness in every state, live like brethren, mutually aid and protect one another, unite to oppose all criminal manifestations, obey the military and municipal authorities, and soon your tears will cease to flow.

In relation to the provisioning of the army, Napoleon gave orders for the troops to take turns in foraging *à la maraude* through the city to procure food, that thus the army might be secured for the future.

In relation to religion, Napoleon ordered that the popes should be brought back — *ramener les popes* — and worship be reëstablished in the churches.

In relation to trade and the provisioning of the army, the following was posted everywhere: —

PROCLAMATION

You, peaceable inhabitants of Moscow, artisans and workmen whom misfortunes have driven from this city, and you, dispersed farmers, who through unfounded terror remain concealed in the fields, — listen!

Peace reigns in this capital, and order is reëstablished within it. Your compatriots are boldly leaving their retreats, finding that they are treated with consideration.

All violence shown to them or their property is immediately punished.

His Majesty the Emperor and King protects them, and considers none among you his enemies except those that disobey his orders.

He desires to put an end to your misfortunes, and restore you to your homes and your families.

Respond to his benevolent intentions, and come to us without fear.

Inhabitants !

Return with confidence to your dwellings ; you will soon find means of satisfying your wants.

Mechanics and laborious artisans !

Come back to your trades ; houses, shops, watchmen, await you, and for your labor you will receive the wage which is your due !

And you, finally, peasants, come forth from the forests, where you have been hiding in fear ; return boldly to your cottages, with the firm assurance that you will find protection.

Grain-shops have been established in the city, where the peasants may bring all their surplus provisions and the products of the soil.

The government has taken the following measures to assure the free sale of these products : —

1. From this date, peasants, farmers, and the inhabitants of the suburbs of Moscow may without danger bring their products, whatever they may be, into town, to the two markets established for the purpose — in Mokhovaya Street, and in the Okhotnui Riad.

2. These products will be purchased of them at such prices as may be agreed on between seller and buyer ; but if the seller cannot obtain the just price demanded, he is free to take his goods back to his village, and no one under any pretext shall prevent him from doing so.

3. Every Sunday and Wednesday are legalized as " chief market days " ; therefore sufficient numbers of soldiers will be placed, Tuesdays and Saturdays, in the principal thoroughfares at such a distance from the city as to protect the provision trains.

4. Similar measures will be taken to expedite the return of the peasants to their villages with their horses and teams.

5. Measures will be taken immediately to reëstablish the ordinary markets.

Inhabitants of the city and the villages, and you workmen and artisans, to whatever nation you may belong !

We urge you to follow the paternal wishes of His Majesty the Emperor and King, and coöperate with him for the general welfare.

Bring to his feet respect and confidence, and hesitate not to unite with us.

To keep up the spirits of the troops and the people, reviews were frequently held and many decorations were distributed. The emperor rode through the streets on horseback and consoled the inhabitants, and in spite of all his devotion to state matters, he visited the theaters established by his orders.

In relation to charity, that best virtue of crowned heads, Napoleon also did all that could be expected of him.

He ordered the words *Maison de ma mère* to be inscribed on the buildings devoted to charity, by this act uniting the sentiment of a loving son with the grand virtue of a monarch.

He visited the Foundling Asylum,[1] and, allowing his white hands to be mouthed by the orphans saved by him, he conversed graciously with Tutolmin.

Then, according to Thiers's eloquent narrative, he ordered his troops to be paid in counterfeit Russian money which he had manufactured !

"Crowning the employment of these measures by an act worthy of him and of the French army, he commanded to give aid to those who had suffered from the fires. But as provisions were too precious to furnish to foreigners, most of whom were enemies, Napoleon preferred to give them money, and let them procure provisions outside, and he ordered paper rubles to be distributed among them."[2]

[1] *Vospitatelnui Dom.*

[2] *Relevant l'emploi de ces moyens par un acte digne de lui et de l'armée française, il fit distribuer des secours aux incendiés. Mais les vivres étant trop précieux pour être donnés à des étrangers, la plupart ennemis,*

In relation to the discipline of the army, he did not cease to issue orders to inflict severe punishments for all infractions of the rules of the service, and to stop pillaging.

CHAPTER X

But, strangely enough, all these arrangements, measures, and plans, which were in no respect inferior to those which he had taken under similar circumstances, did not touch the root of the trouble, but, like the hands of a clock disconnected with the mechanism behind the dial, moved at random and aimlessly, having nothing to do with the wheels.

As for military matters, the plan for the campaign, of which Thiers says, "Napoleon's genius never imagined anything more profound, more skilful, or more admirable," [1] and which, in his argument with M. Fain, he proves was conceived, not on the fourth, but on the fifteenth of October, — this plan, full of genius as it was, was not and could not have been carried out, for it had in it nothing resembling validity.

The fortifying of the Kreml, to accomplish which it was necessary to destroy the mosque, *la mosquée*, — for so Napoleon called the church of St. Basil, — was perfectly unnecessary.

The placing of mines under the Kreml served only to carry out the personal desire of the emperor, who wished, on leaving Moscow, to see the Kreml blown up, — just as a child wants the floor on which he has hurt himself to be beaten.

The pursuit of the Russian army, which so engrossed Napoleon's attention, presented a most unheard-of phenomenon. The French generals lost the Russian army, numbering not less than sixty thousand men, and according to Thiers, it was only through Murat's ability

Napoléon aima mieux leur fournir de l'argent à fin qu'ils se fournissent au dehors, et il leur fit distribuer des roubles papiers." — Thiers, " Histoire du consulat et de l'empire," Tom. xiv.

[1] " ....*que son génie n'avait jamais rien imaginé de plus profond, de plus habile, et de plus admirable.*"

—his genius, one might say—that the French succeeded in finding, like a pin, the Russian army, sixty
thousand strong!

As for diplomatic matters, all Napoleon's declarations
of magnanimity and justice, made to Yakovlef and to
Tutolmin, were chiefly concerned about obtaining cloaks
and teams, and proved without effect.

Alexander did not receive these ambassadors, and did
not reply to their letters.

As for justice, after the execution of the supposed
incendiaries, the other half of Moscow was burned!

As for administration, the establishment of a municipality did not put an end to pillage, and was of service
only to the few individuals who took a part in this
municipal government, and, under the pretext of establishing order, plundered Moscow, or saved their own
property from pillage.

As for religion, the thing he had found so easy to
arrange in Egypt, by visiting a mosque, here in Moscow
produced no results. Two or three priests, found in
Moscow, were compelled to fulfil the emperor's wishes;
but a French soldier struck one of them on the cheeks
while conducting divine service, and of the other the
French official reported as follows :—

"The priest whom I found and commanded to begin
once more the saying of mass, cleaned and locked the
church. That same night certain persons again went
and smashed the doors and the locks, tore the books in
pieces, and committed other disorders." [1]

As for the reëstablishment of trade, the proclamation
to laborious artisans and to all peasants met with no
response. There were no laborious artisans; while the
peasants seized the commissioners who ventured too far
outside the city with the proclamation, and killed them.

As for amusing the people and the troops by theatrical representations, the result was a failure. The thea-

---

[1] *Le prêtre que j'avais découvert et invité à recommencer à dire la
messe a nettoyé et fermé l'église. Cette nuit on est venu de nouveau en-
foncer les portes, casser les cadénas, déchirer les livres et commettre d'autres
désordres.*

ters that were established in the Kreml and in Pozniakof's house were immediately closed because the actors and actresses were robbed.

Even his charities did not bring forth the anticipated results. Counterfeit and genuine assignats were so abundant in Moscow that they were alike valueless. The French, who had gathered in great booty, would have nothing but gold. Not only the false assignats that Napoleon so kindly distributed among the unfortunates were worthless, but silver also fell below its value compared to gold.

But the most striking proof of the inefficiency of all these orders was Napoleon's effort to put an end to pillage and restore discipline.

Here are some of the reports made by the commanding officers : —

Pillage continues in the city in spite of the order that it shall be stopped. Order is not yet reëstablished, and there is not a merchant engaged in legitimate trade. Peddlers alone venture to sell anything, and what they sell are objects pillaged.

A part of my district continues to be pillaged by soldiers of the Third Corps, who, not content with taking from the wretched citizens hiding in the cellars the little that they have, are even brutal enough to strike them with their swords, as I myself have seen in many instances.[1]

There is nothing new; the soldiers still continue theft and pillage. (October 9.)[2]

Theft and pillage continue. There is a band of robbers in our district who ought to be put down by strong measures. (October 11.)[3]

The emperor is greatly displeased because, in spite of his strict orders to restrain pillage, detachments of marauders from the guard are continually entering the Kreml. . . . In the Old

---

[1] *La partie de mon arrondissement continue à être en proie au pillage des soldats du 3 Corps, qui, non contents d'arracher aux malheureux réfugiés dans des souterrains le peu qui leur reste, ont même la ferocité de les blesser à coups de sabre, comme j'en ai vu plusieurs exemples.*

[2] *Rien de nouveau outre que les soldats se permettent de voler et de piller. (Le 9 Octobre.)*

[3] *Le vol et le pillage continuent. Il y a une bande de voleurs dans notre district qu'il faut faire arrêter par de fortes gardes. (Le 11 Octobre.)*

Guard disorder and pillage were renewed yesterday, last night, and to-day more actively, if possible, than ever. The emperor sees with sorrow that his chosen soldiers, detailed to defend his own person, who ought to set an example of subordination, carry disobedience so far as to despoil cellars and warehouses stocked with stores for the army. Others have fallen so low that they have refused to obey the watchmen and sentinels, and have reviled and beaten them.

The grand marshal of the palace complains bitterly, wrote the governor, that, notwithstanding his reiterated commands, the soldiers continue to perform the offices of nature in all the courts, and even under the windows of the emperor.[1]

This army, like a herd let out in disorder, and trampling under its feet the fodder that would have saved it from starvation and death, was each day of its delay in Moscow nearer its disorganization and its destruction.

But it did not stir.

It started in flight only when panic fear suddenly seized it at the capture of the provision train on the Smolensk road, and at the battle of Tarutino.

This same news of the battle of Tarutino, unexpectedly received by Napoleon during a review, inspired in him, Thiers tells us, the desire to punish the Russians, and he gave the order to retreat which the whole army demanded.

On leaving Moscow, the men of this army loaded themselves with all the booty they could get together.

Napoleon also had his own *trésor* to take with him. Seeing the vehicles encumbering the army, Napoleon, as Thiers says, was horror-struck. But, with all his experience in war, he did not order the superfluous wagons to be destroyed, as he had ordered in regard to his marshals' when they were approaching Moscow. He glanced at the calashes and coaches in which the soldiers were traveling, and said that it was very good — that these vehicles would be useful for carrying provisions, the sick, and the wounded.

---

[1] *Le grand maréchal du palais se plaint vivement que malgré les défenses reiterées les soldats continuent à faire leurs besoins dans toutes les cours, et même jusque sous les fenêtres de l'empereur.*

The situation of the whole army was like that of a wounded animal feeling death to be near and not knowing what to do.

To study the artful manœuvers and the purposes of Napoleon and his army, from the time he entered Moscow to the destruction of this army, is like watching the convulsions and the death struggles of an animal mortally wounded. Often the wounded animal, hearing a noise, runs directly into the hunter's fire, turns this way and that way, and hastens its own end.

Thus acted Napoleon, under the pressure of his whole army.

The noise of the battle of Tarutino alarmed the beast, and it threw itself forward directly into the fire, ran toward the hunter, turned back again, and, like every wild beast, suddenly fled by the most dangerous, the most disadvantageous, but the best-known road — its former trail.

Napoleon, whom we imagine to have been the director of all these movements, just as the figure-head on the prow of a ship is supposed by the savage to be the power that moves the ship, — Napoleon, throughout the whole of his activity, was like a child seated in a carriage clasping the straps that hang on the inside, and imagining that he makes it go.

CHAPTER XI

On the eighteenth of October, early in the morning, Pierre stepped out of the *balagan*, or prison-hut, and then, turning back, stood in the doorway, playing with the long-bodied, bandy-legged, little pink puppy, which was gamboling around him.

This puppy had made her home in the hut, sleeping next Karatayef; but sometimes she made excursions out into the city, from which she would always return again. She had evidently never belonged to any one, and now no one was her master, and she had no name. The French called her Azor; the wit of the company called her *Femme-galka* — Jenny Daw; Karatayef and the others called her *Serui* — Gray; sometimes *Vislui* — the Hanger-on.

The fact that she belonged to no one and had no name or breed and no definite color seemed in no wise to trouble the little pink puppy. She held her furry tail like a plume, boldly and gallantly; the crooked bow-legs served her so well that often, as if disdaining to use all four of them, she would lift gracefully one of the hind legs, and run with great agility and adroitness on three. Everything that came along was an object of satisfaction to her. Now grunting with delight she would roll on her back, now she would warm herself in the sun with a thoughtful and significant expression, now she would gambol and play with a chip or a straw.

Pierre's costume now consisted of a torn and dirty shirt, — the only remains of his former dress, — soldier's trousers, by Karatayef's advice tied with string around the ankles for the sake of greater warmth, a kaftan, and his peasant's cap.

Physically, during this time Pierre had greatly changed. He no longer seemed portly, although he still retained that appearance of rotundity and strength which in their nature are hereditary. His beard and mustache had grown, and covered the lower part of his face. His long hair, all in a tangle on his head and full of lice, fell in tangled locks from under his cap. The expression of his eyes was firm, steadfast, calm, and full of an alertness which had never before been characteristic of him. His old-time indolence, manifested even in his eyes, had now given place to an energetic spirit which was ready for activity and resistance.

His feet were bare.

Pierre looked now at the field along which, that morning, teams and mounted men were moving, now far off across the river, now at the puppy which was pretending that she was going to bite him in real earnest, and now at his bare feet, which, for the sport of the thing, he was placing in various attitudes, wagging his dirty, thick toes. And every time he looked at his bare feet, a smile of lively satisfaction illumined his face. The sight of those bare feet reminded him of all that he had been through and had learned to understand in that time, and this recollection was agreeable to him.

The weather for several days had been mild and bright, with light frosts in the morning — the so-called *Babye lieto* — Woman's summer.

In the sun the air felt warm ; and this warmth, together with the invigorating freshness of the morning frost, which left its influence in the air, was very pleasant. Over everything, objects remote and objects near at hand, lay that magical crystalline gleam which is seen only at this time of the autumn. In the distance could be seen the *Vorobyevui Gorui*, — the Sparrow Hills, — with a village, a church, and a great white house. And the leafless trees and the sand and the rocks and the roofs of the houses, the green belfry of the church, and the angles of the distant white house, — everything stood out with unnatural distinctness, with all its delicacy of outline, in the transparent atmosphere.

Near at hand were the well-known ruins of a nobleman's mansion, half burned, occupied by the French, with its still dark-green lilac bushes along by the garden. And even this house, ruined and befouled, which in gloomy weather would have been repulsive from its disorder, now, in the bright, steady light, seemed like something tranquilly beautiful.

A French corporal in undress uniform, in his nightcap, with a short pipe between his teeth, came from behind the corner of the hut, and, with a friendly wink, joined Pierre.

"*Quel soleil, hein! Monsieur Kirill*," — for that was what all the French called Pierre, — "*on dirait le printemps* — you 'd think it was springtime."

And the corporal leaned up against the door-post and offered Pierre his pipe, although whenever he offered it Pierre always declined it.

"*Si l'on marchait par un temps comme celui-là —*

if we should start in such weather as this...." he be‑
gan.

Pierre asked what the news was in regard to a re‑
treat, and the corporal told him that almost all the
troops were beginning to move, and that the order in
regard to the prisoners was to be issued that day.

In the hut in which Pierre was confined a soldier
named Sokolof was sick unto death, and Pierre told the
corporal that something ought to be done about this
soldier.

The corporal replied that Pierre might be easy on
that score, that there were permanent and movable
hospitals, and that the sick would be cared for, and that
the authorities had provided for all emergencies.

"And besides, Monsieur Kirill, you have only to say
a single word to the captain, you know.   Oh, he is a —
he never forgets anything!   Tell the captain when he
makes his tour of inspection, and he will do anything
for you." —

The captain of whom the corporal was speaking had
often talked with Pierre and showed him all manner of
condescension. —

" 'Do you see, St. Thomas,' says he to me the other
day, 'Kirill is a man of education who speaks French ;
he is a Russian seigneur who has been unfortunate, but
he 's a man !   And he knows what.... if he asks for any‑
thing,' says he, 'let him tell me ; I could n't refuse him.
When one has been studying, you see, you like educa‑
tion and the right kind of people.'   It 's for your sake I
tell you this, Monsieur Kirill.   In that affair the other
day, if it had n't been for you, it might have come out
pretty bad !" [1]

[1] *Et puis, M. Kirill, vous n'avez qu'à dire un mot au capitaine, vous
savez.   Oh! c'est un — qui n'oublie jamais rien.   Dites au capitaine
quand il fera sa tournée, il fera tout pour vous. — "Vois-tu, St. Thomas,"
qu'il me disait l'autre jour, " Kirill c'est un homme qui a de l'instruction,
qui parle français ; c'est un seigneur russe, qui a eu des malheurs, mais
c'est un homme.   Et il s'y entend le — s'il demande quelque chose, qu'il me
dise, il n'y a pas de refus.   Quand on a fait ses études, voyez-vous, on aime
l'instruction et les gens comme il faut."   C'est pour vous que je dis cela, M.
Kirill !   Dans l'affaire de l'autre jour si ce n'était grâce à vous, ça aurait
fini mal.*

And after chatting a little while longer the corporal went off.

The "affair" which the corporal mentioned as having taken place a few days before was a squabble between the prisoners and the French in which Pierre had taken it on him to act as peacemaker.

Several of the prisoners had been listening to the conversation between Pierre and the corporal, and they immediately began to ask what had been said. While Pierre was telling his comrades what the corporal had said about the retreat of the French, a lean, sallow, and ragged French soldier made his appearance in the door of the hut. With a quick, timid gesture he addressed himself to Pierre, raising his fingers to his forehead as a salute, and asked him if there were a soldier in that hut named Platoche, to whom he had given a shirt to make.

The week before the French had received leather and linen, and had distributed them among the Russian prisoners to make boots and shirts.

"All ready, all ready, my dear," said Platon Karatayef, coming forth with a carefully folded shirt.

Karatayef, owing to the warmth of the weather, and for convenience of working, wore only his trousers and a torn shirt as black as earth. His hair, after the fashion of master workmen, was tied up with a bast string, and his round face seemed rounder and more good-natured than ever.

"'Agreement's own brother to business.' I promised it for Friday, and here it is!" said Platon, smiling, and unfolding the shirt which he had made.

The Frenchman glanced round uneasily, and, as apparently conquering a doubt, he quickly stripped off his uniform, and put on the shirt. The Frenchman had no shirt on under his uniform, but his bare, yellow, lean body was clad in nothing but a long, greasy waistcoat of brocade silk.

The Frenchman was evidently afraid that the prisoners who were staring at him would make sport of him, and he hastily thrust his head into the shirt. Not one of the prisoners said a word.

"There, it was time," exclaimed Platon, pulling down the shirt. The Frenchman, getting his head and arms through, without lifting his eyes, inspected the fit of the shirt, and scrutinized the sewing.

"You see, my young hawk, this is not a tailor's shop, and I had n't suitable tools ; and the saying is, ' It takes a tool to kill even a louse,' " said Platon, with a round smile, and taking evident delight in his handiwork.

" *C'est bien, c'est bien, merci !* — Very good, thank you ! But you ought to have some of the cloth left over," said the Frenchman.

"It will set on you better when you get it fitted to your body," said Karatayef, continuing to delight in his production. "It will suit you nicely and be very comfortable .... "

" *Merci, merci, mon vieux, — le reste,*" insisted the Frenchman, smiling ; and, getting out an assignat, he gave it to Karatayef, "*mais le reste* — where is the rest of it ? "

Pierre saw that Platon had no wish to understand what the Frenchman said, and, without interfering, he looked at them. Karatayef thanked him for the money, and continued to admire his work. The Frenchman was bound to have the pieces that were left over, and begged Pierre to translate what he said.

" What does he want of the pieces ? " asked Karatayef. " They would come in handy as leg-wrappers. Well, then, God go with him — *Bog s nim !*" and Karatayef, his face suddenly changing to an expression of deep depression, took out from his breast a bundle of rags, and handed them to the Frenchman without looking at him. "Ekh-ma !" exclaimed Karatayef, and he started back into the hut.

The Frenchman looked at the cloth, deliberated a moment, gave Pierre a questioning look, and as if Pierre's look said something to him, —

" *Platoche, dites donc ! Platoche, Platoche !*" cried the Frenchman, suddenly flushing, and speaking in a piping voice. "*Gardez pour vous* — Keep it ! " said he, giving him the rags, and, turning on his heel, went off.

"Good-by," said Karatayef, nodding his head. "They say they're heathens, but that one has a soul. It used to be a saying in old times, 'Sweaty hand's lavish, dry hand close.' That man was naked, but he gave, all the same." Karatayef, thoughtfully smiling and looking at the rags, remained silent for some time.

"But they'll come handy as leg-wrappers, my friend," said he, and returned into the hut.

CHAPTER XII

FOUR weeks had passed since Pierre had been taken prisoner. Although the French had proposed to transfer him from the privates' hut to the officers', he still remained in the one where he had been placed on the first day.

In burned and plundered Moscow Pierre experienced almost the utmost privations which it is in the power of man to endure; but, owing to his vigorous constitution and health, — a blessing which he had never realized till then, — and especially owing to the fact that these privations had come on him so imperceptibly that it was impossible to say when they began, he not only bore them easily but even cheerfully.

And at this very time he began to feel that calmness and self-satisfaction which he had before vainly striven to attain. He had been long seeking in various directions for this composure and self-agreement, the quality that had amazed him so in the soldiers at the battle of Borodino; he had sought it in philanthropy, in Freemasonry, in the diversions of fashionable life, in wine, in the heroic effort of self-sacrifice, in his romantic love for Natasha. He had sought it in the path of thought, and all these efforts and experiments had disappointed him.

And now without any effort or thought he had discovered this calmness and self-contentment only by the horror of death, by privations, and by what he had found in Karatayef.

Those terrible moments which he had passed through at the time of the executions had, as it were, cleared forever from his imagination and his recollection those anxious thoughts and feelings which had formerly seemed to him of consequence. He no longer thought about Russia, or the war, or politics, or Napoleon. It was evident to him that all this concerned him not, that he was not called on to decide, and therefore could not judge about all this.

> "No love is lost
> 'Twixt Russia and frost,"

he would say, quoting one of Karatayef's proverbs, and these words strangely calmed him.

His scheme of killing Napoleon seemed to him now incomprehensible and even absurd, and so also his calculations concerning the cabalistic number and the Beast of the Apocalypse. His indignation against his wife, and his anxiety that his name should not be disgraced, seemed to him now not only insignificant, but even ludicrous. What difference did it make to him whether this woman led the life that best pleased her, or where? Whose business was it and what difference did it make to him whether it were known or not known to the French that their prisoner was Count Bezukhoï.

He now frequently recalled his conversation with Prince Andreï and fully agreed with him, except that he understood Prince Andreï's ideas in a slightly different way.

Prince Andreï thought and declared that happiness is merely negative, but he said this with a shade of bitterness and irony. It seemed as if in saying this he had expressed the corresponding thought, — that all our aspirations for real, positive happiness are given to us merely to torment us, without ever being satisfied.

---

[1] *Rossii da lietu —*
Soyuzu nietu.

A variant of the popular saw, *Rusi i lietu — Soyuzu nietu —* "Winter and summer have no alliance."

But Pierre, without any mental reservation, acknowledged the correctness of this. The absence of pain, the gratification of desires, and consequently the free choice of occupations, in other words, the manner of life, seemed now to Pierre man's indubitable and highest happiness.

Here and now, for the first time, Pierre appreciated the pleasure of eating when he was hungry, of drinking when he was thirsty, of sleeping when he was sleepy, of warmth when he was cold, of converse with his fellow-men when he felt like talking and hearing a human voice. The gratification of desires, — good food, cleanliness, independence, — now that he was deprived of them all, seemed to Pierre perfect happiness; and the choice of occupation, — that is life, — now when this choice was so limited, seemed to him such an easy matter that he forgot that the superfluity of the comforts of life destroyed all the happiness of gratifying the desires, while great freedom in choice of occupations, that freedom which in his case was given him by his culture, his wealth, his position in society, that such freedom is exactly what makes a choice of occupations hopelessly difficult, and destroys the very desire and possibility of occupation.

All Pierre's thoughts of the future were directed toward the time when he should be free. But nevertheless, afterwards, and all his life long, Pierre thought and spoke with enthusiasm of that month of imprisonment, of those strong and pleasurable sensations which would never return again, and above all of that utter spiritual peace, of that perfect inward freedom, which he had experienced only at that time.

When on the first day of his imprisonment he arose early in the morning and went out at daybreak from the hut and saw the cupolas, dim and dark at first, the crosses on the Novo-Dievitchy monastery, saw the frosty dew on the dusty grass, saw the tops of the Sparrow Hills, and the winding woody banks of the river vanishing in the purple distance; when he felt the contact of the fresh, cool air, and heard the cawing of the daws flying from Moscow across the field; and when, after-wards, suddenly flashed forth the light from the east, and the disk of the sun arose solemnly from behind the cloud, and the cupolas and the crosses, and the dew and the distance and the river, were all bathed in glad-some light, — then Pierre felt a new sense of joy and vital vigor such as he had never before experienced.

And this feeling not only did not once leave him during all the time of his imprisonment, but, on the contrary, it grew more and more, according as the diffi-culties of his position increased.

This feeling of readiness for anything, of moral eleva-tion, was still more enhanced in Pierre by that lofty recognition which immediately on his incarceration in the hut he began to enjoy among his companions.

Pierre, by his knowledge of languages, by the respect which was shown him by the French, by the simplicity with which he gave anything that was asked of him, — he received three rubles a week, the same as the officers, — by the strength which he manifested before the soldiers by driving in the pegs in the wall of the hut, by the sweetness of disposition which he showed in his treatment of his companions, by his power, which they could not understand, of sitting motionless, thinking, seemed to the soldiers a somewhat mysterious and superior being.

Those very characteristics of his which had been, if not injurious, at least a hindrance, in that society where he had moved before, — his strength, his scorn for the amenities of life, his fits of abstraction, his simplicity, — here, among these people, gave him the position almost of a hero. And Pierre felt that this view imposed responsibilities on him.

CHAPTER XIII

THE French troops started to retreat on the night of the eighteenth of October. Kitchens and huts were dismantled; wagons were loaded, and the troops and trains set forth.

At seven o'clock in the morning, in marching trim, in shakoes, with muskets, knapsacks, and huge bundles, the convoy of the French stood in front of the huts, and a lively interchange of French talk, interspersed with oaths, rolled along the whole line.

In the hut all were ready, clothed, belted, shod, and only awaiting the word of command to start.

The sick soldier, Sokolof, pale and thin, with livid circles under his eyes, was the only one unshod and un-clad; and he lay in his place, and his eyes, bulging from his very leanness, looked questioningly at his comrades, who paid no heed to him or his low and regular groans. Evidently it was not so much his sufferings — he was ill with dysentery — as it was the fear and grief at being left alone that caused him to groan.

Pierre, with his feet shod in slippers fabricated for him by Karatayef out of remnants of goatskin which a Frenchman had brought him to make into inner soles for his boots, and belted with a rope, came to the sick man and squatted down beside him on his heels.

"Now, see here, Sokolof, they're not absolutely all going away. They're going to have a hospital here. Maybe you'll be better off than the rest of us," said Pierre.

"Oh, Lord, oh! The death of me! Oh, Lord!" groaned the soldier, louder than ever.

"There, I'll go directly and ask them," said Pierre, and, getting up, he went to the door of the hut.

Just as Pierre reached the door, the very corporal who, the day before, had offered Pierre his pipe, appeared at the outside with two soldiers. The corporal and the soldiers also were in marching trim, with knapsacks, and wore shakoes with chin-straps. This gave a new appearance to their well-known faces. The corporal approached the door for the purpose of locking it, according to the order of the authorities. Before letting out the prisoners they had to call the roll.

"Corporal, what is to be done with the sick man?" .... Pierre began to say; but at the instant that he said this, the doubt arose in his mind whether this was the corporal whom he had known, or an entirely different man — the corporal was so unlike himself at that instant. Moreover, at the instant Pierre spoke, on two sides the rolling of drums was suddenly heard.

The corporal scowled at Pierre's words, and, uttering a meaningless oath, he clapped the door to.

In the hut there was semi-darkness; on two sides the sharp rattle of the drums drowned the sick man's groans.

"Here it is!.... here it is again!" said Pierre to himself, and an involuntary chill ran down his back.

In the changed face of the corporal, in the tone of his voice, in the exciting and deafening rattle of the drums, Pierre recognized that mysterious, unsympathetic power which compels men against their wills to murder their kind, that power the working of which he had seen during the executions.

To fear this power, to try to escape it, to address with petitions or with reproaches the men who served as its instruments, was idle.

Pierre now realized this. It was necessary to wait and have patience.

Pierre did not go back to the sick man, or even look in his direction. Silent, scowling, he stood at the door of the hut.

When the doors of the hut were thrown open, and the prisoners, crowding against each other, came flocking out, Pierre threw himself in front of them and went to the very captain who, according to the corporal's account, was ready to do anything for him.

This captain was in marching trim, and from his cold face looked forth that same "it" which Pierre had recognized in the corporal's words and in the rattle of the drums.

"*Filez, filez* — on with you!" commanded the captain, frowning sternly as he looked at the prisoners crowding past him. Pierre knew beforehand that his effort would be wasted, but still he went up to him.

"*Eh bien, qu'est-ce-qu'il y a?* — What do you want?"

asked the officer, coldly, scanning Pierre as if he did not recognize him.

Pierre told him about the wounded.

" He can walk, the devil take him ! " replied the captain. *" Filez, filez ! "* he went on saying, not looking at Pierre.

" No, but he is dying," began Pierre.

" Go to the —— ! " cried the captain, scowling wrathfully.

Dram-da-da-dam-dam-dam went the rattle of the drums. And Pierre realized that this mysterious force was already in full possession of these men, and that to say anything now was useless.

The officers among the prisoners were separated from the privates and ordered to go forward. The officers, including Pierre, numbered thirty, the privates three hundred.

The officers who were taken out of the other prison-balagans were otherwise and far better dressed than Pierre, and they looked at him and his foot-gear with distrust and even repulsion.

Not far from Pierre marched a stout major in a fine Kazan khalat, belted with a towel, with a puffy, sallow, cross face, who evidently enjoyed general distinction among his fellow-prisoners. He kept one hand holding his tobacco-pouch in his breast ; in the other he clutched his pipe. This major, puffing and breathing hard, growled and scolded at everybody because it seemed to him they were pushing him, and were in a hurry when there was no sense in being in a hurry, and were wondering at everything when there was nothing to wonder at.

Another officer, a little lean man, was chattering with every one, expressing his suppositions as to where they were to be taken now, and how far they would succeed in moving that day.

A chinovnik, in felt boots and wearing the uniform of the commissariat department, ran from one side to another and gazed at the burned city, loudly communicating his speculations in regard to the buildings burned, or how it was with this or that part of Moscow visible from where they were.

A third officer, of Polish origin, judging by his accent, disputed with the commissariat chinovnik, arguing that he was mistaken in his identification of the different parts of Moscow.

"What are you disputing about?" angrily asked the major. "Whether Nikola or Vlas, 't is all one; can't you see .'t is all burnt, and that 's the end of it?.... What are you pushing so for? is n't there room enough?" he exclaimed, turning wrathfully on the one next to him, who had not even touched him.

"Aï! aï! aï! what have they done!" was heard on all sides as the prisoners gazed at the devastation wrought by the fires.

"The ward across the river[1] and Zubovo and even in the Kreml!"

"Look! half of the city's gone!"

"Yes, and I told you that the ward across the river was burnt, and there! you see, it is so!"

"Well, now you know it's burnt, and what's the use of talking about it?" grumbled the major.

As they passed through Khamovniki,[2] one of the few unscathed quarters of Moscow, and went by a church, the whole throng of prisoners suddenly swerved to one side, and exclamations of horror and disgust were heard:—

"Oh, the scoundrels!"

"Are n't they heathens?"

"Oh, it 's a corpse, it 's a corpse!"....

"They 've smeared it with something."

Pierre also moved toward the church, where the object that had called forth the exclamations was, and he vaguely discerned something leaning up against the walls of the church.

From the words of his comrades who could see better than he did, he made out that this object was a man's

[1] The *Zamoskvorietchye*.
[2] The Weavers'. Count Tolstoï's present Moscow residence is in Khamovniki.

dead body, placed in a standing posture by the fence, and with its face smeared with lampblack.

"*Marchez! Sacré nom! Filez!.... trente mille diables!*" shouted the soldiers of the guard ; and the French soldiers, with fierce objurgations and abuse, applied their sabers to drive on the throng of the prisoners, who had stopped to gaze at the dead man.

CHAPTER XIV

ON the streets that crossed Khamovniki, the prisoners marched along with their convoy and the wagons and teams that belonged to the soldiers composing it, and followed behind them ; but when they reached a storehouse of provisions, they found themselves in the midst of a vast detachment of artillery, moving in close order, which had got mixed up with a number of private conveyances.

On the bridge itself all halted, and waited for those in the van to move on. From the bridge the prisoners could see before them and behind them endless lines of moving vehicles.

At the right, where the Kaluga road bends away past Neskutchnoye, stretched endless files of troops and trains, disappearing in the distance. These were the troops belonging to Beauharnais's corps, which had left the city before the others.

Behind, along the Naberezhnaya quay and across the Kamennui Most or Stone Bridge, stretched the troops and trains of Ney.

Davoust's troops, in whose charge the prisoners were, had crossed the Kruimsky Brod, or Crimean Ford Bridge, and already some of the divisions were debouching into Kaluga Street. But the teams stretched out so endlessly that the last ones belonging to Beauharnais's division had not yet left Moscow to enter Kaluga Street, while the head of Ney's troops had already left Bolshaya Orduinka.

After the prisoners had crossed the Crimean Ford

Bridge, they moved on some little distance, and were halted, and then moved on again, while from all sides equipages and men were crowded together more and more. After consuming more than an hour in marching the few hundred steps that separated the bridge from Kaluga Street, and reaching the square where Kaluga Street and the Trans-Moskva Streets meet, the prisoners, closely squeezed into one group, were halted again and kept standing for some hours at the cross-way.

In every direction was heard the incessant roar of carriages like the tumult of the sea, and trampling of feet and incessant angry shouts and curses. Pierre stood crushed up against the wall of a house which had been exposed to the flames, and listened to this uproar, which blended in his imagination with the rattle of the drum.

Several of the officers in the group of prisoners, in order to get a better view, climbed up on the wall of the burned house next which Pierre was standing.

"What crowds of people! oh, what crowds!".... "They're even riding on the guns! See the furs!" they exclaimed. "Oh, the carrion-eaters! what thieves!" .... "Look yonder, on that telyega!".... "Do you see that, they've got an ikon, by God!"....

"Those must be Germans.".... "And our muzhiks, by God!"....

"Akh! the scoundrels!".... "See how they're loaded down, as much as they can do to get along! And there's one's got a drozhsky—they stole even that!"....

"See! he's sitting on the trunks! Ye saints!".... "There, they're having a fight."....

"See! he hit him in the snout, right in the snout!"

"At this rate they won't get through till night!"....

"Look! Just look! Those must be Napoleon's! See what fine horses! With monogram and crown!"....

"This was a fine house!".... "See, he's dropped a bag and didn't notice it!"....

"There! they're fighting again!"....

"There's a woman with a baby! Not so bad-looking either!"....

"See! There's no end to it. Russian wenches! there's the wenches for you, by God!"....

"They're having an easy time in that carriage there, hey!"

Again the wave of general curiosity, just as had been the case at the church of Khamovniki, drove all the prisoners into the street; and Pierre, thanks to his stature, could, over the heads of the others, see what had so awakened the curiosity of the prisoners: in three calashes, jammed in among some artillery caissons, rode several women, sitting close together, adorned with bright colors, painted, and shouting at the top of their sharp voices.

Since the moment Pierre had recognized the reappearance of that mysterious power, nothing seemed to him strange or terrible: neither the corpse smeared with lampblack for a joke, nor these women hastening no one knew where, nor the conflagration that had destroyed Moscow. All that he now saw produced scarcely any impression on him — as if his soul, preparing for a hard struggle, refused to submit to any impressions that might render it weaker.

The teams with the women drove past. Again behind them stretched on telyegas, soldiers, baggage wagons, soldiers, powder trains, carriages, soldiers, caissons, soldiers, and here and there women.

Pierre could not distinguish faces, but he could make out the general movement of the masses.

All these people and these horses seemed to be driven forth by some invisible force. All of them, during the course of the hour that Pierre spent in watching them, came pouring forth from different streets with one and the same wish, to get along as rapidly as possible; all of them were alike apt to interfere with one another, to quarrel, even to come to blows. White teeth were displayed, brows scowled, oaths and curses intermingled, and all faces bore one and the same youthfully resolute and cruelly cold expression which, that morning, had struck Pierre in the corporal's face at the sound of the drum.

Some time before nightfall the *chef* of the convoy mustered his command, and with shouts and disputes marched them in amongst the teams, and the prisoners, guarded on every side, debouched into the Kaluga road.

They proceeded very rapidly, without stopping to rest, and only halted at sunset. The teams ran into one another, and the men prepared for their night encampment. All seemed angry and dissatisfied. It was long before the curses and shouts and blows ceased on all sides. A private carriage, which had been following the prisoners' guard, came up against one of the wagons belonging to the same, and the pole ran into it. Several soldiers ran up from various sides; some struck the heads of the horses that drew the private carriage, and tried to turn them aside; others squabbled among themselves, and Pierre saw a German severely wounded in the head with a short saber.

It seemed as if all these people, now that they found themselves in the open country in the chill twilight of an autumn evening, experienced the same feeling of disagreeable reaction which had come on after the haste and excitement that had occupied them all during the march. They halted all as if they realized that it was inevitable that they should still move forward somewhere, and that in this march there would be much that was hard and trying.

During this halt, the soldiers in charge of the prisoners treated them even worse than they had during the march. At this halt horse-flesh was for the first time served out to the prisoners.

From officers down to humblest soldiers, all seemed alike to feel, as it were, a personal sense of anger against each one of the prisoners, all the more noticeable from the unexpected change from their former friendliness.

This ill-will grew more and more pronounced, when, at calling the roll of the prisoners, it transpired that during the bustle attendant on leaving Moscow a Russian soldier, feigning to be ill with colic, had escaped.

Pierre saw a Frenchman strike a Russian soldier for

having strayed away from the road too far; and he heard the captain, his friend, reprimand a non-commissioned officer for the escape of the Russian soldier, and threaten him with court-martial.

At the corporal's excuse that the soldier was ill, and could not march, the officer replied that the orders were to shoot those who had to be left.

Pierre felt that that fateful power which had taken possession of him during the executions, and which had been in abeyance during the time of his imprisonment, now once more ruled his existence.

It was terrible to him; but he felt that in proportion to the efforts made by this fateful force to crush him, in his own soul waxed and strengthened the force of life that was independent of it.

Pierre made his supper of rye-meal porridge and horse-flesh, and chatted with his comrades.

Neither Pierre nor any of his companions said a word of what they had seen in Moscow, or about the cruelty of the French, or about the order to have stragglers shot, which had been explained to them; all of them were especially cheerful and lively, as if to counteract the wretchedness of their position. They called up their personal recollections, and the comical incidents which they had seen during the march, and avoided all mention of their actual position.

The sun had long ago set; the bright stars were everywhere glittering in the sky; along the horizon spread the ruddy glow of the rising full moon like the glare of a conflagration, and soon the huge red globe hung swaying wonderfully in the grayish mists. It grew light. The evening was over, but the night had not fairly begun.

Pierre left his new comrades, and, stepping among the watch-fires, started to cross to the other side of the road, where he had been told the privates of the prisoner party were encamped. He wanted to have a talk with them. But a sentinel halted him on the road and ordered him back.

Pierre returned, but not to the watch-fire, to his com

panions, but to an unharnessed wagon where there was no one. Doubling up his legs and dropping his head, he sat down on the cold ground by the wagon-wheel, and remained there long motionless, thinking.

More than an hour passed in that way. No one disturbed him.

Suddenly he burst out into a loud and burly peal of jovial laughter, so loud that men gathered round from various directions in amazement, to see what caused this strange and solitary fit of laughter.

"Ha! ha! ha!" roared Pierre, and he went on talking aloud to himself. "The soldier would not let me pass. I was caught, I was shut up. They still keep me as their prisoner. Who am I? I? I?.... my immortal soul! Ha! ha! ha!" and he laughed until the tears ran down his cheeks.

Some one got up and came over to see what this strange, big man found to laugh at all alone by himself. Pierre ceased to laugh, got up, went off to some distance from the inquisitive man, and glanced around him.

The huge, endless bivouac, which shortly before had been noisy with the crackling of camp-fires and the voices of men, was now silent; the ruddy fires were dying down and paling. High in the bright sky stood the full moon. Forest and field, before invisible beyond the confines of the bivouac, could now be seen stretching far away. And still farther beyond these forests and fields the eye followed the bright, quivering, alluring, infinite distance.

Pierre gazed up into the sky, into the depths of the marching host of twinkling stars.

"And all that is mine, and all that is in me, and all that is *me*," thought Pierre. "And they took all that and shut it in a hut made of boards!"

He smiled, and went back to his comrades, and lay down to sleep.

CHAPTER XV

TOWARD the middle of October, a messenger came to Kutuzof with still another letter from Napoleon, and a proposal for peace. It was deceitfully dated from Moscow, since at that time Napoleon was not far in advance of Kutuzof on the old Kaluga highway.

Kutuzof replied to this letter exactly as he had replied to the first one with which Lauriston had been sent : he declared that there could be no question of peace.

Shortly after this, word was received from Dolokhof, who was in command of a band of "partizans" operating at the left of Tarutino, that the enemy had appeared in Fominskoye, that these troops consisted of Broussier's division, and that this division, being separated from the rest of the army, might be easily destroyed.

Soldiers and officers again demanded offensive operations. The staff generals, animated by their remembrance of the easy victory at Tarutino, brought all their influence to bear on Kutuzof to grant Dolokhof's proposal.

Kutuzof considered it unnecessary to make any attack. A middle course was adopted : a small detachment was sent to Fominskoye, charged to attack Broussier.

By an odd coincidence, this operation — most difficult and most important, as it turned out, in its consequences — was intrusted to Dokhturof — that same modest little Dokhturof whom no one ever thought of describing for us as making plans for engagements, flying at the head of regiments, scattering crosses on the batteries, and so on ; who was considered and counted irresolute and lacking in penetration, but nevertheless that same Dokhturof whom, during all the wars between the Russians and the French, from Austerlitz until 1813, we find always in command where there was anything difficult to do.

At Austerlitz, he stays until the last on the dike of Augest, re-forming the regiments, saving what he can, when all are fleeing and perishing, and not one general is left in the rear.

Though ill with fever, he goes to Smolensk with twenty thousand men to defend the city against the whole army of Napoleon. At Smolensk, he has just caught a wink of sleep at the Malakhof gates, during a paroxysm of his fever, when he is awakened by the cannonade of the city, and Smolensk holds out the whole day.

In the battle of Borodino, when Bagration is struck down, and nine men in every ten from among the troops of our left flank are killed, and all the force of the French artillery fire is concentrated in that direction, no one else but Dokhturof, irresolute and lacking in penetration, is sent there, and Kutuzof makes haste to retrieve the blunder which he had made in sending some one else there. And the little, mild Dokhturof goes there, and Borodino becomes the brightest glory of the Russian arms. And many heroes have been celebrated by us in verse and prose, but of Dokhturof scarcely a word!

Again, Dokhturof is sent to Fominskoye and from there to Malo-Yoroslavetz, to the place where the last battle with the French took place, and where evidently the destruction of the French began; and again many heroes and geniuses have been celebrated by us at that period in the campaign, but of Dokhturof never a word, or almost nothing, or half-heartedly. This silence concerning Dokhturof more palpably than aught else proves his merit.

Naturally, for a man who understands not the working of a machine, it seems, on first seeing it in motion, that the most important part of it is the shaving which accidentally got into it, and, while interfering with its movement, makes a buzzing noise. The man, not knowing the virtues of the machine, cannot comprehend that not this shaving, vitiating and deranging the works, but that little distributing cog-wheel which turns noiselessly, is the most essential part of the machine.

On the twenty-second of October, the same day on

which Dokhturof traversed the half of the road toward Fominskoye, and had halted in the village of Aristovo, preparing himself accurately to carry out the orders that had been given him, the whole French army, in its spasmodic motion moving down as far as Murat's position, as if for the purpose of giving battle, suddenly, without any reason, swerved to the left to the new Kaluga highway, and moved toward Fominskoye, where shortly before only Broussier had been.

Dokhturof, at this time, had under his command, with the exception of Dolokhof's men, only the two small divisions of Figner and Seslavin.

On the afternoon of October twenty-third, Seslavin came to the commander at Aristovo with a French guardsman, who had been taken prisoner. The prisoner said that the troops which had that day occupied Fominskoye consisted of the vanguard of the main army, that Napoleon was there, that the whole army had left Moscow on the seventeenth.

That same evening a domestic serf, who had come from Borovsko, declared that he had seen an enormous host entering the town.

The Cossacks of Dolokhof's division brought word that they had seen the French guard marching along the road to Borovsko.

From all these rumors it was evident that at that place where they expected to find a single division was now the whole army of the French, which had marched out of Moscow in an unexpected route — along the old Kaluga highway.

Dokhturof was loath to make any demonstration, since it was not now at all clear to him what it was his duty to do. He had been commanded to attack Fominskoye.

But where, before, Broussier had been alone in Fominskoye, now there was the whole French army.

Yermolof wanted to act on his own judgment, but Dokhturof insisted that it was necessary to have orders from his serene highness. It was determined to send a messenger back to headquarters.

For this duty was chosen a highly intelligent officer, Bolkhovitinof, who, in addition to the written report, was to give a verbal report of the whole matter. At midnight Bolkhovitinof, having received the envelop and the verbal message, galloped off, accompanied by a Cossack, with extra horses, to headquarters.

CHAPTER XVI

IT was a dark, warm, autumn night. There had been a steady rain for four days. After changing horses twice, and riding thirty versts in an hour and a half over the muddy, sticky road, Bolkhovitinof reached Letashevko at two o'clock in the morning. Dismounting in front of an izba on the wattled fence of which was the sign, "GLAVNUI SHTAP," — "Headquarters," — and leaving the horse, he went into the dark entry.

"The general on duty, instantly! Very important!" he exclaimed to some one, who had been snoring in the darkness of the entry and started up.

"He was very unwell last evening; he has n't slept for two nights," whispered a denshchik's voice, apologetically. "Better wake the captain first."

"Very important — from General Dokhturof," said Bolkhovitinof, entering the door, which was held open for him. The denshchik led the way, and tried to awaken some one.

"Your nobility! your nobility! — A courier!"

"What, what is it? From whom?" exclaimed some one's sleepy voice.

"From Dokhturof and from Aleksei Petrovitch. Napoleon is at Fominskoye," said Bolkhovitinof, not being able to make out, by reason of the darkness, who it was that was questioning him, but judging by the sound of the voice that it was not Konovnitsuin.

The man who had been aroused yawned and stretched himself.

"I don't like to wake him," said he, fumbling about

for something. "He's a pretty sick man. Maybe it's a rumor."

"Here is the despatch," said Bolkhovitinof. "I was ordered to hand it instantly to the general on duty."

"Wait, I will strike a light. Where are you, you scamp, always asleep!" he cried, addressing the denshchik.

This was Shcherbinin, Konovnitsuin's aide. "I have found it, I have found it," he added.

The denshchik struck a light. Shcherbinin had been searching for the candlestick. "Akh! the wretched business!" he cried, with disgust.

By the candlelight Bolkhovitinof saw Shcherbinin's youthful face, and in the opposite corner a man still sound asleep. This was Konovnitsuin.

When the tinder flared up first with blue and then with ruddy flame, Shcherbinin lighted the tallow candle, from which the cockroaches that had been feasting on it dropped to the ground. He stared at the messenger.

Bolkhovitinof was covered with mud, and in wiping his face on his sleeve he smeared it all over.

"Who brought the news?" asked Shcherbinin, taking the envelop.

"The news is trustworthy," replied Bolkhovitinof. "The prisoners and the Cossack and the scouts are all unanimous in saying the same thing."

"It is unavoidable — must wake him," said Shcherbinin, getting up and going over to the man asleep in a nightcap, and covered with a cloak.

"Piotr Petrovitch!" he called.

Konovnitsuin did not stir.

"Headquarters!" he cried, with a smile, knowing that that would assuredly waken him. And, in fact, the head in the nightcap was immediately lifted. In Konovnitsuin's handsome, resolute face, with the cheeks aflame with fever, there remained for an instant the expression of the visions of sleep, far enough removed from the reality; but suddenly he shivered; his face assumed its ordinarily calm and resolute expression.

"Well, now, what is it? From whom?" he asked,

not hastily, but without unnecessary delay, blinking his eyes at the light.

On hearing the officer's report, Konovnitsuin broke the seal and read the letters. He had hardly finished reading them before he set his feet in woolen stockings down on the earth floor, and began to put on his shoes. Then he took off his cap, and, running the comb through the locks on his temples, he put on his forage-cap.

"Did you come quickly? Let us go to his serene highness."

Konovnitsuin immediately realized that this news was of the greatest importance, and that it brooked no delay. He did not take into consideration, or even ask himself, whether it was good news or bad news. This did not interest him. He looked on the whole business of war, not with his intellect or with his reason, but with something else. His soul had a deep but unexpressed conviction that all would be well; but the confession or expression of this faith that was in him seemed to him entirely unnecessary; he had only to do his duty. And his duty he did, giving to it all his powers.

Piotr Petrovitch Konovnitsuin, just like Dokhturof, seemingly out of mere formality, had his name inscribed on the list of the so-called heroes of 1812, — the Barclays, the Rayevskys, the Yermolofs, the Platofs, the Miloradovitches; just like Dokhturof, enjoyed the reputation of being a man of very limited capacity and talent; and again, like Dokhturof, Konovnitsuin never made plans of battles, but he was always found where the greatest difficulties were to be met. Ever since his appointment as general on duty he had slept with an open door, insisting that he should be awakened whenever a courier should come; in battle he was always under fire, so that Kutuzof chided him for exposing himself recklessly, and for that reason dreaded to send him into service; and thus again, like Dokhturof, he was one of those invisible springs which, without fuss or racket, constitute the most essential part of the machine.

On coming out from the izba into the damp, dark night, Konovnitsuin scowled, partly because his head·

ache had grown worse, and partly from the disagreeable thought that occurred to him, that now, at this news, would be aroused all that nest of influential men connected with the staff, and especially Benigsen, who since Tarutino had been at swords' points with Kutuzof. How they would propose, discuss, give orders, interfere! And this presentiment was disagreeable to him, although he knew that it was inevitable.

In point of fact, Toll, to whom he went to communicate this news, immediately began to lay down his ideas for the benefit of the general who shared his lodgings with him; and Konovnitsuin, after listening in silence until he was tired, reminded him that they ought to go to his serene highness's.

CHAPTER XVII

KUTUZOF, like all old people, slept little at night. In the daytime he frequently dozed at unexpected times; but at night, throwing himself, still dressed, down on his couch, he would lie awake and think.

Thus it was at this time. He was lying on his bed, leaning his heavy, big, scarred head on his fat hand, and thinking, his one eye staring out into the darkness.

Since Benigsen, who was in correspondence with the sovereign, and had more influence with the staff than any one else, had kept out of his way, Kutuzof was more at ease in reference to his being urged again to let the troops take part in useless offensive movements. The lesson of the battle of Tarutino and of the day before it, ever memorable to Kutuzof, must have its effect, he thought.

"They must understand that it can only be a losing game with us to act on the offensive. *Patience* and *Time*, they are my warrior-heroes," said Kutuzof to himself.

He knew that it is not best to pluck the apple while it is green. It will fall of itself when it is ripe; but if you pluck it green, then it spoils the apple and the tree, and sets your teeth on edge as well.

Like an experienced huntsman, he knew that the wild beast was wounded, — wounded as only the whole force of Russia could wound; but whether the wound was mortal or not was as yet an undecided question.

Now, by the sending of Lauriston and Berthémi, and by the reports of the guerrillas, Kutuzof was almost certain that the wound was mortal.

But proofs were still requisite; it was necessary to wait.

"They want to rush forward and see how they have killed him. Wait, and you'll see. Always 'manœuvers,' always 'offensive movements'!" he said to himself. "What for? So as to gain distinction. One would think there was something jolly in this fighting. They are just like children, from whom you can't expect reason, for the whole business lies in the fact that they all want to prove how well they can fight. But that is not the case now. And what fine manœuvers they are always proposing to me! It seems to them that when they have devised two or three chances" — he was thinking about the general plan sent from Petersburg — "they have exhausted the list, but there's no end to them."

The vexed question whether the wild beast was mortally wounded or not at Borodino had been for more than a month suspended over Kutuzof's head.

On the one hand, the French had taken possession of Moscow; on the other, Kutuzof undoubtedly felt in his whole being that that terrible blow, in the dealing of which had been concentrated the force of the united Russian people, must have been mortal.

But, in any case, proofs were required, and he had been waiting for them for more than a month; and in proportion as time slipped away, the more impatient he became.

As he lay on his couch during those sleepless nights of his, he did the same thing that the younger element among his generals did, — the very thing for which he

reproached them.   He thought out all possible con-
tingencies, just as the younger generals did, but with
this difference only, that he placed no dependence on
these prognostications, and that he saw them, not in
twos or threes, but in thousands.

The more he thought about them, the more abundantly they arose before him.   He imagined every kind
of diversion which the Napoleonic army might make,
whether as a whole, or in divisions, against Petersburg,
against himself, against his flank.   There was one con-
tingency which he imagined, and that he dreaded
more than any other: it was that Napoleon might turn
against him his own weapon, — that he might settle
down in Moscow and wait for him.

Kutuzof even imagined Napoleon's army marching
back to Meduin and Yukhnof, but the one thing that he
could not have foreseen was the very thing that happened, that senseless, cautious doubling to and fro of
Napoleon's army during the first eleven days after it
left Moscow; that indecision which rendered possible
what Kutuzof had not till then dared even to think about
— namely, the absolute destruction of the French.

Dolokhof's report about Broussier's division, the information imparted by the "partizans" in regard to the
distresses of Napoleon's army, the rumors of preparation
for evacuating Moscow, all taken together, confirmed
the presumption that the French army was worsted and
was preparing to flee.   But these presumptions appealed
to the younger men only, not to Kutuzof.

He, with his sixty years' experience, knew how much
dependence was to be put on hearsay, knew how prone
men who wished anything were to group all the indica-
tions in such a way as to conform with their desire, and
he knew how in such a case as this they are glad to
drop out of sight anything that may seem opposed to it.

And the more Kutuzof desired this the less he permitted himself to put any trust in it.   This question
engaged all the energies of his mind.   Everything else
was for him merely the ordinary business of life.   And
such subordinate business of life included his conversa-

tion with his staff-officers, his letters to Madame Stahl written from Tarutino, the reading of novels, the granting of rewards, his correspondence with Petersburg, and the like.

But the destruction of the French, which he had been the only one to foresee, was the only real desire of his soul.

On the night of the twenty-third of October, he was lying down, his head resting on his hand, and was thinking about this.

There was a commotion in the next room, and the steps of Toll, Konovnitsuin, and Bolkhovitinof were heard.

"Eï! who is there? Come in, come in! What news?" cried the field-marshal to them.

While the servant was lighting a candle, Toll told the gist of the news.

"Who brought it?" asked Kutuzof, his face amazing Toll, when the light was made, by its cold sternness.

"There can be no doubt about it, your serene highness."

"Bring him in, bring him in."

Kutuzof sat down, stretching out one leg on the bed, and resting his huge paunch on the other, which he doubled up. He blinked his sound eye, in order to get a better sight of the messenger, as if he expected in his features to read the answer to what was occupying him.

"Go on, tell us about it, friend," said he to Bolkhovitinof, in his low, senile voice, gathering together over his chest his shirt, which had fallen open. "Come here, come nearer. What is this bit of news you have brought me? What! Napoleon left Moscow? And his army too? Ha?"

Bolkhovitinof gave him a detailed account, from the very beginning, of all that had been intrusted to him.

"Speak faster, faster; don't torment my very soul," exclaimed Kutuzof, interrupting him.

Bolkhovitinof told the whole story and then remained silent, awaiting orders.

Toll began to make some remark, but Kutuzof interrupted him. He wished to say something, but suddenly
his face wrinkled and frowned. Waving his hand to
Toll, he walked across the room, to the "red corner"
of the izba, where the holy pictures were ranged black
against the wall.

"Lord, my Creator! Thou hast heard our prayer...."
said he, in a trembling voice, folding his hands. "Saviour
of Russia! I thank thee, O Lord."

And he burst into tears.

CHAPTER XVIII

From the time that this news came until the end of
the campaign, all Kutuzof's activity is confined to exercising his power, shrewdness, and persuasion to prevent
his troops from useless attacks, manœuvers, and encoun-
ters with an enemy already doomed.

Dokhturof goes to Malo-Yaroslavetz; but Kutuzof
dawdles along with his whole army, and gives orders for
the evacuation of Kaluga, retreat behind that town
seeming to him perfectly practicable.

Kutuzof falls back; but the enemy, not waiting for
his retreat, takes to flight in the opposite direction.

The historians of Napoleon describe for us his clever
manœuvers at Tarutino and Malo-Yaroslavetz, and indulge in hypotheses as to what would have happened if
Napoleon had succeeded in entering the rich southern
provinces.

But, not to mention the fact that nothing prevented
Napoleon from entering these southern provinces, since
the Russian army gave him a free road, the historians
forget that nothing could have saved the French army,
for it carried within itself the already inevitable elements of its own destruction.

How could an army which had found an abundance
of provisions at Moscow, and, instead of keeping them,
had trampled them under its feet, an army which, on
arriving at Smolensk, had, instead of gathering stores,

given itself up to pillage,—how could this army have
saved itself in the province of Kaluga, inhabited by Russians the same as Moscow was and where fire had the
same property of burning up whatever was set on fire?

This army could nowhere have retrieved itself.   After
Borodino and the pillage of Moscow it henceforth bore
in itself the chemical conditions of decomposition.

The men of what was once an army ran, like their
leaders, knowing not whither, having—Napoleon and
every soldier—but one desire, to escape as soon as
possible from this situation, which they all, though
vaguely, realized was inextricable.

This was the only reason that at Malo-Yaroslavetz,
when Napoleon's generals pretended to hold a council,
and various opinions were offered, the last opinion of all,
General Mouton's, who, being a simple-minded soldier,
spoke what all thought, that they must get away as
quickly as possible, closed all mouths ; and no one, not
even Napoleon, could say anything against a truth recognized by all.

But though all knew that they must depart, there still
remained the shame of confessing that they must take
to flight.   Some external impulse was needed to overcome this shame.   And the impulse came at the proper
time.   It was what the French called "the emperor's
ambush."[1]

Early the next morning, after the council, Napoleon,
pretending that he was going to inspect his troops and
examine the field of battle, past and to come, rode to
the center of his lines, accompanied by his suite of marshals and by his guard.

Some Cossacks, prowling about in search of plunder,
stumbled on the emperor, and almost made him prisoner.

If the Cossacks failed this time to capture Napoleon,
he was saved by the very thing that proved the destruction of the French : love of booty, which on this occasion, as at Tarutino, led the Cossacks to neglect men,
and think only of pillage.   They paid no attention to the

---

[1] *Le hourra de l'empereur.   Hourra :* "the cry of the Cossacks going
against an enemy; a sudden and unexpected charge of irregulars."

emperor, but flung themselves on the spoils, and Napoleon succeeded in escaping.

When the "children of the Don" — *les enfans du Don* — were able to lay hold on the emperor himself in the midst of his army, it became clear that there was nothing else to be done but beat a retreat by the shortest known road.

Napoleon, with the rotund abdomen of his forty years, no longer felt his former agility and courage, and accepted the omen. Under the influence of the fright given him by the Cossacks, he immediately sided with Mouton, and, as the historians say, gave the order to retreat along the road to Smolensk.

The fact that Napoleon agreed with Mouton and that the French troops retreated does not prove that Napoleon ordered the movement, but that the forces which were acting on the army to push it in the direction of Mozhaïsk had at the same time exerted their influence on Napoleon himself.

CHAPTER XIX

WHEN a man undertakes any movement he has always an object in view. If he has a journey of a thousand versts before him, he must expect something good at the end of those thousand versts. He must imagine a promised land, in order to have strength enough to cover the distance.

When the French invaded Russia their promised land was Moscow; when they began their retreat it was their native land. But their native land was far, far away; and when a man starts out on a journey of a thousand versts, he must surely forget the end in view and say to himself, "To-day I will go forty versts, and there find rest and lodging;" and during this first stage of his journey this resting-place becomes for the time being his ultimate destination, and he concentrates on it all his hopes and desires.

Aspirations found in any isolated man are always intensified in a body of men.

To the French, returning over the old Smolensk high·
way, the final end in view — the return to the fatherland — was too far off ; and the immediate goal towards
which all their desires and hopes, magnified to enormous
proportions in the whole body of men, were directed,
was Smolensk.

It was not because they expected to find in Smolensk
many provisions or fresh troops, or because they had
been told any such thing ; on the contrary, all the generals of the army, and Napoleon as well, knew that there
was very little to be found at Smolensk, — but because
this was the only thing that could give the soldiers the
power to march and to endure the privations of the
moment, that those who knew the truth and those
who knew it not, alike deceiving themselves, struggled
toward Smolensk as their promised land.

Once on the highroad, the French hurried toward
this fictitious destination with a remarkable energy
and unprecedented velocity.

Besides the general yearning for a single object, on
which the whole body of the French army was united
and which imparted a certain additional energy, there
was still another cause uniting them. This cause was
found in their aggregation.

This enormous multitude, as if obedient to the physical law of attraction, drew to itself all isolated atoms
of men. These hundred thousand men moved on in
a compact mass like a whole empire !

. Each man among them wished for but one thing —
to fall into captivity, and so to be delivered from all
their horrors and sufferings. But, on the one hand,
the power of the common impulse toward their goal,
Smolensk, carried each one in the same direction.

On the other hand, it was impossible for an entire
corps to surrender to a single company, and, although
the French took advantage of every convenient occasion to separate from their fellows, and at even the
slightest pretext surrendered to the Russians, these pre-
texts did not always offer.

The great numbers of them, and their hard, rapid

march, deprived them of these possibilities, and made it not only difficult, but impossible, for the Russians to arrest this movement in which was concentrated the entire energy of such a mass of the French.

The mechanical disruption of the body could not hasten, beyond a certain limit, the process of decomposition in progress.

It is impossible to melt a snowball in an instant. There exists a certain limit of time before which no power of heat can melt the snow. On the contrary, the greater the heat the more solidified is the snow which remains.

With the exception of Kutuzof, none of the Russian generals understood this. When the retreat of the French army took the definite shape of flight along the Smolensk road they began to realize the truth of what Konovnitsuin had foreseen on the night of October 23.

All the superior generals of the army wished to distinguish themselves, to cut the French off, to take them prisoners, to set upon them; and all demanded offensive operations.

Kutuzof alone employed all his powers — the powers of any commanding general are very small — to resist offensive operations.

He could not say what we can say to-day — why fight battles, why dispute the road, why lose your own men, and why inhumanly kill unfortunate wretches? why do all this, when from Moscow to Viazma, without any combat whatever, a third of this army has disappeared? but drawing from his wisdom what they might have understood, he told them about "the golden bridge"[1]; and they mocked him, slandered him, and hurled themselves on the dying beast to rend it and cut it in pieces.

At Viazma, Yermolof, Miloradovitch, Platof, and others, finding themselves near the French, could not restrain themselves from cutting off and destroying two French army corps. Kutuzof they derided by sending

---

[1] "Let them cross the golden bridge;" that is, "Give them every chance of self-destruction."

him a sheet of blank paper in an envelop, instead of a report of their undertaking.

And, in spite of all Kutuzof's efforts to restrain our troops, the troops assailed the French, and endeavored to dispute their way. Regiments of infantry, we are told, with music and drums, boldly advanced to the attack, and killed and lost thousands of men.

But they could not cut off the fugitives, or exterminate the enemy. And the French army, drawing its ranks more closely together, because of the danger, and regularly melting away, advanced along this — its fatal road to Smolensk.

END OF VOL. V.

THE DEATH OF PETYA.

Original Drawing by E. H. Garrett.

WAR AND PEACE

VOL. VI

CONTENTS

PART XIV

CONTENTS

CONTENTS

EPILOGUE. — PART I

CHAPTER I. Page 152 (1819)

The storm-tossed historical sea. Reaction and progress. Alexander I. Reproaches on his reactionary tendencies. The welfare of humanity. The activity of Napoleon and Alexander.

CHAPTER II. P. 156

Chance. Genius. The parable of the fattened sheep. Facts and objects.

CHAPTER III. P. 158

The movements of the nations. *Résumé* of Napoleon's life. The man needed. The readiness of the forces. The movement from West to East. The counter-movement.

CHAPTER IV. P. 163

The new upheaval. The return of the man of destiny. The last act. Fate. *Résumé* of Alexander's career. Dual relationship of man. The final object of bees.

CHAPTER V. P. 167

Natasha's marriage. The Rostof family. The count's death. His debts. Nikolaï's sense of honor. Inclemency of the debtors. Hard days. Sonya's character. Nikolaï misanthropic.

CHAPTER VI. P. 171

Princess Mariya's call at the Rostofs'. Nikolaï's reserve. The countess urges Nikolaï to call on the princess. Nikolaï's call. The princess's abstraction. A personal turn to the conversation. An explanation.

CHAPTER VII. P. 176

Nikolaï's marriage. His mode of conducting his estate. His confidence in the muzhik. His rule of conduct. His world apart. Countess Ma riya's jealous amazement. His theories.

CONTENTS

CONTENTS xiii

and Causality. Reason and consciousness. Substance and form. Comparison between Gravity and the force of Free Will. The *Force* of Free Will the substance. Vital force.

WAR AND PEACE

PART FOURTEENTH

CHAPTER I

THE battle of Borodino, with the successive occupation of Moscow and the flight of the French army without further battles, is one of the most instructive events of history.

All historians agree that the external activity of states and peoples, in their mutual collisions, is expressed by war; that immediately after great or petty military successes the political power of states and nations is increased or diminished.

Strange as it seems in reading history to find that such and such a king or emperor, on quarreling with other emperors or kings, gets his troops together, attacks the enemy's army, wins the victory, kills three thousand, five thousand, ten thousand men, and in consequence of this vanquishes a whole state and a whole population of millions of men; hard as it is to understand why the defeat of an army — the loss of a hundredth part of all a nation's forces — should compel the submission of the entire nation, — yet all the facts of history, as far as it is known to us, confirm the justice of the assertion that the greater or less success of the army of any nation at war with another is the cause, or at least the essential indication, of the increase or decrease of the power of those nations.

When an army has won a victory, instantly the "rights" of the victorious nation are increased to the detriment of the vanquished. When an army has suffered defeat, immediately the nation is deprived of "rights" in proportion to the defeat; and when the army has been completely defeated, the nation is completely vanquished.

This has been the case, according to history, from the most ancient to the most recent times. All of Napoleon's wars serve to confirm this rule.

In proportion as the Austrian troops were defeated, Austria lost its "rights," while the rights and powers of France were magnified.

The victories of the French at Jena and Austerlitz destroyed the independence of Prussia.

But suddenly in 1812 the "battle of the Moskva" was won by the French, and Moscow was captured; after that no more battles were fought, Russia ceased not to exist, but an army of six thousand men did cease to exist, and subsequently the France of Napoleon.

To force facts to fit the rules of history, to say that the battle-field of Borodino was won by the Russians, or that, after the occupation of Moscow, battles were fought which exterminated Napoleon's army, — is impossible.

After the victory of the French at Borodino, not only was there no general battle, but no battle of any importance; and yet the French army ceased to exist.

What does this fact signify?

If such a thing had occurred in the history of China, we might say that it was not a historical event — the favorite loophole of historians when facts do not fit theories; if it were a question of a conflict of short duration in which small forces took part, we might declare the event an exception to the general rule.

But this event took place under the eyes of our fathers, for whom the question of the life or death of their country was decided, and this war was the most momentous of all known wars.....

That period in the campaign of 1812, from the battle of Borodino to the retreat of the French, proved not only that a battle won is not always a cause of conquest, but also that it may not be even a sign of

conquest, — proved that the force which decides the
destiny of nations consists not in conquerors, or even
in armies and battles, but in something different.

The French historians, describing the condition of
the troops before the evacuation of Moscow, assure us
that everything was in good order in the "Grand
Army," excepting the cavalry, the artillery, and the
wagon-trains, — forage being also lacking for the horses
and cattle. There was no help for this evil, for the
muzhiks of the region around burned their hay, and
would not let the French have it.

The victory won by the French did not bring the
usual results, because of the muzhiks Karp and Vlas,
who, after the departure of the French, went to Moscow with carts to plunder the city, and who personally,
as a rule, manifested no heroic sentiments; and yet the
whole innumerable throng of similar muzhiks refused
to carry hay to Moscow in spite of the money offered
to them, but burned it.

Let us imagine two men engaged in a duel with
swords according to all the rules of the art of fencing.
For a considerable time the parrying has continued;
then suddenly one of the contestants, feeling that he
has been wounded, realizing that the affair is no joke,
but that his life depends on it, throws aside his sword,
and, seizing the first club that comes to hand, begins to
wield it.

Now let us imagine that this man, who so wisely
employs the best and simplest method for attaining his
object, is at the same time imbued with the traditions of
chivalry, and, wishing to conceal the truth, should insist
that he was victorious over the sword according to the
rules of the art of fencing. It may be imagined what
confusion and lack of clearness would arise from such
a description of a past duel.

The duelist who demands an encounter according to
the rules of the art is the French; his enemy, who
throws away his sword and takes up a club, is the Russians; those who try to explain everything according

to the rules of fencing are the historians who have described these events.

From the time of the burning of Smolensk began a form of war which does not belong to any of the former traditions of war.

The burnings of towns and villages, battles followed by retreats, the blow at Borodino and the retreat, the burning of Moscow, the hunting down of marauders, the intercepting of provision-trains, the "partizan" warfare, — all this was contrary to the rules.

Napoleon felt this; and from the very time when he stood in Moscow, in the regular position of fencing, and discovered that the hand of his opponent held a club over him instead of a sword, he did not cease to complain to Kutuzof and the Emperor Alexander that the war was conducted contrary to all rules — as if there were rules for the killing of men!

But, in spite of all the complaints of the French about the breaking of rules, in spite of the fact that the Russians highest in position were ashamed of fighting with the cudgel and desired to stand in a position where, according to all the rules, they could fight, — *en quarte, en tierce*, and make the clever thrust, *en prime*, and so on, — the club of the popular war was lifted in all its threatening and majestic power, and, caring nothing for good taste and rules, with stupid simplicity but sound judgment, not making distinctions, it was lifted, and fell, and pounded the French until the whole army of invaders perished.

And honor be to that people who did not as the French did in 1813, who saluted the enemy according to all the rules of the art, and, reversing their swords, politely and gracefully handed them to their magnanimous conqueror. Honor be to that people who in the moment of trial, not asking how others had acted in conformity to rules in similar circumstances, simply and quickly seized the first club at hand, and wielded it until the feeling of anger and vengeance in their hearts gave way to contempt and pity!

CHAPTER II

ONE of the most obvious and advantageous infractions of the so-called rules of war is the action of isolated individuals against troops crowded together into a mass.

This sort of activity is always seen in wars which assume a popular character. This form of warfare consists in this, that, instead of one compact body meeting another compact body, men disperse, attack separately, and instantly retire when threatened by superior forces, and then reappear at the first favorable opportunity.

Thus did the Guerrillas in Spain, thus did the mountaineers in the Caucasus, thus did the Russians in 1812.

Warfare of this sort is called "partizan" warfare, and people suppose that when it is thus named its meaning is explained.

This sort of warfare, however, not only fails to come under any rules, but is directly opposed to a well-known law of tactics regarded as infallible. This law demands that the assailant shall concentrate his troops so as to be, at the moment of combat, stronger than his enemy.

Partizan warfare (always successful, as history proves) is directly opposed to that law.

This contradiction arises from the fact that military science takes the strength of armies to be identical with their numbers. Military science says: The more troops, the greater the strength. Great battalions are always right: *Les gros bataillons ont toujours raison.* In making this assertion, military science is like the science of mechanics, which, considering the momenta of moving bodies only in relation to their masses, affirms that these forces will be equal or unequal as their masses are equal or unequal.

Momentum (the *quantity* of movement) is the product of the mass into the velocity.

In war the momentum of troops is likewise the product of the mass multiplied by some unknown quantity, x.

Military science, seeing in history an infinite collection of examples of the fact that the mass of armies does not coincide with the strength, and that small detachments have conquered large ones, confusedly recognizes the existence of this unknown factor, and tries to discover it, now in geometrical combinations, now in differences of armament, now, and this most generally, in the genius of the commanders.

But the values given to all these factors do not suffice to account for the results in accordance with historical facts.

Meantime it is sufficient for us to rid ourselves of the false idea, invented for the pleasure of heroes, that in the effect of the arrangements made by the commanders in time of war, we shall find this unknown x.

This x is the spirit of the army; in other words, the more or less intense desire of all the men composing the army to fight and expose themselves to perils, independently of the question whether they are under the command of men of genius or otherwise, whether they fight in three or two ranks, whether they are armed with clubs or with guns delivering thirty shots a minute.

Men who have the most intense desire to fight always put themselves in the most advantageous position for fighting.

The spirit of the army is the factor, multiplied by the mass, which gives the product, power. To determine and express the meaning of the spirit of the army — that unknown factor — is the problem of science.

The problem is possible only when we cease to put arbitrarily, in place of this unknown x, the conditions under which the momentum is produced, such as the dispositions of the commander, the armament, and so on, and disregarding them as the significant factor, realize this unknown quantity in all its integration as the more or less active desire animating the men to fight and confront danger.

Only when we express known historical facts by means of equations can we, by a comparison of the relative value of this unknown factor, determine the unknown factor.

Ten men, battalions, or divisions, fighting with fifteen men, battalions, or divisions, conquer the fifteen, that is, kill them or take them all prisoners without exception, themselves losing only four. On one side fifteen have been exterminated, on the other four. In reality the four were equal to the fifteen, and consequently

$$4x = 15y;$$

consequently

$$x:y = 15:4.$$

This equation does not give the value of the unknown factor, but it expresses the relations between the two unknown factors, and, by putting into the form of similar equations historical units taken separately, — battles, campaigns, periods of war, — a series of numbers will be obtained in which laws must exist and may be discovered.

The rule of tactics commanding troops to act in masses during an attack, and separately in a retreat, is an unconscious expression of the truth that the strength of troops depends on their spirit. Better discipline is required to lead men into fire than to induce them to defend themselves against assailants, and is obtained exclusively by movements in masses.

But this rule, which takes no account of the spirit of the troops, constantly proves fallacious and particularly opposed to the reality, when there is an increased or diminished spirit among the troops — in all popular wars.

The French, in retreating in 1812, though they should, according to tactics, have defended themselves separately, drew into closer masses, because the spirit of the troops had fallen so low that the army could be maintained only by holding the men in mass.

The Russians, on the contrary, ought, according to tactics, to have attacked in mass; but in fact they scattered their forces, because the spirit of their troops had risen so high that isolated men attacked the French without waiting for orders, and had no need of constraint to induce them to expose themselves to fatigues and perils.

CHAPTER III

THE so-called partizan or guerrilla war [1] began with the arrival of the French at Smolensk.

Before this guerrilla warfare was officially recognized by our government, thousands of the hostile army — marauders left behind and foraging parties — had been exterminated by Cossacks and muzhiks, who killed these men as instinctively as dogs worry to death a mad dog that has run astray.

Denis Davuidof, with his keen Russian scent, was the first to understand the significance of this terrible cudgel, which, without regard to the rules of military science, annihilated the French; and to him belongs the glory of taking the first step toward formulating this sort of warfare.

On the fifth of September, Davuidof's first partizan squad was organized; and after the example of his, others were organized. The longer the campaign continued, the greater became the number of these bands.

The partizans demolished the "Grand Army" in detachments. They trampled down the fallen leaves which came off from the dried tree — the French army — and now and again shook the tree itself.

In October, when the French were on their way back to Smolensk, there were hundreds of these bands, of various sizes and characters. There were bands which had all the appurtenances of a regular army — infantry, artillery, staff-officers — and many of the comforts of life; others consisted solely of Cossacks — cavalry; there were others of insignificant size, gathered at haphazard, infantry and cavalry mixed; there were those composed of muzhiks, and those organized by landowners, and others that owed no allegiance to any commander.

A *diachok*, or sacristan, was the leader of one band, which, in the course of a month, took several hundred

[1] *Partizanskaya voïna.*

prisoners; and there was the wife of a village starosta, named Vasilisa, who killed hundreds of the French.

The early days of November saw the greatest development of this partizan warfare. Ended was the first period of this kind of war — during which the "partizans" themselves were amazed at their own audacity, were afraid every moment of being surprised and surrounded by the French, and kept hid in the forests, not unsaddling, and scarcely venturing to dismount from their horses, expecting to be pursued at any moment.

By this time this kind of warfare had taken definite form; it had become clear to all what they could do and what they could not do in grappling with the French.

The leaders of bands, who had regular staffs and followed rules, kept at a respectful distance from the French, and regarded certain things as impossible. Petty partizans who had been engaged for some time in the business and had gained a close acquaintance with the French, considered feasible what the leaders of the large bands would not dare even to think of.

Cossacks and muzhiks who slipped easily in and out among the French reckoned that everything was possible.

On the fourth of November, Denisof, who was one of these partizan leaders, found himself, with his band, in the very brunt of partizan excitement. Since morning, he and his band had been on the march. All day long, keeping under shelter of the forest that skirted the highway, he had been following a large French convoy of cavalry baggage and Russian prisoners, isolated from the other troops, and under a powerful escort, on its way to Smolensk, as was known from scouts and prisoners.

The existence of this train was known, not only to Denisof and Dolokhof, — who was also a partizan leader with a small band, and was advancing close by, — but to the heads of several large bands, with their staffs. All knew about this train, and, as Denisof expressed it, "were whetting their teeth for it."

Two of these large bands, one commanded by a Polyak, the other by a German, almost simultaneously sent to Denisof to join forces, each inviting him to help them attack the "transport."

"No, thank you, bwother, I gwow my own whiskers," said Denisof, as he read their letters; and he replied to the German that, in spite of the heartfelt desire which he had of serving under the command of such a valiant and distinguished general, he should have to deprive himself of that pleasure, because he had already joined the command of the Polish general.

And to the Polish general he wrote the same thing, assuring him that he had already joined the command of the German.

Having thus disposed of these matters, Denisof made his plans without reference to these high officials, to join in company with Dolokhof, and attack and capture this train, with the small force at their command.

The "transport" was proceeding, on the fourth of November, from the village of Mikulina to the village of Shamsheva. On the left-hand side of the road between the two villages ran a dense forest, in places approaching the road, in places receding from the road a verst and more.

Under the cover of this forest, now hiding in its depths, now approaching its edge, Denisof had been advancing all day long with his band, not once losing the French from sight.

In the morning, not far from Mikulina, where the forest came nearest to the road, the Cossacks of Denisof's band had seized two of the French wagons, loaded with cavalry saddles, which had got stuck in the mud, and made off with them into the forest.

From that time until evening, the band, without attacking, followed the French in all their movements.

It was necessary to allow them, without being alarmed, to reach Shamsheva in safety; there Denisof would unite with Dolokhof, who was to come for a consultation, that evening, to a designated spot in the forest, about a verst from Shamsheva, and at daybreak they would fall on them from two sides at once quite unexpectedly, —

"like snow on the head," — and defeat and capture the whole host at one fell blow.

In the rear, two versts from Mikulina, where the forest approached the road, six Cossacks had been left, who were to report instantly in case new columns of the French appeared.

In front of Shamsheva, Dolokhof was to scour the road so as to know at what distance other French troops might be.

The "transport" mustered fifteen hundred men. Denisof had two hundred, and Dolokhof had perhaps as many. But the preponderance of numbers did not deter Denisof. The only thing that he cared now to know was what sort of men composed these troops, and, with this end in view, Denisof wanted to capture a "tongue," — that is, a man from the enemy's ranks. In the morning, when they fell on the two wagons, the affair was accomplished with such celerity that all the French in charge of the two wagons had been killed, and the only one taken alive was a drummer boy who had remained behind, and was incapable of giving any definite information about the kind of men that formed the column.

To make a second descent, Denisof considered, would be at the risk of arousing the whole column, and therefore he sent forward to Shamsheva the muzhik Tikhon Shcherbatof, one of his band, to pick up, if possible, one of the French quartermasters who would be likely to be there in advance.

CHAPTER IV

IT was a mild, rainy, autumn day. The sky and the earth blended in the same hue, like that of turbid water. At one moment it was precipitated in the form of fog; at the next, round, slanting drops of rain would suddenly fall.

Denisof, in his *burka*, or felt cloak, and *papakh*, or Cossack cap, from which the water was streaming, was riding along on a lean thoroughbred, with tightened girths. Like his horse, he kept his head bent and ears alert, and, scowling at the slanting rain, peered anxiously ahead. His face was somewhat thinner than of yore, and, with its growth of thick, short black beard, looked fierce.

Abreast of Denisof, also in burka and papakh, on a plump, coarse-limbed Don pony, rode a Cossack esaul,[1] Denisof's ally.

A third, the Esaul Lovaïski, likewise in burka and papakh, was a long-limbed, light-complexioned man, as flat as a plank, with narrow bright eyes and a calmly self-confident expression both of face and pose. Although it was impossible to tell wherein consisted the individuality of horse and rider, still at a glance, first at the esaul and then at Denisof, it was evident that Denisof was wet and uncomfortable, that Denisof was a man who merely rode his horse; while, on looking at the esaul, it was evident that he was as comfortable and confident as he always was, and that he was not a man who merely rode the horse, but a man who was one being with his horse and thus possessed of double strength.

A short distance ahead of them walked their guide, a little peasant in a gray kaftan and a white cap, wet to the skin.

A little behind them, on a lean, slender Kirgiz pony with a huge tail and mane, and with lips torn and bloody, rode a young officer in a blue French capote.

Next him rode a hussar, who had taken up behind him, on his horse's crupper, a lad in a torn French uniform and blue cap. This lad clung to the hussar with hands red with cold, and rubbed his bare feet together to warm them, and gazed around him in amazement with uplifted brows. This was the French drummer boy whom they had taken prisoner that morning.

Behind them, three and four deep, stretched the line of hussars along the narrow, winding, and well-worn

[1] *Esaul* at the present time is the Cossack title corresponding to captain of a *sotnya* or hundred ; *sotnik* (centurion) was the former term.

forest path ; then came Cossacks, some in burkas, some in French capotes, some with cavalry housings thrown over their heads. Their horses, whether roan or bay, seemed all black as coal in the rain which was streaming from them.

The horses' necks seemed strangely slender from their soaked manes. From the horses arose a steam. The clothes and the saddles and the bridles, — everything was wet, slippery, and limp, just like the ground and the fallen leaves which covered the path. The men sat with scowling faces, trying not to move, so as to warm the water that had trickled down their backs, and not to allow any fresh invasion of cold water to get under their saddles, on their knees, or down their necks.

In the midst of the long train of Cossacks the two wagons drawn by French and Cossack horses (the latter harnessed in with their saddles on) rattled over the stumps and roots and splashed through the ruts full of water.

Denisof's horse, avoiding a puddle which covered the road, sprang to one side and struck his knee against a tree.

"Oh, the devil!" cried Denisof, wrathfully, and, showing his teeth, he gave the horse three blows with the whip, spattering himself and his comrades with mud. Denisof was not in good spirits, owing to the rain and his hunger, — he had eaten nothing since morning, — and principally because nothing had been heard from Dolokhof, and because the man sent to capture the "tongue" had not returned.

"We shan't be likely to find another chance like to-day's to stwike the twansport twain. To attack them alone is too much of a wisk ; and to wait till another day — some of those big bands of partizans will be sure to snatch it away from under our vewy noses," said Denisof, who kept his eyes constantly toward the front, thinking that he might see the expected messenger from Dolokhof.

On coming out into a vista where there was a clear

view extending to some distance toward the right, Denisof reined in.

"Some one's coming," said he.

The esaul looked in the direction indicated by Denisof.

"There are two of them — an officer and Cossack. Only you don't *presuppose* that it is the sub-lieutenant himself, do you?" said the esaul, who liked to bring in words that were not in use among the Cossacks.

The riders who were coming toward them were lost from sight, and after a little while reappeared again. The officer, with disheveled hair, wet to the skin, and with his trousers worked up above his very knees, came riding in advance at a weary gallop, urging his horse with his whip. Behind him, standing up in his stirrups, trotted his Cossack. This officer, a very young lad, with a broad, rosy face, and alert, merry eyes, galloped up to Denisof and handed him a wet envelop.

"From the general," said the officer. "Excuse its not being perfectly dry.".…

Denisof, frowning, took the envelop and started to break the seal.

"Now they all said it was dangerous.... dangerous," said the young officer, turning to the esaul while Denisof was reading the letter. "However, Komarof" — he pointed to the Cossack — "Komarof and I made all our plans. We each had two pist.... But who is that?" he asked, breaking off in the middle of the word on catching sight of the French drummer boy. "A prisoner? Have you had a fight? May I speak with him?"

"Wostof! Petya!" cried Denisof, at that instant having run through the letter that had been given him. "Why didn't you say who you were?" and Denisof, with a smile, turning round, gave the young officer his hand.

This young officer was Petya Rostof!

All the way Petya had been revolving in his mind how he should behave toward Denisof as became a full-fledged officer, and not give a hint of their former acquaintance.

But as soon as Denisof smiled on him, Petya imme-

diately became radiant, flushed with delight, and forgot
the formality which he had stored up against the occasion, and began to tell him how he had galloped past
the French, and how glad he was that such a commission had been intrusted to him, and how he had been
in the battle near Viazma, where a certain hussar greatly
distinguished himself.

"Well, I'm wight glad to see you," said Denisof,
interrupting him, and then his face assumed again its
anxious expression. "Mikhaïl Feoklituitch," said he,
turning to the esaul, "you see this is fwom the German
again. He insists on our joining him."

And Denisof proceeded to explain to the esaul that
the contents of the letter just received consisted in a
reiterated request from the German general to unite
with him in an attack on the transport train. "If we
don't get at it to-mowow, he will certainly take it away
fwom under our vewy noses," he said in conclusion.

While Denisof was talking with the esaul, Petya,
abashed by Denisof's chilling tone, and supposing that
the reason for it might be the state of his trousers,
strove to pull them down under shelter of his cloak, so
that no one would notice him, and did his best to
assume as military an aspect as possible.

"Will there be any order from your excellency?"[1]
he asked of Denisof, raising his hand to his vizor, and
again returning to the little comedy of general and aide
for which he had rehearsed himself. "Or should I
remain with your excellency?"

"Orders?" repeated Denisof, thoughtfully. "Can
you wemain till to-mowow?"

"Akh! please let me. .... May I stay with you?"
cried Petya.

"I suppose your orders fwom the genewal were to
weturn immediately — were n't they?" asked Denisof.

Petya reddened.

"He said nothing at all about it; I think I can," he
replied, somewhat doubtfully.

"Well, all wight!" said Denisof.

---

[1] *Vuisokoblagorodiye*, high well-born-ness.

And, turning to his subordinates, he made various arrangements for the party to make their way to the place of rendezvous at the watch-house in the forest that had been agreed upon, and for the officer on the Kirgiz horse — this officer performed the duties of aide — to ride off in search of Dolokhof, and find whether he would come that evening or not.

Denisof himself determined to ride down with the esaul and Petya to the edge of the forest nearest to Shamsheva to reconnoiter the position of the French, and find the best place for making their attack on the following day.

"And now, gwaybeard," said he, turning to the muzhik who was serving as their guide, "take us to Shamsheva."

Denisof, Petya, and the esaul, accompanied by a few Cossacks and the hussar who had charge of the prisoner, rode off to the left, through the ravine, toward the edge of the forest.

CHAPTER V

It had ceased to rain; there was merely a drizzling mist, and the drops of water fell from the branches of the trees.

Denisof, the esaul, and Petya rode silently behind the muzhik, who, lightly and noiselessly plodding along in his bast shoes over the roots and wet leaves, led them to the edge of the wood.

On reaching the crest of a slope, the muzhik paused, glanced round, and strode toward where the wall of trees was thinner. Under a great oak which had not yet shed its leaves he paused, and mysteriously beckoned with his hand.

Denisof and Petya rode up to him. From the place where the muzhik was standing, the French could be seen. Immediately back of the forest, occupying the lower half of the slope, spread a field of spring corn. At the right, beyond a steep ravine, could be seen a small village and the manor-house[1] with dilapidated roofs. In this hamlet, and around the mansion-house, and over the whole hillside and in the garden, around the well and the pond, and along the whole road up from the bridge to the village, which was not more than quite a quarter of a mile, throngs of men could be seen in the rolling mist. Distinctly could be heard their non-Russian cries to the horses that were dragging the teams up the hill, and their calls to one another.

"Bwing the pwisoner here," said Denisof, in a low tone, not taking his eyes from the French.

A Cossack dismounted, helped the lad down, and came with him to Denisof. Denisof, pointing to the French, asked what troops such and such divisions were. The little drummer, stuffing his benumbed hands into his pockets, and lifting his brows, gázed at Denisof in affright, and, in spite of his evident anxiety to tell all that he knew, got confused in his replies, and merely said yes to everything that Denisof asked him. Denisof, scowling, turned from him, and addressed the esaul, to whom he communicated his impressions.

Petya, moving his head with quick gestures, looked now at the little drummer boy, now at Denisof, and from him to the esaul, then at the French in the village, and did his best not to miss anything of importance that was going on.

"Whether Dolokhof comes or does not come, we must make the attempt — hey?" said Denisof, his eyes flashing with animation.

"An excellent place," replied the esaul.

"We'll attack the infantwy on the low land — the swamp," pursued Denisof. "They'll escape into the garden. You and the Cossacks will set on them fwom that side." Denisof pointed to the woods beyond the village. "And I fwom this, with my hussars. And when a gun is fired ...."

"You won't be able to cross the ravine .... there's a quagmire," said the esaul. "The horses would be mired .... you'll have to strike farther to the left."

[1] *Barsky domik.*

While they were thus talking in an undertone, there
rang out below them, in the hollow where the pond was,
a single shot; a white puff of smoke rolled away, then
another, and they heard friendly, as it were jolly, shouts
from hundreds of the French on the hillside.

At the first instant both Denisof and the esaul drew
back. They were so near that it seemed to them that
they were what had occasioned those shots and shouts.

But the shots and shouts had no reference to them.
Below them across the swamp a man in something red
was running. Evidently the French had shot and were
shouting at this man.

"Ha! that 's our Tikhon," said the esaul.

"So it is, so it is."

"Oh! the wascal!" exclaimed Denisof.

"He 'll escape 'em!" said the esaul, blinking his
eyes.

The man whom they called Tikhon ran down to the
creek, plunged into it, spattering the water in every
direction, and, disappearing for a moment, he crawled
out on all fours, and, black with water, dashed off once
more.

The French who had started in pursuit paused.

"Cleverly done!" exclaimed the esaul.

"What a beast!" snarled Denisof, with the same expression of vexation as before. "And what has he been
up to all this time?"

"Who is it?" asked Petya.

"Our *plastun*.[1] We sent him to catch a 'tongue.'"

"Oh, yes," said Petya, at Denisof's first word, nodding his head as if he understood, although really he
did not comprehend a single word.

Tikhon Shcherbatui was one of the most useful men
of the band. He was a muzhik from Pokrovskoye —
near Gzhatya.

When Denisof, near the beginning of his enterprise,
reached Pokrovskoye, and, according to his usual cus-

---

[1] *Plastun* (plastoon), the name of a sharpshooter who lies in ambush
or a scout, among the Black Sea Cossacks.

tom, summoned the starosta, or village elder, and asked
him what news they had about the French, the starosta
had replied, as all starostas always reply, as if called to
account for some mischief, that they had not seen or
heard anything.

But when Denisof explained to him that his aim was
to beat the French, then the starosta told him that
miroders had only just been there, but that only one
man in their village, Tishka Shcherbatui, troubled himself about such things.

Denisof ordered Tikhon to be summoned, and, after
praising him for his activity, spoke to him, in the starosta's presence, a few words about that fidelity to the
Tsar and the fatherland, and that hatred toward the
French, which the sons of the fatherland were in duty
bound to manifest.

"We haven't done any harm to the French," said
Tikhon, evidently confused by this speech of Denisof's.
"We only amused ourselves, as you might say, with the
boys. We killed a few dozen of the *miroders*, that was
all; but we haven't done 'em any harm."....

On the next day, when Denisof, who had entirely forgotten about this muzhik, was starting away from Pokrovskoye, he was informed that Tikhon had joined the
band, and asked permission to stay. Denisof gave
orders to keep him.

Tikhon, who at first was given the "black work" of
making camp-fires, fetching water, currying horses,
quickly displayed great willingness and aptitude for
partizan warfare. He would go out at night after booty,
and every time he would return with French clothes and
arms, and when it was enjoined upon him he would even
bring in prisoners.

Denisof then relieved Tikhon from drudgery, began
to take him with him in his raids, and enrolled him
among the Cossacks.

Tikhon was not fond of riding horseback, and always
traveled on foot, but he never let the cavalry get ahead
of him. His weapons consisted of a musket, which he
carried as a joke, a lance, and a hatchet, which he used

as a wolf uses his teeth, with equal facility eliciting a flea out of his hair, or crushing stout bones. Tikhon, with absolute certainty, would split a skull with his hatchet at any distance, and, taking it by the butt, he would cut out dainty ornaments, or carve spoons.

In Denisof's band Tikhon enjoyed an exclusive and exceptional position. When there was need of doing anything especially difficult and obnoxious, — to put a shoulder to a team stuck in the mud, or to pull a horse from the bog by the tail, or act as knacker, or make his way into the very midst of the French, or travel fifty versts a day, — all laughed and gave it to Tikhon to do.

"What harm will it do him, the devil? He's tough as a horse!" they would say of him.

One time a Frenchman, whom Tikhon had taken prisoner, fired his pistol at him, and wounded him in the buttocks. This wound, which Tikhon treated with nothing but vodka, taken internally and externally, was the object of the merriest jokes in the whole division, and Tikhon put up with them with a very good grace.

"Well, brother, how's it coming on? Does it double you up?" the Cossacks would ask mockingly; and Tikhon, entering into the fun of the thing, would make up a face, and, pretending to be angry, would abuse the French with the most absurd objurgations. The only impression that the affair made on Tikhon was that, after his wound, he was chary of bringing in prisoners.

Tikhon was the most useful and the bravest man in the band. No one was quicker than he was in discovering the chances of a raid; no one had conquered and killed more of the French; and, in consequence of this, he was the buffoon of the whole band, and he willingly accommodated himself to this standing.

Tikhon had now been sent by Denisof the evening before to Shamsheva to capture a "tongue." But either because he had not been satisfied with one single Frenchman, or because he had slept that night, during daylight he had crept among the bushes in the very midst of the French, and, as Denisof had seen from the brow of the ravine, had been discovered by them.

CHAPTER VI

AFTER talking with the esaul for some little time longer about the morrow's raid, which Denisof, it seemed, having got a view of the French near at hand, was fully disposed to make, he turned his horse and rode back.

"Well, bwother, now we'll go and dwy ourselves," said he to Petya.

As they rode up to a forest watch-house, Denisof reined in, and gazed into the woods. Along the forest, among the trees, came, at a great swinging gait, a long-legged, long-armed man, in a *kurtka*, or roundabout, bast boots, a Kazan cap, with a musket over his shoulder, and a hatchet in his belt. On catching sight of Denisof, this man hastily threw something into the thicket, and, removing his wet cap, with its pendent brim, he approached his leader.

This was Tikhon.

His face, pitted with smallpox and covered with wrinkles, and his little, narrow eyes, fairly beamed with self-satisfied jollity. He lifted his head high, and, as if trying to refrain from laughing, looked at Denisof.

"Where have you been all this time?" asked Denisof.

"Where have I been? I went after the French," replied Tikhon, boldly and hastily, in a hoarse but sing-song bass.

"Why did you keep out of sight all day? Donkey! Well, why didn't you bring him?"

"I brought what I brought," said Tikhon.

"Where is he?"

"Well, I got him, in the first place, before sunrise," pursued Tikhon, setting his legs, high-wrapped in lapti, wide apart. "And I lugged him into the woods. But I see he's no good. I thinks to myself, 'I'll try it again; I'll have better luck with another.'"

"Oh, you wascal! — what a man he is!" exclaimed Denisof, turning to the esaul. "Why didn't you bwing him?"

"Yes, why did n't I bring him!" exclaimed Tikhon, angrily. "No good! Don't I know what kind you want?"

"What a beast!.... Well?"

"I went after another one," resumed Tikhon. "I crept this way into the woods, lying flat!"—Tikhon here unexpectedly and abruptly threw himself on his belly, watching their faces while he did so. "Suddenly one shows up," he went on to say; "I collar him.... this way." Tikhon swiftly, lithely leaped to his feet. "'Come along,' says I to the colonel. What a racket he made! And there were four of 'em! They sprang on me with their little swords. And I at 'em in this way with my hatchet: 'What's the matter with you! Christ be with you!' says I," cried Tikhon, waving his arms and, putting on a frightful scowl, swelling his chest.

"Yes, we just saw from the hill what a tussle you had with 'em, and how you went through the swamp!" exclaimed the esaul, squinting up his glistening eyes.

Petya felt a strong inclination to laugh, but he saw that all the others kept perfectly sober. He swiftly ran his eyes from Tikhon's face to the esaul's and Denisof's, not understanding what all this meant.

"Cease playing the fool!" cried Denisof, angrily coughing. "Why did n't you bwing in the first one?"

Tikhon began to scratch his back with one hand and his head with the other, and suddenly his whole mouth parted in a radiant, stupid smile, which exposed the lack of a tooth (that was what had given him the name of Shcherbatui, the gap-toothed). Denisof smiled, and Petya indulged in a hearty laugh, in which Tikhon himself joined.

"Oh, well, he was entirely no good!" said Tikhon. "His clothes were wretched, else I'd have brought him. And besides he was surly, your nobility. Says he, 'I am an *anaral's* son myself,' says he, 'and I won't come,' says he."

"What a bwute!" exclaimed Denisof. "I wanted to question him...."

"Well, I questioned him," said Tikhon. "'Hard to talk *by signs!*' says he. 'Lots of us,' says he, 'but a poor lot. Only,' says he, 'they are all the same kind. Groan a little louder,' says he, 'you'll get 'em all,'" said Tikhon, in conclusion, looking gayly and resolutely into Denisof's eyes.

"I'll have you thwashed with a hot hundwed, and then you'll perhaps cease playing the fool," said Denisof, severely.

"What's there to get mad about?" asked Tikhon. "Because I didn't see your Frenchmen. Wait till after it's dark, and then, if you want some, I'll bring in three of 'em."

"Well, come on," said Denisof; and he rode away, angrily scowling, and uttered not a word until he reached the watch-house.

Tikhon followed, and Petya heard the Cossacks laughing with him and at him about the pair of boots that he had flung into the bushes. When he had recovered from the fit of laughing that overmastered him on account of Tikhon's words and queer smile, and he understood in a flash that Tikhon had killed a man, Petya felt uncomfortable.

He glanced at the little drummer, and something wrung his very heart. But this sense of awkwardness lasted only for a second. He felt that he must lift his head again, pluck up his courage, and he asked the esaul with an air of great importance in regard to the morrow's enterprise, so as to be worthy of the company in which he found himself.

The officer who had been sent to find Dolokhof met Denisof on the road with the report that Dolokhof would be there immediately, and that, as far as he was concerned, all was favorable.

Denisof suddenly recovered his spirits, and beckoned Petya to himself.

"Now, tell me all about yourself," said he.

CHAPTER VII

PETYA, on leaving Moscow and saying farewell to his parents, had joined his regiment, and soon after had been appointed orderly to a general who had a large detachment under his command.

Since the time of his promotion to be an officer, and especially his transfer into the active army, with which he had taken part in the battle at Viazma, Petya had been in a chronic state of excitement and delight, because he was now "grown up," and in a chronic state of enthusiastic eagerness not to miss the slightest chance where heroism was to be displayed.

He was much delighted with what he saw and experienced in the army, but, at the same time, it seemed to him that all the chances of heroism were displayed, not where he was, but where he was not. And he was crazy to be on the move all the time.

When, on November second, his general had expressed the desire to send some one to Denisof's division, Petya pleaded so earnestly to be sent, that the general could not refuse. But, the general, remembering Petya's reckless escapade in the battle of Viazma, when, instead of taking the road that had been recommended to him, he galloped off in front of the lines and under the French fire, shooting his pistol twice as he rode, in now letting him go expressly forbade Petya to take part in any of Denisof's enterprises.

That was the reason why Petya had flushed and become confused when Denisof asked him whether he could stay with him.

Until he reached the edge of the forest, Petya had promised himself that he should immediately return, strictly fulfilling his duty as he should do. But when he saw the French, when he saw Tikhon, and learned that during the night there would infallibly be a raid on them, he, with the swift changeableness of youth from one view to another, decided in his own mind that his general, whom till then he had highly respected, was a rubbishy German, that Denisof was a hero, and that the esaul was a hero, and that Tikhon was a hero, and that it would be shameful of him to desert them at such a critical moment.

It was twilight by the time Denisof with Petya and the esaul reached the watch-house. Through the twilight could be seen saddled horses, Cossacks, hussars, shelter-huts set up on the clearing, and the scattered glow of fires built in the forest ravine, so that the smoke might not betray them to the French.

In the entry of the little hovel, a Cossack with sleeves rolled up was cutting up mutton. In the izba itself were three officers of Denisof's band constructing a table out of a door. Petya pulled off his wet clothing, giving it to be dried, and immediately offered his services in helping to set the dinner-table.

Within ten minutes the table was ready, and spread with a cloth and loaded with vodka, a bottle of rum, white bread, and roasted mutton and salt.

Sitting down with the officers at the table, tearing the fat, fragrant mutton with hands from which dripped the tallow, Petya found himself in an enthusiastic, childlike state of affectionate love to all men, and consequently of belief that all men felt the same love toward him.

"Say, what do you think, Vasili Feodorovitch," he asked, turning to Denisof, "should I get into trouble if I stayed with you for a single little day?" And, without waiting for an answer, he went on answering himself, "For you see I was ordered to find out, and I shall find out. .... Only you must send me into the most .... into the chief .... I don't want any reward .... but I want ...."

Petya set his teeth together, and, lifting his head erect, glanced around and waved his hand.

"Into the chief?" .... repeated Denisof, smiling.

"Only please let me have a company; let me command it myself," pursued Petya. "Now, what difference will it make to you? — Akh! would you like a knife?" he asked, turning to an officer who was trying to dissect the mutton. And he handed him his case-knife.

The officer praised the knife.

"Pray keep it. I have several like it...." said Petya, blushing. "Ye saints! I forgot all about it," he suddenly cried. "I have some splendid raisins; quite without seeds, you know. We had a new sutler, and he brought some magnificent things. I bought ten pounds. I like something sweet. Would you like them?".... And Petya ran into the entry where his Cossack was, and brought back a basket containing five pounds of raisins. — "Take them, gentlemen, take them. — I wonder if you want a coffee-pot?" he asked, addressing the esaul. "I bought a splendid one of our sutler. He had magnificent things. And he was very honest. That is the main thing. I will send it to you without fail. And perhaps you are out of flints? Do you need some? I've got some here" — he pointed to his basket — "a hundred flints. I bought them very cheap. Take them, I beg of you, as many as you need, take them all...."

And, suddenly frightened lest he was talking too much, Petya stopped short and colored.

He began to recall whether he had said anything silly, and, while passing the events of the day in review, his mind recurred to the little French drummer. "We are very comfortable here, but how is it with him? What have they done with him? Have they given him anything to eat? I hope they haven't been abusing him," he wondered; but, recognizing that he had gone too far in his offer with the flints, he was now afraid.

"Might I ask?" he queried. "Won't they say, 'He's a boy himself, and of course he pities another boy'? But I'll show them to-morrow what kind of a boy I am. Ought I to be ashamed to ask?" queried Petya. "Well, then, what difference does it make?" and, on the spur of the moment, flushing and giving a timid look at the officers to see whether they would laugh at him, he said : —

"May I call in that lad whom you took prisoner, and give him something to eat?.... May I?"....

"Yes, poor little fellow!" replied Denisof, evidently

seeing nothing to be ashamed of in thus speaking of him. "Call him in. His name is Vincent Bosse. Call him."

"I 'll call him," cried Petya.

"Call him, call him, poor little fellow!" said Denisof.

Petya was already at the door when Denisof said this. Petya made his way among the officers, and swiftly returned to Denisof.

"Let me kiss you, dear,"[1] said he. "Akh! how splendid of you! How kind!" And, after giving Denisof a hearty kiss, he ran out of doors.

"Bosse! Vincent!" called Petya, standing at the door.

"Whom do you want, sir?" asked a voice from the darkness. Petya explained that it was the French lad whom they had taken that day.

"Oh! *Vesennui?*" inquired the Cossack. The lad's name, Vincent, had been already changed by the Cossacks into Vesennui,[2] by the soldiers and muzhiks into Visenya. In each of these variations the reference to spring seemed to have a special appropriateness to the young lad.

"He's there by the fire, warming himself. Hey, Visenya! Visenya! Vesennui!" sounded the voices, passing the call on, mingled with laughter.

"Oh, he's a likely lad," said a hussar standing near Petya. "We just gave him something to eat. He was half starved."

Steps were heard in the darkness, and the drummer boy, with his bare feet slopping through the mud, came up to the door.

"Ah, *c'est vous,*" said Petya. "*Voulez-vous manger? N'avez pas peur! On ne vous fera pas de mal.*— Don't you want something to eat? Don't be afraid; they won't hurt you," he added timidly and cordially, laying his hand on his arm. "*Entrez, entrez.*"

"*Merci, Monsieur!*" replied the drummer, in a trembling voice, almost like that of a child, and he proceeded to wipe his muddy feet on the threshold.

[1] *Galubchik.* [2] The adjective from *Viesna*, spring.

Petya felt like saying many things to the drummer, but he dared not. Passing beyond him, he stood next him in the entry. Then in the darkness he seized his hand and pressed it. "*Entrez, entrez,*" he repeated in an encouraging whisper.

"Akh! what can I do for him, I wonder?" Petya asked himself, and, opening the door, he let the lad pass in front of him into the room.

After the drummer entered the izba, Petya sat down at some distance from him, considering it undignified to pay him too much attention. He merely fumbled the money in his pocket, and was in doubt whether it would not be shameful to give it to the drummer boy.

CHAPTER VIII

FROM the drummer, who, by Denisof's direction, was served with vodka and mutton, and dressed in a Russian kaftan, so that he might remain in his band, and not be sent off with the other prisoners, Petya's attention was diverted by Dolokhof's arrival. He had heard many stories in the army about Dolokhof's phenomenal gallantry, and cruelty to the French, and therefore, from the moment that Dolokhof came in, Petya gazed at him without taking his eyes from him, and held his head high, so as to be worthy even of such society as Dolokhof.

Dolokhof's outward appearance struck Petya strangely, from its simplicity.

While Denisof was dressed in a *chekmen*, or Cossack kaftan, wore a beard, and on his chest a picture of St. Nicholas the Miracle-worker, — *Nikola Chudotvorets*, — and in his manner of speech, in all his ways, manifested the peculiarity of his position, Dolokhof, on the contrary, who had before worn a Persian costume in Moscow, now had the air of a most conceited officer of the Guards.

His face was smooth-shaven, he wore the wadded uniform coat of the Guards, with the George in the buttonhole, and his forage-cap set straight. He re-

moved his wet burka in the corner, and, going directly
up to Denisof, without exchanging greetings with any
one, immediately proceeded to inquire about the business in hand.

Denisof told him about the projects which the large
detachment of troops had formed of attacking the transport train, and about the message which Petya had
brought, and how he had replied to the two generals.

Then Denisof related all that he knew about the position of the French escort.

"So far, so good; but we must know what sort of
troops, and how many they are," said Dolokhof. "We
must enter their lines. If we don't know exactly how
many of them there are, it's no use to attempt the
thing. I like to do such business in good style. Here,
I wonder if any of these gentlemen will go with me
into their camp. I have an extra uniform with me."

"I .... I .... I will go with you!" cried Petya.

"You are pwecisely the one who shall not go," said
Denisof, turning to Dolokhof. "I would not let him
go on any account."

"That's a great note!" cried Petya. "Why can't I
go?"

"Why, because there's no weason why you should."

"Well, now, you will excuse me because .... because
.... but I will go; that's all there is of it!.... You will
take me, won't you?" he asked, addressing Dolokhof.

"Why not?" .... replied Dolokhof, absent-mindedly,
staring into the face of the French drummer.

"Have you had this young lad long?" he asked of
Denisof.

"Took him to-day, but he knows nothing; I kept him
with me."

"Well, now, what do you do with the others?" asked
Dolokhof.

"What should I do? I send them in and get a we-
ceipt," replied Denisof, suddenly reddening. "And I'll
tell you fwankly, that I have not a single man on my
conscience. What's the twouble in sending thirty or
thwee hundwed under escort to the city? I tell you

honestly it's better than to stain the honor of a soldier."

"Let this sixteen-year-old countlet have all these fine
notions," said Dolokhof, with icy ridicule, "but it's time
you gave them up."

"Well, I say nothing of the sort, I only say that I am
certainly going with you," timidly interrupted Petya.

"Yes, it's high time you and I, brother, gave up these
fine notions," insisted Dolokhof, as if he found especial
delight in dwelling on this point which was annoying to
Denisof. "Now, for instance, why did you keep this
one?" he asked, shaking his head. "Why, it was because
you pitied him, wasn't it? We know well enough what
your receipts amount to! You will send a hundred men,
and thirty'll get there! They'll die of starvation or be
killed. So why isn't it just as well not to take any?"

The esaul, snapping his bright eyes, nodded his head
in approval.

"It's all wight; no need of weasoning about it here.
I don't care to take the wesponsibility on my soul. You
say they die on the woad. Well and good. Only 'tisn't
my fault."

Dolokhof laughed. "Haven't they been told twenty
times to take me? And if they should .... or you,
either, with all your chivalry, it would be an even game
.... a rope and the aspen tree!" He paused. "However, we must to work. Have my man bring in my
pack. I have two French uniforms. So you are going
with me, are you?" he asked of Petya.

"I? I?.... yes, certainly!" cried Petya, reddening
till the tears came, and glancing at Denisof.

Again at the time while Dolokhof was discussing with
Denisof as to what should be done with the prisoners,
Petya had that former sense of awkwardness and pre-
cipitancy; but, again, he did not succeed very well in
comprehending what they said. "If grown-up, famous
men have such ideas, of course it must be so, it must be
all right," he said to himself. "But the main thing is
that Denisof must not think that I am going to
listen to him, that he can give orders to me! Certainly

I 'm going to the French camp. If *he* can, of course I can."

To all Denisof's urgings not to go, Petya replied that he was accustomed to do things properly—*akkuratno*—and not at haphazard, and he never thought about personal danger.

"Because — you yourself must acknowledge this — if we don't know pretty well how many there are, the lives of hundreds of us may depend upon it, while here we are alone.... and, besides, I am very anxious to do this, and I am certainly, certainly going, and you must not try to keep me from it," said he; "that would only make it the worse." ....

CHAPTER IX

HAVING put on the French uniforms and shakoes, Petya and Dolokhof rode to the vista from which Denisof had reconnoitered the camp, and, emerging from the forest in absolute darkness, they made their way down into the ravine. On reaching the bottom, Dolokhof ordered the Cossack who accompanied them to wait for them there, and started off at a round trot along the road to the bridge; Petya, his heart in his mouth with excitement, rode by his side.

"If we fall into their clutches, I won't give myself up alive; I have a pistol," whispered Petya.

"Don't speak in Russian!" exclaimed Dolokhof, in a quick whisper, and, at that instant, they heard in the darkness the challenge " *Qui vive ?* " and the click of the musket.

The blood rushed into Petya's face, and he grasped his pistol.

" *Lanciers de 6ᵐᵉ,*" cried Dolokhof, neither hastening nor checking his horse's pace.

The dark figure of the sentinel stood out upon the bridge.

" *Mot d'ordre !* "

Dolokhof reined in his horse, and rode at a foot-pace.

"Tell me, is Colonel Gérard here?" he demanded.

"The countersign," insisted the sentinel, not answering the question, and blocking the way.

"When an officer is making his round, the sentinels do not ask the countersign," cried Dolokhof, suddenly losing his temper, and spurring his horse against the sentinel. "I ask you if the colonel is here?"

And, without waiting for an answer from the sentinel, whom he shouldered out of the way, Dolokhof rode up the slope at a foot-pace.

Perceiving the dark figure of a man crossing the road, Dolokhof halted him, and asked where the commander and the officers were. This man, who had a basket on his shoulder, paused, came close up to Dolokhof's horse, laid his arm on her, and told, in simple, friendly way, that the commander and the officers were higher up on the hill, at the right-hand side, at the "farm," as he called the estate.

After riding along the road, on both sides of which were the bivouac fires, where they could hear the sounds of men talking French, Dolokhof turned into the yard of the manorial mansion. On riding into the gates, he slid off his horse, and went up to a great blazing camp-fire around which sat a number of men talking loudly. In a kettle at the edge of it, something was cooking, and a soldier in a cap and blue capote was on his knees in front of it, his face brightly lighted by the flames, and was stirring it with his ramrod. "*Oh, c'est un dur à cuire* — It's a tough one to cook!" cried one of the officers who were sitting in the shadow in the opposite side.

"*Il fera marcher les lapins* — He'll make the rabbits fly," said another, with a laugh. Both relapsed into silence, and looked out into the darkness at the sounds of Dolokhof and Petya's footsteps, who came up to the fire, leading their horses.

"*Bonjour, messieurs,*" cried Dolokhof, in a loud tone, saluting the officers politely. The officers made a little stir in the shadow by the watch-fire, and a tall man with a long neck, coming around the fire, approached Dolokhof.

"C'est vous, Clément?" he began. *"D'où diable* — where the deuce?" but he did not finish his question, recognizing his mistake, and, slightly frowning, he exchanged greetings with Dolokhof, as with a stranger, asking him in what way he might serve him.

Dolokhof told him that he and his comrade were in search of their regiment, and, addressing the officers in general, he asked them if they knew anything about the sixth regiment.

No one knew anything about it, and it seemed to Petya that the officers began to look suspiciously and with animosity at him and Dolokhof. For several seconds all were silent.

"Si vous comptez sur la soupe du soir, vous venez trop tard — You are too late if you expect soup this evening," said a voice with a suppressed laugh from behind the fire.

Dolokhof explained that they were not hungry, and that they had to go still farther that night. He handed over his horse to the soldier who had been busy over the stew, and squatted down on his heels by the fire, next the long-necked officer. This officer stared at Dolokhof, without taking his eyes from him, and asked him for a second time what regiment he belonged to.

Dolokhof made no reply, affecting not to hear his question; and, as he puffed at the short French pipe which he got out of his pocket, he inquired of the officers how far the road in front of them was free from danger of the Cossacks.

"Les brigands sont partout — They're everywhere!" replied an officer from the other side of the camp-fire.

Dolokhof remarked that the Cossacks were dangerous only for those who were alone, as he and his companion were, but that certainly they would not venture to attack a large detachment — "Would they?" he added dubiously.

All the time Petya, who was standing in front of the fire and listening to the conversation, kept saying to himself, "Now surely he will start."

But Dolokhof once more took up the thread of the conversation which had been dropped, and began to ask them up and down how many men there were in their battalion, how many battalions, how many prisoners. And while asking his questions about the Russian prisoners whom they had in their escort Dolokhof said : —

"Wretched business to drag these corpses around with us. We'd much better shoot this trash," [1] and he laughed aloud with such a strange laugh that it seemed to Petya as if the French would then and there discover the imposition, and he involuntarily took a step from the fire.

No one responded to Dolokhof's remark or his laugh, and a French officer who till then had not showed himself (he had been lying down wrapped up in his capote) raised himself up and whispered something to his comrade. Dolokhof got up and beckoned to the soldier who held his horse.

"Will they let us have the horses or not?" wondered Petya, involuntarily moving nearer to Dolokhof.

The horses were brought.

"*Bonjour, messieurs*," said Dolokhof.

Petya wanted to say "*Bonjour*" as well, but he could not pronounce a word. The officers said something among themselves in a whisper. Dolokhof sat for some time on his horse, which was restive ; then he rode out of the gates at a foot-pace. Petya rode after him, wishing, but not daring, to glance around to see if the French were following him or not.

On striking the road, Dolokhof did not ride back into the fields, but along the village street. In one place he stopped and listened.

"Hark!" said he.

Petya recognized the sound of Russian voices, and saw by the watch-fires the shadowy forms of the Russian prisoners. On reaching the bridge again, Petya and Dolokhof rode past the sentinel, who, not saying a word, was moodily pacing back and forth across the bridge ; and then they plunged into the ravine, where their Cossacks were waiting for them.

---

[1] *La vilaine affaire de trainer ces cadavres après soi. Vaudrait mieux fusiller cette canaille.*

"Well, good-by for now. Tell Denisof at daybreak, at the sound of the first shot," said Dolokhof, and he started to ride away; but Petya seized him by the arm.

"Oh," he cried, "you are such a hero! Akh! how splendid! how glorious! How I like you!"

"All right, all right!" said Dolokhof, but Petya did not let go of him, and in the darkness Dolokhof could just make out that Petya was leaning over toward him. He wanted to kiss him. Dolokhof kissed him laughingly, and, turning his horse, disappeared in the darkness.

CHAPTER X

ON returning to the forest hut, Petya found Denisof in the entry. He had been waiting for him, full of excitement, uneasiness, and self-reproach that he had let him go.

"Thank God — *Slava Bohu!*" he cried. "Now, then, thank God!" he repeated, on hearing Petya's enthusiastic story. "The devil take you. I have n't had a wink of sleep on account of you," exclaimed Denisof. "Well, thank God. Now go and get some sleep. We'll have time for a nap before morning."

"Yes, — but no," said Petya, "I don't want to go to sleep. I know myself too well. If I once get to sleep that's the end of it. And besides, I'm not in the habit of sleeping before a battle."

Petya sat some time in the izba, gleefully recalling the details of his visit, and vividly picturing what would happen on the morrow. Then, observing that Denisof had fallen asleep, he got up and went out of doors.

It was still perfectly dark. It had ceased raining, but the drops were still falling from the trees. Near the hut could be seen the dark forms of the Cossack shelters and their horses picketed together. Behind the hut the dark forms of the two wagons were visible, and next them the horses, and in the gully the dying fire was still glowing red. Not all the Cossacks and hussars

were asleep; occasionally could be heard, together with the sound of the pattering drops, and the horses champing their teeth, low voices, which seemed to be whispering together.

Petya stepped out of the entry, glanced around in the darkness, and approached the wagons. Some one was snoring under the wagons, and near them stood the horses saddled and eating oats.

Petya in the darkness recognized his horse, which he called Karabakh, though it was a Little Russian horse, and he went to him.

"Well, Karabakh, to-morrow we shall see service," said he, putting his face to the horse's nose and kissing it.

"What! barin, are n't you asleep?" asked the Cossack sitting under the wagon.

"No, I .... your name 's Likhatchef,[1] is n't it? You see I 've just come back. We 've been to visit the French."

And Petya gave the Cossack a detailed account, not only of his expedition, but also why he had taken it, and why he considered it much better to risk his own life than to work at haphazard.

"Well, you 'd better get some sleep," said the Cossack.

"No, I 'm used to it," replied Petya. "I wonder if you are out of flints for your pistol? I brought some with me. Wouldn't you like some? Take them!"

The Cossack put his head out from under the wagon to get a closer look at Petya.

"Because I 'm used to doing everything carefully .... *akkuratno* ...." said Petya. "Some never think of making ready beforehand, and they are sorry for it afterwards. I don't like that way."

"That's a fact," said the Cossack.

"I wonder if you 'd be kind enough to sharpen my saber? It got dull " — but Petya could not tell a lie — "it's never been sharpened. Can't you do it for me?"

"Why, of course I can."

Likhatchef got up, fumbled in his pack, and soon

[1] From *Likhatch*, a good driver of horses. Greek, *hippokrates*.

Petya heard the warlike sound of the steel on the stone. He climbed upon the wagon and perched on the edge. The Cossack was sharpening the saber under the wagon.

"Well, are the boys asleep?" asked Petya.

"Some of 'em are asleep, some ain't."

"Well, how about the lad?"

"Who? Vesennui? He's crawled into the hay yonder. Asleep out of sheer fright. I was glad of it."

For a long time after that, Petya said nothing, but listened to the various sounds. Steps were heard approaching in the darkness, and a dark form appeared.

"What are you whetting?" asked a man, coming up to the wagon.

"Whetting this barin's saber."

"Good thing," said the man, whom Petya took to be a hussar. "I wonder if a cup was left over here with you?"

"There it is by the wheel."

The hussar took the cup.

"It'll be daylight soon," he added, yawning, and went off.

Petya might have been supposed to know that he was in the woods with Denisof's party, a verst from the highway, that he was perched on the wagon taken from the French, while around the horses were tethered, and under it sat the Cossack Likhatchef sharpening his saber,—that the great black spot at the right was the guard-house, and the bright red spot below at the left was the dying watch-fire, that the man who came after the cup was a hussar who wanted a drink; but he did not realize this, and had no desire to realize it.

He was in a magic realm, in which nothing resembled the reality.

The great black spot, perhaps, was simply the guard-house, but perhaps it was a cavern leading down into the depths of the earth.

The red spot, perhaps, was a fire, but perhaps it was the eye of a huge monster.

Perhaps he was really perched on the wagon, but very possibly he was sitting not on the wagon, but on a terribly high turret, from which, if he fell, it would take him a whole day, a whole month, to reach the earth — he might fall forever, and never reach it!

Perhaps it was merely the Cossack Likhatchef sitting under the wagon, but very possibly it was the best, kindest, bravest, most glorious, most admirable man in the world, and no one knew it!

Perhaps it was merely a hussar who came after water, and went down the ravine; but perhaps he had disappeared from sight, and vanished absolutely into nothingness.

Nothing that Petya might have seen at that moment would have surprised him. He was in a magic realm, in which everything was possible.

He glanced at the sky. And the sky was as magical a thing as the earth. The sky had begun to clear, and over the tree-tops swiftly scurried the clouds, as it were, unveiling the stars. Sometimes it seemed as if the sky were clearing, and the black depths of clear sky were coming into sight. Sometimes it seemed as if those black spots were clouds. Sometimes it seemed as if the sky were lifted high, high above his head; sometimes the sky stooped down absolutely so that his hand could touch it.

Petya's eyes began to close, and he swayed a little.

Raindrops dropped.[1] Men were talking in low tones. The horses neighed and shook themselves. Some one snored.

Ozhik, zhik, ozhik, zhik — sounded the saber on the whetstone; and suddenly Petya heard a harmonious orchestra playing a solemnly exquisite hymn, which he had never heard before.

Petya had a gift for music, just as Natasha had, and greater than Nikolaï's; but he had never taken music lessons. His mind was not occupied with music, and consequently the themes that entered his mind were to him absolutely new and fascinating.

The orchestra played louder and louder. The air was resolved, transferred from one instrument to another.

[1] *Kapli kapali.*

The result was what is called a fugue, although Petya had not the slightest idea what a fugue was. Each instrument, the one corresponding to the violin, and the one corresponding to the horn, — only better and purer than violin or horn, — each instrument played its own part, and before it had played to the end of the *motif*, blended with another, which began almost the same way, and then with a third, and with a fourth, and then all of them blended in one, and again separated, and again blended, now into something solemnly ecclesiastical, now into something brilliant and triumphant.

" Oh, yes, I must be dreaming," said Petya to himself, as he pitched forward. " It was in my ears. But perhaps it is *my* music! Well, then, once more! Go on, music mine! Now!"

He closed his eyes. And from different directions, as if from a distance, the sounds came trembling, began to fall into rhythmical form, to run into variations, to coalesce, and once more they united in the same sweet and solemn triumphal hymn.

"Akh! this is so exquisite. Truly as I wish and what I wish," said Petya to himself. He tried to direct this vast orchestra of instruments.

" Now, more softly, more softly; let it almost die away!"

And the sounds obeyed him.

" Now, then, fuller, more gayly. Still more, still more jollity!"

And from unknown depths arose the triumphant strains in vastly fuller volume.

" Now, voices, join in!" commanded Petya.

And at first far away he heard the voices of men, then of women. The voices grew in regular gradations into solemn power. Petya felt a mixture of terror and joy in recognizing their extraordinary loveliness.

With the solemn strains of the triumphal march blended the song, and the raindrops dropped, and with its *Vzhik, zhik, zhik*, rang the saber, and again the horses stirred and neighed, not disturbing the chorus, but rather blending with it.

Petya knew not how long this lasted; he enjoyed it, was all the time amazed at his enjoyment of it, and regretted that there was no one to share it with him.

He was awakened by Likhatchef's affectionate voice.

"Ready, your nobility; you can split two Frenchmen[1] with it."

Petya grew wide awake.

"It's getting light; truly it's growing light!" he cried. The horses, before invisible, could now be plainly seen, and through the bare limbs of the forest trees gleamed a watery light.

Petya shook himself, sprang down, got a silver ruble out of his pocket, and gave it to Likhatchef, and, after brandishing his sword, he examined the blade, and pushed it into the sheath.

The Cossacks were beginning to untie their horses and tighten their girths.

"Here is the commander," said Likhatchef.

From the guard-house came Denisof, and, nodding to Petya, gave orders to get ready.

CHAPTER XI

IN the twilight of the dawn the horses were speedily brought out, saddle-girths were tightened, and the men fell into line.

Denisof stood by the hut, giving the final directions. The infantry detachment, with their hundreds of feet splashing at once, marched ahead along the road, and were soon hidden from sight among the trees in the dawn-lighted mist.

The esaul gave some command to his Cossacks. Petya held his horse by the bridle, impatiently await-ing the signal to mount. His face, which had been laved in cold water, and especially his eyes, glowed with fire; a cold shiver ran down his back, and his whole body shook with a rapid, nervous trembling.

---

[1] He calls *Frantsus, Khrantsus.*

"Well, are you all ready?" asked Denisof. "To horse!"

The horses were brought out. Denisof scolded his Cossack because his saddle-girth was loose, and, after tightening it, he mounted. Petya put his foot in the stirrup. His horse, as was his wont, tried to bite his leg; but Petya, not conscious of his weight, quickly sprang into the saddle, and, looking at the long line of hussars stretching away into the darkness, rode up to Denisof.

"Vasili Feodorovitch, you'll give me some charge, won't you? Please .... *vadi Boga* — for God's sake!" .... said he.

Denisof seemed to have forgotten about Petya's existence. He glanced at him.

"I'll ask you one thing," said he, severely, "to obey me and to mind your own business."

During all the march Denisof said not a word further to Petya, and rode in silence.

When they reached the edge of the forest the morning light was spreading over the fields. Denisof held a whispered consultation with the esaul, as the Cossacks rode past Petya and him. When they had all filed by, Denisof turned his horse and rode down the slope. The horses, sitting back on their haunches, and sliding, let themselves and their riders down into the ravine. Petya rode by Denisof's side. The trembling over his whole frame kept increasing.

It was growing lighter and lighter. Only distant objects were still concealed in the fog. On reaching the bottom, Denisof, after glancing back, nodded to a Cossack standing near him.

"The signal," he cried.

The Cossack raised his hand. A shot rang out, and at the same instant they heard the trampling hoofs of the horses simultaneously dashing forward, and yells in different directions, and more shots.

At the instant that the first sounds of the trampling hoofs and the yells broke upon the silence, Petya, giving a cut to his horse, and letting him have full rein, galloped forward, not heeding Denisof, who called him back.

It seemed to Petya that at the moment he heard the musket-shot it suddenly became perfectly light, like mid-day. He galloped up to the bridge. In front of him, along the road, the Cossacks were dashing ahead. On the bridge he knocked up against a Cossack who had been left behind, but still he galloped on. In front of him he saw some men — they must be the French — running from the right side of the road to the left. One fell in the mud under the feet of Petya's horse.

Around one izba a throng of Cossacks were gathered doing something. From the midst of the throng arose a terrible shriek. Petya galloped up to this throng, and the first thing that he saw was a Frenchman's white face, his lower jaw trembling. He was clutching the shaft of a lance directed at his breast.

"Hurrah!.... boys. .... Ours!" yelled Petya, and, giving free rein to his excited horse, he flew up the street.

In front of him shots were heard. Cossacks, hussars, and tattered Russian prisoners, running from both sides of the road, were incoherently shouting something at the top of their voices. A rather youthful Frenchman, with-out his cap, and with a red, scowling face, in a blue ca-pote, was defending himself with his bayonet from the hussars.

When Petya reached there he was already fallen.

"Too late again!" flashed through Petya's head, and he dashed off where the shots were heard the thickest. This was in the yard of the manor-house, where he had been the night before with Dolokhof. The French had intrenched themselves behind the hedge and in the park, where the bushes had grown up dense and wild, and they were firing at the Cossacks clustering around the gates. On reaching the gates, Petya, through the gunpowder smoke, saw Dolokhof, with a pale greenish face, shouting something to his men.

"At their flank! Wait for the infantry!" he was yelling, just as Petya rode up.

"Wait?.... Hurra-a-a-ah!" yelled Petya; and he,

without waiting a single instant, rode up to the very place where the shots were heard, and where the gunpowder smoke was densest. A volley rang out; the bullets fell thick and fast, and did their work. The Cossacks and Dolokhof followed Petya through the gates. The Frenchmen could be seen through the thick, billowing smoke, some throwing down their arms and coming out from behind the bushes to meet the Cossacks, others running down the slope to the pond.

Petya still rode his horse at a gallop around the manor-house dvor, but, instead of guiding him by the bridle, he was waving both his hands in the strangest, wildest manner, and was leaning more and more to one side of the saddle. His horse, coming on the camp-fire, which was smoldering in the morning light, stopped short, and Petya fell heavily on the wet ground. The Cossacks saw his arms and legs twitch, although his head was motionless. A bullet had struck him in the head.

Dolokhof, after a moment's conversation with an old French officer, who came out of the house with a handkerchief on his sword, and explained that they surrendered, dismounted and went to Petya, lying there motionless, with outstretched arms.

"Done up," he said, scowling; and he went to the gates to meet Denisof, who was coming toward him.

"Killed!" cried Denisof, seeing, while still at a distance, the unquestionably hopeless position, only too well known to him, in which Petya's body lay.

"Done up," repeated Dolokhof, as if the repetition of this word gave him some satisfaction; and he hastened to the prisoners around whom the Cossacks were crowding. "We can't take him," he called back to Denisof.

Denisof made no reply. He rode up to Petya, dismounted, and with trembling hands turned Petya over, looked at his face, already turned pale, and stained with blood and mud.

"I like something sweet. Splendid raisins, take them all," occurred to him. And the Cossacks, with amazement, looked around as they heard the sound,

like the barking of a dog, with which Denisof quickly
turned away, went to the hedge, and clutched it.

Among the Russian prisoners released by Denisof
and Dolokhof was Pierre Bezukhoï.

CHAPTER XII

CONCERNING the party of prisoners to which Pierre belonged at the time of the general exodus from Moscow,
the French commanders had made no new dispensation.

On the third of November this party found itself with
a different escort and with a different train of wagons
from the one with which they had left Moscow.

One half of the provision train, which had followed
them during the first stages of the march, had been
captured by the Cossacks; the other half had gone on
ahead. The cavalrymen without horses, who had
marched in the van, had every one disappeared; not one
was left. The artillery, which during the first stages
had been visible in front of them, was now replaced by
Marshal Junot's huge baggage wagons, under the escort
of Westphalians. Behind the prisoners rode a train of
cavalry appurtenances.

After leaving Viazma the French troops, which before had marched in three columns, now proceeded in
perfect confusion. The symptoms of disorder which
Pierre had observed in the first halting-place out of
Moscow had now reached its final stage. The road
along which they had passed was strewn on both sides
with dead horses. Ragged men, stragglers from the
different commands, constantly shifting about, now
joined, then again fell out of, the moving columns.

Several times during the march there were false
alarms, and the soldiers of the convoy raised their muskets, fired them, and ran headlong, pushing one another; but then again they would form and revile each
other for the needless panic.

These three divisions which proceeded in company —
the cavalry stores, or *dépôt*, the detachment of the

wounded, and Junot's baggage — still constituted a separate and complete body, but each of them was rapidly melting away.

In the department, to which at first one hundred and twenty teams belonged, now remained no more than sixty ; the rest had been captured or abandoned. A number of wagons of Junot's train had also been left behind and captured. Three teams had been rifled by stragglers from Davoust's corps.

From the talk of the Germans, Pierre gathered that this train was more strongly guarded than that of the prisoners, and that one of their comrades, a German soldier, had been shot by order of the marshal himself because he had been found with one of the marshal's silver spoons in his possession.

The number of prisoners had melted away more than any of the three divisions. Out of three hundred and thirty men who had left Moscow, now remained less than one hundred. The prisoners were more of a nuisance to the soldiers of the convoy than were the saddles of the cavalry stores or than Junot's baggage.

The saddles and Junot's spoons, they understood, might be of some advantage to some one ; but why cold and hungry soldiers should stand guard and watch over equally cold and hungry Russians, who died and were abandoned on the way, whom they were commanded to shoot down, was not only incomprehensible, but even repulsive.

And the men of the convoy, as if they were apprehensive that in the cruel position in which they found themselves they should give way to the real feeling of pity which they felt for the prisoners, and thus make their own condition harder, treated them with peculiar gruffness and severity.

At Dorogobuzh, while the soldiers of the convoy went off to plunder some of their own stores, and locked the prisoners in a barn, several of the Russian soldiers dug out under the walls and escaped; but they were caught by the French and shot.

The order which had been observed on the departure

from Moscow, of keeping the officers from the other prisoners, had for some time been disregarded : all those who could march went together, and Pierre after the third march was again brought into the company of Karatayef and the short-legged pink dog, which had chosen Karatayef as her master.

Karatayef, on the third day out from Moscow, had a relapse of the same fever from which he had suffered in the Moscow hospital, and as he grew worse Pierre avoided him. He knew not why it was, but from the time that Karatayef began to fail, Pierre found himself obliged to exercise great self-control to be near him. And when he approached him, and heard the low groans which he kept up all the time when they were in camp, and smelt the odor which now more powerfully than ever exhaled from Karatayef, Pierre avoided him as far as possible, and kept him out of his mind.

During his imprisonment in the hut, Pierre was made aware, not by his reason, but by his whole being, by life, that man is created for happiness, that happiness is in himself, in the satisfaction of the simple needs of humanity, and that all unhappiness arises, not from lack, but from superfluity.

But now, during these last three weeks of the march, he had learned still another new and consoling truth — he had learned that there is nothing terrible in the world. He had learned that just as there was no position in the world in which a man would be happy and absolutely free, so also there was no position in which a man would be unhappy and unfree.

He had learned that suffering has its limits, and that freedom has its limits, and that these limits are very near together; that the man who suffered because one leaf on his bed of roses was crumpled, suffered just as much as he now suffered sleeping on the cold, damp ground, one side roasting, the other freezing; that when he used to wear his dancing-pumps too tight, he suffered just as much as he suffered now in going barefooted, — his shoes were entirely worn out, — with his feet covered with sores.

He had learned that when he, as it seemed to him by his own free will, married his wife, he was not really any more free than now, when he was shut up for the night in a stable.

Of all that which he afterwards called sufferings, but which at the time he scarcely felt, the worst was from his bare, bruised, scurvy-scarred feet.

The horse-flesh was palatable and nourishing, the salt-peter odor of the gunpowder which they used instead of salt was even pleasant; the weather was not very cold; in the daytime while marching it was even warm, but at night they had bivouac fires; the vermin which fed upon him warmed his body.

The one thing hard at that time was the state of his feet.

On the second day of the retreat, Pierre, examining his sores by the fire, felt that it was impossible to take another step on them; but when all got up, he went along treading gingerly, and afterwards, when he was warmed to it, he walked without pain, though when evening came it was more terrible than ever to look at his feet. But he did not look at them, and turned his thoughts to other things.

Now for the first time Pierre realized all man's power of vitality, and the saving force of abstracting the attention, which, like the safety-valve in the steam-engine, lets off the excess of steam as soon as the pressure exceeds the normal.

He saw not and heard not how the prisoners who straggled were shot down, although more than a hundred had perished in this way. He thought not of Karatayef, who grew weaker every day, and was evidently fated to suffer the same lot. Still less Pierre thought of himself. The more trying his position, the more appalling the future, the more disconnected with the position in which he found himself, the more joyful and consoling were the thoughts, recollections, and visions which came to him.

CHAPTER XIII

At noon of the third, Pierre was climbing up a muddy, slippery hill, looking at his feet and at the inequalities of the road.

Occasionally his eyes glanced at the familiar throng around him, and then back to his feet again. Both the one and the other were peculiarly connected with his individual impressions.

The pink, bandy-legged Sierui was frolicking by the side of the road, occasionally lifting up her hind leg, as a sign of her agility and jollity, flying along on three legs, and then again on all four darting off to bark at the crows, which were feasting on the carrion. Sierui was more frolicsome and in better condition than she had been in Moscow. On all sides lay the flesh of various animals — men as well as horses — in various degrees of putrefaction, and the constant passing of people did not permit of the wolves approaching, so that Sierui was able to get all that she wanted to eat.

It had been raining since morning, and if for a moment it seemed that it was passing over and the skies were going to clear, instantly after such a short respite the downpour would be heavier than ever. The road was perfectly soaked, and could not absorb any more water, and little brooks ran along the ruts.

Pierre plodded along, looking at one side, counting his steps by threes, and doubling down his fingers. Apostrophizing the rain, he kept repeating mentally, "Rain, rain, please not come again." [1]

It seemed to him that he was not thinking of anything ; but in the depths of his mind, remote, there were grave and comforting thoughts. They were the direct spiritual outcome of his yesterday evening's conversation with Karatayef.

The evening before, while they were halting for the night, Pierre, after half freezing at a fire that had gone out, had got up and gone over to a neighboring camp-

[1] *Nu ka, nu ka, yeshcho, yeshcho naddai !*

fire that was burning more brightly. Near this fire to which Pierre went, Platon was sitting with his head wrapped up in his cloak as if it were a chasuble, and was telling the soldiers, in his fluent, agreeable, but weak and sickly voice, a story which Pierre had often heard.

It was already after midnight. This was the time when Karatayef usually recovered from his paroxysms of fever, and became peculiarly lively.

On approaching the camp-fire and hearing Platon's weak, sickly voice, and seeing his pathetic face brightly lighted up by the fire, something unpleasantly pricked Pierre's heart. He was alarmed by his feeling of pity for the man, and wanted to go away; but there was no other camp-fire, and Pierre, trying not to look at Platon, sat down by the bivouac fire.

"Well, how is your health?" he asked.

"Health? Even if you weep for illness, God does not send death," said Karatayef, and instantly resumed the story he was telling.

"So, then, my dear brother," Platon went on, with a smile illumining his thin, pale face, and with a gleam of peculiar delight in his eyes, — "so, then, my dear brother...."

Pierre had heard this story a long time before; Karatayef had related it half a dozen times to him alone, and always with a peculiar feeling of pleasure. But, well as Pierre knew it, he now listened to it as if it were something new, and that genial enthusiasm which Karatayef evidently felt in relating it communicated itself to Pierre.

It was the story of an old merchant who lived a moral, God-fearing life with his family, and who once set out with a friend of his, a rich merchant, on a pilgrimage to the shrine of St. Makarii.

They put up one night at an inn, and the two merchants retired to bed; and the next morning, the merchant's companion was found robbed and with his throat cut. The bloody knife was found under the old merchant's pillow. The old merchant was tried, knouted, and after his nostrils had been slit — "as was proper according to the law," said Karatayef — was sent to hard labor.

"So, then, my brother," — it was at this place that Pierre had interrupted Platon's story, — "ten years or more passed. The good old man lives in the mines. He submits as in duty bound; never does any one any harm. Only he prays to God to let him die. Very good. One time the convicts were gathered together — it was night — just as if it had been you and I, and the good old man was with 'em. And they were telling each other what they had been punished for, and of what they were guilty before God. They began to confess, one that he had murdered a man[1]; another, two; a third that he had set a house on fire; another that he had been a deserter, and so on. Then they began to ask the old man: 'And you, grandsire, what are you being punished for?' — 'I, my dear friends,'[2] says he, 'am punished for my own sins, and for the sins of others. I never killed a soul, I never stole from any one; instead, I used to give to any needy brother. I, my dear friends, was a merchant, and I had a large property.' And so on and so on, he tells the whole story, of course, just as it happened. 'I don't complain,' says he. 'Of course, God did it to search me. Only,' says he, 'I am sorry for my old woman and my children.' And then the old man began to cry. It happened the very man who had murdered the merchant, you know, was there in that company. 'Where was it, grandsire, it happened? When? What month?' He asked all about it. His heart stung him. And so he goes up to the old man and falls at his feet. 'You were punished all on my account, you good old man,' says he. 'That's the truth, the honest truth. It's a fact, boys[3]; this man is innocent, and has been punished for my crime,' says he. 'I did it myself,' says he, 'and I put the knife under your pillow while you was asleep. Forgive me, grandsire,' says he, 'for Christ's sake!'"

[1] *Dusha*, a soul.   [2] *Bratsui moï milenkiye*, brothers mine dear.
[3] *Rebyatushki*, little children.

Karatayef paused, joyously smiling, and as he gazed into the fire he straightened the logs.

"And the good old man says, 'God will forgive you, but we are all of us,' says he, 'sinners before God. I suffer for your sin.' He wept bitter tears. And what think you, friend,[1]" exclaimed Karatayef, with a radiant, beatific smile lighting his face more and more, as if what he had now to relate included the main charm and all the significance of the story, "what think you, friends! this murderer revealed the whole thing to the authorities. 'I,' says he, 'I have killed six souls,' — he was a great villain! — 'but what I regret more than all is this good old man. Let him not weep any longer on my account.' He explained the whole matter; they took it down, sent off the paper in proper shape. It's a long way off, and it was a long time before the matter was decided, and before all the papers were written as they had to be, as it always is with the authorities. It reached the Tsar. And then came the ukase: 'Let the merchant go; give him a present, whatever they may decide.' The document came; they tried to find the poor old man. Where is the poor old man who was innocent and suffered so long? A document has come from the Tsar. They began to search for him." Karatayef's lower jaw trembled. "But God had forgiven him — he was dead. That was the way of it, friends,"[2] concluded Karatayef, and for a long time he sat looking into the fire, with a smile on his lips.

It was not so much this story itself, but its mysterious meaning, the solemn joy that irradiated Karatayef's face as he related it, the mysterious significance of this joy, which filled Pierre's soul with a vague sense of joy.

[1] *Sokolik*, a hawk.
[2] "A Long Exile" is a variant of this same story, told by Count Tolstoï for children.

CHAPTER XIV

"*À vos places!*" suddenly cried a voice.

A glad stir and expectation of something good and solemn awoke among the prisoners and convoy. On all sides were heard shouts of command, and at the left suddenly appeared handsomely dressed cavalrymen, trotting by the prisoners, on handsome horses. All faces wore that expression of tension which is usually seen in the neighborhood of important personages.

The prisoners were collected and pushed out of the road; the soldiers formed in line.

"*L'empereur! l'empereur! Le maréchal! Le duc!*" and as soon as the plump horses of the mounted escort dashed by, a coach drawn by six gray steeds thundered past. Pierre, as by a flash, caught sight of the calm, handsome, plump but pale face of a man in a three-cornered hat.

This was one of the marshals.

The marshal's eye rested on Pierre's rotund, noticeable figure, and the expression with which the marshal scowled and turned away his face made it evident to Pierre that he felt sympathy and wanted to hide it.

The general in charge of the division galloped after the carriage, with a red, frightened face, spurring on his lean horse. Several officers gathered together; the soldiers pressed around them. All faces wore an expression of excitement and tension.

"*Qu'est-ce qu'il a dit? qu'est-ce qu'il a dit?*—What did he say?" Pierre heard them asking.

While the marshal had been passing, the prisoners had been gathered in a clump, and Pierre noticed Karatayef, whom he had not seen since early that morning. Karatayef in his short cloak was leaning up against a birch tree. While his face still bore that expression of joyful emotion which it had had the evening before, when telling the story of the merchant's unmerited punishment, it was lighted up by an expression of gentle solemnity.

Karatayef looked at Pierre out of his kindly round

eyes, which were now full of tears, and he seemed to be calling him to him, as if he wanted to say something. But Pierre felt quite too terribly about himself. He affected not to see him, and hastened away.

When the prisoners were set on their march again, Pierre glanced back. Karatayef was sitting by the edge of the road, under the birch tree, and two Frenchmen were discussing about something over him. Pierre did not look longer. He passed on his way, limping up the hill.

From the place where Karatayef had been left behind, the report of a musket-shot was heard. Pierre distinctly heard this report, but at the instant he heard it he recollected that he had not finished his calculation how many stages there were to Smolensk, a calculation in which he had been interrupted by the arrival of the marshal. And he proceeded with his counting.

The two French soldiers, one of whom held the smoking musket which he had just discharged, ran past Pierre. Both of them were pale, and in the expression of their faces — one of them looked timidly at Pierre — there was something that reminded him of the young soldier who had been executed.

Pierre looked at this soldier, and remembered how this private, a few days before they had started, had burned his shirt as he was drying himself by the campfire, and how they had made sport of him.

The dog stayed behind, and was howling around the place where Karatayef was left.

"What a fool! what is she barking about?" Pierre exclaimed inwardly.

The soldiers, Pierre's comrades, walking in file with him, like him did not look back to the place where first the shot and then the howl of the dog was heard, but a stern expression settled on all their faces.

CHAPTER XV

THE provision train and the prisoners and the marshal's baggage wagons were halting at the village of Shamsheva. All gathered in groups around the bivouac fires. Pierre went to a camp-fire, and, after eating some roasted horse-flesh, lay down with his back to the fire and instantly fell asleep. He slept the same kind of sleep which he had slept at Mozhaïsk after Borodino.

Once more real events mingled with visions, and once more some one, either himself or some other person, uttered thoughts, even the same thoughts which had been spoken to him at Mozhaïsk.

"Life is everything. Life is God. Everything changes and is in a state of flux, and this movement is God. And as long as there is life, there is enjoyment of the self-consciousness of the Divinity. To love life is to love God. More difficult and more blessed than all else is it to love this life in its sufferings, in undeserved sufferings."

"Karatayef!" occurred to Pierre.

And suddenly there seemed to be standing before Pierre, as if alive, a dear little old man, long forgotten, who in Switzerland had taught Pierre geography.

"Wait," said the little man. And he showed Pierre a globe. This globe was a living, rolling ball, and had no natural divisions. The whole surface of the globe consisted of drops closely squeezed together. And these drops were all in motion, changing about, sometimes several coalescing into one, sometimes one breaking up into many. Each drop tried to expand, to occupy as much space as possible; but others, striving for the same end, crushed it, sometimes annihilated it, sometimes coalesced with it.

"Such is life," said the little old teacher.

"How simple and how clear," thought Pierre. "Why is it I never knew this before?"

"In the center is God, and each drop strives to spread out, to expand, so as to reflect Him in the largest pos-

sible proportions.   And each expands, and coalesces,
and is pressed down, and is to all outward appearance
annihilated, and sinks into the depths and comes out
again."

"That was the case with Karatayef ; he overflowed
and vanished."

"*Vous avez compris, mon enfant*—you understand now,
my boy!" said the teacher.

"*Vous avez compris !   Sacré nom !*—You understand?
The devil take you!" cried a voice, and Pierre awoke.

He sat up.   Squatting on his heels by the camp-fire
sat a Frenchman who had just been pushing away a
Russian soldier, and was now broiling a piece of meat
stuck on a ramrod.   His muscular, red hand, covered
with hairs, with short fingers, was skilfully twirling the
ramrod.   His cinnamon-colored, scowling face and
knitted brows could be clearly seen in the light of the
coals.

"*Ça lui est bien égal*—It's all the same to him," he
growled out, addressing the soldier standing near him.
"*Brigand !   Va !*"

And the soldier, twirling the ramrod, glared gloomily
at Pierre.   Pierre turned away and gazed into the darkness.

A Russian soldier, one of the prisoners, the very same
whom the Frenchman had pushed away, was sitting by
the fire and was patting something with his hand.
Looking closer, Pierre recognized that it was the little
bandy-legged, pink dog, which was wagging her tail as
she crouched down next the soldier.

"Ah!   She's come, has she?" said Pierre, "but
Plat...." he began, but did not finish the name.

Suddenly in his imagination, all blended together, —
the recollection of the look which Platon had given him
as he sat under the tree, the shot which he had heard at
that same place, the howling of the dog, the guilty faces
of the two Frenchmen who hastened past him, the
empty, smoking musket, Karatayef left behind at that
halting-place, — and this now made him realize that
Platon was dead, but at the same instant, suggested by

God knows what, there arose in his mind the recollection of an evening that he had spent in company with a Polish beauty one summer, on the balcony of his mansion at Kief. And, nevertheless, without making any effort to coördinate his recollections, and drawing no conclusions from them, Pierre closed his eyes, and the vision of the summer scene mingled with his recollections of bathing, of the fluid, rolling globe, and he seemed to be sinking in water, so that the water went over his head.

Before sunrise he was wakened by loud and frequent firing and shouts. The French were flying past him.

"*Les Cosaques!*" cried one of them, and in a moment Pierre was surrounded by a throng of Russians.

It was some time before Pierre could realize what had happened to him. On all sides he heard the joyful vociferations of his comrades. "Brothers! comrades! friends!" shouted old soldiers, and burst into tears as they embraced Cossacks and hussars. Cossacks and hussars surrounded the prisoners and made haste to offer them, — one man, clothes; another, shoes; another, bread.

Pierre stood in the midst of them, sobbing, and could not speak a word. He threw his arms around the first soldier whom he met, and kissed him, weeping.

Dolokhof stood at the gates of the dilapidated mansion, watching the throng of the disarmed French file past him. The Frenchmen, excited by all that had occurred, were talking loudly among themselves; but when they passed Dolokhof, who stood lightly flecking his boots with his *nagaïka*, or short whip, and watched them with his cool, glassy glance, that boded them nothing good, their voices were hushed. On the other side stood Dolokhof's Cossack, and counted the prisoners, scoring them in hundreds on the gate with a bit of chalk.

"How many?" asked Dolokhof of the Cossack who was counting the prisoners.

"Into the second hundred," replied the Cossack.

"*Filez, filez !* — Step on, step on!" exclaimed Dolo-khof, who had learned this expression of the French; and, as his eyes met those of the prisoners who filed past, they lighted with a cruel gleam.

Denisof, with a gloomy face, walked bareheaded behind the Cossacks who were carrying the body of Petya Rostof to a grave which they had dug in the garden.

CHAPTER XVI

AFTER the ninth of November, when hard frosts began, the flight of the French assumed a still more tragic character, because of the many who perished of the cold or were burned to death at the camp-fires, while the emperor, kings, and dukes continued to pursue their homeward way wrapped in furs and riding in carriages, and carrying the treasure that they had stolen.

But in its real essence, the process of flight and dissolution of the army had not really changed.

From Moscow to Viazma the seventy-three thousand composing the French army, not counting the Guard, — which throughout the whole war had done nothing except pillage, — the seventy-three thousand of the army were reduced to thirty-six thousand. Out of the number lost, not more than five thousand perished in battle. This is the first term of a progression whereby, with mathematical accuracy, the succeeding terms are determined.

The French army melted away and was destroyed in the same proportion from Moscow to Viazma, from Viazma to Smolensk, from Smolensk to the Beresina, from the Beresina to Vilna, independently of the greater or less degree of cold, the pursuit of the Russians, the obstruction of the road, and all other conditions taken singly.

After Viazma, the French armies, instead of marching in three columns, went in one crowd, and thus proceeded to the end.

Berthier wrote to his sovereign (it is well known how far commanders allow themselves to depart from the truth in describing the position of their armies). — He wrote : —

I think it my duty to acquaint your majesty with the condition of the troops in the different army corps that I have observed during these last three days in the various stages. They are almost disbanded.   Less than a fourth of the soldiers, at most, remain under the standards.   This proportion holds in nearly all the regiments.   The others are straggling off by themselves in different directions, trying to find provisions and to escape from discipline.   All of them look to Smolensk as the place where they will retrieve themselves.   During the last few days many soldiers have been noticed throwing away their cartridges and muskets.   In this condition of things, the interests of your majesty's service require that, whatever your ultimate plans may be, the army should be rallied at Smolensk, and rid of non-combatants, of unmounted cavalrymen, of superfluous baggage, and of a portion of the artillery, since it is no longer in proportion to the effective of the army.   Moreover, the soldiers require some days of rest and supplies of food, for they are worn out by hunger and fatigue ; many in the last few days have died on the road or in bivouac.   This state of things is constantly growing worse, and there is danger that, if remedies are not promptly applied, the troops could not be controlled in case of battle. — November 9, at thirty versts from Smolensk.[1]

---

[1] *'Je crois devoir faire connaître à Votre Majesté l'état de ses troupes dans les différents corps d'armée que j'ai été à même d'observer depuis deux ou trois jours dans différents passages.   Elles sont presque débandées.   Le nombre des soldats qui suivent les drapeaux est en proportion du quart au plus dans presque tous les regiments, les autres marchent isolément dans différentes directions et pour leur compte, dans l'espérance de trouver des subsistances et pour se débarrasser de la discipline.   En général ils regardent Smolensk comme la point où ils doivent se refaire.   Ces derniers jours on a remarqué que beaucoup de soldats jettent leurs cartouches et leurs armes. Dans cette état de choses, l'interêt du service de Votre Majesté exige, quelles que soient ses vues ultérieures, qu'on rallie l'armée à Smolensk en commençant à la débarrasser des non-combattants, tels que hommes demontés et des bagages inutiles et du matériel de l'artillerie qui n'est plus en proportion avec les forces actuelles.   En outre les jours de repos, des subsistances sont nécessaires aux soldats qui sont extenués par la faim et la fatigue ; beaucoup sont morts ces derniers jours sur la route et dans les bivacs.   Cet état de choses va *oujours en augmentant et donne lieu de craindre que si l'on n'y prête un prompt remède, on ne soit plus maître des troupes dans un combat. — Le 9 Novembre, à 30 verstes de Smolensk.*

Rushing into Smolensk, which was to them like the promised land, the French fought with one another for food, pillaged their own stores, and, when everything had been plundered, they hurried on.

All fled, not knowing whither or why; and Napoleon, with all his genius, knew less than others why they did so, for no one ordered him to fly.

But, nevertheless, he and those around him observed their old habits: wrote orders, letters, reports, *ordres du jour*, and they addressed one another as — *Sire, Mon Cousin, Prince d'Eckmühl, Roi de Naples*, etc.

But these orders and reports were only on paper; nothing was done according to them, because they could no longer be carried out; and though they continued to call each other Majesty, Highness, and Cousin, they all felt that they were miserable wretches, who had done much evil, and that expiation had begun. And, though they pretended to be very solicitous about the army, each of them thought only of himself and how he might get off and escape as speedily as possible.

CHAPTER XVII

THE actions of the Russian and French troops during the retreat from Moscow to the Niemen were like the game of *zhmurki*, or blind-man's-buff, where the two players have their eyes bandaged, and one of them rings a bell from time to time, to call the attention of the "catcher."

At first, the one who is to be caught sounds his bell without fear of the enemy; but when the pursuer is coming close to him, he seeks to evade his pursuer by going noiselessly, and often, when he thinks he is escaping, he runs directly into his arms.

At first Napoleon's troops let themselves be heard from — this was during the first period of their movement on the Kaluga road; but afterwards, when they had gone back to the Smolensk road, holding the clapper of the bell, they fled, and, while believing that they were escaping, they ran straight into the hands of the Russians.

Owing to the speed with which the French ran and the Russians pursued, and the consequent exhaustion of the horses, the chief method of ascertaining the position of an enemy — reconnoissance by cavalry — became impossible. Moreover, owing to the numerous and rapid changes of position in both armies, information, such as it was, always came too late.

If the news came on one day that the enemy's army was at such and such a place the night before, on the next day, by the time that anything could be undertaken, this army would have already made a two days' march and occupied an entirely different position.

One army fled, the other pursued. From Smolensk the French had a choice among many different routes, and it would seem as if, during their four days' halt there, they might have found out where the enemy was, and might have adopted some advantageous plan, and tried some other way.

But after the four days' rest the army hastened on in throngs, turning neither to the right nor to the left, and without manœuvers or combinations following the beaten track along their former route — the worst of all — that of Krasnoye and Orsha.

Thinking always that the enemy was behind and not before them, the French hastened on, spreading out and scattering often twenty-four hours' march from one another.

At the head of the whole army ran the emperor, then the kings, then the dukes.

The Russian army, believing that Napoleon would turn to the right toward the Dnieper, which was the only reasonable route, themselves turned to the right, and followed the main road toward Krasnoye.

And here, just as in the game of blind-man's-buff, the French ran against our advance-guard.

Having thus unexpectedly caught sight of the enemy, the French were confused, and paused in astonishment and fright, only to resume their flight, abandoning their comrades who followed them. There, for three days, the separate fragments of the French army, first the viceroy's, then Davoust's, then Ney's, one after the other, as it were, ran a gauntlet of the Russian troops.

They all abandoned one another, they all abandoned their heavy possessions, — the artillery, half of their forces, — and took to flight, marching only by night and in detours, so as to avoid the Russians.

Ney, who came last (because, in spite of their wretched condition, or rather in consequence of it, since, like the boy, he wanted to beat the floor on which he had been hurt, he had stopped to blow up the unoffending walls of Smolensk), — Ney, coming last, rejoined Napoleon at Orsha with only one thousand men out of the ten thousand of his corps. Having abandoned all his soldiers and all his artillery, he had succeeded in secretly making his way through the woods by night, and crossing the Dnieper.

From Orsha they hastened onward, taking the road to Vilna, in exactly the same way, playing blind-man's-buff with the pursuing army.

At the Beresina again they were thrown into confusion. Many were drowned, many gave themselves up; but those who got across the river still hastened on.

Their chief commander wrapped himself up in his furs, got into a sledge, and, abandoning his companions, galloped off alone.

Those who could escaped the same way; those who could not surrendered or perished.

CHAPTER XVIII

It would seem as if, during this period of the campaign, while the French were doing everything possible to ruin themselves, while in no single movement of this mass of men, beginning with its detour on the Kaluga road up to the flight of Napoleon, was there one gleam of sense, — it would seem as if those historians who consider the action of the masses subservient to the will of

a single man might find it impossible to make this retreat fit in with their theory.

But no! Mountains of books have been written by
historians about this campaign, and Napoleon's plans
and dispositions, the manœuvers executed by the troops,
and the genius shown by the marshals in their measures
have been characterized as profound.

The retreat from Malo-Yaroslavetz — that useless
retreat by a devastated route, when he was offered one
through a well-supplied region, when he might have
taken the parallel road by which Kutuzof afterwards
pursued him — is explained for us according to various
profound considerations. According to similar profound
considerations his retreat from Smolensk to Orsha is
described. Then they describe his bravery at Krasnoye,
where, we are led to believe, he was ready to put himself at the head of his troops and to give battle, and
where he marched with a birchen cane, saying: —

"I have been emperor long enough; it is time to be
the general." [1]

And yet, immediately after this, he fled, leaving to
their fate the defenseless fragments of his army struggling after him.

Then they describe for us the grandeur of soul displayed by the marshals, especially by Ney, whose grandeur of soul was shown by his sneaking through the
forest, and passing the Dnieper by night, and escaping
into Orsha without his standards and artillery, and with
a loss of nine-tenths of his troops.

And, finally, the great emperor himself abandoning
his heroic army is represented by historians as something grand, as a stroke of genius. Even this last
miserable trick of running away, which in ordinary
language would be called the lowest degree of mean-
ness, which every child is taught to consider a shameful
deed, even this vile trick finds justification among the
historians.

For, when it is no longer possible to stretch out the
attenuated threads of historical arguments, when actions

[1] *J'ai assez fait l'empereur, il est temps de faire le général.*

flagrantly contradict what humanity calls good and even right, the historians bring up the saving idea of greatness. Greatness seems to exclude the possibility of applying the standards of good and evil. In the great, nothing is bad. He who is great is not charged with the atrocity of which he may have been guilty.

"It is great! — *C'est grand!*" say the historians; and then there is no more good or evil, but only *great* and *not great.*

Great is good; *not great* is bad.

Greatness is, according to them, the quality of certain peculiar beings, whom they call heroes.

And Napoleon, fleeing to his own fireside, wrapped in his warm furs, and leaving behind his perishing companions, and those men whom, according to his idea, he had led into Russia, feels that he is great, and his soul is tranquil.

"There is only one step," he says, "from the sublime to the ridiculous." (He sees something sublime in himself!) And for fifty years everybody has repeated it: "*Sublime! Great! Napoléon le grand!*" Truly, there is only one step from the sublime to the ridiculous![1]

It has never entered the mind of any man that by taking greatness as the absolute standard of good and evil, he only proclaims his own emptiness and immeasurable littleness.

For us who have the standard of right and wrong set by Christ, there is nothing incommensurate. And there is no greatness where there is not simplicity, goodness, and justice.

CHAPTER XIX

WHAT Russian is there who, reading the descriptions of the last period of the campaign of 1812, has not experienced a profound feeling of annoyance, dissatisfaction, and perplexity?

---

[1] *Du sublime au ridicule il n'y a qu'un pas.*

Who has not asked himself : Why did we not capture or destroy all the French, when they were surrounded by our three armies, each of superior numbers ; when, dying of starvation and cold, they surrendered in throngs; and when, as history tells us, the aim of the Russians was precisely this — to cut off the French, to stop them, and to take them all prisoners ?

How was it that this army, — which, when weaker in numbers, fought the battle of Borodino, — how was it that this army, when it surrounded the French on three sides, and intended to take them prisoners, did not accomplish its purpose ?

Had the French such immense preëminence over us that we, though possessing superior numbers, and having surrounded them, could not defeat them ?

How was it that this failed of execution ?

History, — or what is called history, — in reply to these questions, declares that it failed of execution because Kutuzof, and Tormasof, and Chitchagof, and this one and that one, and the other, did not execute such and such manœuvers.

But why did they not execute these manœuvers ? If these generals were to blame because the end in view was not attained, why were they not court-martialed and put to death ?

But even if we admit that Kutuzof and Chitchagof and the others were to blame for the Russian *non-success*, it is still impossible to understand why the Russian troops, under the conditions which obtained at Krasnoye and at the Beresina (for in both cases the Russians had a preponderance of numbers), did not capture the French troops, with their marshals, kings, and emperors, if such was the object of the Russians.

This strange phenomenon cannot be explained — as is done by the Russian military historians — by saying that it was because Kutuzof prevented offensive operations, for we know that Kutuzof's will was unable to restrain the troops from attacking at Viazma and at Tarutino.

If the Russian army, which with inferior forces was

able at Borodino to wrest a victory from an enemy then at the zenith of its strength, why could it not conquer the demoralized throngs of the French at Krasnoye and at the Beresina, when its forces had become superior?

If the object of the Russians had been to cut off and capture Napoleon and his marshals, and this object not only was not attained, but all attempts in that direction failed in the most shameful manner, then the French were perfectly right in representing the last period of the campaign as a series of victories, and Russian historians are perfectly wrong in representing that we were victorious.

Russian military historians, if they have any regard for logic, must involuntarily come to this conclusion, and, in spite of their lyrical effusions about courage and patriotism, and the like, must in spite of themselves confess that the retreat of the French from Moscow was for Napoleon a series of victories, and for Kutuzof a series of defeats.

But, if we put absolutely aside national pride, it would seem that this conclusion involves a contradiction, since this series of victories on the part of the French brought them to complete destruction, while the series of defeats on the part of the Russians led them to the absolute overthrow of their enemy, and the evacuation of their own country.

The source of this contradiction lies in the fact that historians who study events in the correspondence of kings and generals, and in official narratives, reports, and plans, have taken for granted the entirely false and unjustifiable idea that the object of the last period of the campaign of 1812 was to cut off and to capture Napoleon and his marshals and his army.

This object never existed, and could not exist, because it had no sense, and it was absolutely impossible of attainment.

The object had no sense, in the first place, because Napoleon's demoralized army was flying from Russia with all possible speed; in other words, was fulfilling the very wish of every Russian. What reason in direct ing various military operations against the French, who were running away as fast as they could go?

Secondly, it was senseless to try to stop men on the road who were employing all their energy in running away.

In the third place, it was senseless to sacrifice troops in destroying the French armies, who were going to destruction without external causes, and at such a rate that even when every road was given them undisputed, they could carry across the frontier only the small number that remained to them in the month of December — a hundredth part of their whole army.

In the fourth place, it was senseless to wish to make prisoners of the emperor, the kings, and the marshals, and the men, for their captivity would have been to the highest degree embarrassing to the Russians, as was recognized by the ablest diplomatists of the time, J. Maistre and others.

Still more senseless was the desire to capture whole regiments of the French, when the Russian army had been reduced one-half by the time it reached Krasnoye, and whole divisions would have been needed to guard the troops of prisoners, and when their own soldiers were not all the time receiving full rations, and when the French already captured were dying of starvation!

All of this profound plan of cutting off and seizing Napoleon and his army was like the plan of the gardener who, in trying to drive out of his inclosure the cattle that were trampling down his garden, should run to the gates and strike them on the head when they passed out. The only thing that could be said in the gardener's justification would be that he was very angry. But this excuse could not be made for those who devised this plan, for they were not the ones who suffered from the trampled garden.

The idea of cutting off Napoleon and his army, besides being senseless, was impossible.

It was impossible, first, because, since experience has shown that the movement of columns of soldiers in battle for a distance of five versts can never be made in accordance with plans, the probability that Chitchagof, Kutuzof, and Wittgenstein would effect a junction at a designated place on time was so slight that it amounted to an impossibility, as Kutuzof felt, who, on receiving the sovereign's plan, declared that operations at great distances never gave the desired results.

Secondly, it was impossible because, in order to neutralize that momentum with which Napoleon's army was recoiling, incomparably larger forces would have been necessary than those which the Russians had.

Thirdly, it was impossible because the military phrase "to cut off" an enemy has no sense. We may cut off a piece of bread, but not an army.

To cut off an army, to dispute its road, is never possible, for there are always many places where detours can be made, and there is the night, when nothing can be seen, as military students may convince themselves from the example of what took place at Krasnoye or the Beresina.

It is just as impossible to take a person prisoner, unless the person taken prisoner consents to be seized, as it is to catch a swallow, although it is possible to catch it if it comes and lights on your hand.

Armies can be captured only when they surrender, as the Germans do — according to the rules of strategy and tactics. But the French troops, with perfect correctness, found this unfit, since death by cold and starvation awaited them alike in flight and in captivity.

Fourthly, — and chiefly, — this was impossible because not since the world began had a war ever been waged under such terrible conditions as those which characterized the campaign of 1812; and the Russian troops, in pursuing the French, strained every effort, and could do no more without going to destruction themselves.

During the movement of the Russian army from Tarutino to Krasnoye fifty thousand men — in other words, a number equivalent to the population of a large provincial city — were sick and disabled.

Half of the men left the army without engaging in a battle.

And in regard to this period of the campaign, — when the troops, without boots or greatcoats, with insufficient food, and without vodka, for months spent the nights in the snow, in a temperature fifteen degrees below freezing; when the days were only seven or eight hours long, and all the rest of the twenty-four were night, discipline being in such circumstances impossible; when, not as in battle, men for a few hours only enter the domain of death where there is no discipline, but lived for months in an incessant struggle with death from cold and starvation; when in a single month half of the army perished, — in regard to this period of the campaign, historians tell us how Miloradovitch ought to have made a flank movement in this direction, and Tormasof in that, and Chitchagof in another (struggling through snow that was knee-deep), and how such and such a one "destroyed" and "cut off" — and so on, and so on!

The Russians, of whom one-half perished, did all that they could or ought to have done to attain an end worthy of the people, and they are not to blame if other Russians, sitting in warm apartments, proposed what it was impossible to do.

All this strange and at the present time incomprehensible contradiction between the fact and the historical account arises simply from this: the historians who have written about these events have described the fine sentiments and the fine speeches of different generals, and not the history of the event.

Very important to them seem the speeches of Miloradovitch, the rewards received by this, that, and the other general, and their proposals; but the question about the fifty thousand Russian soldiers who were left behind in the hospital or in the grave does not interest them, because it is outside of their studies.

And yet all it requires is for them to turn their attention from the study of the reports and plans of the generals, and to follow the movements of these hundred thousand men who took an active, immediate part in the event, and all the questions that before seemed unsolvable will at once be solved with extraordinary ease and simplicity.

The aim of cutting off the retreat of Napoleon and his army never existed except in the imaginations of a dozen men. It could not exist, because it was absurd and its realization was impracticable.

The Russian people had only one object in view: to rid their soil of the invaders.

This object was attained, in the first place, of its own accord, because the French ran away, and afterwards it was only necessary not to check that movement. In the second place, this object was attained by means of that popular warfare which destroyed the French; and, in the third place, because a great Russian army followed the enemy, ready to employ force in case the movement of the French was suspended.

The Russian army acted like the knout on a running animal. And the experienced cattle-driver knew that it was most advantageous to hold the knout upraised, threatening it, but not to strike the running animal on the head.

PART FIFTEENTH

CHAPTER I

WHEN a man sees a dying animal, horror seizes him: what he himself is, — his own essence, — is evidently perishing before his very eyes, — ceasing to exist.

But when the dying one is a human being, and a person beloved and tenderly cherished, then, over and above the horror at the cessation of the life, there is felt a rending and wounding of the soul. This wound, like a physical wound, sometimes kills, sometimes heals, but it is always painful, and shrinks from any external, irritating touch.

After Prince Andreï's death, Natasha and the Princess Mariya felt this in the same way. Their souls had quailed and bowed under the threatening cloud of death that hung over them, and they dared not look into the face of life. They were extremely cautious not to expose their wounds to humiliating, painful contact.

Everything — a swiftly passing carriage on the street, the announcement of dinner, the maid's question as to what gowns she should get ready for them; still worse, a word of perfunctory, feeble sympathy — made the wound throb painfully, seemed an affront, and profaned that urgent silence in which they both were striving to listen to that stern, terrible choir which ceased not, in their imagination, to chant, and prevented them from looking into those mysterious, infinite distances which, for an instant, opened out before them.

Only when they were together alone, they felt no sense of pain and humiliation. They talked together very little. When they talked, it was on the most in-

significant topics. And both of them alike avoided all
reference to anything concerning the future.

To recognize the possibility of a future seemed to
them an offense to his memory. All the more sedu-
lously they avoided in their talk everything that had
reference to the departed. It seemed to them that what
they experienced and felt could not be expressed in
words. It seemed to them that every verbal reference
to the separate events of his life disturbed the majesty
and sacredness of the mystery which had been accomplished before their eyes.

Their continual self-restraint, their constant, strenuous
avoidance of all that might lead to mention of him, these
halting-places that stood in the way of every possible
approach to the subject which they had tacitly agreed
to leave untouched, brought up before their imaginations with all the greater clearness and distinctness that
which they felt.

But pure, unmitigated grief is as impossible as pure
and unmitigated joy.

The Princess Mariya, by her position as sole and independent mistress of her fate, as guardian and instructor
of her nephew, was the first to be brought, by the exi-
gencies of real life, forth from that world of tribulation
in which she had been living for the past fortnight.
She received letters from her relatives, which had to be
answered; the room which Nikolushka occupied was
damp, and he began to have a cough. Alpatuitch came
from Yaroslavl with his accounts to be rectified, and
with his proposal and advice for her to go back to
Moscow, to her house on the Vozdvizhenka, which had
remained intact and needed only small repairs.

Life would not stand still, and it was necessary to
live.

Hard as it was for the Princess Mariya to emerge
from that world of solitary contemplation in which she
had been living till then, sorry as she was, and almost
conscience-stricken, to leave Natasha alone, the labors
of life demanded her participation, and she, in spite of
herself, had to give way.

She verified Alpatuitch's accounts, consulted with Dessalles in regard to her nephew, and made arrangements and preparations for her journey to Moscow.

Natasha was left to herself, and, since the Princess Mariya had begun to get ready for her departure, avoided even her.

The Princess Mariya proposed to the countess to let Natasha go to Moscow with her, and both father and mother gladly consented, since each day they noticed a decline in their daughter's physical vigor, and hoped that a change of scene would do her good, and that the physicians of Moscow would help her.

"I will go nowhere," replied Natasha, when this matter was proposed to her. "All I ask is to be left in peace," said she, and she hastened from the room, scarcely able to restrain her tears, — tears not so much of grief as of vexation and anger.

Since she had felt herself abandoned by the Princess Mariya, and left alone with her grief, Natasha, for the most of the time, sat in her room with her feet in the corner of the divan, and, while her slender, nervous fingers kept tearing or bending something or other, her eyes would remain obstinately fixed on whatever happened to attract her attention.

This solitude exhausted, tortured her; but it was something that she could not help. As soon as any one came to her, she would quickly get up, change her position and the expression of her eyes, and take up her book or her sewing, and make no attempt to conceal her desire that the one who came to disturb her should go.

It constantly seemed to her that she was on the very point of discovering, of penetrating that terrible, unendurable problem on which her mental eye was directed.

About the beginning of January, Natasha, thin and pale, and dressed in a black woolen dress, with her braid carelessly knotted up in a pug, was sitting with her feet up on the divan, concentratedly puckering and folding out the ends of her sash, and gazing with her eyes fixed on the door.

She was looking at the place where he had vanished, at that side of life. And that side of life, of which she had never thought in the days gone by, which hitherto had always seemed to her so distant and unreal, was now nearer and more familiar, more comprehensible, than the ordinary side of life, where everything was either emptiness and decay, or suffering and humiliation.

She looked at the place where she knew he had been; but she could not make it out that he was not there still. She saw him once more as he had been at Muitishchi, at Troïtsa, at Yaroslavl.

She saw his face, heard his voice, repeated his words and the words that she had said to him, and sometimes imagined words which they might have spoken.

There he is lying in the easy-chair, in his velvet shubka, with his head leaning on his thin white hand. His chest is terribly sunken and his shoulders raised. His lips are firmly set, his eyes are gleaming, and on his pallid brow a wrinkle comes and goes. One leg trembles almost imperceptibly with a rapid motion.

Natasha knows that he is struggling with tormenting pain. "What is that pain like? Why that pain? How does he feel? How does it pain him?" she wonders.

He noticed her fixed gaze, he raised his eyes, and without a trace of a smile began to speak:—

"There is one thing terrible," said he, "to be bound forever to a suffering man. This is eternal torment!"

And he looked at her with a scrutinizing glance. Natasha replied then, as she always did, before she had time to think what she should reply. She said:—

"This cannot continue so, it will not be so always; you will get well—entirely well."

She now saw him as he had been from the first, and lived over in her memory all that she had then experienced. She recalled that long, melancholy, stern look which he had given her at those words, and she realized the significance of the reproach and despair expressed in this protracted look.

"I agreed with him," said Natasha to herself, "that it would be terrible if he should remain always suffering so. I said this at that time, simply because I meant that for him it would be terrible, but he understood it in a different way. He thought that it would be terrible for me. At that time he was still anxious to live, was afraid to die. And I said this so crudely, so stupidly! I did not think of that. I meant something entirely different. If I had said what I meant, I should have said: 'If he were to perish by a living death before my eyes, I should be happy in comparison with what I feel now.' Now — there is no one, nothing! Could he have known this? No! He knew it not, and he will never know! And now it is too late, too late to set this right."

And once more he said to her those same words, but this time Natasha, in her imagination, answered him in a different way. She stopped him and said: "Terrible for you, but not for me. You know that for me life without you would be nothing, and to suffer with you is the dearest happiness."

And he seized her hand and pressed it just as he had pressed it that terrible evening four days before he died. And in her imagination she spoke to him still other tender, loving words which she might have uttered then, but did not, and which now she could and did say: "I love thee!.... thee.... I love, I love!" she repeated, convulsively wringing her hands, clinching her teeth, with set determination. ....

And the bitter sweetness of grief took possession of her, and her eyes filled with tears, but suddenly she asked herself to whom she was saying that. "Where is he and what is he now?" And once more everything grew dark with hard and cruel doubt, and, once more closely drawing her brows into a frown, she looked at the place where he had been. And now, now it seemed to her that she was going to fathom the mystery....

But at the very instant when it seemed to her that the incomprehensible was already about to reveal itself to her, a loud rattling of the door-knob painfully struck upon her ears. With hasty, incautious steps, with a frightened expression never before seen on her face, Dunyasha the maid came running into the room.

"Please come to your papa as quick as possible," said Dunyasha, with that peculiar and excited look. "Bad news.... about Piotr Ilyitch.... a letter," she cried, with a sob.

CHAPTER II

BESIDES the general feeling of aversion for all people, Natasha at this time experienced a peculiar feeling of aversion for the members of her own family. All her relatives — father, mother, Sonya — were so near to her, so familiar, so *every-day*, that all their words, their sentiments, seemed to her a disrespect to that world in which she had been lately living, and she looked upon them not only with indifferent but even with hostile eyes. She heard Dunyasha's words about Piotr Ilyitch, about bad news, but she did not take them in.

"What misfortune can have happened to them? what bad news can it be? Everything with them goes on calmly, as it always has," said Natasha, mentally.

As she went into the hall her father was coming hastily out of the countess's room. His face was wrinkled and wet with tears. He was evidently hastening from her room so as to give free course to the affliction that overmastered him. When he saw Natasha he waved his hands in despair, and burst into painfully convulsive sobs, which distorted his round, placid face.

"Pet.... Petya.... go to her, go.... she.... she is.... calling for you...."

And, crying like a child, swiftly shuffling along on his feeble legs, he went to a chair and almost fell into it, burying his face in his hands.

Suddenly something like an electric shock ran over Natasha's whole being. A terribly acute pain struck her heart. She experienced a cruel agony. It seemed to her that something within her snapped and that she was dying. But immediately succeeding this agony there came a sense of deliverance from the torpor that had been weighing down her life. Seeing her father, and hearing her mother's terribly agonized cry in the next room, she instantly forgot herself and her own sorrow.

She ran up to her father, but he, feebly waving his arm, pointed to her mother's door.

The Princess Mariya, pale and with her lower jaw trembling, came out of the room, and, taking Natasha by the hand, said something to her.

Natasha saw her not, heard her not. With swift steps she passed through the door, paused for an instant, as if struggling with her own inclinations, and ran to her mother.

The countess lay in her easy-chair, in a strangely awkward and stiff position, and was beating her head against the wall. Sonya and the maids were holding her by the arms.

" Call Natasha ! Natasha ! " .... cried the countess. " It is false ! false ! .... He lies ! .... Call Natasha ! " she cried, trying to tear herself away from those holding her. — " Go away, all of you. It is false ! .... Killed ? .... Ha ! ha ! ha ! .... 'T is false ! "

Natasha leaned her knee on the chair, bent over her mother, threw her arms around her, lifted her up with unexpected strength, turned her face around, and pressed her cheeks against hers.

" Mamenka ! .... Darling ! .... I am here, dearest ! Mamenka ! " she kept whispering, without a second's intermission.

She kept her arms firmly around her mother, gently struggled with her, called for cushions and water, and unbuttoned and began to take off her mother's gown.

" Darling, dearest .... mamenka .... dearest heart ! " [1] she kept all the time whispering, while she kissed her head, hands, and face, and felt how her tears, like rivulets, tickling her nose and her cheeks, kept flowing.

The countess pressed her daughter's hand, closed her eyes, and was calm for an instant. Then suddenly, with unnatural swiftness, she raised herself up, glared around wildly, and, seeing Natasha, pressed her head with all her might. Then she turned toward her Na-

---

[1] *Druk moï, galubushka, mamenka, dushenka.*

tasha's face, convulsed with the pain, and long scrutinized it.

"Natasha, you love me," she said, in a low, confiden-
tial whisper. "Natasha, you would not deceive me?
Tell me the whole truth."

Natasha looked at her with eyes brimming with tears,
and her face expressed only a prayer for forgiveness
and love.

"Dearest, mamenka," she repeated, exerting all the
energies of her love, in order to take upon herself some
of the excess of woe that had become too heavy for her
mother to bear.

And again, in that unequal struggle against the reality, the mother, refusing to believe that she could still
exist when her darling boy, treasured far more than life,
was killed, she relapsed from the reality into the world
of unreason.

Natasha could not have told how that first day passed,
that night, the following day, and the following night.
She did not sleep, and did not leave her mother's side.
Natasha's love, faithful, patient, every second, as it were,
wrapped the countess round about, not with consolation,
not with explanation, but with something like a summons back to life.

On the third night the countess grew calm for several
minutes, and Natasha closed her eyes, and rested her
head on the arm of the chair. The bed creaked;
Natasha opened her eyes. The countess was sitting
up in bed, and speaking in a low tone: —

"How glad I am that you have come! You are
tired; wouldn't you like some tea?"

Natasha went to her.

"You have grown handsome and strong!" continued
the countess, taking her daughter's hand.

"Mamenka, what are you saying?"....

"Natasha! he is dead, he is dead!" And, throwing
her arms around her daughter, the countess for the first
time began to weep.

CHAPTER III

THE Princess Mariya had postponed her departure.

Sonya and the count tried to take Natasha's place, but they found it impossible. They saw that she was the only one that could keep the mother from wild despair. For three weeks Natasha lived constantly by her mother's side, slept in a chair in her room, gave her food and drink, and talked to her unceasingly, talked because her tender, caressing voice was the only thing that calmed the countess.

A wound in the heart of a mother cannot heal. Petya's death had torn away the half of her life. At the end of a month, after the news of Petya's death had arrived, though it had found her a fresh and well-preserved woman of fifty, she crept out of her room an old woman, half dead, and no longer taking any interest in life. But the same wound which had half killed the countess, — this new wound brought Natasha back to life.

A spiritual wound, arising from the laceration of the spiritual body, exactly like a physical wound, strange as it may seem, after the deep wound has cicatrized, and its edges have come together, — the spiritual wound, like the physical one, heals only through the inward working of the forces of life.

Thus healed Natasha's wound. She had thought that life for her was finished. But suddenly her love for her mother proved to her that the essence of her life — love — was still alive within her. Love awoke and life awoke.

Prince Andreï's last days had brought Natasha and the Princess Mariya close together. This new misfortune still more united them. The Princess Mariya postponed her departure, and for three weeks tended Natasha like an ailing child. The weeks spent by her in her mother's room had been a severe drain on her physical energies.

One time, toward noon, the Princess Mariya, observing that Natasha was trembling as if she had a fever, took her to her room, and made her lie down on her bed. Natasha lay down, but when the princess, pulling down the blinds, started to go, Natasha called her back.

"I don't care to sleep, Marie; sit down with me!"

"You are tired; try to go to sleep."

"No, no! Why did you bring me here? She will be asking for me!"

"She is much better. She talked so naturally to-day," said the Princess Mariya.

Natasha lay on the bed, and in the semi-darkness of the room studied the Princess Mariya's face.

"Is she like him?" Natasha asked herself. "Yes, like him and not like him. But she is peculiar, strange, entirely original, unlike any one else. And she loves me! What is in her heart? Nothing but goodness! But what, what does she think of me? How does she regard me? Yes, she is beautiful!"

"Masha!" said she, timidly, drawing her hand to her. "Masha, don't think that I am bad. You don't, do you? Masha! darling, how I love you! Let us always, always be friends!"

And Natasha, throwing her arms around the Princess Mariya, began to kiss her hands and face. The princess was both embarrassed and delighted at this expression of Natasha's feelings.

From that day forth began between the Princess Mariya and Natasha that passionate and tender friendship which only exists between women.

They were constantly kissing each other, calling each other affectionate names, and spent the larger part of the time together. If one went out the other was restless, and hastened to rejoin her friend. Each felt more at peace with herself when the two were together than when they were alone. There existed between them a stronger feeling than friendship: this was that exclusive feeling that life was possible only when they were together.

Sometimes they sat without speaking for hours at a time; sometimes while in bed they would begin to talk, and talk till morning. Their conversation ran mainly on their earliest recollections.

The Princess Mariya would tell about her childhood, about her mother, about her father, about her hopes and fancies; and Natasha, who in times gone by, in the serene thoughtlessness of her joyous nature, would have been repelled by this life of devotion, of humility, by this poetry of Christian self-sacrifice, now feeling herself bound in affection to the princess, loved also the princess's past life, and began to comprehend the hitherto incomprehensible side of her life.

She had no idea of applying in her own case the principles of this humility and self-abnegation, because she was accustomed to find other pleasures, but she comprehended and loved in her friend this formerly incomprehensible virtue.

For the Princess Mariya also, when she heard Natasha's stories of her childhood and early youth, a formerly incomprehensible phase of life — faith in life itself and in the joys of life — was revealed.

Neither of them liked to speak of *him*, for fear they should in words desecrate what seemed to them those lofty heights of feeling which were in their hearts; but this reticence concerning him was causing them, little by little, — though they would not have believed it, — to forget him.

Natasha grew thin and pale, and feeble physically, so that they kept talking about her health; but this was agreeable to her. But sometimes, unexpectedly, there came over her not so much a fear of death as a fear of pain, weakness, loss of beauty; and, in spite of herself, she sometimes attentively contemplated her bare arm, marveling at its thinness, or in the morning she gazed into the mirror at her pinched and, as it seemed to her, ugly face. It seemed to her that this was unavoidable, and at the same time it was terrible and melancholy to her.

One time she ran quickly up-stairs, and found herself breathing hard. The next moment she involuntarily invented some excuse to go down again, and then once more ran up-stairs to test her strength and experiment on herself.

Another time she called Dunyasha, and her voice sounded weak. She tried it once more; she called her, although she heard her coming — called her in those chest tones which she used to use in singing, and listened to them.

She did not know it, she would not have believed it, but under what seemed to her the impenetrable crust of mold with which her soul was covered, already the delicate, tender, young shoots of grass were starting, which were bound to grow, and thus, by their life-giving, victorious force, hide from sight the sorrow which she had suffered, so that it would soon be forgotten. The wound was healing inwardly.

Toward the beginning of February the Princess Mariya went to Moscow, and the count insisted on Natasha's going with her, so as to consult with the doctors.

CHAPTER IV

AFTER the encounter at Viazma, where Kutuzof could not restrain his troops from the desire to overthrow, to cut off, the enemy, the further movement of the fleeing French and the pursuing Russians took place without a battle until they reached Krasnoye.

The flight of the French was so rapid that the Russian army chasing them could not catch up with them, that the horses in the cavalry and artillery came to a standstill, and that information in regard to the movements of the French was always untrustworthy.

The men of the Russian army were so worn out by these uninterrupted marches of forty versts a day, that they could not move onward any faster.

To appreciate the degree of exhaustion which the Russian army suffered, it is only necessary to realize the significance of this fact, that, while the Russian army, on leaving Tarutino, had a hundred thousand men, and lost during the whole march not more than five thousand in killed and wounded, and less than a hundred taken prisoners, they had only fifty thousand men when they got to Krasnoye.

The swift pursuit of the Russians after the French was as destructive in its effect on them as the retreat was to the French. The difference was only that the Russian army moved at will, without that threat of destruction which hung over the French army, and that, while the stragglers and the sick from among the French would fall into the hands of the enemy, the Russians who were left behind were at home.

The principal cause of the diminution of Napoleon's army was the rapidity of its flight, and indubitable proof of this is furnished by the corresponding diminution of the Russian troops.

All Kutuzof's efforts, just as had been the case at Tarutino and at Viazma, were directed — as far as lay in his power — solely to the preventing of interference with that destructive movement of the French (though this was contrary to desires expressed in Petersburg and in the Russian army by his own generals), but to coöperate with it, and to facilitate the movement of his own troops.

But, moreover, ever since the troops had begun to suffer from fatigue, and from the tremendous losses due to the rapidity of the movement, Kutuzof had discovered still another reason for slackening the exertions of the army, and for delay. The object of the Russian troops was pursuit of the French. The route of the French was unknown, and therefore the more closely our troops followed on their heels, the greater was the distance which they covered. Only by following at a considerable interval and taking the most direct road could they have avoided the zigzags made by the French.

All the intricate manœuvers proposed by the generals involved an increase for the troops in their marches, while the only reasonable course was to minimize these marches ; and, to this end, all Kutuzof's efforts were directed throughout the campaign from Moscow to Vilna, not as a matter of accident or caprice, but so consistently that he did not for a moment relax them.

Kutuzof knew, not by reason or science, but by his whole Russian nature, — knew and felt what every Russian soldier felt, that the French were conquered, that the enemy were running away, and that it was necessary to escort them; but at the same time he felt with his soldiers the burden of a campaign unprecedented for the rapidity of the marches and the time of the year.

But it seemed to the other generals, especially those who were not Russian, — being anxious to distinguish themselves, to astonish the world, for some reason or other to take some duke or king prisoner, — it seemed to these generals that now, when any battle was odious and absurd, it was the very time to give battle and conquer some one.

Kutuzof merely shrugged his shoulders when, one after another, they laid before him their plans for manœuvers to be accomplished by these badly shod, half-famished soldiers, without greatcoats, who, during a month, had been reduced one-half, though they had not fought a battle, and with whom, under the most favorable conditions of a prolonged retreat, he must go to the frontier, — a distance greater than that already traversed.

This desire to gain personal distinction, to manœuver, to harass and cut off the enemy, was especially manifested when Russian troops encountered French troops.

That was the case at Krasnoye, where the Russian generals thought that they had found one of the three columns of the French, and hurled themselves on Napoleon himself with sixteen thousand men. In spite of all the means employed by Kutuzof to avoid this destructive engagement and to save his troops, for three days an indiscriminate attack on the demoralized mob of the French was kept up at Krasnoye by the weary troops of the Russian army.

Toll wrote out a plan: *"Die erste Colonne marschirt —*

The first column will march," etc., — and, as always
happens, everything took place contrary to the plan.

Prince Eugene of Würtemberg saw from a hilltop a
number of French fugitives fleeing past him down the
road, and asked for reinforcements, which did not
arrive.

The French, managing during the night to avoid the
Russians, scattered and hid through the woods, and
made their way onward each as best he could.

Miloradovitch, who declared that he cared nothing
whatever about the provisioning of his troops, who could
never be found when he was wanted, — a "*chevalier
sans peur et sans reproche*," as he called himself, — and
was fond of talking with the French, sent a flag of truce,
demanding their surrender, and lost time and failed to
execute the orders intrusted to him.

"Boys, I make you a present of that column," he
said, riding up to his troops, and pointing out the French
to his cavalry.

And his troops, mounted on horses that could barely
move, urged them with spur and sword-pricks into a
trot, and, after intense efforts, advanced against the
column that had been given to them, — in other words,
against a crowd of benumbed Frenchmen half dead with
hunger and cold; and this column, which had been
given to them, threw down its arms and surrendered, —
as it long had been wishing to do!

At Krasnoye they took twenty-six thousand prisoners,
and captured hundreds of cannon and a kind of a stick
which they called "the marshal's baton"; and they quarreled as to who had distinguished themselves, and they
were contented with this, but much regretted that they
had not captured Napoleon or some hero, some one
of the marshals, and they blamed one another, and
especially Kutuzof.

These men, carried away by their passions, were only
the blind agents of the most grievous law of necessity,
but they considered themselves heroes, and imagined
that what they had done was a most worthy and noble
work.

They blamed Kutuzof, and declared that ever since the beginning of the campaign he had prevented them from conquering Napoleon, and thought only of his own personal pleasures, and that he had been unwilling to leave Linen Mills [1] because he was comfortable there; that at Krasnoye he stopped the movement because, on learning that Napoleon was there, he had entirely lost his presence of mind, and that it was quite supposable that he had an understanding with Napoleon, that he had been bought over, etc. [2]

Because contemporaries, carried away by their passions, spoke thus, posterity and history call Napoleon "great," while Kutuzof is regarded by foreigners, only as a sly, weak, and debauched old courtier; by Russians as an indefinite sort of person, a puppet useful because of his Russian name. ....

CHAPTER V

IN 1812–1813, Kutuzof was openly accused of serious mistakes.

The sovereign was displeased with him; and in the history of the campaign, written not long since, by imperial orders,[3] it is declared that Kutuzof was a crafty court liar, who trembled at the name of Napoleon, and who, by his blunders at Krasnoye and the Beresina, deprived the Russian troops of the glory of a complete victory over the French.

Such is the fate of men who are not *great* — not *grand homme;* or, since the Russian intellect never recognizes them, such is the fate of those rare and always solitary men who, being able to comprehend the will of Providence, subordinate their own wills to it.

The hatred and scorn of the multitude punish these men for their comprehension of the higher laws.

---

[1] *Polotniani Zavodui.* [2] Wilson's Memoir.
[3] " History of the Year 1812," by Bogdanovitch; characteristics of Kutuzof, and dissertation on the unsatisfactory results of the battles at Krasnoye.

To Russian historians — a strange and terrible thing to say! — Napoleon, that insignificant instrument of history, who never anywhere, even in exile, showed human dignity, — Napoleon is the object of admiration and enthusiasm; he is great — *grand!*

Kutuzof, on the other hand, the man who from the beginning to the end of his activity in 1812, from Borodino to Vilna, not once, by a single act or word, proved a traitor to himself, but offers an example unique in history, of self-sacrifice and present insight into the future significance of an event, — Kutuzof is to them something vague and pitiable, and when they speak of him and of 1812 they seem to be somewhat ashamed.

And yet it is hard to conceive an historical personage whose activity was so faithfully and so constantly devoted to a single aim. It is hard to imagine an aim more worthy or more consistent with the will of a whole people.

Still more difficult it would be to discover another example, in history, where an aim set by an historical personage was so completely realized as the aim to the attainment of which Kutuzof's whole activity was devoted in 1812.

Kutuzof never talked about the forty centuries that looked down from the Pyramids, of the sacrifices he had made for his country, of what he intended to accomplish or had already accomplished.

As a general thing, he spoke little of himself, never played any part, seemed always a most simple and ordinary man, and said only the most simple and the most ordinary things.

He wrote letters to his daughters and to Madame Stahl, read romances, liked the society of pretty women, jested with generals, officers, and soldiers, and never contradicted those that tried to prove anything to him.

When Count Rostopchin galloped across the Yauza bridge up to Kutuzof and loaded him with personal reproaches for the loss of Moscow, and said, "How was it that you promised not to give up Moscow without a battle," Kutuzof replied : —

"I shall not give up Moscow without a battle."

And yet Moscow was already abandoned.

When Arakcheyef came to him from the sovereign and said that Yermolof must be appointed chief of artillery, Kutuzof replied : —

"Yes. Only just now I was proposing that myself."

And yet, a few moments before, he had expressed himself quite differently.

What was it to him, who alone amid the foolish throng about him understood all the mighty significance of the event, what was it to him whether Count Rostopchin attributed to him or any one else the abandonment of the capital? Still less could he be concerned with the question who should be named chief of artillery.

Not only in these circumstances, but on all occasions, this old man, who by experience of life had come to the conviction that thoughts, and the words whereby thoughts are expressed, do not stir men to action, spoke words absolutely without meaning, saying whatever came into his head.

But this same man, who so scorned speech, never once, throughout the whole period of his activity, uttered a single word which would not have agreed with the one object toward the attainment of which he moved throughout the course of the war.

With evident reluctance, with a painful assurance that he would not be understood, again and again in the most varied circumstances he expressed his thought.

From the time of the battle of Borodino, when his quarrel with those around him began, he alone declared that *the battle of Borodino was a victory,* and he repeated it both orally and in his letters, as well as in his reports, until his death.

He alone declared that *the loss of Moscow was not the loss of Russia*.

He, in reply to Lauriston, who was sent to offer terms of peace, said that *peace could not be made, because such was not the will of the people*.

He alone, during the retreat of the French, declared that *all our manœuvers were useless, that everything would come out of itself better than we could wish, that it was only necessary to give the enemy the "golden bridge"* [1] *; that neither the battle of Tarutino, nor that of Krasnoye, nor that of Viazma, was necessary; that, to reach the frontier, troops were needed; that he would not sacrifice a single Russian soldier for ten Frenchmen.*

And he alone, this deceitful courtier, as he is represented to us, this man who to please his sovereign lied to Arakcheyef, he alone, this courtier, at the risk of winning his sovereign's ill-will, declared, at Vilna, that *war prolonged beyond the frontier would be dangerous and useless.*

But words alone would not prove that he grasped the significance of the event. His acts — all without the slightest variation — were all directed to one and the same threefold object: —

1. To concentrate all his forces for any encounter with the French.

2. To vanquish them, and

3. To drive them from Russia, while alleviating, so far as was possible, the sufferings of the people and the troops.

He, this Kutuzof, the temporizer, whose device was "patience and time," the enemy of decisive actions, he gives battle at Borodino, clothing the preparation for it with unexampled solemnity.

He, this Kutuzof, who at Austerlitz, before the battle began, declares that it will be lost; and at Borodino, in spite of the conviction of the generals that it was a defeat, protests up to the time of his death that the battle of Borodino was a victory, though the example of an army that had won a victory being obliged to retreat was unheard of in history, — he alone, during all the time of the retreat, insists on refraining from further battles, since they were now useless — from beginning a new war, and from crossing the frontier.

It is easy at the present time to comprehend the significance of the event, provided we do not concern ourselves with the mass of plans fermenting in the heads

---

[1] That is, give them every facility to destroy themselves.

of a dozen men, since the whole event, with all its consequences, lies before us.

But how was it that at that time this old man, alone,
against the opinions of many, was able to divine so accurately the significance of the national impression of the
event, that he did not once through his whole activity
prove false to it?

This extraordinary power of insight into the import
of the events accomplishing had its source in that
national sentiment which he carried in his heart in all
its purity and vigor.

Only the recognition of this sentiment in Kutuzof
compelled the people by such strange paths to choose
this old man, in disgrace as he was, against the will of
the Tsar to be their representative in the national war.

And only this sentiment elevated Kutuzof to the high
pinnacle of humanity from which he, the general-in-
chief, employed all his efforts, not to kill and exterminate men, but to save and have pity on them.

This simple, modest, and therefore truly majestic figure
could not be cast in the counterfeit mold employed by
history for the European hero supposed to have governed the nations.

For the valet there can be no great man, because the
valet has his own conception of greatness.

CHAPTER VI

THE seventeenth of November was the first day of
the so-called battle of Krasnoye. Before dark, when
after many disputes and blunders caused by generals
who did not reach the places where they should have
been, after much galloping about of aides with commands and counter-commands, when it was already self-
evident that the enemy were everywhere running away,
and that a battle could not and would not take place,
Kutuzof set forth from Krasnoye and rode to Dobroye,
where headquarters had been established for that day.

The day was clear and frosty. Kutuzof, with a big

suite of generals, most of whom were dissatisfied with him and were whispering behind his back, rode to Do-broye, mounted on his stout white cob.

The road all along was crowded with a party of French prisoners captured that day — seven thousand of them had been taken — who were trying to warm themselves around the bivouac fires.

Not far from Dobroye a huge throng of ragged pris-oners, wearing whatever they happened to have laid their hands on, were loudly talking, as they stood in the road near a long row of unlimbered French cannon.

As the commander-in-chief approached, the talking quieted down, and all eyes were fixed on Kutuzof, who, in his white hat with red band, and wadded cloak hunched upon his stooping shoulders, slowly moved along the road. One of the generals was reporting to Kutuzof where the prisoners and cannon had been captured.

Kutuzof seemed preoccupied and did not hear the general's words. He blinked his eyes with displeasure and kept gazing attentively and fixedly at the figures of the prisoners, who presented a particularly melancholy spectacle. · Most of the French soldiers were maimed, with frost-bitten noses and cheeks, and almost all of them had red, swollen, and festering eyes.

One group of the French was near the roadside, and two soldiers—the face of one was covered with scars — were tearing a piece of raw meat. There was some-thing terrible and bestial in the wild glances which they cast on the newcomers and in the ugly expression with which the scarred soldier, after gazing at Kutuzof, im-mediately turned away and went on with his operations.

Kutuzof gazed long and attentively at these two soldiers; frowning still more portentously, he blinked his eyes and thoughtfully shook his head.

In another place he observed a Russian soldier, who, with a laugh, gave a Frenchman a slap on the shoulder and made some friendly remark to him. Kutuzof, again with the same expression, shook his head.

"What were you saying?" he asked of the general,

who had gone on with his report and was calling the commander-in-chief's attention to the captured French colors which were bunched in front of the Preobrazhensky regiment.

"Oh, the colors," said Kutuzof, finding it evidently hard to turn his mind from the object that occupied his thoughts. He looked around absent-mindedly. Thousands of eyes, from every side, looked at him, expecting his reply.

He reined in his horse in front of the Preobrazhensky regiment, drew a heavy sigh, and closed his eyes. One of the suite made a signal to the soldiers who had charge of the standards to advance and group the flagstaffs around the commander-in-chief.

Kutuzof said nothing for some seconds, and then, with evident reluctance, yielding to the necessity of his position, raised his head and began to speak.

The officers gathered around him in throngs. With an attentive glance he surveyed the circle of officers, some of whom he recognized.

"I thank you all," he said, addressing the soldiers and then the officers again. In the silence which reigned around him his slowly spoken words were perfectly distinct. "I thank you all for your hard and faithful service. The victory is complete, and Russia will not forget you. Your glory will be eternal."

He was silent and looked around.

"Bend down, bend down its head!" said he to the soldier who held the French eagle and had unexpectedly inclined it toward the Preobrazhensky standard. "Lower, lower still, — that's the way. Hurrah, boys!" he cried, with a quick movement of his chin, turning to his soldiers.

"Hurrah, rah-rah!" roared forth from thousands of voices.

While the soldiers were cheering, Kutuzof bent down to his saddle, inclined his head, and his eyes gleamed with a gentle, perceptibly ironical gleam.

"Well, boys!"[1] he began when the cheering had ceased.

[1] *Bratsui*, brothers; he generally calls them *rebyata*, children.

And suddenly his voice and the expression of his face changed; no longer the commander-in-chief spoke, but a simple old man, who evidently had something of importance to communicate to his comrades.

Through the crowd of officers and the ranks of the soldiers ran a stir, as they pressed forward to hear more distinctly what he should now have to say: —

"Well, boys! I know it's hard for you, but what's to be done? Have patience; it is not for long. When we have escorted our guests out of the country we will rest. The Tsar will not forget your labors, will not forget you. It is hard for you, but you are at home all this time, while they — see what they have come to," said he, indicating the prisoners, — "worse than the lowest beggars. While they were strong we had no pity on them, but now we may pity them. They, too, are men. Isn't that so, boys?"

He glanced around him, and in the earnest, respectfully perplexed glances fixed on him he read their sympathy with what he had said. His face was constantly more and more illumined by the benevolent smile of old age, by the starlike lines irradiating from the corners of his mouth and eyes.

He remained silent for a little, and in apparent perplexity dropped his head: —

"Of course it may be said, who invited them to come to us? They deserve it, t.... d.... s.... b...." said he, suddenly raising his head. And, cracking his whip, he rode off at a gallop, for the first time in the whole campaign followed by roars of laughter and a bellowing hurrah ringing down the long lines of the soldiers as they broke ranks.

The words spoken by Kutuzof could have been scarcely understood by the troops. No one would have been able to report accurately, either the solemn words which the field-marshal had spoken first, or the kindly simplicity of the old man's words at the last; but not only was the tone of sincerity that rang through the whole speech comprehensible, but that peculiar sense of majestic solemnity in union with compassion for their

enemies, and with the feeling of the righteousness of
their cause, expressed, if in nothing else, in that old-
fashioned, good-natured execration, this feeling found
an echo in every man's breast, and found utterance in
that joyful, long-undying shout.

When afterwards one of the generals came and asked
Kutuzof if he would not prefer to ride in his calash, in
his reply he unexpectedly broke into sobs, evidently
being overcome by powerful emotion.

CHAPTER VII

On the twentieth of November, the last day of the
battles of Krasnoye, it was already twilight when the
troops reached their halting-place for the night. The
whole day had been calm and cold, with an occasional
light fall of snow. Toward evening it had begun to
clear off. Even while the last flakes were falling the
dark-purple starry sky could be seen and the cold grew
more intense.

A regiment of musketeers, which had left Tarutino
three thousand strong, and now mustered nine hundred,
was one of the first to reach the place of bivouac, — a
village on the highway.

The billeters, who met the regiment, explained that
all the cottages were occupied by sick and dying Frenchmen, cavalrymen, and staff-officers. There was only
one izba for the regimental commander.

The regimental commander went to his quarters.
The regiment marched through the village and stacked
their arms near the last houses on the highway.

Like a monstrous many-limbed animal, the regiment
at once set to work to provide for itself a lair and food.
One squad of the men, plowing through snow above
their knees, went to a birch grove, at the right of the
road, and immediately from the grove were heard the
sounds of axes, cutlasses, the crashing of falling limbs,
and gay voices.

A second detachment was gathered around the place

where the regiment's carts and horses were drawn up, noisily busy in getting out kettles and hardtack and in foddering the horses.

A third detachment was scattered through the village, preparing quarters for the staff-officers, clearing away the dead bodies of the French that lay in the izbas, and dragging off beams, dry wood, and straw from the roofs for their fires, and wattled hedges for shelter.

A dozen or more soldiers behind a row of cottages at the edge of the village, with a jocund shout, were pulling at the high wattling of a shed from which the roof had already been torn.

"Now then! once more, all together!" cried the voices, and under the darkness of the night the fabric of the wattling, laden with snow, rocked with a frosty, crackling sound.

The lower posts gave way more and more, and at last the wattling started to give way, taking with it the soldiers who were pushing against it. There were heard loud, coarse shouts and laughter.

"Look out there, you two!"

"Give the hand-spike[1] here!"

"There, that's the way!"

"What are you climbing up there for?"

"Now, all together..... Now wait, boys!.... With a chorus!"

All became silent, and a mellow, velvety, sweet voice struck up the song. At the end of the third stanza, as the last note died away, a score of voices took up the refrain in unison: —

"*U—u—u—u! idyot! Razom! Navalis dyetki!* — She falls! once more — a long pull and a strong pull, boys!"

But, in spite of their united efforts, the wattling gave but little, and in the silence that ensued was heard their heavy breathing.

"Ho there, Company Six! Fiends! Devils! Lend a hand!.... We'll do as much for you some day!"

---

[1] The speaker, a man from Tula perhaps, says *rotchag* instead of *ruitchag*.

A score of men from Company Six, who were passing
through the village, joined forces with the others, and
the wattling, five sazhens long and a sazhen, or seven
feet, wide, bending under its own weight, and crushing
and bruising the shoulders of the panting soldiers who
carried it, moved along the village street. " Keep step
there !.... There you are stumbling !.... Can't you keep
your balance ? "....

There was no cessation of the jovial though sometimes
coarse objurgations.

" What is the matter with you ? " suddenly rang out
the imperious voice of a soldier, who came hastening
toward them.

" There are gentlemen here ! The *anaral* himself is
in that izba, but you are devils, fiends incarnate, foul-
mouthed wretches ! I 'll give it to you ! " yelled the
sergeant, and, with all his might, he struck the first
soldier he encountered a blow on the back. " Can't you
keep quiet ? "

The soldiers ceased their noise. The soldier who had
been struck grunted, and began to rub his face, which
was lacerated and covered with blood. He had been hit
by the wattled branches.

" The devil ! How he made me smart for it ! See
how it made my whole mug bleed ! " said he, in a timid
whisper, when the sergeant had gone back.

" And so you don't like it ! " said a mocking voice,
and, moderating their tones, the soldiers went on their
way. When once they were beyond the village, they
once more began to talk as loud as ever, punctuating
their conversation with the same aimless objurgations.

In the cottage by which the soldiers had been passing
were collected some of the higher officers, and, as they
drank their tea, the conversation waxed lively over the
events of the past day and the proposed manœuvers of
the following day. It was proposed to make a flank
march to the left, to cut off the viceroy and take him
prisoner.

When the soldiers brought in the wattling, the fires
for cooking were already merrily burning in various

directions. The wood was snapping, the snow was melting, and dark shadows of soldiers were moving up and down over the whole space, trampling down the snow.

Axes and cutlasses were busy at work in various directions. Everything was done without special orders. Wood was brought for the night supply, wigwams were prepared for the officers, kettles were set to boiling, arms and ammunition were put into order.

The wattling brought in by the men of the Eighth Company was set up in the form of a semicircular screen toward the north, and propped up with stakes, while the fire was kindled under its shelter. The drums beat the tattoo, the roll was called, the men took their supper, and disposed themselves for the night around the bivouac fires — one repairing his foot-gear, another smoking his pipe, another (stripped to the skin) roasting his lice!

CHAPTER VIII

IT would seem as if in those almost unimaginably difficult conditions of existence in which the Russian soldiers were brought at this time, — lacking warm boots, lacking overcoats, without shelter over their heads, in the snow, with the temperature at eighteen degrees of frost,[1] lacking a sufficiency of provisions, which frequently failed to arrive, — it would seem as if these soldiers might by good rights have presented a most pitiable and melancholy spectacle.

On the contrary, never, even in the very most favorable material conditions, did the army present a more gay and animated spectacle. It was due to the fact that each day the army lost out of its ranks all those who began to show signs of weakness or depression, all who were physically or morally feeble had long since been left behind; the very flower of the army remained — through strength of spirit and of body.

[1] Réaumur.

The Eighth Company, which had set up the shelter of the wattling, had more than its share of men. Two sergeant-majors had come behind it, and their fire blazed up brighter than any of the others. They demanded in exchange for the right to sit behind the shelter a contribution of firewood.

"Hey, Makayef! what's the matter with you?.... Did you get lost, or did the wolves eat you? Bring us some wood," cried one, a rubicund-faced, red-haired soldier, scowling and winking from the smoke, but not stirring from the fire. "Come here, you crow, bring us some wood," cried this soldier, addressing another.

The red-headed man was neither a non-commissioned officer nor an exempt, but was simply a sound, healthy private, and therefore he ordered around those who were weaker than he.

A thin little soldier with a sharp nose, the one they called "Crow," — Vorona, — submissively got up and started to obey the command; but at this time the fire-light fell on the slender, graceful figure of a soldier lugging an armful of fagots.

"Give it here, that's first-rate."

The wood was broken up and thrown on, and the men blew it with their mouths and fanned it with their coat-tails, and the flame began to hiss and crackle. The soldiers, gathering closer, lighted their pipes.

The handsome young soldier who had brought the fagots put his arms akimbo and, in order to warm his frozen feet, began swiftly and skilfully to dance a shuffle where he stood.

> "*Akh, mamenka,*
> *kholodnaya rosa*
> *Da khorosha —*
> *Da f mushkatera* ...."[1]

He sang it out loud, making a sort of hiccoughing sound at every syllable of the song.

"Hey, there, your soles are flying off," cried the red-

[1] Ah, dear little mother, cold is the dew and beautiful, but to the musketeer....

haired man, observing that one of the young soldier's soles was hanging loose. "That makes it poison to dance."

The dancer paused, tore off the loose leather, and flung it into the fire.

"That's so, brother," said he, and, sitting down, he got out of his knapsack a piece of blue French cloth and proceeded to wrap it around his foot and leg. "It will do for a pair," he added, stretching his feet out toward the fire.

"We'll soon have new ones. They say, when we've killed 'em all off, we'll all have enough for a couple of pairs."

"But, say, did you see that son of a dog Petrof? He straggled behind, did n't he?" asked one of the sergeant-majors.

"I saw him some time ago," said another.

"So, then, the soldier boy...."

"They say that in the Third Company yesterday nine men missed roll-call."

"Well, but how's a man to walk when his feet are frozen off, tell me that!"

"Eh, it's idle to talk about it," said the sergeant-major.

"Well, how would you like it?" asked an old soldier reproachfully, addressing the one who had spoken about feet being frozen off.

"What's your idea about it?" cried, in a shrill, trembling voice, the sharp-nosed soldier whom they called Vorona, the crow, suddenly getting up from the farther side of the fire. "The fat grows lean, and lean ones has to die. That's my case. My strength's all gone," said he, suddenly taking a resolute tone and addressing the sergeant-major. "Have me sent to the hospital. The rheumatiz has got the upper hand o' me. And, besides, what difference does it make?"....

"There, now, that'll do, that'll do," said the sergeant-major, calmly.

The little soldier relapsed into silence, and the general conversation went on.

" To-day they took a good number of these French-men, but as for boots, it 's safe to say not one had any good for anything — not one worth naming," began one of the soldiers, with the purpose of starting a new subject.

"The Cossacks got all their boots. When they cleaned out the izba for the colonel, they dragged 'em out. It was a pity to see, boys," said the dancer. "How they flung them around. One was so alive that, would you believe it, he muttered something in his own lan-guage ! "

"They 're a clean people, boys," said the first. "White as a white birch, and some fine fellows among them, I tell you, — noblemen."

"Well, why should n't there be ? They 've recruited all sorts."

"But they can't talk with us in our language," said the dancer, with a smile of perplexity. "I says to one of 'em, 'Under what crown — *cheï koronui ? ' — who 's your king — and he talks back in his own gibberish. A wonderful people ! "

"There 's something odd about it, brothers," pursued the one who had been amazed at their whiteness; "the peasants told me at Mozhaïsk that when they started to clear up the dead where the battle was and where their bodies had been laying most a month, and what do you think, says he, theirs was as white as white paper and just as clean, and there was n't the slightest bit of smell about them."

"Well, don't you suppose 't was from the cold ? " sug-gested one man.

"Well, you are smart ! From the cold ! Why, it was hot weather. Besides, if it had been from the freezing, then ours would n't have spoiled either. But no, says he, when they came to one of ours, he 'd be all eaten up with worms, says he. And so, says he, we had to put a handkerchief round our noses and turn away our heads and get 'em off — could n't stand it. But theirs, says he, was like white paper; and not a grain of smell about 'em."

All were silent.

"Must be from their victuals," said the sergeant·major. "They feed like gentlemen."

No one replied to this.

"This muzhik told me at Mozhaïsk that they came out from a dozen villages and worked twenty days cart·ing 'em off, and did n't get the job done even then.... the dead, I mean. .... The wolves too, says he...."

"That battle amounted to something," said an old soldier. "That was a thing to remember; but those since, why, they've been nothing but a torment to the boys."

"Well, little uncle, day before yesterday, we gave it to 'em. But they won't let us catch up with 'em. They've been throwing down their muskets lively. Down on their knees! '*Pardon,*' they say. Now take one example. Platof twice took 'Poleon himself. He did not know a word about it. He gets him, gets him. That's the way, has the bird in his hands, lets him go .... and off he flies, off he flies. And so no chance to kill him."

"What a healthy liar you are, Kiselyef. I'm looking at you."

"Why liar? Honest truth!"

"If I'd had the chance, I'd given it to him. I'd knocked him down with an aspen cudgel. See how he's ruined us."

"We'll do it before we get through. No way of his escaping," said the old soldier, yawning.

The conversation died away; the soldiers began to get ready for the night.

"Just see the stars, terrible lot of them! One would say the women had been spreading out clothes," said a soldier, pointing to the Milky Way.

"Signs of a good year, boys."

"Will any more fuel be needed?"

"My back's scorching, but my belly's frozen. Queer things happen."

"O Lord ...."

"What are you jabbering about? Are you the only

one, pray, that's burning? There .... stretch yourself out."

Amid the gradually established silence was heard the snoring of several sleepers; the rest kept turning from side to side in their efforts to keep warm, and occasionally uttered exclamations.

From a bivouac fire a hundred paces distant was heard a burst of jovial, good-natured laughter.

"Hark! What a noise they're making in the Fifth Company," said one soldier. "And what a terrible lot of men!"

One soldier got up and went over to Company Five.

"Great fun!" said he, when he came back. "They've got a couple of Frenchmen:[1] one's half frozen; but t' other one's lively enough. He's singing."

"O-o! let's go and see!"....

Several of the soldiers went over to **Company Five.**

CHAPTER IX

THE Fifth Company was stationed near the grove. A huge bivouac fire was brightly blazing in the midst of the snow, casting its light on the branches of the trees, weighed down with their burden of frost.

In the midst of the night the soldiers of Company Five had heard steps in the snow, and the cracking of dry branches in the forest.

"Boys, a bear!"[2] cried one soldier.

All raised their heads and listened; and forth from the forest, into the bright light of the fire, pushed two human forms, strangely clad, and holding each other by the hand.

They were two Frenchmen, who had hidden in the forest. Hoarsely speaking something in a tongue unknown to the soldiers, they approached the fire.

One was tall and wore an officer's hat, and seemed

---

[1] *Khrantsusa.*

[2] *Rebyata, vyedmed'!* The speaker is from Southern Russia, and says *vyedmed'* for *medvyed'*.

perfectly fagged.   Approaching the fire, he tried to sit down, but fell flat.

The other, a small, dumpy private, with his ears tied up in a handkerchief, was stronger.   He lifted his comrade, and, pointing to his mouth, said something.

The soldiers gathered around the Frenchmen, spread down a cloak for the sick one, and gave them both kasha-gruel and vodka.

The enfeebled French officer was Ramball; the one with the handkerchief tied around his ears was his servant Morel.

When Morel had drunk the vodka and eaten a small kettle of kasha, he suddenly grew painfully jolly, and kept talking all the time, though the soldiers could not understand a word he said.

Ramball refused the food, and lay silently leaning on his elbow by the fire, with dull red eyes, staring at the Russians.   Occasionally he uttered a long, low groan, and then relapsed into silence.

Morel, pointing to his shoulders, made the soldiers understand that he was an officer, and that he needed to be warmed.

A Russian officer who came up to the bivouac fire sent to ask the colonel if he would not take in a French officer; and when the messenger said that the colonel ordered the officer to be brought to him, Ramball was invited to go.

He got up and tried to walk, but tottered, and would have fallen if a soldier who happened to be standing near had not supported him.

" What?   Can't you come it?" asked one soldier, turning to Ramball with a wink and a grin.

"Oh, you idiot! durak!".... "Can't you have some decency?".... "What a muzhik! Truly a muzhik!" were heard from all sides in accents of reproach to the jesting soldier.

They gathered round Ramball; two of them lifted him up in their arms and bore him to the izba. He threw his arms around their necks and kept repeating in piteous tones: " *Oh! mes braves, oh mes bons, mes bons amis! Voilà des hommes! oh mes braves, mes bons amis!* — Oh my good friends, you are true men!" and like a child rested his head on the shoulder of one of the soldiers.

Meantime Morel sat in the seat of honor, surrounded by the soldiers.

Morel, a little squat Frenchman, with inflamed, teary eyes, with a woman's handkerchief tied over his cap, was dressed in a woman's shabby sheepskin shubyonka. The vodka had evidently gone to his head, and he, while holding the hand of the soldier who sat next him, was singing, in a hoarse, broken voice, a French song.

The soldiers held their sides as they looked at him.

"Now then, now then, teach us that. How does it go? I'll catch it in a moment. How is it?" asked the jester, who was a singer, and whose hand Morel had seized.

> *" Vive Henri Quatre!*
> *Vive ce roi vaillant!"*

sang Morel, winking one eye.

> *" Ce diable à quatre!"....* [1]

"*Vivarika Vif seruvaru! Sidiobliaka!*" repeated the soldier, beating time with his hand, and actually catching the tune. "See how clever! ho! — ho! — ho! — ho! — ho!" arose the coarse, jocund laughter from every side. Morel, frowning, laughed also.

"Well, give us some more, more!"

> *" Qui eut le triple talent*
> *De boire, de battre,*
> *Et d'être un vert galant!"* [2]

"Now that goes well, too!".... "Now, then, Zale-tayef!"....

"*Kiu!*" repeated Zaletayef, with a will, — "*kiu .... iu .... iu*" — he dwelt on the diphthong, trying to stick out

[1] Live Henry IV.! Long live the gallant king, etc. French song. — AUTHOR'S NOTE.

[2] Who had the threefold talent of drinking, of fighting, and of being loved.

his lips, — "*letriptala de bu de ba i detravagala,*" he sang.

"Aï! splendid! He's a real Frenchy!"

"Oï — ho! ho! ho! ho!"

"Don't you want something more to eat?"

"Give him some more kasha! It'll take some time to fill up his hunger."

They gave him another bowl of the gruel, and then Morel, laughing, took still a third. Jovial smiles broadened the faces of all the young soldiers as they looked at Morel. The old veterans, counting it unseemly to descend to such trivialities, lay on the other side of the fire, but occasionally raised themselves on their elbows and stared at Morel with a smile.

"They're men like us," said one of them, as he wrapped himself up in his cloak. "Even wormwood has roots to grow by."

"Oo! Lord! Lord! What a terrible lot of stars! It's going to be a cold night." ....

And all grew silent again.

The stars, as if they knew that now no one was looking at them, played merrily in the dark sky. Now flashing out, now dying down again, now twinkling, they seemed to be busily engaged in communing among themselves concerning something pleasant but mysterious.

CHAPTER X

The French troops melted away in a regular mathematical progression.

Even that passage of the Beresina, about which so much has been written, was only one of the intermediate steps in the destruction of the French army, and not at all a decisive episode of the campaign.

If so much has been written and still is written about the Beresina, it is, so far as concerns the French, simply because the misfortunes which the French army had, up to that time, endured coming steadily, here suddenly accumulated in one moment at the broken bridge on the river — one tragic disaster, which remained in the memory of all.

On the part of the Russians so much has been talked and written about the Beresina, simply because at Petersburg, far away from the theater of war, a plan was made (by Pfuhl) for drawing Napoleon into a strategical snare on the river Beresina.

All were persuaded that everything would be carried out in conformity with the plan, and therefore they insisted that the passage of the Beresina was the destruction of the French.

In reality, the results of the passage of the Beresina were far less disastrous to the French in loss of artillery and prisoners than the battle of Krasnoye, as is proved by statistics.

The only significance of the passage of the Beresina lies in this, that it proved beyond a doubt the absurdity of all plans for cutting off the retreat of the French, and the correctness of the only feasible operation, that demanded by Kutuzof and all the troops (as a whole), — the idea of simply pursuing the enemy.

The throngs of the French hurried on with constantly increasing velocity, with all their energies concentrated on the attainment of their goal. They fled like a wounded animal, and it was impossible to stop them in their course.

This is proved not so much by the arrangements made for the passage as by what occurred at the bridges.

When the bridges were destroyed, — soldiers without weapons, natives of Moscow, women and children, who were in convoy of the French, all carried away by the force of inertia, instead of giving themselves up, pushed on, throwing themselves into boats or into the icy waters.

This impetus was a matter of course.

The situation of the fugitives and of the pursuers was equally bad. Each one being in company with his fellows in misfortune had hope of their help from the definite place which he held among his fellows.

If he surrendered to the Russians, he would be in the same condition of wretchedness, would indeed be far worse off as far as all the requirements of living were concerned.

The French did not need exact information of the fact that half of the prisoners whom the Russians did not know what to do with, in spite of their desires to save them, had died of hunger and starvation. They felt that this was inevitable.

The most compassionate Russian generals, those well disposed toward the French, Frenchmen in the Russian service, could do nothing for the prisoners. The French perished of the miseries which attended the Russian army.

It was an impossibility to take from their famished, needy soldiers bread and clothes in order to give them to the French, however inoffensive, friendly, and even innocent they might be.

A few even did this, but they were only exceptions.

Behind the French was certain destruction; before them was hope. They had burned their ships, there was no other safety than in associated flight; and on this associated flight all the energies of the French were concentrated.

The farther the French fled and the more pitiable the condition of their remnants became, especially after the Beresina, — on which, in consequence of the Petersburg plan, especial hopes were rested, — the more frantically excited waxed the passions of the Russian generals, who indulged in recriminations of each other and especially of Kutuzof.

Taking for granted that the failure of the Petersburg plan at the Beresina would be attributed to him, their discontent with him, their scorn of him, and their sarcasms at his expense were expressed with greater and greater violence. Their sarcasms and scorn, of course, were couched under the form of respect, so that Kutuzof could not demand in what way and why he was blamed.

They never talked with him seriously; while making their reports to him and asking his advice, they affected to conform with the gravest ceremony, but behind his back they winked at one another and at every step tried to deceive him.

All these men, from the very reason that they could not understand him, were convinced that there was nothing to be said to this old man, that he would never penetrate into all the wisdom of their plans, that he would simply repeat his phrases — it seemed to them they were nothing but phrases — about "the golden bridge," and how he could not think of crossing the border with a troop of vagabonds, and the like.

This was all that he had ever been heard to say. And all that he said, — for example, that it was necessary to wait for provisions, that the men were unprovided with boots, — all this was so simple, and all that they proposed was so complicated and deep, that it was a self-evident truth for them that he was stupid and old, and they were the commanders of genius, who were only lacking in power.

Especially after that brilliant admiral and hero, Wittgenstein, from Petersburg, joined the army, this disposition and this disaffection reached its height. Kutuzof saw it, and, sighing, simply shrugged his shoulders. But one time — after the Beresina — he lost his temper, and wrote the following note to Wittgenstein, who had made a special report to the sovereign.

Owing to your severe attacks of illness, your excellency[1] will be kind enough on receipt of this to retire to Kaluga, where you will await his imperial majesty's further commands and orders.

But after the retirement of Benigsen came the Grand Duke Konstantin Pavlovitch, who had been present at the beginning of the campaign and had been removed from Kutuzof's army. The grand duke, as soon as he reached the army, assured Kutuzof of his majesty the emperor's dissatisfaction at the insufficient successes of our troops and the slowness of our movements, and informed him that his majesty the emperor, himself, intended shortly to be present with the army.

[1] *Vashe vuisokoprevoskhodityelstvo.*

This old man, who was no less experienced in the affairs of courts than in affairs military, this Kutuzof, who had been appointed commander-in-chief the previous August against the sovereign's will, this man who sent the heir-apparent and the grand duke away from the army, who by the power invested in him had signed the abandonment of Moscow, this same Kutuzof now instantly realized that his time was come, that his part was played, and that the semblance of power which he had held was his no more.

And not by his court instinct alone did he realize this. On the one hand, he saw that the war in which he had played his part was ended, and he felt that his calling was fulfilled. On the other hand, at the same time, he began to feel physical weariness in his old frame and the absolute need of physical rest.

Kutuzof, on the eleventh of December, arrived at Vilna — " his good Vilna," as he called it. Twice during his career Kutuzof had been governor of Vilna. In the rich city, which had not suffered from the devastation of war, Kutuzof found, besides the amenities of life, of which he had been deprived so long, old friends and pleasant recollections. And suddenly, casting off all military and governmental cares, he plunged into this calm, equable life as far as he was allowed to do so by the passions seething around him, as if all that was occurring and about to occur in the historical world concerned him not.

Chitchagof, one of the most disaffected and volatile of men, — Chitchagof, who had at first been anxious to make a diversion into Greece and afterwards against Warsaw, though he was never willing to go where he was sent, — Chitchagof, who was famous for his audacious speech to the sovereign, — Chitchagof, who considered himself Kutuzof's benefactor, because when, in 1811, he had been sent to conclude peace with Turkey, without Kutuzof's knowledge, he, on discovering that the peace was already concluded, acknowledged before the sovereign that the credit of concluding the peace belonged to Kutuzof, — this same Chitchagof was the first to meet Kutuzof at the castle of Vilna, where Kutuzof was to be lodged. Chitchagof, in naval undress uniform, holding his forage-cap under his arm, gave Kutuzof his report and handed him the keys of the city.

That scornfully respectful demeanor of the young to Kutuzof, who was regarded as in his dotage, was shown in the highest degree in all the behavior of Chitchagof, who knew of the charges made against his senior.

In his conversation with Chitchagof, Kutuzof told him, among other things, that the carriages with plate which had been captured from him at Borisovo were safe and would be restored to him.

"You wish to insinuate that I have nothing to eat on..... On the contrary, I can furnish you with everything even in case you should wish to give dinner-parties," replied Chitchagof, angrily, in every word that he spoke wishing to prove his correctness of style, and therefore supposing that Kutuzof was occupied with the same.

Kutuzof smiled his peculiar, shrewd smile, and, shrugging his shoulders, replied, " *Ce n'est que pour dire ce que je vous dis* — It was only to tell you, that I told you."

Kutuzof, contrary to the sovereign's wish, kept the larger part of the army at Vilna. Kutuzof, according to those who had most to do with him, was greatly shaken and was very weak physically during his stay at Vilna. He occupied himself with military affairs with a very bad grace; he intrusted everything to his generals, and, while waiting for the sovereign, gave himself up to a life of dissipation.

When, on the twenty-third of December, the sovereign with his suite, — Count Tolstoï, Prince Volkonsky, Arakcheyef, and others, — after a four days' journey from Petersburg, reached Vilna, he drove in his traveling sledge directly to the castle. In spite of the severe cold, a hundred generals and staff-officers, in full-dress uniform, and the guard of honor of the Semyonovsky regiment, were waiting at the castle.

A courier, dashing up to the castle in a sledge drawn

by a sweaty troïka, cried, " He 's coming!"   Konovnitsuin hurried into the vestibule to inform Kutuzof, who
was expecting him in the Swiss's pretty little room.

In a moment the old general's stout, portly form, in
full-dress uniform, his full regalia covering his chest,
and with a scarf tied around his abdomen, came tottering and swaying to the head of the stairs.   Kutuzof
put his three-cornered hat on, point front, took his
gloves in his hand, and, letting himself painfully, toil-
somely sidewise down the stairs, stepped forth holding
in his hand the report which had been prepared to give
to the sovereign.

There was a running to and fro, a sound of hurried
talking, another troïka came unexpectedly dashing by,
and all eyes were fixed on a sledge which came flying
up.   In it could be already seen the figures of the sovereign and Volkonsky.

All this had its physically exciting effect on the old
general, though he had been used to it for half a century.   With a hasty, nervous movement he adjusted his
decorations and straightened his hat, and the instant
that the sovereign, stepping out of the sledge, raised
his eyes to him, taking courage and lifting himself up
to his full height, he handed him the report and began
to speak in his measured, ingratiating voice.

The sovereign, with a swift glance, measured Kutuzof
from head to feet, frowned for an instant, but, instantly
mastering himself, stepped forward, and, stretching out
his arms, embraced the old general.

Once more, owing to the old familiar impression
and to the thoughts that came surging into his mind,
this embrace had its usual effect upon Kutuzof : he
sobbed.

The sovereign greeted the officers and the Semyonovsky Guard, and, having once more shaken hands
with the old general, he went with him into the castle.

After the sovereign was left alone with his field-
marshal, he freely expressed his dissatisfaction with the
slowness of the pursuit, with the mistakes made at
Krasnoye and on the Beresina, and gave him his ideas

as to what should be the coming campaign beyond the frontier.

Kutuzof made no reply or remark. That same submissive and stupid expression with which seven years before he had listened to his sovereign's comments on the field of Austerlitz rested now on his face.

When Kutuzof left the cabinet and was passing along the hall with his heavy, plunging gait and with sunken head, some one's voice called him back.

"Your serene highness," cried some one.

Kutuzof raised his head and looked long into the eyes of Count Tolstoï, who, with a small trinket on a silver platter, stood before him.

Kutuzof apparently knew not what was wanted of him.

Suddenly he came to himself; a scarcely perceptible smile flashed across his pudgy face, and, making a low and respectful bow, he took the object lying on the platter.

It was the George of the first degree.

CHAPTER XI

The next day the field-marshal gave a dinner and a ball which the sovereign honored with his presence.

Kutuzof had received the George of the first degree, the sovereign had paid him the highest honors; but the sovereign's dissatisfaction with the field-marshal was noticeable to every one. The proprieties were strictly observed, and the sovereign set the first example of this; but all knew that the old general was considered blameworthy and unfit for further employment.

When, at the ball, Kutuzof, in accordance with an old custom of Catherine's time, commanded the standards captured from the enemy to be inclined before the sovereign as he entered the ball-room, the sovereign frowned with annoyance, and muttered certain words, among which some overheard the expression, — " *Starui Komediant* — the old actor !"

The sovereign's dissatisfaction with Kutuzof was in-creased in Vilna, especially because Kutuzof evidently would not or could not understand the significance of the campaign before him.

When, on the following morning, the sovereign said to the officers who came to pay their respects to him, "You have saved not Russia alone : you have saved all Europe," every one very well understood that the war was not ended.

Kutuzof was the only one who would not see this, and he openly expressed his opinion that a new war could not improve the position or increase the glory of Russia, but could only weaken her position and diminish the already lofty pinnacle of glory on which Russia, in his opinion, was now standing. He endeavored to show the sovereign the impossibility of recruiting fresh armies ; he spoke about the difficult position of the inhabitants, and hinted at the possibility of failure and the like.

Having such ideas, the field-marshal naturally made himself only a hindrance and a stumbling-block in the way of the coming war.

A convenient way of avoiding collisions with the old man presented itself. This was: just as at Austerlitz, and as at the beginning of the campaign when Barclay was commander-in-chief, to take out from under the commander-in-chief the ground of the power whereon he stood, without disturbing him, or even letting him realize it, and to transfer it to the sovereign himself.

With this end in view, the staff was gradually re-formed, and all that constituted the strength of Kutuzof's staff was destroyed or transferred to the sovereign's.

Toll, Konovnitsuin, Yermolof, received other appoint-ments. All openly expressed the opinion that the field-marshal was becoming very weak, and that his health was in a precarious condition.

It was necessary for him to be in "feeble health," so that he might transfer his place to his successor. And the truth was his health was feeble.

Just as naturally and simply and gradually as Kutuzof had been summoned from Turkey to appear in the court of the exchequer at Petersburg to take charge of the militia and afterwards of the army, so now when it was necessary it came about just as naturally, gradually, and simply, when Kutuzof's part had been played to the end, that his place should be filled by the new actor that was required.

The war of 1812, besides accomplishing the national object so dear to every Russian heart, was destined to have another significance still — one European.

The movements of the nations from west to east was to be followed by a movement from east to west, and for this new war a new actor was needed, who had other qualities and views from those of Kutuzof, and was moved by other impulses.

Alexander the First was as necessary to move the nations from east to west and to establish the boundaries of the nations as Kutuzof had been for the salvation and glory of Russia.

Kutuzof had no notion of the meaning of Europe, the Balance of Power, Napoleon. He could not understand this. For the representative of the Russian people, after the enemy had been annihilated, Russia saved and established on the highest pinacle of her glory, for him, a Russian, as a Russian, there was nothing left to do. For the representative of the national war there was nothing left except death.

And he died.

CHAPTER XII

PIERRE, as is generally the case, felt the whole burden of his physical deprivations and the long strain to which he had been subjected while a prisoner, only when the strain and the privations were at an end.

After his liberation he went to Orel[1]; and on the second day after his arrival, just as he was about to start for Kief, he was taken ill, and remained in Orel for three months.

[1] Pronounced Ayról.

He had what the doctors called bilious fever.

The doctors treated him, bled him, and made him swallow drugs ; nevertheless he recovered.

All that happened to him between the time of his liberation and his sickness left scarcely the faintest impression on him. He remembered only gray melancholy, sometimes rainy, sometimes snowy days, internal physical distress, pain in his legs, in his side ; he had a general impression of unhappy suffering people ; he recollected the annoying inquisitiveness of officers and generals, who asked him all sorts of questions ; his difficulties in finding carriages and horses ; and above all he recalled his disconnected thoughts and his feelings at the same time.

On the day that he was liberated, he saw Petya Rostof's dead body. On the same day he learned that Prince Andreï had lived more than a month after the battle of Borodino, and had died only a short time previously at Yaroslavl, at the Rostofs' house.

On that same day, also, Denisof, who had given Pierre this piece of news, spoke of Ellen's death, supposing that Pierre had known about it long before.

All this, at that time, had seemed merely strange to Pierre. He felt that he could not take in the significance of all this news.

His sole desire at that time was to get away as speedily as possible from those places where men were killing one another, to some quiet refuge, and there to collect his senses, to rest, and to think over all that was so strange and new that he had learned in those days.

But as soon as he reached Orel he was taken ill. When he regained his consciousness, he saw two of his servants, — Terentii and Vaska, — who had come from Moscow, and the oldest of the princesses, who had been residing at Yelets, on one of Pierre's estates, and, hearing of his liberation and illness, had come to take care of him.

During his convalescence, Pierre only gradually got rid of the impressions which the preceding months had made on him, and accustomed himself to the thought that no one would drive him forth the next morning, that no one would dispossess him of his warm bed, and that he was certain to have dinner and tea and supper. But in his dreams he still, for a long time, continued to see himself in the same conditions of captivity.

In the same way Pierre gradually realized the significance of the news which he had heard on the day of his liberation : Prince Andreï's death, the death of his wife, the annihilation of the French.

The joyous feeling of freedom, that perfect, inalienable freedom inherent in man, a realizing sense of which he had for the first time experienced at the first halting-place, when he was carried away from Moscow, filled Pierre's soul during his convalescence. He was amazed that this inner freedom, which had been independent of all external circumstances, now that he had a superfluity, even luxury, seemed to remain still as external freedom.

He was alone in a strange city, where he had no acquaintances. No one wanted anything of him, no one forced him to go anywhere against his will. He had everything that he wanted ; the thought about his wife, which had formerly tormented him, had vanished as if she had never existed.

"Ah, how good! how glorious!" he would say to himself, when a table with a clean cloth was moved up to him with fragrant bouillon, or when, at night, he lay stretched out on the soft, clean bed, or when he remembered that his wife and the French no longer existed. "Ah! how good! how glorious!" And out of old habit he would ask himself the questions : "Well, what next? what am I going to do?" and instantly he would answer himself, "Nothing at all! I'm going to live. Oh! how glorious!"

The very thing that he had formerly tormented himself about, and constantly sought in vain, — an object in life, — now no longer existed for him.

This long-sought-for object of life was not merely absent by chance for the time being, but he felt that it did not exist and could not exist. And this very absence of an object in life gave him that full joyous sense of free-dom which at this time constituted his happiness.

He could have no object, because now he had a faith —not a faith in any rules or creed or dogmas, but faith in a living, everywhere perceptible God.

Hitherto he had sought for Him in aims which he had set for himself. This searching for an aim was only the seeking for God, and during his captivity he had suddenly learned, not from words, not from reason-ing, but from his immediate consciousness, what his old nurse had used long, long before to say, that God was here, there, and everywhere.

He had learned, during his captivity, that God in Karatayef was more majestic, endless, and past finding out than in what the Masons called the Architect of the Universe.

He had a similar experience to that of the man who should find under his very feet the object of his search, when he had been straining his eyes in looking far away. All his life long he had been looking over the heads of the surrounding people, while all the time there had been no need to strain his eyes, but merely to look straight ahead.

He had not been able hitherto to see the Great, the Incomprehensible, the Infinite, in anything. He had only felt that It ought to be somewhere, and he had searched for it.

In all that was near and comprehensible, he had seen only what was limited, the narrow, finite, meaningless. He had provided himself with a mental telescope, and looked out into the distance, yonder, where this narrow, finite object, concealed in the murky distance, seemed to him great and infinite, simply because it was not clearly seen.

In this way European life, politics, Masonry, philoso-phy, philanthropy, had presented themselves to him.

But at the very moments when he had accounted him-self most weak his mind had leapt forth into that same distance, and then he had seen how small and narrow, how finite and meaningless, it all was.

Now, however, he had learned to see the Great, the Eternal, and the Infinite in everything, and therefore, naturally, in order to see it, in order to enjoy the contemplation of it, he had thrown away his telescope, through which he had, till then, been looking over men's heads, and he now joyfully contemplated the ever changing, incomprehensible, and eternal life all around him. And the more closely he looked, the more serene and happy he became.

The terrible question which hitherto had overturned all his mental edifices — the question *Why* — no longer existed for him. Now to that question *Why*, his mind had always ready the simple answer : *Because God is*, that God without whose will not a hair falls from the head of a human being.

CHAPTER XIII

Pierre had scarcely changed in his outward habits.

At first sight he was just the same as he had been before. Just as before he was absent-minded, and seemed inly absorbed, not in what was before his eyes, but in his own thoughts. The difference between his former and his present self lay in this : hitherto, when he had forgotten what was before him, or paid no attention to what was said to him, he would wrinkle his brows with a martyr-like air, as if striving, but without success, to study into something that was far away. Now in the same way he was oblivious of what was said to him, and of what was before him ; but now with a scarcely perceptible smile, which one might almost have thought satirical, he looked at what was before him, he listened to what was said to him, although it was evident that his eyes and his mind were concerned with something entirely different.

Hitherto he had seemed to be a good man, but unhappy, and therefore people could not help being repelled by him. Now a smile, called forth by the mere pleasure of living, constantly played around his mouth, and his eyes were lighted up by a sympathetic interest in people, — in the question, "Were they as happy as he was?"

And people liked to be with him.

Hitherto he had talked much, got easily excited when he talked, and was a poor listener; now he was rarely carried away by the heat of an argument, and had become such a good listener that people were glad to tell him the deepest secrets of their hearts.

The princess, who had never liked Pierre and had cherished a peculiar feeling of animosity against him ever since that time when, after the count's death, she had found herself under obligations to him, greatly to her annoyance and surprise, after a short stay at Orel, whither she came with the intention of showing Pierre that, in spite of his "ingratitude," she considered it her duty to take care of him, — the princess quickly felt that she was growing fond of him.

Pierre did nothing for the sake of winning her good graces. He merely studied her with curiosity. Hitherto the princess had felt that only indifference and irony were expressed in his view of her, and she shrank into herself before him, just as she did in the presence of other people, and showed only her harsh and disagreeable side; now on the contrary she felt that he had, as it were, penetrated into the most intimate and secret recesses of her existence, and she, at first with distrust, but afterwards with gratitude, showed him the good side of her character, which she had kept hidden.

The craftiest of men could not have been more skilful in winning the princess's confidence, than he was in eliciting her recollections of the happiest days of her youth, and in expressing his sympathy. But meantime Pierre's whole craft consisted in his finding his own pleasure in calling out humane feelings in the spiteful, acidulous, and in her own way haughty princess.

"Yes, he is a very, very good man when he is under the influence of people who are not bad — of people like myself," thought the princess.

The change that had taken place in Pierre was remarked, in their own way, by his servants Terentii and Vaska. They found that he had grown vastly more simple.

Terentii oftentimes, while undressing his barin, and while he had his boots and his clothes in his hand, and had wished him good-night, would hesitate about leaving the room, thinking that his barin might like to engage him in conversation. And it was a very common occurrence for Pierre to call Terentii back, noticing that he was in a mood for talking.

"Well, now, tell me — how did you manage to get anything to eat?" he would ask.

And Terentii would begin to relate about the destruction of Moscow, or about the late count, and would stand for a long time with the clothes in his hand, telling stories, or sometimes listening to Pierre's yarns, and then, with a pleasing sense of nearness to his barin and of friendliness to him, go into the anteroom.

The doctor who had charge of Pierre's case, and who visited him every day, in spite of the fact that, in accordance with the custom of doctors, he felt it his duty to assume the mien of a man every minute of whose time was precious in the care of suffering humanity, would spend hours with Pierre, relating his favorite stories and making his observations on the peculiarities of the sick in general, and the ladies in particular.

"Yes, there is something delightful in talking with such a man — very different from what one finds in our province," he would say.

In Orel there were several French officers who had been taken prisoner, and the doctor brought one of them, a young Italian, to see Pierre.

This officer began to be a frequent visitor, and the princess laughed at the sentimental affection which the Italian conceived for Pierre.

The Italian was happy only when he could be with Pierre and talk with him, and tell him about his past, about his home life, about his love-affairs, and pour out in his ears his indignation against the French and particularly against Napoleon.

"If all the Russians are in the least like you," he would say to Pierre, "it is a sacrilege to wage war on a people like yours — *c'est un sacrilège que de faire la guerre à un peuple comme le vôtre!* Though you have suffered so much from the French, yet you seem to have no ill-will against them."

This passionate love shown by the Italian, Pierre had won only because he had brought out in him the best side of his nature, and took pleasure in him.

During the latter part of Pierre's stay in Orel, he received a visit from his old acquaintance, the Freemason Count Villarski — the same one who had introduced him into the lodge in 1807. Villarski had married a rich Russian lady, who had a great estate in the government of Orel, and he held a temporary position in the commissariat department in the city.

Learning that Bezukhoï was in Orel, Villarski, though his acquaintance with him had been far from intimate, came to call on him with the same manifestations of friendship and neighborliness which men are apt to show each other when they meet in a wilderness. Villarski was bored to death in Orel, and he was delighted to meet a man of the same social rank as himself, and with similar interests, as he supposed.

But Villarski quickly discovered, to his amazement, that Pierre was far behind the times and had fallen into a state of apathy and egotism, as he expressed it in criticizing Pierre to his face.

"*Vous vous encroutez, mon cher* — You are becoming a fossil," he would say to him. Nevertheless Villarski was more at home with Pierre than he had ever been in times past, and he came to see him every day.

As Pierre looked at Villarski and listened to him now, it was strange and almost incredible to think that he himself had been like him only such a short time before.

Villarski was a married, family man, occupied with the business connected with his wife's estate, and with his public duties and with his family. He looked on all these occupations as a hindrance to life, and felt that they were all worthy of contempt, because their end and aim was the personal advantage of himself and his family. Military, administrative, political, and Masonic affairs constantly engrossed his attention. And Pierre, without making any effort to change Villarski's views, and not blaming him, studied this strange but only too well-known phenomenon, with his now constantly gentle and pleasant smile of irony.

In Pierre's relations with Villarski, with the princess, with the doctor, with all the people with whom he was now brought in contact, he displayed a new characteristic, which won for him the good-will of all men : this was the recognition of the possibility that every one may think and feel for himself, and look on things in his own way ; the recognition of the impossibility of convincing any one of anything by mere words ; this legitimate, lawful prerogative of every man, which formerly had excited and annoyed him, now gave him ground for the sympathy and interest which he felt in people. The variance and sometimes the perfect contradiction between the views of people and his life, and among themselves, delighted Pierre, and brought to his lips a gentle, satirical smile.

In practical affairs Pierre now unexpectedly felt that he had a center of gravity that had been lacking before. Hitherto, every question concerning finance, especially demands on him for money, to which he, as a very rich man, was often subjected, aroused in him helpless worry and perplexity.

To give, or not to give ? that was the question with him. " I have it, but he needs it. But another one needs it still more. Which needs it the most ? But perhaps both are frauds."

And in days gone by, out of all these hypotheses he had found no exit, and was in the habit of giving to all indiscriminately, as long as he had anything to give. He used to find himself in precisely the same quandary at every question which concerned his estate, when one would say that he must do this way, and another would recommend another way.

Now he found, to his amazement, that he was troubled

no longer with doubts and perplexities. He now seemed to have some sense of judgment, which, by some laws unknown to himself, decided what was necessary and what was unnecessary for him to do.

He was no less than before indifferent to pecuniary matters; but now he knew infallibly what he ought to do and what not. The first time that this new sense of justice had to decide a question was in the case of one of the prisoners, a French colonel, who came to him, told him many stories of his great exploits, and, finally, almost demanded that Pierre should give him four thousand francs to send to his wife and children.

Pierre, without the slightest difficulty or effort, refused him, amazed afterward to find how simple and easy it was to do what had always before seemed to him unutterably difficult.

At the very time, however, that he refused the colonel, he made up his mind that it required the utmost shrewdness in order, on the eve of his departure from Orel, to induce the Italian officer to take some money, which he evidently needed.

A new proof for Pierre of the greater soundness in his views of practical affairs was his decision of the question concerning his wife's debts, and whether his houses in Moscow and his villas should be rebuilt or not.

While he was at Orel, his head overseer came to him, and he and Pierre made out a general schedule of his altered income. The conflagration of Moscow had cost Pierre, according to the overseer's reckoning, about two millions.

The head overseer, as a measure of relief for his losses, proposed a scheme whereby, notwithstanding the losses, his income would be not only not diminished, but rather increased, and this was that he should refuse to honor the debts left by the late countess, for which he could not be held accountable, and should not rebuild his Moscow houses and pod-Moskovnaya datcha, which cost him, to keep up, eighty thousand a year, and brought him in nothing.

" Yes, yes, that is true," said Pierre, smiling cheerfully. Yes, yes, I don't need it at all. The fire has made me vastly richer ! "

But in January, Savelyitch came from Moscow, told him about the condition of the city, about the estimate which the architect had made for rebuilding the Moscow mansion and the pod-Moskovnaya, and spoke about it as if it were a matter already decided.

At the same time Pierre received letters from Prince Vasili and other acquaintances in Petersburg. These letters mentioned his wife's debts. And Pierre decided that the scheme proposed by his head overseer, which had pleased him so much at first, was not right, and that he must go to Petersburg to wind up his wife's business affairs, and must rebuild his Moscow houses. Why this was necessary he knew not ; he only knew beyond a peradventure that it was necessary. His income, in consequence of this decision, would be reduced to three-fourths ; but it was a case of necessity, he felt it.

Villarski was going to Moscow, and they agreed to travel together.

Pierre had experienced during all the time of his convalescence, in Orel, a sense of delight, of freedom, of life ; but when, during his journey, he came out into the free world and saw hundreds of new faces, this feeling was still further intensified.

During all the time of his journey he felt as happy as a school-boy at having his vacation. All the faces, — the postilion, the watchman, the peasants along the road or in a village, — all had a new meaning for him.

The presence of Villarski, with his observations and his constantly expressed regret at the poverty, barbarism, and backwardness of Russia compared with Europe, only heightened Pierre's delight.

Where Villarski saw only deadness, Pierre saw the extraordinary fecund power of life, that power which, in the snow, in that expanse of plains, upheld the life of this united, peculiar, and unique people. He did not contradict Villarski, and affected to agree with him —

since pretended agreement was the shortest means of avoiding arguments from which there was no escape — and joyously smiling, listened to him.

CHAPTER XIV

JUST as it is hard to explain why and whither the ants rush from a scattered ant-hill, some dragging away little fragments, eggs, and dead bodies, others hurrying back to the ant-hill again, why they jostle one another, push one another, and fight, — so would it be hard to explain the causes that compelled the Russian people, after the departure of the French, to throng back to that place which had formerly been called Moscow.

But just as when one looks at the ants tearing in wild confusion around their despoiled abode, notwithstanding the complete destruction of the ant-hill, one can see by the activity and energy, by the myriads of insects, that everything is utterly destroyed, except the something indestructible and immaterial, which constitutes the whole strength of the ant-hill, — so, in Moscow, in the month of October, though there was an absence of authorities, of churches, of priests, of riches, of houses, still it was the same Moscow as it had been in the month of August.

Everything was destroyed except the something immaterial, but potent and indestructible.

The motives of the people who flocked from all sides into Moscow after its evacuation by the enemy were the most various and personal, and, for the most part, savage, animal. One motive, only, was common to all: that was the attraction toward the place which had once been called Moscow, for the employment there of their activity.

Within a week Moscow already had fifteen thousand inhabitants; in a fortnight twenty-five thousand, and so on. Constantly rising and rising, the population, by the autumn of 1813, reached a figure exceeding that which it had in 1812.

The first Russians to enter Moscow were the Cossacks of Winzengerode's division, the muzhiks from the neighboring villages, and citizens that had fled and concealed themselves in the environs.

Returning to ruined Moscow, the Russians, finding it plundered, began also to plunder. They continued the work begun by the French. Muzhiks brought in carts, in order to carry back to their villages whatever was to be found abandoned in the houses or streets of ruined Moscow.

The Cossacks carried off what they could to their tents; proprietors of houses took possession of whatever they could lay their hands on in other houses, and carried it home under the pretext that it was their own property.

But the first comers were followed by other plunderers, and they by still others; and pillage each day, in proportion as the numbers increased, became more and more difficult, and was conducted under more definite forms.

The French found Moscow, though deserted, yet provided with all the forms of a city the life of which flowed in accordance with organic laws, with its various functions of trade, handicraft, luxury, imperial administration, religion. These forms were lifeless, but they still existed. There were markets, shops, magazines, grain-stores, bazaars, — most of them provided with wares; there were manufactories and workshops; there were palaces, noble mansions filled with objects of luxury; there were hospitals, prisons, court-rooms, churches, cathedrals.

The longer the French stayed, the less these forms of city life were kept up, and toward the end everything was resolving itself into one common dead level of pillage.

The longer the pillage conducted by the French continued, the more it diminished the wealth of Moscow and the strength of the pillagers.

The pillage conducted by the Russians (and the occupation of the capital by the Russians began with this) — the longer it lasted, and the more freely it was shared by the people, the more rapidly it increased the wealth of Moscow and restored the regular life of the city.

Besides the pillagers, the most varied sort of people, attracted, some by curiosity, some by their duties in the service, some by interest, — householders, clergymen, officials of high and low degree, tradesmen, artisans, muzhiks from various parts, — flowed back into Moscow like blood to the heart.

At the end of a week, already, peasants who drove in with empty carts in order to carry away things, were halted by the authorities and compelled to carry away dead bodies from the city.

Other muzhiks, hearing of the lack of commodities, came in with wheat, oats, hay, by competition with one another reducing prices even lower than they had been before. Master carpenters, hoping for fat jobs, each day flocked to Moscow, and in all directions new houses began to go up and the old burned mansions to be restored.

Merchants displayed their wares in huts. Restaurants and taverns were established in mansions which had been through the flames. The clergy conducted divine service in many churches which had escaped the conflagration. People contributed ecclesiastical furniture which had been stolen.

Chinovniks spread their tables and set up their bureaus in little rooms. High officials and the police made arrangements for restoring property which had been abandoned by the French. The owners of houses in which were found many articles brought from other houses complained of the injustice of the order to bring everything to the court of the exchequer. Others urged that, as the French had brought things from different houses into one place, it was therefore unfair to allow the owner of that house to keep whatever was found in it. They abused the police; they tried to bribe them. Estimates were received, tenfold too high, for building crown edifices that had been burned. Pecuniary assistance was asked for. Count Rostopchin wrote his proclamations.

CHAPTER XV

TOWARD the beginning of February, Pierre came to Moscow and established himself in a wing which remained intact. He paid visits to Count Rostopchin and various acquaintances who had returned to Moscow, and he planned to go two days later to Petersburg.

All were enthusiastic over the victory. There was a ferment of life in the ruined and revivified capital. All welcomed Pierre warmly. All were anxious to meet him, and plied him with questions in regard to all that he had seen.

Pierre felt drawn by special ties of sympathy and friendship to all whom he met; but he now treated every one guardedly, so as not to bind himself to any one. To all questions which he was asked — whether important or the most trivial — where he was going to live? was he going to rebuild? when was he going to Petersburg, and should he try to take his trunk with him? — he would answer "Yes," or "Perhaps so," or "I think so," or the like.

He heard that the Rostofs were in Kostroma, and the thought of Natasha rarely occurred to him. If it came to him, it was only as a pleasant recollection of something long past. He felt himself freed not only from the conditions of life, but also from that sentiment which, as it seemed to him, he had wittingly allowed himself to cherish.

On the third day after his arrival at Moscow, he learned from the Drubetskoïs that the Princess Mariya was in Moscow. Prince Andreï's death, sufferings, and last days had often recurred to Pierre's mind, and now they came back to him with fresh force. When, after dinner, he learned that the Princess Mariya was in Moscow, and was residing in her own house, which had escaped the conflagration, he went, that same evening, to call upon her.

On the way to the mansion on the Vozdvizhenka, Pierre constantly thought about Prince Andreï, about his friendship for him, about his various meetings with him, and especially their last meeting at Borodino.

"Can he have died in that same sardonic mood in which he then was?" Pierre asked himself. "Can the explanation of life have been revealed to him before his death?"

He remembered Karatayef and his death, and involuntarily he began to compare these two men, so antipodal, and, at the same time, so alike in the love which he had felt for them, and then from the fact that both had lived and both were dead.

In the most serious frame of mind, Pierre reached the old prince's mansion. This house remained intact. It bore traces of wear and tear, but the character of the house was the same as before.

Pierre was met by an old butler,[1] with a stern face, who seemed to wish it to be understood that the prince's absence did not affect the strictness of the *régime*, and said that the princess had been pleased to retire to her room, and received on Sundays.

"Carry her my name; perhaps she will receive me," said Pierre.

"*Slushayu-s* — I obey," replied the butler. "Please come to the portrait gallery."

In a few moments the butler returned to Pierre with Dessalles. Dessalles, in the name of the princess, informed Pierre that she would be very glad to see him, and begged him, if he would excuse her for the lack of ceremony, to come up-stairs to her room.

The princess was sitting in the low-studded room, lighted by a single candle. There was also some one else, in a black dress. Pierre remembered that the princess had always with her lady-companions,[2] but who and what these lady-companions were, Pierre knew not and could not remember.

"That is one of her lady-companions," he said to himself, glancing at the lady in the black dress.

The princess quickly arose, came forward to meet him, and shook hands with him.

[1] *Ofitsiant.*   [2] *Kompanyonki.*

"Yes," said she, as she looked into his altered face, after he had kissed her hand. "So we meet again at last. He often used to speak about you during the last days of his life," said she, turning her eyes from Pierre to the "kompanyonka" with an embarrassment that for an instant struck Pierre. "I was so glad to know of your rescue. That was truly the best piece of news we had received for a long time."

Again the princess looked still more anxiously at the "kompanyonka," and wanted to say something, but Pierre did not give her an opportunity.

"You may imagine I knew nothing about it," said he. "I thought he was killed. All that I knew, I knew from others, and that at third hand. All I know is that he fell in with the Rostofs....what a strange good fortune!"

Pierre spoke rapidly, with animation. He looked once into the "kompanyonka's" face, saw an apparently flattering, inquisitive glance fastened on him, and, as often happens during a conversation, he gathered a general idea that this "kompanyonka" in the black dress was a gentle, kindly, good creature, who would not interfere with the sincerity and cordiality of his conversation with the Princess Mariya.

But when he said the last words about the Rostofs, the embarrassment expressed on the princess's face was even more noticeable than before. She again turned her eyes from Pierre's face to the face of the lady in the black dress, and said : —

"But don't you recognize her?"

Pierre once more looked into the "kompanyonka's" pale, delicate face, with the dark eyes and strange mouth. Something near and dear, something long forgotten and more than kind, was looking at him from those attentive eyes.

"But no, it cannot be," he said to himself. "That face so stern, thin, and pale, and grown so old. That cannot be she! It is only something that reminds me of her!" But at that instant the Princess Mariya said:

"Natasha!"

And the face with the attentive eyes, with difficulty, with an effort, — just as a rusty door opens, — smiled, and from the opened door suddenly breathed forth and surrounded Pierre the perfume of that long-forgotten happiness, of which he had rarely thought, especially of late. Forth breathed the perfume, seized his senses, and swallowed him up entirely. When she smiled, all doubt ceased; it was Natasha, and he loved her!

At the first minute, Pierre involuntarily told both her and the Princess Mariya, and, chief of all, himself, the secret that he long had not confessed even to his own heart. He reddened with delight and passionate pain. He tried to hide his agitation. But the more he tried to hide it, the more distinctly — more distinctly than in the most definite words — he told himself and her and the Princess Mariya that he loved her!

"No, of course, it is only from the surprise," said Pierre to himself; but in spite of all his efforts to prolong the conversation that he had started with the Princess Mariya, he could not help looking again at Natasha, and a still deeper flush suffused his face, and a still deeper agitation of joy and pain clutched his heart. He hesitated in his speech, and stopped short in the midst of what he was saying.

Pierre had not remarked Natasha for the reason that he had not in the least expected to see her there, but the reason he did not recognize her was because of the immense change that had taken place in her since he had seen her last.

She had grown thin and pale. But it was not that that had changed her identity; it was impossible that he should have recognized her on the first moment of his entrance, because that face from whose eyes hitherto had always gleamed forth the secret joy of living, now when he came in and for the first time glanced at her, had not even the shadow of a smile; they were merely attentive, kindly, and pathetically questioning eyes.

Pierre's confusion did not waken any answering confusion in Natasha, but only a contentment which lighted up her whole face with an almost imperceptible gleam.

CHAPTER XVI

"She has come to make me a visit," said the Princess Mariya. "The count and countess will be here in a few days. The countess is in a terrible state. But Natasha herself had need of consulting the doctor. They sent her with me by main force."

"Yes, is there a family without its own special sorrow?" said Pierre, addressing Natasha. "You know that it happened on the very day that we were set free. I saw him. What a charming boy he was!"

Natasha looked at him, but in answer to his words her eyes dilated and a shade crept over them.

"What consolation can be given in either thought or word?" exclaimed Pierre. "None at all! Why should such a glorious young fellow, so full of life, have to die?"

"Yes, indeed, in these days it would be hard to live, if one had not faith...." said the Princess Mariya.

"Yes, yes! That is the real truth," interrupted Pierre, hastily.

"Why?" asked Natasha, gazing attentively into Pierre's eyes.

"How can you ask 'why'?" exclaimed the Princess Mariya. "The mere thought of what awaits us there ...."

Natasha, without hearing the Princess Mariya to the end, again looked at Pierre with questioning eyes.

"Why, because," continued Pierre, "only that man who believes that there is a God who directs our ways can endure such a loss as hers — and yours," added Pierre.

Natasha had her lips parted to say something, but suddenly stopped. Pierre quickly turned from her, and again addressed the princess with a question concerning his friend's last days.

Pierre's embarrassment had now almost disappeared, but at the same time he felt that all his former freedom had also disappeared. He felt that his every word and act had now a critic, a judge, who was dearer to him than the opinion of all the people in the world.

When he spoke now, he measured at every word the impression which his words produced on Natasha. He did not purposely say what would have pleased her; but whatever he said he judged from her standpoint.

The Princess Mariya, reluctantly at first, as is always the case, began to tell him about the state in which Prince Andreï had come to them. But Pierre's questions, his evidently troubled eyes, his face trembling with emotion, gradually induced her to enter into particulars which she would have been afraid to call back to her recollection for her own sake.

"Yes, yes, indeed it is so...." said Pierre, leaning forward with his whole body toward the Princess Mariya, and eagerly listening to her story, — "Yes, yes, and so he grew calmer? more softened? He so earnestly sought with all the powers of his soul for the one thing: to be perfectly good. He could not have feared death. The faults that he had — if he had any — came from other sources than himself. And so he grew softened?" exclaimed Pierre. "What good fortune that he met you again," he added, turning to Natasha and looking at her, his eyes brimming with tears.

Natasha's face twitched. She frowned, and for an instant dropped her eyes. For a minute she hesitated: should she speak, or not speak.

"Yes, it was good fortune," said she, in a low chest voice. "For me indeed it was a happiness." She became silent. "And he .... he .... he said that it was the very thing that he was longing for when I went to him...."

Natasha's voice broke. She clasped her hands together on her knees, and suddenly, evidently making an effort to contain herself, raised her head and began to speak rapidly :—

"We knew nothing about it when we left Moscow. I had not dared to ask about him. And suddenly Sonya told me that he was with us. I had no idea, I could not imagine, in what a state he was. I only wanted one thing—to see him, to be with him," said she, trembling and choking. And without letting herself be interrupted, she related what she had never before told a living soul: all that she had lived through in those three weeks of their journey and their sojourn at Yaroslavl.

Pierre listened to her with open mouth and without taking from her his eyes full of tears. In listening to her he thought not of Prince Andreï or of death, or even of what she was telling him. He heard her, and only pitied her for the suffering which she underwent now in telling the tale.

The princess, frowning with her endeavor to keep back her tears, sat next Natasha, and listened for the first time to the story of these last days that her brother had spent with Natasha.

This tale, so fraught with pain and joy, it was evidently necessary for Natasha to relate.

She spoke, commingling the most insignificant details with the intimate secrets of the heart, and it seemed as if she would never reach an end. Several times she repeated the same things.

Dessalles's voice was heard outside the door, asking if Nikolushka might come and bid them good-night.

"And this is the whole story .... all ...." said Natasha.

When Nikolushka came in she quickly sprang up and almost ran to the door, and, hitting her head against the door, which was hidden by a portière, flew from the room with a groan caused partly by pain, partly by grief.

Pierre gazed at the door through which she had disappeared, and could not understand why he seemed suddenly left alone and deserted in the world.

The Princess Mariya aroused him from his fit of abstraction by calling his attention to her nephew, who had come into the room.

Nikolushka's face, which resembled his father's, had such an effect on Pierre, in this moment of soul-felt emotion into which he had come, that after he had kissed the lad he quickly arose, and, getting out his handkerchief, went to the window.

He wanted to bid the Princess Mariya good-night and go, but she detained him.

"No, Natasha and I often sit up till three o'clock; please stay a little longer. I will order supper served. Go down-stairs, we will follow immediately."

But before Pierre left the room the princess said to him : —

"This is the first time that she has spoken so of him."

CHAPTER XVII

PIERRE was conducted into the large, brightly lighted dining-room. In a few minutes steps were heard, and the princess and Natasha came into the room. Natasha was now calm, although a grave expression, untouched with a smile, still remained on her face.

The Princess Mariya, Natasha, and Pierre alike experienced that sense of awkwardness which is sure to follow after a serious and intimate conversation. To pursue the former subject is no longer possible ; to talk about trifles does not seem right ; and silence is disagreeable because such silence seems hypocritical, especially if one wishes to talk.

They silently came to the table. The butlers drew the chairs back and pushed them forward. Pierre unfolded his cold napkin, and, making up his mind to break the silence, looked at Natasha and the Princess Mariya.

Each of them had evidently at the same time made the same resolve ; the eyes of both shone with the satisfaction of life, and the avowal that, if sorrow exists, so also joy may abound.

"Will you have vodka, count?" asked the Princess Mariya, and these words suddenly drove away the shadows of the past.

"Tell us about yourself," said the Princess Mariya. "We have heard such incredible stories about you."

"Yes?" replied Pierre, with that smile of good-humored irony which was now habitual with him. "I too have been told most marvelous things — things that I have never even dreamed of seeing. Marya Abramovna invited me to her house, and told me all that ever happened to me or was supposed to have happened. Stepan Stepanuitch also gave me a lesson in the way that I should tell my story. As a general thing, I have observed that it is a very comfortable thing to be an 'interesting person' (I am now an interesting person)! I am invited out and made the subject of all sorts of stories."

Natasha smiled, and started to say something.

"We were told," said the Princess Mariya, forestalling her, "that you lost two millions here in Moscow. Is that true?"

"But still it made me three times as rich as before," replied Pierre.

Pierre, in spite of his wife's debts and the necessity which he felt of rebuilding his houses, which would alter his circumstances, continued to tell people that he had grown three times as rich as before.

"What I have undoubtedly gained," said he, "is this freedom which I enjoy" — he had begun seriously, but he hesitated about continuing, observing that the topic of the conversation was too egotistical.

"And you are going to rebuild?"

"Yes; Savelyitch advises it."

"Tell me, you did not know at all about the countess's death when you were in Moscow?" asked the Princess Mariya, and instantly reddened, noticing that in having put this question immediately after what he had said about his freedom, she might have given a sense to his words which perhaps they had not.

"No," replied Pierre, evidently not discovering anything awkward in the interpretation which the Princess Mariya had given to his remark about his freedom. "I first heard about it in Orel, and you cannot imagine how it surprised me. We were not a model husband and wife," he quickly added, with a glance at Natasha, and observing in her face a gleam of curiosity as to what he would have to say about his wife. "But her death gave me a terrible shock. When two persons quarrel, always both are at fault. And a person's fault suddenly becomes awfully serious when the other party comes to die. And then such a death!.... without friends, without consolation! I felt very, very sorry for her," said he, in conclusion, and noticing with a sense of satisfaction a look of joyful approval in Natasha's face.

"Well, and so you are a single man and marriageable again," said the Princess Mariya.

Pierre's face suddenly grew livid, and for long he tried not to look at Natasha. When at length he had the courage to look at her, her face was cold, stern, and even scornful as it seemed to him.

"And did you really see Napoleon and talk with him? That's the story they tell us," said the Princess Mariya.

Pierre laughed.

"Not once, never! It always seems to every one that to have been a prisoner was to have been Napoleon's guest. I not only never saw him, but did not hear him talked about. I was in far too humble company."

Supper was over, and Pierre, who at first refused to tell about his captivity, was little by little drawn into stories about it.

"But it is true, isn't it, that you remained behind for the purpose of killing Napoleon?" asked Natasha, with a slight smile. "I imagined as much when we met you at the Sukharef Tower, — do you remember?"

Pierre acknowledged that this was true; and with this question as a starting-point, and gradually led on by the Princess Mariya's questions, and especially by Natasha's, Pierre was brought to give them a detailed account of his adventures.

At first he told his story with that gentle, ironical expression which he now used toward other people and especially himself; but afterwards, when he came to tell about the horrors and sufferings which he had beheld, he, without being himself aware of it, was carried away, and began to talk with the restrained excitement of a man who was re-living, in his recollections, the most vivid impressions.

The Princess Mariya, with a gentle smile, looked now at Pierre, now at Natasha. Throughout all this narration, she saw only Pierre and his goodness.

Natasha, leaning her head on her hand, with her face reflecting in its expression all the varying details of the story, gazed steadily at Pierre without once taking her eyes from him, evidently living with him through all the dreadful scenes of which he told.

Not only her looks, but her exclamations and the brief questions which she asked, showed Pierre that, from his story, she took to heart exactly what he wanted to convey. It was evident that she understood not merely what he told her, but also that which he would have wished but was unable to express in words.

Concerning his adventure with the child and the woman the protection of whom had led to his capture, Pierre told in the following manner : —

" It was a horrible sight : children deserted, some in the flames .... one child was dragged out before my very eyes .... women who were robbed of their possessions, their ear-rings snatched away ...."

Pierre reddened and stammered.

"Then came the patrol and arrested all those who were not engaged in pillage — all the men. — And myself ! "

" You certainly are not telling the whole story ; you certainly did something," said Natasha, and paused a moment, — " something good ! "

Pierre went on with his narration. When he came to tell about the execution, he wished to avoid the horrible details, but Natasha insisted that he should not omit anything.

Pierre began to tell about Karatayef. By this time he had risen from the table, and was walking back and forth, Natasha's eyes following him all the time. But he paused.

" No, you cannot understand how I learned from that illiterate man — half an idiot ! "

" Yes, yes, go on," cried Natasha. " What became of him ? "

"He was shot almost in my very presence."

And Pierre began to tell about the last period of the retreat of the French, Karatayef's illness (his voice constantly trembled) and his death. Pierre, in relating his adventures, put them in an entirely new light.

He now found what seemed to be a new significance in all that he had experienced. Now, while he was telling all this to Natasha, he experienced that rare delight afforded by women — not *intellectual* women, who, in listening, try either to remember what is said for the sake of enriching their minds, and, on occasion, of giving it out themselves, or to apply what is said to their own cases, and to communicate with all diligence their intellectual remarks elaborated in the petty workshops of their brains — but the delight afforded by genuine women gifted with the capacity to bring out and assimilate all that is best in the manifestations of a man.

Natasha, without knowing it, was all attention; she did not lose a word or an inflection of his voice, or a glance, or the quivering of a muscle in his face, or a single gesture made by Pierre.

She caught on the wing the word as yet unspoken, and took it straight to her generous heart, divining the mysterious meaning of all the spiritual travail through which Pierre had passed.

The Princess Mariya comprehended his story and sympathized with him, but now she saw something else which absorbed all her attention : she saw the possibility of love and happiness for Pierre and Natasha. And this thought, occurring to her for the first time, filled her heart with joy.

It was three o'clock in the morning. The butlers, with gloomy, stern faces, came to bring fresh candles, but no one heeded them.

Pierre finished his story. Natasha, her eyes gleaming with excitement, continued to look steadily and earnestly at Pierre, as if wishing to read the portions of his story that he had perhaps not told.

Pierre, with a shamefaced but joyous sense of embarrassment, occasionally looked at her, and wondered what to say next in order to change the conversation to some other topic.

The Princess Mariya was silent. It occurred to none of them that it was three o'clock in the morning and time to go to bed.

"We talk about unhappiness, sufferings," said Pierre. "Yet, if now, this minute, I were asked, 'Would you remain what you were before your imprisonment, or go through it all again?' I should say, 'For God's sake, the imprisonment once more and the horse-flesh.' We think that when we are driven out of the usual path, everything is all over for us; but it is just here that the new and the good begins. As long as there is life, there is happiness. There is much, much before us! I tell you so," said he, addressing Natasha.

"Yes, yes," said she, answering something entirely different. "And I should wish nothing better than to live my life all over again."

Pierre looked at her keenly.

"No, I could ask for nothing more."

"You are wrong, you are wrong," cried Pierre. "I am not to blame because I am alive and want to live; and you also."

Suddenly Natasha hid her face in her hands, and burst into tears.

"What is it, Natasha?" asked the Princess Mariya.

"Nothing, nothing."

She smiled at Pierre through her tears.

"Good-by, it is bedtime."

Pierre got up and took his departure.

The Princess Mariya and Natasha, as usual, met in their sleeping-room. They talked over what Pierre had told them. The princess did not express her opinion of Pierre. Neither did Natasha speak of him.

"Well, good-night, Marie," said Natasha. "Do you know I am often afraid that, in not speaking of him — of Prince Andreï — for fear of doing wrong to our feelings, we may forget him?"

The Princess Mariya drew a deep sigh, and by this

sigh confessed to the justice of Natasha's words; but when she spoke, her words expressed a different thought: — "How could one forget him?" she asked.

"It was so good for me to-day to talk it all over; and hard too, and painful and good — very good," said Natasha. "I was certain that he loved him so. That was why I told him..... There was no harm in my telling him, was there?" she asked, suddenly reddening.

"To Pierre? Oh, no! What a lovely man he is!" exclaimed the Princess Mariya.

"Do you know, Marie," suddenly broke out Natasha, with a roguish smile, which the Princess Mariya had not seen for a long time on her face, "he has grown so clean, neat, fresh, just as if he were out of a bath. Do you know what I mean — morally out of a bath! Isn't that so?"

"Yes," said the Princess Mariya. "He has gained very much."

"And his jaunty little coat,[1] and his neatly cropped hair; exactly — yes, just exactly as if he were fresh from his bath! Papa used...."

"I remember that *he* — Prince Andreï — liked no one so well as Pierre," said the Princess Mariya.

"Yes; and yet they were so different. They say that men are better friends when they are not alike. It must be so. Don't you think that they were very different?"

"Yes, and he's splendid."

"Well, good-night," replied Natasha; and the same mischievous smile, as if she had forgotten it, long remained in her face.

CHAPTER XVIII

It was long before Pierre went to sleep that night. He strode back and forth through his chamber, now scowling, now burdening himself with heavy thoughts, then suddenly shrugging his shoulders and starting, and then again smiling.

[1] *Surtoutchek korotenkii.*

He was thinking about Prince Andreĭ, about Natasha, and their love; and sometimes he felt jealous of her for what was past, sometimes he reproached himself for it, sometimes he justified it.

It was already six o'clock in the morning, and still he kept pacing through his room.

"Well, what's to be done? Is it still impossible? What is to be done? Of course it must be so," said he to himself, and, hastily undressing, he got into bed, happy and excited, but free from doubt and irresolution. "Yes, strange and impossible as this happiness seems, I must do everything, everything, to make her my wife," he said to himself.

Several days previously, Pierre had fixed on Friday for the day of his departure for Petersburg. When he woke up it was Thursday, and Savelyitch came to him for orders in regard to the packing of his things for the journey.

"Petersburg? What about Petersburg? Who is going to Petersburg?" he could not help asking of himself! "Oh, yes, some time ago, before ever this happened, I had some such thought — I was going to Petersburg for some reason or other," he remembered. "Why was it? Yes, perhaps I shall go as it is. How good and attentive he is! How he remembers everything," he said to himself, as he looked into Savelyitch's old face. "And what a pleasant smile," he thought.

"Are n't you always longing to have your freedom, Savelyitch?" demanded Pierre.

"Why should I wish my freedom, your illustriousness? While the late count was alive — the kingdom of heaven be his — we lived with him, and now we have nothing to complain of from you."

"Well, but your children?"

"The children will live also, your illustriousness; one can put up with such masters."

"Yes, but my heirs," suggested Pierre. "I may suddenly marry..... You see, that might happen," he added, with an involuntary smile.

"And may I be bold enough to say, a very good thing, too, your illustriousness!"

"How easy it seems to him," thought Pierre. "He cannot know how terrible, how perilous, a thing it is. Too early or too late.... terrible!"

"What orders do you please to give? Do you wish to start to-morrow?" asked Savelyitch.

"No, I am going to postpone it for a few days. I will tell you when the time comes. Forgive me for putting you to so much trouble," said Pierre, and, as he saw Savelyitch's smile, he said to himself, "How strange it is that he does n't know that Petersburg is now nothing to me, and that this matter must be decided before anything is. Of course he must know — he 's only pretending! Shall I talk with him about it? How will he like it?" wondered Pierre. "No, I will wait a little."

At breakfast Pierre informed his cousin, the princess, that he had been the evening before to call upon the Princess Mariya, and whom did she suppose he found there? Natasha Rostova!

The princess pretended that she saw nothing more extraordinary in this than if he had seen Anna Semyonovna.

"Do you know her?" asked Pierre.

"I have met the princess," she replied. "I have heard that she has become engaged to young Rostof. That would be a very good thing for the Rostofs; they say their affairs are in perfect confusion."

"No, but do you know the Countess Natasha?"

"I have heard something about her story. It 's very sad."

"Either she does not understand, or she is pretending not to understand," said Pierre to himself; "I 'd better not tell her, either."

The princess also had been making some preparations for Pierre's journey.

"How kind they all are," thought Pierre, "when now there can be nothing at all interesting to them in all this, to take so much trouble with my affairs. And all for me! truly it 's wonderful!"

On that same day Pierre went to the chief of police to tell him that he would send a trusty servant to receive the property that was to be restored to the citizens that day at the *granavitaya palata*, or court of the exchequer.

"And now this man, also," thought Pierre, as he looked into the officer's face. "What a splendid, fine-looking officer, and how kind he is! Now he is occupied with such trifles! And yet they say that he is not honest, and is making use of his opportunities! What nonsense! Besides, why should he not take advantage? He was educated to do so. And that's the way they all do. But he had such a pleasant, good face! and smiled so agreeably when he looked at me."

Pierre went that evening to dine at the Princess Mariya's.

As he went along the streets, lined with the blackened ruins of houses, he was amazed at the beauty that he discovered in these ruins. The chimney-stacks, the fallen walls, vividly reminding Pierre of the Rhine and the Colosseum, stretched along one behind another, all through the burnt districts. The hack-drivers and passers-by, the carpenters hewing timbers, merchants and shop-keepers, all with jovial, shining faces, gazed at Pierre, and seemed to say, 'Ah, there he goes. Let us see what will come of it.'

Before he reached the Princess Mariya's, the doubt occurred to Pierre's mind whether it were true that he had been there the evening before, and seen Natasha and talked with her.

"Perhaps I was dreaming. Perhaps I shall go in and find no one."

But he had no sooner entered the room, than, in his whole being, by the instantaneous loss of his freedom, he realized her presence. She wore the same black dress with soft folds, and her hair was done up in the same way as the evening before, but she herself was entirely different. If she had been like that the evening before, when he went into the room, he could not for a single instant have failed to recognize her.

She was just the same as she had been when almost

a child, and afterwards, when she was Prince Andreï's affianced bride. A merry questioning gleam flashed in her eyes; her face had a genial and strangely roguish expression.

Pierre dined with them, and would have spent the whole evening, but the Princess Mariya was going to vespers, and Pierre accompanied them.

The following day, Pierre went early, dined with them, and spent the whole evening.

Although the Princess Mariya and Natasha were evidently glad of his company, although all the interest of Pierre's life was now concentrated in this house, still, as the evening wore away, they had talked everything out, and the conversation constantly lagged from one trivial subject to another, and often flagged altogether.

Pierre stayed that evening so late that the Princess Mariya and Natasha exchanged glances, evidently feeling anxious for him to go. Pierre saw it, and yet could not tear himself away. He felt embarrassed and awkward, but still he stayed because he *could not* get up to go.

The Princess Mariya, not seeing any end to it, was the first to get up, and, pleading a headache as an excuse, started to bid him good-night.

"And so you are going to Petersburg to-morrow?" she asked.

"No, I don't expect to go," hastily replied Pierre, with surprise and apparent annoyance. "Yes, ... no, ... oh, to Petersburg? Day after to-morrow, perhaps. Only I won't say good-by now. I will call to see if you have any commissions," said he, standing in front of the Princess Mariya, with flushed face and embarrassed manner.

Natasha gave him her hand, and left the room. The Princess Mariya, on the contrary, instead of going, resumed her chair, and, with her luminous, deep eyes, gazed gravely and earnestly at Pierre. The weariness which she had really felt just before had now entirely passed away. She drew a long and deep sigh, as if nerving herself for a long conversation.

All Pierre's confusion and awkwardness instantly disappeared the moment that Natasha left the room, and gave place to an agitated excitement.

He swiftly drew his chair close to the Princess Mariya.

"Yes, I wanted to have a talk with you," said he, responding to her look, as if it were spoken words.

"Princess! help me! What am I to do? Have I reason to hope? Princess, my friend, listen to me. I know all about it. I know that I am not worthy of her. I know that it is wholly impossible, at the present time, to speak about it. But I wish to be like a brother to her. .... No, I do not, I cannot wish that .... I cannot...."

He paused and rubbed his face and his eyes with his hands.

"Now, here!" he pursued, evidently making an effort to command himself to speak coherently. "I don't know when I first began to love her. But she is the only one in all my life I have loved, and I love her so that I cannot imagine life without her. I cannot make up my mind to sue for her hand now; but the thought that perhaps she might be mine, and that I had lost this possibility .... possibility .... is horrible to me. Tell me, have I reason to hope? Tell me what I must do. Dear princess," said he, after a little silence, and he touched her hand when she did not reply.

"I was thinking of what you have told me," returned the Princess Mariya. "Now .... hear what I have to say. You are right that to speak to her now of love .... "

The princess paused. She meant to say, to speak to her of love was impossible now; but she paused because for two days past she had observed, from the change that had taken place in Natasha, that Natasha would not only not be offended if Pierre should confess his love for her, but that this was the very thing that she was longing for him to do.

"To tell her now .... is impossible," said the Princess Mariya, nevertheless.

"But what am I to do?"

"Leave it all to me," said the Princess Mariya. "I know .... "

Pierre looked into the Princess Mariya's eyes. "Well .... well ...." said he.

"I know that she loves you .... will love you," said the Princess Mariya, correcting herself.

She had scarcely spoken these words before Pierre sprang up, and, with a frightened face, seized the Princess Mariya's hand.

"What makes you think so? Do you really think that I may hope? Do you think so?"....

"Yes, I think so," said the Princess Mariya, with a smile. "Write to her parents. And trust it all to me. I will tell her when the suitable time comes. I am desirous of it. And my heart tells me that it will be."

"No, it cannot be! How happy I am! .... But it cannot be!" repeated Pierre, kissing the princess's hand.

"Go to Petersburg; that is best. And I will write to you," said she.

"To Petersburg? Go away? Yes, very good, I will go. But may I come to call to-morrow?"

On the following day, Pierre went to say good-by. Natasha was less animated than on the preceding days; but to-day when Pierre occasionally looked into her eyes he felt that his existence was nothing, that he was not and that she was not, but that one feeling of bliss filled the world.

"Can it be? No! impossible!" he said to himself at each glance, word, motion of hers, so filling his heart with joy.

When, on saying "good-by," he took her delicate, slender hand, he involuntarily held it rather long in his.

"Can it be that this hand, this face, these eyes, — all this marvelous treasure of womanly beauty, — can it be that it will be mine forever, as familiar to me as I am to myself? No, it is impossible!"

"Good-by, count — *prashchaïte, graf!*" said she to him aloud. "I shall wait your return with impatience," she added in a whisper.

And these simple words, the look and the expression of her face that accompanied them, constituted the basis of inexhaustible recollections, memories, and happy dreams during Pierre's two months' absence.

" 'I shall await your return with impatience.' Yes, yes, how did she say ? — Yes, 'I shall await your return with impatience.' Akh! how happy I am! How can it be that I am so happy?" Pierre kept saying to himself.

CHAPTER XIX

In Pierre's soul nothing now took place like what had taken place in similar circumstances at the time of his engagement with Ellen.

He did not repeat as before, with a sickening sense of shame, the words that he had said; he did not ask himself : "Akh! why did I not say that, and why, why did I say, *Je vous aime ?*"

Now, on the contrary, every word that she said, every one of his own words, he repeated in his imagination with all the various details of her face and her smile, and he had no wish to take away or add a single one. His sole desire was to repeat them.

There was now not the slightest shadow of doubt as to whether what he was going to do was right or wrong. Only one terrible doubt ever occurred to his mind : Was it not all a dream? Was not the Princess Mariya mistaken? "Am I not too proud and self-conceited? I believe I am; but this surely might happen — the Princess Mariya might tell her, but she would smile and reply, 'How strange! He is surely mistaken! Does he not know that he is a man, a simple man? while I .... I am entirely different, vastly superior.' "

This was Pierre's only doubt, and it frequently recurred to him. He now even ceased to make plans. His actual happiness seemed to him so incredible that the accomplishment of this seemed enough of itself, and anything more was a work of supererogation. All was over.

A joyous, unexpected insanity, of which Pierre be-

lieved himself incapable, possessed him. All the meaning of life, not for himself alone, but for the whole world,
seemed to him to be included only in his love for her
and the possibility of her love for him.

It sometimes seemed to him that all men were occupied with only one thing — his future happiness. It
sometimes seemed to him that they were all rejoicing,
just as he was, and were only trying to hide this happiness, while pretending to be absorbed in other interests.
In every word and action he discovered hints pointing
toward his happiness. He often surprised the people
who met him by his blissful looks and smiles, which
expressed some secret, inward harmony.

But when he realized that these people could not know
about his happiness, he pitied them with all his heart,
and experienced a keen desire somehow to explain to
them that all that occupied their time was perfect rub-
bish and trifles not worthy of their attention.

When it was proposed to him to take some office, or
when criticisms were made on the general course of
political events or the war, and suppositions were advanced that such and such a method of procedure would
bring happiness to all men, he listened with his gentle,
compassionate smile, and amazed those who were talking with him by his strange observations.

But as those men who seemed to Pierre to comprehend the real meaning of life, that is, his own views of
it — as well as those who were unfortunate enough
apparently not to comprehend it — in fact, all men at
this particular time were brought into such a brightly
concentrated light, radiating from his own heart, that
without the slightest difficulty he at once on meeting
with any one saw in him whatever was good and worthy
of love.

On examining his late wife's affairs and papers, he, in
his memory of her, experienced nothing, no other feeling than one of pity, that she knew not the happiness
which he now knew. Prince Vasili, who was now
especially proud of a new place and new decorations,
seemed to him a touchingly good and pitiable old man.

Pierre often in after days remembered this time of happy folly. All the judgments which he formed for himself of men and events at this time remained forever established in his mind. He not only did not afterward renounce these views of men and things, but, on the contrary, in all his inward doubts and contradictions, he came back to that view which he had during this time of folly, and this view always seemed correct.

"Perhaps," he would say to himself, "I seemed strange and absurd at that time. But I was not so foolish as it might appear. On the contrary, I was wiser and more sagacious than ever before, and I understood all that is worth understanding in life, because.... I was happy."

Pierre's folly or unreason consisted in this, that he did not as before wait for the personal reasons — the merits of people, as he called them — to be displayed before he loved them, but love filled his heart, and he, by constantly loving his fellow-men, found undoubted reason for making it worth his while to love them.

CHAPTER XX

FROM that first evening when Natasha, after Pierre had left them, had told the Princess Mariya with a joyously mischievous smile that he was just as if he had come out of his bath, and called attention to his jaunty coat and his closely cropped hair, from that moment something in her heart awoke that had lain dormant, and was unknown even to her, but irresistible.

Everything about her suddenly underwent a change — her face, her gait, her look, her voice. Unexpectedly to herself the power of life and hope of happiness flashed forth outwardly and demanded satisfaction. From that first evening Natasha seemed to have forgotten all that had happened to her. Henceforth she never once complained of her situation or said one single word about the past, and she had no hesitation even in forming pleasant plans for the future.

She had little to say about Pierre; but when the Princess Mariya mentioned him, the long-extinguished gleam was kindled in her eyes, and her lips were curved with a strange smile.

The change that took place in Natasha at first amazed the Princess Mariya; but when she understood the significance of it she was grieved.

"Can it be that she loved my brother so little that she is so ready to forget him?" mused the Princess Mariya, when by herself she pondered over this change that had come over Natasha.

But when she was with Natasha she neither felt angry with her nor reproached her. The awakening powers of life, which had taken such hold of Natasha, were evidently so uncontrollable, so unexpected to herself, that the Princess Mariya while in her presence felt that she had no right to reproach her even in her heart.

Natasha gave herself up with such completeness and frank honesty to this new feeling, and made so little pretense to hide it, that now she became glad and merry instead of sad and sorry.

When the Princess Mariya, after that midnight declaration of Pierre's, returned to her room, Natasha met her on the threshold.

"He has spoken? Yes? He has spoken?" she insisted, and an expression, joyous, and at the same time pathetically pleading for forgiveness for her joy, came into Natasha's face. "I was tempted to listen at the door; but I knew that you would tell me."

Thoroughly as the princess understood the look which Natasha gave her, touching as it was, much as she pitied her emotion, still Natasha's words, at the first instant, offended the Princess Mariya. She remembered her brother, his love for her.

"But what is to be done? She cannot be otherwise than what she is," reasoned the Princess Mariya, and with a melancholy and rather stern face she told Natasha all that Pierre had said to her.

When she heard that he was going to Petersburg, Natasha was surprised.

"To Petersburg?" she repeated, apparently not taking it in. But when she observed the melancholy expression which the Princess Mariya's face wore, she surmised the reason for her melancholy, and suddenly burst into tears.

"Marie," said she, "tell me, what must I do? I am afraid I am doing wrong. I will do whatever you say; teach me...."

"Do you love him?"

"Yes," whispered Natasha.

"What makes you cry, then? I am glad for you," said the Princess Mariya, already, because of these tears, completely pardoning Natasha's joy.

"It will not be very soon, if ever. .... Just think what happiness when I am his wife and you marry Nicolas."

"Natasha, I have asked you never to speak about that. We will talk about yourself."

Both were silent.

"But why must he go to Petersburg?" suddenly exclaimed Natasha, and made haste to answer her own question. "Well, well, it is best so. .... Yes, Marie, it is best so."....

EPILOGUE

PART FIRST

CHAPTER I

SEVEN years had passed. The storm-tossed histori-cal sea of Europe lay sleeping on its shores. It seemed at peace; but the mysterious forces which move humanity — mysterious because the laws that govern their movements are unknown to us — were continually at work.

Though the surface of the historical sea seemed motionless, humanity was pressing onward with a motion as continuous as the passage of time.

Distinct groups of men were organized and disorgan-ized; causes for the formation and disintegration of empires and the migrations of nations were set to work.

The historical sea no longer, as before, swayed in vast swells from shore to shore. It boiled in its secret depths.

Historical characters no longer, as before, rode on the crest of the billows from shore to shore; they now seemed to be gathered together in one place. Histori-cal personages, who before, at the head of armies, had reflected the motion of the masses by calls to war, by campaigns and battles, now reflected this movement by political and diplomatic combinations, laws, treaties. ....

This activity of historical personages historians call *reaction*.

Historians, in describing the activity of these histori-cal personages, who, according to their judgment, were the cause of what they call the *reaction*, are very severe in their strictures upon them. All the famous people of that time, from Alexander and Napoleon to Madame de Staël, Fothier, Schelling, Fichte, Châteaubriand, and the like, are haled before this stern court of justice, and justified or condemned, from the standpoint of whether they helped *progress* or *reaction*.

In Russia, also, according to their writings, reaction set in about this same time, and the one principally to blame for this reaction was Alexander I. — that same Alexander I. who, according to their writings, was the principal cause of the liberal tendencies of his reign and the salvation of Russia.

In Russian literature at the present time there is no one, from the school-boy to the accomplished historian, who would not cast a stone at Alexander for his faulty behavior at this period of his reign.

" He ought to have done this or done that."

" In such and such a case he did well, in something else he did ill."

" He behaved splendidly at the beginning of his reign and during 1812; but he did wrong in giving a constitution to Poland, in establishing the Holy Alliance, in granting power to Arakcheyef, in encouraging first Golitsuin and mysticism, and afterwards encouraging Shishkof and Fothier."

" He made an error in employing the van of the army; he blundered in disbanding the Semyonovsky regiment," and so on and so on.

One might fill a dozen pages with the enumeration of all the reproaches which the historians have made against him on the ground of that knowledge of the welfare of humanity which they possess.

What is the significance of these reproaches?

The very same actions for which the historians praise Alexander I., — for instance, the liberal tendency of his reign, his quarrel with Napoleon, the firmness which he displayed in the year 1812 and during the campaign of 1813, — do they not flow from exactly the same sources — the conditions of blood, education, life, which made Alexander's personality what it was — from which also flowed the actions for which the historians blame him; for instance, the Holy Alliance, the restoration of Poland, the reaction of the twenties?

What constitutes the essence of these reproaches?

In this, — that such an historical personage as Alexander I., a personage standing on the highest possible pinnacle of human power, as it were in the focus of the dazzling light of the historical rays concentrated on him; a personage subjected to the most potent influences in the world, in the form of intrigues, deceptions, flatteries, inseparable from power; a personage who, every moment of his life, bore the responsibility of all that took place in Europe; and not an imaginary personage, but as much alive as any other man, with his own individual peculiarities, passions, aspirations for the good, the beautiful, the true, — that this personage, fifty[1] years ago, lacked not virtue (the historians do not reproach him for that), but those views concerning the welfare of humanity which are now held by any professor who from early youth has been occupied with science, that is, with the reading of books and lectures and the copying of these books and lectures into a note-book.

But even if it be granted that Alexander I. fifty years ago was mistaken in his views as to what constitutes the true welfare of nations, it cannot but be taken for granted that the historian also who criticizes Alexander will, in exactly the same way, after the lapse of some time, prove himself incorrect in his view as to what is the welfare of humanity.

This proposition is all the more natural and inevitable from the fact that, in the development of history, we see that every year, with every new writer, the standard as to what is the welfare of humanity changes: thus what once seemed good becomes evil in the course of ten years, and *vice versa*. Still, we find occurring, at one and the same time, perfectly contradictory views as to what is good or what is evil: some regard the constitution granted to Poland and the Holy Alliance as creditable, others as disgraceful, to Alexander.

[1] "War and Peace" was written between 1864 and 1869.

As to the activity of Alexander and Napoleon, it is impossible to declare that it was advantageous or harmful, since we cannot say wherein it was advantageous or wherein it was harmful. If this activity fails to please any one, then it fails to please simply in consequence of its failure to coincide with this person's limited comprehension as to what is good.

Apart from the question whether the preservation of my father's house in Moscow in 1812, or the glory of the Russian troops, or the weal of the Petersburg or any other university, or the freedom of Poland, or the might of Russia, or the balance of Europe, or a certain state of European enlightenment — progress — appear to me advantageous, I must acknowledge that the activity of every historical personage had, besides these ends and aims, still others, more universal and beyond my comprehension.

But let us grant that so-called science has the capacity of reconciling all contradictions, and has for all historical personages and events an invariable, absolute standard of right and wrong.

Let us grant that Alexander might have done everything in a different way. Let us grant that he might, according to the prescription of those who accuse him, those who profess to have a knowledge of the final causes of the movements of humanity, — that he might have acted in accordance with the program of nationality, liberty, equality, and progress, which his present-day accusers would have laid down for him. Let us grant that this program might have been possible and might have been laid down, and that Alexander might have acted in accordance with it. What, then, would have become of the activity of all those men who at that time were in opposition to the tendency of the administration? — of that activity which, according to the opinion of the historians, was good and profitable?

This activity would not have existed; there would have been no life; there would have been nothing.

If it is admitted that human life can be directed by reason, then the possibility of life is annihilated.

CHAPTER II

IF it is admitted, as the historians do, that great men lead humanity toward the attainment of certain ends, such as the greatness of Russia or France, or the balance of Europe, or the propagation of the ideas of the Revolution, or progress in general, or anything else, then it is impossible to explain the phenomena of history without the concept *chance* or *genius*.

If the object of the European wars at the beginning of the present century had been the greatness of Russia, this object might have been attained without the preliminary wars and without the invasion.

If the object had been the greatness of France, this object might have been attained without the Revolution and the empire.

If the object had been the propagation of ideas, the printing-press would have accomplished it far better than soldiers.

If the object had been the progress of civilization, it is perfectly easy to suppose that there are ways for the propagation of civilization more expedient than the destruction of men and their property.

Why did it happen this way and not that?

Simply because it happened so.

"*Chance* created the situation, *genius* profited by it," says history.

But what is chance, and what is genius?

The words "chance" and "genius" represent nothing that actually exists, and therefore cannot be defined.

These words only indicate a certain degree of comprehension of phenomena.

I know not the cause of a certain phenomenon; I believe that I cannot know it; therefore I do not try to know it, and I say *chance*.

I see that a force has produced an action disproportionate to the ordinary human qualities : I cannot understand the cause of this force, and I cry *genius*.

To the flock of sheep, the sheep that is driven off

every evening by the shepherd to a separate pen, and given extra food, and becomes twice as fat as the others, must seem to be a genius. The very fact that every evening this particular sheep, instead of going to the common fold, has a special pen and extra food, and that this sheep, this particular sheep, once fattened, is killed for mutton, doubtless impresses the other sheep as a remarkable combination of genius with a whole series of extraordinary chances.

But if the sheep will only stop thinking that everything that happens to them results solely for the attainment of their sheepish welfare, if they grant that the events happening to them may have objects which they cannot comprehend, they will immediately perceive a unity and logic in what happened to the fattened sheep.

Even if they cannot know why it was fattened, they will, at least, know that nothing that happened to the sheep happened by chance, and they will not need either the concept of *chance* or the concept of *genius*.

Only when we rid ourselves of the idea of the proximate and visible object, the end of things, and recognize that the ultimate end is wholly unattainable by us, can we see a logical connection in the lives of historical personages; there will be revealed to us the cause of that disproportion between the capacities of ordinary men and the deeds they perform, and we shall not need the words *chance* and *genius*.

It is sufficient only to admit that the object of the movements of European nations is unknown to us, and that we know only facts, such as the butcheries first in France, then in Italy, in Africa, in Prussia, in Austria, in Spain, in Russia, and that the movement from west to east and from east to west constituted the essence and object of events, and we shall not only no longer need to find *genius* or anything exceptional in the characters of Napoleon and of Alexander, but it will be impossible for us to imagine these personages as anything else than men like all other men, and we shall not only not need to explain on the score of *chance* the little events that made these personages what they were, but it will be evident to us that all these little events were necessary.

When we rid ourselves of the knowledge of the ulti-mate end, we clearly understand that, just as it is impos-sible to imagine on a given plant other flowers and other fruits than those which it produces, so is it impos-sible to imagine two other men with all that they did who would have been fitted to such a degree and in the smallest details to the mission which they were called upon to fulfil.

CHAPTER III

THE fundamental, essential fact in European events at the beginning of the nineteenth century is the warlike movements of masses of the nations of Europe from west to east, and then from east to west.

The first element of this movement was the movement from west to east.

In order that the nations of the West might push their warlike advance as far as Moscow — and this they succeeded in accomplishing — it was necessary : —

1. That they should be concentrated into a warlike mass of sufficient magnitude to endure a collision with the warlike mass of the East ;

2. That they should renounce all their long-founded traditions and habits ; and

3. That, when this warlike movement was accom-plished, they should have at their head a man of their own sort, who could justify himself and them for the lies, the pillage, and the slaughter which, as an essential concomitant, accompanied this movement of theirs.

And, beginning with the French Revolution, the primitive group, which is not large enough, disperses ; old habits and traditions come to naught ; little by little, a group of new precedents, new habits, and new tradi-tions is formed, and the man who is to take his place at the head of the coming movement, and bear all the responsibility of the events to follow, is prepared for his mission.

A man without convictions, without habitudes, without traditions, without name, not even a Frenchman, — by what seems strange chances, — glides through all the parties agitating France, and, taking part with none, is borne to his destined place.

The stupidity of his associates, the weakness and inanity of his rivals, his own frankness in lying, and his brilliant and self-confident narrow-mindedness place this man at the head of the army.

The excellent quality of the soldiers in his Italian army, the disinclination of the enemy to fight, his childish audacity and self-confidence give him military glory.

An infinite number of so-called chances meets him everywhere.

The disfavor into which he falls with the authorities of the French serves to his advantage.

His attempts to change his predestined career are failures; he is not received into the Russian service, the appointment to Turkey is not given to him.

During the war in Italy, he several times comes to the very brink of destruction, and every time escapes in some unexpected way.

The Russian troops, the very ones who have the power to extinguish his glory, through various diplomatic combinations do not enter Europe while he is there.

On his return from Italy, he finds the government at Paris in a state of decomposition so far advanced that the men forming it are inevitably doomed to ruin; and an escape from this dangerous situation offers itself to him in the senseless, unreasonable expedition to Africa.

Again so-called chances accompany him. Impregnable Malta surrenders without the firing of a shot; the most foolhardy plans are crowned with success.

The hostile fleet, which afterwards would not allow a single rowboat to pass, allows his army to pass!

In Africa, a whole series of atrocities are committed on the almost unarmed inhabitants. And the men who unite with him in these atrocities, and especially their chief, persuade themselves that this is admirable, that this is glory, that this is like Cæsar and Alexander of Macedon, and that this is great !

This ideal of *glory* and *greatness*, which consists in the not only considering nothing wrong for him, but of being proud of every crime, attributing to it an inconceivable and supernatural significance, — this ideal, which is destined to be the guide of this man and of those allied with him, has full field for increase in Africa.

All that he undertakes prospers. The plague touches him not. The cruelty of massacring prisoners is not imputed to him as a fault.

His puerile, senseless, unreasonable, dishonorable departure from Africa, from his companions in distress, is accounted to him as meritorious, and again, the second time, the hostile fleet allows him to pass.

When, dazzled by the fortunate crimes committed by him, and ready to play his part, but without any definite object in view, he reaches Paris, the republican government, which a year before might still have put an end to him, has now attained the last degree of disintegration, and the fact that he, a man belonging to no party, is on hand, can now only exalt him.

He has no plan; he fears every one; but the parties resort to him, and beg his support.

He alone, with his ideal of glory and greatness built up in Italy and Egypt, with his senseless self-adoration, with his audacity in crime, with his frankness in' falsehood, — he alone is able to direct the events about to take place.

He is needed for the place that is waiting for him, and therefore, almost independently of his own will, and notwithstanding his irresolution, his lack of any determined plan, and all the blunders that he makes, he is drawn into a conspiracy the aim of which is the possession of power, and the conspiracy is crowned with success.

He is thrust into a session of the Directorate. Alarmed, he wishes to escape, counting himself lost; he pretends that he is faint; he utters senseless things which ought by good rights to have been his destruction.

But the directors of France, once so bold and haughty, now feeling that their part is played, and being more confused than he is, say just the words they should not have said to retain their power and overthrow him.

Chance, millions of *chances* give him power, and all men, as if by common agreement, agree to confirm this power.

Chances form the characters of the members of the Directorate of France, at that time subservient to him.

Chances form the character of Paul I., who recognizes his power.

Chance forms against Napoleon a conspiracy which, instead of being prejudicial to him, confirms his power.

Chance brings the Prince d'Enghien into his hands, and unexpectedly compels him to assassinate him, this very act, more than any other, proving to the multitude that he had the right, since he had the might.

Chance brings it about that he gives all his powers to an expedition against England which would evidently have ruined him, and never carries out the plan, but falls unexpectedly upon Mack and the Austrians, who surrender without a battle.

Chance and *genius* give him the victory at Austerlitz, and, by *chance*, all men, not only the French but all Europe (with the exception of England, which takes no part in the events about to occur), all men, in spite of their former horror and repulsion at his crimes, now recognize his power, his title, which he has given himself, and his ideal of glory and greatness, which seems to them all reasonable and beautiful.

As if practising and preparing for the impending movement, the forces of the West several times push toward the East in 1805, 1806, 1807, and 1809, all the time strengthening and increasing.

In 1811 a group of men formed in France unites into an enormous group with the nations of Central Europe.

While this group of men goes on increasing, the man at the head of the movement and directing it finds his powers more and more developed.

During the ten years' preparatory period preceding this great movement, this man has been the leader of all the crowned heads of Europe. Dethroned rulers of the world have no reasonable ideal to oppose to the senseless Napoleonic ideal of *glory* and *greatness*. One after another they strive to show him their own insignificance.

The king of Prussia sends his wife to solicit the great man's favor; the emperor of Austria considers it a favor if this man will take to his bed the daughter of the Kaisers; the Pope, holy guardian of the nations, makes use of his religion to raise the great man higher.

Napoleon does not prepare himself for the fulfilment of his part so much as it is his whole environment, which makes him assume all the responsibility for what is taking place and for what is about to take place.

No act, no crime, no petty deception which he essays fails to be instantly hailed by those around him as some mighty deed.

The best entertainment for him which the Germans can think of is the celebration of Jena and Auerstädt.

Not alone is he great: his ancestors, his brothers, his stepsons, his brothers-in-law are also great.

Everything conspires to take from him the last vestige of reason, and to make ready for his terrible career.

When he is ready, the forces are also ready.

The invasion rushes toward the East, reaches its final goal — Moscow.

The capital is taken. The Russian army is more completely shattered than ever were the hostile armies in former battles from Austerlitz to Wagram.

But suddenly, instead of the *chances* and that *genius* which have borne him so steadily till now through an uninterrupted series of successes to the predestined end, appears an incalculable quantity of contrary *chances*, from the influenza at Borodino, to the frosts, and the spark that set fire to Moscow; and instead of *genius* appear unexampled stupidity and baseness.

The invasion runs away, turns back, again runs away,

and all the chances are now not in his favor but against him.

There occurs a counter-movement, from east to west, bearing a close resemblance to the preceding movement from west to east.

The same symptoms of the movement from east to west as occurred in 1805–1807 and 1809 precede the great movement: the same union into a group of colossal proportions; in the same way the nations of Central Europe rally to this movement; the same irresolution in the midst of the way, and the same velocity in proportion as the goal is approached.

Paris, the ultimate goal, is reached. The Napoleonic government and army are overthrown.

Napoleon himself no longer has any of his former significance; all his actions strike men as pitiable and disgusting: but once more an inexplicable chance supervenes; the allies hate Napoleon, in whom they see the cause of their misfortunes; deprived of prestige and power, convicted of crimes and perfidy, he ought to have been regarded as he had been ten years before, and as he was a year later, as a bandit and outlaw. But, by a strange chance, no one sees this.

His *rôle* is not yet finished.

The man who, ten years before and a year later, men held to be a bandit and outlaw, is sent two days' distance from France to an island, which is given to him as a domain, with a guard, and millions which are paid to him, for some reason!

CHAPTER IV

THE movement of the nations begins to calm itself along the shores. The waves of the great uprising fall back, and on the tranquil sea are formed various eddies on which float diplomatists, imagining that they have brought about the cessation of the commotion.

But the sea grown so calm suddenly rises again. The diplomatists imagine that they, their dissensions, are the cause of the new access of violence; they expect another war among their sovereigns. The situation seems to them inextricable.

But the billow the approach of which they feel arises not from the source from which they expect it.

It is the same billow arising from the same point of departure, Paris. The last recoil of the movement from the West takes place — a recoil which is destined to solve the diplomatic difficulties, which have seemed inexplicable, and to put an end to the warlike movement of that period.

The man who has devastated France returns to France alone, without the aid of a conspiracy, without soldiers. Any guardsman may capture him, but, by a strange chance, not only does no one touch him, but all run with enthusiasm to meet this man whom they had cursed the day before, and whom they will curse a month later.

This man is still needed for the completion of the last act.

The act is ended.

The last *rôle* is played. The actor is told to remove his costume, and wash off the antimony and the rouge.

He is no longer needed.

And several years pass while this man, in solitude on his island, plays by himself and for himself a miserable comedy, intrigues and lies, justifying his actions, when justification is no longer necessary, and shows to the whole world what it was that men took for a force when the invisible Hand made use of it.

The Manager, having ended the drama and unmasked the actor, exposes him to us.

"See in whom you have believed! Here he is. Do you see now that not he, but I, moved you?"

But blinded by the violence of the movement, men long failed to understand this.

Even greater logical sequence and necessity is shown by the life of Alexander I., that personage who was at the head of the counter-movement, from east to west.

What qualities should the man possess who should take precedence of others and be placed at the head of this movement from east to west?

He must have the sense of justice, distant and perfectly disinterested participation in the affairs of Europe.

He must have a loftier moral character than any of his contemporaries, — sovereigns of that time. He must have a sweet and captivating personality. And he must have a personal grievance against Napoleon.

And all this is found in Alexander I.; all this was produced by innumerable so-called chances throughout his past life: his education, his liberal beginnings, and the counselors by whom he was surrounded, by Austerlitz and Tilsit and Erfurt.

Throughout the patriotic war, this personage is inactive, because he is not needed.

But, as soon as the necessity of a general European war becomes evident, this personage is found at the given moment in his place, and, rallying the nations of Europe, he leads them to their goal.

The goal is reached.

After the final war of 1815, Alexander finds himself at the highest pinnacle of human power.

What use does he make of this power?

Alexander I., the pacificator of Europe, the man who from his youth had striven only for the welfare of his people, the first to introduce liberal innovations in his country, now, it seems, when he possesses unlimited power, and therefore the ability to bring about the welfare of his people at the very time that Napoleon, in exile, is making childish and fictitious plans how he would benefit humanity if he had the power, — Alexander I., who has fulfilled his mission, and feels the hand of God upon him, suddenly comes to a realizing sense of the nothingness of this presumable power, renounces it, and surrenders it into the hands of despicable men whom he scorns, and merely says: —

"'Not unto us, not unto us, but unto Thy name!' I am a man like other men. Let me live like a man, and think of my soul and of God."

As the sun and every atom of ether is a sphere per-fect in itself, and at the same time only an atom in the mighty All inaccessible to man, so each individual has within himself his own objects, and at the same time serves the common object inaccessible to man.

The bee, poising on a flower, stings a child.   And the child is afraid of bees, and declares that the end of the bee is to sting people.

The poet admires the bee sucking from the calyx of a flower, and declares to us that the end of the bee is to absorb into itself the aroma of the flowers.

The bee-keeper, observing that the bee gathers pollen and brings it home to the hive, declares that the end of the bee is the manufacture of honey.

Another bee-keeper, observing more closely the habits of the swarm, declares that the bee gathers pollen for the nourishment of the young bees and the exploitation of the queen, and that the object of the bee is the prop-agation of the species.

A botanist observes that the bee, in flying with the dust of a diœcious flower to the pistils of another, fer-tilizes it; and the botanist sees in this the object of the bee.

Another, observing the transmigration of plants, sees that the bee assists in this transmigration; and this new observer may say that in this consists the object of the bee.

But the final object of the bee is not wholly included in the first or the second or the third of the objects which the human mind is able to discover.

The higher the human mind rises in its efforts to discover these objects, the more evident it is that the final object is inaccessible to man.

Man can only observe the correlation existing between the life of the bee and the other phenomena of life. The same is true in regard to the objects of historical personages and nations.

CHAPTER V

NATASHA'S marriage to Bezukhoï, which took place in 1813, was the last happy event for the older generation of the Rostofs. That same year Count Ilya Andreyevitch died, and, as always happens, his death brought about the end of the former family.

The events of the preceding year, the conflagration of Moscow and the family's flight from the city, the death of Prince Andreï and Natasha's despair, Petya's death, the countess's grief, all taken together, blow upon blow, fell on the old count's head.

It seemed as if he could not comprehend, and as if he realized that he had not the strength to comprehend, the significance of all these events; he morally, as it were, bent his old head, as if he expected and invited the new blows which would finish him.

He appeared sometimes frightened and abstracted, sometimes unnaturally excited and alert.

Natasha's marriage, for the time being, gave him something to think about outside of himself. He ordered dinners and suppers, and evidently tried to be cheerful; but his gayety was not contagious as of yore; on the contrary, it aroused compassion in people who knew and liked him.

After Pierre and his bride had taken their departure, he fell into a very feeble condition, and began to complain of not feeling well. In a few days he grew really ill and took to his bed. From the first days of his illness, in spite of the doctor's encouragement, he felt certain that he should not recover.

The countess, without undressing, spent a fortnight in her arm-chair by his bedside. Every time she gave him his medicine, he would sob and silently kiss her hand. On the last day he wept and begged the forgiveness of his wife and his absent son for the dissipation of their property, the chief blame for which, he felt, rested on himself.

Having taken the last communion and final unction,

he died peacefully, and on the following day a throng of acquaintances, who came to pay their duties to the late lamented, filled the Rostofs' lodgings. All these acquaintances, who had so many times dined and danced at his house, who had so many times made sport of him, now, with a unanimous feeling of inward reproach and emotion, said, as if in justification of themselves before some one : —

"Yes, whatever may be said, he was, after all, one of the best of men. We don't often find such men these days. .... And who has not his failings?" ....

Just at the very time when the count's affairs had become so entangled that it was impossible to see what the end would be if they were allowed to go on for another year, he had unexpectedly died.

Nikolaï was with the Russian troops in Paris when the news of his father's death reached him. He immediately tendered his resignation, and, without waiting for it to be accepted, took a furlough and hastened to Moscow.

The state of the family finances within a month after the count's death were completely scheduled, and surprised every one by the magnitude of the sum to which the various little debts amounted, the existence of which no one had even suspected.

The property would not half pay the debts.

Nikolaï's relatives and friends advised him to renounce the inheritance. But Nikolaï saw in this suggestion the implication of a reproach to his father's memory, which he held sacred, and therefore he refused to hear anything said about renouncing the inheritance, and accepted it with all the obligations to settle the debts.

The creditors, who had been so long silent, being kept good-natured during the count's lifetime by the vague but powerful influence which his easy-going generosity had exerted on them, now all suddenly began to clamor for their debts to be paid. As always happens, there sprang up a regular competition as to who should be the first to be paid; and those very persons, like Mitenka and others, who held accommodation notes — gratuities often — now showed themselves as the most pressing of the creditors.

Nikolaï was given no rest or respite; and those who apparently had had pity on the old man — the cause of their losses, if losses they·were — were now pitiless toward the young heir, who was evidently innocent toward them, but had honorably assumed his father's debts.

Not one of the speculations which Nikolaï tried to engineer was successful: the real estate was sold by auction, but did not bring half its value, and still half the debts remained unliquidated. Nikolaï took thirty thousand rubles which his brother-in-law, Bezukhoï, offered him to pay that portion of the debts which he considered most pressing. And, in order that he might not be sent to jail for the remaining obligations, as the other creditors threatened, he again entered the service.

To return to the army, where at the first vacancy he would be promoted as regimental commander, was impossible, because his mother now clung to her only son as the last joy of her life; and therefore, in spite of his disinclination to remain in Moscow, in the circle of those who had always known him, notwithstanding his distaste for the civil service, he stayed in Moscow and accepted a place in the civil section, and, giving up the uniform which he so loved, he settled down with his mother and Sonya in a modest apartment on the Siv-tsevoï Vrazhek.

Natasha and Pierre were at this time living at Peters-burg, and had not a very definite idea of Nikolaï's posi-tion. Nikolaï, who had already had some money from his brother-in-law, strove to hide from him his unhappy situation. His position was rendered peculiarly hard because, with his twelve hundred rubles salary, he was not only obliged to support himself, Sonya, and his mother, but he was obliged to live in such a way that his mother would not suspect that they were poor. The countess could not conceive of any existence without those conditions of luxury to which she had been accus-tomed from childhood; and without a suspicion that it was hard for her son, she was continually requiring a carriage, though they had none, to send for a friend, or some rich delicacy for herself or wine for her son, or money to provide some gift for a surprise to Natasha, Sonya, or Nikolaï himself. ·

Sonya had charge of the domestic arrangements, waited on her aunt, read aloud to her, endured her whims and her secret ill-will, and aided Nikolaï in hiding from the old countess the condition of poverty to which they were reduced.

Nikolaï felt that he owed Sonya a heavier debt of gratitude than he could ever repay for all that she had done for his mother; he admired her patience and devotion, but he tried to avoid her.

In the depths of his heart, he, as it were, reproached her for her very perfection, and because there was nothing for which to reproach her. She had every quality which people prize; but still there was lacking the something which would have compelled him to love her. And he felt that the more he prized her, the less he loved her. He had taken her at her word when she wrote the letter releasing him from his promise, and now he treated her as if all that had taken place between them had been long, long forgotten, and could never by any chance return.

Nikolaï's condition grew worse and worse. The idea of saving something from his salary became a dream with him. Instead of laying up anything, he was driven by his mother's constant demands on him to incur petty debts. There seemed to be no way out of his difficulties.

The idea of making a wealthy marriage, such as had been proposed to him by his relatives, was repugnant to him. The only other escape from his situation — the death of his mother — never occurred to him. He had no wishes, and he had no hope, and in the deepest depths of his heart he experienced a stern and gloomy enjoyment in thus resignedly enduring his situation. He tried to avoid his old acquaintances, their condolence and humiliating offers of assistance; he avoided every sort of amusement and dissipation, and did not even do anything at home except play cards with his mother, or pace in gloomy silence up and down the room, smoking pipe after pipe.

He cherished, as it were, this gloomy state, in which alone he felt himself capable of enduring his position.

CHAPTER VI

EARLY in the winter the Princess Mariya came to Moscow. From the current gossip of town she learned of the position of the Rostofs, and how "the son was sacrificing himself for his mother," for so it was said in the city.

"I should have expected nothing else from him," said the Princess Mariya to herself, feeling a joyful confirmation of her love for him.

When she remembered her relations of friendship, almost of kinship, to the whole family, she felt it her duty to go to see them. But when she remembered her relations to Nikolaï at Voronezh, she dreaded to do so. At length, several weeks after her return to the city, she made a powerful effort and went to the Rostofs'.

Nikolaï was the first to meet her, for the reason that the countess's room could be reached only by passing through his. When he first caught sight of her, his face, instead of showing that joy which the princess had expected to see, assumed a cold, haughty, and repellent expression which the princess had never before seen in it. Nikolaï inquired after her health, conducted her to his mother, and, after remaining five minutes, left the room.

When the princess left the countess, Nikolaï again met her, and with especial ceremony and reserve ushered her into the anteroom. He answered never a word to her remark about the countess's health.

"What have I to do with you? Leave me in peace," his look seemed to say.

"Now, what makes her come round? What does she want? I can't endure these fine ladies and all their inquisitive ways," he said aloud in Sonya's presence, evidently not able to restrain his annoyance after the princess's carriage had rolled away.

"Oh! how can you say so, Nicolas!" said Sonya, who could scarcely restrain her joy. "She is so good, and *maman* loves her so."

Nikolaï made no answer, and would have preferred not to say anything more about the princess. But from that time forth the old countess kept talking about her a dozen times a day.

The countess praised her, insisted on her son going to return her call, expressed her anxiety to see her more frequently, but at the same time, whenever she spoke of her, she always got out of sorts.

Nikolaï tried to hold his tongue when his mother spoke of the princess; his silence annoyed his mother.

"She is a very worthy and lovely girl," she would say, "and you must go and call upon her. At all events, you will see somebody. It seems to me it must be tedious for you with us."

"I don't care to see anybody, mamenka!"

"A little while ago you wanted to see people, but now it's — 'I don't care to.' Truly, my dear boy, I don't understand you. You have been finding it tedious, but now suddenly you don't wish to see any one!"

"But I have not said it was tedious to me."

"Did you not just say that you did not want to see her? She is a very worthy girl and you always liked her, but now you find some excuse or other. It's all a mystery to me!"

"Why, not at all, mamenka!"

"If I had asked you to do something disagreeable — but no, all I ask of you is to go and return this call! It would seem as if politeness demanded it. .... I have asked you, and now I shall not interfere any more, since you have secrets from your mother."

"But I will go, if you wish it."

"It's all the same to me. I wish it for your sake."

Nikolaï sighed, and, gnawing his mustache, proceeded to lay out the cards, trying to divert his mother's attention to something else.

On the next day, on the third, and on the fourth, the same conversation was renewed.

After her call upon the Rostofs and the unexpectedly cool reception which Nikolaï had given her, the Princess Mariya confessed to herself that she had been right in not wishing to go to the Rostofs' first.

"I expected as much," said she to herself, calling her pride to her assistance. "I have nothing to do with him, and I only wanted to see the old lady, who has always been good to me, and who is bound to me by so many ties."

But she could not calm her agitation by these arguments; a feeling akin to remorse tormented her when she remembered her visit. Although she had firmly resolved not to go to the Rostofs' again, and to forget all about it, she could not help feeling that she was in a false position. And when she asked herself what it was that tormented her, she had to confess that it was her relation to Rostof.

His cool, formal tone did not really express his feelings, — she knew this, — and this tone only covered something. She felt that it was necessary for her to discover this something. And until she did, she felt that it was impossible for her to be at peace.

One time in midwinter she was in the school-room, attending to her nephew's lessons, when the servant came and announced that Rostof was in the drawing-room.

With a firm determination not to betray her secret and not to manifest her confusion, she summoned Mlle. Bourienne and went down with her into the drawing-room.

At her first glance into Nikolaï's face she perceived that he had come merely to fulfil the duty of politeness, and she firmly vowed that she would keep to the same tone in which he treated her.

They talked about the countess's health, about common acquaintances, and about the latest news of the war, and when the ten minutes demanded by etiquette had passed, at the end of which the caller can take his departure, Nikolaï rose to say good-by.

The princess, with Mlle. Bourienne's aid, had sustained the conversation very well; but at the very last moment, just as he rose to his feet, she had grown so weary of talking about things that interested her not, and the thought why she alone had so little pleasure in life came over her so powerfully, that she fell into a fit of abstraction, and sat motionless with her radiant eyes looking straight ahead and not perceiving that he had arisen.

Nikolaï glanced at her, and, feigning not to notice her abstraction, spoke a few words to Mlle. Bourienne, and again looked at the princess. She sat as before, motionless, and an expression of pain showed itself in her gentle face.

Suddenly he felt a sense of compassion for her, and a dim consciousness that he himself might be the cause of the sorrow that was expressed in her face. He wanted to help her, to say something cheering to her; but he could not think what to say.

"Good-by, princess," said he.

She came to herself, flushed, and drew a long sigh.

"Oh, I beg your pardon," said she, as if awakening from a dream. " Are you going already, count ? Well, good-by. .... Oh, but the pillow for the countess ? "

" Wait, I will fetch it down to you," said Mlle. Bourienne, and left the room.

Both were silent, though they occasionally looked at each other.

"Yes, princess," said Nikolaï at last, with a melancholy smile. "It does not seem very long ago, but how much has happened [1] since you and I met first at Bogucharovo. How unfortunate we all seemed then ; but I would give a good deal for that time to return again .... but what is past is past."

The princess looked steadily into his face with her

[1] Russian : " How much water has flowed."

clear, radiant eyes, while he was saying this. She seemed to be striving to discover some secret significance in his words which might interpret his sentiments toward her.

"Yes, yes," said she. "But you have nothing to regret in the past, count. When I think what your life is now, I am sure that you will always remember it with pleasure, because the self-sacrifice which at the present time you...."

"I cannot accept your words of praise," said he, hastily interrupting her. "On the contrary, I am constantly reproaching myself; but this is not at all an interesting or amusing subject of conversation."

And again his eyes assumed their former expression of reserve and coldness.

But the princess had once more seen in him that man whom she had known and loved, and she was now talking only with that man.

"I thought you would permit me to say this to you," said she. "You and I have been brought so near together.... and your family.... and I thought that you would not consider my sympathy out of place; but I was mistaken," said she. Her voice suddenly trembled. "I do not know why," she continued, correcting herself, "you were so different before, and...."

"There are a thousand reasons *why*"—he laid a special stress on the word *why*—"I thank you, princess," said he, gently. "Sometimes it is hard...."

"So that is the reason, then, that is the reason," said a voice in the Princess Mariya's heart. "No, it was not alone his merry, kind, and open eyes, not alone his handsome exterior, which I loved him for: I suspected his nobility, firmness, and sacrificing heart," said she to herself. "Yes, now he is poor, and I am rich..... Yes, that, then, was the sole reason..... Yes, if it were not that...."

And, as she remembered his former gentleness, and looked now into his kind and melancholy face, she suddenly realized the reason of his coolness.

"Why is it, count, why is it?" she suddenly almost

cried, and involuntarily came closer to him. "Why is it? tell me. You ought to tell me."

He was silent.

"I don't know, count, what your *why* is," she went on to say — "but it is hard for me too, for me.... I confess it to you. For some reason you wish to deprive me of your old friendship. And this pains me."

The tears were in her eyes and in her voice.

"I have so little happiness in life that every loss is hard for me to bear. Excuse me.... good-by."

She suddenly burst into tears, and started to leave the room.

"Princess! Wait! for God's sake!" he cried, trying to detain her. "Princess!"

She looked around. For several seconds they looked into each other's eyes, each in silence, and what had been distant and impossible suddenly became near, possible, and inevitable.

* * * * * *

CHAPTER VII

In the autumn of the year 1813, Nikolaï was married to the Princess Mariya, and went with his wife, his mother, and Sonya to live at Luisiya Gorui.

In the course of four years, without selling any of his wife's property, he settled the last of his debts, and, having inherited a small estate by the death of a cousin, he also paid back what he had borrowed of Pierre.

Three years later still, in 1820, Nikolaï had so managed his pecuniary affairs that he had purchased a small estate adjoining Luisiya Gorui, and was in negotiations for repurchasing Otradnoye, which was one of his favorite dreams.

Having been forced by necessity to manage his own estate, he quickly grew so passionately interested in farming that it came to be his favorite and almost exclusive occupation.

Nikolaï was a farmer of the simple old-fashioned

school;[1] he did not like innovations, especially English ones, which at that time were coming into vogue; laughed at theoretical works on farming, disliked machinery, expensive processes, the sowing of costly grains, and as a general thing had no patience with occupying himself with only one side of farming. He always kept before his eyes the idea of the estate as a whole, and favored no part of it to the exclusion of the rest.

The chief element of success in an estate was not the azote and the oxygen found in the soil and in the atmosphere, or any especial form of plow or manure, but rather the principal instrument by means of which the oxygen and the nitrogen and the manure and the plow act, — the *muzhik* — the working peasant.

When Nikolaï took up the care of his estate and began to study the different parts of it, the muzhik especially attracted his attention. The muzhik seemed to him not only a tool and instrument, but the object and judge. From the very first he studied the muzhik, striving to comprehend what he wanted, what he considered good and bad, and only pretended to give orders and lay out work, while in reality he was learning of the peasants, both from their ways and their words, and their judgment as to what was good or bad.

And only when at last he learned to understand the tastes and aspirations of the muzhiks, learned to speak their speech and comprehend the secret significance of their sayings, when he felt himself one with them, only then did he dare boldly to direct them, that is, to fulfil toward them the duties that were demanded of him.

And Nikolaï's management[2] brought about the most brilliant results.

When he undertook the management of the estate, Nikolaï at once unerringly, by some gift of second sight, appointed as *burmistr*, or village bailiff, or as *starosta*, or as the peasant delegate, the very men who would have been chosen by the muzhiks themselves, if

---

[1] *Khozyaïn prastoï*, simple proprietor, landowner, householder, etc.
[2] *Khozyaïstvo.*

the choice had been in their hands; and his appointees were never changed.

Before he made investigations into the chemical properties of manures, before he entered into the question of "debit and credit," as he laughingly termed it, he learned about the number of cattle that the peasants had, and increased it by all the means in his power.

He tried to keep the families of the peasants as large as possible, not permitting them to break up.[1] He kept a strict oversight upon the lazy, the dissolute, and the feeble, and tried to rid the community of such. During seed-time and haymaking and harvest, he gave the same careful attention to his own fields and those of his muzhiks. And few proprietors got their seed in so early or averaged such good crops as Nikolaï did.

He liked not to have anything to do with the *dvorovuie*, or domestic serfs, called them drones, and, as every one said, neglected them and spoiled them; when it was necessary to do anything, or make any disposition concerning a domestic serf, especially when it was necessary to punish one, he was always undecided, and had to ask the opinion of all in the house; only when it was possible to send a domestic serf as a soldier in place of a muzhik, he would do so without the slightest hesitation.

But in regard to all the dispositions which he had to make concerning the muzhiks, he never experienced the slightest hesitancy. He knew that any disposition that he might make concerning the muzhiks would be approved by all excepting perhaps one or a very few.

Likewise, he never allowed himself to overwork or punish a field-hand out of any personal whim or caprice, nor would he ease a man's labors or reward him simply because such a thing constituted his personal desire. He could not have said where he got his standard for what he ought and what he ought not to do; but this standard was firm and inflexible in his heart.

[1] The communal system of Russia is patriarchal, the head of the family having control of all the sons and daughters, married and single, living under his roof.

Yet often, in vexation at some failure or disorder, he would exclaim: "With this Russian people of ours!" and try to argue to his own satisfaction that he could not put up with the muzhik.

But with all the strength of his heart he loved "this Russian people of ours," and their ways; and this reason alone made him appreciate and adopt the only manner and method of managing his estate which could bring him in good results.

The Countess Mariya was jealous of her husband because of this love of his, and regretted that she could not share in it; but she could not understand the joys and annoyances which for him constituted this world, so foreign and apart from her own. She could not understand why he should be so peculiarly animated and happy, when, having arisen with the dawn and spent the whole morning in the field or the threshing-floor, he came back from the sowing, the mowing, or the harvest, to drink tea with her.

She could not understand what should so kindle his enthusiasm as he told of the wealthy and enterprising muzhik Matvyei Yermishin, who had spent the whole night with his family in carrying sheaves, and who had his corn-stacks all made up, while as yet the others had not touched theirs.

She could not understand why he was so glad, and smiled under his mustaches so joyously, as he came from the window out on the balcony, while the warm frequent showers fell on the dry and thirsty young oats; or why, when during haymaking or harvest-time the wind drove away the threatening clouds, he would come in from the threshing-floor flushed, sunburnt, and sweaty, and with the scent of wormwood and wild gentian in his hair, and, gayly rubbing his hands, exclaim:

"Well, now, one more short day, and my grain and the peasants' will all be in the barn."

Still less was she able to understand why he, with his kindness of heart, with his never failing readiness to anticipate her desires, was almost in despair when she presented to him petitions from peasant women or muzhiks who had applied to her for relief from some drudgery or other, — why he, this good Nicolas, was so obstinate in refusing to do so, and begged her sternly not to interfere in what was not her business. She felt that he had a special world of his own which he passionately loved, and which was governed by laws she could not understand.

When, sometimes, in her endeavors to understand him, she would speak to him of the service he was rendering in doing so much good to his dependents, he would lose his temper and reply: —

" Not in the least; it never entered my head, and I am not doing anything for their good. That is all poetry and old woman's tales, all this talk about kindness to one's neighbor. What I want is, that our children should not become beggars; what I want is, to get our property on a satisfactory basis while I am alive : that is all. And to do that, order is necessary, and so is sternness. .... That 's all there is of it," said he, clenching his sanguine fist, " .... and justice of course," he added. " Because if the peasant is naked and hungry, and has only one little horse, then he will work neither for himself nor for me."

And there can be no doubt that for the very reason that Nikolaï allowed himself not to think that he was doing anything for others, in the way of a benefactor, that all he did was so abundantly successful, his property rapidly increased; neighboring muzhiks came to him and begged him to buy them, and, long after he was dead and gone, a devout memory of his *régime* obtained among the peasantry.

" He was a manager.[1] .... He looked after his peasants' affairs first, and then his own. And he did not show too much indulgence, either. In one word, he was a manager."

[1] *Khozyaïn.*

CHAPTER VIII

ONE thing sometimes troubled Nikolaï in relation to his administration of affairs, and this was his quick temper and a propensity, which was a relic of his old life as a hussar, to enforce his will by means of his hands. At first, he saw nothing reprehensible in this; but in the second year of his married life his views in regard to this form of inflicting punishment underwent a sudden change.

One time during the summer the starosta of Bogucharovo, the successor of Dron, who was now dead, was summoned over to Luisiya Gorui charged with various rascalities and villainies. Nikolaï met him on the porch, and at his first reply the sound of cries and blows rang through the vestibule.

On going into the house for breakfast, Nikolaï joined his wife, whom he found sitting with her head bent low over her embroidery-frame, and began to tell her, as his wont was, about all that occupied him that morning, and, among other things, about the *starosta*, or headman, of Bogucharovo. The Countess Mariya, turning red, then pale, and compressing her lips, sat with her head still bent, and made no reply to her husband's words.

"Such an impertinent scoundrel!" exclaimed he, growing hot at the mere recollection. "If he had only told me that he was drunk .... I never saw .... but what is the matter, Marie?" he suddenly asked.

The countess raised her head and tried to say something, but again hastily drooped her head, and compressed her lips.

"What is it? What is the matter, my darling?"[1] ....

Plain as the Countess Mariya was, she always grew pretty when tears were in her eyes. She never wept because of pain or annoyance, but always from melancholy and pity. And when she wept her liquid eyes acquired an irresistible charm.

[1] *Druzhok moï;* druzhok is a caressing diminutive of *druk*, friend.

The moment Nikolaï took her by the hand, she could no longer restrain herself, but burst into tears.

"Nicolas, I saw .... he is at fault, but, oh, Nicolas, why did you?" ....

And she hid her face in her hands.

Nikolaï said nothing, turned crimson, and, turning away from her, began to pace up and down the room. He understood what made her weep; but at the same time he could not agree with her in his heart, that what he had been used to regarding since childhood as a customary thing was wrong.

"Is it her amiability and feminine weakness, or is she right?" he asked himself. Not being able to decide this question for himself, he once more looked into her suffering, loving face, and suddenly realized that she was right, and that he had been wrong even in his own eyes for a long time.

"Marie," said he, gently, and he came to her, "this shall never happen again; I give you my word. Never!" he repeated, in a trembling voice like a lad asking forgiveness.

The tears rolled faster than ever from the countess's eyes. She took her husband's hand and kissed it.

"Nicolas, when did you break your cameo?" she asked, for the purpose of changing the conversation, and examining his hand, on which he wore a ring with a head of Laocoon.

"To-day; it's all the same story. Akh! Marie, don't speak of it again." He flushed once more. "I give thee my word of honor that this shan't happen again. And let this always be a reminder to me," he added, pointing to the broken ring.

From that time forth, when he had to enter into explanations with the starostas, and the hot blood flew into his face, and he began to clench his fists, Nikolaï would turn the broken ring round on his finger and drop his eyes before the man who was angering him. However, once or twice a year he would forget himself, and then, when he came into his wife's presence, he would confess, and again give his promise that it should be the last time.

" Marie, truly you will despise me," he would say to her.   " I deserve it."

"You should go away, go away as fast as you can, if you find that you have not the strength of mind to restrain yourself," said the Countess Mariya, in a tender voice, trying to console her husband.

Nikolaï was respected but not liked among the gentry of the province.   He did not care about the interests of the nobility.   And on this account some considered him proud, others stupid.

During the summer, he spent all his time in the management of his farms, from the time that the seed was put in until the crops were garnered.

During the autumn, he gave himself up to hunting with the same practical seriousness which he showed in the care of his estates, and, for a month or two, he would ride out with the hounds.

During the winter, he rode off to visit his other villages, and occupied himself with reading.   His reading consisted, principally, of historical works, for the purchase of which he spent a certain amount each year. He was forming for himself, as he said, a "serious library," and he made it a rule to read through every book which he purchased.   With a grave face, he would shut himself up in his library for this reading, which, at first, he imposed on himself as a duty ; but in time it came to be his ordinary occupation, furnishing him with a certain kind of satisfaction, and the consciousness that he was occupied with a serious task.

Except for the time he spent out of doors, in the prosecution of his affairs, during the winter he was mostly in the house, entering into the domestic life of the family, and taking an interest in the every-day relations between the mother and children.   He kept growing closer and closer to his wife, each day discovering in her new spiritual treasures.

Sonya, since the time of Nikolaï's marriage, had been an inmate of his house.   Some time before his marriage, Nikolaï, laying all blame on himself, and praising her, had told the Princess Mariya what had occurred between him and Sonya. He had begged the Princess Mariya to be kind and good to his cousin. The Countess Mariya fully realized her husband's fault. She also felt that she was to blame toward Sonya ; she realized that her own position had influenced Nikolaï's choice, and she could not see that Sonya was in any way blameworthy, and she wanted to love her ; but not only did she not love her, but she often found bitter feelings against her arising in her soul, and she could not overcome them.

One time she was talking with her friend Natasha about Sonya and about her own injustice toward her.

" Do you know," said Natasha, — " you have read the New Testament a great deal, — there is one place that refers directly to Sonya."

"What is that ? " asked the Countess Mariya, in amazement.

" ' *For unto every one that hath shall be given, but from him that hath not shall be taken away even that which he hath.*' Do you remember ? She is the one that hath not. Why, I do not know ; it seems to me she has no selfishness about her. I don't know, somehow, but it is taken away from her — everything has been taken away from her. I am terribly sorry for her sometimes ; I used to be terribly anxious for Nicolas to marry her, but I always had a sort of presentiment that it would never be. She is a sterile flower ; you have seen them in the strawberry patch, have n't you ? Sometimes I am sorry for her, but then, again, I think that she does n't feel it as we should."

And although the Countess Mariya explained to Natasha that these words from the Gospel must have a different meaning, still, as she looked at Sonya, she agreed with the explanation which Natasha gave to them. It really seemed to her that Sonya was not troubled by her uncomfortable position, and was perfectly satisfied with her name of " sterile flower."

It seemed that she did not so much care for any special individual as for the family as a whole. Like a cat, she attached herself, not to the household, so much as to the house itself. She took care of the old countess, she petted and spoiled the children, was always ready to show such little services as she could; but all this was accepted unwittingly, without any special sense of gratitude. ....

The establishment at Luisiya Gorui had now been restored to good order, but not on the same footing as it had been during the late prince's lifetime. The new buildings, begun during the hard times, were more than simple. The enormous mansion-house, erected on the original stone foundations, was of wood, merely plastered on the inside. The great, spacious mansion, with its unpainted deal floors, was furnished with the simplest and coarsest divans and easy-chairs, tables and chairs made from their own lumber by their own carpenters. The house was capacious, with rooms for the domestics, and special suites for guests.

The relatives of the Rostofs and Bolkonskys often came to visit at Luisiya Gorui, with their families and almost a score of horses, with dozens of servants, and would spend months there. Moreover, three or four times a year, on the name-day or birthday festivals of the host and hostess, a hundred guests would be present at once for several days.

The rest of the year the regular life moved in its regular channels with the usual occupations — teas, breakfasts, dinners, suppers, supplied from the resources of the estate.

CHAPTER IX

It was the eve of St. Nicholas Day, in the winter[1]— the seventeenth of December, 1820.

That year Natasha with her children and husband had come early in the autumn to visit her brother. Pierre was in Petersburg, where he had gone on private business for three or four weeks, as he said, but where

---

[1] *Zimnii Nikolina dyen'* or *Nikola zimnii* (as the peasants call it) comes Dec. 6. (O.S.), in contradistinction to *Nikola lyetnii* or St. Nicholas Day in the summer, the 9th (21st) May.

he had already spent seven. They were expecting him at any moment.

On the seventeenth of December the Rostofs had, besides the Bezukhoï family, Nikolaï's old friend, General Vasili Feodorovitch Denisof, who was now on the retired list.

Nikolaï knew that on the eighteenth, the day of the festivity for which the guests had assembled, he should have to take off his *beshmet* or Tatar blouse, put on his dress-coat and tight, narrow-toed shoes, and go to the new church which he had just built, and then receive congratulations and offer lunch, and talk about the elections and the crops; but he felt that on the eve of his name-day he had the right to spend his time in the usual way.

Just before dinner Nikolaï had been verifying the accounts of the *burmistr*, or bailiff, from the Riazan estate of his wife's nephew, had written two business letters, and had made the round of the granaries, the cattle-yard, and his stables. Having taken precautions against the general drunkenness which was to be expected on the morrow in consequence of its being a capital festival, he came in to dinner, and, without having had a chance for a few moments of private conversation with his wife, he took his seat at the long table set with twenty covers for his whole household.

At the table were his mother, the old dowager Countess Byelova, who was still living, his wife, his three children, their governess, their tutor, his nephew with his tutor, Soñya, Denisof, Natasha, her three children, their governess, and the little old Mikhaïl Ivanuitch, the prince's architect, who lived at Luisiya Gorui on a pension.

The Countess Mariya was sitting at the opposite end of the table. As soon as her husband took his place she knew by the gesture with which he took his napkin and quickly pushed away the tumbler and wine-glass that were set before him, that he was in bad humor, as was sometimes the case with him especially before soup, and when he came directly from his work to dinner.

The Countess Mariya knew perfectly well this disposition of his, and, when she herself was in her usual good spirits, she would calmly wait until he should finish his soup, and not till then would she begin to talk with him and make him realize that his ill temper was groundless; but on the present occasion she had entirely forgotten this observation of hers; it hurt her to feel that he was angry with her without cause, and she felt that she was innocent.

She asked him where he had been.

He told her.

Then again she asked him if he found everything in good order. He scowled disagreeably at her unnatural tone, and answered hastily.

"So I was not mistaken," thought the Countess Mariya. "Now, why is he vexed with me?"

By the tone in which he answered her the Countess Mariya detected what she thought was ill-will toward herself, and a wish to cut short the conversation. She realized that her own words had been unnatural, but she could not refrain from asking several other questions.

The conversation during dinner, thanks to Denisof, quickly became general and animated, and the Countess Mariya had no chance to say anything to her husband. When they left the table and went to thank the old countess, the Countess Mariya, offering her hand, kissed her husband and asked him why he was vexed with her.

"You *always* have such strange ideas! .... I had no thought of being vexed with you," said he. But this word *always* said with sufficient clearness to the Countess Mariya: "Yes, I am angry, and I won't tell you."

Nikolaï lived so harmoniously with his wife that even Sonya and the old countess, who out of jealousy might have been happy to see some discord between them, could not find any excuse for reproach; but still they had their moments of hostility. Sometimes, especially after their happiest times, they were suddenly assailed by the feeling of repulsion and animosity; this feeling was particularly liable to occur when the Countess Mariya was with child. She was now in this condition.

"Well, *messieurs et mesdames*," said Nikolaï, in a loud and apparently gay tone, — it seemed to the Countess Mariya that it was on purpose to hurt her feelings, — "I have been on my feet ever since six o'clock. To-morrow I shall have to endure a good deal, and now I'm going to rest."

And, without saying anything more to the Countess Mariya, he went into the little divan-room and lay down on the divan.

"That's the way it always is," thought the Countess Mariya. "He talks with all the rest, but not with me. I see, I see that I am repulsive to him, especially when I am in this condition."

She looked at her changed figure, and caught sight in the mirror of her yellowish-pale, thin face, with her large eyes more prominent than ever.

And everything seemed disagreeable to her, — Denisof's shouts and laughter, and Natasha's talk, and especially the look which Sonya hastily threw after her.

Sonya was always the first pretext which the Countess Mariya took to excuse her irritation.

After sitting down for a little while with her guests, and not comprehending a word of what they said, she softly got up and went to the nursery.

The children were on chairs, "going to Moscow," and they begged her to join them. She sat down and played with them, but the thought of her husband and his causeless vexation tormented her without ceasing. She got up and went to the little divan-room, painfully trying to walk on her tiptoes.

"Perhaps he is not asleep; I will have a talk with him," said she to herself.

Andryusha, her oldest boy, imitating her, followed her on his tiptoes. The Countess Mariya did not notice him.

"*Chère Marie*, I think he is asleep; he is so tired," said Sonya, from the large divan-room; it seemed to the countess as if she met her everywhere! "Andryusha might wake him."

The Countess Mariya looked round, saw Andryusha at her heels, and felt that Sonya was right; this very thing made her angry, and it was evidently with difficulty that she restrained herself from a sharp reply.

She said nothing, and, affecting not to have heard her, she made a gesture with her hand to Andryusha not to make a noise but to follow her, and went to the door.

Sonya passed through another door.

From the room where Nikolaï was sleeping could be heard his measured breathing, so well known to his wife, even to its slightest shadow of change.

As she listened to his breathing she could see before her his smooth, handsome brow, his mustache, his whole face, at which so often she had gazed in the silence of the night, while he was asleep.

Nikolaï suddenly started and yawned. And at that same instant Andryusha cried from the door: —

"Papenka, mamenka is there!"

The Countess Mariya grew pale with fright, and started to make signs to her son. He became still, and for an instant the silence, so terrible to the Countess Mariya, continued. She knew how Nikolaï disliked being awakened.

Suddenly in the room were heard fresh yawns, rustling, and Nikolaï's voice said in a tone of annoyance: —

"Can't I have a moment's rest! Marie, is it you? What made you bring him here?"

"I only came to see if.... I did not see him .... forgive me ...."

Nikolaï coughed, and said nothing more. The Countess Mariya went away from the door, and led her son to the nursery.

Five minutes later, the little, dark-eyed, three-year-old Natasha, her father's favorite, hearing her brother say that her papenka was asleep and her mamenka was in the divan-room, ran to her father unobserved by her mother. The dark-eyed little maid boldly pushed the door open with a slam, ran on her energetic little stumpy legs up to the divan, and, after attentively looking at her father, who was lying with his back turned toward her, raised herself on her tiptoes and kissed his hand, on which his head was resting. Nikolaï, with a fond smile, turned over.

"Natasha! Natasha!" the Countess Mariya was heard saying in a terrified whisper outside the door, "papenka wants to get a nap."

"No, mamma! he does n't want a nap," replied the little Natasha, in a tone of settled conviction. "He's laughing."

Nikolaï put down his feet, sat up, and took his daughter in his arms. "Come in, Masha," said he to his wife.

The Countess Mariya went in and sat down near her husband.

"I did not see that he was tagging behind me," said she, timidly. "That's the way with me."

Nikolaï, holding his daughter in one arm, looked at his wife, and, perceiving the apologetic expression in her face, he put his other arm around her and kissed her on the hair.

"May I kiss mamma?" he asked Natasha.

Natasha smiled shyly.

"Again!" said she, with an imperative gesture designating the spot where Nikolaï had kissed his wife.

"I don't know why you should think that I am out of sorts," said Nikolaï, answering the question which he knew was in his wife's heart.

"You cannot imagine how unhappy, how lonely, I feel when you are so! It seems to me all the time...."

"Marie, stop! What nonsense! Are n't you ashamed of yourself?" he asked gayly.

"It seems to me that you cannot love me, that I am so plain.... always.... but now.... in this con...."

"Akh! how absurd you are! Beauty does not make sweetness, but sweetness makes beauty! It is only such women as the Malvinas who are loved for their beauty. Do I love my wife? I don't love her in that way.... but I can't explain it. Without thee.... or even if a cat should run between us, I should be quite lost and should n't know what to do. Well, then, do I love my little finger? I don't love it, but .... just try it .... cut it off .... "

" No, I 'm not like that, but I understand you. And so you are not vexed with me ? "

" Oh, yes, I am .... horribly vexed," said he, smiling; then, getting up, and smoothing his hair, he began to pace up and down the room. " You know what I was thinking about," he began, now that peace had been made, immediately beginning to think aloud in his wife's hearing. He did not ask whether she were ready to listen to him; it was all the same to him. If he had any thoughts she *must* have the same. And he told her his intention of inviting Pierre to remain with them till spring.

The Countess Mariya listened to him, made some observation, and began in her turn to think her thoughts aloud. Her thoughts were about her children.

" How the woman can be seen in her already ! " said she in French, alluding to the little Natasha. " You accuse us women of being illogical. Well, she is our logic personified. I say, ' Papa wants to get a nap,' but she says, ' No, he is laughing.' And she is right," said the Countess Mariya, with a happy smile.

" Yes, yes," and, taking his daughter by his strong hands, he lifted her up in the air, set her on his shoulder, holding her by the feet, and began to walk up and down the room with her. The faces of father and daughter alike expressed the most absurd happiness.

" But you know you are apt to be partial. You love this one more than the others," whispered the Countess Mariya in French.

" But how can I help it ? .... I try not to show it." ....

At this instant sounds of slamming doors and steps were heard in the vestibule and anteroom, as if there was an arrival.

" Some one has come."

" I think it must be Pierre. I 'll go and find out," said the Countess Mariya, and she left the room.

During her absence Nikolaï permitted himself to give his little daughter a gallop around the room.

All out of breath, he quickly set down the laughing child, and pressed her to his heart. His gambols reminded him of dancing, and, as he gazed into the little maid's round, radiant face, he thought of the future, when he should be a nice old man and lead her out and dance the mazurka with her, as his own father had once danced " Daniel Cooper " with his daughter.

" Yes, 't is he, 't is he, Nicolas," said the Countess Mariya, returning to the room after a few minutes. " Now our Natasha has got back her spirits. You ought to see how happy she is ! and how he caught it for having been away so long ! But come quick, let us go and see him, come ! Do let him go," said she, looking with a smile at her daughter, who clung to her father.

Nikolaï started off, holding the little girl by the hand.

The Countess Mariya remained in the divan-room.

" Never, never, would I believe that I could be so happy," she whispered to herself. Her face was radiant with a smile ; but at the same time she sighed, and a gentle melancholy showed itself in her deep eyes. It was as if over and above that happiness which she now experienced there were another kind of happiness, unattainable in this life, and she at that moment involuntarily remembered it.

CHAPTER X

NATASHA had been married in the early spring of 1813, and in 1820 she had already three daughters and one son — the child of her desires, whom she was now suckling.

She had grown plump and fleshy, so that it would have been difficult to recognize in the strong matron the slender, vivacious Natasha of yore. The features of her face had grown more marked, and bore an expression of sedate gentleness and serenity. Her face had lost all of that ever flashing light of animation which had formerly constituted her chief charm. Often now you would see only her face and her bodily presence and nothing of the animating soul. All you could see was a healthy, handsome, fruitful female.

Very rarely now the old fire flashed forth. This happened at times when, as now, her husband returned from a journey, or when a sick child was convalescing, or when she and the Countess Mariya talked over old memories of Prince Andreï (she never talked about him with her husband, imagining that he might be moved by some jealousy of such memories), and at the very rare times when something happened to make her sing, though, since her marriage, she had entirely abandoned this accomplishment. And at these rare moments, when the old fire flashed forth, she, with the beauty of her mature development, was even more fascinating than before.

Since the time of her marriage, Natasha and Pierre had lived at Moscow, at Petersburg, and their pod-Moskovnaya estate, and with her mother, or rather with Nikolaï.

The young Countess Bezukhoï was seen little in fashionable society, and those who met her were not attracted by her. She was neither genial nor careful of pleasing. It was not that Natasha liked solitude, — she knew not whether she liked it or not, it even seemed to her that she did not, — but while engaged in the bearing and nursing and rearing of children, and sharing in each moment of her husband's life, she could not satisfy these demands otherwise than by denying herself society.

All who had known Natasha before her marriage were amazed at the change that had taken place in her, as if it were something extraordinary. Only the old countess, who knew by her maternal insight that all Natasha's impulses of enthusiasm had their origin merely in the need of having a family, of having a husband, as she had cried more in earnest than in jest that winter at Otradnoye. The mother was amazed at the amazement of people who did not understand Natasha, and she insisted that she had always known that Natasha would be a model wife and mother.

"Only she carries her love for her husband and children to extremes," the countess would say, "so that it even seems stupid in her."

Natasha did not follow that golden rule preached by clever men, especially the French, to this effect, that when a young lady marries she must not neglect, must not abandon, her talents, must even more zealously than when she was a girl cultivate her personal adornment, must charm her husband as much after as she did before marriage.

Natasha, on the contrary, abandoned all at once all her accomplishments, even the one that was most of an accomplishment — her singing. She abandoned it for the very reason that it was an accomplishment.

Natasha took no pains either with her deportment or the elegance of her language, nor did she try to give herself graces before her husband, or think about her toilet, or dream of not imposing irksome exactions on her husband.

She proceeded in direct opposition to this rule.

She felt that those witcheries which instinct had taught her to employ before would now be absurd in the eyes of her husband, to whom she had surrendered entirely from the first minute — that is, with her whole soul, not leaving one single corner secret from him. She felt that the bond between her and her husband was held, not by those poetic feelings which had attracted him to her, but by something else, vague and undefined, but irresistible, like the union of her own soul and body.

To shake her curls, to put on *robronui*,[1] and to sing romances in order to attract her husband to her, would have seemed to her as ridiculous as to adorn herself for the purpose of giving herself pleasure.

To adorn herself to please others, possibly, might have been pleasing to her, — she knew not, — but she never did such a thing. The chief reason that she did

---

[1] French, *robe ronde*, a kind of dress, fashionable many years ago.

not indulge in singing or the witcheries of the toilet, or in using elegant language, was that she had absolutely no time to indulge herself in these things.

It is a well-known fact that a man has the capacity of completely immersing himself in any object, no matter how insignificant that object may be. And it is a well-known fact that any such object, however insignificant, through the attention concentrated on it, may expand into infinite proportions.

The object in which Natasha was absolutely absorbed was her family, that is to say, her husband, whom she had to hold so that he would cling to her and his home, — and her children, who had to be born, nursed, and reared and educated.

And the more she studied, not with her intellect but with her whole soul, her whole being, into this object which absorbed her, the more this object waxed in her estimation, and the weaker and more insignificant seemed to her her own powers, so that she concentrated them on one and the same thing, and still did not succeed in accomplishing what seemed to her so necessary.

The discussions and criticisms on the rights of women, on the relations of marriage, on the liberty and the rights of husband and wife, although at that period they had not yet begun to be called questions, were nevertheless just the same as they are at the present time; but not only did these questions not interest Natasha, but she really failed to understand them.

These questions, even then just the same as at the present time, existed only for those who looked for nothing but that sensual gratification in marriage which husband and wife afford each other: that is, merely the beginning of marriage, and not its whole significance — the family.

These arguments and the present-day questions are analogous to the question how can one get the most possible enjoyment from dinner? and at that time did not exist any more than they do now for men whose object in eating dinner is nourishment, and in marriage is raising a family.

If the object in eating dinner is the nourishment of the body, then the person who should eat two dinners at a sitting would perchance attain great enjoyment, but would not attain his object, since his stomach would not digest the two dinners.

If the object of marriage is a family, then the person who should wish many wives (or husbands) would perhaps get much enjoyment, but would not in any case be likely to have a family.

The whole question, provided the object of a dinner is nourishment, and the object of marriage is a family, is settled simply by not eating more than the stomach can digest, and by a person not having more husbands or wives than are necessary for a family; that is, one.

Natasha wanted a husband. The husband was given to her. And the husband gave her the family. And she not only saw no need of any better husband, but, since all the energies of her soul were directed toward serving her husband and family, she could not imagine, and saw no possible amusement in imagining, what would have been if things had been otherwise.

Natasha cared not for society in general, but she clung all the more to the society of her relatives — the Countess Mariya, her brother, her mother, and Sonya.

She took delight in the society of those whom she could run in to see, with unkempt hair, in her morning gown, right from the nursery, with happy face, to show them the yellow instead of green stain on the baby linen, and to hear the comforting words that now the baby would soon be much better.

Natasha was so neglectful of herself that her dresses, her mode of doing up her hair, her carelessly spoken words, her jealousy, — she was jealous of Sonya, of the governess, of every woman, whether pretty or plain, — were a common subject for amusement for the whole family.

The general impression was that Pierre was "under his wife's slipper," as the saying goes, and this was really so.

During the very first days of her married life, Natasha laid down her demands. Pierre was greatly amazed at this idea of his wife's, which was so absolutely new to him; she insisted that every minute of his life belonged to her and his children; Pierre was amazed at his wife's demand, but he was flattered by it and submitted to it.

Pierre's submission lay in his acceptance of the implied prohibition not merely of paying attentions to other women, but even of talking and laughing with them, of going to the club to dinner or for the purpose of merely passing away the time, of spending his money on whims, or taking long journeys except on business, — and in this category his wife included his interest in scientific pursuits, to which she attributed great importance, though she had no understanding of such things.

In return for this, Pierre had a perfect right to dispose of himself and his whole family as he might please — Natasha, in her own home, placed herself on the footing of a slave toward her husband, and the whole house went on tiptoes when he was busy reading or writing in his library. Pierre had only to manifest any desire, and his wish would be instantly fulfilled. He had only to express a desire, and Natasha would make haste to have it carried out.

The whole house was conducted according to the husband's supposititious commands, in other words, in accordance with Pierre's wishes, which Natasha tried to anticipate. The style, the place of living, their acquaintances, their intercourse with society, Natasha's occupations, the education of their children, — everything was done not merely in accordance with Pierre's expressed will, but Natasha strove to find out what would elicit hints of his ideas when he was talking. And she actually discovered what constituted the essence of Pierre's desires, and when she thus did, she firmly clung to what she had once adopted. When Pierre himself showed signs of changing his mind, she would turn his own weapons against him.

Thus, during the trying time, which Pierre never forgot, after the birth of their first child, which was ailing, and they were obliged three times to change wet-nurses, and Natasha fell ill from anxiety, Pierre one time told her of the ideas of Rousseau, with whom he was always in perfect concord, as to the unnaturalness and harmfulness of wet-nurses.

When the next child was born, Natasha, in spite of the opposition of her mother, the doctors, and her husband himself, who revolted against her suckling the child, as at that time something unheard-of and harmful, insisted on doing so, and from that time forth she always nursed all her children.

Very often, in moments of irritation, it would happen that husband and wife would have animated discussions; but long after the quarrel was forgotten, Pierre would find, to his joy and amazement, not only in what his wife said, but in what she did, his own ideas, against which she had rebelled. And not only would he find his own idea, but find it purified of everything superfluous that had been elicited by the excitement of the argument.

After seven years of married life, Pierre felt a joyous, settled consciousness that he was not a bad man, and this consciousness arose from the fact that he saw himself reflected in his wife. In himself he felt that all that was good and bad was mixed together and confused. But, in his wife, only that which was truly good found expression; all that was not absolutely good was purged away in her. And this reflection resulted, not along the line of logical thought, but from another mysterious, proximate reflection.

CHAPTER XI

PIERRE, two months before, while he was still visiting the Rostofs, received a letter from Prince Feodor, urging him to come to Petersburg to help decide some weighty questions that were agitating the members of a society of which Pierre was one of the most influential members.

On reading this letter, Natasha, — for she always read

her husband's letters, — hard as it was for her to bear her husband's absence, herself was the first to urge him to go to Petersburg. · Every intellectual, abstract interest of her husband's she considered of immense importance, even though she did not understand it, and she was constantly afraid of being a hindrance to this activity of her husband's. In reply to Pierre's timid, questioning look, on reading this letter, she begged him to go, but to make the time of his return as definite as possible. And leave of absence of a month was given him.

After this leave of absence had expired, a fortnight before, Natasha found herself in a state of constant alarm, depression, and irritation.

Denisof, now a general on the retired list, and greatly dissatisfied with the actual state of affairs, had been visiting at the Rostofs' for the past fortnight, and looked upon Natasha in amazement and grief, as on an unlike portrait of some once beloved face. Dejected, melancholy looks, haphazard replies, and perpetual talk about the children were all that was left of his former enchantress.

Natasha was melancholy and irritable all the time, especially when her mother, her brother, Sonya, or the Countess Mariya tried to excuse Pierre and find reasons for his delay.

"All nonsense, trivial nonsense," Natasha would say; "all these considerations of his, — leading to nothing, — and all these foolish societies," she would say, in regard to those very things of the immense importance of which she was firmly convinced. And off she would go to the nursery to nurse her only son, the little Petya.

No one could tell how consoling, how reasonable, this little creature of only three months was when he lay at her breast, and she felt the motion of his mouth and the snuffling of his little nose. This being said to her: "Thou art cross, thou art jealous, thou desirest vengeance, thou hast thy fears; but here .... I am! Oh, yes, here I am!" ....

And there was no answer to be made. It was more than the truth !

Natasha, during those two weeks of anxiety, went so many times to her baby for consolation, she made such a to-do over him, that she overfed him, and he had an ill turn. She was horror-struck at his illness, and at the same time it was the very thing that she needed. In caring for him, she more easily endured her husband's absence.

She was nursing him when a commotion, caused by Pierre's arrival, was heard; and the nurse, who knew how much it would delight her mistress, came running in noiselessly but swiftly, with a beaming face.

" Has he come ? " asked Natasha, in a hurried whisper, afraid to move lest she should awaken the sleeping infant.

" He 's come, matushka ! " whispered the nurse.

The blood rushed into Natasha's face, and her feet made an involuntary movement, but it was impossible to jump up and run. The child again opened his eyes and looked up at her. ' Art thou here ? ' he seemed to say, and again smacked his lips.

Cautiously withdrawing the breast, Natasha rocked him a little, and then handed him to the nurse and ran swiftly to the door. But at the door she paused, as if her conscience reproached her for having, in her joy, too hastily given up the child, and she looked round. The nurse, with her elbows in the air, was just putting the baby safely into its cradle.

" Yes, go right along, go right along, matushka, have no fears, go right along," whispered the nurse, smiling with the familiarity which always exists between nurse and mistress.

And Natasha with light steps ran to the anteroom.

Denisof, with his pipe, coming from the library into the hall, now for the first time recognized the Natasha of yore. A bright, gleaming light of joy poured forth in streams from her transfigured face.

" He 's come ! " she called to him, as she flew along, and Denisof felt that he was enthusiastic over Pierre's arrival, though he had never had any great love for him.

As Natasha came running into the anteroom, she caught sight of the tall form in a shuba, untying his scarf.

"Here he is! Here he is! Truly, he is here!" she said to her own heart, and, flying up to him, she threw her arms around him, pressed him to herself with her head on his breast, and then, pushing him away, she gazed into Pierre's frost-covered, ruddy, happy face. — "Yes, here he is! happy and satisfied!"....

And suddenly she recalled all the torments of disappointed expectation which she had endured during the last two weeks; the radiance of joy beaming from her face was suddenly clouded; she frowned, and a stream of reproaches and bitter words was poured out upon Pierre.

"Yes, it's very fine for you; you are very glad, very happy!.... But how is it with me? You've had a great longing for your children! I nurse them, and the milk was spoilt because of you...... Petya almost died. And you are very gay.... yes, you are very gay."....

Pierre knew that it was not his fault, because it was impossible for him to return sooner; he knew that this explosion of hers was unbecoming, and he knew that within two minutes it would be all over; he knew, chief of all, that he himself felt gay and happy. He would have preferred to smile, but he had no time to think about it. He put on a scared, timid face, and stooped down to her.

"By all the powers, I could not help it.... but how is Petya?"

"He is all right now! Let us go to him. But aren't you ashamed? Didn't you know how I missed you, how I was tormented without you?"....

"Are you well?"

"Come, let us go, come," said she, not letting go of his hand.

And they went to their rooms.

When Nikolaï and his wife came to inquire after

Pierre, he was in the nursery, and was holding on the huge palm of his right hand his babe, now awake, and was tending him. A jolly smile hovered over its broad face with its toothless mouth. The storm had long since passed over, and the bright sun of joy shone in Natasha's eyes as she gazed tenderly at her husband and son.

"And so you talked everything over satisfactorily with Prince Feodor," Natasha was saying.

"Yes, admirably."

"Do you see, he's holding it up!" — Natasha meant the baby's head. — "Well, how he startled me!"

"And did you see the princess? Is it true that she's in love with that ...."

"Yes, you can imagine ...."

At that instant, Nikolaï and the Countess Mariya came in. Pierre, not putting down his little son, stooped down and kissed them, and replied to their questions.

But evidently, notwithstanding the much that was interesting that they had to talk over, still the baby in its cap, with its vain efforts to hold up its head, absorbed all Pierre's attention.

"How sweet!" exclaimed the Countess Mariya, looking at the child and beginning to play with it. "There's one thing I can't understand, Nicolas," said she, turning to her husband, "and that is, why you can't appreciate the charm of these marvelous little creatures."

"I don't and I can't," said Nikolaï, looking at the baby with indifferent eyes. "A lump of flesh. Come, Pierre."

"But really he is such an affectionate father," said the Countess Mariya, apologizing for her husband. "Only at that age, before they are a year old ...."

"No, but Pierre makes a splendid nurse," said Natasha. "He says that his hand was made on purpose for a baby's back. Just look!"

"Well, not for that alone," said Pierre, suddenly, with a laugh, and, seizing the baby, he handed him over to the nurse.

CHAPTER XII

At the Luiso-Gorsky home, as in every genuine family, there lived together several absolutely distinct microcosms, which, while each preserved its own individuality and made mutual concessions, united into one harmonious whole.

Every event that happened to the household was alike glad or sad — alike important — for all these microcosms; but each one had its own personal, independent reasons for joy or sorrow at any particular event.

Thus, Pierre's coming was one of these happy, important events, and it affected the members of the household in somewhat this way : —

The servants (who are always the most reliable judges of their masters, because they judge not by words and the expressions of feelings, but by actions and the manner of life) were glad of Pierre's return, since they knew that, when he was there, the count would cease to make the tour of the estate every day, and would be jollier and kinder, and still more because all would receive rich presents on the holidays.

The children and governesses were delighted at Pierre's return, because there was no one like Pierre to keep up the general life of any occasion. He alone was able to play on the harpsichord that "*Écossaise*" — his one piece! — to which they could dance, as he said, all possible dances, and then besides he would probably make them, too, holiday presents.

Nikolenka, who was now a thin, sickly, intellectual lad of fifteen, with curling flaxen hair and handsome eyes, was glad, because "Uncle Pierre," as he called him, was the object of his admiration and passionate love. No one had tried to instil in the lad a special love for Pierre, and he had only seen him a few times. His aunt and guardian, the Countess Mariya, exerted all her energies to make Nikolenka love her husband as she loved him; and Nikolenka did love his uncle, but his love had an almost perceptible tinge of scorn

in it. He worshiped Pierre. He had no desire to be
a hussar or a cavalier of St. George; he preferred to
be a learned, good, and intellectual man like Pierre.
In Pierre's presence, his face always wore a look of
radiant delight, and he flushed and choked when Pierre
addressed him. He never lost a word that Pierre
uttered; and afterwards, when with Dessalles or even
alone by himself, he recalled and pondered over the
meaning of every word.

Pierre's past life, his misfortunes before 1812 (concerning which he had formed a vague poetic idea from
hints that had been dropped), his adventures in Moscow,
his imprisonment, Platon Karatayef (of whom he had
heard from Pierre), his love for Natasha (whom also the
boy loved with a peculiar love), and, above all, his friendship for his father, whom Nikolenka did not remember,
— all this made of Pierre a hero and a sacred being for
the boy.

From snatches of conversation concerning his father
and Natasha, from the emotion which Pierre always
showed when he spoke of the lamented prince, from
the guarded tone of veneration and affection with which
Natasha spoke of him, the lad, who was only just beginning to have an idea of love, gathered that his father
had loved Natasha, and in dying had bequeathed her to
his friend.

This father of his, whom the lad did not remember,
seemed to him a divinity whom it was impossible to
picture to himself, and he never thought of him except
with an oppression of the heart and with tears of
tenderness and enthusiasm.

And this boy was glad at Pierre's return.

The guests were glad, because Pierre was always a man
full of life, and a bond of union in any sort of society.

The adult members of the household, to say nothing
of his wife, were glad of a friend who made life easier
and smoother.

The old women were glad, because of the presents
which he brought, and principally because his coming
gave Natasha new life.

Pierre felt the effect on himself of these varying views of the varying microcosms, and hastened to give to each what each expected.

Pierre, the most abstracted, the most forgetful, of men, now, by the advice of his wife, took a memorandum, and, without forgetting a single item, executed the commissions of her mother and brother, buying such things as the dress for Madame Byelova and toys for his nephews.

When he was first married, this demand of his wife that he should do all her errands and not forget a single thing that he had undertaken to purchase seemed very strange to him, and he was greatly amazed at her grave displeasure when, on his first journey from home, he forgot absolutely everything. But afterwards he became used to it. Knowing that Natasha never ordered anything for herself, and ordered for the others only when he himself suggested it, he now took a boyish enjoyment, quite unexpected to himself, in these purchases of gifts for the whole household, and he never forgot anything any more. If he deserved reproaches from Natasha, it was solely because he bought needless and over-expensive gifts. In addition to her slackness and negligence, — faults, as they seemed to the majority ; qualities, as they seemed in Pierre's eyes, — Natasha had also that of excessive frugality.

From the time Pierre began to live on a grand scale, and his family demanded large outlays, he noticed, much to his surprise, that he spent only half as much as before, and that his affairs, which had been in great confusion of late, especially by reason of his first wife's debts, were beginning to improve.

It was cheaper to live, because his life was tied down ; since the most expensive luxury consists in a style of life that can at any minute be changed, Pierre no longer went into this extravagance, and had no longer any wish to do so. He felt that his style of life was determined now until death, that to change it was not in his power, and consequently this style of life was cheap.

Pierre, with a jovial, smiling face, unwrapped his purchases.

"How much do you suppose?" he asked, as, like a shopkeeper, he unwrapped a roll of cloth.

Natasha was sitting opposite him holding her oldest daughter on her lap, and swiftly turning her shining eyes from her husband to what he was exhibiting.

"Is that for Byelova? Splendid!" She examined the niceness of the material. "That cost about a ruble, didn't it?"

Pierre told her the price.

"Too dear," said Natasha. .... "Well, how glad the children and *maman* will be. .... Only 'twas of no use to buy that for me," she added, unable to restrain a smile, as she looked at a gold comb set with pearls, which were just then becoming fashionable.

"Adèle tried to dissuade me; I didn't know whether to buy it or not."

"When should I wear it?"

Natasha took it and put it in her braid. "And you brought this for Mashenka: perhaps they'll wear them again. Come, let us go."

And, having decided on the disposition of the gifts, they went first to the nursery, and then to the countess's room.

The countess was sitting as usual with Madame Byelova, playing *grand-patience*, when Pierre and Natasha, with their parcels under their arms, came into the drawing-room.

The countess was now sixty years old. She was perfectly gray, and wore a cap which framed her whole face in ruching. Her face was wrinkled, her upper lip sunken, and her eyes were dimmed.

After the loss of her son, followed so quickly by that of her husband, she felt herself unexpectedly forgotten in this world, — a being without aim or object. She ate, drank, slept, sat up, but she did not live. Life left no impression on her.

She asked nothing from life except repose, and this repose she could find only in death. But till death should come she had to live, in other words, she had to employ all her vitality. She exemplified in a high degree what is noticeable in very young children and very old people. Her life had no manifest outward aim, but was merely, so far as could be seen, occupied in exercising her own individual proclivities and peculiarities. She had to eat and drink, sleep a little, think a little, talk, shed a few tears, do some work, lose her temper occasionally, and so on, simply because she had a stomach, brains, muscles, nerves, and a liver.

All this she did, not because action was called forth by anything external, not as people in the full vigor of life do, when above and beyond the object for which they are striving is the unnoticeable object of putting forth their strength.

She talked, simply because she felt the physical necessity of exercising her lungs, her tongue. She wept like a child, because she had to blow her nose and the like. What for people in the full possession of their faculties was an object and aim, was evidently for her only an excuse.

Thus in the morning, especially if the evening before she had eaten anything greasy, she manifested a disposition to show temper, and then she would choose the handiest pretext, Madame Byelova's deafness. She would begin to say something in a low tone of voice from the other end of the room.

" It seems warmer to-day, my love," she would say in a whisper, and when Madame Byelova would reply, " What, has he come?" she would grumble : —

" Oh, dear me,[1] how stupid and deaf!"

Another pretext was her snuff, which she complained of, as being now too dry, now too damp, now badly powdered.

After these displays of temper her face would show that there had been an effusion of bile, and her maids had infallible signs to know when it would be the deaf Byelova, and when it would be that the snuff was too damp, and when she would have a bilious countenance.

Just as it required some preparations for her bilious

[1] *Bozhe moï.*

fits, so also she had to exert herself for her other peculiarities, — the pretext for thinking would be "patience."

When she had occasion to shed tears, then the pretext would be the late count.

When she wanted to be anxious, her pretext was
Nikolaï and his health.

When she wanted to speak sarcastically, then her pretext was the Countess Mariya.

When she wanted to exercise her voice, — this was
generally about seven o'clock, after her *digesting nap*,
in her darkened room, — then the pretext was forever
the same old stories, which she would always tell to the
same audience.

This state of second childhood was understood by all
the household, though no one ever mentioned it, and all
possible endeavors were made to gratify her desires.
Only occasional glances, accompanied by a melancholy
half-smile, exchanged between Nikolaï and Pierre, Natasha and the Countess Mariya, would express the reciprocal comprehension of her state. But these glances
also said something else : they declared that she had
already played her part in life, that what was now to be
seen in her was not wholly herself, that all would at last
come to be the same, and that it was a pleasure to yield
to her, to restrain ourselves for this poor creature who
was once so dear, who was once as full of life as we
ourselves.

Memento mori, said these glances. Only utterly depraved and foolish people and little children failed to
understand this, and avoided her.

CHAPTER XIII

WHEN Pierre and his wife came into the drawing-
room, the countess found herself, as usual, absorbed in
what she considered the intellectual labor of working out
her *grand-patience*, and therefore, according to her custom,
she spoke the words which she was sure to speak on the
return of Pierre or her son, namely, " Late, late, my dear;

we have been expecting you. Well, thank the Lord;"
and when she was given the presents, she said other
perfunctory words: "Wasn't it too expensive a present
for me, my dear boy? Thanks for remembering the
old lady."....

But it was evident that Pierre's intrusion was distaste-
ful to her at that moment because it distracted her attention from her unfinished game of *grand-patience*.
She completed the laying out of the cards, and then
only turned her attention to her gifts.

The gifts consisted of a beautifully carved card-casket,
a bright blue Sèvres cup with a cover and adorned with
a pastoral scene, and, finally, a gold snuff-box with a
portrait of the late count, which Pierre had commissioned a Petersburg miniaturist to paint. The countess
had been long wishing for one.

She was not now in one of her tearful moods, and
therefore she looked with indifference on the portrait,
and took more interest in her card-case. "Thank you,
my dear; you have cheered me up," said she, just as
she always said. "But, best of all, you have brought
yourself back. But you can't imagine how naughty it
was, you ought to give your wife a good scolding. Why!
she was like a crazy person while you were away! She
had n't any eyes or any memory for anything!" said the
countess, in the usual strain. "Look, Anna Timofeyevna,
see what a beautiful case my dear son has brought to us."

Madame Byelova lauded the gifts, and felt of the silk
that was her gift.

Although Pierre, Natasha, Nikolaï, the Countess
Mariya, and Denisof were anxious to talk over many
things which they were not in the habit of discussing in
her presence, not because they wanted to keep anything
from her, but because she was so out of the ordinary
current of life that when any topic of conversation was
brought up in her presence, it was always necessary to
answer her questions, however untimely, and repeat for
her benefit what had already been many times repeated,
— tell her who was dead, who was married, and other
things that she could not seem to comprehend, — they

sat down as usual to tea in the drawing-room, around the samovar, and Pierre replied to all the countess's questions, which were wholly unnecessary to her, and uninteresting to every one else: as to whether Prince Vasili began to show his age, and whether the Countess Marya Alekseyevna sent any message to her, and the like.

Conversation of this sort, though interesting to no one, was unavoidable, and lasted all through their tea-time. All the adult members of the family were gathered for tea at the round table, over which Sonya presided.

The children, the tutors, and the governesses had already finished drinking their tea, and their voices were heard in the adjoining divan-room.

While the elders were at tea, all sat in their accustomed places: Nikolaï near the stove, at the small table, where they handed him his glass. The old *Borzaya Milka* — Milka the swift, daughter of Milka I., — lay on the chair near him, with her perfectly gray face, from which occasionally bulged forth a pair of great black eyes. Denisof, with his curly hair, his mustaches, and side whiskers fast turning gray, sat next the Countess Mariya, with his general's coat unbuttoned. Pierre sat between his wife and the old countess. He was relating what, as he knew, would greatly interest the old lady and be comprehensible to her. He was telling her of the superficial events of the society and about those people who had once formed the circle of the old countess's intimate friends, who, in days gone by, had been an active, lively, distinct "coterie," but who now were, for the most part, scattered here and there, like herself waiting for the final summons, gathering the last gleanings of what they had sowed in life.

But these were the very ones, these contemporaries of hers, who seemed to the old countess the only important and actual world.

Natasha knew by Pierre's excitement that his journey had been interesting, that he had much he wanted to talk about but dared not mention in the old countess's presence.

Denisof, who had not been a member of the family

long enough to understand the cause of Pierre's reserve, and, moreover, as a "malcontent" was greatly interested in what was going on in Petersburg, kept urging Pierre to tell about the trouble in the Semyonovsky regiment, which had just then broken out, and about Arakcheyef, and about the Bible Society. Pierre was occasionally drawn away and would begin to tell about these things, but Nikolaï and Natasha would always bring him back to the health of Prince Ivan or the Countess Marya Antonovna.

"Now tell me, what is all this nonsense about Hosner and Tatarinof?" asked Denisof. "Is it going to last always?"

"Last always?" screamed Pierre; "it's worse than ever. The Bible Society is in full control of the government."

"What is that, *mon cher ami?*" asked the countess, who had finished drinking her tea, and was now evidently anxious to find some excuse for peevishness after her meal. "What is that you said about the government? I don't understand."

"Yes, you know, *maman*," put in Nikolaï, who knew how to translate what was said into language suitable for his mother's comprehension, "Prince A. N. Golitsuin has started a society, and he is now a man of great influence, they say."

"Arakcheyef and Golitsuin," said Pierre, incautiously, "are now the real heads of the government. And what a government! They affect to see plots in everything; they are afraid of their own shadows."

"What! Prince Aleksandr Nikolayevitch [1] in any way blameworthy! He is a very fine man. I met him once at Marya Antonovna's," said the countess, in an offended tone, and she grew still more offended because no one made any further reply. She went on, "Nowadays, they're always criticizing everybody. What harm is there in the Gospel Society?"

And she got up (all the rest also arose), and, with a stern face, sailed into the divan-room, to her own table.

---

[1] Golitsuin (Galitzin).

Amid the gloomy silence that ensued could be heard the talking and laughter of the children in the adjoining room. Evidently there was some joyous excitement going on among the little ones.

"It's done! It's done!" rang out little Natasha's merry shriek above all the others.

Pierre exchanged glances with the Countess Mariya and Nikolaï (his eyes were always on Natasha), and smiled gayly.

"That is wonderful music!" said he.

"Anna Makarovna must have finished a stocking," said the Countess Mariya.

"Oh, I'm going to see!" cried Pierre, jumping up. "You know," he added, as he paused by the door, "why I specially love that kind of music — they make me know for the first time that everything is well. To-day, on my way home, the nearer I come, the more afraid I am. As soon as I come into the anteroom, I hear little Andryusha's voice, and of course I know that all's well." ....

"I know, I know what that feeling is," said Nikolaï in corroboration. "But I can't go with you, for you see those stockings are to be a surprise for me!"

Pierre joined the children, and the shouts and laughter grew still louder.

"Well, Anna Makarovna," Pierre's voice was heard saying, "now I'll stand in the middle here, and at the word — one, two — and when I say three, you come to me. Clap your hands! Now, then, one — two...." cried Pierre.

There was perfect silence. "Three!" and a rapturous shout of children's voices rang from the room. "Once more! once more!" cried the children.

There were two stockings which, by a secret process kept to herself, Anna Makarovna had been knitting at the same time, and it was always her habit triumphantly to produce the one out of the other, in the children's presence, when the stockings were done.

CHAPTER XIV

SHORTLY after this the children came in to say good-night. The children kissed every one, the tutors and governesses bowed and left the room. Dessalles and his charge were alone left. The tutor whispered to his charge to go down-stairs.

"No, M. Dessalles, I will ask my aunt to let me stay," replied Nikolenka Bolkonsky, also in a whisper. — "*Ma tante*, let me stay," pleaded Nikolenka, going to his aunt. His face was full of entreaty, excitement, and enthusiasm.

The Countess Mariya looked at him and turned to Pierre.

"When you are here, he cannot tear himself away," said she. ....

"M. Dessalles, I will bring him to you very soon; *bon soir*," said Pierre, giving the Swiss gentleman his hand; and then, turning with a smile to Nikolenka, he said: "Really, we haven't had a chance to see each other. Marie, how much he is growing to resemble...." he added, turning to the Countess Mariya.

"My father?" asked the boy, flushing crimson, and surveying Pierre from head to foot with enraptured, gleaming eyes. Pierre nodded, and went on with his story, which had been interrupted by the children.

The Countess Mariya was working on her embroidery; Natasha, without dropping her eyes, gazed at her husband. Nikolaï and Denisof had got up, asked for their pipes, were smoking, and getting an occasional cup of tea of Sonya, who sat downcast and in gloomy silence behind the samovar, and kept asking questions of Pierre.

The curly-headed, sickly lad, with gleaming eyes, sat, unobserved by any one, in the corner, and merely craned his slender neck from his turned-down collar, so as to look toward Pierre, occasionally starting, or whispering something to himself, and was evidently under the influence of some new and powerful emotion.

The conversation turned on the contemporary gossip

about the higher members of the government, in which the majority of people usually find the chief interest in internal politics.

Denisof, who was dissatisfied with the government on account of his lack of success in the service, was rejoiced to learn of the follies which, in his opinion, were being committed at that time at Petersburg, and his comments on Pierre's remarks were made in keen and forcible language.

"Once upon a time you had to be a German : now you must dance with Tatawinova and Madame Kwüdener, and wead Eckarsthausen and the like. Okh! if we could only set our bwave Bonaparte upon 'em! He would dwive the folly out of 'em! Now, I'd like to know what's the sense of giving the Semyonovsky wegiment to a man like Schwartz?" he cried.

Nikolaï, though he had no wish at all to find fault with everything, as Denisof did, felt that it was a thoroughly dignified and suitable thing to make some criticisms on the government, and he felt that the fact that A had been appointed minister in this department, and that B had been appointed governor-general of this city, and that the sovereign had said this or that, and this minister something else, and all these things, were very significant. And he considered it necessary to take an interest in these things, and to ask Pierre questions.

Owing to the questions of the two men the conversation did not get beyond that general character of gossip concerning the upper spheres of the administration.

But Natasha, who knew her husband's every habit and thought, saw that Pierre had been long vainly wishing to lead the conversation into another path, so that he might speak his mind and tell why he had gone to Petersburg to consult with his new friend, Prince Feodor, and she tried to help him with a question : —

How had his business with Prince Feodor succeeded?

"What is that?" asked Nikolaï.

"Oh, it's all one and the same thing," said Pierre, glancing around him. "All see that affairs are so rotten that they cannot be allowed to remain so, and that it is the duty of all honorable men to oppose them to the best of their ability."

"What can honorable men do?" asked Nikolaï, slightly contracting his brows. "What can be done?"

"This can ...."

"Come into the library," suggested Nikolaï.

Natasha, who had been for some time expecting to be called to suckle the baby, heard the nurse's call, and went to the nursery. The Countess Mariya went with her.

The men went into the library; and Nikolenka Bolkonsky, unobserved by his uncle, went with them, and sat down in the shadow by the window, at the writing-table.

"Well, then, what are you going to do?" asked Denisof.

"Forever visionary!" exclaimed Nikolaï.

"This is what," began Pierre, not sitting down, but striding through the room, occasionally pausing and making rapid gestures while he spoke. "This is the way of it: the state of affairs in Petersburg is like this: the sovereign takes no part in anything. He is wholly given over to mysticism [Pierre could not pardon mysticism in any one now]. All he asks for is to be left in peace, and this peace can be given him only by the men *sans foi ni loi*, who are perfectly unscrupulous in their rough and cruel treatment of every one: Magnitsky, Arakcheyef, *e tutti quanti*. .... You must admit that if you yourself were not busy with your management of the estate, but merely wanted comfort and peace, the crueler your bailiff was, the more quickly you would attain your aim," said he, addressing Nikolaï.

"Well, now, why do you say that?" demanded Nikolaï.

"Well, everything's going to pieces. Robbery in the courts; the army under the rod; harsh discipline — deportation — torturing the people — civilization crushed. All the young men and the honorable are persecuted. All see that this cannot go on so. The strain is too great, and there must be a break," said Pierre (as men, regarding the deeds of any government, have always said

and will always say as long as governments shall last).
" I told them one thing at Petersburg...."

" Told whom?" asked Denisof.

" Why, you know whom," exclaimed Pierre, giving
him a significant look from under his brows. " Prince
Feodor and all of them. To make rivals of enlightenment and charity is a fine thing, of course. The aim is
admirable and all that, but something else is necessary
in the present circumstances."

At this moment, Nikolaï noticed that his nephew was
present. His face clouded; he went over to him : —

" Why are you here?"

" Why, let him stay," said Pierre, taking Nikolaï by
the hand and proceeding : " ' That 's not all,' said I to
them, ' something else is necessary. While you stand
and wait, this strained cord breaks; while we are all expecting some imminent change, we ought to be gathering closer together, and taking hold of hands, more and
more of us, in order to prevent the general catastrophe.
All that is young and vigorous is crowding there and
becoming corrupt. One is seduced by women; another,
by ambition and grandeur ; a third, by vanity or money ;
and then they go over to the other camp. There are
getting to be no independent, free men at all, like you
and me. I say — widen the circle of the society ; let the
mot d'ordre be not merely virtue, but also independence
and activity.' "

Nikolaï, who had let his nephew remain, angrily moved
his chair, sat down in it, and while he listened to Pierre
he involuntarily coughed and scowled still more portentously.

" Yes, but what is to be the object of this activity?"
he cried. " And what position do you hold toward the
government?"

" What position? The position of helpers. The society might not remain a secret one if the government
would give us its favor. It is not only not hostile to the
government, but this society is composed of genuine
conservatives. It is a society of gentlemen [1] 'n the full

---

[1] *Dzhentelmenof.*

meaning of the word. We exist merely to prevent Pugachof [1] from coming to cut the throats of my children and yours, and Arakcheyef from sending me to one of his military colonies; for this purpose we have banded together, with the single aim of the general welfare and the general safety."

"Yes, but a secret society must necessarily be harmful and prejudicial — is bound to produce nothing but evil."

"Why so? Did the *Tugendbund*, which saved Europe," — even then they dared not imagine that it was Russia that saved Europe, — "did that produce anything harmful? *Tugendbund* — that means a society of the virtuous; it was love, mutual aid, it was what Christ promised on the cross .... "

Natasha, who had come into the room in the midst of the discussion, looked joyfully at her husband. It was not that she was pleased with what he said. It did not even interest her, because it seemed to her that it was all so perfectly simple, and that she had known it all long before, — it seemed so to her because she knew so well the source from which it all came, from Pierre's mind, — but she was pleased because she looked into his lively, enthusiastic face.

With still more joyful enthusiasm, the lad, who again had been forgotten by all, gazed at Pierre, craning his thin neck from his turned-down collar. Every word that Pierre spoke made his heart glow, and, with a nervous motion of his fingers, without knowing what he was doing, he broke the pens and pieces of sealing-wax on his uncle's table.

"But I beg of you not to think that the German *Tugendbund* and the one to which I belong are at all alike."

"Come, now, bwother, this *Tugendbund* is well enough for the sausage-eaters, but I don't understand it, and I don't say anything against it," cried Denisof, in his loud, decisive tones. "Everything's wotten, and going

---

[1] Emilian Pugachof, a vagabond Cossack, during the reign of Catherine the Great, gave himself out for Peter III., and, after about a year of varying success, was captured and quartered in January, 1775.

to wuin, I admit, but as for your *Tugendbund*, I know nothing about it, and I don't like it — give us a weai wevolt,[1] that's the talk! *Je suis vot'e homme.*"

Pierre smiled, Natasha laughed, but Nikolaï still further knitted his brows and tried to prove to Pierre that there was no revolution to be apprehended, and that all the danger of which he spoke existed only in his imagination.

Pierre argued to the contrary; and, as his powers of reasoning were stronger and better trained, Nikolaï felt that he was driven into a corner. This still further incensed him, since, in the bottom of his heart, not through any process of reasoning, but by something more potent than logic, he knew the indubitable truth of his opinion.

"Well, this is what I tell you," he cried, rising, and with nervous motions putting his pipe in the corner and finally throwing it down. "I can't prove it to you. You say that everything is all rotten, and that there will be a revolution, I don't see it; but you say that an oath of secrecy is an essential condition, and in reply to this I tell you: You are my best friend, — you know it, — but if in founding a secret society you should undertake anything against the administration, whatever it was, — I know that it would be my duty to obey it. And if Arakcheyef should order me to go against you with a squadron instantly, and cut you down, I should not hesitate a second, but should start. So, then, decide as you please."

An awkward silence followed these words.

Natasha was the first to speak; she took her husband's side and opposed her brother. Her defense was weak and clumsy, but her object was attained. The discussion was renewed on a different topic, and no longer in that hostile tone with which Nikolaï's last words had been spoken.

When all got up to take supper, Nikolenka Bolkonsky went to Pierre with pale face and gleaming, luminous eyes.

---

[1] A pun in the original : *bunt* (a revolt), from German *Bund*, and pronounced the same.

"Uncle Pierre .... you .... no .... if my papa were alive .... he would agree with you, would n't he ? " he asked.

Pierre suddenly realized what a peculiar, independent, complicated, and powerful work must have been operating in this lad's mind during this discussion; and when he recalled what had been said, he felt a sense of annoyance that the lad had listened to them. However, he had to answer him.

"I think so," said he, reluctantly, and left the library.

The lad bent his head, and then for the first time seemed to realize what mischief he had been doing on the writing-table. He flushed, and went to Nikolaï.

"Uncle, forgive me for what I have done. I did not mean to," said he, pointing to the broken pens and pieces of sealing-wax.

Nikolaï gave an angry start.

"Fine work, fine work," said he, flinging the fragments of pens and wax under the table. And, evidently finding it hard to restrain the anger that overmastered him, he turned away.

"You ought never to have been here at all," said he.

CHAPTER XV

At supper, the talk no longer turned on politics and secret societies, but, on the contrary, proved to be particularly interesting to Nikolaï, owing to Denisof's bringing it round to reminiscences of the war of 1812, and here Pierre was particularly genial and diverting. And the relatives parted for the night on the most friendly terms.

When, after supper, Nikolaï, after having changed his clothes in his library and given orders to his overseer, who was waiting for him, returned in his khalat to his sleeping-room, he found his wife still at her desk; she was writing something.

"What are you writing, Marie ? " asked Nikolaï.

The Countess Mariya reddened. She feared that what she was writing would not be understood and

approved by her husband. She would have preferred
to conceal from him what she had been writing, but at
the same time she was glad that he had found her and
that she had to tell him.

"It is my diary, Nicolas," said she, — showing him
a bluish note-book written in a fair round hand.

"A diary!" exclaimed Nikolaï, with just a shade of
irony in his tone, and he took the note-book. It was
written in French.

Dec. 16. To-day, Andryusha [her oldest son], when he
woke up, did not wish to be dressed, and Mlle. Luise sent for
me. He was capricious and wilful, and when I tried to threaten
him, he only grew the more obstinate and angry. Then I took
him to my room, left him alone, and began to help the nurse
get the rest of the children up, but I told him that I should
not love him. He was silent for a long time, as if in amazement; then he jumped up, ran to me in nothing but his little
night-shirt, and sobbed so that it was long before I could pacify
him. It was evident that he was more grieved because he had
troubled me than by anything else! Then, when I put him to
bed this evening, and gave him his card, he again wept piti-
fully, and kissed me. You can do anything with him through
his affections.

"What do you mean by 'his card'?" asked Nikolaï.

"I have begun to give the older children cards in the
evening, when they have been good."

Nikolaï glanced into the luminous eyes that gazed at
him, and continued to turn the leaves and read. In the
diary was written everything concerning the children's
lives that seemed important in the mother's eyes as
expressing the character of the children, or that suggested thoughts concerning their education. These
were, for the most part, the most insignificant trifles,
but they seemed not such to the mother, or the father
when now, for the first time, he read this journal about
his children.

The entry for the seventeenth of December was: —

Mitya played pranks at table; papa would not let pastry be
given to him. It was not given to him, but he looked so

eagerly and longingly at the others while they were eating ! I think that the punishment of not letting him have a taste of the sweets only increases his greediness. Must tell Nicolas.

Nikolaï put down the book and looked at his wife. Her radiant eyes looked at him questioningly: did he approve, or disapprove, of the diary? There could be no doubt of his approval or of his admiration for his wife.

"Perhaps there was no need of doing it in such a pedantic manner, perhaps it was not necessary at all," thought Nikolaï; but this unwearied, everlasting, sincere effort, the sole end and aim of which was the moral welfare of the children, roused his admiration. If Nikolaï could have analyzed his feelings, he would have discovered that the chief basis of his firm, tender, and proud love for his wife was found in his amazement at her cordial sincerity and her spiritual nature, at that lofty moral world in which his wife always lived, but which was for him almost unattainable.

He was proud that she was so intelligent and so good, acknowledging his inferiority to her in the spiritual world, and rejoicing all the more that she in her soul not only belonged to him but formed a part of him.

"I approve and thoroughly approve, my dear," said he, with a meaning look. And, after a little silence, he added: "I have behaved very scurvily to-day. You were not in the library. Pierre and I had a discussion, and I lost my temper. Yes, I can't help it. He's such a child. I don't know what would become of him if Natasha did not hold him in leading-strings. Can you imagine why he went to Petersburg? .... They have started there a ...."

"Yes, I know," interrupted the Countess Mariya; "Natasha told me about it."

"Well, then, you must know," pursued Nikolaï, growing hot at the mere memory of the quarrel, "he wanted to make me believe that it is the duty of every honorable man to go against the government, even though he has taken the oath of allegiance. .... I am sorry that you were not there. But they were all against me, — Denisof and Natasha. .... Natasha is ludicrous. You know how she keeps him under her slipper, but when there is anything to be decided, she can't speak her own mind at all. She simply says what he says," added Nikolaï, giving way to that vague tendency which men have to criticize their nearest and best friends. Nikolaï forgot that, word for word, what he said about Natasha might be said about him and his wife.

"Yes, I have noticed it," said the Countess Mariya.

"When I told him that my duty and my oath of allegiance were above everything, he tried to prove Heaven knows what. Pity that you were n't there, I should like to know what you would have said."

"In my opinion, you were perfectly right. I said so to Natasha. Pierre says that all are suffering, persecuted, corrupt, and that it is our duty to render help to our neighbors. Of course he is right," said the Countess Mariya; "but he forgets that we have other obligations, nearer still, which God Himself has imposed on us, and that we may run risks for ourselves but not for our children."

"There, there, that is the very thing I told him," cried Nikolaï, who actually thought that he had said that very thing. "But they made out that this was love to the neighbor, was Christianity, and all that, before Nikolenka, who stole into the library and broke up everything on my table."

"Akh! do you know, Nicolas, Nikolenka so often makes me anxious," said the Countess Mariya. "He is such an extraordinary boy. And I am afraid that I am too partial to my own children and neglect him. Our children have both father and mother, but he is absolutely alone in the world. He is always alone with his own thoughts."

"Well, now, it seems to me that you have nothing to reproach yourself with in regard to him. All the most affectionate mother could do for her son, you have done and are doing for him. And of course I am glad of it.

He is a splendid, splendid boy. To-day, he listened to Pierre, and had no ears for anything else. And you can imagine; as we were going out to supper, I look, and lo! he has broken into flinders everything on my table, and he instantly told me. I never knew him to tell an untruth. Splendid, splendid boy," repeated Nikolaï, who really, at heart, did not like the lad, though he always took pains to call him *slavnui*, — splendid.

"Well, I am not like a mother to him," said the Countess Mariya; "I feel that I am not, and it troubles me. He's a wonderful lad, but I'm terribly anxious about him. More society would be a good thing for him."

"Well, it won't be long; this summer I'm going to take him to Petersburg," said Nikolaï. "Yes, Pierre always was and always will be a visionary," he went on to say, returning to the discussion in the library, which had evidently greatly agitated him. "Now, what difference does it make to me that Arakcheyef is not good and all that? What difference did it make to me when I was married and had so many debts that I might have been put into the sponging-house, and mother, who could not see it and understand? And then you and the children and my affairs? Is it for my own enjoyment that I spend the whole day from morning till night in attending to business and in the office? No, I know that it is my duty to work in order to soothe my mother's last days, to pay you back, and so as not to leave the children in such a condition of beggary as I was!"

The Countess Mariya wanted to tell him that not by bread alone is manhood nourished, that it was possible to set too great store in these affairs of his, but she knew that it would be unnecessary and unprofitable to say this.

She only took his hand and kissed it. He accepted this act of his wife's as approval and confirmation of his words, and, after some little time of silent meditation, he went on aloud with his thoughts.

"Do you know, Marie," said he, "Ilya Mitrofanu-itch" — this was their man of business — "came to-day from our Tambof estate, and told me that they would give eighty thousand for the forest there."

And Nikolaï, with animated face, began to speak about the possibilities of being very soon able to buy back Otradnoye. "If only I live ten years longer, I shall leave the children .... in a splendid position."

The Countess Mariya listened to her husband and understood all that he said to her. She knew that when he thus thought aloud, he sometimes asked her what he had said, and was vexed to find that she had been thinking of something else. But she had to use great effort over herself, for she was not in the least interested in what he said.

She looked at him, and, if she was not thinking of something else, she had other feelings. She felt an obstinate, tender love for this man, though he would never be able to understand what she understood, and, as it were, for this very reason she loved him all the more, with a touch of passionate affection.

Besides this feeling, which entirely absorbed her, and made her enter into all the details of her husband's plans, her mind was filled with ideas which had no connection with what he was talking about. She was thinking of her nephew — the story that her husband told of his excitement at Pierre's remarks had powerfully impressed her — and the various characteristics of his tender, sensitive nature arose to her mind, and the thought about her nephew made her think of her own children. She made no comparison between her nephew and her own children, but she compared her respective feelings toward them, and found to her sorrow that there was something lacking in her feeling for Nikolenka.

Sometimes the thought came to her that this difference arose from the difference in their ages, but she felt that she was blameworthy toward him, and in her heart she vowed that she would do better and would make every effort; that is, that during her life she would love her husband and her children and Nikolenka and all her neighbors as Christ loved the human race.

The Countess Mariya's soul was always striving toward the Infinite, the Eternal, and the Absolute, and therefore she could never rest content. Her face always wore the stern expression of a soul kept on a high tension by suffering, and becoming a burden to the body.

Nikolaï gazed at her.

"My God! what would become of us if she should die, as it sometimes seems must be when her face has that expression?" he said to himself, and, stopping in front of the holy pictures, he began to repeat his evening prayers.

CHAPTER XVI

Natasha and her husband, left alone, also talked as only wife and husband can talk, namely, with extraordinary clearness and swiftness, recognizing and communicating each other's thoughts, by a method contrary to all logic, without the aid of reasoning, syllogisms, and deductions, but with absolute freedom. Natasha had become so used to talking with this freedom with her husband that the surest sign, in her mind, that there was something wrong between her and him was for Pierre to give a logical turn to his arguments with her. When he began to bring proofs and to talk with calm deliberation, and when she, carried away by his example, began to do the same, she knew that they were surely on the verge of a quarrel.

From the moment that they were entirely alone, and Natasha with wide, happy eyes went quietly up to him, and, suddenly, with a swift motion, taking his head between both her hands, pressed it to her breast, and said: "Now, thou art all mine, mine! Thou wilt not go!" — from that moment began that intimate dialogue, contrary to all the laws of logic, — contrary simply because the talk ran at one and the same time upon such absolutely different topics.

This simultaneous consideration of many things not only did not prevent their clearly understanding each other, but, on the contrary, was the surest sign that they understood each other.

As in a vision everything is illusory, absurd, and incoherent except the feeling which is the guide of the vision, so in this intercourse, so contrary to all the laws of logic, the phrases uttered were not logical and clear, while the feeling that guided them was.

Natasha told Pierre about her brother's mode of life, how she had suffered and found it impossible to live while he, her husband, was absent, and how she had grown fonder than ever of Marie, and how Marie was in every respect better than she was.

In saying this, Natasha was genuine in her acknowledgment that she saw Marie's superiority, but, at the same time, in saying this she claimed from Pierre that he should still prefer her to Marie and all other women, and now again, especially after he had been seeing many women in Petersburg, that he should assure her of this fact.

Pierre, in answering Natasha's words, told her how unendurable it was for him to go to dinners and parties with ladies.

"I had really forgotten how to talk with the ladies," said he. "It was simply a bore. Especially when I was so busy."

Natasha gazed steadily at him and went on : —

"Marie! she is so lovely!" said she. "How well she knows how to treat the children! It seems as if she read their very souls! Last evening, for example, little Mitenka began to be contrary .... "

"But how like his father he is!" interrupted Pierre.

Natasha understood why he made this remark about the likeness between Mitenka and Nikolaï : the remembrance of his discussion with his brother-in-law was disagreeable to him, and he wanted to hear her opinion in regard to it.

"Nikolenka has the weakness of not accepting anything unless it is received by every one. But I apprehend you set a special value on this *pour ouvrir une carrière*," said she, repeating words once spoken by Pierre

"No; the main thing is, Nikolaï looks on thought and reasoning as amusement, almost as a waste of time," said Pierre. "Now he is collecting a library, and he has made a rule for himself never to buy a new book until he has read through what he has already bought — Sismondi and Rousseau and Montesquieu," added Pierre, with a smile. "Why, you know him as well as I do." He began to modify his words, but Natasha interrupted him, giving him to understand that this was unnecessary.

"So you think that he considers pure thought mere trifling." ....

"Yes, and for me everything else is mere trifling. All the time that I was in Petersburg it seemed to me as if I saw all men in a dream. When I am engaged in thinking, then everything else seems a sheer waste of time."

"Akh! what a pity that I did not see you greet the children!" said Natasha. "Which one do you love most of all? — Liza, I suspect."

"Yes," said Pierre; and he went on with what was engrossing his attention. .... "Nikolaï says that we have no business to think. Well, I can't help it. Not to mention that I felt in Petersburg — I can tell *you* — that if it were not for me, everything, all our scheme, would go to pieces, every one was pulling in his own direction. But I succeeded in uniting all parties, and, besides, my idea is so simple and clear. You see, I don't say that we ought to act in opposition to this one or that one. We may be deceived. But I say: let those who love what is right join hands, and let our whole watchword be action and virtue. Prince Sergii is a splendid man and very intelligent."

Natasha had no doubt that Pierre's idea was grand, but one thing confused her. This was that he was her husband. "Can it be that a man so important, so necessary to the world, can at the same time be my husband! How did this ever come about?"

She wanted to express this doubt to him. "No matter who should decide this question, he would be so much more intelligent than them all, would n't he?" she asked herself, and in her imagination she reviewed the men who were very important to Pierre. None of all these men, judging by his own story, had such an important effect on him as Platon Karatayef.

"Do you know what I was thinking about?" she asked. ..... "About Platon Karatayef! How about him? Would he approve, now?"

Pierre was not at all surprised at this question. He understood the trend of his wife's thoughts.

"Platon Karatayef?" he repeated and pondered, apparently honestly endeavoring to realize what Karatayef's opinion concerning this matter would be. "He would not understand, but still I think he would approve — yes!"

"I love thee awfully!"[1] said Natasha, suddenly. "Awfully! Awfully!"

"No, he would not approve," said Pierre, after a little reconsideration. "What he would approve would be this domestic life of ours. He so liked to see beauty, happiness, repose, in everything, and I should be proud if I could show him ourselves. — Now you talk about parting! But you cannot understand what a strange feeling I have for you after being separated from you." ....

"Why, — was it .... " began Natasha.

"No, not that. I shall never cease to love thee. It would be impossible to love thee more; but this is peculiar. .... Well, yes!" ....

But he did not finish his sentence, because their eyes met and said the rest.

"What nonsense," suddenly cried Natasha, "that the honeymoon and real happiness are only during the first part of the time! On the contrary, now is the best of all. If only you would never go away from me! Do you remember how we quarreled? And I was always the one at fault. Always I. But as to what we quarreled about, I am sure I don't remember!"

"Always about one thing," said Pierre, smiling. "Jealo...."

---

[1] *Ushazno:* literally, horribly.

"No, don't mention it, I can't endure it," cried Natasha, and a cold, cruel light flashed into her eyes. "Did you see her?" she added after a little silence.

"No, and if I had seen her I should not have recognized her."

They were both silent.

"Akh! do you know, when you were talking in the library, I was looking at you," pursued Natasha, evidently trying to drive away the cloud which had suddenly risen. "Well, you and our little lad are as alike as two drops of water." "Our little lad"—*malchik*—was what she called her son. "Akh! it is time for me to go to him.... I'm sorry to have to go!"

They were silent for several seconds. Then suddenly they turned to each other, and each began to make some remark at the same instant.

Pierre began with self-confidence and impulsive warmth, Natasha with a quiet, blissful smile. Their words colliding, they both stopped to give each other the road, so to speak.

"No, what was it? tell me! tell me!"

"No, you tell me,—what I was going to say was only nonsense," said Natasha.

Pierre went on with what he had begun to say. It was a continuation of his self-congratulatory opinion concerning the success of his visit at Petersburg. It seemed to him at that moment that he was called to give a new direction to all Russian society and to the whole world.

"I was only going to say that all ideas which have portentous consequences are always simple. My whole idea consists in this: that if all vicious men are bound together and constitute a force, then all honorable men ought to do the same. How simple that is!"

"Yes."

"And what were you going to say?"

"Only a bit of nonsense!"

"No, tell me what it was!"

"Oh, nothing, a mere trifle!" said Natasha, beaming with a still more radiant smile. "I was only going to say something about Petya: To-day the nurse was going to take him from me. He began to laugh, then scowled a little and clung to me.... evidently he thought that he was going to play peek-a-boo.... awfully cunning..... There, he is crying! Well, good-night!" and she left the room.

At the same time below in Nikolenka Bolkonsky's apartment, in his sleeping-room, the night-lamp was burning as always, — the lad was afraid of the darkness and they could not break him of this fault, — Dessalles was sleeping high on his four pillows, and his Roman nose gave forth the measured sounds of snoring.

Nikolenka, who had just awakened from a nap, in a cold perspiration, with wide-opened eyes sat up in bed and was looking straight ahead.

A strange dream had awakened him. In his dream he had seen himself and Pierre in helmets such as the men wore in his edition of Plutarch. He and his Uncle Pierre were marching forward at the head of a tremendous army. This army was composed of white, slanting threads, filling the air, like the cobwebs which float in the autumn, and which Dessalles called *le fil de la Vierge* — the Virgin's thread.

Before them was glory, just exactly like these threads, only much stouter. They — he and Pierre — were borne on lightly and joyously, ever nearer and nearer to their goal. Suddenly the threads which moved them began to slacken, to grow confused; it became trying. And his Uncle Nikolaï Ilyitch stood in front of them in a stern and threatening posture.

" What have you been doing? " he demanded, pointing to his broken sealing-wax and pens. " I loved you, but Arakcheyef has given me the order, and I shall kill the first who advances."

Nikolenka looked around for Pierre, but Pierre was no longer there. In place of Pierre was his own father, Prince Andreï, and his father had no shape or form; but there he was, and in looking at him Nikolenka felt the weakness of love: he felt himself without strength.

without bones, — as it were, liquid. His father petted him and pitied him. But his Uncle Nikolaï Ilyitch came ever closer and closer to him. Horror seized Nikolenka and he awoke.

"Father," he thought. "Father!" (although there were in the house two excellent portraits, Nikolenka had never imagined Prince Andreï as existing in human form). "My father was with me and caressed me. He approved of me. He approved of Uncle Pierre. Whatever he says I will do. Mucius Scævola burnt his hand. But why should I not do as much in my life? I know they want me to study, and I will study. But when I am grown up then I will do it. I will only ask one thing of God : that I may have in me what the men in Plutarch had, and I will do likewise. I will do better. All will know me, all will love me, all will praise me."

And suddenly Nikolenka felt the sobs fill his chest, and he burst into tears.

"*Êtes-vous indisposé?*" asked Dessalles's voice.

"*Non*," replied Nikolenka, and he lay back on his pillow. "He is good and kind, I love him," said he of Dessalles, "but Uncle Pierre! Oh, what a wonderful man! But my father! my father! my father! Yes, I will do whatever *he* would approve."

PART SECOND

CHAPTER I

'THE object of history is the life of nations and of humanity. To grasp and express proximately in words — that is, to depict the life, not of humanity, but merely of a single people, is an impossibility.

All the historians of former times employed exactly the same way of describing and apprehending what seems incapable of apprehension — the life of a nation. They described the actions of the individuals who ruled over a nation, and the actions of these individuals, they supposed, were an epitome of the activity of the nation.

To the questions, How could individuals make a whole nation act in accordance with their wills? and How was the will of these men themselves controlled? the historians of old answered the first by proclaiming a divine will which subordinated nations to the will of a single chosen man; and the second question, by declaring that this divinity directed the will of the chosen man toward a predestined end.

For those of old times all such questions were answered by a belief in the immediate interference of the Divinity in human affairs.

The new school of history has in its theory abandoned both these positions.

It would seem that, after having abandoned the old faith in the subordination of man to the Divinity, and in the doctrine of predestined ends to which nations are led, the New History ought to study, not the manifestations of power, but the causes which are the source of power.

But the New History has not done this.

After theoretically abandoning the views of the old school, it follows them in practice.

In place of men clothed with divine power and governed directly by the will of the Divinity, the New History represents either heroes endowed with extraordinary, superhuman qualities, or simply men of the most varied talent, from monarchs to journalists, directing the masses.

Instead of finding in the special, divinely preordained objects of any nation — Jewish, Greek, or Roman — the object of human action in general, as was the custom of the historians of old, the New History discovers its objects in the welfare of the French, the English, the Germans — and, in its loftiest abstraction, in the welfare of the civilized world and of the whole of humanity, by which is meant especially the nations occupying the little north-west corner of the continent.

Modern history has abandoned the old theories without establishing any new views in place of them, and the logic of their position has compelled the very historians who have rejected the hypothesis of the divine right of kings and the *Fatum* of the ancients to reach by a different route the same point: the assertion (1) that nations are guided by individuals, and (2) that there is a special object toward which the nations and humanity are moving.

In all the works of the most recent historians, from Gibbon to Buckle, notwithstanding their apparent disagreement and the apparent novelty of their views, at bottom lie these two old theories, from which they could not escape.

In the first place, the historian describes the activity of men who, in their opinion, have guided humanity. One counts as such only monarchs, generals, and statesmen; another, besides monarchs, takes orators, men of science, reformers, philosophers, and poets.

In the second place, the historian believes he knows the end toward which humanity is guided: to one, that end is the greatness of the Roman, the Spanish, or the French empires; to another it is liberty and equality, or the kind of civilization that obtains in the little corner of the globe called Europe.

In 1789 a fermentation begins at Paris; it grows, spreads, and results in a movement of peoples from west to east. Several times this movement is directed toward the east; it meets with a counter-movement from east to west.

In 1812 it reaches its final limit, Moscow, and with remarkable rhythmic symmetry occurs the counter-movement from east to west, which, like the former, carries with it the nations of Central Europe. This return movement reaches to the departing point of the preceding wave, — Paris, — and subsides.

During this twenty-years period a vast number of fields remain unplowed, houses are burned, trade changes its direction, millions of men are ruined, are enriched, emigrate, and millions of Christians who profess to obey the law of love to their neighbors kill one another.

What does all this signify? What is the cause of this? What forced these men to burn houses and kill their fellow-men? What were the reasons for these events? What force compelled men to act in this way?

Such are the ingenuous, involuntary, and most legitimate questions that humanity propounds to itself on meeting with the memorials and traditions of this movement in the past.

For a solution of these questions the common sense of humanity looks to the science of history, the aim of which is to teach the nations and humanity self-knowledge.

If history should assume the old point of view, it would reply, "The Divinity, as a reward or as a punishment of His people, gave power to Napoleon, and guided his will to the accomplishment of the divine purposes."

And this reply would be, at any rate, full and clear. One may or may not believe in the divine mission of Napoleon; for one who does believe in it, everything in the history of that time would be intelligible, and there would be no contradiction.

But the New History cannot reply in this way. Science does not recognize the view of the ancients as to the direct interference of the Divinity in human affairs, and consequently must give another reply.

The New History, in answering these questions, says, — "You wish to know what the significance of this movement was, why it took place, and what forces produced these events? Listen : —

"Louis XIV. was a very proud and self-confident man; he had such and such mistresses, and such and such ministers, and he governed France badly.

"The successors of Louis XIV. were also weak men, and they also governed France badly, and they also had such and such favorites, and such and such mistresses.

"Moreover, at that time, certain men wrote certain books.

"Toward the end of the eighteenth century, there came together at Paris a score of men who began to declare that all men were free and equal. The result of this was that all over France men began to slaughter and ruin each other. These men killed the king and many others.

"At this same time there was a man of genius, named Napoleon. He was everywhere successful; that is to say, he killed many people, because he was a great genius.

"And he went off to kill the Africans, for some reason or other, and he killed them so well, and was so shrewd and clever, that when he came back to France, he ordered every one to submit to him.

"And every one submitted to him.

"Having made himself emperor, he again went off to kill the people in Italy, Austria, and Prussia.

"And there he killed many.

"But in Russia there was an emperor, Alexander, who determined to reëstablish order in Europe, and, consequently, waged war with Napoleon. But in 1807 they suddenly became friends; then in 1811 they quar-

reled again, and again they began to kill many people;
and Napoleon led six hundred thousand men into Russia, and conquered Moscow, but afterwards he suddenly
fled from the city, and then the Emperor Alexander, by
the advice of Stein and others, united Europe into a
coalition against the disturber of the peace.

"All Napoleon's allies suddenly became his enemies,
and this coalition marched against Napoleon, who had
got together new forces.

"The allies defeated Napoleon; they entered Paris;
they compelled the emperor to abdicate the throne, and
sent him to the island of Elba, without depriving him of
his dignities as emperor, or failing to show him all possible respect, although five years before and a year after
that time all regarded him as a bandit and outlaw.

"Then Louis XVIII. began to reign, though up to
that time the French, and also the allies, had only made
sport of him.

"Napoleon, having melted into tears in presence of
his Old Guard, abdicated the throne and went into exile.

"Thereupon astute statesmen and diplomatists (especially Talleyrand, who managed to sit down before any
one else did in a certain arm-chair, and thereby magnified the boundaries of France) held a discussion at
Vienna, and by their discussions made nations happy or
unhappy.

"Suddenly the diplomatists and monarchs almost
quarreled; they were about to set their armies to killing each other again, but at this moment Napoleon, with
a battalion, came back to France, and the French, who
had been hating him, immediately all submitted to him.

"But the allied monarchs were indignant at this, and
once more set out to fight with the French.

"And they defeated and sent Napoleon, the genius,
to the island of St. Helena, having suddenly begun to
call him a bandit.

"And there, an exile, separated from those dear to his
heart and from his beloved France, he died a lingering
death on the rock, and bequeathed his great deeds to
posterity.

"Meanwhile, in Europe, a reaction was taking place, and all the sovereigns began once more to oppress their peoples."

You should not think that this is a parody or caricature of historical writings. On the contrary, it is the mildest expression of the contradictory answers which fail to answer, and are given by *all* History, whether in the form of Memoirs and histories of various kingdoms, or Universal Histories, and the new kind, Histories of *Culture*, in vogue at the present time.

The strangeness and absurdity of these replies are due to the fact that the New History is like a deaf man who answers questions that no one has asked him.

If the object of history is to describe the movements of nations and of humanity, then the first question, and the one which, if left unanswered, makes all the rest unintelligible, will be as follows : —

"What force moves the nations?"

To this question the New History replies elaborately either that Napoleon was a great genius, or that Louis XIV. was very proud, or that such and such writers published such and such books.

All this may, perhaps, be very true, and humanity is ready to assent, but it did not ask about that.

All this might be interesting if we acknowledge the divine power, self-established, and always the same, which governs its nations by means of Napoleons, Louises, and the writers, but we do not recognize this power, and, therefore, before talking about Napoleons, Louises, and the writers, it is necessary to show the connecting link between these men and the movements of the nations.

If, in place of the divine power, a new force is to be substituted, then it is necessary to explain in what this new force consists, since all the interest of history is concentrated precisely in this force.

History seems to take it for granted that this force is a matter of course, known to all. But, in spite of all desire to recognize this new force as known, he who studies very many of the historical writings will, involuntarily, come to doubt whether this new force, which is understood in so many different ways, is wholly clear to the historians themselves.

CHAPTER II

WHAT force moves the nations?

Ordinary biographers and the historians of distinct nations understand this force as the power inherent in heroes and rulers. According to their writings, events take place exclusively in accordance with the wills of the Napoleons and the Alexanders, or, in general, of those individuals whom the private biographer describes.

The answers given by historians of this class to the question, What force moves events? are satisfactory only as long as each event has but one historian. But as soon as historians of different nationalities and views begin to describe one and the same event, then the answers given by them immediately become nonsensical; since this force is understood by each one of them not merely in a different way, but often in an absolutely contradictory way.

One historian affirms that an event took place by means of the power of Napoleon; another affirms that it took place by means of the power of Alexander; according to a third, it took place by means of the power of some third person.

Moreover, the historians of this class contradict one another even in their explanations of that force whereon is based the power of one and the same man.

Thiers, a Bonapartist, declares that Napoleon's power was due to his virtue and genius. Lanfrey, a Republican, declares that it was due to his rascality and skill in deceiving the people.

Thus the historians of this class, by mutually destroying each other's position, in the same process destroy the conception of force producing the events, and give no answer to the essential question of history.

General historians, who treat of all nations, seem to

recognize the fallacy of the views held by the special historians in regard to the force that produces the event. They will not admit that force to be a power inherent in heroes and rulers, but consider it to be the resultant of many forces variously applied.

In describing a war or the subjugation of a nation, the general historian seeks for the cause of the event, not in the power of any one individual, but in the reciprocal influence on each other of many individuals who took part in the event.

According to this view, the power of historical personages who themselves represent the product of many forces, it would seem, cannot be regarded as the force which in itself produces the events.

And yet the general historians, in the majority of cases, make use of a concept of power as a force which in itself produces events and holds the relation to them of first cause.

According to their exposition, the historical personage is only the product of various forces; next, his power is a force producing the event.

Gervinus and Schlösser, for example, and others try to prove that Napoleon was the product of the Revolution, of the ideas of 1789, and so forth; and then they say up and down that the campaign of '12, and other events which they disapprove of, were simply the results of Napoleon's misdirected will, and these very ideas of the year 1789 were hindered in their development in consequence of Napoleon's opposition.

The ideas of the Revolution, the general state of public opinion, brought about Napoleon's power. But Napoleon's power stifled the ideas of the Revolution and the general state of public opinion.

This strange contradiction is not accidental. Not only is it met with at every step, but from a continuous series of such contradictions all the writings of general history are composed. This contradiction results from the fact that on getting into the region of analysis the general historians stop half-way on their route.

In order to find the component forces equal to the

combination or the resultant, it is necessary that the sum of the factors should equal the resultant.

This condition is never observed by the general historian, and, therefore, in order to explain the resultant force, they are necessarily compelled to admit in addition to their inadequate components a still unexplained force, which acts supplementary to the resultant.

An ordinary historian describing the campaign of '13 or the restoration of the Bourbons says in so many words that these events were brought about by the will of Alexander.

But the general historian, Gervinus, refuting this view held by the ordinary historian, endeavors to prove that the campaign of '13 and the restoration of the Bourbons had for their causes, not the will of Alexander alone, but also the activity of Stein, Metternich, Madame de Staël, Talleyrand, Fichte, Châteaubriand, and others.

The historian evidently resolved Alexander's power into its factors: Talleyrand, Châteaubriand, and the like. The sum of these factors — that is, the mutual influence of Châteaubriand, Talleyrand, Madame de Staël, and the others — evidently does not equal the whole resultant; in other words, the phenomenon that millions of Frenchmen submitted to the Bourbons.

The fact that Châteaubriand, Madame de Staël, and others said such and such words to each other shows merely their mutual relations, but not the submission of millions. And, therefore, in order to explain how from this fact of their reciprocal relations resulted the submission of millions, that is from factors equal to A alone comes a resultant equal to a thousand times A, the historian is inevitably bound to admit that same force of personal power, which he rejects by calling it the resultant of forces; that is, he is bound to admit an unexplained force acting on the factors.

This is the very thing which the general historians do. And consequently they contradict, not only the special historians, but themselves.

Inhabitants of the country districts, judging by their desires for rain or fine weather, and having no clear comprehension of the causes of rain, say, "The wind has scattered the clouds," or "The wind has brought the clouds."

In exactly the same way the general historians : sometimes, when they want a certain thing, when it fits in with their theory, they say that the power is the result of events ; but at other times, when it is necessary to prove the opposite, they will say that the power produces the events.

A third class of historians, called the historians of *culture*, following on the track laid down for them by the general historians, recognizing sometimes writers and ladies as forces producing events, reckon this force in an entirely different way still. They see it in so-called culture, in intellectual activity.

The historians of culture are thoroughgoing partizans in relation to their kinsfolk, the general historians, since if historical events can be explained by the fact that certain men had such and such an effect upon one another, then why not explain them by the fact that certain men wrote certain books ?

These historians, from the whole vast collection of manifestation accompanying every phenomenon of life, select the manifestation of intellectual activity and say that this manifestation is the cause !

But, notwithstanding all their endeavors to prove that the cause of the event lay in intellectual activity, we can agree only by great concessions that there is anything in common between intellectual activity and the movements of the nations, but we cannot admit in any case that intellectual activity directs the activity of men, since such phenomena as the cruel massacres of the French Revolution, which were the outcome of the doctrine of the equality of men, and wicked wars and reprisals, which have been the outcome of the doctrine of love, do not support this proposition.

But even granting that all the ingenious hypotheses with which these histories are filled are correct, granting that the nations are led by some undetermined force called the *idea*, the essential question of history still either remains unanswered, or to this original power of monarchs, and the influence of contemporaries and other individuals adduced by the general historians, must still be added this new force of the *idea*, the relation of which to the masses demands an explanation.

We may conceive that Napoleon had power and therefore an event took place; with some concessions, we may also conceive that Napoleon, together with other influences, was the cause of an event; but how the book "Contrat Social" influenced Frenchmen to destroy one another cannot be understood without an explanation of the connection between this new force and the event.

Undoubtedly, there exists a connection between all things existing at the same time, and therefore there is a possibility of finding some connection between the intellectual activity of men and their historical movements, just as this connection may be found between the movement of humanity and trade, handicrafts, horticulture, and what not.

But why the intellectual activity of men furnishes the historians of culture with the cause or the expression of every historical movement, it is hard to comprehend. Only the following reasoning can bring historians to such a conclusion : —

(1) That history is written by wise men, and it is natural and agreeable for them to think that the activity of their guild is the ruling element in the movement of all humanity, just as it is natural and agreeable for the merchant, the agriculturist, the soldier, to think the same.

This fails to find expression simply because merchants and soldiers do not write histories.

And (2) that intellectual activity, enlightenment, civilization, culture, the idea, — all these things are indeterminate concepts under which it is very convenient to employ words still more vague and therefore easily adapted to any theory.

But, not to reckon the intrinsic value of this class of historians, perhaps they may be useful for some people and for some purposes, — the histories of culture, to which all general histories are beginning more and more to conform, are significant for this reason, that in developing seriously and in detail various religious, philosophical, and political doctrines, as the causes of the events, every time when it becomes necessary for them to describe some actual historical event, as, for example, the campaign of '12, they involuntarily describe it as the result of power, saying in so many words that this campaign was the result of Napoleon's will!

Speaking in this way, the historians of culture unwittingly contradict themselves, or prove that the new force which they have discovered does not explain historical events, but that the only means of understanding history is to admit that very same power which they affect to disclaim.

CHAPTER III

A LOCOMOTIVE is in motion.

The question is asked, What makes it move?

The muzhik answers, 'T is the devil moves it.

Another says that the locomotive goes because the wheels are in motion.

A third affirms that the cause of the motion is to be found in the smoke borne away by the wind.

The peasant sticks to his opinion. In order to confute him, it must be proved to him that there is no devil, or another peasant must explain to him that it is not the devil, but a German, that makes the locomotive go.

Only then because of the contradictions will it be seen that they cannot both be right.

But the one who says that the cause is the movement of the wheels contradicts himself, since, if he enters into the region of analysis, he must go farther and farther; he must explain the cause of the motion of the wheels. And until he finds the ultimate cause of the motion of the locomotive in steam compressed in the boiler, he will not have the right to pause in his search for the cause.

The one who accounted for the motion of the loco-motive by the smoke borne back had noticed that the explanation regarding the wheels did not furnish a satis-factory cause, and so took the first manifestation which attracted his attention and in his turn offered it as the cause.

The only concept capable of explaining the motion of the locomotive is the concept of a force equivalent to the observed movement.

The only concept capable of explaining the movement of nations is the concept of a force equal to the whole movement of the nations.

And yet the forces assumed by the different his-torians to satisfy this concept are perfectly different, and in every case are not equal to the movement under observation.   Some see in it a force independently in-herent in heroes, as the peasant sees a devil in the loco-motive.   Others see a force proceeding from certain other forces, like the motion of the wheels.   A third class — an intellectual influence, like the smoke borne away.

As long as histories of individuals are written, — whether Cæsars and Alexanders, or Luthers and Vol-taires, — and not the histories of *all*, without a single exception of *all* the men that took part in events, there is no possibility of describing the movements of hu-manity without the conception of a force which obliges men to direct their activity toward a common end.

And the only concept of this sort known to historians is Power.

This concept is the only handle by means of which it is possible to manage the materials of history in the present state of the subject ; and the one who should break this handle, as Buckle did, and not know any other way of dealing with historical material, would be deprived of his last chance of dealing with it.

The unavoidableness of the concept of Power in explaining historical events is shown better than any other way by the authors of universal histories and histories of civilization, who affect to renounce the idea of power, and yet, inevitably, at every step, make use of it.

Historical science, at the present time, in its relation to the questions of humanity, is like money in circulation, — bank-notes and coin. Biographies and the ordinary histories of nations are like bank-notes. They may pass and circulate, satisfying their denomination without injury to any one, and even be of service as long as the question does not arise whether their value is assured.

If only we forget the question how the will of heroes brings about events, the histories of the Thierses will be interesting, instructive, and, moreover, will have a touch of poetry.

But, just as doubt with regard to the actual value of bank-notes arises either from the fact that, since it is so easy to make them, many of them are made, or because there is a general desire to exchange them for gold, in exactly the same way doubt concerning the actual significance of historical works of this sort arises from the fact that they are too numerous, or because some one, in the simplicity of his heart, asks, "By what force was Napoleon able to do this?" In other words, wishes to have his bank-notes exchanged for the pure gold of the genuine concept.

General historians and the historians of culture are like men who, recognizing the inconvenience of assignats, should resolve, in place of paper, to make coin out of some metal which had not the density of gold. And their money would actually have the ring of metal, but only the ring.

Paper notes may deceive the ignorant, but coin which is spurious can deceive no one.

Now, as gold is only gold when it can be used, not merely for exchange, but in practical business, so universal histories will become gold only when they will be able to reply to the essential question of history: "What is power?"

Authors of universal histories contradict one another in their replies to this question, and historians of culture ignore it entirely, and reply to something entirely different.

And as tokens resembling gold can be used only among men who agree to take them for gold, or who know not the properties of gold, so the general historians and the historians of culture who do not respond to the essential questions of history have currency only at the universities, and among the throng of readers who are fond of "serious books," as they call them.

CHAPTER IV

HAVING renounced the views of the ancients as to the divinely ordained submission of the will of the people to the one chosen man, and the submission of this one will to the Divinity, history cannot take another step without being involved in contradictions, unless it make choice between two alternatives : either to return to the former belief in the immediate interference of the Divinity in human affairs, or definitely to explain the meaning of this force which produces historical events and is known as Power.

To return to the first is impossible ; the belief has been overthrown, and it is therefore necessary to explain the meaning of Power.

Napoleon gave orders to raise an army, and go to war. This notion is so familiar to us, we have become to such a degree wonted to this view of things, that the question why six hundred thousand men should go to war because Napoleon said such and such words seems to us foolish. He had the power, and consequently his orders were obeyed.

This answer is perfectly satisfactory if we believe that the power was given to him by God. But, as soon as we deny it, we must decide what that power is that one man has over others.

That power cannot be the direct power of the physical superiority of a strong being over the weak, — a superiority based on the application, or threatened application, of physical force, — like the power of Hercules. It cannot be founded either on the superiority of moral force, though certain historians, in the simplicity of their hearts, declare that historical actors are heroes — that is, men gifted with a peculiar force of soul and intellect, called genius.

This power cannot be based on the superiority of moral force, since, without speaking of popular heroes like Napoleon, concerning whose moral qualities opinions are completely at variance, history shows us that neither the Louis XI.'s, nor the Metternichs, who governed millions of men, had any special qualities of moral force, but, on the contrary, were, for the most part, morally weaker than any one of the millions of men whom they ruled.

If the source of Power lies in neither the physical nor the moral qualities of the individual exercising it, then evidently the source of this Power must be found outside the individual, — in those relations between the masses governed and the individual possessing the Power.

In exactly this way Power is understood by the science of Law, the selfsame exchange bank of history which promises to change the historical concepts of Power into pure gold.

Power is the accumulation of the wills of the masses, transferred, avowedly or tacitly, to the rulers chosen by the masses.

In the domain of the science of Law, which is composed of dissertations on the requisite methods of building up a State and Power, if it were possible to do all this, this explanation is all very clear; but in its application to history this definition of Power demands explanation.

The science of Law regards a State and Power as the ancients regarded fire, as something existing absolutely. For History the State and Power are only phenomena, just as in the same way as for the "Physics" of our day fire is not an element but a phenomenon.

From this fundamental divergence of view between History and the science of Law, it follows that science of Law can relate in detail how, in its opinion, it would be necessary to build up Power, and to tell what Power is, existing immovably outside of time; but to the historical questions about the significance of Power modified by time, it can give no reply.

If Power is the accumulation of wills transferred to a ruler, then is Pugachof the representative of the wills of the masses? If he is not, then why is Napoleon I. such a representative? Why was Napoleon III., when he was apprehended at Boulogne, a criminal, and why were those whom he afterwards apprehended criminals?

In palace revolutions, in which sometimes only two or three men take part, is the will of the masses also transferred to the new monarch?

In international relations, is the will of the masses of the people transferred to their conqueror?

In 1808 was the will of the Rhine Convention transferred to Napoleon?

Was the will of the Russian people transferred to Napoleon in 1809 when our troops, in alliance with the French, went to fight against Austria?

These questions may be answered in three ways:—

Either (1) by acknowledging that the will of the masses is always unconditionally handed over to this or that ruler whom they have chosen, and that consequently every outbreak of new Power, every struggle against the Power once given over, must be regarded as an infringement of the real Power;

Or (2) by acknowledging that the will of the masses is transferred to the rulers conditionally, under known and definite conditions, and by showing that all signs of restlessness, all collisions, and even the destruction of Power, proceed from non-fulfilment of the conditions under which the Power was given to them;

Or (3) by acknowledging that the will of the masses is transferred to the rulers conditionally, but under un-

known and undefined conditions, and that the outbreak
of many new Powers, their conflict and fall, arise only
from the more or less complete fulfilment of those unknown conditions according to which the will of the
masses was transferred from some individuals to others.

In these three ways the historians explain the relations of the masses to their rulers.

Some historians, not comprehending, in the simplicity
of their souls, the question of the meaning of Power, —
the same special and " biographical historians " of whom
mention has been made above, — seem to acknowledge
that the accumulated will of the masses is transferred
unconditionally to the historical personages, and therefore, in describing any Power whatever, these historians
suppose that this selfsame Power is the one absolute
and genuine, and that any other force rising in opposition to this genuine Power is not a Power, but a breach
of Power — violence !

Their theory, satisfactory for the primitive and peaceful periods of history, has, when it comes to be applied
to the complicated and stormy periods in the life of the
nations, — during which simultaneously various Powers
rise up and struggle together, — the disadvantage that
the Legitimist historian will try to prove that the
Convention, the Directory, and Bonaparte were only
infringements of Power, while the Republican and
Bonapartist will try to prove, the one that the Convention, and the other that the Empire, was the genuine
Power, and that all the rest were only infringements of
Power.

Evidently since the explanations of Power given by
these historians mutually contradict each other, they
can prove satisfactory only for children of the tenderest
growth !

A second class of historians, recognizing the fallacy
of this view of history, say that Power is founded on
the conditional transfer of the accumulated wills of the
masses to the rulers, and that historical personages have
the Power only on condition of carrying out the program which with tacit consent has been prescribed by

the will of the nation. But what goes to make up this program, these historians fail to tell us, or, if they tell us, they constantly contradict one another.

To every historian, according to his view of what constitutes the object of the movement of the nations, this program presents itself in the grandeur, liberty, enlightenment, of the citizens of France or some other state.

But not to speak of the contradictions of the historians, or of what this program is, even granting the existence of one program common to all, still the facts of history almost universally contradict this theory.

If the conditions under which Power is granted consist in riches, liberty, the enlightenment of the nation, why, then, were such men as Louis XIV. and Ivan IV.[1] allowed to live to the end of their reigns, while such men as Louis XVI. and Charles I. were put to death by their nations?

These historians answer this question by saying that the activity of Louis XIV., being contrary to the program, met with its punishment in the person of Louis XVI.

But why was not the punishment inflicted on Louis XIV. and Louis XV.? Why should it have been inflicted especially on Louis XVI.? And what is the length of time required for such a repercussion?

To these questions there is and can be no answer. In the same way this view fails to explain the cause of the fact that the accumulated will of the people for several centuries is preserved by the rulers and their successors, and then suddenly, in the course of fifty years, is transferred to the Convention, to the Directory, to Napoleon, to Alexander, to Louis XVIII., to Napoleon again, to Charles X., to Louis Philippe, to the Republican administration, to Napoleon III.

In their explanations of these rapidly occurring transfers of will from one individual to another, and especially in international relations, conquests, and treaties, these historians must, in spite of themselves, acknowledge that a part of these phenomena are not regular transfers of will, but accidental chances, dependent now on cun-

---

[1] Ioann or Ivan the Terrible, of Russia, reigned from 1546 till 1584.

ning, now on the mistakes or the deceitfulness or the weakness of diplomat or monarch or party director.

So that the greater part of the phenomena of history — civil wars, revolutions, conquests — appear to these historians certainly not as the products of the transfers of free wills, but as the products of the misdirected will of one man or several men, in other words, again infringements of Power.

And consequently historical events, even to historians of this class, appear as exceptions to the theory.

These historians are like a botanist who, observing that certain plants come from seeds with dicotyledonous leaves, should insist upon it that everything that grew must grow in this bifoliate form, and that the palm and the mushroom and even the oak, which develop to their full growth and have no more resemblance to the dicotyledons, are exceptions to their theory.

A third class of historians acknowledge that the will of the masses is conditionally transferred to the historical personages, but assert that these conditions are not known to us. They say that the historical characters possess the power simply because they have to fulfil the will of the masses, which has been transferred to them.

But in such a case, if the force that moves the nations is not inherent in the historical individuals, but in the nations themselves, then what constitutes the significance of these historical personages?

Historical personages, these historians say, are in themselves the expression of the will of the masses; the activity of the historical personages serves as the representative of the activity of the masses.

But in this case the question arises: Does all the activity of the historical characters serve as the expression of the will of the masses, or only a certain side of it?

If all the activity of historical personages serves as the expression of the will of the masses, as some think, then the biographies of the Napoleons, the Catherines, with all the details of court gossip, serve as the expression of the life of the nations, which is evidently absurd.

If only one side of the activity of the historical personage serves as the expression of the life of the nations, as is thought by other so-called philosopher-historians, then in order to determine what side of the activity of the historical personage expresses the life of the nation, it is necessary first to determine what constitutes the life of the nation.

Having met with this difficulty, the historians of this sort have invented a most obscure, intangible, and universal explanation, under which to bring the greatest possible quantity of events, and they say that this abstraction covers the object of the movements of humanity. The most ordinary abstractions which are selected by the historians, almost without exception, are : liberty, equality, enlightenment, progress, civilization, culture.

Having thus established as the object of the movement of humanity some abstraction or other, the historians study the men who have left behind them the greatest quantity of memorials — tsars, ministers, commanders, authors, reformers, popes, journalists, according as these personages, in their judgment, have contributed to help or to oppose the given abstraction.

But since it has not been shown by any one that the object of humanity consisted in liberty, equality, enlightenment, or civilization, and as the connection of the masses with the rulers and enlighteners of humanity is based only on an arbitrary assumption that the accumulation of the wills of the masses is always transferred to those individuals who are known to us, therefore the activity of millions of men, who are marching forth, burning houses, abandoning agriculture, exterminating one another, is never expressed in the description of the activity of a dozen men who have never burned houses, had nothing to do with agriculture, and did not kill their fellow-men.

History shows this at every step.

Can the fermentation of the nations of the West at the end of the last century, and their eager rush toward the East, be expressed in the activity of Louis XIV., Louis XV., or Louis XVI., or their mistresses and ministers, or in the lives of Napoleon, Rousseau, Diderot, Beaumarchais, and the others ?

Was the movement of the Russian people toward the East, to Kazan and Siberia, expressed in the details of the sickly character of Ivan IV. and his correspondence with Kurbsky?

Is the movement of the nations at the time of the crusades explained in the life and activity of the God-freys and the St. Louises and their ladies? For us it remains still incomprehensible what moved the nations from west to east, without any object, without leader-ship, — a crowd of vagrants, with Peter the Hermit.

And still more incomprehensible remains the discon-tinuance of that movement at a time when the reason-able and holy object of the crusades — the liberation of Jerusalem — was so clearly set forth by the historical agents. Popes, kings, and knights incited the people to rally for the liberation of the Holy Land; but the people would not go, for the reason that the unknown cause which before had incited them to the movement was no longer in existence.

The history of the Godfreys and the Minnesingers evidently cannot comprise in itself the life of the nations. And the histories of the Godfreys and the Minnesingers remain the history of the Godfreys and the Minnesingers, but the history of the lives of the nations and their mainsprings of action remain un-known.

Still less is the life of the nations explained for us by the histories of authors and reformers.

The history of culture explains for us the awakening of the conditions of life and the thoughts of writers and reformers. We know that Luther had an irascible nature and uttered such and such sayings; we know that Rousseau was a skeptic and wrote such and such books; but we know not why, after the Reformation, men cut one another's throats, or why, at the time of the French Revolution, they put one another to death. If these two kinds of history are welded together, as some of the most recent historians have done, it will still be the histories of monarchs and writers, but not the history of the life of the nations.

CHAPTER V

THE life of the nations cannot be summarized in the lives of a few men, for the bond connecting these few persons with the nations has not been discovered. The theory that this bond of union is based on the will of the masses transferred to historical personages is an hypothesis not confirmed by the experience of history.

The theory of the transference of the will of the masses to the historical personages perhaps explains many things in the domain of Law, and is very possibly essential for its objects; but in relation to history, as soon as revolutions, civil wars, conquests, make their appearance, as soon as history begins, this theory no longer explains anything.

This theory seems to be irrefutable, simply because the act of transference of the will of the nation cannot be verified, since it never existed.

No matter what the event may be, or what personage may stand at the head of it, theory can always say that the personage in question was at the head of the affairs for the reason that the accumulated will of the masses was transferred to him.

The answers afforded by this theory to historical questions are like the answers of a man who, watching a herd of cattle moving about, and not taking into consideration the varying quality of the feed in different parts of the field or the whip of the drover, should attribute their movement in this or that direction to the animal at the head of the herd.

"The herd go in that direction because the animal at the head leads them there, and the accumulated will of all the other animals is transferred to this leader of the herd."

Thus reply the first class of historians — those that believe in the unconditional transference of power.

"If the animals moving at the head of the herd change their direction, it is because the accumulated will of all the animals is transferred from one leader to another according as this or that animal conducts them in the direction chosen by the herd."

Thus reply the historians who hold that the accumulated will of the masses is transferred to rulers under certain conditions which they consider indeterminate.

In such a method of observation it would often come about that the observer, drawing his conclusions from the direction taken by the herd, would consider certain animals at the side or even at the rear as the leaders, owing to changes of direction taken wholly by chance!

"If the animals at the head of the herd constantly change about, and if the course of the whole herd constantly varies, it is from the fact that, in order to attain the direction which we observed, the animals transfer their will to those other animals observed by us; and, in order to study the movements of the herd, we must study all the animals under whose influence the herd is led from side to side."

Thus argue the historians of the third class, who believe that all historical personages, from monarchs to journalists, are the expressions of their own time.

The theory of the will of the masses being transferred to historical personages is merely a periphrase.... only the question expressed in other words!

What is the cause of historical events? Power.

What is Power?

Power is the accumulated wills of the masses transferred to a given personage.

Under what conditions are the wills of the masses transferred to a given personage?

On condition that the personage expresses the will of the masses.

That is, Power is Power. That is, Power is a word, the meaning of which is incomprehensible to us.

If all human knowledge were comprehended within the domain of abstract reasoning, then humanity, having subjected to criticism the idea of Power that *science* gives, would come to the conclusion that Power is only a word, and does not, in reality, exist at all.

For the knowledge of phenomena, however, man has, besides abstract reasoning, the tool of experience, by which he tests the results of reasoning. And experience declares that Power is not a mere word, but a thing actually existing.

Aside from the fact that without the concept of Power it is impossible to describe the united action of men, the existence of Power is proved, not only by history, but by the observation of contemporary events.

Always, when an historical event takes place, there appears one man or several men, in accordance with whose will the event apparently takes place.

Napoleon III. gives his orders, and the French go to Mexico.

The king of Prussia and Bismarck give their orders, and the troops enter Bohemia.

Napoleon I. gives his orders, and the troops march into Russia.

Alexander I. gives his orders, and the French submit to the Bourbons.

Experience shows us that whatever event has come to pass is always connected with the will of one man or several men, who gave the commands.

Historians who, according to the old custom, recognize the participation of the Divinity in the affairs of humanity, try to find the cause of an event in the expression of the will of the individual who is clothed with the Power, but this conclusion is confirmed neither by reason nor by experience.

On the one hand, reason shows us that the expression of the will of a man — his words — is but a part of the general activity expressed in an event, for example, a war or a revolution ; and, therefore, without the acknowledgment of the existence of an incomprehensible, supernatural force — a miracle — it is impossible to grant that mere words can be the proximate cause of the movement of millions of men; on the other hand, if we grant that words can be the cause of an event, then history proves that in many cases the expression of the will of historical personages has been productive of no effect whatever — that is, not only have their decrees been often disobeyed, but some-times the exact opposite of what they ordered has been brought to pass.

Unless we grant that the Divinity participates in human affairs, we cannot regard Power as the cause of events.

Power, from the standpoint of experience, is merely the relationship existing between the expressed will of the individual and the accomplishment of that will by other men.

To explain the conditions of this relationship, we must first of all establish the idea of the expression of will by referring it to man and not to the Divinity.

If the Divinity gives commands, expresses his will, as the history written by the ancients would have us believe, then the expression of this will is not dependent on time, or conditioned by any determining cause, since the Divinity is wholly disconnected with the event.

But when we speak of decrees as the expression of the will of men who, in their acts, are subject to time and dependent on one another, in order to understand the connection between decrees and events, we must establish : —

(1) The condition under which everything happens : continuity in time of action, both of the historical move-ment and the person who gives the command; and

(2) The condition of the inevitable connection between the personage who gives the command and the men who carry out his command.

CHAPTER VI

ONLY the expression of the will of the Divinity, which is independent of time, can be related to the whole series of events extending over a few years or centuries, and only the Divinity, which is unconditioned by anything, can by its own will alone determine the direction of the movements of humanity; man, however, acts in time, and himself participates in events.

Having established the first neglected condition — the condition of Time — we shall see that no command can be executed without the existence of some previous command, making the fulfilment of the latter possible.

Never is a single command produced spontaneously, and it never includes in itself a whole series of events; but each command has its source in another, and is never related to a whole series of events, but only to the one moment of an event.

When we say, for instance, that Napoleon commanded his armies to go to war, we combine in one simultaneous expression, "command," a series of consecutive orders, dependent one upon another.

Napoleon could never have decreed the campaign to Russia, and he never did decree it.

He gave orders one day to write such and such letters to Vienna, to Berlin, and to Petersburg; the next day certain decrees and "orders" to the army, the navy, and the commissariat department, and so on and so on, — millions of commands, forming a series of commands corresponding to a series of events, which brought the French army into Russia.

If Napoleon throughout the whole course of his reign issues commands concerning the expedition against England, and if on no single one of his designs he wastes so much time and energy, and yet during the whole course of his reign not once attempts to carry out his intention, but makes the expedition to Russia, with which as he expressed himself repeatedly, he considered it advantageous to be in alliance, then this results from the fact that the first orders do not correspond to any series of events, whereas the second do.

In order that a command should be genuinely carried out, it is necessary that a man should express an order which can be carried out. To know what can and what cannot be carried out is impossible, not merely in case of a Napoleonic expedition against Russia in which millions participate, but even in the simplest event; since for the accomplishment of the one or the other, millions of obstacles may be encountered.

For every command that is carried out, there are always enormous numbers that are not carried out.

All infeasible commands have no connection with the event, and are not carried out. Only those that are feasible become connected with consecutive series of commands accompanying whole series of events, and are carried out.

Our false premise that the command preceding the event is the cause of the event, arises from the fact that when an event has taken place, and out of a thousand commands only those that are connected with the event are carried out, we forget those that were not carried out because they could not be carried out.

Moreover, the chief source of our error in this way of thinking arises from the fact that in historical narratives a whole series of numberless, various, petty events, as for example, all the things that brought the French armies into Russia, is generalized into one event according to the result produced by this series of events, and, corresponding with this generalization, the whole series of commands is also generalized into one expression of will.

We say: Napoleon planned and made an expedition against Russia.

In reality, we never find in all Napoleon's career anything like the expression of this will, but we find a series of commands or expressions of his will in the most varied and indeterminate sort of direction.

Out of the numberless series of Napoleonic decrees that were never executed proceeded a series of commands concerning the campaign of '12 which were executed, not because these commands were in any respect different from the other commands that were not executed, but because the series of these commands coincided with a series of events which brought the French army into Russia, — just as by a stencil this or that figure is designed, not because it makes any difference on what side or how the color is applied, but because the color was smeared over the whole side, including the figure that had been cut out of the stencil plate.

So that, by considering the relation of the commands to the events in time, we shall find that in no case can the command be the cause of the event, but that between the two exists a certain definite connection.

In order to comprehend what this connection is, it is necessary to establish a second neglected condition of every command which proceeds, not from the Divinity, but from a man; and this is the fact that the man who gives the command must himself be a participant in the event.

This relationship between the person giving the command and the one to whom the command is given is precisely that which is called Power.

This relationship consists in the following: —

In order to undertake action in common, men always form themselves into certain groups in which, notwithstanding the variety of the objects impelling them to united action, the relation between the men who participate in the action is always the same.

Having united into these groups, men always establish among themselves such a relationship that the greater number of the men take the greatest direct part, and the smaller number take the smallest direct part, in the mutual action for which they have united their forces.

Of all such groups into which men have ever joined themselves for the accomplishment of a common activity, the most definite and clearly defined is the army.

Every army is composed of the lower members, "the rank and file" in military parlance, the privates, who always form the majority; then of those who in military parlance hold higher rank — corporals, non-commissioned officers, less in number than the first; then those still higher, the number of whom is still less, and so on up to the highest power of all, which is concentrated in a single individual.

The organization of an army may be expressed with perfect accuracy under the figure of a cone, in which the base, having the greatest diameter, is represented by the privates, the higher and smaller plane sections representing the higher ranks of the army, and so on up to the very top of the cone, the apex of which will be represented by the commander-in-chief.

The soldiers forming the majority constitute the lowest portion of the cone and its base. The soldier himself directly does the killing, stabbing, burning, pillaging, and in these actions always receives commands from those who stand above him; he himself never gives commands.

The non-commissioned officer — the number of non-commissioned officers is still less — more seldom than the soldier takes part in these acts, but he gives commands.

The officer still more rarely takes part in the action himself, and gives orders still more frequently.

The general only commands the troops to march, and tells them where they are to go, but he almost never uses weapons.

The commander-in-chief never can take a direct part in the action itself, but merely issues general dispositions concerning the movements of the masses.

The same mutual relationship of individuals is to be noted in every union of men for common activity — in agriculture, trade, and in every other enterprise.

Thus, without elaborately carrying out all the complicated divisions of the cone and the grades of the army or of any calling and establishment of any kind whatever, or of any common business, from highest to lowest, the law everywhere holds by which men, for the accomplishment of mutual activities, join together in such a relationship that in proportion as they take a greater direct share in the actual work, and the more they are in numbers, the less they give orders, and in proportion as they take a less direct part in the work itself, the more they give orders and the fewer they are; thus passing up from the lowest strata to the one man standing alone, taking the smallest possible direct part in the work, and more than all the others directing his activity to the giving of commands.

This relationship of the individuals who command

to those who are commanded is the very essence of the concept which we call Power.

Having established the conditions in time under which all events are accomplished, we have found that the command is executed only when it bears some relation to the corresponding series of events.

Having established the inevitable condition of the connection between the commander and the commanded, we have found that by its very nature those who most issue the commands take the least part in the event itself, and that their activity is exclusively directed toward commanding.

CHAPTER VII

WHEN any event whatever is taking place, men express their various opinions and wishes concerning the event, and, as the event proceeds from the united action of many men, some one of the expressed opinions or wishes is sure to be executed, even though it may be approximately.

When one of the opinions expressed is fulfilled, this opinion seems to be connected with the event as a command preceding it.

Men are dragging along a beam. Each expresses his opinions as to how and where it should be dragged. They drag the beam to its destination, and it is shown that it has been done in accordance with what one of them said.

He gave the command.

Here the command and the power are seen in their primitive form.

The man who labored hardest with his arms could not so well think what he was doing, or be able to consider what would be the result of the common activity, or to command.

The one who gave the most commands could, by reason of his activity with his words, evidently do less with his arms.

In a large concourse of men who are directing their activity to one end, still more sharply defined is the class of those who, in proportion as they take a less active part in the general business, direct their activity all the more toward giving commands.

A man, when he acts alone, always carries with him a certain series of considerations which seem to him to have guided his past activity, and serve to facilitate his activity at the moment and to assist him in his plans for his future enterprises.

In exactly the same way assemblages of men act, leaving those who take no part in the actual work to do their thinking for them, and to justify their operations, and to make their plans for their future activity.

For reasons known or unknown to us, the French begin to ruin and murder one another, and conformably to the event its justification is found in the expressed will of the people, who declare that this was essential for the well-being of France, for liberty, for equality!

The French cease to murder one another, and this finds justification in the necessity for the unity of Power, for resistance to Europe and the like.

Men march from the West to the East, killing their fellow-men, and this event is accompanied by the words: "the glory of France," "the humiliation of England," and the like.

History shows us that these justifications of events have no common sense, are mutually contradictory, like the murder of a man in consequence of the recognition of his rights, and the massacre of millions in Russia for the humiliation of England. But these justifications have a necessary significance at the time they are made.

These justifications free from moral responsibility the men who brought these events about. These temporary objects are like the "cow-catchers," which serve to clear the road along the rails in front of the train: they clear the road of the moral responsibility of men.

Without these justifications we could not answer the simplest questions which stand in the way of the examination of every event: "How did millions of men commit wholesale crimes — wars, massacres, and the like?"

Would it be possible in the present complicated forms of political and social life in Europe to find any event whatever that would not have been predicted, prescribed, ordained, by sovereigns, ministers, parliaments, newspapers? Could there be any united action which would not find justification for itself in National Unity, in the Balance of Europe, in Civilization?

So that every accomplished event inevitably corresponds to some expressed wish, and, having found justification for itself, appears as the fulfilment of the will of one or several men.

When a ship moves, whatever may be her course, there will always be visible, in front of the prow, a ripple of the sundered waves. For the men who are on board of the ship the movement of this ripple would be the only observable motion.

Only by observing closely, moment by moment, the movement of this ripple, and comparing this movement with the motion of the ship, can we persuade ourselves that each moment of the movement of the ripple is determined by the motion of the ship, and that we were led into error by the very fact that we ourselves were imperceptibly moving.

We see the same thing in following, moment by moment, the motion of historical personages — that is, by establishing the necessary condition of everything that is accomplished — the condition of uninterrupted motion in time — and by not losing from sight the inevitable connection of historical personages with the masses.

Whatever has happened, it always seems that this very thing has been predicted and preordained. In whatever direction the ship moves, the ripple, which does not guide or even condition its movement, boils in front of her, and will seem, to an observer at a distance, not only to be spontaneously moving, but even directing the movement of the ship.

Historians, regarding only those expressions of the will of historical personages which bore to events the relation of commands, have supposed that events are dependent on commands.

Regarding the events themselves, and that connection with the masses by which historical personages have been bound, we have discovered that historical personages and their commands are dependent on the events.

An undoubted proof of this deduction is given by the fact that, no matter how many commands are uttered, the event will not take place if there be no other causes for it; but as soon as any event — no matter what it is — is accomplished, then out of the number of all the continuously expressed wills of the various individuals, there will be found some which in meaning and time will bear to the event the relation of commands.

In coming to this conclusion, we are able to give a direct and circumstantial reply to the two essential questions of history : —

(1) What is Power ?

(2) What force causes the movement of the nations ?

(1) Power is a relationship established between a certain person and other persons, in virtue of which this person, in inverse proportion to the part which he takes in action, expresses opinions, suppositions, and justifications concerning the common action to be accomplished.

(2) The movement of the nations is due, not to Power or to intellectual activity, or even to a union of the two, as some of the historians have thought, but to the activity of *all* the men that took part in the event, and always group themselves together in such a way that those that take the greatest direct share in the event assume the least responsibility, and *vice versa*.

In the moral relation Power is the cause of the event; in the physical relation it is those who submit to the Power. But since moral activity is meaningless without physical activity, therefore the cause of an event is found neither in the one nor in the other, but in a combination of the two.

Or, in other words, the concept of a cause is inapplicable to the phenomenon which we are regarding.

In last analysis we reach the circle of Eternity, that ultimate limit to which in every domain of thought the human intellect must come, unless it is playing with its subject.

Electricity produces heat; heat produces electricity. Atoms attract one another; atoms repel one another.

Speaking of the reciprocal action of heat and electricity and about the atoms, we cannot say why this is so, but we say that it is, because it is unthinkable in any other way, because it must be so, because it is a law.

The same holds true also about historical phenomena.

Why are there wars or revolutions? We know not; we only know that for the accomplishment of this or that action men band together into a certain group in which all take a share, and we say that this is so because it is unthinkable otherwise, that it is a law.

CHAPTER VIII

IF history had to do with external phenomena, the establishment of this simple and evident law would be sufficient, and we might end our discussion.

But the law of history relates to man. A particle of matter cannot tell us that it is wholly unconscious of the attraction or repulsion of force, and that it is not true.

Man, however, who is the object of history, declares stoutly, " I am free, and therefore I am not subjected to laws."

The presence of the unacknowledged question of the freedom of the will is felt at every step in history.

All serious-minded historians have had, in spite of themselves, to face this question. All the contradictions, the obscurities, of history, that false route by which this science has traveled, are based on the impossibility of solving this question.

If the will of every man were free, that is, if every

one could do as he pleased, then history would be a series of disconnected accidents.

If even one man out of millions, during a period of thousands of years, had the power of acting freely, that is, in conformity with his own wishes, then evidently the free action of that man, being an exception to the laws, would destroy the possibility of the existence of any laws whatever for all humanity.

If there were one single law which directed the activities of men, then there could be no free will, since the will of men must be subjected to this law.

In this contrariety is included the whole question of the freedom of the will, a question which from the most ancient times has attracted the best intellects of the human race, and which from the most ancient times has loomed up in all its colossal significance.

The question, at bottom, is this : —

Looking at man as an object of observation from any standpoint that we please, — theological, historical, ethnical, philosophical, — we find the general law of Fate or necessity to which he, like everything else in existence, is subjected. Yet, looking at him subjectively, as on something of which we have a consciousness, we feel ourselves to be free.

This knowledge is a perfectly distinct source of self-consciousness, and independent of reason. By means of reason man observes himself ; but he knows himself only through consciousness.

Without consciousness there could be no such thing as observation or application of the reason.

In order to understand, to observe, to reason, man must first recognize that he is existent.

As a living being, man cannot recognize himself other than as a wishing one ; that is, he recognizes his own will.

His will, which constitutes the essence of his life, man conceives and cannot conceive otherwise than as free.

If, on subjecting himself to study, man sees that his will is always directed in accordance with one and the same law, — whether he observe the necessity of taking food or the activity of the brain, or anything else, — he cannot understand this invariable direction of his will otherwise than as a limitation of it.

Whatever should be free could not be also limited. The will of man appears to him limited for the very reason that he can conceive of it in no other way than as free.

You say, "I am not free, yet I raised and dropped my hand." Every one understands that this illogical answer is an irrefutable proof of freedom.

This answer is the expression of consciousness, which is not subordinate to reason.

If the consciousness of freedom were not a separate source of self-consciousness independent of reason, it would be subjected to reason and experience, but in reality such subordination never exists and is unthinkable.

A series of experiments and judgments shows every man that he, as an object of observation, is subordinate to certain laws, and man submits to them and never quarrels with the laws of gravity or impenetrability when once he has learned them.

But this series of experiments and arguments proves to him that the perfect freedom of which he is conscious within himself is an impossibility, that his every act is dependent on his organization, his character, and the motives that act on him; but man will never submit himself to the deduction from these experiments and arguments.

Knowing from experiment and argument that a stone always falls, man infallibly believes in this, and in all circumstances he expects to see the fulfilment of this law which he has learned.

But, though he has learned just as indubitably that his will is subject to laws, he does not believe it and cannot believe it.

However many times experience and reason have shown a man that in the same circumstances, with the same character, he will always act in the same way as before, he for the thousandth time coming, under the same conditions, with the same character, to a deed which always ends in the same way, nevertheless indubitably feels himself just as firmly convinced that he can act as he pleases, as he did before the experiment.

Every man, whether savage or cultivated, however irrefragably reason and experiment have taught him that it is impossible to imagine two different courses of action in the same circumstances, feels that without his unreasoning idea — which constitutes the essence of freedom — he could not imagine life possible.

He feels that, however impossible it is, still it is true, since without this notion of freedom he would not only not understand life, but could not live a single instant.

He could not live, because all the aspirations of men, all the incitements to living, are only the aspirations toward enhancement of freedom.

Riches, poverty; fame, obscurity; power, subjection; strength, weakness; health, sickness; knowledge, ignorance; labor, leisure; feasting, hunger; virtue, vice, — are only greater or less degrees of freedom.

For a man himself to imagine not having freedom is impossible except as being deprived of life.

If the concept of freedom seem to reason as a senseless contradiction, like the possibility of accomplishing two courses of action at one and the same time, or an effect without a cause, then this only goes to prove that consciousness does not belong to reason.

This immovable, incontestable consciousness of freedom, which is not subject to experiment and reason, recognized by all thinkers and admitted by all men without exception, a consciousness without which any conception of man is nonsense, constitutes another side of the question.

Man is the work of an omnipotent, omniscient, and infinitely good God. What is the sin the notion of which takes its origin from the consciousness of the freedom of man?

Such is the question of theology.

The actions of men are subject to invariable general laws expressed by statistics. What constitutes man's responsibility to society, the notion of which takes its origin from the consciousness of free will?

Such is the question of law.

The actions of man flow from his natural temperament and the motives acting on him. What is conscience and the consciousness of the good and evil of the acts that arise from the consciousness of free will?

Such is the question of ethics.

Man, relatively to the general life of humanity, seems to be subject to the laws that determine this life. But this same man, independently of this relation, seems to be free. Must the past life of nations and of humanity be regarded as the product of the free or of the unfree acts of men?

Such is the question of history.

But in these self-confident days of the popularization of knowledge by that great instrument of ignorance, the diffusion of literature, the question of the freedom of the will has been taken into a field where it cannot be a question at all.

In our time, most of the men who call themselves advanced — that is, a mob of ignoramuses — accept the work of the naturalists, who look at only one side of the question, as the solution of this question.

"There is no soul, no free will, because the life of man is expressed by muscular movements, but these muscular movements are conditioned by nervous action; there is no soul, no free will, because, in some unknown period of time, we came from monkeys."

This is spoken, written, and printed by men who do not even suspect that for thousands of years all religions, all thinkers, have not only recognized, but have never denied, this same law of necessity which they have been striving so eagerly to prove, with the aid of physiology and comparative zoölogy.

They do not see that in regard to this question the natural sciences are only to serve as a means of throwing light on one side of it.

Since, from the standpoint of observation, reason and will are only secretions of the brain, and man, following the general law, may have developed from lower animals in an indeterminate period of time, it only explains from a new side the truth, which has been recognized for thousands of years by all religions and all philosophical theories, that from the standpoint of reason man is subject to the laws of necessity, but it does not advance by a single hair's-breadth the solution of the question which has another and contradictory side, based on the consciousness of liberty.

If men could have come from monkeys in an indeterminate period of time, it is just as comprehensible that they could have been formed from a handful of clay during a determined period of time (in the first supposition, x is the time; in the second, it is descent); and the question as to how far man's consciousness of freedom can be reconciled with the law of necessity to which man is subject, cannot be solved by physiology and zoölogy, for we can observe only the muscular activity of the frog, the rabbit, or the monkey, while in man we can observe neuro-muscular activity and consciousness.

The naturalists and their disciples, who think they have solved the question, are like masons commissioned to stucco one side of the walls of a church, and who, in a fit of zeal, taking advantage of the absence of the overseer, should put a coat of plaster over the windows, the sacred pictures, the scaffolding, and the walls as yet uncemented, and should be delighted from their plasterers' standpoint, at having made the whole so even and smooth!

CHAPTER IX

In the decision of the question of Free Will and Necessity, History has the advantage over all the other branches of knowledge which have taken this question in hand, that for History this question touches not the very essence of man's will, but the manifestation of the display of this will in the past and under certain conditions.

History, by its decision of this question, stands toward other sciences in the position of an empirical science toward speculative sciences.

History has for its object not the will of man, but our representation of it.

And therefore the impenetrable mystery of the reconciliation of the two contradictories, Free Will and Necessity, cannot exist for History — as it does for theology, ethics, and philosophy.

History examines that manifestation of the life of man, in which the reconciliation of these two contradictions is already effected.

In actual life, every historical event, every act of man, is understood clearly and definitely, without any sense of the slightest inconsistency, although every event appears in part free and in part necessitated.

For deciding the question how Freedom and Necessity are united, and what constitutes the essence of these two concepts, the philosophy of History can and must pursue a route contrary to that taken by the other sciences. Instead of defining the concepts of Free Will and Necessity, and then subjecting the phenomena of life to the definitions prepared, History, from the enormous collection of phenomena at her disposal, and which always seem dependent on Free Will and Necessity, is obliged to deduce her definition from the concepts themselves of Free Will and Necessity.

However we may regard the manifestation of the activities of many men or of one man, we cannot fail to understand it as the product, in part of the Freedom of man, in part of the laws of Necessity.

When we speak of the transmigrations of nations and the invasions of barbarians, or of the arrangements of Napoleon III., or of a man's act performed an hour ago, and consisting in the fact that from various directions for his walk he chose one, we detect not the slightest contradiction. The measure of Free Will and Necessity involved in the actions of these men is clearly defined for us.

Very often, the manifestation of greater or less freedom varies according to the standpoint from which we regard the phenomenon; but always and invariably every action of man presents itself to us as a reconciliation of Free Will and Necessity.

In every act that we take under consideration we see a certain share of Freedom and a certain share of Necessity. And always the more Freedom we see in any action, the less is there of Necessity, and the more Necessity the less Freedom.

The relation between Freedom and Necessity diminishes and increases according to the standpoint from which the action is viewed; but this relation always remains proportional.

A drowning man, who clutches another and causes him to drown; or a starving mother, exhausted in suckling her baby, who steals food; or a soldier in the ranks, subjected to army discipline, who kills a defenseless man by command of his superior, — all appear less guilty, that is, less free, and more subjected to the law of Necessity, to one who knows the conditions in which these people were brought, and more free to the one who knows not that the man himself was drowning, that the mother was starving, that the soldier was in line, and so on.

In exactly the same way, a man who, twenty years ago, should have committed a murder, and after that should have lived peaceably and harmlessly in society, appears less guilty; his action is more subordinated to the law of Necessity for the one who should consider his crime after the lapse of twenty years, and more free to the one who should consider the same action a day after it had been perpetrated.

And exactly in the same way every action of a lunatic, of a drunken man, or of a person under strong provocation, seems less free and more inevitable to the one who knows the mental condition of the person committing the act, and more free and less inevitable to the one who knows not.

In all these cases the conception of Free Will is increased or diminished, and proportionally the conception of Necessity is increased or diminished, according to the standpoint from which the action is viewed. The greater appears the Necessity, the less appears the Freedom of the Will.

And *vice versa.*

Religion, the common sense of humanity, the science of law, and history itself, accept in exactly the same way this relationship between Necessity and Free Will.

All cases without exception in which our representation of Free Will and Necessity increases and diminishes may be reduced to three fundamental principles:—

(1) The relation of the man committing the act to the outside world;

(2) To time; and

(3) To the causes which brought about the act.

The first principle is the more or less palpable relation of the man to the outside world, the more or less distinct concept of that definite place which every man occupies toward every other man existing contemporaneously with him.

This is the principle which makes it evident that the drowning man is less free and more subject to Necessity than a man standing on dry land; the principle which makes the acts of a man living in close connection with other men, in densely populated localities, the acts of a man bound by family, by service, by engagements, seem less free and more subjected to Necessity than the acts of a single man living alone.

(1) If we examine an isolated man without any relations to his environment, then his every act seems to us free. But if we detect any relation whatever to what surrounds him, if we detect any connection with anything whatever,—with the man who talks with him, with the book he reads, with the labor he undertakes, even with the atmosphere that surrounds him, even with the light that falls on surrounding objects, we see that each one of these conditions has some influence on him, and governs at least one phase of his activity.

And so far as we see these influences, so far our

representation of his freedom diminishes and our representation of the necessity to which he is subjected increases.

(2) The second principle is the more or less visible temporal relation of man to the outside world, the more or less distinct conception of the place which the man's activity occupies in time.

This is the principle whereby the fall of the first man, which had for its consequences the origin of the human race, seems evidently less free than the marriage of a man of our day.

This is the principle in consequence of which the lives and activities of men who lived a century ago and are bound with me in time cannot seem to me so free as the lives of contemporaries, the consequences of which are as yet unknown to me.

The scale of apprehension of the greater or less Freedom or Necessity in this relation depends on the greater or less interval of time between the accomplishment of the action and my judgment on it.

If I regard an act which I performed a moment before under approximately the same conditions in which I find myself now, my action seems to me undoubtedly free.

But if I judge an act which I performed a month back, then finding myself in different conditions, I cannot help recognizing that if this act had not been performed, many things advantageous, agreeable, and even indispensable would not have taken place.

If I go back in memory to some act still farther back, — ten years ago and more, — then the consequences of my act present themselves to me as still more evidently necessitated, and it is hard for me to imagine what would have happened if this act had not taken place.

The farther back I go in memory, or, what is the same thing, the longer I refrain from judgment, the more doubtful will be my decision as to the freedom of any act.

In history we find also exactly the same progression of persuasion as to the part that Free Will plays in the actions of the human race. A contemporary event tak ing place seems to us undoubtedly the product of all the eminent men; but, if the event is farther away in time, we begin to see its inevitable consequences, other than which we could not imagine flowing from it. And the farther we go back in our investigation of events, the less do they seem to us spontaneous and free.

The Austro-Prussian war seems to us the undoubted consequence of the acts of the astute Bismarck and so on.

The Napoleonic wars, though with some shadow of doubt, still present themselves to us as the results of the will of heroes; but in the crusades we see an event definitely taking its place, an event without which the modern history of Europe would be meaningless, and yet in exactly the same way this event presented itself to the chroniclers of the crusades as merely the outcome of the will of certain individuals.

In the migration of the nations, it never occurs to any one, even in our time, that it depended on the pleasure of Attila to reconstitute the European world.

The farther back into history we carry the object of our investigation, the more doubtful appears the freedom of the men who brought events about, and the more evident grows the law of Necessity.

(3) The third principle is the greater or less accessibility to us of that endless chain of causes, inevitably claimed by reason, in which every comprehensible phenomenon, and therefore every act of man, must take its definite place, as the result of what is past, and as the cause of what is to come.

This is the principle which makes our deeds and those of other men seem to us, on the one hand, the more free and the less subjected to Necessity, according as we know the physiological, psychological, and historical laws to which man is subject, and the more faithfully we examine the physiological, psychological, and historical causes of events; and, on the other hand, in proportion as the action under examination is simple and uncomplicated by the character and intellect of the man whose act we are examining.

When we absolutely fail to comprehend the reasons of any act, — in the case of a crime, or an act of virtue, or even an act which has no reference to good and evil, — we are apt to attribute the greatest share of Freedom in such a case.

In the case of a crime, we demand especially for such an act the extreme penalty; in the case of a good action we especially reward such a virtuous deed.

In the case of something unique, we recognize the greatest individuality, originality, freedom.

But if a single one of the innumerable motives be known to us, we recognize a certain degree of necessity, and are not so eager in our demand for the punishment of the crime; we recognize less service in the virtuous action, less freedom in the apparently original performance.

The fact that a criminal was brought up among evildoers mitigates his fault. The self-denial of a father or mother — self-denial in view of a possible reward — is more comprehensible than self-denial without reason, and therefore seems to us less deserving of sympathy, — less free.

The founder of a sect or of a party, an inventor, surprises us less when we know how and by whom his activity was prepared beforehand.

If we have a long series of experiment, if our observation is constantly directed to searching into the correlation between cause and effect in the actions of men, then the acts of men will seem to us proportionally more necessitated and less free, the more accurately we trace causes and effects in events.

If the acts under consideration are simple, and we have for our study a vast number of such acts, then our notion of their necessity will be still more complete.

The dishonorable act of a man whose father was dishonorable, the evil conduct of a woman who has fallen in with low associates, the return of the drunkard to his drunkenness, and the like, are cases which will seem to us less free the clearer we comprehend their causes.

If, again, a man whose actions we are examining

stands on the lowest plane of mental development, —
as a child, a lunatic, an idiot, — then we who know the
causes of his activity and lack of complexity in his character and intellect see forthwith a decidedly large proportion of Necessity and so little Freedom of Will that
as soon as we know the cause that must have produced
the act we can foretell the act.

These three principles alone make possible the theory of irresponsibility for crime that is recognized in all
codes, and that of extenuating circumstances.

Responsibility seems greater or less in proportion to
our greater or less knowledge of the conditions in which
the man whose crime is under judgment found himself
in proportion to the longer or shorter interval of time
between the perpetration of the crime and our judgment of it, and in proportion to our more or less complete comprehension of the causes of the act.

CHAPTER X

THUS our recognition of Free Will and Necessity in
the phenomenon of the life of man is less or more in proportion as we look at the greater or less connection with
the outer world, in proportion to the greater or less interval of time, and the greater or less dependence on the
motives.

So that if we consider the position of a man in whose
case the connection with the external world is best
known, when the period of time between our judgment
and the act is the very greatest possible, and the causes
of the act most accessible, then we shall gain a conception of the most perfect Necessity and the least possible
Freedom.

But if we consider a man who shows the least dependence on external conditions, if his act is consummated
at the nearest possible moment to the present time, and
the motives of his act are inaccessible to us, then we
have a presentation of the least possible Necessity and
the greatest possible Freedom.

But neither in the one case nor in the other, however we might change our standpoint, however clear we might make the connection between the man and the outer world, or however inaccessible it might appear to us, however remote or however near might be the period of time, however comprehensible or incomprehensible for us the motives, we could never formulate to ourselves the idea of perfect Freedom or of complete Necessity.

(1) However hard we might endeavor to imagine a man freed from all influence of the external world, we could never conceive of such a thing as Freedom in space.

Every act of a man is inexorably conditioned also by the fact that he is bounded by the very nature of his body.

I raise my arm and drop it again. My action seems free, but, on asking myself, "Can I raise my arm in every direction?" I see that I have raised my arm in that direction where there would be the least resistance to such an action — either by the human bodies around me or by the organization of my own body.

If among all possible directions I choose one, then I choose it because there were less obstacles in that direction.

In order that my action should be free, it would be indispensable that it should meet no obstacles at all. In order to conceive of a man as being free, we should imagine him outside of space, which is evidently impossible.

(2) However close we may approximate the time of an event to the present, we can never gain the notion of Freedom in time.

For if I witness an act which was accomplished a second ago, I am nevertheless obliged to recognize that the act was not free, since the act is conditioned by that very moment of time in which it took place.

Can I raise my arm?

I raise it, but I ask myself, "Can I have not raised my arm at that moment of time already past?"

In order to convince myself, at the next moment I do not raise my arm. But I did not refrain from raising my arm at that former moment when I asked the question about Freedom.

The time has passed, and to retain it was not in my power; and the arm which I then raised, and the atmosphere in which I made the gesture, are no longer the atmosphere which now surrounds me, or the arm with which I now refrain from making the motion.

That moment in which the first gesture was made is irrevocable, and at that moment I could make only one gesture, and, whatever gesture I made, that gesture could have been only one.

The fact that in the subsequent moment of time I did not raise my arm is no proof that I might have refrained from raising it then. And since my motion could have been only one, at one moment of time, then it could not have been any other. In order to represent it as free, it is necessary to represent it at the present time, at the meeting-point of the past and the future, that is to say, outside of time, which is impossible; and

(3) However much we may magnify the difficulty of comprehending motives, we can never arrive at a representation of absolute Freedom, that is, to an absence of motive.

However unattainable for us may be the motive for the expression of will as manifested in an action performed by ourselves or others, the intellect first demands an assumption and search for the motive without which any phenomenon is unthinkable.

I raise my arm for the purpose of accomplishing an act independent of any motive, but the fact that I wish to perform an act without a motive is the motive of my act.

But even if, representing to ourselves a man absolutely freed from all influences, regarding merely his momentary action as of the present, and not called forth by any motive, if we grant that the infinitely small residuum of Necessity is equal to zero, even then we should not arrive at the notion of the absolute Freedom of man; since a being that does not respond to any influences from the outside world, exists outside of time, and is independent of motives, is no longer man.

In exactly the same way we can never conceive of the acts of a man without a share of Freedom, and subjected only to the law of Necessity.

(1) However great may be our knowledge of the conditions of space in which man finds himself, this knowledge can never be perfect, since the number of these conditions is infinitely great, in the same way as space is limitless. And consequently, as long as all the conditions that influence man are not known, there can be no absolute Necessity, but there is a certain measure of Freedom.

(2) However much we may lengthen out the period of time between the act which we are examining, and the time when our judgment is passed, this period will be finite; but time is endless, and therefore in this relation there can never be absolute Necessity.

(3) However accessible may be the chain of motives for any act whatever, we should never know the whole chain, since it is endless, and again we should never have absolute Necessity.

But, moreover, even if, granting a residuum of the least possible Freedom, equal to zero, we were to recognize, in any possible case, as for example a dying man, an unborn child, an idiot, absolute lack of Freedom, then by that very act we should destroy our concept of man which we were examining; for without Freedom of the Will man is not man.

And therefore our perception of the activity of man, subordinated only to the law of Necessity, without the slightest trace of Free Will, is just as impossible as the conception of the absolute Freedom of the acts of man.

Thus, in order to represent to ourselves the act of a man subjected only to the law of Necessity without any Freedom of the Will, we must have knowledge of an *infinite* number of the conditions in space, an *infinitely* long period of time, and an *infinite* series of motives.

In order to represent a man absolutely free and un-subordinated to the law of Necessity, we must represent him as one *outside of space, outside of time, and outside of all dependence upon motives.*

In the first case, if Necessity were possible without Freedom, we should be brought to define the laws of Necessity by .Necessity itself; that is, a mere form without substance.

In the second case, if Freedom without Necessity were possible, we should arrive at absolute Freedom outside of space, time, and cause, which, for the very reason that it would be unconditional and illimitable, would be nothing, or substance without form.

We should have arrived in general terms at those two fundamental principles on which man's whole conception of the world depends, the incomprehensible essence of life, and the laws which condition this essence.

Reason says : —

(1) Space, with all its forms, which are given to it by its quality of *visibility*, — matter, — is infinite, and can-not be conceived otherwise.

(2) Time is endless motion without a moment of rest, and it cannot be conceived otherwise.

(3) The chain of cause and effect can have no begin-ning and can have no end.

Consciousness says : —

(1) I am one, and all that happens is only I ; conse-quently I include space ;

(2) I measure fleeting time by the motionless moment of the present, at which alone I recognize that I am alive; consequently I am outside of time; and

(3) I am outside of motives, since I feel conscious that I myself am the motive of every manifestation of my life.

Reason expresses the laws of Necessity. Conscious-ness expresses the essence of Free Will.

Freedom, unconditioned by anything, is the essence of life in the consciousness of man.

Necessity without substance is the reason of man in **its** three forms.

Freedom is that which is examined. Necessity is that which examines.

Freedom is substance. Necessity is form.

Only by sundering the two sources of knowledge which are related to each other, as form and substance, do we arrive at the separate, mutually excluding, and inscrutable concepts of Free Will and Necessity.

Only by uniting them is a clear presentation of the life of man obtained.

Outside of these two concepts, mutually by their union defining one another, — form and substance, — any representation of man's life is impossible.

All that we know of the life of man is merely the relation of Freedom to Necessity; that is, an avowal of the laws of Reason.

All that we know of the outer world of Nature is only a certain relationship of the forces of Nature to Necessity; that is, the essence of life related to the laws of reason.

The life-forces of Nature lie outside of us, and are unknown to us, and we call these forces gravity, inertia, electricity, vital force, and so on; but the life-force of man is recognized by us, and we call it Freedom.

But just as the force of gravitation, in itself unattainable, inscrutable, though felt by every man, is only comprehensible to us as far as we know the laws of Necessity to which it is subject (from the first consciousness that all bodies are heavy up to the laws of Newton), in exactly the same way incomprehensible, inscrutable in itself, is the force of Freedom, though recognized by every one, and is only understood by us so far as we know the laws of Necessity to which it is subject — beginning with the fact that every man must die, up to the knowledge of the most complicated laws of political economy and history.

All knowledge is but the bringing of the essence of life under the laws of Reason.

Man's Freedom is differentiated from every other force by the fact that man is conscious of this force; but Reason regards it as in no respect different from any other force.

The forces of gravitation, electricity, chemical affinity, are only in this respect differentiated from one another, that these forces are differently defined by Reason. Just so the force of man's Freedom in the eyes of Reason differs from other forces of nature merely by the definition which this very Reason gives it.

Freedom without Necessity, that is, without the laws of Reason which define it, is in no respect different from gravity, or heat, or the forces of vegetation; for Reason it is a transitory, undefined sensation of life.

And as the undefined essence of force moving the heavenly bodies, the undefined essence of the force of electricity and the force of chemical affinity and vital force, constitute the substance of astronomy, physics, chemistry, botany, zoölogy, and so on, in exactly the same way the essence of the force of Freedom constitutes the substance of History.

But just as the object of every science is the manifestation of this indeterminate essence of life, while this same essence may be only a subject for metaphysics, so the manifestation of the force of the Free Will of man in space, time, and causality constitutes the object of History, while Free Will itself is the subject of metaphysics.

In the empirical sciences that which we know we call the laws of Necessity; that which we do not know we call vital force. Vital force is only the expression of the unknown reserve of what we know of the essence of life.

Just so in History: that which is known to us we call the laws of Necessity, that which is unknown we call Free Will.

Free Will or History is only the expression of the unknown reserve from what we know about the laws of the life of man.

CHAPTER XI

HISTORY observes the manifestations of the Freedom of man in their relations with the external world, with time, and with causality; that is, it determines this Freedom by the laws of Reason, and therefore History is a science only in so far as it determines Freedom by these laws.

For History to regard the Free Will of men as a force able to exert influence on historical events, that is, as not subject to law, is the same thing as for astronomy to recognize freedom in the movement in the heavenly forces.

This admission would destroy the possibility of the existence of laws, that is, of any knowledge whatever.

If a single body existed endowed with freedom of movement, then the laws of Kepler and Newton would no longer exist, and we could have no conception of the movements of the heavenly bodies.

If a single human action were free, there would be no historical laws, no conception of historical events.

History is concerned only with the lines of the movement of human wills, one end of which disappears in the unseen, while at the other end appears consciousness of the Free Will of man in the present, moving in space, time, and causality.

The more the field of movement opens out before our eyes, the more evident become the laws of this movement.

To grasp and define these laws is the object of History.

From the standpoint from which science now looks at the object of its investigations, along that route which it traverses in seeking the causes of events in the Free Will of men, the formulation of laws is impossible, for, however carefully we limit the Free Will of men, as soon as we recognize it as a force not subjected to laws the existence of the law is impossible.

Only by reducing this Freedom to an infinitesimal, that is, regarding it as an infinitely small quantity, do we believe in the absolute accessibility of causes, and only then, instead of seeking for causes, History takes as its problem the search for laws.

The search for these laws has been undertaken in times past, and the new methods of thought which History must appropriate are elaborated simultaneously with the self-destruction toward which the "old History" moves with its constant differentiation of the causes of phenomena.

Along this route all the human sciences have traveled.

Mathematics, the most exact of sciences, having reached the infinitely small, abandons the process of differentiation, and makes use of a new process, that of summing up the unknown — the differential or infinitesimal calculus.

Mathematics, giving up the concept of causes, seeks for laws; that is, the qualities common to all of unknown, infinitesimal elements.

Though in another form, the other sciences have followed the same route of thought.

When Newton formulated the law of gravitation, he did not say that the sun or the earth had the property of attracting; he said that all bodies, from the largest to the smallest, possessed the property of attracting one another; that is, putting aside the question of the cause of the movement of bodies, he simply formulated a quality common to all bodies, from the infinitely great to the infinitely small.

The natural sciences do the same; putting aside the question of causation, they seek for laws.

History also stands on the same path, and if History has for its object the study of the movements of peoples and of humanity, and not a description of episodes in the lives of men, it must put aside the notion of cause, and search for the laws common to all the closely united, infinitesimal elements of Freedom.

CHAPTER XII

FROM the time the law of Copernicus was discovered and demonstrated, the mere recognition of the fact that the sun does not move, but the earth, overturned the entire cosmography of the ancients.

It was possible, by rejecting the law, to hold fast to the old view of the motion of bodies; but unless the law was rejected, it became impossible, apparently, to continue in the teaching of the Ptolemaic worlds. And yet, even after the discovery of the law of Copernicus, the Ptolemaic worlds were still for a long time taught.

From the time when man first said and proved that the number of births or crimes was subject to mathematical laws, and that certain geographical and politico-economical conditions determined this or that form of government, that certain relations of the population to the soil produce the movements of the nation, hence-forth the fundamental principles whereon History was based were entirely subverted.

It was possible, by rejecting the new laws, to hold to the former views of History; but, unless they were rejected, it was impossible, apparently, to continue to teach that historical events were the product of the Free Will of men.

For if any particular form of government was established, or any movement of a nation took place, as a consequence of certain geographical, ethnographical, or economical conditions, the wills of those men who appeared to us to have established the form of government can no longer be regarded as the cause.

But still the old style of History continues to be taught side by side with the laws of statistics, of geography, of political economy, comparative philology, and geology, which directly contradict its tenets.

Long and stubbornly the struggle between the old view and the new went on in the domain of physical philosophy.

Theology stood on guard in behalf of the old view,

and denounced the new for its destruction of Revela·
tion. But when Truth won the day, Theology intrenched
herself just as solidly in the new ground.

Just as long and stubbornly at the present time rages
the struggle between the old and the new view of His·
tory, and, just as before, Theology stands on guard in
behalf of the old view, and denounces the new for its
subversion of Revelation.

In the one case, just as in the other, passions have
been called into play on both sides, and the truth has
been obscured. On the one hand, fear and sorrow for
all the knowledge elaborately built up through the centuries; on the other, the passion for destruction.

For the men who opposed the rising truth of physics,
it seemed as if by their acknowledgment of this truth
their faith in God, in the creation of the universe, in the
miracle of Joshua the son of Nun, would be destroyed.

To the defenders of the laws of Copernicus and Newton, to Voltaire, for instance, it seemed that the laws
of astronomy were subversive of religion, and he made
the laws of gravitation a weapon against religion.

In exactly the same way now it is only necessary to
recognize the law of Necessity, and the idea of the soul,
of good and evil, and all state and church institutions
that revolve around these concepts would be subverted.

Now, just as Voltaire in his time, the uninvited defenders of the law of Necessity employ this law against
religion; and exactly the same way as the law of Copernicus in astronomy, so now the law of Necessity in
History not only does not subvert, but even strengthens,
the foundation on which are erected state and ecclesiastical institutions.

As at that time in the question of astronomy, so now
in the question of History, every variety of view is based
on the recognition or non-recognition of the absolute
unit which serves as the standard measure of all visible
phenomena. In astronomy this standard was the immovability of the earth; in History it was the independence of the individual — Freedom of the Will.

As for astronomy, the difficulty in the way of recog·

nizing the immovability of the earth consisted in having to rid one's self of the immediate sensation that the earth was immovable, and of a similar sense as to the motion of the planets; so also in History the difficulty in the way of recognizing the subjection of personality to the laws of space, time, and causality consisted in being obliged to rid one's self of the sense of the independence of one's personality.

But, as in astronomy, the new theory says : —

"It is true we are not conscious of the motion of the earth, but if we grant its immobility, we arrive at an absurdity; whereas, if we admit the motion of which we are not conscious, we arrive at laws," in the same way, in History the new view says : —

"It is true we are not conscious of our dependence, but, by admitting the Freedom of the Will, we arrive at an absurdity; whereas, by admitting our dependence on the external world, time, and causality, we arrive at laws."

In the first case it was necessary to get rid of the consciousness of non-existent immobility in space, and to recognize a motion which was not present to our consciousness; in the present case, in exactly the same way, it is essential to get rid of a Freedom which does not exist, and to recognize a dependence which is not present to our consciousness.

THE END